THE Decadence AFTER DARK SERIES

M. NEVER

DECADENCE AFTER DARK

Decadence Series Cover Design and Photography By:
Sara Eirew

Individual Cover Designs By:
Marisa Shor, Cover Me, Darling

Editing By:
Jenny Carlsrud Sims, Editing 4 Indies

Copy Editing for Ruined By:
Candice Royer

Proofreading By:
Nichole Strauss, Perfectly Publishable

Interior Design and Formatting By:
Christine Borgford, Perfectly Publishable

M. NEVER

DEDICATION

This book is dedicated to the victims of sexual abuse and human trafficking. You are true survivors, inspirations and fighters.

"What lies behind you and what lies in front of you, pales in comparison to what lies inside of you."

~ Ralph Waldo Emerson

PROLOGUE

I LIKE YOU COLLARED, BABY. I like you naked. I like you mine.

ELLIE

I HURRY OUT OF THE subway.

Of all days for me to be late, I choose this one.

My phone rings, and I know exactly who it is. My boss, Mark. My anal retentive, no nonsense, perfectionist boss—whom I adore.

He drives me nuts, but he is the most supportive man I have ever met, so I'm giving him a pass this morning. I know why he's wound tight. His biggest client is coming in for a meeting and everything needs to be just right. Which is part of the reason I'm late in the first place. I couldn't decide what to wear! Every time Kayne Roberts walks into the building my pulse races, my heart rate spikes, and my knees go weak. He's a walking god in an Armani suit.

"Hello?" I answer as I turn the corner, picking up the pace.

"Where are you?" Mark snaps.

"I'll be in the office in five minutes."

"Three minutes. Roberts will be here any second. The conference room needs to be prepped and coffee needs to be made."

I sigh. "I prepped last night, and the coffee is on a timer." Okay, so maybe I knew I was going to be late.

"You're magic glitter in high heels," he says then hangs up. Did I mention Mark is flaming gay? Makes him that much more fun to work for.

There's a pedestrian traffic jam right outside of my building's entrance. Of course. I push through the mass, battling my way to the double doors I have in sight. I emerge from the throng, but not before my heel gets caught in a crack in the sidewalk, and I fly face first onto my hands and knees. Shit. Everyone saw that. I allow myself to feel humiliated for just a second, and then proceed to pick myself up.

"Okay down there?" A smooth, masculine voice vibrates through my limbs. I look up to find Kayne Roberts himself holding his hand out to help me. I'm stuck. Kneeling at his feet as my brain forgets how to command my body.

He frowns. "Ellie, are you hurt badly? Do you need me to carry you inside?"

Carry me? *Yes please!*

"No." I finally find my wits. "I'm okay."

Kayne plucks me up, and I'm caught staring into his beautiful crystal blue eyes. Well, one beautiful crystal blue eye. His right eye has a large patch of brown that looks like a lightning bolt is striking his pupil.

It makes them even more of a spectacle to stare at.

He smiles down at me and then drops his gaze a little lower, smirking wickedly. I look down immediately to find the top button of my shirt popped open and my cleavage fully exposed.

I want to crawl into a hole and die of embarrassment, mortification, and shame.

"Nice," Kayne quips.

I grab my shirt and yank it closed.

"Thank you." It's the only thing I can think to say and makes my embarrassment burn brighter, right on the apples of my cheeks. I right myself as Kayne opens the door for me, and we walk to the elevator together. Him haughty, me abashed.

As we ride to the tenth floor in silence, I pull my black pencil skirt up and check my knees. Kayne watches with entertained eyes as I expose more leg. I feel claustrophobic under his gaze. My right one is scraped and stings slightly, but I don't notice the pain. All I can think about is that old expression *you should be careful what you wish for.* Because ever since he strolled into this company, I have lusted after him. Wishing that just once he would notice me. Well, today he did. And all I want to do is die.

Mark is waiting by the elevators when we arrive. I swear if he could stick his whole head up Kayne's ass instead of just his nose, he would. I guess I can't blame him. Kayne is his number one client. Expo is an import/export company and Mark's baby. He hired me straight out of high school and I have worked my way up from novice secretary to irreplaceable personal assistant during that four year time. My family couldn't afford to send me to college, and I didn't want to rack up one hundred thousand dollars worth of debt by going to the top-ten school of my dreams. So, I decided to forgo college until I could save up enough to attend. Mark has been overly generous with my paychecks and bonuses ever since he found out I had half a brain. Coming from the poor family I did, I learned quickly that I am the master of my own destiny. If I want something out of life, the only person who can afford it to me, is me. My upbringing wasn't all bad though. Contrary to the bottom line of their bank account, my family had a wealth of love to give.

Mark is wearing his power suit—a dark grey jacket and matching pants with a bright purple shirt and printed tie. Despite the way Mark dresses, he is brilliant, and I have learned an abundance since he took me under his wing.

"Kayne." He and Mark shake after we walk out of the elevator.

"Mark."

"Everything is set up. Ellie, please escort Mr. Roberts to the conference room. And tend to whatever he needs."

I suddenly flush. Whatever he needs? My mind races with erotic images. I'll tend to *anything* he needs.

"Yes, Mark," I answer dutifully.

Kayne gazes down at me with vigilant eyes. His glare heats my skin. It's as hot as the sun.

I walk Kayne to the conference room with him trailing slightly behind me, and if I didn't know any better, I'd swear he's stealing glimpses of my ass. It turns me on and makes me uncomfortable all at the same time. I guess that's what I get for wearing the tightest pencil skirt I own.

"Do you need to clean your knee?" Kayne asks.

"It will be fine. I'll take care of it after you're settled."

He nods.

Kayne relaxes himself in one of the large leather office chairs adjacent to where Mark usually sits.

"Coffee?" I ask.

"Yes, please." He smoothes his tie. "Milk"

"No sugar." I finish his sentence.

"You remembered." He smiles brightly, and I almost dissolve.

"It's my job not to forget." Jesus, is that even my voice? It sounds husky, thick with desire. *Can I be any more desperate?*

"Rare quality. Attentiveness," he muses.

"I guess." I shrug, backpedaling toward the door. "I'll be right back."

I flee the room, seriously needing to pull my shit together.

By the time I return with Kayne's coffee, a tea for Mark, and the tray of baked goods Mark always requests, the meeting is already under way. I hand Kayne his coffee first. He winks at me and our fingers brush during the exchange. The contact feels like an electrical current.

I shakily place Mark's tea in front of him as he reads through the agenda, and then set the silver platter of muffins, scones, and miniature cupcakes in the middle of the table. After that, I leave the room, stealing a glance at Kayne right before I exit.

I clean my knee, then spend the rest of the morning spying into the conference room, swooning over the very desirable and even more unattainable Mr. Roberts.

"I see your boyfriend's back." Susie, one of Mark's logisticians, bumps my hip.

"I don't know what you're talking about," I say with a huge smile. Everyone in the office knows how bad I have it for Kayne.

"Yeah right." She laughs with her throaty voice. "You're standing there with your tongue unraveled."

"Am I that obvious?" I scrunch my face.

"You're like a white dot on a wall of red."

"Is the red because I heat up every time I see him?" I ask chewing my lip and twirling the end of my light brown hair compulsively.

"Not just you, honey. The building."

"I'm a desperate loser." I drop my face into my hands.

"Don't beat yourself up about it. That man is walking sex with a side of pheromones. No one blames you." She stirs her coffee with the thin orange plastic stick.

"He'll never notice me." I sigh as I eye him through the glass. He's engrossed in whatever Mark's talking about. I'm engrossed by his body, his face, his hands and his hair.

I finally look back at Susie. She's smiling, chewing on her coffee stirrer. "You want him to notice you? Give him something to look at. You'll never know if he's interested if you don't put yourself out there."

"He's Mark's most important client. I wouldn't want to mess anything up for him by mixing business with pleasure."

Susie shrugs. "A risk comes with every reward."

She throws her stirrer in the trash. "See if he's going to the party tonight. If not, invite him," she advises before she saunters away.

Ask *him* out?

I glance up to find the meeting coming to an end. Everyone is slowly but surely clearing out of the conference room. Except Kayne. He's still sitting, jotting notes.

"Ellie. Can you clean up in there? I'm heading to lunch," Mark calls.

"Yes, Mark," I once again dutifully respond, and Kayne looks up.

His stare makes the insides of my thighs heat up. *Get a grip!*

I head into the conference room, steeling my nerves.

"How was the meeting?" I ask Kayne sweetly as I begin to collect the information folders left behind.

"Excellent. Mark is a genius at logistics. He found an alternate flight route out of Mexico that will save a few hundred thousand over the next year. I'm pleased."

Kayne utilizes Expo to import limes and his own personal brand of tequila out of Mexico. He's making a fortune right now on that little green fruit. Because of weather conditions and poor crops, the price per bushel of limes has quadrupled. Mark sees dollar signs every time we have margaritas after work.

"That's good." I smile. "No lunch for you?" I ask casually.

"I have another meeting in an hour. I'll be having lunch then. Mark said I could utilize the conference room to do some work to kill time."

"I see," I say as I pick up the last folder.

"What about you?" He tracks my movements with his majestic blue eyes. They remind me of a wild jungle cat.

"My lunch is sitting right in front of you. I'll be dining on miniature cupcakes."

"Healthy," he mocks.

"I know, but they're little. So ... less calories?" I shrug playfully.

"I guess that's one way to spin it." He smiles, pulling the silver tray toward him. "Which flavor is your favorite?" Kayne looks up at me like *I'm* a confection sweet enough to eat. I swallow hard.

"It's a toss-up between the red velvet and lemon drop."

"Well, I'm a red velvet man myself." He picks up the lone red velvet cupcake on the plate. "Would you mind sharing your lunch with me, Ellie?"

"Of course not. It's only polite to share." I fiddle with the collar of my dress shirt.

Kayne pulls the wrapper off of the dyed cake, and then splits it in two. "Sit."

I take a seat next to him, still clutching the file folders in my arms.

He offers me one half of the cupcake, and I take it with trembling fingers.

"Do I make you nervous, Ellie?" he asks as he lightly licks the cream cheese frosting.

"No." I try to play it cool. "Just too much coffee."

"I see." He stares at me intensely as he laps the top of the cupcake clean. I think I just came watching his tongue work the icing. "Aren't you going to eat?" he asks enticingly, right before he stuffs the naked cupcake into his mouth. I just sit there frozen, trying not to squish the dessert still in my hand.

This man could write a handbook on seduction. Chapter one: Cupcakes.

Kayne looks at me expectantly. Without even thinking, I shove my half into my mouth. Not seductively at all. I'd be the first one to buy that handbook. Kayne smirks, his eyes alight. Then he brushes a crumb off my bottom lip. I nearly pass out.

"Did you decide what school you're going to attend in the fall?" he asks as he lounges back in his chair. I can't believe it. We had that conversation over three months ago, the last time he was here.

"You remembered?" I can't stop the smile from spreading across my face.

"I'm in the business of not forgetting." He skims his tie slowly between his thumb and index finger. Lucky tie.

"It's between the University of Miami, NC State, and Hawaii," I tell him.

"Inclined to warm weather."

I pout my lip. "I've never been away from the East Coast. I wanted a change. I plan to visit Europe next summer."

"Ambitious."

His responses are so simple, so controlled, yet so inveigling it feels like I'm falling into a trance.

"I want more than a two-bedroom apartment shared by four people," I divulge meekly.

"I admire your aspirations. Do you know what you're going to study?"

"Logistics."

"Thinking about starting your own import/export? I'd hire you." His gaze is heavy, probing almost. Is it suddenly hot in here?

"Well, thank you for the vote of confidence. But I'm not sure what I want to do yet. I just know it's an open field. And something I've come to learn."

"Do what you know?"

"Something like that."

Kayne nods, glancing at his watch. "Crap, Ellie, I have to go."

"I understand." We both stand up, our chests landing an inch apart. I stop breathing.

Kayne stares down at me with those mesmerizing eyes. "Thank

you for sharing your lunch with me."

"Anytime," I breathe. Inhaling the clean scent of his expensive cologne. The smell is heady.

"Kayne?"

"Mmmm hmmm, Ellie?" He leans a little closer.

"Are you going to Mark's party tonight?" I ask, a little lightheaded from his scent and his proximity.

A smile plays on his lips. "I was invited."

"And are you going?"

"Will you be there?" he counters.

"It depends."

"On what?"

"If I'll be spending the evening alone or not." I stare straight up at him, trying not to waver.

"Are you asking me out, Ellie?"

Am I?

"Maybe." I bite my lip.

"Then maybe I'll be there."

Did he just accept?

With that, Kayne picks up his phone from the table and drops it into his pocket. I just watch him like a dumbstruck fool.

"Until tonight," he says, then steps away from me and starts for the door. "Oh, and Ellie." He stops short right next to me so we are shoulder to shoulder. "The next time you want to get my attention. Bend over. Your tits are nice, but I'm more of an ass man."

He then leaves.

With me nailed to the floor.

AYNE

I SHOULD HAVE SAID NO.

I should've just blown Ellie off then apologized for it the next time I saw her. Blaming it on a business issue that needed my immediate attention. But I didn't. Because right now I'm standing at the bar in the middle of a trendy downtown restaurant waiting for Ellie the way a dog would wait for a bone.

I'll give it to Mark. He knows where to throw a party. You had to walk through a pawn shop to get into the place. The first floor is a lounge. The second is where dinner is served. The diners can look down over the railing at the patrons mingling on the white leather couches shrouded in florescent light. Like a legal peep show.

Only in fucking Manhattan.

I've already said hello to Mark and some other employees of his. I was introduced to some of his other clients as well. Very kissy kissy, shaky shaky business shit. It goes with the territory. Now I'm sucking down bourbon like a drain in a distillery, regretting that I'm here. I regret even more that I told Ellie she has nice tits. Good going. Then, just to add fuel to the fire, I told her I was an ass man. If she only knew how true that was. It's exactly why I shouldn't be here. Ellie is too sweet. Too playful. I would never want to take those traits away from her. She reminds me of a frisky kitten tangled in a strand of yarn. She has no idea how tangled she'll be if she gets involved with me.

I slug some more bourbon. If she's not here by the time I finish this drink, I'm out. I suck down the last drops of alcohol in the glass and get ready to jet.

That's when I spot her. I stop dead in my tracks as she walks toward me. She's wearing a scrap of material I think she's trying to pass off as a dress. It's all skintight, long-sleeved, and super short.

"Hi." She greets me with a bright smile. "Are you leaving?"

I jingle the keys in my hand. I should say yes. I should bolt out of this room and never look back. But instead I say, "I was beginning to think you stood me up."

"Never. I'm a woman. We're always fashionably late." She bats her eyelashes flirtatiously.

Not if you were my woman.

"Buy you a drink?" I ask as I greedily ingest every sexy inch of her in that skintight dress.

"Yes please, a vodka and tonic with lemon."

"Lemon?" I curl my lip.

"Yes." She giggles.

"Most people drink it with a lime."

Ellie shrugs. "I'm not most people."

You certainly are not.

I order our drinks just as Mark appears from the masses. "There she is. My magic glitter in high heels." He holds out his arms like she's a Broadway diva who just gave the performance of her life.

He's definitely a little trashed. It's only when Ellie turns to kiss Mark hello do I notice the back of her dress; a huge oval cut-out is exposing her bare skin. Holy shit. It's provocative as hell, and I nearly choke.

"So glad you could make it, Kayne." He shakes my hand and tells me again—for the third time. "Take care of my little Ellie here. She's leaving us soon, and I won't be able to find my ass without her."

"Aww," Ellie coos. "That is the sweetest thing you've ever said to me."

"Hold on to your knickers, kid. If you're even wearing any under that dress. It barely covers your bottom," he muses.

And I love it.

Mark pauses, looking between us with his bloodshot eyes. "What was I saying?"

"Goodbye," I chime in.

He lifts his glass to cheer us and goes on his merry way. I shake my head as he gets lost in the crowd. He is a character. Brilliant, but still a character.

"When do you start school?" I ask Ellie as the bartender serves us our drinks.

"September. I finally made my decision."

"And where are you going?"

"Hawaii. I mailed the deposit check on my way here." She's practically glowing.

"Definitely the school I would have picked," I say, excited for her, yet at the same time I suddenly feel sad. I shake off the odd sentiment. Maybe the bourbon is going to my head. I raise my glass. "To rainbows, surfing, and getting lei'd."

Ellie laughs freely, clinking my glass. "To getting lei'd." Our eyes linger long after we take a sip of our drinks. I feel the heated stare radiate through the whole room.

"Do you want to sit?" I finally ask her.

"Sure." She bites on her little red straw enticingly. *Don't look at me like that Ellie.* I want to tell her. I want to warn her. It will only get you into trouble. Who am I kidding? Just by me being here, she's in trouble.

It's putting us both in trouble.

"I like your dress." I lean into her, glancing down at her barely covered ass. She smells sweet. Like cotton candy. "Did you wear it to get someone's attention?"

"Yes."

"Whose?"

"Yours." She looks straight into my eyes.

"You've got it," I murmur in her ear. "Undividedly."

Aww, shit. If I'm going to hell, I might as well have some fun getting there. Presently in the form of a playful little kitten named Ellie. I take her hand and lead her to the darkest, most hidden corner of the room. We sit on one of the white leather couches, and she snuggles into me as the catchy tune of *Sing* by Ed Sheeran resonates around us. It's the perfect match for the trendy atmosphere and flirtatious vibe.

Trouble. So much trouble.

Ellie and I talk about this and that. Nothing of utter importance. I can't remember the last time I had a mundane conversation. She tells me how much she hates spiders because one crawled into her shirt when she was child and scared her half to death. I tell her how I hate cinnamon but can chew an entire pack of Big Red gum.

By our second drink, my hand is on her knee. By the third, it's on her thigh and we're both having trouble denying the uninhibited attraction kindling between us.

"Kayne?" Ellie sighs as I stroke my thumb right under the hem of her scarcely there dress.

I lean into her, my face an inch away from hers. "Ellie. Do you really want this with me?" I give her one chance for an out. If she consents, I'm taking her back to my penthouse and fucking her till morning.

"Yes." Her voice doesn't waver. Then she spreads her legs a little wider and allows my hand to move farther up her thigh, a whisper away from the sweet spot I have been fantasizing about for over a year.

"There's something you should know about me." I brush my lips against hers.

"What's that?" She returns the affection by sliding her tongue into my mouth. Little lioness.

I like to dominate. I want submission. I'll tie you up and have my way with you until you beg me to stop.

"Kayne?" She breathes my name, and I nearly combust.

"Ellie, I—"

"Amigo?" I'm interrupted by a thick Spanish accent. I glare up at the man standing in front of us, and Ellie shifts uncomfortably away from me. I could decapitate Javier. The homegrown Mexican scumbag—and my house guest for the next I don't know how long—has just ruined a defining moment. I stand menacingly and shake his hand.

"I wasn't expecting you until tomorrow," I say as politely as possible.

"I caught an early flight." He slaps my shoulder. "Too excited to see you."

Ellie watches our exchange. I can't tell if she notices anything is off or not.

"Ellie?" I hold out my hand for her to stand up. "Would you mind getting some water?" I pull out a fifty. She nods with a small smile, acknowledging both of us. She takes the money then slips silently away.

When Ellie is out of earshot, I snap at Javier. "What the fuck are you doing showing your face here?"

"Your driver said you were out for the evening. Sounded like fun." He smiles at me with that wicked grin that I want to wipe right off his face.

"I don't think it's wise to be seen in public together." I speak through clenched teeth.

Javier shrugs. "It's dark in here."

I huff.

"The girl, is she one of yours?" He ogles in the direction of the bar, where Ellie is standing with her back to us, ass on display.

"Not exactly."

"Available then?" He raises his eyebrows.

"For what?" I sneer.

"Something to occupy my time with while I'm here. She looks *entertaining."* His eyes sparkle with something sinister, something that spurs a disturbing memory to flash before me.

It feels like someone just tied a noose around my neck.

"I have plenty of girls to keep your time occupied," I inform him directly.

"Yes, but I want *that* girl. In my room. Tied to my bed, tonight."

Why? So you can rape her repeatedly and beat her within an inch of her life? Like hell.

"I'm afraid that can't happen," I respond coolly, while my blood simmers in my veins.

"And why is that?"

I make a drastic decision.

"Because I've already claimed her. She's mine."

I just fucking hung myself.

"I DIDN'T REALIZE YOU WERE in the business of acquiring slaves."

My heart rate spikes. "I wasn't, but spending time with you has given me a new perspective."

Javier's mouth twists. "Glad to be an influence. Too bad you found her first."

"Yeah, well, you know what they say. Finders keepers and all."

"Yes." He looks at me perversely, and I don't like it one bit. His black eyes are hollow. Soulless. I know all too well what he's capable of. "Better keep her close."

Oh, I will.

I pull my keys out of my pocket and slap them into Javier's hand. "Get out of here. My Maserati is parked in the lot on the corner. Hit Mansion on the GPS. It will direct you where to go."

I watch as Ellie approaches. Completely innocent. Completely unaware her whole life is about to change. Tonight.

Javier lifts her hand and brings it to his mouth when she reaches us. "Señorita."

He sounds so suave. So genuine. I want to punch his goddamn lights out for even touching her.

He doesn't say a word to me when he leaves.

I look down regretfully at Ellie. I knew I put her in danger by being here. I just didn't realize how much fucking danger.

"Are you ready to go?" I ask. My heart twists, but my arousal roars to life.

"Yes." She's so sure, so confident. She has no idea who she's leaving with.

"Leave first. I'll have my driver pick you up in the back alley. I think it will look better if we go separately."

She nods, all blushed cheeks and starry eyes. I wonder if she'll look at me that way in the morning. I watch grimly as Ellie walks away. Then I pull out my phone.

"Jett," I snap at my driver, the house caretaker, and my best friend. "Why the fuck would you bring him here?"

"He whipped out a knife and demanded that I take him wherever you were. Bit mistrusting, don't you think?"

"Coming in a day early unannounced? Nah."

In the business we're in, trust is a nonexistent commodity. "Why didn't you let me know he was here before you picked him up?"

"I called and text, shithead."

I pull the phone away from my ear and check it. It's on silent. Stupid fuck. And sure enough there are several missed calls and texts. I groan in frustration.

"We have a situation," I tell Jett as I hurry through the restaurant. "Meet me out front. I sent Javier back in the Maserati."

"Oh, that was smart. I wonder what kind of trouble he can get into with that," Jett patronizes.

"He better not get in any. It's risky enough he's on American soil."

"True. So what's the situation?"

"Ellie."

"Ellie? The girl you've been obsessing over?"

"I haven't been obsessing!" I snap.

"Mmmm hmmmm," Jett responds. "She rejected you? Need some ice cream?"

"No, cocksucker. Javier. He wants her. I made an executive decision."

"Oh no. Kayne, you and executive decisions are never good." He sounds worried.

"Yeah, well, it was either that or let Javier get his sadistic hands on her. And like hell I was going to let that happen." Another disturbing image flashes across my mind. I shudder. "You have any stuff stashed?"

"Yes."

"Good."

Jett pulls up just as I get outside. I hop in the limo. "Go around to the back alley. Where's the stuff?"

"Under the ice bin," he tells me, looking straight ahead. The back of his blond head is all I can see.

I pull out the ice bin, grab one of the little white pills, and dissolve it in a glass of champagne. Ellie is waiting just where I told her to. I wasn't lying when I said I was going to hell.

She slides in when Jett opens the door. I pull her near me, not wasting a moment, and devour her mouth. I need to taste it just one time with her permission. One time, while she still wants me.

She's gripping my shirt by the time I pull away.

"Where are we going?" she asks, a little breathless as I hand her the champagne.

"My place." I clink our glasses, and she takes a sip. "Drink up," I urge. We both finish our champagne in record time. I only poured a quarter of a glass.

Then I pull her onto my lap, straddling her legs over mine. The sexual chemistry circling the car is potent enough to put an elephant on its ass. Speaking of asses, I grab Ellie's and force her against me. She moans as her hips collide with mine. My cock has been swollen since the moment I saw her in that fucking dress, with her long gold-ish brown hair and sultry green eyes.

"Have you ever fucked in the back of a limo, Ellie?"

She shakes her head.

"Would you let me fuck you right here if I wanted to?"

"Yes." Her eyes are starting to get heavy.

"Right answer. Good girl. Next time though, it's yes, Kayne."

Hell. I am going straight to hell.

"I feel funny." She starts to sway.

"Too much to drink." I steady her as her eyes roll into the back of her head and her body goes limp.

Fuck! Fuck! Fuck!

A moment later she's gone.

Passed out against me.

ELLIE

I WAKE UP WITH THE worst headache I have ever had.

I flutter my eyes open and don't recognize my surroundings. It's cold. I pull my legs up to my chest and realize I still have on the same clothes from last night. Where am I? What happened? The last thing I remember is waiting for Kayne in the alley. I sit up. Why am I in a cage? It looks like a jail cell. What the fuck? I start to panic. I get up and pull on the locked door. "Hello?" my voice echoes. "Hello, is anyone out there?" I yank harder on the door but it won't budge. Don't freak out, don't freak out.

"Morning, Ellie." I hear Kayne's voice from somewhere out of sight.

"Kayne? Kayne! Let me out! Is this some kind of sick joke?"

"It's no joke, Ellie. I'm sorry."

"Sorry for what?" I ask confused and slightly terrified.

He shows himself. Standing in front of the steel bars, he's dressed in black pants and a white button up shirt. His hair is a brown mess on top of his head and his blue eyes are acute. Watchful. Cunning.

"You're mine now, Ellie."

"What the fuck does that mean?"

"It means I have acquired you and you belong to me."

"Like fucking hell. Let me out!"

"I will, Ellie. When you submit."

"Fuck you," I spit.

"Yes, we'll be doing a lot of fucking. Don't you worry about that." He smiles, but the emotion doesn't reach his eyes. "That is what you want, right? To fuck me? Isn't that why you wore that dress and practically threw yourself at me?"

"I didn't throw myself at you. You arrogant asshole!"

"Tomato, tomatoe. Regardless. I know you want me. And I definitely want you." He moves closer to the cell door and I immediately back away. "You're going to do everything I say if you want to get out of that cage."

I stand there staring at him. Angry tears threaten my eyes.

"And what exactly do you want me to do?" I ask spitefully.

"Take your clothes off. All of them."

"Go to hell," I snap.

"You weren't so opposed last night."

"Last night I thought I was with someone sane. Not a psychopath!"

"I won't hold it against you for being a bad judge of character."

I shake my head. "This isn't you."

"It is me. There are so many things you don't know about me, but are going to find out." His voice is so calm, it's eerie.

"Let me out," I demand.

"Strip."

"Never."

"Suit yourself. You'll stay in there until you're ready. I want your submission, Ellie. And I'll get it."

He starts to walk away.

"Kayne!" I throw myself against the bars. "I have a family! I have a life! People will be looking for me! You can't do this!" I scream, sobbing now, yanking on the steel door. What did I get myself into? How did this happen? Is it all my fault? Why kidnap a girl who was willing to give herself freely? I wish I could remember more of last night. When did it all go so terribly wrong?

I'VE WATCHED ELLIE WASTE AWAY for the last three days.

I'm staring at her right now on the security feed in my office. Mansion's ground zero. Nothing happens in this house without Jett or me knowing about it. And that includes every breath Ellie takes.

"How long do you think she's going to hold out?" Jett asks from behind me. There may be seventeen screens on the wall, but he knows exactly which one has my undivided attention.

"I don't think much longer. I could see the desperation in her eyes this morning."

Presently, Ellie is huddled in a ball on the bench in her cell. I know she's cold. There's no heat in the dungeon, and she's only wearing that tiny, sexy-as-sin dress from Mark's party. I also know she's hungry too. I barely feed her.

"What if she doesn't give in?"

"She'll impress me." I laugh. "But I know she will," I respond with inflated certainty. Reading people is what I do. What I've been trained for. And Ellie is crumbling like a cupcake. Prisoner of war tactics: isolation, starvation, sleep deprivation. A slow dismantling of the human psyche.

"Are you sure you're going to be able to do this? She's not like the other girls." Jett uses that probing tone. The one he knows I hate.

"I'll have to, won't I? We've come this far." I rock back in my chair, hitting him square in the nuts.

"You fucker, you did that on purpose," he grunts.

"Prove it." I grin widely, with my eyes glued on Ellie.

ELLIE

I DON'T KNOW HOW LONG I've been in here.

What I do know is that I'm freezing and hungry and have barely slept. Kayne has visited me six times. And each time he has told me the same thing. I belong to him. I'm his property. His pet. He feeds me just enough bread and water to sustain my consciousness, but that's it. And every time I nod off, a loud blaring siren startles me awake. I'm miserable, angry, confused, scared, and worst of all, close to giving in—because being in this dark, damp, isolated cell is making me go mad.

"Morning, Ellie." Kayne greets me the same each time. I have no idea if it's really morning or night. A weekday or a weekend.

I don't respond. I just recoil tighter into my ball on the bench. That's where I sit and attempt to sleep. A wooden bench. No pillow, or cushion or blanket. I'm shivering I'm so cold and covered in goose bumps. My tiny dress gives my body no protection against the elements.

"Are you ready to come out? I know you're cold and hungry and dirty. I'll take you someplace warm. More comfortable. If you agree to come out." For all the times Kayne has come to taunt me, he has never once stepped foot inside my cell. Never once tried to touch me or hurt me. "It doesn't have to be like this."

I trust him about as far as I can throw him. I'm afraid of the unknown if I step out of this cage, and I'm afraid of the unknown if I stay in it.

"Fine," I say feebly, finally breaking down.

"Good." He smiles victoriously. Like he had some bet going or something. "You know what you have to do."

"Why?" I gripe.

"Because that's the way it is. I know this is all new. But you'll learn. I'm going to teach you to be a good kitten."

I look up at him. *Kitten?*

We stare at each other for what seems like an eternity. "Come on, Ellie. Don't keep me waiting."

"Are you going to hurt me?" I ask apprehensively.

"Not if you don't make me."

"What does that mean?"

"It means if you're obedient and give me what I want, no harm will come to you."

I hesitate for just a beat. Then on shaky legs, I stand. Kayne's mouth curves into salacious smile. He knows he has me. I haven't even removed my clothes yet and he's already licking his lips. *Asshole.* I unbutton the clasp at the nape of my neck, hating this dress for what it represents. I bought it to catch Kayne's attention. I wanted to dress as sexy and alluring as I could with high hopes he'd be attracted to me. Right now all I want is to shred the material into a million pieces. Maybe if I'd worn something different, less appealing, things would have turned out different.

I pull my arms through the sleeves, covering my breasts until the very last second. I can't do it.

"Ellie," Kayne urges firmly.

I take a deep breath, trembling, and then in one swift motion, like removing a Band-Aid, I slide the dress completely off. Kayne inhales, staring at me wondrously as I stand there completely naked.

"No panties, Ellie? You did want me."

"*Did* being the operative word." I try to cover my breasts with one arm and cross my legs. But in any position I am completely bare.

"That will change. By the time I'm done with you, you'll beg to come every time you see me."

He lifts something off the wall and it clinks. Then he opens the door.

"Come, Ellie." It's a command, like how you'd call a dog.

"No," I defy him.

"Fine." He glares irritated. "I'll come to you. But I promise that's the one and only time you'll ever say no. And the one and only time I'll ever acquiesce." It's a threat.

He steps inside the cell and I step back; the room feels like it's shrinking. I bump into the wall with Kayne crowding me. He's holding black leather things attached to chains.

"Perfect. Be a good girl and hold still." He reaches up and secures something around my neck. *A collar!*

"No!" I protest, but it's too late. I hear the click of a lock. It's thick and heavy and digs into my skin.

"Mmmm. Perfect fit." Then he grabs my wrists, even though I try to struggle. His strength is Herculean compared to mine. He cuffs them and binds my hands to the hook on the front of the collar.

I'm completely helpless, totally naked, and close to crying. This is a nightmare.

Just when I think it can't get any worse, he attaches a leash.

"Come, kitten."

The tears start to roll.

"I hate you," I expel, my voice thick with emotion.

"I know. But you'll get over that." He yanks the chain and we start walking. He totes me like a puppy through a hallway of cells. *What is this place?* Then up a dark winding staircase with sconces on the wall. When we emerge, I squint at the bright light. We're in a house. An opulent, spacious mansion.

If my fear and humiliation were on red alert before, they're at DEFCON 1 now. The house is eerily quiet but has a sexual undercurrent running through it that shocks you like electricity. There are nude statues everywhere depicting sexual acts and large portraits of naked women in compromising positions hanging on the walls. Dispersed throughout the large hall are curved gold leaf couches and oversized wingback chairs.

As I walk past one of the chairs, I notice hooks sticking out of the folds. What the fuck? We leave the large banquet hall and enter an open, spacious foyer with a grand staircase that has three tiers, pink and cream colored marble stairs, and an intricate black iron railing. The decor is magnificent; a dream home with a stark European flare. The arched doorways and humongous hand-blown glass chandelier reminds me of an expensive hotel or elegant casino.

I try to cover myself with my elbows as I walk stark naked through the enormous house. It's wrong. It's weird. And I know I'm in so much trouble. Kayne ascends the stairs with me in tow, never looking back. It feels like we are climbing forever, my naked skin hyperaware of every subtle draft. When we make it to the top of the never-ending staircase, Kayne leads me right, down a long hallway scattered with doors. It's dimmer than the rest of the house with a dark purple carpet and smaller chandeliers exactly like the one in the immense foyer. The corridor is mysterious with a sense of seductiveness. As we walk I hear muttered noises becoming louder and louder. My skin prickles. One of the doors is cracked open and I sneak a peek inside. I wish I hadn't. What I see shocks me. A woman chained with her hands above her head is being—I don't even know the right word to use—ravished, assaulted, violated by three men at one time. One is sucking her nipple, another has his head between her legs. The third is having sex with her from behind. My insides spin.

"What is this place?!" I cry, pulling at the restraints.

Kayne jerks me forward by the chain. "Your new home."

A daunting sense of dread takes over.

He finally stops at the last door on the end. He unlocks it with a set of keys and ushers me inside. If it were under any other circumstance, I would be in awe. The room is imperial. It looks like a queen's master suite. There's an enormous bed turned down with shiny gold sheets and a headboard made out of vining white iron and pink tufted satin. Decorative molding covers the walls and high vaulted ceilings, giving the decor a very Parisian feel. A large flat screen hangs directly in front of the bed and the armoire right next to it is impossible to ignore. It's stark white with huge ornately decorated doors.

But as magnificent as the space is, it's the semicircular adjoining room with large bay windows that's giving me palpitations. If this was a normal suite, I'd take it for a sitting room. But trust me when I tell you it's not. In its center is a table with thick leather straps and stirrups. A horror movie version of a gynecologist's exam table. Underneath it are several metal drawers. I stop myself from imagining what could be in them. A crop, a flogger, and a wooden paddle are hanging between each window on the wall. My stomach tightens. He's going to hurt me. I know it. I can feel it.

"This way." Kayne flicks the leash, leading me through another doorway into the bathroom. It's a large space with off-white marble floors, matching counters, and a large stone shower. There's also a clawed soaking tub so big you could swim in it. Kayne opens the glass door of the shower and turns a knob, spurring several shower fixtures to spring to life.

Then he strips down to nothing. "Look at me, Ellie."

I keep my eyes closed and my head turned as much as the collar will allow.

"I said look." He tugs the chain hard. "You need to start learning to obey commands."

That gets my attention. I open my eyes and gape at him. Not because he is gloriously naked in front of me. Because the words obey and command rattle my soul. I want to scream, I want to yell. But my emotions are choking me worse than the collar.

Kayne unhooks my wrists, and then unclasps the uncomfortable leather. I rub my sore skin. He then removes my new neck jewelry.

"In," he orders. But I don't move. I can't move. My head is spinning. He slaps me on the ass and I jump. *"In."*

"You hit me!" My eyes water from the sting.

"I'll do it again if you don't listen to me."

I escape immediately into the shower. Not that it's really an escape because Kayne steps in right behind me. I cower into the corner, trying to get as far away from him as possible. Only a world of wrong can happen now, with both of us naked and him looking at me with carnivorous want in his eyes.

"Turn around, put your hands against the wall." I never thought I would wish to be back in that cell. But cold and hungry is way better than being raped.

"Kayne. Don't," I beg, sounding pathetic. Where is my fight?

It's stinging your ass! Resist him, and he'll beat you!

"Now, Ellie." He grabs my arm and faces me away from him, shoving me against the wall. My palms smack against the light colored stone.

Then he juts my hips out and I fray at the seams. My breathing is heavy and my head is light all at the same time. I brace myself against the wall, trying to put my mind anywhere but here.

"I love your ass, Ellie." He smacks me again and I yelp. That smarts. Then he rubs my throbbing cheek. It feels wrong; him touching me.

The warm water rains down on my prickly skin as Kayne runs his hands up my back and over my shoulders. I shudder. Then I hear the pop of a cap. My insides jolt. I'm worse than a spooked cat.

The smell of eucalyptus fills the shower as Kayne begins to wash me, lathering my breasts, my stomach, my arms, and my backside. I hold my breath. I once would have killed for this man to touch me. Now that he is, all I do is cringe. He works his way between my thighs, and I instinctively squeeze them together.

"That's not going to keep me out. You need to get used to me touching you," he murmurs lasciviously into my ear.

"Why are you doing this?" I ask disgusted.

"I have my reasons."

"Want to share them with me?"

"All you need to know is that I want you, Ellie. I want your obedience, I want your submission, and I want your body." He skims my clit with one of his fingers and I jump.

"What the fuck are you waiting for then? Why are you fucking with my head?" I erupt, fear dragging me under.

Kayne chuckles. "Hot for me baby? Want me to take you right here? Think you can handle it?" He presses his body against mine.

I tremble from the inside out. My fright and rage getting the best of me.

"You're a bastard!"

"Name calling doesn't really do it for me." He smacks me again. *That fucking hurts!* "And I'm not in the business of raping women. That doesn't do it for me either. I want you to hand yourself over willingly. Submit. Until then, we'll just play."

"Play?"

"Mmmm hmmm." He goes back to rubbing my clit. "This is mine." He slips one finger inside me and I gasp, digging my fingernails into the tile.

"Who do you belong to, Ellie?"

"No one!"

"Wrong answer." He withdraws his finger. Half of me wants to scream, half wants to cry. "Stay," he commands. *I'm not a fucking dog!*

Kayne turns off the shower, steps out, and towel dries himself, all while I stand there naked and emotionally exposed. Then he opens a towel to me. "Come."

I scowl at him.

"Come, or I'll spank you again. And this time I won't stop." His eyes narrow.

I take a deep breath, trying to control the tears. This can't be happening. Reluctantly, I step out of the shower and into his waiting arms. He dries me off, not missing one part of my body. He touches it like he has license. Like he owns it.

Once I'm dry, Kayne lifts the collar from the floor.

"No." I instinctively step back, but Kayne catches my wrist.

"Yes." He pulls me forward with a dangerous look.

He fastens the collar around my neck and locks it. It's tight and uncomfortable. The chain that's still attached dangles between my naked breasts. I hate it. I hate the way it feels and what it signifies.

Kayne walks me back into the bedroom. There's a plate of food sitting on the modest-size round table underneath the large wagon wheel window that only has one chair.

"Go eat. I'll be back to put you to bed later."

"Don't I get any clothes?"

"Clothes?" He cocks an eye brow at me.

"Yeah, you know, shirt, pants, socks?" I want to spit. I can't just walk around naked in a collar. *Can I?*

Kayne cuts across the plush shag rug to the dresser on the opposite side of the room. He opens a drawer and pulls something out. Then he walks back to me and kneels. "Here." He holds up a sheer pair of panties.

"That's it?" I look down at him.

"That's it. Get used to being naked baby. That's how I want you twenty-four seven."

Twenty-four seven?

Kayne jerks my panties on, and then goes into the bathroom. A few moments later he emerges fully clothed and heads straight for the door.

"You have twenty minutes to eat, then bed. I'll be back." His tone is flat, almost detached.

The door clicks shut behind him, and I'm alone again, in yet another cell.

In a fit of desperation I attack the door, yanking on the handle with some sliver of hope it might open. Tears run down my cheeks. I'm a captive. Going to be forced to do things with a man I once obsessed over and now hate. I pull at the collar and scream. *This can't be happening!* It just can't. I have a family, I have a future. I have a life waiting for me beyond this room. I pound harder, yell louder. But it's no use. Deep down I know it. I can feel it. I'm his.

When my energy is depleted, I slump down onto the floor. I can't stop the tears from flowing as I lie there defeated. That's when Kayne returns. Has it been twenty minutes already?

He opens the door and it jams against my body. "Ellie, what the fuck?" He steps over me and into the room.

"Not hungry?" He takes notice of the untouched food.

"Fuck you," I spit.

"I hope so." He lifts my limp body off the ground. *Keep dreaming.* I will never give my body or my will over to him. "You're going to need your strength." He places me on the enormous bed that can sleep ten.

"For what?" I ask dejectedly.

"Me."

He picks up the end of the chain attached to the collar and locks it around one of the curves of the iron headboard.

"What the fuck!" I yank and pull.

"This is how you'll sleep. New puppies need to be chained up."

"I'm not a fucking puppy!" I erupt.

"No, you're right," Kayne muses. "You're more like a frisky little kitten." He runs one finger down my face the way you would pet a cat. I jerk my head away.

He jerks me back by the collar. Fucking thing. Rage burns a hole through my chest.

"You'll learn, kitten."

"I hate you."

"We've established that. We've also established that you'll get over it." He kisses me quickly on the lips. "Tomorrow we start."

"Start what?" I snarl.

"Obedience training."

AYNE

I LEAVE ELLIE'S ROOM WITH my emotions in a stir. I stand by the door and listen to her scream bloody murder for the second time tonight. Part of me hates myself for doing this. Part of me knows it's the only way.

Part of me can't wait to tie her up and dominate the fuck out of her. I'll have her begging. You just wait.

The only way to keep her safe is to turn her into the one thing I'm trying to protect her from. The last three days have been hell watching her waste away in that tiny cell. They would have been worse if I had to witness her at the mercy of Javier. I may have collared and chained her to the bed, but her screams would be blood-curdling if she were confined to his room. He'd have no sympathy for her pain or tolerance for her disobedience. He'd starve her, torture her, and leave her for dead. Fuck that. I may run an elaborate whore house, but no one has the right to treat another human being like that. Listen to me, righteous motherfucker. I'm the one who has a captive on the other side of this door.

But no one can know. No one can know I had any other reason for taking Ellie than to make her my slave. Not even Ellie. It would be too dangerous. Make me too vulnerable. Make her a target.

And I can't let that happen. There's too much at stake.

I leave Ellie to scream herself to sleep. With the lack of food and earlier outburst, I doubt she'll last much longer.

LLIE

SUNLIGHT BECKONS ME AWAKE.

My mouth is dry and my throat is sore. Where am I? Then I remember. The chain clinks as I move. I'm a prisoner. I pull on the collar and fiddle with the lock. Off. I just want it fucking off.

Suddenly the door opens and I instinctively huddle into a ball, naked and completely defenseless.

"Ah, you're up." A tall, nice looking man with turquoise eyes and a shock of blond hair saunters toward me. I recoil.

"There, there," he coos. Pulling on the chain once he reaches the bed. I resist him. "Aren't you a pretty thing? No wonder Kayne wanted you. Come here."

"No. Who are you?" I fight him.

"Jett." He yanks harder, forcing me closer to him. "I'm your keeper."

"I don't need a keeper. I need to go home!"

Jett grabs my face, ignoring me. He moves it around like he's inspecting me.

"Sweetheart, the only place you're going is into the shower."

"I took a shower last night," I say bitterly, recalling the way Kayne manhandled and spanked me.

"It's time for another. You also need to be groomed."

"Groomed! I'm not an animal!" I try to snap my head back.

Jett looks into my eyes, clutching my face tighter. "Technically you're owned, so you're the equivalent."

Tears threaten.

"Ellie. I will tell you this once. Cooperate with me or I will tie you down and spank you until you do."

"Is that my life now? Beating after beating?"

"It doesn't have to be. But you have to listen and do as Kayne and I say."

"Do I belong to both of you?" The words slice my tongue as they roll out of my mouth.

"No. You're just Kayne's. But I do have the authority to punish you if you don't behave." His pretty eyes flash with something dark. Jett looks like he belongs on a beach with a surfboard. But it's clear he's no laidback surfer.

"So, what's it going to be sweet thing? We can be friends or we can be enemies. It's up to you. Personally, I'd like to be friends. It will make things easier for everyone involved."

I only stare up at him. I can't bring myself to submit. It's not who I am, it's not who I was raised to be. After a few drawn out moments Jett nods, then pulls out a set of keys from his pocket and unlocks the padlock linking the chain to the collar. I just sit until he tells me to move. At this point I don't know what else to do. I don't want to get hurt.

"Bathroom?" he points. I get up and walk into the room. Covering as much of my nakedness as I can.

"Good girl," he says in a condescending tone as he walks behind me. I hate it. Once in the bathroom, he turns on the shower. "We'll groom you first, then breakfast."

"Groom?" I repeat curiously.

"Mmmm hmmm." He pulls out a table from the linen closet and opens it up.

"What's that for?"

"You'll see." He pulls the key ring out from his pocket and unlocks the collar, removing it from my neck. I immediately rub my sore throat. "In you go."

I step into the stall and allow the water to scald my skin. The temperature of my shower is about the only thing I have control over at the moment.

"Wash," Jett instructs. I stick my tongue out at him as I turn for the soap.

"I saw that," he says amused. I guess better amused than pissed off.

I wash my hair and my body slowly, elongating the shower as much as possible. The smell of eucalyptus engulfs my senses, but the calming scent does nothing to unwind the anxiety coiled around me.

"Done," Jett announces. He opens the door and turns the shower off.

"Hey!" I immediately jump and cover myself. He pulls my arms away from chest. "Get over the modesty. And get used to being naked."

"Why?"

"Because that's how Kayne wants you." He wraps me in a towel and dries me off. I feel like I'm losing all self-sufficiency.

"Why me?" I ask forlornly.

"He has his reasons." Jett works to dry my hair.

"I wish someone would share them with me."

"You don't need to worry about his reasons. All you need to do is what you're told."

"What if I can't be submissive? Then what?" I challenge.

"I don't think you want to know."

My lip quivers. "He's going to hurt me, isn't he?" An image of the table in the other room flashes in front of my face.

"Not if you listen."

"What does he want from me?" I demand with my emotions bubbling over.

Jett gives me an *I think you know* look. "Don't be naive, Ellie. It doesn't become you. You know exactly what he wants." *Your obedience, your submission, your body.* "You've been acquired as a sex slave."

"Don't use that word!" I scream with my head in my hands, tears bursting from eyes. The word slave sounds like nails being dragged down a chalkboard. "I can't do this. You have to let me go!" I sob.

"Shhh, Ellie." Jett wraps me in his arms. "You can and you will."

"Why?" I cry into his shoulder.

"Because—" Jett pulls away and looks into my eyes. I see compassion there. "Listen to me Ellie. You need to trust Kayne. I know that might be hard, but he's doing this for a reason."

"How can I trust him?" I ask with my universe in turmoil. "He puts a collar on me and forces me to walk around naked. And soon ..." I wipe my eyes. "Soon ... I don't know what's going to happen."

"The only thing I can tell you is things aren't always as they seem."

I search Jett's eyes. "What does that mean?"

He just shakes his head. "Trust Kayne."

Easy for him to say.

"Enough talk, Ellie. It's time to be strong. Lay on the table."

"What are you going to do?" I sniff.

Jett looks at me with an annoyed expression. "Here's your first lesson in submission. Don't ask questions, don't talk back, and do as you're told."

I frown.

"Now go, or I'll force you down and tie you to it."

His eyes tell me all I need to know: Don't fuck with me.

I lay on the table, naked with my hair still damp and my emotions spiraling out of control.

"Pull your knees up and spread your legs. Put your hands over your head." I do as he says, panting nervously.

"Breathe, Ellie."

"What are you going to do?" I ask again.

"Wax you." He smears warm sticky stuff all over my pubic hair. I flinch. He holds me still with firm hands. "Don't move."

Then he covers the smeared wax with strips of cloth. I breathe heavily, anticipating the pain.

"Have you ever had a Brazilian before?" Jett asks as he rips the first strip off.

"No!" I shriek as scalding pain burns my skin and tears run out of my eyes. God, will I ever stop crying?

Jett rips off strip after agonizing strip, until I am completely bare. Bare physically and bare emotionally. "Aloe," he says showing me a green blob of something on his fingers before he applies it to my sensitive skin. The cool gel eases the pain slightly, but not nearly enough. The way he handles me makes me feel like an object. Like my humanity is being stripped away layer by precious layer.

"Up you go." He takes one of my hands, and I stand, a little wobbly, on my feet.

"Turn around and rest your hands on the table," Jett instructs. "We're not done yet."

Dear God, what now? I reluctantly do as he says. Hating every second of this new life.

"Are you on any birth control?" he asks matter-of-factly.

"No, why?" I look over my shoulder. He's holding a syringe.

"Good." He stabs me in the ass.

"What is that?" I grit my teeth and wince as the needle penetrates my skin. How much more must I endure today?

"Depo-Provera," he informs me, and the realization as to why I need birth control hits home. This is really happening. I'm becoming Kayne's whore. I start to hyperventilate.

"Ellie, calm down." Jett rubs my back. "You need to eat." He takes my arm and leads me back into the bedroom. "Lie down, I'll be right back. Is there anything you're allergic to?"

"No," I cry into the pillow. My ass is sore, my vagina is throbbing, and I feel like a humiliated mess.

I don't know how long Jett is gone. But I'm still suffocating myself with the pillow when he returns.

"Time to eat." He pulls me up and forces me to sit at the small table where a silver dome is waiting for me. Jett lifts it to reveal scrambled eggs and buttered toast.

"Eat it. All of it. It will make you feel better."

I stare at the food with puffy eyes. As much as I don't want to eat, my stomach rumbles loudly, so I pick up the fork and slowly take a bite. It's good, really good, and still warm. I finish everything on the plate while Jett stands over me.

Once satisfied, he covers the dish then lifts the platter off the table.

"I'll be back later to get you ready." *Ready?* "Try to relax. You'll need your strength for Kayne tonight."

I look up at him callously.

"Retain that frame of mind, Ellie. Remember what I told you. Strong."

Then he leaves the room. I hear the lock click and my heart squeezes. I'm supposed to stay cooped up in here all day? I look around, taking in my jail cell. It's a room people like me only dream about—opulent and luxurious, with silk window treatments and expensive furnishings. I stare out the window at the rolling green hills. I'm high in the air with no escape in sight and nothing but trees and grass for miles. I see the future I worked so hard for slipping away. *I'm a slave.* Kayne's slave. Tears roll down my cheeks. But they aren't tears of sadness, they're tears of rage. I'll figure a way out of this mess.

I have to.

Or I'll die trying.

HOURS UPON HOURS ALONE IS a tad bit maddening.

I tried the television, but there was no cable. There was, however, a porno DVD. I shut it off immediately when I heard the moaning and saw a girl being fucked from behind. I tried some books on the shelves, but realized just as quickly it was all erotica. Titles like *Bound by Passion* and *Temptation* were all I could find. It's like he wants me hopped-up on hormones at all times.

My worst mistake was wandering into the adjoining circular room. I'm standing next to a table that reminds me of a torture device. The black cushions look unforgiving. The straps on the sides and on the stirrups are thick leather with silver buckles. They seem implacable. But the things that scare me the most are the whipping tools on the wall; a crop, a flogger, and a wooden paddle with a heart-shape cutout. I shiver with fear just looking at them.

The drawers under the table are full of sex toys. I can't begin to imagine what you do with some of these things. Vibrators of all different shapes and sizes. Small bullet looking things with chains on the end. Belts, handcuffs, and ball gags that remind me of muzzles. I shake just looking at them. When the door clicks, I jump, slamming the drawer shut. I walk quickly back into the bedroom as Jett appears. His aqua eyes are wide as he regards me.

"Exploring?"

I look down timidly. "I was bored."

"I see. Find anything that interests you?"

"No." I wrap my arms around my naked chest begrudgingly.

"There's an old saying. Don't knock it until you try it." Jett pulls my arms away from my body. "No hiding. Your body is beautiful, show it."

"I know an old saying too," I retort. "Easier said than done."

Jett chuckles. "Smartass. Come on, kitten. Time to go back on your leash."

Jett motions to the bed. Then he retrieves the collar and chain from the bathroom. I sort of hoped it was its final resting place.

Jett makes quick work of fastening the thick leather around my neck. The cold steel chain once again brushes between my breasts and dangles down to my knees.

"Stay," he says. Then walks over to the dresser and pulls out a pair of black see-through panties. I have déjà vu as he slides them on me. Underwear seems to be the only article of clothing I'm allowed to wear.

"On the bed, kitten. Kayne will be here soon." My heart rate quickens. I'm not sure I'm ready for this. I climb onto the huge opulent bed covered with rich, plush throw pillows.

"Remember what I told you. Behave. Listen to Kayne and you should be able to walk just fine tomorrow." I pale as he fastens the chain to the elaborate iron and tufted headboard. "See you in the morning, sweet thing."

He closes the door with a light click.

I'm alone again, chained to a bed like a scared puppy about to have her first obedience lesson with her new owner. What could this possibly entail? *Nothing good,* I conclude. I bring my legs up to my chest and curl into a ball, trying to cover up as much of myself as possible. I don't know how long I sit and just stare at the door. The waiting is almost as maddening as the anticipation of what's to come. Then the door clicks and my heart jumps into my throat. Kayne walks in to the room with an air of authority. His face is tight, his eyes are dark, and his presence is oppressive. I stare stoically as he approaches me like he's stalking a wounded animal. I pull my legs tighter to my body.

He's wearing black suit pants and a blood red dress shirt. His collar is open and his shirt sleeves are rolled up to his elbows. I swallow thickly. He's also holding something in his right hand.

"Evening, kitten," he says in an even tone. It's almost chilling. "How was your day?"

I don't respond.

Kayne narrows his eyes. "I asked how your day was, kitten. When I address you directly, you answer. Lesson one."

I stare him down with my defenses up.

"Kitten?" he goads.

"My name is Ellie."

"Your name is whatever I choose to call you. And right now, it's kitten." He grabs me by the collar and pulls me effortlessly across the silken sheets, drawing my face close to his. I pull at his hand as he nearly lifts me off the mattress. "We can do this my way or we can do it yours. I'll be fine with either. The end result will be the same."

I struggle against his grip, my knees barely grazing the smooth fabric underneath me.

With the collar choking me I spit out, "Boring. It was boring."

Kayne releases me, and I drop back down on all fours.

"There. Was that so hard?"

I stare up at him with hatred.

"Save your hostility, kitten. It doesn't intimidate me, and it will only make things worse for you."

He fondles one of my naked breasts. I cower away, but he pulls me closer.

"Time for your first lesson." He grabs my chin and forces me to look at him. "You only speak when you are directly spoken to. And even then it is yes Kayne, please Kayne, more Kayne, can I come Kayne."

I flinch in his grip. "Commands. Kneel. I expect you in this position every time I walk into the room. It doesn't matter where you are or what you're doing. You stop immediately and drop. Sit on your haunches, tuck your feet under your ass, splay your hands on your thighs and bow your head. Let me see."

"No," I snarl.

"No?"

"I will never kneel." My independence roars. I can't do this. I'm not submissive. I'm not a slave.

"Fine." In a flash he grabs me by the collar again and forces me forward. My face is hanging over the side of the bed, my ass is sticking straight up in the air. Then he hits me with the object in his hand. A rolled up newspaper. I cry out when it connects with my bottom. It's concealing a stick of some kind. I can't move in the awkward position as he hits me again. My ass stings painfully as he hits me a third time.

"Please stop!" I scream, and he hits me once more. Then he lifts me back up. Totally dominating my body with the control he has holding the collar.

"Are you ready to submit?" he asks authoritatively.

"Never!" I snap, even though my body is rebelling against my will. "You can beat me all you want. I don't care if you kill me! I'll never be yours!"

Kayne's dark gaze bores into mine. His strange, majestic eyes calculating. He lets go of the collar and I grab at my neck, only feeling the thick leather under my fingertips. He unlocks the chain from the bed. "I would never kill you. But I will break you. I'll give you one last chance to cooperate, Ellie." He winds the chain around his hand. "Kneel."

"Fuck off."

"Fine. We'll do it your way." He drags me off the bed. "Maybe a night with my clients is all you need. I'll string you up, gag you, and blindfold you. Then watch as they have their way with you. Just like you saw the other night."

Images of the naked helpless woman spring unbidden into my mind.

"Kayne, no!" I screech as I fight against him, thrashing my body as he pulls on the chain like I'm a disobedient puppy who doesn't want to go out in the rain.

"I gave you your chance, kitten." He has me almost out the door. I drop to my knees. "No, please," I beg with my forehead pressed against the ground. I would much rather kneel to him than be gang-banged and emotionally destroyed for the rest of my life. Tears stream down my face. I'm pathetic. Naked, on a leash, being commanded by a man who is going to use me as a living sex toy.

"Good girl. Now we're getting somewhere. That position is called drop. Get used to it. You'll be in it a lot. Don't move until I say so." I keep my head down as I hear his footsteps around me. He smacks my ass with the newspaper again and I cry out. The tears streaming harder now.

I whimper on the floor, my butt throbbing and my soul fractured. I stay in this drop position until my knees hurt and my back aches. Fucking prick.

"Very good, kitten. You can get up." I raise my head and look around the room. I find Kayne sitting behind me in the chair at the table. He looks relaxed with his legs spread and large hands resting on his thighs.

"Come," he says, crooking his finger at me. I move to stand.

"Crawl, kitten. Crawl to me."

I pause on all fours. He's being fucking serious.

"I'm waiting." His eyes are cold, hard.

I begin to crawl across the room, over the plush white rug, past the bed, to the chair he's sitting in under the large circular window. The night sky is dotted with stars, and the moon is full and bright behind him. Once I reach him I stare up, still on my hands and knees. He cracks a small smile. I want to spit on him. Then he leans forward and places a finger under my chin, forcing my face up to his.

"That fire in your eyes will dim. I promise you, kitten. I know it's hard. Giving up control. But I want you to understand house rules. Listen carefully, I'll only say this once. I tell you what to do, you say yes, Kayne. You will please me. End of story."

I remain quiet but glare at him callously.

"Kneel," he commands. My stomach rolls, my freedom fraying as I rise to my knees. I sit just the way he described. On my haunches with my hands splayed on my thighs. Right between his legs. An obedient pet. He groans approvingly. "My kitten." He leans forward and fondles both of my breasts. Skimming his thumbs over my nipples until they are straining and hard. I breathe rapidly. I don't want him to touch me, but my body responds involuntarily. The sensations networking straight to my burning core.

"You're so perfect, Ellie." He breathes hard as touches me. It seems my body isn't the only one involuntarily responding. The bulge in his pants is undeniable.

"Another command. On your back. Lay down, bend your knees, spread your legs and place your hands over your head. Do it. Now."

Kayne tracks my every move as I slowly lay on the floor and open my legs wide for him. I want to fight. I want to say no, but my stinging ass and the image of that woman from last night is a constant reminder of what will happen if I resist.

"Now we're getting somewhere."

He stares down at me for a very long time. His gaze feels heavy, and after what feels like forever, he gets up and walks into the semi-circular room with the table of torture. My anxiety spikes tenfold as I hear the opening and closing of drawers. I almost get up and dart into the bathroom, but Kayne returns before I can force my limbs to move. He stands above my mostly naked body. Two pairs of handcuffs dangling in one hand.

"You've been a good girl. Time for a treat." His breath is ragged as he drops to his knees. I squirm away, but he grabs my legs and fastens one handcuff to each ankle.

"Give me your hands." I don't move.

"Ellie." He says my name harshly. "Do you want me to turn you over and spank you instead? Pleasure or pain. Your choice. It doesn't matter to me either way. I like giving both."

He reaches over me and grabs my right hand, securing it to the handcuff on my right ankle.

"Kayne, please," I beg, as he repeats the motion with my left side. I'm bound.

Completely helpless.

No matter which way I move, the restraints act like marionette strings biting into my skin. Pulling one of my wrists up, my leg follows. Pull my ankle down, my arm gets yanked.

I'm gasping with fear.

Kayne hovers over me. My senses on overload.

I tremble as I stare up at him. His eyes are fierce, lustful, wanton, and unrepentant. I know exactly what he wants.

Me.

"Tell me you don't want me to touch you," he dares me.

"I don't want you to touch me." The words flow, but there's no fire behind them.

"Are you sure, kitten?" He massages me over the thin fabric of my panties.

"Yes." *No.*

"I think you do." He slides my panties over and I squirm harder in the restraints. My heartbeat palpitating. The metal clinking as I shift. He circles his finger gently over my clit. I close my eyes trying to reject his touch. When he sinks his finger inside me, I gasp.

"You're so fucking wet for me." He slides his finger in and out, every so often spreading the slickness through my folds. My body tightens and aches, but I fight the urges he's bringing forth. I will not come. I will not give this man my pleasure. Kayne works his hand faster, insistent. The sensations build and I clench my fists, fighting the orgasm he's demanding. As if aware I'm resisting, he simultaneously rubs my swollen clit with his thumb while he fingers me relentlessly. I moan uncontrollably.

No! No! No!

Yes! Yes! Yes!

Just before I explode, Kayne removes his hand, and I nearly weep.

"Not yet, kitten. I didn't give you permission." If I wasn't bound, I'd slap him. "I tell you when to come. Understand?" I'm panting beneath him, burning a hole through his head with my stare. He smirks arrogantly at me. Then leans down and whispers, taunting me, "Ask my permission."

"No."

"You'll regret that." There's amusement in his eyes. This is all just a game. With no warning at all, he rips my panties. The thin material tearing right in two. I jerk, the metal cuffs cutting into my skin. He skims his tongue down the inside of one of my thighs, and then licks a slow hot drag over my slit.

"Fuck, you taste so good. Like cupcakes," he pants. His specific description isn't lost on me. A simple cupcake is how all this began.

Kayne swirls his tongue over my heated flesh, nipping and sucking, driving me mad. My body is bowing in ecstasy, my mind trying to reject the pleasure. If I give in, what will that mean?

Kayne stabs his tongue into my entrance, and I moan loudly. Oh God, an orgasm is looming; hot and fast.

"Ask permission." His hot breath skims against my overly sensitive skin. I resist. Fighting him the only way I can. With my will.

He sinks a finger deep inside me and sucks on my clit, bringing me right to the breaking point. My heart is hammering and so is my core.

"Ask permission. The way I told you," he orders.

I'm writhing in my restraints so hard I know I'm going to have marks, but I need to disperse the buildup somehow. I can barely breathe as he dangles me over the edge again and again, yet another form of torture to get me to obey. I feel the slightest caress of my orgasm, and I fracture, unable to withstand the torment anymore. "Please, Kayne, may I come!" I scream out.

He chuckles. *That fucking bastard.*

"Yes, you may, kitten." He attacks me, fingering me swiftly while lavishing my clit. I splinter in every direction, my climax shredding me to pieces. I pull on the handcuffs—the pain as potent as the pleasure—as I writhe and moan. When the quake dissipates, I'm left limp on the floor, breathing raggedly and close to tears. Kayne brushes his face against my inner thigh, smearing my arousal all over my skin.

"Good, kitten," he patronizes, rising to his knees, unbuttoning his shirt slowly. I stare up at him dazed. Inch by inch, he bares his chest, then tosses his shirt on the floor. He's sculpted and lean, a demonic perfection. Several tattoos adorn his body, a compass on his left pec, barbed wire dripping with blood around his arm, and a quote written across his rib cage. 'A certain kind of darkness is needed to see the stars.'

When he starts to unbuckle his belt, I tense. He doesn't say a word as he sheds the rest of his clothes, but the energy in the room is unmistakable. It's thick with sex and lust.

He said he wouldn't rape me. He said he wouldn't rape me. I repeat the mantra trying to stay calm. Once he's as bare as me, Kayne hovers over my bound body, bracing his hands on each side of my head.

"Who owns you, Ellie?" He stares down at me with his majestic eyes.

"You do," I answer reluctantly.

"That's right." He kisses my jaw softly.

"What do I want?"

I swallow hard. "My obedience, my submission, my body." The words barely come out as a whisper.

"Right again." He brings his mouth to mine, skimming his tongue along my lower lip.

"Can I fuck you, Ellie?"

"No, Kayne." I fight back the tears.

"Fine." He kisses me tenderly. Rolling his tongue against mine, allowing me to taste myself on his lips.

His change in demeanor is unexpected. I don't understand it one bit. My defenses stand at attention. Kayne then shifts, grabbing his erection with one hand and moving down to take one of my nipples into his mouth. Swirling his tongue against me, he strokes himself, lightly at first and then more urgently. As his jerks become stronger, so does the pressure of his mouth, nipping and sucking my nipple as he works himself to a climax. There's nothing I can do. There's no place I can go tethered beneath him. He bites my nipple as he comes, sending a shock of pain straight through my body. I strain, helpless as he comes on my stomach. His groans vibrating against my breast. He releases my abused nipple once he's finished. It's red and swollen.

"Mine," he declares victoriously against my lips, like he just marked his territory. Then he kisses me hard and unapologetically, making my head spin.

When he's finished with my mouth, I drop my head to the side, exhausted. My emotions are a shitstorm inside of me. There are too many to even process at the moment. So I just shove them all away.

Kayne admires his handiwork on my abdomen for a few perverted seconds before he unlocks the handcuffs. Once removed, I immediately stretch my arms and legs. They're stiff. He rubs my ankles then my wrists, kissing the inside of each one softly.

"Go clean up, kitten."

I jump to my feet and disappear into the bathroom, desperate to be alone. I grab a hand towel off the rack and run it under some warm water. When I look into the mirror, what I see startles me. There are red rings around my wrists, my hair is a mess, and my cheeks are flushed. With the collar around my neck and ejaculation on my stomach, my lip quivers uncontrollably as I wipe away Kayne's remnants. I discard the towel on the floor then grab another and clean between my legs. I feel so odd—disconnected, alone, abused—light and heavy all at the same time. I don't understand what's happening.

I prolong going back into the bedroom. I wish I could escape, just hurl myself right out the window. I spy the door to my freedom. It's visible from the bathroom. I wonder idly if it's locked. Could I make a run for it before Kayne grabs me? Where would I go if I made it out alive; collared, chained, and completely naked?

"Ellie?" Kayne calls, pulling me out of my reverie. My legs start moving before I can process what I'm doing. I bolt to the door and grab at the handle, jiggling it for dear life. It opens!

"Son of a bitch!" I hear Kayne bark as I escape down the dark hallway, sprinting toward the staircase. Just as I reach the first landing on the stairs I hear Kayne behind me. I keep my eyes on the front door as we both battle downwards, me strenuously trying not to tumble and fall. I jump the last five steps and hit the foyer floor with a thud, managing somehow to remain on my feet and keep oxygen pumping through my lungs. I dart across the cold marble with my heart beating out of control. When I reach the front door, I haul it open, even though the fucking thing weighs a ton. Just as I feel the cool breeze of outside, the door slams closed.

"No!" I scream as Kayne throws me over his shoulder, kicking the air and punching his back.

"You're a fast little thing. I'll give you that." He smacks my naked, vulnerable ass.

"Oww!" My whole body jolts as the hard slap echoes around the opulent foyer.

"You're going to pay for that, kitten." He huffs up the stairs in bare feet and boxer briefs.

"Kayne, no!" I squirm with tears threatening.

The trek back to my cell is a terrifying one. Kayne doesn't say a word as I dangle over his shoulder, fighting for my life. Once back inside, he marches straight into the circular room with the table of torture.

"Kayne!" I cry.

"You brought this on yourself, kitten." He grabs something off the wall. I nearly go slack from the stress. The only thing keeping my body moving is the spasms of fear.

Kayne tosses me on the bed face down with me begging and pleading, and holds me there by my collar. "Don't do this. You don't have to do this!"

He ignores me as he positions my body; my feet spread on the floor, my chest pressed into the mattress. My behind exposed for the spanking.

"Kayne please! I'll be good!" I implore one last time.

"You're goddamn right you will."

Smack!

He hits my bottom with something hard and the sound rings out through the room. "Ouch!" I yell.

Smack!

"Please! Please!" I beg some more as the object lands straight across my behind.

"You were a bad girl, kitten. You need to be punished. That's how it works around here."

Smack!

Smack!

Smack!

He paddles my ass continuously until I'm choking with tears.

"Please stop!" I fight fruitlessly against him. His grip on my collar impenetrable. My behind on fire.

"What I really want to know, is where do you think you were going to go butt naked and collared?"

Smack!

"Anywhere is better than here! I'd rather be lost in the wilderness!"

"You think so, huh?"

Smack!

"Yes!" I screech.

One more immobilizing hit, then he stops, with me heaving for air. I hear the object fall to the floor.

Kayne yanks at my collar, flipping me over, and then crawls on top of me. My tiny frame nothing more than a weightless rag doll to him. He pins my sore wrists to the mattress with a tight grip, bringing his face an inch from mine. His eyes are wild and scary as hell. My tender butt screaming in agony, pressed against the bed.

"Don't try that shit again," he snaps. "There are monsters way worse than me on the other side of that door. The next time you think about escaping, do it at your own risk."

I stare back at him with choppy breaths, tear-soaked cheeks, and a stinging behind. I have no response. He made his point. I broke the rules; he showed me who's boss.

"You're mine now, Ellie. Just accept it." He lingers over me for a few long beats, our eyes locked, our breathing labored. A zap of something rousing passes between us in that moment. My heart flutters and so does my pussy. Traitorous body.

I hate him. I hate him. I hate him, I remind myself.

"Have you learned your lesson?" he asks still restraining me.

I nod.

"Answer correctly."

My lip quivers. "Yes, Kayne." The words barely leave my mouth.

"Good girl. If I let you up will you behave?"

I nod again, silently. My eyes still locked on his.

Kayne pushes himself off me with a huff.

You're mine now, Ellie. Just accept it.

I'll never accept I belong to him. I belong to no one. Do what you want to this body, hold it captive, beat it, pleasure it. But my mind he can never have. It's the one thing I can still control. The one place he can't penetrate.

"Time for bed." He jerks my leash, forcing me higher on the luxurious bed. I look down and catch a glimpse of what he used to beat me. The wooden paddle with the heart shape cut out. Kayne locks the end of the chain to the white vining iron in the center of the headboard with the padlock. The click pierces through me. It's my reminder I'll never be free.

"Lay down," he orders.

I stretch my body out, placing my head on one of the golden pillows. The satin sheets are a welcoming cold against my heated skin. I'm so tired, completely drained, and totally defeated.

"Listen to me, Ellie, you need to behave," Kayne reiterates. "I'd much rather shower you with pleasure than torture you with pain." He runs his thumb across my bottom lip. "But I'll do what I have to do to make you submit."

He bends and kisses my naked shoulder. The gesture is almost sweet. It makes no sense to me at all. A minute ago he was pummeling my ass. This man is a walking enigma. "Get some sleep."

All I can do is watch as he turns and heads for the door.

"Till tomorrow." He looks back at me with infiltrating blue eyes. Eyes that promise, eyes that threaten. My emotions feel like they're about to capsize.

When the door clicks, I let it all loose. The frustration, the sadness, the emptiness, the rage; sobbing inconsolably in the dark, desperate for slumber to take me.

I BEAT THE CRAP OUT of the punching bag.

My frustration level has reached max capacity. All I keep picturing are Ellie's sad eyes and abused behind. Over and over, I hear the sounds of the strikes ring out.

Smack!

Smack!

Smack!

Foreign sensations swim through my veins, like a straight shot of adrenalin. A euphoric high and a debilitating low.

"A little late to be training?" I hear Jett's voice behind me.

I slam the bag. "Never a bad time to train."

"What was all the commotion earlier?" He comes to stand where I can see him. The gym is dark except for the small light over the boxing ring and heavy bags.

"Ellie and I had a disagreement." I jab with my left then uppercut with my right.

"About?" He drags out the word.

"About whether the wilderness is a dangerous place or not." I kick the bag, and it swings left.

"Excuse me?" Jett raises his eyebrows.

I hit the bag in succession until my biceps hurt. "She tried to run. I punished her." I slam the bag square in the middle.

"Run? Where?"

"The door was unlocked. She made it all the way to the foyer.

She's freakin' quick. She had me sprinting." I catch myself smirking. Jett notices too.

"Bit more of a challenge than you expected, huh?"

"Yeah, you can say that." I concentrate on hitting the black bag, trying to avoid all eye contact with Jett.

"She gave you a run for your money? That's why you're in here punching a defenseless heavy bag at three am?"

I glare at Jett. So much for avoiding eye contact. He's fishing. I hate it when he fishes. I wish he would just let me punch out my emotions and be done with it. But no. Jett believes in talking. Getting your feelings off your chest and all that kumbaya crap. He thinks he's my personal fucking shrink and has been analyzing me since the day we met. *Skinny prick.*

"No, I knew she wouldn't get far," I tell him point blankly.

"So what's the issue?"

"No issue. Can't a man just work out in the middle of the night?"

"A man? Yes. You? No."

"Jett!" I holler as I punch. "I don't want to talk about it."

"Do you remember the last time you didn't want to talk about something? A very innocent fishing boat was blown up."

I stop mid punch. "I take no responsibility for that. The pin on the grenade popped by itself."

"Sure it did." He crosses his arms and looks at me like I'm full of shit. Maybe I am, maybe I'm not.

"Besides, better the fishing boat than us. Right?"

"Yes," he agrees.

"Damn straight." I clam up and go back to slamming the bag. Jett just stands there eyeing me.

When I take a moment of reprieve, he strikes.

"So nothing's bothering you?" the calculating motherfucker questions again.

"Yes, something's bothering me. You." I kick the bag, the frustration blistering under my skin. *I don't want to talk!*

"I always bother you, it's what I live for. And I'll pester you all night until you spill. I don't want another explosive catastrophe."

"Jett," I warn, crackling like a live wire. He needs to lay off.

"Kayne!" he shouts shoving the black bag in my face.

My emotions burst. "I punished her okay! I picked up a goddamn paddle and beat her ass!"

Jett pauses, looking at me funny. "And that's bad because?"

"Because I liked it!" I hit the punching bag so hard my knuckles crunch. Fuck!

"Oh?" He studies me. I growl at him as I rip off my boxing gloves. "What has you conflicted? You've punished women before."

"I've punished a *willing* submissive before. Ellie is different," I clarify.

"She's your slave. You treat her as such. She disobeyed. You delivered the consequences. That's how it works. You knew this when you took her. Yes, she's different, but that's the harsh reality."

"I don't want to become the thing I'm fighting against." I toss the gloves on the ground.

"You won't," Jett says simply. I'm glad one of us is convinced. "Warrior mindset, my friend. Ellie got caught in the crossfire and now you have to protect her by any means possible. Don't overthink it. It will only drive you mad. Just remember, your hand may be firm, but Javier's is deadly. And if you like it, so be it." He shrugs. "Our business is stressful. Being with her is a release. Give her some time, she'll come around."

"You sure about that?" I respond skeptically as I unravel the tape from my hand.

"I am. I've been training girls a long time. Her biggest hang-up is perception. The taboo lifestyle. Break down the barriers of belief and she'll be eating out of your hand."

"I'm trying." I drop my head, concentrating on the rivulets of sweat dripping down my chest.

"Keep it up. She's strong, but you're Master."

"What if she ends up hating me in the end?" I look up at him with just my eyes.

"What if she ends up loving you?" he counters.

"I don't for one second believe that will happen," I scoff.

"You never know. People can surprise you. Ellie never saw you coming."

"That's because I'm trained to be invisible."

"Well you're not transparent anymore. Make her believe what she has to for now. It's for her own good."

I groan. "I'm definitely going to hell."

"I'll be right there with ya, brother. Wearing a hat and sunscreen." He slaps me on the shoulder.

"You're a pain in my ass, you know that?"

"Yup. Someone has to be." Jett glances at his watch and grimaces. "Speaking of pains in the ass."

"Javier?"

"Yes," he seethes. "I don't like the way he's treating the girls. Especially Spice. He's way too rough."

"Warrior mindset, my friend," I throw his words back at him. Jett glares, then slugs me.

ELLIE

THE SUNLIGHT WAKES ME UP.

I'm still in the same position I was lying in when I fell asleep. On my side, hugging the pillow, chained to the bed.

My emotions feel like they've been put in a mixing glass and shaken up. I don't know what to feel, so I choose nothing at all.

I hear the door click, but I don't move. Kayne said I was supposed to kneel every time he came into the room. *Well fuck him*, my subconscious screams. My body, on the other hand, trembles knowing I'll be subjected to punishment if I disobey.

"Morning, sweet thing." I see Jett hovering over me in my peripheral vision.

"Go away," I say petulantly, squeezing the pillow tighter.

"Feeling a little used and abused this morning?"

"Yes!" I yell distraught. I'm not doing a very good job at reining my emotions in. So much for not feeling anything.

"I heard you tried to make a great escape."

"*Tried* being the operative word," I talk into the pillow.

"Didn't go so well, did it?" he mocks.

"Ask my ass, it'll tell you. I hate him."

"Rough night," he muses. I groan in response. I want to punch him in his patronizing mouth.

Jett pulls on my shoulder, rolling me over onto my back. I wince as my tender behind makes contact with the mattress. "It wasn't all bad, was it?" His aqua eyes are wide and sparkling.

I look at him like he's a loon. "He spanked me, hit me with a newspaper, and made me crawl around on all fours. Then he handcuffed me ..." I stop right there.

"Handcuffed you and did what?" Jett probes salaciously.

I stay silent with tears welling in my eyes.

"Made you feel good?" he questions. "Made you come?"

"*Made*. That is exactly the word," I growl.

"And feeling good is a problem because?"

"It's not the fact he made me feel good. It's the fact he treats me less than human. That he forced me!"

"Maybe he's trying to liberate you."

"Maybe that's utter and total horse shit!"

"We can argue the maybes all day. Bottom line, you came and you liked it."

"It's empty," I dispute furiously.

"Sex slave," Jett reiterates. "Power, ownership, pleasure."

I nearly burst into tears.

"Keep your eye on the prize sweetheart. Please him, and he'll please you. It doesn't have to be any more complicated than that."

"It goes against everything I know."

"Then maybe you need to learn a few new things." Jett shrugs.

"And I should let Kayne teach me?" I sneer.

"You said it, I didn't."

I curl my lip at him.

"Come on. Get up. A shower will make you feel better. Then I'm going to pretty you up." He hits my leg good-naturedly.

"Pretty me up?"

"Yes." He pulls the key ring that holds my freedom out of his pocket and unlocks the collar. Once off, I immediately rub my neck. That thing is restrictive as fuck. "This manicure has died and gone to hell." He lifts my hands, pointing out my chipped pink polish.

I begrudgingly roll off the bed. My ass is so sore. I curse Kayne with each step I take—*fucking bastard, asshole, shithead, douchebag*. As Jett turns on the shower, I catch a glimpse of my battered behind in the mirror, and gasp. It's beet red with flesh-colored hearts all over my butt cheeks. "Oh my God."

Jett looks at me through the mirror and smirks. "Kayne spanked you with love."

"I don't think he's capable of love," I bitterly retort.

"Of course he is. Everyone is capable of love."

"He's a monster."

"Maybe, but even beauty loved the beast."

"I'm not living a fairy tale. I'm living an American horror story."

Jett shrugs. "It's whatever kind of literature you make it. If you believe it's a horror story, it is. If you believe it's a dark erotic romance, it is. The choice is yours. The mind is a powerful thing."

I look at him like he's crazy.

"Just trying to help," he states.

"It's not working," I respond flatly.

He rolls his eyes. "No more chitchat. In you go." Jett ushers me into the steaming shower, and as soon as I step under stream, I jump. "It hurts," I whine as the running water hits my abused bottom. It feels like tiny needles stabbing me.

"It's supposed to. It's a reminder of who you belong to and what happens when you disobey. Makes you think twice about running again, huh?"

I stick my tongue out at him. It's the only rebellion I have left.

"Wash, Ellie," Jett instructs curtly.

I do as I'm told. Delicately. Every movement hurts. Once I'm done with the most torturous shower of my life, I dry off carefully. Jett tries to have me sit on the folding table, but that's just not happening. My butt is way too sore. Instead, I stand as he blow dries my hair with a round brush making it smooth. Good thing he's a foot taller than me. After that, he opens a drawer and retrieves two bottles of nail polish. A light peach colored one and a red.

"Which?" he asks.

"You're giving me a choice?"

"Yes. I'm not your owner. I have no interest in dominating you."

I survey the bottles, debating carefully. "Which do you think he'll like?"

Jett cocks an eyebrow at me.

I purse my lips. "I don't want to pick the wrong color and displease him. My ass would like to avoid another beating," I clarify.

Jett shakes the peach color. The bottle jingles. "He won't care. Trust me. He likes anything when it comes to you."

I stare at Jett quizzically. He just smiles and starts removing my chipped polish.

"How long have you known Kayne?" I inquire tactfully as he carefully paints my nails. I don't pretend to believe I have a friend or ally in Jett. But he doesn't come off as threatening as long as I behave. He's shown compassion, and even though I don't trust him completely, it doesn't mean I can't pump him for information.

Jett flicks his eyes up at me. Then starts on a second coat. "A while."

"What's a while?"

"Years."

"How did you meet?" I ask, my gaze jumping between his face and my hand.

"Mutual friends," he says flatly.

"How did you start working *here?*" I don't really even know where here is. I just know Kayne has 'clients' and 'women' who he keeps captive and strings up for their pleasure.

Jett scoffs. "I don't work for him. I work with him. Don't confuse my duties. I may not be the face of the company, but I do my fair share. Actually, I do more."

"What's the 'company' specifically?" It's obviously more than just tequila. "What is this place exactly?"

"The less you know the better." He sidesteps my question.

"Jett, please," I beg with big puppy dog eyes. Hey, if I am going to be compared to a pet, I might as well use the goods. "Tell me something."

He groans under his breath, hesitant to talk. Once he finishes painting my pinky finger with the shimmery peach, he looks up at me with an entertained expression.

"I have a feeling you are going to give Kayne a run for his money in more ways than one." He shoves the brush back into the bottle, and then huffs. "It's a whore house, Ellie. An upscale brothel. We keep women here for pleasure."

"How many women?" My eyes widen.

"A good amount. And I'm responsible for their well-being. All of them."

"Are they all locked up like me?" My voice strains at the image of dozens of women chained to a bed.

Jett looks at me like he's trying to dance around words. "No. They aren't locked up like you."

"They're not? It's just me then?"

Jett nods.

"Why?"

"Because you're special and that's all you need to know."

"Because I'm Kayne's?" I speculate.

"Now you're learning."

I frown. This shit's fucked-up.

Jett rests his hands gently on my shoulders. "I will tell you this one thing about me. I care about each and every one of them. Including you."

KAYNE

I WAIT OUTSIDE ELLIE'S ROOM.

I don't know for how long, because time seems to stand still.

I'm leaning against the wall off to the side, so Jett doesn't notice me immediately when he exits.

"How is she?" I ask as he locks the door. He jumps, snapping his head in my direction.

"Must you lurk?" he scowls.

"Yes. It's what I do. How is she?" I reiterate.

"A little upset, feeling abused, but she'll be okay. This is hard for her. She doesn't understand."

"We agreed that was the best way."

"I still believe it is. But if you're worried, go in and see her."

"You know I can't do that. I have to keep my distance. It's safer for everyone involved."

"I know that too." He puts the key ring holding Ellie's protection and freedom back in his pocket.

"Just make sure ..." I falter, not exactly sure what I'm trying to say. "Make sure—"

"She's taken care of?" Jett answers astutely.

I nod with stern eyes. I haven't been able to think of much else since Ellie was carried into this house. Last night felt like an injection into my veins. I didn't think I could do it—command someone against their will—but it came easier than expected. Fighting her, overcoming her, watching her slow descent into submission. Then tasting my sweet, sweet victory in the end—it changed something in me. And I want more. So much more that I'm counting the seconds until I can go back in that room again.

"It's what I'm here for," he reminds me.

"It's not the only thing you're here for." I punch him in the arm. Don't let his skinny ass fool you. Jett may spend a majority of his time with women, but he can throw down with the best of them. I know, because I fucked with him once. *Once*. The first time I met Jett I couldn't understand what he was doing with a bunch of hooligans like me. He was quiet and reserved and when he looked at you, those aqua eyes felt like they were digging under your skin. At least that's how it felt to me. I didn't like it, and I made it known—I threatened to stab them out. That toothpick motherfucker actually got in my face. He scored a point for formidability. I'm half a foot taller than him, double his weight and muscle mass. But it didn't matter. The minute I lunged at him, he took out my knee, quick as a jackrabbit. Dirty little shit. I ended up on my back with Jett's hand around my throat. For a puny guy, he has a death grip. It was my first lesson in don't judge a book by its cover. I was put on my ass by someone I would normally be able to knock into next week.

It took a little while, but Jett and I finally cleared the air. My ego was bruised and so was my knee, but he never stopped pushing—for some reason he wanted to be friends *with me*. That was a tough concept. I was a loner. Still sort of am I guess. I didn't have the most favorable upbringing; I bounced from foster home to foster home my entire life. Trust is hard to come by when you're verbally and physically abused, starved and locked in closets at seven years old. Most of the time it felt like I was living with a wild pack of wolves. Everyone out for themselves, survival of the fittest. And even though Jett grew up with a loving mother and stable home, his life wasn't much easier. He was a target; a black sheep because of the business his family was involved in. Growing up he fought for his life every day. In and out of hospitals, being treated for concussions and broken bones, after seven guys would gang up on him after school, smashing bottles over his head or breaking two or three of his fingers.

Seven to one? Those are some seriously fucked-up odds.

We had torture in common, and the same torment in our eyes. Except he was the trusting human and I was the untamed animal. He definitely helped shape the man I am today. He taught me about discipline and control. He opened my trust with loyalty, my mind with books, and my body with women. I was a virgin until I was nineteen. No lie. When I said I had trust issues, I wasn't kidding. Especially when it came to women. Having your birth mother promise to come back and save you from the hell you're living in, and then never hear from her again kind of fucks with a little boy's head. So much so it ripples into adulthood.

Jett introduced me to the BDSM lifestyle and was my mentor in all aspects of sexual exploration and dominance. He is not just a business partner or good friend. He's my brother, and the only true family I've ever had.

"Speaking of other things," Jett hints. "Where is our Mexican house guest?"

"Slithering around the mansion like the snake he is." I have eyes on him at all times. I know where he goes and whom he's with, making sure he doesn't slither within a mile of Ellie's room. He asks about her every night.

"How's your whore Kayne?"

I ignore him.

"When she's ready I want a taste," he antagonizes me.

Drop fucking dead, *I want to say. Instead, I bite my tongue till it bleeds.*

"What's mine is mine," is my only reply.

"Has he indicated when the meeting with El Rey will take place?" Jett inquires.

"No. He's still feeling us out. He's not stupid." I cross my arms. "We just have to go on like normal and hope he finds everything kosher."

"Well I hope he hurries up, and then slithers right into some oncoming traffic."

"If everything goes as planned, amigo, he will." We bump fists.

ELLIE

MY OBEDIENCE TRAINING HAS CONTINUED the last five nights. It's always the same. Kayne comes to me as soon as the sun goes down.

He feeds me dinner with his fingers while I kneel between his legs. That's why there's only one chair at the table. He quizzes me with commands, making me roll over and sit up repeatedly. He forces me to lay down at his feet to rest. When I don't obey or move quickly enough, he punishes me.

At times he's ruthless. Other times he's tender. Regardless of his mood, the night always ends the same. He ties me up and makes me come, afterwards asking if he can fuck me. When I refuse, he jerks off and marks me. He allows me to clean up then puts me to bed.

This is the vicious circle my life is becoming. Alone all day, misused at night. I'm nothing more than a pet to play with.

I hear the door click, and I immediately jump to my knees. He's training me whether I want to admit it or not. My body reacts in spite of my brain's objections.

"Evening, kitten." He scratches me under my chin. "How was your day?"

"Boring." I've learned the hard way he wants an honest answer to this.

"That's a shame. We'll have to do something to make up for that. Bend over I want to spank you."

"Kayne, why?" I protest, and instantly know I fucked up. Shit.

He shakes his head at me, vastly disappointed. "That was a test kitten, and you failed. Miserably."

"I'm sorry," I immediately respond.

"Me too. But not really," he gloats. He likes hurting me. The other night he chained me to the bed by the collar. Strategically placing it high enough so I was strained on all fours. Then he proceeded to spank me until I cried. Immediately after, he laid down, put his head between my legs and forced me to come. I was a limp nothing by the time he was done.

"Come, kitten. I'm going to teach you a lesson that will stick tonight."

I balloon with fear. I watch, removed, as he unlocks my chain then drags me into the circular room. The one with the table of torture. We've never been in here before. I know tonight is going to be bad.

"Kayne, please," I beg as he positions me between the stirrups of the table. He turns me around, smacks me hard on the ass then fastens each of my wrists in the straps. He's so quick, and they're so tight, the tears form before I even realize what's happening.

"You don't have to do this." I tug, bent over.

"You need to learn to do as I say, without question, without hesitation." He kisses my shoulder softly, sliding my hair over to one side.

"I'll be good. I'll behave," I whimper.

"I know you will once I'm through with you. I'm going to quiz you so you don't mess up again." He squeezes my stinging behind. I think it's been permanently stained red. "Then I'm going to make you come so hard you'll pass out."

My breathing is ragged, but as fearful as I am, the thought of Kayne's mouth on me makes me instantly wet. My body altogether loves him and hates him. The past few days have broken down so many barriers it's becoming harder and harder to refuse him. The things he can make me feel, the pleasure he can dispense, is unequivocal. And he's only just used his fingers and tongue. I can't begin to imagine what he can do with his body. He wants inside me. It's no secret. But he's never forced himself on me, or forced me to touch him. It's bizarre and maddening all at the same time; it's the ultimate mind game. Because he knows the moment I willingly surrender, I'll truly be his. Irrevocably.

Kayne peels the white lacy panties Jett dressed me in down to my thighs.

My head spins.

I can't see behind me, but I hear the crack against his hand from whatever object he's chosen to use.

"Let's review." He walks in front of me holding the crop, his eyes a smoldering blue. My breathing slows. He positions the end of the crop under my chin and lifts my face. "I will ask you a question. You will provide me with the correct answer."

"And you won't hit me?"

"No. You're getting spanked regardless. But as soon as you answer all the questions correctly, the spanking will cease."

I quiver. Seeing the crop in his hand is terrifying. This is so bad.

He vanishes from my sight and the tears spill.

Whack! He hits me without any warning and I cry out. It stings and bites my bare skin all at the same time.

"Who owns you, Ellie?"

"You do," I answer rapidly.

"Scream, kitten, so the whole house hears. I want everyone to know who owns you."

Whack!

"You do!" I scream like he ordered me to.

Whack!

"When I tell you to kneel, what do you say?"

"Yes, Kayne," I yell.

Whack!

"When I tell you to lie down and open your legs, what do you say?"

"Yes, Kayne." I suck in a deep breath.

Whack!

"When I tell you to bend over so I can spank you, what do you say?"

"Yes, Kayne!" I choke out through sobs.

Whack!

"What do I want from you, Ellie?"

"My obedience."

Whack!

"And?"

"My submission," I cry uncontrollably.

Whack!

"And?"

"My body," I wheeze, my legs nearly giving out.

I hear Kayne drop the crop then feel him wrap his arms around me delicately from behind.

"Shhhh, baby." He kisses my hair as I sob. "You did so good."

I tremble in his arms. My face is soaked and I swear my backside is broken and bleeding. My ass feels so raw. I hate him more in this moment than I have ever hated anyone in my entire life.

He holds me securely, raining soft kisses all over my face and neck until my sobs taper off. It doesn't happen quickly. When I'm calm, he reaches over and opens one of the drawers beneath the table. I watch distantly as he pulls out a tiny silver bullet with a chain attached to the flat end.

"I'm going to make you come so hard," he rasps, then brings the plug to my lips. I shiver, half with fear, half with lust. "Open." I open my mouth. "Suck." I close my lips around the cool metal and do as I'm told. When he tugs on the chain, I release it. He then kneels down behind me, spreads my cheeks, and licks my secret little buttonhole. I jerk forward.

"Ellie," Kayne warns, and I know right then not to test him. When I feel the pressure at my back entrance, my head becomes light and my breathing becomes erratic. No one has ever touched me there.

"Relax, Ellie," he coaxes as he takes his time inching the plug into me, my body battling against the foreign sensation. It feels like decades have passed by the time he's done inserting it. The object is small, but it feels like it's filling me completely, the pressure hitting me right in the core every time I move.

"Fuck. Good, kitten." He kisses my sore behind, and then shifts around me on his knees until his hot breath is tickling my sensitive flesh. He has no idea how much I need this. *To escape.*

He lightly licks between my folds and I moan, desperate for the mental break. I spread my legs wider, my panties ripping, crazy for him to get closer and press harder. Kayne groans as he slashes his tongue against me repeatedly. I pant uncontrollably as I ride his face while he fucks me with his mouth. The feeling is unparalleled.

"Please may I come?" I beg. I don't even care what I sound like, I just need the release; I need to get away.

"Say my name." He grips my thighs tightly, stabbing my throbbing entrance with his tongue over and over. Everything inside me builds, my climax urged on by the spine tingling pressure of the plug and Kayne's expert mouth. I can't hold back much longer.

"Kayne, please may I come!" I implore desperately. Writhing against this face.

"Come, baby." He sucks my clit. "Come as many times as you want." His fingers dig into my skin and I let go. My orgasm blasting through me like dynamite. My mind is blank for a few blissful seconds. There's no pain or chains. Nothing confining me. In the midst of my climax, Kayne yanks out the butt plug and another wave of ecstasy thunders through me. I scream, falling forward as my limbs give out. I'm wrecked. This man demands every ounce I have, and then leaves me with nothing.

"Good girl." I feel him wipe his face on the inside of my leg. Once again smearing my arousal on my own skin.

As he moves from underneath me, I hear him unfasten his belt and unzip his fly. I know what comes next.

"Can I fuck you, Ellie?" he asks, his voice rough and unsteady.

"No." *Yes!* I breathe shallowly, bent over the table.

My ass is bruised, my pussy is swollen, my limbs are as heavy as lead, and he's not through with me yet.

I hear him moan behind me, as he strokes himself. Rubbing my back with jerky movements while my face is pressed against the thin pad of the table and my wrists are bound.

"You have no idea how bad I want you. How bad I want to slide my cock inside you and fuck you senseless."

I think I do.

I hear his discomposed groan, and then feel the warm spurts of his climax shoot all over my back.

"Mine," he declares as he comes.

Kayne leans over and grabs the collar around my neck, jerking it so I look at him out of the corner of my eye. "One day soon, kitten," he licks my face. "I'm going to come in your hot little mouth, in your wet little pussy, and in your tight little ass all in the same night."

I shake because I know he's right. I'm so close to caving. Look at what happened tonight. He beat me mercilessly, and I still ached for his touch.

The last shreds of my resolve are fraying away. I'll soon be his.

Kayne unbuckles my wrists from the table and eases me up. My whole body hurts. My butt especially.

"Go inside and lay on your stomach," he says, kissing the shell of my ear gently. I do as I'm told—like the good little slave-in-training I am—and lie down on the plush white carpet in the middle of the room. I close my eyes and try to relax, but I'm still wound so tight. I feel another piece of myself disappear. Each night we spend together, more and more of me goes. Who will I become the longer he keeps me?

Kayne kneels down beside me, setting a bowl and towels on the floor. Watching in my peripheral vision, he dips one of the towels into the bowl and wipes between my legs, then over my back. The water is warm and soothing and smells like lavender. I inhale the scent as he cleans me.

"Baby, this is going to hurt a little bit."

I blast my eyes open to find him holding a small jar. My body and mind lock up as he rubs some balm over my abused bottom. It's so sore I don't think I'm going to be able sit for a week.

"Go to bed," he orders softly when he's done. I do as I'm told. Yet another one of his commands.

I climb onto the bed and rest on my stomach. Kayne re-chains me to the headboard, the padlock clicking over my head. Back on my leash for the night.

He follows me onto the mattress, kneels next to me, and proceeds to rub my back, kissing my shoulders sweetly every so often.

As much as I hate to admit it, his hands feel good. Consoling almost.

I don't understand how he can be so demonic one minute and so angelic the next?

I feel every whip mark over and over as Kayne massages me well into the night. It takes a long time, but he finally eases some of my tension. I try to clear my mind and not relive every painful moment of tonight, or any other night since he took me. I concentrate on the dark and Kayne's kneading hands until I'm finally lulled fast asleep. Into the darkness where nothing can hurt me.

"UH OH, SOMEONE WAS A bad girl last night," Jett muses as he looks over my abused skin.

"Do you think you're being funny? It hurts!" I snap

"I bet it does. But it doesn't look so bad. He could have done way worse."

Oh God. I smother my face in the pillow. "It was plenty bad for me!" My words are muffled.

"What happened?"

"He whipped me with a crop!"

"I see that, silly. I mean why?"

"He wanted to spank me, and I talked back."

"That unreasonable motherfucker," Jett scolds facetiously. This has become somewhat of a ritual for me and Jett. Kayne spends the night abusing me, and we talk shit about it the next day. I try not to giggle. It isn't funny. I was brutalized last night! But Jett has become the tiny bit of light in my new dark world.

"How was the orgasm?" He pulls out a small jar balm from the nightstand and rubs some on my bruises.

I stay silent.

"That good, huh?"

I turn my head.

"Imagine what fucking him will be like."

I have. Although I'm not going to admit that to him.

"Is that something you fantasize about? Fucking Kayne?" I ask irritably.

"Don't be ridiculous. I may paint nails and do hair, but my dick is gender specific. Lady love only please."

I laugh. If I didn't, I'd cry.

"What about you? Ever partake in any lady loooove?"

I peek up at him from the gold pillow. "I kissed a girl in high school once."

"And you liked it?" he leers lewdly.

I shrug. "I didn't hate it."

Jett smiles, his eyes sparkling like he's intrigued. "Well, aren't you full of surprises."

"Not really," I disagree.

"Same sex is an acquired taste, sweet thing. The fact that you didn't hate it tells me there's more to your sexual appetite than meets the eye."

"If you say so," I answer, not sure I'm buying his presumption.

"I do." He rubs my ass a little harder and I groan. "You'll come to learn, I'm always right.

KAYNE

I FINISH DRESSING IN A daze.

I fasten my sterling silver cufflinks, adjust my tie, and slip on my suit jacket. I have a meeting in the city, but in no way do I want to leave the mansion. Thoughts of Ellie cloud my mind. The vision of her in her room—alone, chained to the bed, waiting to be played with—teases me. I don't know how long this situation is going to last. It depends on Javier. But every night I spend with her is pulling me deeper into a dark place. The lure of power is seductive. I love controlling her. I love punishing her. I love hearing her cry. It's unlike anything I've ever experienced. The women I've been with in the past have all been willingly submissive. They all knew what to expect and vice versa. But with Ellie, it's more than just dominance. The challenge of her will and fundamental breakdown of her mental faculty is addicting. It's wrong. I know it's wrong, but thrilling just the same. I crave my kitten every night. Like the gravitational pull of a lunar tide. My blood roils from just the mere knowledge I'll be back in her room tonight.

I make my way downstairs and find Javier eating breakfast in the formal dining room. To look at him, you wouldn't think much. He's not a very tall or muscular man. With olive skin and black hair, he comes off like an immigrant worker in his khaki pants and polo shirt. But one look in his eyes tells you all you need to know. He's dangerous: approach with caution.

"Amigo." He smiles balefully. I despise it when he calls me that.

"Javier. Have you heard anything from El Rey about my proposal?"

I get right down to business.

"It's under review." He places some scrambled eggs in a warm tortilla, covers it with hot sauce then rolls it up. Ever since he arrived, my kitchen has been inundated with international food staples. If I never see beans and rice again, it will be too soon.

"Do you have any idea when he may respond with a decision?"

Javier shrugs. "When he's ready."

That tells me a lot.

I adjust my shirt collar and check my watch.

"Going somewhere?" he asks a little too interested. It makes me suspicious. But then again, everything Javier says or does makes me suspicious.

"I have a meeting in the city. I'll be back tonight."

"How fun. When the cat's away, the mice will play," he taunts.

I glare at him. "Not too much fun."

Javier just stares back at me. It's no secret our relationship is less than amicable. But we both have something the other one wants. So we play our little pissing game. Tit for tat until one of us ends up on top. And I already know who that's going to be.

I turn to leave.

"¿Cómo está tu puta, Kayne?"

How's your whore, Kayne?

I glance over my shoulder haughtily. "Aún mia."

Still mine.

THE DRIVE INTO THE CITY is tedious. There's traffic through the tunnel and all throughout midtown. I'm dreading this meeting. I tried to blow it off as many times as possible, but Mark is insistent. It's part of the reason I hired him; he gets things done and quickly. But I had hoped to avoid stepping inside Expo until things cooled down. No such luck. The car drops me off in front of the modest-size building with the large hammered metal sign. Mark's little company is doing well for itself.

I take a deep breath and step out onto the sidewalk. It's early May, and the temperature is comfortable. Not so hot you're sweating through your suit; not so cold you need an extra layer.

"I'll call once I'm ready to be picked up," I tell the driver. Usually Jett drives me into the city, but I felt it was safer for Ellie if he stayed behind today, and he agreed. I didn't like that flicker in Javier's eye when I told him I was leaving the house. It's still bothering me. I want to make this meeting quick then get my ass back to Jersey. Mansion is located in an elite country-like suburban community an hour outside the city. It's privately tucked away, inconspicuous to the naked eye, and perfectly situated for my clients all over the metropolitan area and beyond.

I walk into the contemporary-designed building and head toward the elevator. The last time I was here, Ellie was standing right next to me looking a little embarrassed and totally tempting in a tight pencil skirt. What I wouldn't give to live that day over again.

The elevator doors open to a sickly looking Mark. I frown. His skin is pale, his eyes are red, and his clothes are wrinkled. Very unlike the neat as a pin man I've come to know.

"You look awful." I step out of the lift.

"I am awful. I'm a wreck." He doesn't even shake my hand. Instead he pulls out a bottle of Tums and pops two into his mouth. "I haven't slept since Ellie disappeared," he says crunching away.

Oh shit. This is exactly why I wanted to avoid all things Expo.

"Why don't we have some coffee and talk?" I put my hand on his shoulder.

Mark nods. "The conference room is prepared."

I follow Mark down the hall, past numerous employees, to the corner room framed with windows. The energy in the office is different compared to all the other times I've been here. Mark prides himself on having a positive, upbeat work environment. He's always boosting morale and incentivizing his employees. But today, the negative energy is palpable. And I know exactly why that is. It isn't the same without Ellie, and it's affecting everyone. Including me.

Mark plops down in his usual seat at the table as I shut the door behind me. He eats another antacid, leaving the large bottle out on the table.

I decide to pour Mark some tea instead of coffee. I figure it would be easier on a sour stomach or enflamed esophagus or whatever the fuck he has going on.

I place the cup in front of him and proceed to sit across the table.

"Thank you." He lifts the white mug with Expo's rainbow colored logo on it. It's as modern as the sleek building we're sitting in.

"Want to talk about it?" I ask as Mark takes a sip of the steaming tea. I would've at least blown on it first, but by the looks of him, he's not feeling anything but anxiety at the moment.

"It's my fault," he blurts out.

"What?"

"Ellie's disappearance is my fault."

My jaw drops. "Why is it your fault?"

"Because I should have been watching her more closely."

"*Mark—*"

"That beautiful little spitfire is gone. And I'm completely helpless." He puts his head in his hands. This is not good. I knew Ellie being taken would put a strain on her friends and family, but I never imagined Mark would blame himself or fall the fuck apart. I've never really had friends or family who cared about me that much, so maybe I underestimated the impact of her disappearance. She's lucky, and loved, by more people than I realized. I feel a strange twinge in my chest. Jealousy? Envy maybe? Jett is the only person who would give two shits if I ever disappeared. Regardless of the repercussions, Ellie is safer being held captive by me than being tormented at the hands of Javier. I stand by my decision. As deceitful as it is.

"Kayne, you were the last one to see her. What was she like? Was she drunk? Upset? Why did she leave alone?"

As much as I wanted to avoid this conversation, it's clear Mark needs answers. So I will give him *some*.

"Trust me when I tell you, I tried everything in my power to get her to come home with me," I divulge. Although in reality I didn't have to try very hard. I think Ellie would have come home with me even before the alcohol freed her inhibitions. "But Ellie wasn't having it. I think she was playing hard to get," I insinuate.

"She didn't drink that much and seemed fine to leave on her own. I never would have left her side if I thought something might happen to her." It's the exact same thing I told the police when they questioned me. I knew it was going to happen. Luckily for me, the commissioner of New York is a personal friend. You meet a lot of high profile people in my line of work, and sometimes those contacts come in handy. "I offered her a ride several times, but she declined. You know how Ellie is," I lie through my teeth.

"Yes, I do." Mark stares into the light brown liquid. "She's a smart, young girl with a bright future ahead of her. It's breaking my heart to think she'll never have a chance to pursue it."

I sigh. I would never take Ellie's future away from her. If anything, I hope one day to make it brighter. If she'll let me; if she ever speaks to me again after this is all over.

"She's also strong, and I'm sure wherever she is, or whatever she's going through, she'll survive," I try to reassure him.

"I'm trying not to imagine what's she's going through." Mark's eyes water. Damn. I pull out the white handkerchief from my left pocket and hand it to him uncomfortably.

"Thank you." Mark takes it and wipes his eyes. Geez. I'm so bad at the emotions thing. I don't even like my own.

"I wish I could tell you everything is going to be okay. But I'm a realist." And I don't want to look too incriminating. "I can tell you that I care about Ellie just as much as you do. Maybe more." Mark pauses and looks at me for what seems like the first time today. Like he's really seeing me.

"I understand. You two always did have explosive chemistry."

"Explosive?" I widen my eyes. "Was it that obvious?"

"Boyfriend, please." Mark makes a *don't bullshit me* face. "Every time you two were in the same room, I had the bomb squad on speed dial."

I smirk coyly. "Ellie is a bit ... incandescent."

"She used to light up this whole office." Mark smiles sadly.

She will again.

"Try not to be so hard on yourself," I tell him.

"That is easier said than done." He twists the handkerchief in his hands.

There's nothing more I can say or do.

After our conversation, and a little bit of work, I bid Mark goodbye. I wish I could've given him more reassurance. Told him I knew Ellie was going to be okay. But my secrets have to stay hidden, because even I can't guarantee the outcome. I can only proceed with what I'm doing, with hope that Ellie will come around and we'll both come out of this alive.

Before I leave, I meander by Ellie's desk. It's filled with papers and sticky notes. Her keyboard has a thin layer of dust and the green plant she keeps on her filing cabinet is wilting. I spy the pictures on her pin board. She's hugging a girl I don't recognize. They look alike so I assume it's her sister. There's another of her with two older people. They must be her parents. She looks like her father. Their pointy noses are the same, and so is the color of their eyes. A deep mossy green. The one of her and Mark I find the most amusing. It's St. Patrick's Day, and they're both wearing *Kiss me I'm Irish* t-shirts, green sparkly top hats, and have a shot glass in each hand. Looks like whiskey. Ellie's cheeks are a little flushed, and she's smiling brightly. If I had to guess, she's a little tipsy. I catch myself grinning as I stare at her. I wonder if I'll ever have the chance to get to know the girl in that picture. I really want to, almost desperately.

Once back outside, I slip into the town car waiting for me on the street. I slide up the privacy screen and try to relax against the leather seat, loosening my tie and stretching my legs. Why didn't I just rent a driver and take my limo? More room!

I shift around uncomfortably, anxious to get home and play with my kitten. I drop my head back, close my eyes, and dream up numerous ways I can make Ellie come. I get hard just thinking about how she tastes on my tongue. I can't wait to see what she feels like on my cock. I wonder if tonight will be the night she finally gives in. I know she's close, so damn close to being mine. The wait is nearly killing me.

I grab myself and stroke, trying to appease the arousal that is now a living, breathing beast ripping my insides apart.

"Driver!" I kick the back of his seat restlessly. "Hurry the fuck up!"

ELLIE

JETT DUBBED ME HIS BRUNETTE Barbie doll.

Once again he did my nails and straightened my hair.

He fed me ice cream for lunch and indulged me in mindless conversation. It was the least boring and least stressful day so far.

I watch the sun set through the large circular window diagonal from my bed. As soon as the first shred of night appears, I know he'll be here.

I wait on my knees; impatiently, nervously.

Tonight I know I'm going to say yes. My mind has finally lost the war. It will be my descent into darkness. I'll finally be his. I try not to think about what that means. All I know is that I need more. My body needs more. It's becoming dependent, like a junkie hooked on drugs, jonesing for the unparalleled pleasure only Kayne can distribute. It's my escape, my avoidance, my diversion to the reality at hand.

The door clicks and my body reacts, adrenaline rippling through me. I stay perfectly still as I listen to him approach. His footsteps sound different tonight. I flick my eyes up at the figure in front of me. It's not Kayne. I snap my head to attention. The adrenaline previously rippling through me has turned into waves of dread. The man rakes over my naked body with cold black eyes and a twisted grin. I spring back, but he snatches my chain before I can get far. He drags me toward him sinisterly until my face is an inch from his.

"Señorita," he growls. I recognize him then. He's the man who showed up at Mark's party.

"Kayne has to do a better job training his slave. If you were mine, your mouth would already be wrapped around my dick." His accent is thick and his tone is menacing. This man is evil.

He unbuttons his pants with one hand. "No!" I push at him, struggling against the tight hold he has on the chain.

He laughs at me. "That word doesn't exist in my world."

He pulls me forward, forcing me to brace myself on the edge of the bed. I swipe at him with one hand spurring him to squeeze the collar until it's choking me. I gasp for air as he brings the head of his penis to my lips.

"No!" I try to turn my head, but his hold is tight and too restrictive. Tears spring. When I try to fight, he chokes me harder. I wheeze and cough desperate for oxygen as tiny stars cloud my vision.

He lets up once I stop squirming, close to passing out.

"Bite me and I'll beat you unconscious." He grabs a fist full of my hair and shoves his cock so far into my mouth I gag.

Oh God, please no!

KAYNE

IT TAKES ME A MINUTE to register what I'm seeing.

Javier has Ellie bent over the edge of the bed by her collar.

"What the fuck!" I roar as he tosses her aside crying and covered in ... *Oh for Christ's sake.*

"Your whore needs work," he sneers.

I see fucking red. The whole room is bleeding crimson.

You can't fucking kill him. Yet. I restrain myself as my heart tries to punch a hole straight through my chest.

"This fucking room is off-limits, and you know it." I step forward with my fists clenched.

"Apparently not." He zips his fly imperiously with that ridiculous smirk I want to smack right off his face.

Javier brushes past me, and it takes every ounce of control I have not to beat him into the floor. As soon as he slams the door, I bolt to Ellie. She looks like she's in shock.

Our eyes meet for a fleeting moment then she loses it. "Unchain me!" she screams, sobbing irrepressibly. She yanks at her collar, then starts erratically wiping Javier's come off her face and out of her hair. *That fucking rat bastard. He's dead.*

I clumsily release the chain from her collar during her fit. As soon as she's free, she darts into the bathroom and turns on the shower. My anger has reached volcanic proportions. I give Ellie a minute, because truthfully I need one myself. Then I follow her into the bathroom.

The muscle I forgot was in my chest cracks for the very first time in my life as I watch her scrub her face furiously under the water, bawling uncontrollably. *My kitten.* The crack fissures so deep it touches my soul.

That tortilla-eating motherfucker did this to make a point. To flex his superiority. To get to me. *Cocksucker.* I want to scream, but I don't want to upset Ellie more than she already is, so I stuff my amplified emotions away and step into the shower with her, clothes and all. Ellie instinctively cowers away from me, still crying. Her face is red from scrubbing and her body hunched in shame. I thank God for the stream of water running down my face. It masks the tears falling from my eyes. This was never supposed to happen. He was never supposed to get to her. I thought if I kept her close, kept her captive, she'd be safe. I was wrong.

I hate being wrong.

It eats me alive.

So does her suffering.

I pull a defiant Ellie into my arms. She fights me tooth and nail, but I'm bigger and stronger, and she knows it. She submits, wilting against me. Her pain is palpable through her wretched sounds. It guts me.

In a fit of sudden rage, she balls her hands into fists and starts pounding on my chest. "You did this to me! You made me a whore!" Then her legs give out and she slumps into my arms.

"He was never supposed to touch you." I hug her tightly. "You only belong to me." I press my lips to her head. She cries some more and I just hold her until the tears subside. It feels like an agonizing eternity. The only thing reminding me we're still alive is the feel of the scalding water and sound of the strong spray.

When Ellie finally looks up at me, it's with dejected green eyes. It liquefies my soul. I drop my lips to hers, kissing her softly, trying to ease the pain, the shock, the after effect. She grabs at my face and kisses me fiercely, as if I'm the only lifeline she has left.

I tighten my arms around her and allow her into my mouth, giving her what she needs; my body and my newly functioning heart.

"I'm sorry, Ellie." I find my balls. "I'm sorry he touched you. I'm sorry I wasn't here to stop him." She blinks up at me naked, defenseless, and so utterly tempting. "I promise no one will ever hurt you again." It's a vow.

"Except you." Her voice is small, but callous none the less.

Burn.

I drop my forehead to hers. "I won't as long as you behave."

"You promise?" She looks up at me with just her clouded eyes.

"Yes."

"I'm trying," she whispers weakly.

"I know. You're a good girl."

She closes her eyes as if surrendering. Giving up. Giving in. "Kayne, can you touch me?"

The question blindsides me.

"Is that what you want, Ellie?" I smooth my hand over her wet hair.

"Yes. Please. Take it all away." She doesn't even hesitate.

I would take every ounce of her suffering if I could.

I lift her face, brushing my thumb across her raw skin. Then I drop a light kiss against her lips. She darts her tongue out, and I know in that instance I have her. A butterfly trapped in my web. My web of lies, and my web of deception. My web of selfishness, because I've always wanted Ellie. And now I finally have her. *She's Mine.*

I turn off the shower without a sound, pull Ellie's listless body out, and then wrap her in a towel. When I lift her up and cradle her in my arms, she looks at me with hollow eyes. It feels like a piece of her spirit is broken, which is the last thing I ever wanted to happen.

In the bedroom I place her on her feet, and then strip the bed, sending the comforter and sheets flying to the floor. She'll get new bedding tomorrow; that set is being burned. I dry her off in silence, skimming over her breasts and stomach, and rubbing between her thighs. Then I dry her hair, soaking up the droplets of water from scalp to tip. When I'm through, she's left naked in front of me wearing only her collar. The thick leather around her neck makes me hard as fuck. It's a symbol, a statement. It tells the world she belongs solely to me.

"Lie down," I order. "On the carpet." She steels herself, breathing heavily, and then walks to the center of the room.

"Look at me." She turns and raises her head. She is so goddamn beautiful it hurts, with those sultry green eyes and light brown hair. "On your back. Spread your legs."

Breathing erratically, she drops to her knees, and then lies on her back. Just like I taught her. My cock throbs. She props her feet up and opens her legs as wide as they can go. I nearly combust in my pants.

"Good girl."

I stalk the seven steps it takes to get to her then unhook my belt, while standing above her. We never take our eyes off each other as I pull my wet shirt over my head and shed my pants. I'm completely naked, same as her.

I kneel down between her legs; her enticing little pussy wide open and on display. I moan deep and guttural in my throat as its soft pink folds call to me. Tease me. Tell me they're finally mine.

I'm going to attempt to be gentle. I don't exactly do gentle. But I can try for Ellie's sake.

"Tell me again that you want me to touch you." I kiss the inside of her thigh.

Ellie closes her eyes and grips the plush rug.

"I want you to touch me." Her voice is raspy from fighting back tears.

"I have wanted you for so long." And now that I have her, I'm going to make sure I bury myself so deep inside her, the only thing she'll feel, taste, smell, breathe, or even think about is me. I know I've said I want her obedience, and her submission, and her body, but what I want most of all is her mind. I want to cloud it, consume it, rule over it. Have her thoughts only be of me. I never knew how deep my affections for Ellie ran until the night of Mark's party. That first small kiss sparked it all. It ignited something between us, something that's been smoldering ever since.

Ellie closes her eyes as I run one finger down her slit, shaking like a leaf as I circle the tip of my finger over her clit. Her body springs to life as I slide it inside her. She gasps, grabbing onto the rug tighter as I push all the way in. I finger her slow and deep, after a while adding a second digit then a third. She moans loudly, her body bowing from the pleasurable intrusion.

I drop my head and suck her clit between my teeth causing her to whimper. I love that sound. I've come to live for that sound.

I work my mouth while simultaneously fucking her with my fingers. I know what she likes. I know what gets her off. She writhes beneath me, flexing her hips, begging for more. For a fleeting second I regret not tying her down. I withdraw my fingers and Ellie groans in protest. I crawl over her, licking my way up her body until we're nose to nose, mouth to mouth. "Tell me you want me to fuck you."

She's panting and flushed, the fear evident in her smoky green eyes. But there's also something more, something dark and desirous.

"I want you to fuck me."

I grab her by the collar and yank, pulling her face to mine. I kiss her hard, forcing her mouth open, giving her no choice but to accept my tongue. I plunge in deeply and swirl it all around, sucking the oxygen right out of the room. Then I shove her back down. My need spiraling.

"Stay still."

I spread her legs wider with my hands and Ellie emits an uncomfortable sound. Then I line the head of my cock up to her entrance and tease her with shallow thrusts. Her pussy tightens, begging for more. I slide into her, taking her all at once. She sighs insufferably as a tear trickles down her cheek. I lean in and lick it off.

I'll swallow every salty emotion she sheds tonight.

Taking her wrists I pin her down, fucking her as slow and as leisurely as I can. As controlled as my body will allow.

"How do I feel?" I ask as I thrust.

"Big," she responds, her fists clenching.

I chuckle not expecting that response.

She starts to shift. "Kayne—"

"Keep those fucking legs open. And no talking. Unless you're asking permission to come." I grit my teeth. The Dom is never far. It's a ramification of this life.

She obeys, crying a little harder. I hold her wrists tighter as I lick her face.

"Cry all you need. It won't be the last time," I tell her as I pump into her harder. Her pussy tight and wet, constricting around me. I nearly see stars.

Ellie's breathing speeds up, becoming erratic and disjointed, as our hips clash together.

"Please, may I come?!" she erupts. Her eyes are screwed shut, her body is tense.

I want to say no, but I'll be nice. Tonight, Ellie needs nice.

"Come, baby. Come as many times as you need."

She lets go as soon as I consent. A flood of warm heat saturates my cock as she clamps down around me. Fuck, Ellie feels better than I could have ever imagined, could have ever conjured in my wildest dreams.

She cries out, struggling against me as her orgasm tears her apart. I watch transfixed as her face strains in ecstasy, her breasts swell, and nipples harden. I suck one into my mouth during the height of her pleasure and another little ripple of arousal washes over me. The sensation makes me crazy. Makes me crave blood.

Her body gives out as soon as her tremors subside.

"Turn over," I order. Ellie immediately rolls onto her stomach. I pull her hips up, forcing her on all fours then slam into her, burying myself to the hilt.

"Oh!" she screams. My desire has me drunk, lustful, and unrepentant. I beat into her, holding on tight, sprinting after my orgasm.

"Who do you belong to, Ellie?"

"You," she strains.

I grab her collar, fucking her harder.

"If I tell you to spread your legs for me, what do you say?

"Yes, Kayne."

"If I tell you to bend over so I can fuck you, what do you say?

"Yes, Kayne."

"What do I want?" I ask as my climax circles like a cyclone.

"My obedience. My submission. My body."

I have all three. I pull out right before I explode and come all over her abused ass. The crop marks still red and fresh. I love it.

I drop back, panting wildly once the oscillating sensations subside and drink Ellie in on all fours.

MINE.

"Lie down," I command. She slides forward onto her stomach, stretching out like a tired little kitten. *My tired little kitten.*

I crawl over her. "Did I hurt you?"

She looks up at me. Her eyes are red and her cheeks are puffy.

"No."

"Are you telling me the truth, or what you think I want to hear?"

She bites her lip. "It hurt a little. You're big."

I hold back a grin. Her response just stroked my ego. Big time.

"I don't ever want you to lie to me, understand? If I ask you a question, tell me the truth."

She nods, pressing her cheek into the plush white rug. I kiss her softly on the corner of her mouth then grab the towel on the floor next to the bed. I wipe my come off her ass then pull her to her feet. She stands like she's supposed to, with her head bowed. Just like I trained her to. It's arousing and odious all at the same time. I draw her face up. "Mine, Ellie."

"Yes, Kayne," she answers, and my insides go berserk. I will never get tired of hearing her say that.

I walk over to the armoire and open the intricately decorated doors with Ellie standing where I left her. I grab what I'm looking for, and then return to the center of the room.

"Look at me."

Ellie lifts her head. I unlock the thick black training collar and remove it from her neck.

"I don't have to wear it anymore?" Her voice pitches.

"No. Not that one." I drop it on the floor.

Her face falls. I lift the new collar to show her. This one is less harsh, more feminine. With rhinestones. It also has a padded inside so it won't rub uncomfortably against her skin. I slide it around her neck and lock it in place. I yank her forward by it and give her a kiss. "I like you collared, baby. I like you naked. I like you mine."

I STAY WITH ELLIE UNTIL she falls asleep.

It seemed wrong to just leave after the night she had. I didn't exactly know what to do with myself once I put her to bed. Should I lie down with her? Sit next to her? Hold her? Holding her seemed a little too close for comfort. Although, if I had to choose, it would be option number three. But I can't cross that line. For all our sakes. An arm's length is where I have to keep her. Owner/pet. Master/slave. That is as far as the relationship can go.

Sitting in the chair at the table, I watch as she drifts off. The moonlight shining through the wagon wheel window is illuminating her face, highlighting the streaks of tears running down her cheeks. The rhinestones on her new collar reflecting off the light every time she shifts.

Beautiful is too inferior a word to describe Ellie. Inside and out. Even when she's crying, she's the most captivating thing on the face of the Earth. At least to me. I could watch her sleep for hours. Watch her move and laugh and come apart in my arms. She's mine.

Once her breathing levels off and she's sleeping peacefully, I silently slip out of the room.

I thought I had fucked all the murderous rage out of me, but as I walk down the dimly lit hallway, my fury returns.

My legs bring me to the exact place my brain forbids me to go. With extreme force I kick open the door to Javier's room. The lock splinters straight through the wood. That felt good. I walk in to find Javier once again with Spice. He's taken a pathological liking to her. It irks me. She looks too much like Ellie. Same green eyes and brown hair. It heightens the turmoil blistering beneath my skin. I grab the switchblade out of my pocket and pop the knife as I stalk toward Javier. His black eyes widen, and then turn hard. He's not afraid of me. He should be. I slam him up against the wall next to the bed. "Next time you decide to stick your dick where it doesn't belong, I'll cut your nut sack open and watch your balls fall to the floor." I dig the tip of the blade into his crotch. He goes up on his toes. "This is my fucking house. You will respect me and my girls.

"Vivas bajo mi techo, obedeces mis reglas. Comprende?"

You live under my roof, you obey my rules. Understand?

Javier sneers, staring me down. "I obey no one."

This is an all-around dicey situation. One wrong move or one wrong word and I could fuck everything up. All the years of hard work and money spent. All the sacrifices and all the lies, good for nothing.

But at the moment I just don't give a fuck. All I know is if Javier ever lays a hand on Ellie again, the whole compound is going to go up in smoke. "It doesn't look like you have much of a choice at the moment." I twist the knife deeper.

Javier's mouth curves up into a taut deranged smile, despite the compromising position I have him in. "You amuse me, amigo."

"Glad to know I'm good for something."

"You're good for many things," he says cryptically.

"Stay away from what's mine," I warn one last time, then shove myself away from him. I cut Spice loose, she's bound and gagged and has been whimpering the whole time. Javier tied her up so tightly to the four poster bed she's suspended over the mattress. Her wrists are rubbed raw from the abrasive rope and there's hot red wax drizzled all over her body. Both of her nipples are completely covered. It looks like the poor girl is bleeding to death. She scrambles up once she's free and rushes out of the room. Fear and relief are both evident in her eyes. She doesn't even bother to remove the ball gag stretching her mouth. My heart lurches. If I hadn't walked in, who knows what else he might have done.

"You cut my fish loose."

"Your gaming privileges have been revoked. No more playtime for you. You've had your fun." The words feel like battery acid burning my tongue. Ellie's horrified face flashes in front of me. It's an image that has been permanently branded into my brain.

"I don't like boundaries, amigo."

"I don't like you," I spit.

I leave Javier's room after that, praying to almighty God I didn't just destroy everything I've worked the last six years for. I don't stop walking until I reach the gym. I lift my hands, not even bothering with gloves, and pound away, seeing Javier's face every time my fist connects with the punching bag.

ELLIE

I WAKE UP ON A bare mattress.

The sheets and comforter are still on the floor and I am back on my leash. My legs hurt, and so does my core. I think this kind of pain is something I'll need to get used to. I handed myself over last night. My obedience, my submission, and my body. I am officially Kayne's. Officially owned.

I huddle into a ball and shiver, but not because I'm cold. Because I'm numb. The image of evil black eyes haunt me. What if Kayne hadn't come in when he did? What if ... I push the crippling, abominable thought away. There's no point in what-ifs. That's what my mother always says. I miss my family terribly. Just the thought of them fragments my pain and loneliness further. I can't imagine what they're going through—not knowing where I am, if I'm dead or alive.

What would they think if they found out I was owned?

I fight back the tears, put my loved ones in a box, and shove it into the darkest depths of my mind. I need to be strong, and missing my family makes me weak. Makes me vulnerable. I have to survive.

I try not to think. I try not to feel. I'm alone, and my existence is abhorrent.

I concentrate solely on something small. The need to pee. I hope Jett comes soon.

I look around my prison cell and idle thoughts take over. Is this where I'll live forever? Will I ever be able to go outside again? Will I always be a dog chained to the bed? A sexual object, to use as he pleases.

Before I'm sucked into a rabbit hole of despair, the door opens. I jump to my knees, never knowing if it's Kayne or not. And now that I officially belong to him, I have to act accordingly. A little piece of my hope dies.

"Heel, it's just me." I relax my body and lift my head. Tears streaming down my face.

"Don't cry." Jett embraces me. "It's going to be okay. How do you feel?" he asks as he unlocks the chain from my new collar. There's no fun, lighthearted banter today.

"Numb, abused. Confused."

"I could kill that shithead for laying a finger on you."

"Kayne or the other guy?" I sniff.

Jett's lip twitches. "Nice to know you haven't lost your sense of humor."

"Someone told me I need to be strong." I look up at him drained of life.

He hugs me. "You're rising to the occasion."

"I feel like I'm falling apart."

"You're not alone. You can talk to me about whatever you want. You can cry, you can let it all out."

I take him up on his offer. I melt into Jett and sob, crying every single sickening emotion out. Every one I tried and failed miserably to suppress. Jett just holds me for as long as I need and after what feels like a lifetime's worth of tears, I pull myself together.

"That's a girl." Jett pats me. "Let's get you cleaned up. A hot shower and something sinful for lunch will make you feel better."

"How sinful?" I look up at him with puffy eyes.

He leers. "Something a priest can't even forgive you for."

I smile weakly.

Jett removes my collar. "Sparkly new jewelry," he comments offhandedly.

"It's definitely more comfortable than the other one." I rub my neck.

"Prettier too."

I pee, take a long shower, and eat the most decadent lunch I've ever had in my life; a giant portion of crème Brulee French toast with a side of vanilla ice cream drowned in chocolate syrup. After that, I just stare at myself in the mirror for most of the day. Who is this girl I've become? I still have the same eyes and nose and hair. Except now I'm someone's sex *slll ... pleasure kitten.* I can't even bring myself to use the other term.

"Time to go back on your leash." Jett pops his head into the bathroom, vaporizing my scattered thoughts. "You've been in here all day."

I frown.

"I laid your clothes out. Kayne will be here soon. Wear your hair up, it's a mess." He winks.

With a heavy heart, I pull my long, light brown hair up into a loose bun. It's sort of sexy with tendrils falling down around my face. I wonder briefly if Kayne will like it. *Why do you care!?*

My 'clothes' consist of a pair of black, lace-trimmed boy shorts, knee-high stiletto boots, and my collar. That's it. I don't think I'll ever wear real clothes again. I slip on the underwear and boots, right after Jett secures my new neck jewelry. Then back on my chain I go. "You look sexy enough to eat," Jett comments once I'm perched back on my bed.

"Thank you?"

"You're welcome. We need to work on makeup with you though."

I raise my eyebrows. I never was one for makeup. A little mascara and some blush. I'm even less inclined since I've been here.

"Tomorrow." Jett taps me on the nose. "I'll be back with dinner later."

He closes the door to my prison, leaving me alone to just wait. Minutes tick by. I fiddle with my hands, the chain, and the collar.

I can only so go far. To the edge of the bed is all my leash allows. I shift this way and that, nervously, curious about how tonight will play out. Kayne has full range of me now. What will he do?

I stare mindlessly at my new bedding. I like it, despite the circumstances. It's all shimmery creams and sparkly whites with matching decorative throw pillows. It looks like I'm sitting on a cloud of diamonds. It makes me think of Mark and how he used to call me his magic glitter in high heels. I push the thought away and place him in the box with the rest of my loved ones. I miss him too much. I miss them all too much.

The lock clicks and I bound onto my knees like I'm supposed to. Like a good girl. An obedient girl. An owned girl.

I see Kayne's shoes in front of me as I keep my head down and my hands on my thighs. My heart hammering in my chest. He stands there for what seems like an eternity. My back starts to cramp.

"Hello, kitten, how was your day?" he finally asks.

"Fine, Kayne," I answer like I'm supposed to.

"Look at me." I sweep my head up and look directly into his crystal blue eyes.

"How was your day? Answer honestly."

I frown. "I was lonely. And I feel conflicted." I tear my gaze away from him.

"Honesty, Ellie. I always want honesty. It will get easier. I promise." He runs one finger softly under my chin. "You're beautiful."

I blush, still not looking at him. Does he mean that or does he say it just to play with my mind?

Kayne pulls at my collar bringing me up onto my knees and cups one of my breasts, massaging it gently.

My heart beats wildly. I flashback to last night. My legs still ache from being spread so wide. My lips tender from being kissed so hard. "On a scale of one to ten, how sore are you?" He hooks one finger into my panties and peeks down inside.

"Six," I answer, holding perfectly still.

"I'd prefer four, but six is fuckable."

My pulse races. I remind myself that I handed my body over to him. Freely and willingly. It's his to do with as he pleases. Whatever that may be. Before Kayne has a chance to pounce on me, Jett appears with dinner. He walks through the room with a large platter covered by a silver dome. He places it on the table by the window then leaves without a word. The door clicks behind him and my heart is suddenly in my throat. I stare at Kayne, and he stares back at me. His eyes are roaring with some unnamed desire. My stomach flips.

"Are you hungry?"

Honestly, no. So much for giving him what he wants.

"Yes, Kayne," I answer.

"Good girl." He snaps my underwear.

Kayne unhooks me from the headboard and leads me by my leash to the table. He sits with the chair facing out, his legs spread wide. "Kneel."

I drop in front of him. Then he begins to feed me from his hand. "Open."

I open my mouth and he slips a piece of steak inside. I chew. It's cooked perfectly and tastes delicious. Then he scoops some mashed potatoes onto one finger. I open my mouth again and suck them off. He feeds me like this until almost everything on the plate is gone.

"Enough." His voice is gruff and thick with lust. The bulge in his pants straining against his zipper.

"Lie down." I lie at his feet. Just how I'm supposed to. Minutes tick by, as he gazes at me on the floor, feasting on every naked inch of my body with his mesmerizing eyes.

"Stand," he commands. So I do. He loves to boss me around. Kayne continues to drink me in as I stand before him. My bare breasts on display. The stiletto boots giving me four extra inches of height.

"You are so fucking sexy," he admires darkly. Something inside me twinges. "Pull your underwear down your thighs."

With shaky hands and erratic breaths, I obey. Once my panties are where he wants them, Kayne runs his large hands over my body, feeling my curves, cupping my breasts, squeezing my ass. He moans with satisfaction. Then traces his fingers over my hipbones, down to the middle of my thighs. When he inserts his thumb into me, I wince and moan all at the same time. He's menacingly quiet as he fingers me, concentrating solely on my face. His stare is burdensome, but I endure it as I let the effect of his ministrations play out on my face. After a few heat-induced minutes, he withdraws his thumb and replaces it with his middle finger. It's only a few seconds before he smears my wetness away from my pussy, and up toward my ass. I gasp. "Shhh." He grabs onto one of my legs with his free hand steadying me. "Remember when I told you I was an ass man?"

"Yes." I tremble.

He slowly sinks his thumb back inside me as his middle finger works its way into my button hole. I tense, remembering how the butt plug felt. Full and intrusive. Kayne's finger is twice as long.

"Relax, Ellie." Kayne tries to pacify me as his finger sinks steadily into my tight little entrance.

The intrusion bites, but every now and again the pain subsides and I'm shocked with a small amount of pleasure. It takes a few slow minutes, but his entire finger finally makes its way deep inside me.

I feel so full as Kayne proceeds to simultaneously fuck my pussy and my ass with his thumb and middle finger. His thrusts are relentless. I start to shake as an orgasm builds so hot inside of me, I fear I might turn to ash.

"Do you like the way I touch you, Ellie?" I want to say no just to be spiteful. But I reply the way I should.

"Yes, Kayne."

"You know I'm going to fuck you here." He pushes hard into my behind. It hurts; heavenly pleasure mixed with hellish pain.

"Yes, Kayne." I'm panting now, my climax is so close.

"Don't you dare come." He works his hand faster, harder. I'm going to crumble.

"Kayne, please," I beg.

"Please, what?"

"Please." I can barely say the words.

"You want to come baby?

"Yes, please." I breathe heavily.

"Say it. Say you want me to fuck you until you come."

I swallow hard. I've never talked like that before.

"Say it, Ellie."

"I want you to fuck me until I come." My voice is a whisper.

"You'll have to do better than that, kitten." He withdraws his fingers, leaving me empty and frustrated. "You need to learn to control your urges. And you're going to have to start talking dirty, baby. I like it." He leans over and sucks my clit. I nearly die.

"What do you say when I tell you to bend over so I can fuck you?"

"Yes, Kayne."

"Good girl. Turn around and grab your ankles." I obey his command like the good little pet I agreed to be. I turn, bend, and grab my ankles. My leg muscles scream. Kayne gets up and moves around the room. In this position, I can't see what he's doing, leaving me raging with anticipation and an overdose of fear. He could have taken me as soon as I bent over, but instead he's shuffling around the room. I tremble from the need and the unknown. When Kayne returns he grabs my hips, and grinds his hard-on firmly against me. I moan. So does he. Then he bends and grabs the chain dangling from my collar. He winds it around my right ankle and locks it in place. Holy shit. Then he attaches another chain to my collar, mirroring his actions on the other ankle. I can't stand up straight. He's literally restrained me bent over. I start to hyperventilate. "Kayne?"

"Shush, Ellie. You look fucking amazing like this." He slaps my ass, and I have no choice but to accept the pain. I'm trapped. I can't lift my head, and every time I try the chains restrict me. I hear him undo his zipper, and see his trousers drop to the floor. My hearts is fluttering like a bird trapped in a cage. "Relax." He rubs my backside gently. Then he slaps me again. My whole being tenses.

"I thought no more punishments." I grit my teeth.

"Only if you behave. And spanking isn't off the table completely." He hits my bare behind hard again. I clench my teeth. I didn't realize there was fine print on our agreement. "Mouth closed, legs open." He rubs the head of his erection against my entrance. "My sexy girl. Who do you belong to?"

"You, Kayne."

"That's right, baby, all mine. No one else's." He slips his cock inside me. Taking my body quickly, inch by combustible inch. In this position he's able to get deeper than he did last night. He fills and stretches me to my breaking point. "Kayne" I whimper, as he completely controls my body.

"How do I feel baby?"

"Big."

He laughs. "Any other description you want to use?" He pumps easily, my muscles tightening around him involuntarily. "I think I feel good. You're squeezing the shit out of me." He digs his fingers into my hips as he starts to move faster.

"Fuck you're so wet, so tight." I'm completely at Kayne's mercy, bent over with my black lacy panties around my thighs, my legs spread wide and my collar chained to my ankles. He tied me up like he owns me, because he does.

He relentlessly slides in and out, hitting my core in the same spot over and over. My orgasm burning brightly within me. "Kayne," I moan insufferably as our hips clash together.

"Ask permission." He slams into me ruthlessly. "Ask me if you can come."

Desperate for the release, I do. "Please, can I come!?"

"I own you, Ellie; don't forget that."

"Yes, Kayne," I answer willingly, trying to keep my orgasm from ripping me to shreds.

"Come, baby. Right fucking now."

And I do. As soon as permission is granted I let go, becoming nothing but sensation, and Kayne's living, breathing sex toy. My climax nearly buckles my knees. But Kayne's tight grip keeps me upright. I suck in air greedily as he pounds away at me, finally finding his own release. He pulls out and ejaculates on my ass, moaning and groaning as he spurts hot come all over my backside. My legs are screaming, my pussy is throbbing, and I'm pretty sure Kayne left fingerprints on my hips.

"Fuck, you're amazing," he sighs, the physical gratification evident in his voice. I guess I should feel flattered, but all I feel like is a dolled-up pretzel, twisted for his pleasure.

After a minute, I feel him wipe himself off me with the cloth napkin from dinner.

How chivalrous.

He then walks around and drops to his knees right in front of me, breathing hard. He lifts my chin with one finger, the chains restricting how far I can look up.

"You're fucking incredible." He's just full of compliments tonight. "I'm going to keep you forever." He kisses me chastely. The word forever rocks my existence. I almost burst into tears. Then he unlocks the chains around my ankles. "Go clean up." I stand up straight, my muscles in agony. I walk into the bathroom and wipe away the arousal dripping down my leg. That's when I catch a glimpse of myself in the mirror. My face is red, my hair is a mess, and both chains are still dangling from my collar. I don't know what to make of myself. Only one word fits. Whore. Kayne's whore.

"Ellie," Kayne summons me.

Fuck.

I clean up quickly then hurry back into the bedroom and stand in front of him.

"Go to bed," he orders. I crawl onto the mattress. Kayne's fully dressed and jingling a set of keys in his hand. The keys that can liberate me.

"How do you feel?" he asks as I kneel in front of him.

"Tired."

"That was only the beginning."

I inhale a steadying breath. "Beginning of what?"

"Your new life." He removes one of the chains from my collar, and then shackles the remaining one back to the headboard. A puppy played with then put back on her leash. He yanks me toward him and kisses me brutally on the mouth. My lips swell he sucks so hard. "Fucking all mine. Stay kneeling until I leave."

I place my hands on my thighs and drop my head. "Such a good girl." He runs his thumb under my jaw. I grind my teeth. I despise that fucking patronizing tone. Kayne silently exits the room. Once I hear the door click, I collapse onto the comforter an exhausted, misused mess.

And weep.

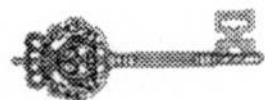

SUNLIGHT FLOODS THE ROOM. I squint as my eyes adjust to the brightness. This time of the morning, when it's quiet and I'm alone, I pretend my prison is a fairy-tale dream. The room is beautiful, open, and airy. The furniture modern but still feminine and the large white rug blanketing the hardwood floor brings a sense of warmth. A princess residing in her castle in the sky. Then I move and my fairy-tale dream turns into a nightmarish reality. I remember I'm trapped, like Rapunzel, chained to the bed. My energy is drained, my limbs hurt, and I feel empty.

And everything that happened last night is going to happen all over again. And again, and again.

I am owned. A pleasure kitten to be touched and prodded and fucked as my owner sees fit. He demonstrated his ownership last night when he chained my collar to my ankles and had his demonic way with me, bent over and helpless. I wish I could get up on my own accord and move around the room. But I'm at the mercy of others, always at the mercy of others in this house. I have a ridiculous fear that one day Jett won't show up and I'll be trapped on this bed forever. My fears are put to rest when the door clicks and Jett appears with breakfast.

"I could have been Kayne," he reminds me. I didn't shoot to my knees when the door opened.

"My legs hurt." And I don't care to obey at the moment.

"That doesn't matter. If he wants you kneeling when he walks into the room, you kneel. Don't cross him. He doesn't like to hurt you."

"Could have fooled me," I say bitterly, rubbing my ass. I still have red marks from when he whipped me.

"Cranky this morning. Last night wasn't satisfying?"

Physically yes. Mentally, no.

This whole situation is utterly fucked-up. No one deserves to live like this. At the mercy of others. Beaten if they don't obey. Treated like an object, a pet, a ... *slave*. I used the word. It's sickening. I can't believe it's become my life.

"I hate him sometimes," I confess, as Jett removes my collar.

"That's fine, just tell me, not him. Release your aggression when you fuck. It's one of the few outlets you have."

I sigh. Sure, sex is a great stress reducer and anxiety reliever. And sex with Kayne can have your blood pressure skyrocketing one minute, and taking a nosedive the next. That's how physically demanding he is. But emotionally? It means nothing. It's empty. I'm empty. When I used to fantasize about Kayne Roberts, his mischievous personality and charismatic smile were always center stage. He was nothing like the tyrant who keeps me captive. Whenever he came into Expo, his demeanor was always professional, but every now and again I would catch a twinkle in his eye or a roguish smirk. I always suspected under that tailored suit was a man with a secret life—someone extreme who liked BASE jumping or race car driving. Never did I surmise his private life entailed an upscale prostitution ring and client list. Or kidnapping and sexual slavery in the first degree.

"Take a shower. Then we're going to do some yoga," Jett says.

"Are you serious?"

"Deadly. Kayne complained you're not limber enough."

"What? Does he tell you what we do in here?" I flush crimson.

"Not graphic details, but I know some things. It's not much different than when we talk."

I think I'm going to die. "It's completely different!"

"How so?" Jett questions.

"It just is!" I spring off the bed and retreat to the bathroom. It's one thing for me to talk about Kayne with Jett, it's a whole other thing for Kayne and Jett to talk about me! Images of my panties around my thighs, my collar chained to my ankles, and a gloating Kayne makes me turn beet red. I can feel the heat actually scorching my skin. I wish there was a door to the bathroom, I'd lock myself in.

I take a quick shower, eat some breakfast, and then am further tortured with downward dog and flying crane. I would never admit this out loud, but I secretly enjoy spending the day with Jett, even if I am naked and mortified half the time. He's funny, easy to be around, and always tries to cheer me up. On some jacked-up level I see him as a friend.

I take another shower—because really what else do I have to do? A nice long hot one that helps ease the tension in my muscles. As I wash my hair I wonder ruefully what compromising position Kayne will put me in tonight. I half dread it, half crave it. Two nights together and my body is already calling out to his.

I dry off, pull my damp hair up into a bun, and walk into my room fully expecting to find clothes laid out for me. Alright, really just a new pair of underwear. But Jett just hooks my collar back on and leads me to the bed.

"Hang out, sweet thing," he says as the padlock clicks.

"Like I have anywhere else to go," I answer snidely, pulling at the chain.

Jett just snickers at me and taps me on the nose. "See you in the morning."

Then he takes his leave, and I am once again a puppy left waiting to be played with. Night has fallen and moonlight is shining brightly through the large wagon wheel window. My owner is late.

When I hear the door click, I pop onto my knees. Kayne's footsteps command the room. "How's my kitten?" He makes quick work of unlocking my leash from the bed.

"A downward dog expert," I reply flatly.

Kayne pauses. "Excuse me?"

"Jett made me to do yoga today."

Kayne's lip twitches. "Did he?"

"Yes, Kayne."

"Good girl." He rubs me under my jaw. He unhooks the chain from the front loop and re-clasps it to the one on the back of my collar. Red flags fly up.

"Go kneel on the floor. Make sure you face the TV." I scramble off the bed and into the middle of the room. I fall to my knees, look down, and rest my hands on my thighs. I'm breathing heavily, and he hasn't even touched me yet. I hear him shed his clothes then click on the television. The familiar sounds of sex fill the room. Only one thing plays on that flat screen—porn.

"Fours, Ellie." I feel him yank on the chain. I lean forward on my hands and knees as Kayne straddles me, the leash pulled so tight in his hand that the collar is forcing me to look up. On the television, two people are heavily engaged in intercourse. A man and a woman going at it on a white leather couch. The camera is at the perfect angle displaying every thrust of the man's large cock into the woman's bare pink pussy. My heartbeat quickens and my core throbs the longer I'm subjected to the erotic display. I've never watched porn before and its effects are startling.

"I hear you breathing, kitten. Like what you see?" Kayne asks lewdly.

I stay silent. I don't want to answer. I don't want to say yes. I don't even know if yes is the right answer. All I know is my body is responding indecently to the visual stimulation.

"Kitten?" Kayne yanks my chain, provoking a response.

"Yes, Kayne." I can barely expel the words.

"Good, kitten," he replies smugly.

I don't know how long we watch, but it's well into the night. Couple after couple partaking in explicit, untamed sex. Kayne just stands over me, holding my leash as my arousal winds tighter and tighter around me.

I'm close to begging when he finally moves, kneeling behind me. I rock lightly, as he massages my backside with a taut grip on my leash. He runs his finger from the top of my ass along my slit and tickles my clit. I'm so over-stimulated, his touch feels like pins and needles. I pant like the pet I am.

"Need me, baby?" He inserts one finger into me and my body electrifies.

"Yes, Kayne." I don't even recognize my own voice.

"Let's see how much." He withdraws, then rolls my clit between his fingers; I nearly convulse. He quickly pulls away.

"Not yet, kitten, not even close." I don't know what he's talking about, but the tone of his voice sends an ominous shiver down my spine.

Kayne grabs my hip with one hand, clamping down as hard as he can. With the other he keeps a tight grip on my leash, the collar straining against my neck.

"Don't take your eyes off that screen." He pumps the head of his cock against my entrance but never fully penetrates me. I'm dying, I need him so bad it feels like I'm going to tear in two. He just rocks lightly, slipping only a quarter of his erection inside me. I try to move my hips to gain more of him, but he holds me steady with his hand and the firm grip he has on my leash, pulling harder every time I move, the collar constricting me.

"Kayne, please." His shallow pumps do nothing but crank my arousal with no offer of relief in sight.

"When I say you're ready." He withdraws completely, just as the woman on the screen climaxes, the man pounding into her relentlessly as he extracts every drop of her desire. I'm about ready to combust.

Then Kayne slams into me without any warning. "Oh!" I cry out, as the collar stops me from jutting forward. The tip of his cock hitting me exactly where I need, in the deepest, most tender part of my body. He thrusts again and again, sending me soaring.

"Kayne, please may I come!" I cry out as my orgasm breaks loose.

"No," he denies me.

"Kayne, please!" I beg as he picks up his rhythm, as if trying to drive me mad.

"I have to come!"

"Don't you dare." He slams so deep inside me that I implode, losing all control.

I feel him everywhere, through every cell and every synapse in my body. The extreme release is heaven sent. Then, right in the middle of my highest peak, he pulls out, deflating the rigorous orgasm that threatened to destroy me.

"No, why!" I collapse, nearly crying.

"Because I didn't give you permission." He yanks on the chain. I want to murder him. I've never felt so high then crash so low in my entire life.

"Lie down," he growls. I drop to my side, my body quivering from the starved arousal still snaking its way through my system. "Bad girl." He spanks me hard. The sensations inside me rattle. He pushes me onto my stomach while the sounds of exaggerated sex still fill the room. His breathing increases from behind me, and I immediately recognize the sound. He's jerking off. A few hellish moments later, he comes on my ass. I feel the spurts and hear his grunts all at the same time. I'm livid as my core throbs, demanding what he just afforded himself.

"Stay." His voice is hard and for some reason it makes me feel ashamed. Why?

"Go to bed," he instructs after he wipes himself off of me. I lift myself up off the floor.

"I don't remember granting you permission to stand," he snaps. He's being so mean!

I glance at him over my shoulder before I sink back down onto all fours. He eyes my every move with a cold expression. I crawl across the room toward the bed. Then climb on it once I reach it. If I had a tail, it'd be between my legs. I kneel on the mattress as Kayne stalks into the table of torture room. My anxiety spikes. God only knows what he's getting out of there. He returns with a pair of handcuffs.

"Lie down."

I lie on my back.

"Put your hands over your head."

I put my hands up, never taking my eyes off him. He cuffs me to the vining iron. "So you can't touch yourself," he informs me.

My eyes water. Cruel bastard. He repositions my leash after that, locking it to the front of my collar then securing it back to the headboard.

Shackled doesn't even begin to describe me.

Kayne gets dressed, shoving his legs into his pants and jerking his brown pinstripe button up over his head.

He then comes to stand over me. "This is a lesson, kitten. I control your pleasure." He circles the tip of his finger around my inflamed clit. I push my hips off the bed and moan insufferably. I need to come so bad, my head is pounding and my body is shaking.

"Kayne, please," I beseech one last time.

"Sorry, Ellie, you have to learn. Would you rather I whip you instead?"

"No." I shake my head vigorously. He did this on purpose just to torment me. Punishment in one form or another.

He leaves me with my suffering and the porn still playing on the TV.

KAYNE

I SIT IN THE SHADOWS of my office, monitoring the security feed.

The house is quiet this time of night. Most everyone is asleep, except for Ellie. My frisky little kitten. She's squirming uncomfortably handcuffed to her bed. I know she's achy and miserable, just as she should be. Orgasm control, or denial in this case, is a fundamental technique used to bond dominant and submissive. Or with us, Master and slave. It creates intense arousal and physiological need. Need only I can fulfill.

It's close to sunrise when I catch Spice leaving Javier's room on one of the monitors. She's crying, naked, and has whip marks all over her back. They look above and beyond the normal sexual role play. Son of a bitch is at it again. I stand, about to go to her, when Jett steps onto the feed. I swear, if I didn't know any better, he was waiting outside that door all night. I watch as he gently puts his arm around her and she melts against him, sobbing as they walk off the screen. He has a way with women I will never understand. Each and every one in this house adores him. Me, they respect. But him? It's just different.

I catch Ellie jerking and rubbing her thighs together on screen. She's in agony.

So much for not becoming the one thing I'm fighting against. I may not pour hot wax all over her body, or whip or beat her until she's bleeding, but I am torturing her in my own way.

I run my hands through my hair and groan. Time to go see my kitten. I love what I'm doing to her and I hate it. I know it's wrong even when it feels so right, so good, and is so irresistible.

The sounds of explosive sex and Ellie's heavy breathing circle the darkness as I sneak into her room. The dawn hasn't quite peaked over the horizon, so the only light present is the glare from the television. It doesn't offer much illumination considering the large expanse of the room.

"Please, please, please," Ellie begs once she sees me. "I'll control it. I'll learn to control it."

"Shhh." I pet her head, then shrug off my clothes. It never fails, one look at Ellie chained up wearing my collar, and my arousal roars to life. I don't even need to touch her. I grab the key to the handcuffs off the nightstand and crawl onto the bed, situating myself right between Ellie's welcoming knees. "Don't move," I instruct as I release her hands. She grabs onto the white iron as I remove the handcuffs. "Need me, baby?" I ask while she whimpers feebly.

"Yes," she responds with choppy breaths.

"Say it. Say you need me, Ellie." I hoist her hips up.

"Kayne, I need you." As soon as the sentence leaves her lips I drive my cock into her as deep as it can go.

"Ahh!" Her body twists with ecstasy as she grips the iron, her muscles clamping down around me like a metal trap.

"Shit," I grind out, but don't move as I succumb to the need of her body. Ellie is squirming desperately, but I steady her with a firm hold on her waist. "I want you to touch yourself."

Ellie stills, staring at me like I just told her to jump off a cliff without a parachute.

"Touch myself?"

"Come on, kitten." I encourage her with a tiny thrust. The way she moans you'd think I was fucking her mercilessly. All in good time.

"I've never done that before," she squeaks out.

"Really? Never?" I question her.

She shakes her head.

"Well, there's a first time for everything." I reach for her hand and bring it to my lips. I suck two of her fingers into my mouth, making sure to get them nice and wet, then place them over her swollen clit. Ellie tenses. "Come on, baby, touch yourself. It will turn me on," I encourage her.

"You're already turned on." She sucks in a deep breath. I pinch her ass cheek.

"Oh!"

"Remember who you're talking to, kitten."

"Yes, Kayne."

"Good girl. Now, I want to watch you make yourself come." I rock my hips and Ellie nearly fragments.

It takes several long seconds, but she finally starts to massage herself. Her movements are vapid at first, but after a few minutes, she closes her eyes and begins to explore herself with some enthusiasm. I watch and feel every gesture as her fingers slide easily between her wet folds and around her sensitive clit. She quickly finds a rhythm she likes and her breathing takes off, as does mine. Fuck, she feels amazing. I hold on to Ellie tightly, making sure to subdue her jerky hip movements so that all her pleasure is contained between her legs. She's so close, panting hard while rubbing herself into an orgasm.

"Please may I come?" she nearly cries, her face tight with sexual tension.

"Yes, come, now." I'm close to combusting myself. My heart rate spikes, as she crunches up and makes herself come all over my cock. So fucking good. As soon as Ellie drops down on to the bed, I cover her with my body. She's somewhere far away as she wraps her arms around my neck and her legs around my waist. The sounds of over-the-top sex still constantly streaming from the TV. I begin to rock, pulling all the way out then driving as deep as I can back in. She moans emphatically as I work both our bodies.

Ellie feels like nothing else in this world. Soft, wet, warm, and all fucking mine. I don't think I'll ever get enough.

"Fuck, Ellie, your pussy is so sweet." I thrust my hips as my climax intensifies, Ellie's muscles squeezing all the blood to the head of my erection, making me crazy.

"Open those fucking legs," I nearly snarl. Ellie immediately drops her knees and spreads her thighs. I fasten my arm underneath her back as I piston into her.

I lose all control being with Ellie, feeling her bare skin flush against mine, and her soaking wet pussy engulfing every inch of my rock hard cock. The sensations skyrocket my body and my mind.

It consumes me, changes me.

"Kayne!" She cries my name, and I know just what she needs. The exact same thing I do. To come.

"Ellie, let go. Let go and come with me."

She flutters her eyes open and for a split second just stares. The look is invasive. I feel it permeate all the way to my soul. My rhythm dies down, and I slide in and out painstakingly slow.

"*Ohhhh* ..." Ellie closes her eyes, bows her body, snaps her head back, and comes. Every single inch of me hums as she saturates me with her arousal, and for the first time in my life the euphoric look on a woman's face spurs me to break. I still at the tail end of Ellie's orgasm, my whole existence screeching to a grinding halt as I spill inside her. My entire body is ablaze and Ellie is the cause of the inferno. I drop down on top of her once the ensnaring sensations let go and wrap her in my arms. *What the fuck is happening to me?* She feels so perfect, so right, like she really is meant solely for me. An unnamed emotion suddenly surges within me and I grab her by the collar.

"I want you to understand something." She looks up at me with a penetrating stare. "Every morsel of food you eat, every breath of air you take is because of me. Because I allow it." Her eyes widen. "You live because of me. You live *for* me. Remember that when you fall asleep with my come inside you."

Ellie focuses on me silently. A mountain of power shifting between us.

"Yes, Kayne," she succumbs, and suddenly so do I. I kiss her forehead, her eyes, her cheeks, and her lips for a few elongated minutes, lulling her to relax. She inhales a deep breath with her eyes closed on the brink of falling asleep. I, on the other hand, feel like I can run a marathon. The beast is pacing inside me, like a caged animal demanding to be set free. Once never seems to be enough when it comes to Ellie. I want her all night and every second the shrouded darkness can afford us. I'm wildly tempted to fuck her again, but I don't. Instead, I withdraw from her gingerly just before she dozes off. She winces then frowns, tightening her arms. She's so close to passing out that I wonder if she even realizes she did it. On some absurd level I convince myself she really wants me to stay. *Keep dreaming dickhead.*

I lie wrapped in Ellie's arms a little longer than I should. For the first time in my life, I want to stay tangled in a woman's embrace. In Ellie's embrace. What would it be like to fall asleep next to her? To wake up and have her be there instead of an empty side of the bed. It's such a dangerous curiosity on all accounts, but compulsory all on its own. It spurs me to remove Ellie's arms from my neck and climb off the mattress. I can't get close. I *shouldn't* get close.

I turn off the television then dress quietly; all the while watching my kitten sleep. *What is she doing to me?* She's affecting me in ways I don't understand. Burrowing herself deep within a part of me that I never knew existed.

I grab the door handle with one last glance at Ellie's sleeping form; naked and vulnerable, yet passionate and strong. Everything she is, is everything I'll never be.

With all the will I have, I open the door to leave and run right smack into Jett. It's early morning now, and I know he's come to check on her. He looks at me with questioning eyes as he tries to slip past me into her room.

"Let her sleep," I say authoritatively as I step into the hallway, closing the door behind me. It clicks, locking her inside.

"Is she okay?" Jett asks concerned.

"She's fine." *I think.* Jett gazes at me impassively. I know he wants to check on her. I also know she needs her rest. It's been a long night for everyone.

"How's Spice?" I ask.

Jett responds with a pissed off expression. "She's been better."

"Shit."

"Yeah." He folds his him arms crossly. This living situation sucks for all of us.

I sigh as I settle myself against Ellie's thick wooden door.

"Going to stand there all day?" Jett asks irritably.

I shrug. "Maybe."

Probably.

I'm just not ready to leave her yet.

ELLIE

I'VE TAKEN UP READING, BECAUSE really what else do I have to do when Jett isn't stretching me into next week with yoga or Kayne isn't tying me up and fucking me into oblivion. I'm particularly intrigued—but mostly disturbed—by my current title. Almost all of the dirty adult books on the shelf are mindless sex stories. If you need to get in the mood you read one of those, but this one is different. It's about a girl who was abducted at a young age and sold into sexual slavery to numerous buyers. To say it doesn't strike a chord would be lying. The thought of Kayne selling me never occurred to me until this very moment. It's a terrifying realization. I'm an object, not a person. My rights and identity have been stripped away and my sole purpose for living is to serve another. I haven't forgotten Kayne's assertion *You live because of me. You live for me*. A chill runs down my spine. I want to take the book and chuck it across the room, but I keep my head and continue reading, morbidly engrossed in this girl's horrific story of rape, torture, and forced servitude. She addresses all of her owners as Master. It's creepy. I thank God for small favors that Kayne doesn't make me do that.

I read until Jett comes back into the room, close to dusk.

"Evening, sweet thing."

"Hi." I curl my knees up to my chest on the mattress. Not because I'm embarrassed of being naked, but because of the conflicting feelings running rampant inside of me. My mind knows this is all wrong, but my body doesn't care. It's ready for its fix.

Jett takes my book and places it back on the shelf then returns to the bed. He hooks one end of the listless chain back onto my collar and then commands me to drop.

I look at him strangely before I crawl into the position. Completely naked. This is new.

"Good girl." Jett uncoils my leash out from under me.

"No panties?" I ask, my voice elevating.

"Not tonight, Kayne requested you completely naked. And just like this."

I'm on my stomach with my knees pulled up to my chest and my hands over my head. It looks like I'm worshipping a shrine. It reminds me of my first obedience lesson. I shudder.

"When will he be here?" I ask with my face against the sheet.

"I don't know, Ellie, but stay like that until he comes in." I nod slightly.

"See you in the morning, sweet thing."

Jett leaves and it's just me and my thoughts in a compromising position. I'm not alone long. I hear the door click and immediately the room is engulfed with Kayne's dominant presence. My insides quiver.

"Hey, beautiful." He caresses my back and kisses my shoulder. "How was your day?"

"Jett made me do more yoga." I speak into the mattress.

"Good. Limbering you up for me." He spanks me lightly. I tense.

"Apparently."

"I want you as flexible as possible so I can bend you whichever way I want." He drops a soft kiss on the ass cheek he just smacked. In this position, I am overly exposed.

"You look to fucking die for like this."

He massages me in the same place he kissed me. "Ellie, I want to warn you up front. Tonight is going to be intense." He rubs his already erect cock against me.

"How intense?" I can barely utter the words. I'm already sick with anxiety and excited with arousal. I'm turning into a fucking whack job.

"You're not going to be able to walk tomorrow."

"What?" I go to lift my head but Kayne grabs my chain Jett left dangling between my legs, he never secured me to the headboard. My face is pressed firmly to the mattress as Kayne subdues me tight.

"You're mine, Ellie," he reminds me. "I can do to you as I please." I squeeze my eyes shut and swallow the thick fear threatening to choke me. He's going to hurt me.

He yanks my chain. "How do you reply?"

"Yes, Kayne," I say hoarsely.

"Yes, Kayne, please fuck me."

I repeat, "Yes, Kayne, please fuck me." Tears threaten, but I hold them back. I need to be strong, even if I am scared out of my mind.

"Good girl."

I want to slap him. I hope one day I get the chance.

Kayne drops something heavy onto the bed next to me; it bounces slightly on the mattress.

"Bring your hands down Ellie, put them by your sides."

I immediately do what he says. Swiftly, he takes each of my wrists and clamps them down, as something cold and metal runs across the back of my legs.

"Kayne?" I say shaky.

"Shhh." Then he takes my chain and secures it to the rod so I'm tied up tightly. I can't lift my head because of the chain and I can't move my legs or arms because of the cuffs and the bar. I'm scared shitless.

"Relax, Ellie." Kayne starts rubbing my ass that's now sticking high in the air. "You're going to need to trust me. And you're going to need to keep your body loose. The more you squirm and wriggle, the more uncomfortable you'll become."

More uncomfortable? Is that possible?

I can't see Kayne behind me. So I have to rely on my other senses. I feel him brush against me as he takes off his shirt and I hear his zipper lower as he removes his pants. I suddenly feel his tongue against my pussy. I jump trying to snap my head up, but the chain restricts me, acting like a pulley, forcing my knees forward and jutting my ass further into the air. "Told you to hold still."

Kayne begins licking me relentlessly, from the tip of my behind to the bottom of my clit. I'm soaking wet and dizzy with desire within a few short minutes. Then he takes his hands and spreads my ass cheeks as far as they can go, sliding his tongue into my little puckered hole. I shake uncontrollably.

I want to move.

I want more.

I want less.

I want the ache he's commanding quelled. *Now*!

"I'm going to fuck you here, Ellie."

I feel his warm breath brush against me. "I'm going to stretch you with my fingers then bury myself inside you. And that's where I plan to stay. All night." I tremble at his words, terrified of the pain. Recalling how he said I won't be able to walk tomorrow.

"Kayne, please be gentle," I beg in my shackles.

"I won't hurt you, baby. Unless you disobey me, or ask for it."

Like hell I would ever do that.

When Kayne feels he's lubricated me enough, he starts to inch his thumb inside me. The initial intrusion hurts and is so intense, but once he's fully inside, the pain starts to taper.

"Fuck, you're so tight. I can't wait to be inside you." He withdraws his thumb and replaces it with one of his fingers. I'm dying. It hurts, and it doesn't. I like it, and I don't. My body is caught in a feverous mix of pleasure and pain, and it's only the beginning. I don't know if I'm going to survive this night. Just as Kayne slips another finger into me and begins scissoring me open, there's a pounding on the door.

"Kayne!" Jett calls through the wood.

"Jett, the fucking house better be on fire," he growls, continuing his assault.

"There's a situation that needs your immediate attention."

"What kind of situation?" He halts his ministrations but doesn't withdraw his fingers. My body is strung so tight, I could snap at any second.

"A delicate one," Jett relays, and that seems to get Kayne's full attention.

"Motherfucker," he grinds out. "Give me a sec," he barks.

"Hurry up." Jett fumes through the door.

Kayne leans over my subdued face. "I'm sorry, baby, we're going to have to put this on hold for a few minutes." He kisses my cheek, withdraws his fingers then disappears. My body deflates, as I'm left helpless on the bed.

I hear metal sliding across tracks as drawers are opened and closed. My adrenaline spikes. Then I feel Kayne standing behind me once again.

"I really wanted to prime you myself, but this will have to do in my absence. Open." He shoves something hard and metal into my mouth. I know exactly what it is. It's the exact same object he used after he whipped me, except this one is much larger; longer and fatter. My stomach twists. "Ellie, relax." He yanks on the chain attached to the plug and I release it. He then works the extra-large plug into my ass. No inching or easing, just one fluid motion. I groan loudly as it fills me completely. So much more than his fingers did. I'm panting wildly by the time he's through. It fucking hurts. Is this what it's going to feel like when he fucks me? Kayne then tells me to open again. He inserts something hard and rubbery into my mouth. "Suck."

I wrap my lips around the object and do as I'm told. Good little pleasure kitten. He removes it when he's satisfied, then slowly slides it into my pussy. Holy fuck, if I thought I was full before, I'm overflowing now. Then I hear a click and it starts to vibrate gently. The pulse reaches all the way into my womb. My breathing goes from panting to gasping in a nanosecond. He can't leave me like this!?

"You'll be good and ready for me when I get back." Kayne smacks my ass and a simultaneous bolt of pleasure and pain shoots through me. I moan, incapacitated, as the butt plug and vibrator wage war on my body, pushing me to the edge and dangling me there. An orgasm is brewing, but coming nowhere close to where I need to find release. Why did he do this? Why is he torturing me?!

AYNE

I DRESS QUICKLY WITH MY cock as hard as a stone slab and Ellie squirming uncomfortably on the bed.

Whatever the fuck is going on, it better be a red level terror alert. I open the door to find Jett quivering.

"What the fuck?" I ask.

"Just follow me." He hauls ass down the hall. I follow with the same quickness as we fly down one flight of stairs to the second floor and beeline it straight for Javier's room. Crap, this definitely isn't good. Once inside, I see the situation. Spice is flailing all over Javier's bed. She holding her arm, tears pouring down her face.

"That motherfucker dislocated her shoulder," Jett explodes. "I need help popping it back into place."

Son-Of-A-Bitch.

Spice whimpers as Jett and I both climb onto the bed without delay. Me, on Spice's injured side, Jett by her head. She looks up at me in distress. "Okay, baby, we're going to fix it." I talk to her serenely. The last thing I want is her feeling more tension. There's enough radiating off Jett to light up the whole house. "Spice, take a deep breath." I glance up at Jett, his stare is removed, and his face flushed. "Stay with me, brother."

"I'm here," he says, eerily composed. Eerily composed Jett is never a good sign.

"Kayne, please," Spice begs. Her voice is so small. Usually the sound of a woman begging sends me into a state of sexual frenzy. At the moment, it's not eliciting anything sexual from me at all. Unless you count homicidal thoughts as sexually exciting.

"Okay, on the count of three I'm going to pop it back in." I stare into her eyes. The dark green ones that look exactly like Ellie's. My chest aches. This could have easily been her. This and so much worse. I fight to keep my head and concentrate on helping the suffering brunette. "One." I stand up and pull her arm over the edge of the bed. Spice screams. I wait a few seconds for her muscles to relax. I glance at Jett and he nods. "Two." I pull, slow and steady, catching her off guard. She screams again as I roll her arm until I hear her shoulder pop back into place.

As soon as I'm finished, she passes out; I conclude half from stress, half from the pain. Shit. Poor thing. She's been put through the damn wringer ever since Javier stepped foot in this house. I blame myself. Maybe I shouldn't, maybe there's no reason, but nevertheless I do.

"It's okay now, you're okay." Jett kisses her head and caresses her hair. It's a paternal reaction.

"Where is he?" I ask Jett.

"Gone," he replies, not even looking at me. I know he won't drag his attention away from Spice.

"Gone where?" I ask.

"Who cares?" he boils.

"I do, and you better too."

"I heard him say something about wanting a *cerveza.*"

"Great, at the local bar, just what we need. A drunk, belligerent abusive Mexican." I run my hands down my face.

Jett lifts Spice off the bed. "I'm taking her to my room. She needs ice. And I'm putting all the other girls on lockdown for the night."

I nod in agreement. "Is there anyone here?"

"One room is occupied. As soon as Spice is comfortable they're getting kicked the fuck out."

"That should be good for business," I comment back handedly.

Jett shoots me a dangerous look.

"I need to get back to Ellie," I pop off, the mere mention of her name should chill him out.

"Fine, go." Jett walks toward the door. I pull on his arm.

"Don't do anything stupid."

He glances down at my hand and then back up at my face. He curls his lip in warning, his aqua eyes ice cold. "If you can handle it, I can handle it."

I know exactly what he means. If I didn't kill Javier after what he did to Ellie, Jett won't kill him for what he did to Spice.

As Jett and I walk the expansive hall in opposite directions, I'm struck with a lifetime's worth of jarring memories. *My lifetime.* It all comes back, the isolation, the fear, and inability to trust. *You're nothing but a paycheck you little fuck. Slam!*

For as long as I can remember, abuse has always been at the forefront of my life. Whether direct or indirect, it affects you all the same.

I start to breathe heavily as the memories swarm like angry bees. I've spent years trying to suppress the hostility, and sometimes uncontrollable rage, if for nothing more than the simplicity of sleeping at night. But with Ellie and Spice and the situation at hand, my past resurfaces like an underwater eruption.

By the time I reach Ellie's door, I'm wound so tight I don't know what I'm capable of.

ELLIE

TEARS START TO WELL IN my eyes long before Kayne returns. The sensations are way too much. I need to move, to satisfy the ache eating away at my insides. If I shift even a fraction of an inch, I feel it everywhere. Between my legs, up my ass, along my spine. I mewl insufferably, needing relief. The tears spill, wetting my face, and all I can do is let them fall. Kayne is the only one who can release me from this prison.

Just when I think my heart is going to explode from the unrelenting stress, Kayne returns.

"Please, please," I beg. "Please let me come. I can't take anymore."

He doesn't say a word, but I can feel the tension rippling off of his body. It scares the living shit out of me.

"You want to come?" His voice is menacing, and I know I'm in for something brutal. He yanks the vibrator out and I nearly fall apart. A second later he slams into me with such force I scream and slide forward on the bed. "Stay fucking still." He pulls me back and begins to pound into me. In a split second, I come apart. Freefalling into oblivion. Then, right in the middle of my orgasm, he ruthlessly rips out the butt plug, sending another crippling wave of ecstasy crashing through my body. I cry uncontrollably, completely destroyed, drained of all energy as I gasp for air on the bed. I'm still seeing stars when he finally comes. He grits his teeth as he stabs into my hips with his fingers and into my pussy with his cock.

Heaven help me.

When it's finally over, I feel like I'm going to break apart. The man can be so vicious.

I start to nod off when Kayne pokes me with his still hard erection. "Sorry, Ellie." He almost sounds remorseful. "I'm not done with you yet." His voice is calmer now. But still dark and thick with desire. "I told you I was going to fuck you here." He pushes the head of his cock against my sore rose bud. "And that's exactly what I intend to do." How is he still hard? I brace myself for the bite. Then feel something cold and slippery against my skin.

"What's that?" I ask, my voice muffled against the mattress.

"Lubrication." He smears it all over me, and then pushes against my entrance again. I groan as he fights his way in inch by agonizing inch, until he's buried deep inside.

Holy fuck! He's triple the size of the industrial butt plug.

"I knew you were going to feel this way," he expels euphorically, completely still. "I used to jerk off to this exact image. Do you know that? After I would leave Mark's office, I would fantasize about what it would be like to tie you down and make you scream." Kayne starts to move in and out in small, controlled thrusts. I feel him everywhere, governing my entire existence. He's infiltrating my body, compelling my mind, and contorting my soul.

Another gargantuan orgasm starts to bloom. My cheeks flush, my muscles clench, my neck strains, and my wrists hurt as he takes his movements from small and controlled to elongated and deep. Every thrust ripping me open, every withdrawal sewing me closed. "All night. I'm going to fuck you like this all night." And there's not a damn thing I can do about it. I'm tied up, at his mercy.

"You're mine, Ellie, and I want to hear you scream."

And I do, over and over, orgasm after orgasm, until our fluids are soaking the bed, my voice is gone, and my body is limp.

ELLIE?" JETT SHAKES ME LIGHTLY. "Ellie, wake up."

I crack open my eyes but don't move my body. It feels like I've been in a car accident. I hurt all over. I groan. Kayne said I wasn't going to be able to walk today. He wasn't kidding.

"Come on, love, it's late. You need to get up."

"How late?" My eyes flutter to the window.

"Five in the evening. You've been asleep all day. Kayne put a punishing on you last night, huh?"

That is definitely one way to put it.

Kayne didn't leave my room until nearly dawn. When he was finished with me, he discarded me like nothing more than an overused rag doll. He chained me back to the headboard, kissed me on the lips and left silently. That was it. I was his sex toy and he used me as such. An object to play with and then toss back on the shelf. Or in my case, the bed. It fucking hurts. I feel empty and used. This life is hard, nothing like the one I dreamed of having.

"Kayne will want to see you soon. Get up."

"I don't think I can walk." My voice is small and hapless.

"Come on, I'll help you." Jett unlocks me and lifts me into his arms. The ache in my back and between my legs is excruciating. I moan miserably.

He carries me into the bathroom. "How about a hot bath?"

I nod.

"Do you think you can stand?"

I nod again. I'm not in a very talkative mood.

Jett places me on my feet and I wince, the contact with the floor vibrates all the way up my body. He turns on the faucet and squeezes some soap into the water. The now familiar scent of eucalyptus fills the room. Jett turns to me once the enormous soaking tub is halfway filled. As soon as he reaches out to me, I crack. I don't even know where it comes from. The emotion wasn't there a second ago, but now tears are falling like an unstoppable rainstorm from my eyes.

"Ellie!?" Jett wraps me in his arms and the embrace hurts. "Are you in that much pain?"

"Yes. No. I don't know. It's just ... how am I supposed to survive like this? I feel empty. How am I supposed to live with no emotion? No love? As just someone's pet? To be taken off its leash and played with." I sob inconsolably. "I didn't work my ass off for four years so I could end up like this. As nothing. No one. I was supposed to start school in the fall. Travel. See everything my parents couldn't afford me. And now it's all gone. All my hopes, all my dreams."

"Oh, honey." Jett hugs me tighter and I whimper. "I know this isn't your ideal situation. But there are things going on you know nothing about. Trust Kayne."

"Trust him? He did this to me!"

"What? Gave you several nights of unbelievable pleasure? So you're in a little pain. It will subside."

"No, it's not that." I wipe my eyes. "He's isolated me. Emotionally exiled me."

Jett sighs, as if conflicted. "Get in the tub."

He helps me step in, and I sink into the cathartic hot water. Then

Jett crouches beside me. "Let me tell you something about Kayne," he whispers. "When it comes to you, his emotions are more present than you think."

I skeptically look into Jett's aqua eyes. "Are you trying to tell me he cares about me?"

"In his own way. Not everything is always black and white. And some things need to be revealed in their own time."

"What does that mean?" I press.

"It means patience is a virtue and submission is your salvation."

I have no idea what he's talking about. Kayne won't always treat me like an object? That underneath he actually cares? It's hard to believe. He looks at me, treats me, and handles me like I'm nothing but a sexual vessel for his use and abuse. I shift in the tub and my muscles wail.

"How can anyone go that long? He never got soft. What did he do, take Viagra?" I grimace.

Jett whistles pseudo-innocently at my accusation.

I widen my eyes. "He took Viagra?! *Why?*"

Jett shrugs. "He can't get enough of you. You're the first woman I've ever seen him like this with."

"Animalistic?" I snap.

"Infatuated."

"Is that what you call it so you can sleep better at night?"

"Sweet thing, I sleep just fine." Jett kisses me on the head. "Enough talk. Just relax for a while. Okay?"

"Yes, Jett," I sneer submissively.

He rolls his eyes.

AYNE

I WALK SILENTLY INTO ELLIE'S room and hear her crying. The sound shreds me apart. As her voice carries from the bathroom, I listen to her tell Jett everything she's feeling. She opens up to him, and I'm stung with jealousy. I want her to confide in me. Trust me. *I* own her. Not Jett.

I'm tempted to kick him out and join Ellie in the tub but decide against it. It's clear she needs some space. And some time alone.

When I came to check on her, I wasn't expecting to find her like this. Tears. I hate them and I love them. I know she has to be sore. I wasn't nice last night. I planned to fuck her for hours, but our little interruption sent me over the edge, and I ended up taking my frustrations out on her. It wasn't fair, I know that. But on some sick, sadistic level—it was the best sex of my life. If I'm honest, every time with Ellie is the best sex of my life.

Javier, that walking piece of shit, treating Spice like one of his fucking slaves. I have news for him. *No bueno.* His arrogance is festering under my skin. And someday soon I'm going to return all his little favors.

I lean on the wall outside Ellie's room and wait impatiently while Jett tends to her.

"She's upset," I say, startling him once he finally he exits.

"For fuck's sake, Kayne," he snaps. "Yes, she is. Why are you?"

"I don't like it when she's upset. I like it even less that she confides in you."

"Why do you have a problem with her confiding in me? She needs someone to talk to," he argues.

"She has me. *I* own her."

"How is she supposed to confide in someone who treats her like a whore on a leash?"

I growl. "You know that's not how I see her." Even though I love her on that leash.

"*She* doesn't know that. Treat her like the tin man and you get a steel heart."

"What the fuck does that mean, Riddler?"

Jett bristles. "You know, for a smart guy, you're a dumb dumb sometimes. You want her to confide in you, you want her to trust you. You want her to love you, then show her how you feel. Don't just stick your dick in her and walk out of the room."

I inwardly groan. "You know that's dangerous given the circumstances."

"Well, it's a choice you have to make. She's either your whore or your lover. She can't be both."

Why not?

I pinch the bridge of my nose. This is a sticky situation all the way around. I can't let anyone, even Ellie, know how deep my feelings go. But I don't want her to feel unloved. Or like she's slipping away. Especially from me.

"How should I handle this?" I exhale, banging the back of my head against the wall.

Jett smiles deviously, his aqua eyes gleaming.

"Give me two hours. You and Ellie are going on your first date."

ELLIE

JETT REENTERS TO MY ROOM in a rush.

I watch confused as he unlocks my collar and ushers me off the bed. "What's going on?"

"You need to take a shower and get dressed," he says in a hurry, pushing me toward the bathroom.

"But I just spent all day in the tub." Or at least what was left of the day.

"I know." Jett flicks on the water then opens the linen closet and pulls out a bottle. "In you go." He hands me some new soap. "Wash quickly. Hair and everything. I'll be right back."

I do as I'm told. Enjoying the new scent of lemongrass filling the stall. By the time I'm done with the shower, Jett has the folding table opened up and an array of makeup spread out by the sink.

"What's going on?" I ask as he sits me down. I wince. I'm still so sore.

"I'm getting you ready."

"For what?"

"A date." He picks up the comb and a pair of scissors sitting next to me on the table.

"With who?"

"Kayne."

"What?" I look up at him as he begins to part my hair.

"Yup." There's a snip and a chunk of my hair falls to the floor.

"Jett!"

"Trust me, Ellie, I wouldn't let you look anything other than gorgeous."

I suck in a deep breath as he snips away, strands of hair falling all around me. When he's done, he blow dries my hair with the round brush he loves so much. The ends are now falling over my right eye. I try to tuck them behind my ear.

"Don't touch," he scolds playfully. Then he turns his attention to my face, using all the makeup he has spread out on the counter.

"Damn I'm good," he gloats as he lifts my chin and inspects his handiwork. There's a sudden knock at the door and I jump. "Relax, Ellie. That's just dinner." Jett rubs my arms reassuringly. "Stay here."

He leaves the bathroom to answer the door. From where I'm sitting, I can't see into the bedroom, but I can hear everything.

"Perfect, put it on the table," Jett instructs. I lean over to try and see who he's talking to but am only met by a wall.

I hear footsteps then, "Don't we even get to meet her?" a soft, young female voice asks. I freeze.

"Not tonight," Jett responds nicely, but in a hurry. "Now shoo."

There are giggles and then the door closes. Jett walks back into the bathroom with a large smile.

"Who was that?" I inquire, still perched uncomfortably on the table.

"Personnel." He winks. "Come on. Time to get dressed." He helps me stand up with care. I'm slow moving at the moment. The bath and the shower helped relax my back muscles, but my core and behind are still sensitive as hell. Every step reminds me of the brutality from last night.

On the bed are several articles of 'clothing,' sheer white panties, matching thigh highs, garters, and patent leather heels. Jett dresses me quickly, first slipping the satiny low-rise underwear on and then the garters, clipping the thigh highs in place. Finally, he helps me step into the stiletto heels I could use as a weapon, and refastens my collar. He stands back and admires me, but I can tell he thinks something's off. "Ah!" He snaps, and turns for the armoire. After rummaging around it for a few seconds, he returns to me. He holds up a long string of crystals and I look at them curiously. Jett just smirks as he attaches one end to the front loop of my collar, the other end he wraps around my waist and clasps it like a belt. "Body jewelry." He tugs lightly on the strand.

I look down at myself, I feel like I should be modeling for Frederick's of Hollywood.

"Jett?" I ask sadly. "Why are you wasting your time?"

"First, let's get something straight. I never waste my time. Second, sweet thing, I know there is more to you and Kayne than just a Master/ slave relationship, and I think it's time we exploit it."

I glare at him cynically. "All I am is a pet to him."

"Do you really believe that?" he questions me.

"Has he given me a reason not to believe it?"

"Maybe that's what tonight is for." Jett raises his eyebrows.

I highly doubt it. I'm sure the minute Kayne tries to touch me, I'm going to erupt into tears. The mere thought of any kind of sexual interaction has me falling apart. And I know any protest will only lead to a punishment. My foreseeable future fucking sucks.

"Come on, kitten." Jett nudges me. "Get up on that bed and be your sexy little self. Once Kayne sees you, he'll be wrapped around your pinky finger in record time."

"You think it's going to be that easy, huh?" I ask as I crawl onto the mattress.

"I know it," Jett confirms as he fixes me to the headboard. "He's halfway there as it is."

Sure he is.

"Wanna know a secret?" He leans into my face. I nod. "You may not believe it, but you hold all the power."

I stare back at him like he's downright nuts.

Jett winks, and then coils the strand of crystals resting between my naked breasts around his index finger. "Kayne is going to love this."

"How do you know?" I inquire.

"Because I know what he likes. I know what all men like."

"A blow job?" I reply dryly.

"Yes, definitely that." Jett laughs. "And a woman who's all their own."

AYNE

TWO HOURS LATER I'VE CHANGED into a new button up shirt and dress pants, per the request of Jett. I have no idea what he has planned, and I have no idea how this night is going to turn out, but a large piece of me hopes well. I want so many things from Ellie that sometimes I wonder if I'm asking too much. Actually, I know I am because I do want her to be both. *My lover, and my pet.*

I arrive back at Ellie's door precisely one hundred and twenty minutes later. When I walk inside her room, I find her exactly where she should be. Perched on her knees, naked and chained to her bed. Her honey brown hair is falling down over her bare chest and now part of her face, too. She cut, what are those things called? Bangs, I think. I stand in front of her and notice something sparkly around her waist. "Look at me, Ellie." I put my finger under her chin and she sweeps her head up. Her eyes are lined with thick dark pencil, her cheeks are pink and so are her lips. Jett played dress-up. Her hair is cut into chunky layers, and she's wearing diamond body jewelry. A thin string of crystals is attached to her collar, which run along her front, between her naked breasts, and belts around her waist. Her panties are a white, see-through material with garters holding up matching pantyhose. White patent leather stilettos finish her unbelievably sexy, temptress look. She's fucking to die for; my cock is banging inside my pants already, begging to be set free.

"You look stunning."

"Thank you, Kayne," she replies in a lackluster tone. Her

submission usually turns me on, but tonight I just want Ellie. I want the girl who shared her cupcake with me. Who used to laugh and ramble. *Who used to want me.*

I unlock the chain from her collar, drinking her in a few seconds more. "I'm sorry if I hurt you last night. Are you in pain?" I want to touch her but refrain. I don't want her to think I'm just here for sex. *Treat her like the tin man and you get a steel heart.*

"No, Kayne." Her voice breaks a little bit, and so does my newly functioning heart.

"Get up, Ellie." I draw her off the bed. She eases up with grace, even though I see the agony she's trying to hide on her face. I lead her over to the table hand-in-hand, no chains tonight. Jett put out a spread. There's enough food to keep us locked up for three days. I wonder if that was his intention. I sit in the chair and Ellie kneels on the floor between my legs. She's such a good girl. I let her stay for just a second before I pull her onto my lap. "Sit on me, Ellie."

She blinks curiously but remains silent. *Speak only when you are spoken to.*

"How do you feel? Answer honestly."

She looks up into my eyes with her head still bowed. "I'm hurting."

"I'm sorry. I didn't mean to take it that far."

"What happened last night?" Her voice strains. The sound nearly kills me.

"Just a situation I have no tolerance for."

"So you took your frustration out on me?"

"I did. And I'm sorry."

She looks at me surprised, maybe because my apology is genuine. Maybe because I apologized at all.

"I like it rough, but I didn't mean for my anger to translate." I put my hand on her lower stomach. I know she had to feel it deep in her core when I slammed into her that first time.

"Why are you telling me this? Why do you even care? You made it very clear what I'm here for." There are tears brimming in her eyes.

"I'm telling you because I want you to be able to trust me. To be able to talk to me."

She shakes her head incredulously at me. "How am I supposed to talk to you, when you don't allow me to speak? Or look at you, or touch you?"

"I am trying to figure that out." I grab one of her breasts and start massaging it. I can't be this close without touching her. Her nakedness and her sultriness makes me pine for her, even when she's just an inch away. "But I want to know when you're hurt or upset or lonely. I want you to be able to confide in me. Find comfort with me." I drop a kiss on her shoulder. She smells amazing; whatever soap Jett makes her use is intoxicating.

"How am supposed to be open and submissive at the same time? We can barely have this conversation without you groping me."

"I can't help it. I won't lie. I want you all the fucking time. Even now, I wish we were having this conversation with you riding me. If you weren't in so much pain I'd plant you on my cock."

"Kayne," she admonishes.

"What? I'm only telling the truth. It doesn't feel good when I touch you?" I tease her nipple.

"Yes, Kayne," she answers vacantly. She's made her point.

"Be honest. I'll always want honesty." I tease her nipple a little harder. She stifles a moan.

"Yes. It feels good," she finally confesses.

"Good." I inhale her fresh scent. "Because that's what I want. I want to make you feel as good as you make me feel."

"Then I can't be just your pet on a leash." Her smoky green eyes infiltrate mine.

"I like you on a leash. That's not going to change. I want to dominate you, and I want you submissive."

"Then I don't know how anything's going to change." There's defeat in her voice.

"We'll have a safe word." I think quickly on my feet.

"A what?"

"A safe word." I keep massaging her firmly. "For our emotions. Use it when you feel upset or want to talk. Or just need me to make love to you. Say it. And I'll give you whatever you need." I suck on her collarbone, my cock straining painfully against my zipper. "I'll use it so you know you mean more to me than just sex."

Ellie stays silent while I kiss up her neck and then back down, restraining myself from moving to her breasts even though my mouth is begging to suck on the little pink pebbles her nipples have become.

"Do I?" she whispers softly, the moonlight flooding through the window is giving her smooth skin a silver glow.

"Yes, baby. So much more." I lick her.

"What word?" she asks stretching her neck to give me better access.

"Cupcake." I nip at her skin.

She giggles to herself. "That's perfect." Then sighs into me.

"I thought so." I grope her firmly, more urgently. Shit, my control is completely unraveling.

"Ellie, get on the floor." I can't stand it anymore.

"But Kayne—"

"We'll talk more later, I promise. Right now I need you to lie on the floor."

"I don't think I can tonight." She frowns, pleadingly.

"I know. That's why I'm going to fuck your mouth." I grab her face and kiss her ardently on the lips, sucking as much oxygen as I can from her lungs. She's breathing hard, tears dripping down her face.

"Don't think of him, Ellie. Just me. Replace his memory with me."

I won't let fucking Javier get in her head. "I'm going to make him pay for what he did." I trap her face close to mine. "And I'm not going to let him steal what rightfully belongs to me. Now lie on the floor." Maybe I'm being a little harsh. But, tough love and all. It will only make her stronger in the end. I've learned that lesson the hard way, repeatedly.

And I swear, after all this, after everything, I'll make it up to her. *Repeatedly.*

Ellie lies down on the soft rug, bends her knees and draws her hands over her head. I stand, gazing down at her perfect little body dressed only in diamonds, panties, garters, and heels. I discard my clothes in record time, leaving them in a pile on the floor. I kneel between her legs and unhook one garter then the other. Her body goes rigid. "I want you to relax, Ellie. This isn't going to hurt. I promise. I know you're sore." I leave on the thigh highs but remove her clingy underwear, exposing her little pink pussy. It's sticking its tongue out at me, just tempting me to tease it. I lean down and suck on her clit; she bows her body and moans.

I love that reaction. It ignites something inside me. I lick languidly, coaxing her to relax. When she's breathing heavily and her body is loose, I shift, moving around her until I'm kneeling over her head, looking down her elongated body.

"Open your mouth, baby."

She does without hesitation. I lean over and brace myself on the floor with one hand. With the other I skim the head of my erection along her bottom lip. "I want you to suck me, Ellie. And don't stop no matter what I do." She whimpers as I slide my cock into her mouth. "Think of me, Ellie, only me." I lean forward so she can take more of me into her mouth. I support myself above her on my forearms and knees as she begins to suck. Fuck, I already feel it at the base of my tailbone. I grab onto her thighs. "Cupcake." I rasp just before I drop my head between her legs and drag my tongue over her slit. She moans, pulling harder on me as I lick around her clit. I keep her thighs spread as I simultaneously fuck her pussy with my tongue and her mouth with my cock. She's pinned beneath me with her hands still over her head, completely at my mercy, just the way I like her. She starts to rock her hips, no doubt chasing an orgasm. I'm not too far behind her. Her mouth is just as wet and tight as the sweet spot between her knees. Nirvana. Her tongue swirls around me as I pump in and out. Her breath becomes heavy as her muffled moans grow more intense. She tries to squirm, but she trapped. Then in a rush, she comes. The rattling of her body throttles me, and I thrust deeper, sliding all the way in until I touch the back of her throat. The suction and vibrations spur me to crack. My muscles tighten as I come in her mouth, forcing her to swallow every single drop.

My kitten never disappoints.

I make sure to lick Ellie clean before I kiss my way back up her body. She's flushed and panting by the time I get to her face.

"How was that? Did I hurt you?"

"No, Kayne," she answers a little starry eyed.

"Good girl." I grin upside down at her. She smiles back.

I pull Ellie up. "Hungry?"

"Yes, Kayne." Her answer is more playful than serious. I like that tone so much better.

I sit down in the chair and haul Ellie onto my lap. I tug on her little diamond chain with approval. "I think I'll keep this on you."

"Jett said you would like it." She lifts her shoulder to her cheek, half flirty, half shy.

She's never responded to me that way before. It makes my insides flip.

"Jett knows me pretty well," I divulge.

"I'm discovering that."

I feed Ellie a decadent dinner of duck a l'orange. She in turn feeds me back. I've never had a woman feed me before, and Ellie looks like she's enjoying it just as much as I am, giggling when I nip her fingers and moaning when I French kiss food from her mouth.

"Tell me one of your dreams, Ellie."

"I want to see paradise," she answers as I kiss her shoulder. Then her demeanor altogether changes—she withdraws and looks away. Shit.

"Hey." I draw her face back to mine. I know what's made her upset. She thinks she's owned and her freedom is gone. It's the truth. And that's the way it has to stay, for now.

"It's only ever going to be a dream," she says, her voice small and discouraged.

"Don't, Ellie," I respond sterner than I mean to. "Don't ruin tonight," I beseech her.

"Yes, Kayne," she submits.

I shake my head. I don't want to lose playful Ellie. I cup her face firmly, meaningfully. "Cupcake," I whisper against her mouth, right before I claim it.

When I'm done licking, kissing, and sucking her, I lift Ellie into my arms.

"Bed."

She doesn't protest. She looks beat, which is totally my fault. I lay her down, unroll her thigh highs, and remove her shoes. I leave on the diamond jewelry. Then I hook her back on her leash. Every time I see her lying here collared and chained to the bed, it does insane, indescribable things to me. My loins actually throbs.

I crawl next to her and rest my head on her chest, wrapping her tightly in my arms.

"Are you staying?" She sounds surprised. I know why that is. It will be the first time I spend an entire night with her.

"If you don't mind." I nuzzle my face against her soft skin.

"No." She yawns softly, snuggling up to me. Just like she did that night at Mark's party. It felt good then, it feels even better now.

"Sleep," I instruct.

And in no time at all, she is.

ELLIE

I WAKE UP TO KAYNE wrapped snugly around me and sunlight pouring into the room. Morning already.

I try to decipher exactly what happened last night. Did we actually establish an emotional safe word? A word that represents more? I like the idea. I like not feeling empty.

The door clicks and Jett comes to a screeching halt when he realizes what he's walked in on. Or what he thinks he's walked in on. Which is nothing really, but Kayne sleeping soundly on top of me. He backtracks out the door with a smirk on his face.

I lie there silently listening to Kayne breath, inspecting his beautiful features, desperately trying to figure out what makes this complicated man tick. I trace the thick black barbed wire tattoo dripping with blood lightly with the tip of my finger. I've never had the chance to touch him freely before. Kayne stirs ever so slightly, then again. He runs his hand over my body until he reaches one of my breasts.

"Mmmm." He squeezes with his eyes still closed. Then he shifts, digging his erection into my thigh.

"Put your hands over your head."

I do as I'm told. Kayne's eyes pop open, the blue a shock of intensity. He smiles wickedly at me, and then wraps my leash around my wrists, somehow securing me to the bed with it. *Boy Scout*. Then he starts licking his way down my body. "How do you feel?" He sucks one of my nipples into his mouth, and the sensation shoots straight to my groin.

"Better." I sigh, completely at his mercy.

"Good. Because I really need to fuck you."

My heartbeat accelerates as he works his way down to my thighs, kissing the inside of each one. I moan, lifting my hips. I want him to lick me. *Oh, did I really just think that?* My body is a lecherous traitor.

He teases me with his tongue, never going near the pulsating spot between my legs.

The most I get is the tickle of his warm breath as he moves from one thigh to the other.

Why does he need to torture me? I find myself begging.

"Kayne, please." I feel empty and exposed, my body pleading to be touched, to be filled. By him. What's happening to me?

"Beg me. Beg me to be inside you."

"Please, Kayne, please," I whimper, as he sucks harder on my skin.

"Please what? Lick you? Fuck you? Beg for what you want, Ellie."

"I don't care! Either! Both! But please just touch me."

God, when did I become so needy? When did this become okay?

Kayne nestles himself between my thighs forcing them further apart. He rests on top of me, pinning me under his body, the head of his cock pushing against my entrance.

"Open wider, Ellie," he orders.

I inch my legs farther apart, as he slowly, mind numbingly, slides inside me. I let out a low moan as he works his hips languidly. Pushing all the way in and withdrawing all the way out. My muscles clench on their own accord, desperate to keep him inside.

"Wider," he commands.

"I can't," I protest.

"Shhhh ... Don't talk back and spread your legs." He shifts one of his thighs so it presses against mine, forcing my already straining legs wider. I pull on my restraints as Kayne pushes the limits of my body. The wider my legs, the deeper he gets. It's trying pain mixed with unbelievable pleasure. It feels like I'm tearing apart.

He grabs me by my collar as he thrusts harder, more erratic.

"Do you like the way I fuck you, Ellie?"

"Yes, Kayne." I barely have any breath to speak, as an orgasm brews deep inside me. It comes on faster with every driving thrust while my wrists start to burn from fighting against the chains. I have no outlet for my restrained body to absorb the sensations, so it all concentrates between my legs, spasming up my center and punching its way into my stomach. This orgasm is going to rock me.

"Kayne, please may I come?" I ask desperately.

"Not yet." He denies me.

"Please!"

"Wait." His chest tightens as he moves inside me. "Now."

With a solid strike of his hips, Kayne kicks me over the edge. I scream, tears pricking my eyes as he exploits the helplessness of my body, reaping every drop of my climax he can. Moments later he grips my collar strenuously as he comes violently inside me.

My small reprieve from physical pain evaporates. Everything is throbbing again; my legs, my arms, my stomach, my vagina.

I struggle to move as Kayne lies sated on top of me, his hand still gripping my collar.

"Where do you think you're trying to go?"

"Nowhere while you're laid out on top of me. I just need to shift." I wince as I shimmy my butt and attempt to close my legs.

Kayne yanks on my collar. "Remember who you're talking to. I'm the only one who says when you can move." His tone isn't threatening, but there is a shroud of reminder that he is still Master and I am still slave. No matter the understanding we came to last night.

Kayne lies on top of me for a while longer, kissing my neck while massaging my shoulders and breasts. I lay perfectly still, my hands still bound, powerless, just the way he likes me.

"Are we ever going to have sex without you tying me up?" I ask.

"Doubtful," he answers, squeezing my breast hard. "Only speak when spoken to," he reminds me harshly. "Vanilla is nice, but kink is king in my world. And now yours, too."

My heart sinks a little. This room, this fifty-by-fifty space, is my domain. Kayne is my ruler, collars and chains my boundaries.

A little while later, after he's finished feeling me up and making me come a second time with his mouth, he releases my bound hands. "Over and drop." He nudges me onto my stomach. I roll over and pull my legs up underneath me, my arms straight over my head. "I want to look at your ass while I get dressed." He kisses my back with my forehead pressed to the mattress. I hear him pull on his pants and zip up his fly. When he finished ogling me, he orders me to my knees. I sit before him naked, sore and chained to the bed. He sighs contently, bringing my face up.

"You're beautiful and sexy and all fucking mine. I vow to keep you safe."

Thoughts of Javier come unwelcome into my mind. I fight back tears. That experience will haunt me forever. Kayne leans in and kisses me, soft and tender, licking the seam of my mouth before he pulls away.

"Cupcake," he says gruffly. Then leaves.

"I NEED TO GET OUT of this room." I splash in the tub. The aromatherapy soap Jett makes me use works wonders. The spa-like scent mixed with the hot bath literally uncurls the tension in my abused muscles.

"And where would you like to go? You're a kept woman, remember?" he snarks from the bedroom.

"These walls and my body never let me forget," I snark back. "I'd just like some fresh air. I've been stuck in here for ... how long have I been here?" I realize I have no concept of time.

"If you want fresh air, we'll open the window," Jett says as he walks into the bathroom, grabs the towel from the rack, and holds it open. Bath time is over.

"It's not the same," I gripe as I pull myself up reluctantly. I could soak all day. "Can't you talk to him for me?" I plead with puppy dog eyes as he wraps me in the towel. "I would ask him myself, but I'm not allowed to address him directly unless he's asking if I like the way he fucks me."

Jett vibrates with laughter. "You're terrible."

"I only speak the truth." I bat my eyelashes. "Please, Jett."

"Those green eyes are lethal," he huffs.

Jett pulls out his phone begrudgingly and adversely types away.

A few moments later his phone pings. He reads the message and snickers as he responds.

"What did he say?" I ask a little too hopeful.

"He said he'll be here to walk you in a little while."

I make a face. I don't like the allusion one bit. But I'm dying to get out of this room. So I'll deal with it. I'm close to scratching at the walls.

Jett dresses me for my outing. A black pair of lace panties with frilly ruffles on the butt, the black stiletto boots Kayne fucked me in, and a sheer black top that reminds me of a sexy beach cover up. The hem barely covers my ass and the plunging neckline barely covers my breasts. *Why even bother?* Complete with blingy body jewelry, my collar, and leash, I'm fit to be walked. Jett pulls my hair up into a messy bun, rims my eyes with black kohl liner and applies several coats of heavy mascara to finish off my dark sexy look. At least, that's what he calls it.

As we emerge from the bathroom, Kayne walks into the room. I drop to my knees immediately, splaying my hands on my bare thighs while keeping my head bowed. Just like I'm supposed to. Kayne growls in approval as he stands above me; menacing, intimidating, domineering. All things Kayne. All things my proprietor.

"I love that you know what I like," he says to Jett, pleased. Something inside me hiccups at his approval. He grabs my leash and commands me to rise. "Let's go, kitten. I'll show you the house."

AYNE

ELLIE LOOKS FUCKING GOOD ENOUGH to eat. When Jett text me asking if he could take her out of her room for a while, I was completely against it at first. I don't want her to know or see too much. For Ellie, the dark is the safest place. But she's been cooped-up in that room for almost three weeks and I knew the request was inevitable. The word no when it comes to Ellie is never an option, even if she's unaware of it. I wasn't going to let Jett be the one to take her though. My kitten. My responsibility.

I also wanted to be close in case Javier got any stupid ideas seeing her out of her cage.

I failed her once, I wouldn't do it again. I wanted to kill him right on the spot. I wanted to tear out his fucking throat and watch him bleed the white carpet in Ellie's room red. But that wasn't an option. At least not right then. But soon. Very fucking soon.

I tug Ellie's leash. It's time to go. I lead her out of the room and down the hall. She's walking two steps behind me with her head down, dressed in that fucking little outfit and those boots that drive me absolutely insane. But right now isn't about me. It's about Ellie and keeping her sane. But fuck man, does Jett know what he's doing when it comes to dressing her.

I tow Ellie down the long corridor of doors. I put her in the very last room for a reason. I know she has questions, I know she's remembering what she saw the last time she walked this hall and my threat to string her up and feed her to the wolves. That's all it was too, a threat. I would never have done it. I would never let anyone else touch what's mine.

The main staircase is a sweeping three-level butterfly affair made out of white, pink, and black marble. The decor at the mansion is over-the-top, ostentatious, and impressive. It's supposed to be that way. The clientele who come here are top of the line, prestigious, and expect nothing less than luxury and complete and utter anonymity. I walk Ellie into the west wing and through a long, glass enclosed entryway that leads to the utmost back of the house. Once at the end, I unlock the lavishly decorated doors carved out of wood and push them open.

"Ellie, look up." I jiggle her chain.

She raises her head and gasps. This is my favorite part of the mansion, a botanical garden that holds dozens upon dozens of exotic flowers and wild birds. We enter together and I watch as Ellie's face lights up. I grab her hand and she jumps from the contact. Then she relaxes and gives me a small smile. It twists my heart. I stayed far away from Ellie for a reason. My life, my world, is dangerous. I never wanted to bring her into that. But when the opportunity presented itself, I couldn't resist. Having her here these last few weeks, owning her, a slave to my bed, is my most vivid fantasy come to life. And, being the selfish bastard I am, I'm going to take advantage of every second I have with her. I'm going to push every limit, because when it's over, I'm confident Ellie will never want to see me again.

"It's not exactly paradise, but it comes damn close," I say as we walk farther into the conservatory.

"I love it," she replies as we stroll through a field of orchids sprouting purples, pinks, and whites out of the ground. Then she frowns and I know exactly what's upset her. She still thinks she'll never see paradise. She still thinks her freedom is gone. And for now, it is. I have to let her keep believing that. I squeeze her hand tighter as we make our way deeper into the gardens. Cranes dance by us and cockatoos display their colorful feathers as we come to the waterfall in the middle of the room.

"This is amazing," she breathes as she watches the water trickle down and pour into the clear blue pond below.

After a while of standing hand-in-hand among the peaceful surroundings, I catch Ellie glancing at me out of the corner of her eye.

"Ask me, Ellie."

She turns her head. "I'm just trying to understand. This place, you."

"All you need to know is that I'm an entrepreneur who owns you."

"An entrepreneur who deals in women?" There's a hard edge to her tone. I let it go, this time.

"Not everything is as it seems. You'd do best to remember that. And every woman in this house is here of her own free will."

She glares. "Except me."

Shit, she's got me there. "Except you," I confirm callously. "And that isn't up for discussion."

She huffs with tears in her eyes. Those deep green, hypnotizing eyes. I yank her to me, capturing her in my arms. "Don't make me bend you over and give you something to really cry about."

She sucks in a breath, fighting the urge to unleash her emotions.

"Let's not ruin the moment." I dip my head and whisper in her ear. "Mine, Ellie," I remind her.

She nods, composing herself, but the tears are still evident.

We spend the rest of the afternoon wandering the gardens in silence. I never let go of her hand, and she never tries to pull it away. It sprouts a small seed of hope inside me.

Once we leave, Ellie's relaxed energy shifts as we climb the staircase toward her ivory tower.

Her attention catches when she hears music coming from one of the rooms in the hallway. She really is like a curious cat. I stop, licked with an idea. I drop Ellie's hand and take her leash. Her anxiety spikes as I grab the door handle and turn the knob. She resists, but I yank, pulling her into the room. She flushes cherry red once inside. The room is occupied by two women and a man. One of the women is tied to the bed, arms and legs spread eagle. The man is straddling her head, thrusting his cock in and out of her mouth while the other woman has her face between her legs. Ellie tries to look away, but I grab her chin and force her to watch. Her chest expanding and contracting swiftly as her breathing picks up.

"We shouldn't be in here," she states in a low, uneasy tone.

"Of course we should. And no talking."

I pull her over to the couch against the wall directly across from the bed and command her down to her knees. We both sit facing the threesome with Ellie perched between my legs. It's fucking hot. Besides taking part in it, nothing gets me harder than watching two women go at it. Except maybe if Ellie was one of those women.

We spy together, as the three partake in their sexual acts. I scoot closer to Ellie, slipping my hand under her collar, grabbing it tight, straightening her posture. My erection digs into the middle of her back. She's panting heavily and her skin is heated. I shove my free hand into her shirt and grope her breast as we watch the chained girl writhe frenziedly as she climaxes.

I run my nose along her neck, breathing her in. "Do you like watching?" I ask her. "Do you like seeing two women together?"

Ellie doesn't answer. I know her voice is caught in her throat. The energy in the room is highly erotic and thick with sex. The music evocative. We observe, as the red-haired girl, Sugar, is unchained and the brunette, Cinnamon, takes her place, lying face down on the bed. She's shackled tightly, arms and legs spread wide.

"Have you ever been with a woman, Ellie?"

She shakes her head, as Sugar positions herself underneath Cinnamon's face. I rock my erection against Ellie as Cinnamon begins to lick Sugar. All my girls have pet names; it keeps things ambiguous and fantasy-like. These are two of my best girls, most naughty and adventurous.

Sugar drops her head back and moans as the man slides a condom on and impales Cinnamon from behind. She groans loudly as her tongue works Sugar.

"Would you do that, Ellie? Would you let me watch another woman eat your pussy?" She shivers but doesn't answer. I squeeze her bare breast, her flesh is on fire. "I think you would. I think you like watching, and secretly wish it was you." I slip my hand down into her panties and circle her clit with the tip of my middle finger.

"Will you let me fuck you while you go down on her?" I ask, and Ellie whimpers. I thrust my finger inside her, just as Sugar begins to come, jerking her hips and mewling loudly. "Answer, Ellie." I tug on her collar.

"Yes, Kayne."

"Yes, Kayne what? I can fuck you with another woman?"

"Yes." Her voice is barely recognizable it's so thick with lust.

"Who do you want? If you had to choose. Which girl do you want to fuck?" I ask still working my hand. She's soaking wet.

"The redhead." She strains to answer, her muscles clenching around my finger. There's no way I'm letting her come. Not in front of another man, even if he is balls deep in another woman. I withdraw, leaving Ellie empty and wanton.

She makes a protesting sound. Frustrated is just the way I want her. I drag her out of the room and push her face forward against the wall, pinning her wrists above her head, and grind my throbbing cock into her ass. The thought of Ellie with another woman launches my arousal into outer space.

"Tonight," I promise her.

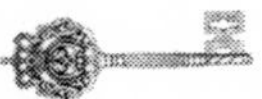

I PACE ELLIE'S ROOM LIKE a wild animal. She is chained to the bed, naked, and sitting like a good girl. I never dreamed of putting Ellie in a threesome situation, but once the idea presented itself, and she consented, I had to pull the trigger. I arranged with Jett to have Sugar prepared. She was bathed, freshened, and informed of the details. She is not to touch me. Not in front of Ellie. I am merely a spectator. Until I take Ellie. She's the only one I will fuck.

The door clicks open and Sugar appears. She's dressed only in lacy panties, stiletto heels, and a black collar. Perfect.

I send her to stand in the middle of the room, on the white shag rug. Then I go to Ellie. I unchain her from the headboard and lean into her face. "Ellie, I want you to know. I will be the only man who ever touches you. But you can fuck as many women as you want."

Her breath hitches. "Yes, Kayne."

"Tell me this is okay. Tell me the truth."

She peeks up at me through her thickly coated lashes and blushes. "Yes, Kayne."

My dick hardens to almost painful and my insides feel like they're going to overheat. I urge Ellie off the bed and walk her over to Sugar who's standing submissively in the middle of the room. I hook the end of Ellie's chain to Sugar's collar so the two are linked. Arousing does not begin to describe the sight of two collared women linked together for the sole purpose of pleasing you.

"Ellie, Sugar belongs to you tonight. You can touch her, lick her, suck her anywhere you want. Anywhere I tell you to."

"Yes, Kayne," Ellie answers, breathing erratically; Sugar is cool as a cucumber.

I step back and take a seat in the chair at the table under the wagon wheel window. Then I pull my shirt off. It's fucking stifling in here.

I stare at the girls momentarily then speak.

"Ellie, touch her." I don't want to waste a moment. I'm about to burst.

Ellie tentatively reaches up with a shaky hand. Is it wrong her inexperience is turning me on even further?

Ellie runs her hand down Sugar's arm, as if saying hello. Not good enough.

"Ellie, touch her breasts."

Ellie slowly puts her hand on Sugar's left breast and fondles her. My desire spins like a high-speed cylinder.

"Both breasts," I insist. "Tease her nipples, make them hard."

Ellie lifts her other hand, squeezing and kneading both of Sugar's breasts. Rolling her nipples between her thumb and index finger, the exact same way I do to her. My fucking cock has a heartbeat, as I watch my little pleasure kitten feel up another woman. The two girls are a stark contrast. Sugar is tall, red-headed, and buxom, while Ellie is petite in every sense of the word. Salivating for more, I order Ellie, "Suck her tits."

Ellie hesitates.

"Don't make me wait." My tone is authoritative as I bore my lust-filled gaze into her.

Ellie leans in and takes one of Sugar's nipples into her mouth. I nearly combust on the chair. I watch as she swirls her tongue and sucks Sugar with more force than I was expecting. Sugar moans. Still standing with her arms by her side and head lowered, her thick red hair dangling over her face.

"Touch her back, Sugar."

Sugar lifts her hands without delay, sliding her fingers into Ellie's hair as she laves her with her tongue. I unzip my pants and stroke my cock. It can't be ignored any longer as the two women touch each other under my strict advisement. Sugar takes the reins, pulling Ellie's mouth to hers, kissing her softly at first, and then darting her tongue between her lips. They both brush and caress and fondle each other as they become more comfortable.

"Ellie, how does Sugar feel?"

"Soft," she responds between kisses.

"How does she taste?"

"Sweet."

"How does she smell?"

"Sexy."

I have come to learn Ellie likes monosyllables when she's describing sexual associations. I have also come to learn, I like it.

"Sugar, get on your knees. Lick my kitten."

I can hear Ellie's sharp intake of breath as Sugar drops in front of her, the chain connecting their collars dangling between them.

"Ellie, spread your legs for Sugar." She glances at me with an unsure expression. Her green eyes wild with something penetrative. Something hot, like unsure desire.

"Go on kitten. I'm right here." I stroke myself as she looks at me. As if telling her *I'm all yours. This is what you do to me. Make me fucking rock hard and yearn for you.*

Sugar puts her mouth on Ellie as she looks at me, taking her by sweet surprise.

"Oh!" Her eyes widen, and then shut as her head drops back. She opens her stance and I see Sugar's tongue take charge. Ellie looks blindsided, and it's fucking incredible. I have to stop stroking myself; if I keep it up I'm going to come. And my hand is an unacceptable place to ejaculate when I have two beautiful women right in front of me. One all mine for the fucking.

"Ellie, how does that feel?" I ask as she runs her fingers through Sugars deep red hair.

"So good." She breathes hard, sounding a little disoriented. Her cheeks are flushed and her eyes are fluttering. She's close to the brink.

I almost can't stand it as I heave low breaths.

"Enough." Sugar halts immediately. The power is intoxicating. Commanding two gorgeous women—nothing else compares. "Sugar, stand up."

She complies immediately. Good little robin. That's what Jett calls her.

"Ellie, remove Sugar's underwear," I direct.

With delicate fingers Ellie lowers Sugar's black panties down her long legs, sliding them over her smooth thighs and toned calves.

My arousal roars.

"Sugar, get down on the ground and spread your legs."

She immediately complies, the chain connecting their two collars forcing Ellie down with her. Sugar puts her hands straight over her head and opens her legs wide with Ellie sprawled out on top of her.

"Ellie, pleasure her. Lick her body, suck her cunt."

The room is so thick with sex, I'm suffocating from the sight. She looks at me with wide green eyes.

"Go on." My response is clipped.

With mild trepidation, Ellie assails Sugar, licking down her neck to her breasts, drawing each nipple into her mouth and unleashing her tongue. Sugar moans and wriggles, her reaction to Ellie prompts me to start stroking again as my wildest dream comes to life.

Ellie keeps making her way down, over Sugar's tight stomach until she lands right at the apex of her thighs. She hesitates, and I instinctively order, "Do it, Ellie."

Her mouth makes contact with Sugar's pussy, and I nearly see stars. She licks Sugar with such ferocity she causes the redhead to moan loudly with pleasure. I watch the two of them completely spellbound. When I see Ellie's tongue dart out and swirl over Sugar's clit, my control completely crumbles.

I discard what's left of my pants and drop to the floor, crawling on all fours to get to Ellie.

I kneel behind her, lining myself up at her entrance. I watch entrapped as my little kitten laps up Sugar like she's a bowl of sweet milk. My body is trembling with overpowering need. And the only one who can satisfy it is Ellie; the only way is to bury myself deep inside her. Deep, deep inside her.

I dig my fingers into her hips. "Don't take your mouth off her pussy, no matter how hard I fuck you, understand?"

"Yes, Kayne," Ellie whimpers, and I immediately shove her face back between Sugar's legs. "What did I tell you?"

She mewls in reply.

I slam into her without any sort of warning and she cries out.

My cock thanks me.

I repeat the motion over and over, rearing all the way back and then blasting forward into her. Every strangled, strained sound she makes is muffled as she eats away at Sugar.

"Make her come, Ellie." I mercilessly thrust. "I won't let you come until she does."

Ellie frantically licks Sugar as she writhes and moans, chasing after an orgasm that's just out of reach. Then Ellie does something that nearly makes my head pop off. She begins to finger her. The little extra pressure was all Sugar needed to fall apart. She arches her body in ecstasy as her orgasm seizes her.

"Come," I command.

Fucking Ellie while she makes another woman splinter is my undoing. Trapping her hips, I beat into her with a punishing rhythm until she's screaming my name. It doesn't take long.

My orgasm holds me hostage as I bury myself to the hilt in Ellie over and over, restraining her as the force of each impact bucks her body forward. "Fuck, fuck." I grind out the words as the feel of her tight wet pussy pulsates around me, tearing me to shreds. I come like a man possessed, because that's exactly what I am. A man possessed by a little pleasure kitten who wears my collar and purrs my name.

I collapse on the floor as soon as the sensation dissipates, drawing a wildly panting Ellie close. The three of us lie spent, recuperating from the sexual overload.

I let the girls fall asleep still chained to each other on the shag rug. It's the sexiest thing I've seen in a long time.

I love all that shit. Sex toys, submission, and bondage.

But I love it even more when it's with Ellie. She blows me away. Her strength. Her playfulness. Her willingness. All the things that drew me to her in the first place have manifested tenfold. My little kitten is a force to be reckoned with.

I slip my hand under her collar and feel her soft pulse. The rhythm settles me.

It's quickly become the sole reason for my existence.

ELLIE

I DON'T KNOW WHAT I was thinking when I agreed to have a threesome with Kayne.

All I know is, I was about to tear at the seams as I watched two women and one man have sex while he fingered me.

I stare mindlessly out the window remembering. It's such a beautiful, clear day; the grass and leaves almost seem to gleam.

Who is this person I'm becoming? Every day I seem to inch further and further away from my old life. My old self. I live to please another. Someone who treats me rough, but at the same time is tender. Someone who makes me forget everything, but him.

"What are you doing in here, kitten?" Kayne asks suddenly from behind me. Shit. I immediately drop to my knees. I didn't even hear him come in. It's the middle of the afternoon; he never comes to see me during the day.

"Turn around. Face me," he orders. Dom dickhead is back.

I shift sideways, still kneeling.

"Look up."

I lift my head.

"Answer."

"Just staring out the window."

The room with the table of torture gives me a more panoramic view of the outside with its circular shape and large paned windows. Ironically, I don't feel so trapped when I'm in here.

"I see." He stares at me for a heartbeat, then commands, "Come."

Since I'm still kneeling and he hasn't ordered me to stand. I crawl on all fours, like he trained me to do. Like a cat. Like the pet that I am.

He watches me salaciously as I come to sit by his feet.

"Lie down."

I drop to my side, stretching out my body, resting my head on my arm. I stare up at Kayne, as he stares down. The look on his face is indescribable; there are so many emotions showing. At the forefront arousal and satisfaction. His eyes are wild as he rakes over my naked form.

"I have something for you," he says while still standing over me, the corners of his mouth turned up. He pulls something out of his pocket, a small silver charm. "Get on the table. Kneel in front of me."

I get up and climb onto the table, kneeling submissively on the firm black cushion. Kayne lifts his hand and shows me the trinket. It's a small heart on a clasp that reads 'Kayne's kitten.'

"Now everyone will know exactly who you belong to." He fastens it to my collar. "Me." Holy shit, I'm now tagged, collared, and owned by him.

"Mine." He leans in and kisses me, trapping my face in his hands. He swirls his tongue around roughly, thrusting it in and out of my mouth. "I want to do that to your pussy." He breathes heavily against my lips. Here we go. My body responds without delay, becoming instantly wet. I've lost all control.

"Lie down. Hands by your sides."

On the table?!? The last time we utilized this room, he beat me, then nearly destroyed me with his sexual prowess. And it's about to happen all over again.

I comply, the slave that I am. Kayne restrains both of my wrists in the cuffs with my pulse flying high. Then he moves to the end of the table and grabs one of my ankles. He deftly secures my leg to one of the stirrups with the thick black leather straps—one over my thigh, one around my calf, and one on my ankle. Then he does the same to my other leg. I'm tied down, helpless, and battling for breath.

"Mmm," he expels as he drinks in my incapacitated state. He then rests his hands on the inside of my thighs and pushes, causing the stirrups to click as he spreads me wide. One, two, three, four. My back is arching and my hands are fisting from the torturous stretch. "Ugh," I heave, trying to channel the pain.

"Perfect." Kayne licks his bottom lip as I pant. He loves working me out.

He walks around to my side, never taking that maniacal stare off me. The room is filled with bright sunlight, making me feel more exposed and more on display than ever before; my nakedness and tethered body at the forefront of my insecurity and fear.

"You are so beautiful, Ellie." Kayne rubs my breasts, my shoulders, my arms. He leans down and kisses me, kneading small, firm circles into my biceps. I release a contented moan against his mouth as he lulls me into submission.

He pulls away once I'm relaxed, and then opens one of drawers. I startle my eyes open and track every move he makes, watching with morbid fascination as he pulls out a thin chain with two little clamps on each end. He dangles it front of my face, his expression carnal, hedonistic almost. I look quickly between his luminous eyes on fire with lust, and the tiny torture device he's holding in his hand.

He grins wickedly, then leans over and sucks one of my nipples into his mouth, lashing his tongue against the little pebble as it hardens. I release a heavy breath, then without any warning, he places the clamp on my nipple. It bites, shooting a sharp sensation straight to the apex of my over-stretched legs. *Oh*. Then he does the same thing to the other nipple, vibrating a moan against my breast, just to tease me. The clamp bites down and I groan in protest.

"Fuck, you look so hot." He grabs both my breasts from underneath and squeezes them hard. The clamps pinch at the same time and my eyes roll into the back of my head.

"Oh, God."

"Oh, Kayne," he corrects arrogantly as he massages me, arousal flaring through my entire being. "I'm your maker now."

Not just my maker—my captor, my owner, my ruler.

He's barely touched me and I'm already breathing rapidly and soaked between my thighs. After he's finished rubbing me into restlessness, he picks up the chain connecting the clamps. With an impish gleam, he somehow ties it to the loop on the front of my collar. The chain is pulled so tight, that every time I move my head the clamps nip at my nipples, straining them, elongating them, driving me crazy with pleasure and pain. My heart is beating, my hands are shaking, and my pussy is throbbing.

Kayne jingles my new tag with one finger as I lie confined to the table, unravelling at the seams.

"Mine," he says haughtily.

I just stare up at him with glassy eyes, trying to remain as still as possible. He unbuttons his light blue shirt; the color makes his eyes pop in the sunlight, the brown lightning bolt looking more pronounced. God, for being the devil, his features are divine. Once he's removed his shirt and dropped it on the floor, he leans over me semi-naked and kisses me on the stomach. I try to breathe steadily, but every time he touches me it feels like a volcanic eruption. "Baby, you don't have to ask permission to come." He slowly kisses down my torso until his head is between my widespread legs. Then he licks me lightly, dragging his tongue unhurriedly over my slit. He does this over and over like a lazy lion until I'm vainly wriggling in my restraints. I snap my head back without thinking and the clamps unapologetically jerk my nipples sending a bolt of white hot heat straight to my blistering pussy.

"Oh!" I try not to move, but he's pushing me right to my breaking point, slowly, painstakingly, licking me into an orgasm.

"Kayne, Kayne." I breathe labored. It's a plea, it's an appeal, it's a demand. My insides are wound so tight they're ready to fracture. He just keeps licking though, ignoring my chants, and my body just keeps winding.

Lick, twist, lick, twist.

I'm an elastic band ready to snap.

Then he inserts one finger into my assailable entrance and I combust. My hips buck and I scream. It feels like I am being electrocuted. It looks like I'm being electrocuted. My hands fisted, my body bowed, my head dropped back, my nipples aching and straining as a current of ecstasy speeds through my veins.

I collapse back onto the table when the climax releases me, moaning feebly. My head rolling all over the place like it's barely attached to my body. The nipple clamps still tugging relentlessly.

"Whoa." Kayne chuckles as he wipes his face against my inner thigh.

I'm glad he finds my soul-shredding orgasms so funny. *Asshole.*

He kisses his way back up to my mouth as I come around. I crack open my eyes as he kisses me, to find him staring back at me.

"Hi, kitten." He smiles.

I grunt.

He laughs. "My turn. You ready?"

"No," I say sarcastically.

He yanks on the chain and my nipples yelp. "Excuse me?

"Yes, Kayne," I correct myself.

"Good, kitten." He brushes his lips against mine. "My kitten." He jingles the tag on my collar again, proudly displaying his satisfaction with my new token of ownership.

I watch withdrawn as he positions himself between my legs. The stirrups have my knees high and legs wide. They're starting to ache from being confined and overstretched. Kayne unbuttons his pants and unzips his fly. He doesn't even bother to remove them, only lowering them enough to release his cock.

"Come if you have to come baby." He teases my wet entrance with its head. Then he braces himself on the table, leaning forward, preparing for total body domination. "You have no idea how fucking sexy you look, wearing that tag." He slams into me, and I feel it all the way to my belly button.

"Ah!" I crunch forward and scream out.

"How much it turns me on. You belong to me." He slams into me again and again. The manic desire is clear on his face.

His relentless thrusts combined with the pinching of the clamps catapult me toward another orgasm before I even see it coming. All at once, my muscles are clenching, my neck is straining and my pussy is pulsating as he rams fast and furiously in and out of me; my nipples are in glorious agony as my breasts bounce from the relentless force of his hips' impact.

"I'm going to come!" I cry out.

"Come!" Kayne snaps, as my orgasm unleashes itself, a torrent of arousal drenching us both as my body splits in two. Kayne stills, arching his back as he comes savagely inside of me.

In the daylight, I can see all the cuts of his body, the definition of his chest and strength of his presence. Like a Roman soldier. Suddenly I'm very aware of my unclothed, tethered state. I blush all over. It's not like he hasn't had me in compromising positions before, or even done worse, but the fact that it's the middle of the day and I'm strapped to a table with my nipples clamped makes me feel awkwardly on display.

"Ellie, what's wrong?" Kayne asks, as he pumps his semi-hard cock into me, sighing satedly.

"Nothing." I drop my head to the side then immediately right it, the clamps reminding me who's in control.

"Ellie," Kayne says more firmly, completely nestled inside me.

"I feel a little ... exposed." I chew my lip.

Kayne smiles. Widely. "I like you exposed baby." He withdraws, and then pulls up his pants that are still hanging on his hips. "Exposed and open and only for me." He hoists himself onto the table and crawls up my body like the predator he is, his eyes sparkling with something dark and triumphant. "See, it says it right here." He jingles my tag. "Mine."

"Yes. We've established that numerous times," I quip.

Kayne pulls at the nipple chain playfully and I wince. "Don't sass me," he says still smiling.

"I can't help it, it's reflexive," I answer.

"You know what else is reflexive?" He drops his head and kisses me torridly, his tongue circling and owning my mouth. I moan softly, then strain as he releases my nipples from the clamps. I breathe through the abrasive sensation as the blood runs through my body. Subdued, little sounds escape my throat as he continues to kiss me through the pain.

Pleasure and pain. Pleasure and pain. Definitely two words synonymous with him.

Kayne slips his hand under my collar and strokes my neck lightly with his thumb. My arms are still strapped down and my legs are still buckled to the stirrups. I wonder if he plans to keep me here all day.

"Don't ever feel ashamed or embarrassed with me, Ellie. Your body is perfect. You're perfect." He kisses me tenderly.

"Yes, Kayne," I answer, kissing him back.

"Good, kitten. Cupcake."

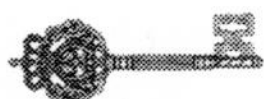

I STARE AT MY SHINY new jewelry sitting on the bathroom counter as I soak my sore muscles in a steaming hot tub. A tag for my collar, a delicate white gold heart with the inscription 'Kayne's kitten'. He gave it to me yesterday, right before he strapped me to the table of torture and fucked me senseless with clamped nipples.

I am collared. I am tagged. I am utterly owned by him.

The man is a sexual carnivore. His appetite insatiable. I have bruises on my hips from where he holds me, hickeys on my body from where he bites me, and handprints on my ass from where he spanks me. I look abused. I feel abused. I feel conflicted. My brain keeps telling me this whole thing is wrong. I'm a victim, a pet, a captive. But my body craves Kayne the same way it would crave water in the desert. It has quickly become the slave to him that he wanted, succumbing to all his devious desires and demands.

I take my time getting out of the tub, knowing Jett is in the bedroom ready to torture me with more yoga. It's doing its job and stretching my muscles, which is pleasing Kayne to no end. It also helps loosen my stiff joints the morning after his brutal punishings.

You love it, don't complain. I shove my subconscious into a dark closet.

I get out of the tub, dry myself off, and allow Jett to torment my body further with more downward dog and lord of dance poses. By the time we're finished and he's fed me, it's late in the evening.

I notice thick chains and leather cuffs dangling off one of the stirrups on the table of torture in the other room.

"What are those for?" I ask as he fastens my collar and chains me stark naked back to the bed.

Jett shrugs. "Kayne requested them. He has something planned."

My heart rate takes off. Jett leaves me with my racing thoughts. Always something new, always something kinky. Always something that leaves my body depleted and my soul stirring. Ever since we established cupcake, I've felt different. Yes, he's a domineering prick sometimes. But when he touches me, when he's inside me there's an undeniable connection. The same connection I felt to him before. When we would steal a look or flirt privately in the conference room. The same red hot connection we had that night he took me.

The door clicks and I shoot to my knees. My sitting position. My submission. The heavy steps of Kayne's presence makes my pulse pound and my most private places throb.

He lifts my chin with one finger so I can look him in the eye. The eyes that are crystal blue with a lightning bolt of brown. He tickles my tag with an arrogant smirk.

"Evening, kitten, how was your day?"

"I missed you." The words just roll right out of my mouth. I stiffen and Kayne's jaw drops. His sharp intake of breath is like a vacuum. Then a wide salacious smile spreads across his tantalizing mouth. The mouth that is capable of so many things. My thighs tingle just looking at it.

"I missed you too." He squeezes one of my breasts. "And these." He runs his hand down my torso and cups my pussy. "And this. But," he leans in to kiss me, "I missed this most of all." I moan as his tongue rolls slowly against mine and he pushes his middle finger deep inside of me.

"I hope Jett gave you carbs for dinner, because it's going to be another all-nighter." He breathes against my lips, almost apologetically.

"Come to think of it. He fed me pasta." I sigh as he fingers me slowly. "Did you take another Viagra?"

He halts all movement. "How did you know I took Viagra?"

"Because no human male is capable of lasting as long as you, unless he's medically enhanced. And Jett confirmed my suspicions," I confess coquettishly.

"Did he?"

"We have to talk about something," I say as Kayne stabs me with his finger.

"Well then," he replies cockily, withdrawing his hand leaving me aching. "You want something to gossip about. I'll give you something to gossip about." He pulls me forward by my collar and smacks my ass hard, making me yelp. "No more talking. Lie on your front." His Dom alter ego has sprung to life.

I do as I'm told with a knot in my stomach.

I watch excited, scared, and turned on as hell, as he picks up the chains and cuffs from the table. He stalks back over to me and without delay, secures my ankles and wrists to the bed. I'm spread wide and at his mercy once again. Just as he desires me. Just like he craves me. He then shortens the length of my leash, removing most of the slack. An inch and a half off the mattress is all I can lift my head. My heart rate goes berserk as I hear him shuffling in the drawers under the table of torture. His treasure chest of sex toys.

Oh God.

I feel him drop multiple items onto the bed, and then I hear the sound of clothes being shed. Kayne crawls on top of me, straddling my parted legs.

"Do you know why I take Viagra, Ellie?" he asks.

"No, Kayne." I reply, panting like the pet I am.

"Because having you once or twice is never enough." He shifts, spreading my ass cheeks, then licks my little puckered hole. I clench instinctually. "I hunger to be inside you all the time and the only way to satisfy the beast is to give it what it wants. Hours and hours submerged in your wet pussy and tight little ass."

I hear the pop of a cap and then feel a cold squirt. I try to crane my head to see behind me, but it's a vain attempt. Then I feel something hard and round push on my behind.

"Pussy first," he says, slowly working the large, lubricated butt plug into my tiny rosebud. I moan and groan as it bites and stretches me, Kayne kneading one of my butt cheeks the entire time. When it's finally all the way in, he twists it, causing my entire body to spasm and work against my restraints. *"Oh!"* Afterwards, Kayne props up my pelvis with a medium-size throw pillow, stretching my arms, my legs, my neck and my ass to the max. The silk soft and smooth against my flaming skin

Kayne flutters light kisses over my back as he mounts me.

"You're so fucking sexy. Beautiful, bewitching," he says as he presses the head of his cock against my entrance and enters me slowly, making sure I feel every hard inch of him. He fucks me unhurriedly, keeping a tempered rhythm that rocks the butt plug deep every time he thrusts.

"You're mine, Ellie," he reminds me. "Do you see? I can do whatever I want to you." He starts to pump harder, my insides overflowing with his thick cock and large plug. I lose my mind as the sensations take over, drowning me in a sea of ecstasy.

"I own you. I own your pleasure." He strains as he hits my core square on and my orgasm peaks.

"Oh God, Kayne!" It's the only words I'm capable of at the moment. I need to move, I need to squirm, but he's right, he owns my pleasure. Commands it with his body.

"Kayne, please!" I'm begging now. Always begging. Just like he wants. A slave to him. "Please! Please!"

He pushes deeper, challenging my body as everything south of my navel quakes.

"Please!" I scream, pulling at my restraints.

"I love to hear you beg." His cock swells, punching me exactly where I need. Once, twice, three times and I combust. My climax tearing me open from the inside out. He bucks once more then slams still inside me, groaning animalistically as he comes. I'm left limp as a noodle on the bed with Kayne lying on top of me, both of us breathing like all the oxygen has dissipated in the room. After a few long minutes, he pushes up and kisses me on the cheek. "Round two." My body trembles. Round one just knocked me on my ass. He withdraws, still erect. I know what I'm in for. We've done this before, him taking me all night.

Straddling above me, he bends to grab something.

"Open," he commands with a purple rubber vibrator in front of my mouth. I open and he shoves it in.

"Suck."

I move my head the little it can go and suck on the extremity.

"Good girl," he says in that condescending, domineering tone, as I lubricate the vibrator. Kayne removes the butt plug still inhabiting my ass, and my muscles contract, sighing with relief. Then he pulls the vibrator from my mouth, clicks it on, and inserts it into me.

Oh! It's not quite as big as him, but it still makes me feel full, the vibrations prickling my already sensitive parts.

I hear the pop of a top again and a squeeze. It makes my heart rate jolt. Then he pushes one finger into my ass, all the way to the knuckle. Fuck, round two. I buck and gasp. "Still, Ellie."

I try, but my body involuntarily shakes. Then he slides another finger inside me and starts to scissor me open, as if I haven't been elasticized enough. I shudder as he simultaneously stretches the already sensitive muscle and my core quakes from the hum of the vibrator.

"So fucking ready," Kayne utters as he removes his fingers, and I don't know if he's referring to me or him.

I feel him shift on the bed, quickly positioning himself directly above me. He nips at my shoulder as he pokes his cock into my behind, pushing into me in one smooth, fluid motion. It forces a moan out of me that sounds like a cat in heat. The size of his erection supersedes both his fingers and the plug. My air supply feels thin as I'm filled to capacity once again. The last all-nighter he only fucked me once, then spent the rest of the night balls deep in my butt. Tonight is completely different. Both holes packed, over and over. I don't know if I'll survive.

Would he spare me if I begged him to stop? I'll soon find out, because he wastes no time fucking me, moving in small thrusts at first, then increasingly pushing harder. I feel every jab in my center as his cock bites my ass while at the same time kissing it with pleasure. The vibrator keeping a steady stream of pulsation against my clit and all around my pussy.

I'm dying.

The monumental speed with which my orgasm is building has me petrified. It's too big, too strong, and the only place it has to escape is between my legs. My arms and legs lend no help to the absorption of the impending tremor while I'm restrained like this.

"God, Ellie, your body. It's so good. So perfect. So tight." He thrusts into me, making me wail. "I'm going to fucking come. You're going to make me fucking come," he says through clenched teeth. I can't hold back as both the force of his cock and the vibrator hit my g-spot all at once. "Kayne!" I detonate, my climax ripping me open right down the middle. I break out into a fit of tears. It's the only other outlet my body has for the energy-sucking sensation to escape. I'm mentally removed as Kayne spills inside me, crying into the pillow until the aftershocks of ecstasy taper off.

I have no life left. Two earth-shattering orgasms are all I can take.

I feel Kayne shift, bringing his face to mine and licking up my tears.

"That's exactly the reaction I want every time."

I just lie there panting. I have nothing left in me to respond.

Kayne gives me a few minutes of reprieve, massaging my back, my legs, even my scalp. But a few minutes is all I get, because all too soon I hear the top of the lubricant bottle pop again, and my whole body locks up. What the fuck is he doing now?

I feel him push against my ass, this time with the butt plug. I tremble. No more. "Kayne," I protest. But he ignores me, pushing the plug all the way in.

"Kayne." I strain against my restraints. My rosebud on fire. "Please."

"Shhh, Ellie," he reprimands me. "The only time I want to hear you is when you're moaning in pleasure or screaming my name."

I'm going to be screaming all night. I clench my cuffed fists as he props my pelvis back on the pillow and lines up behind me. I'm on the brink of tears already, my body begging please while howling no all at the same time. My head is spinning without any end in sight.

"All night, Ellie. I'm going to alternate fucking you like this all night," he murmurs in my ear as he buries himself to the hilt. "And I'm not going to stop until my dick is limp and my come runs dry." I draw in a sharp breath as his cock and the butt plug continuously hammer away at me.

Again.

And again.

Putting demands on my body I'm not sure it's capable of withstanding.

"Kayne!"

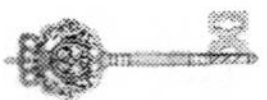

"I HOPE ONE DAY YOU can forgive me, Ellie." I hear Kayne's voice in the distance. I don't know if it's a dream or reality, but when I flutter my eyes open, I'm in his arms. I shift. No cuffs or chains or collar. For a split second I wonder if it was all a dream. Then I look around the room and realize I'm still confined to my prison in the sky.

"You stayed?" I blink, finding his dazzling blue eyes.

"Mmm hmm." He nuzzles my neck and breathes me in. "How do you feel?"

Crazy conflicted.

"My limbs feel like Jell-O, my wrists are rubbed raw, and there's a pain in my ass." I grimace as I move.

"All a reminder of who owns you." He sucks my earlobe. "You're so soft."

"So are you," I reply as my hips rub against his.

"Don't be a wise ass, I'll spank you." He hugs me tighter.

He's acting weird.

"Why are you still here? Where is my collar?"

"Because I wanted to stay, and on the nightstand," he answers straightforwardly.

"I don't have to wear it anymore?" I stretch in his arms.

Kayne snorts. "Of course you do. How would I find you if you got lost?" He kisses me tenderly. "I just thought after last night, you could use some room."

"You weren't wrong in assuming." I touch the compass tattoo on his chest. I don't know why. I guess just to feel it. I never get to touch him. He moans softly, almost like a purr. Last night was the most intense, excruciating, amazing night of my life. Kayne pushed every physical, emotional, and spiritual limit I have. I didn't think I was going to come out alive.

Someone really needs to steal his bottle of Viagra.

"More," he says. It's a request, not a demand. I touch him tentatively, exploring my newfound freedom. We melt into each other, the same way new lovers would; cuddling, snuggling, stealing soft embraces.

Who is this man? Who is he really? The charismatic businessman or the ruthless Dom? The one who holds me affectionately or brings me to tears? I wish I knew. I wish I could figure him out. Why did he have to take me when I offered myself up willingly?

"Do you remember the first time we met?" he asks, rubbing his nose against my cheek.

"Oh, God. Why are you bringing that up?" I hide my face in the crook of his neck so he can't see the embarrassment.

"Because." Kayne chuckles. "You spilt hot coffee in my lap."

I'll never forget that day. The way he strolled into Expo like he owned it, wearing a light brown power suit and aviator sunglasses. He was intimidating and intriguing, and I was drawn to him unlike anyone or anything else on earth. My body and mind just responded. It was a primitive, carnal response. Then he took his sunglasses off and my inner axis tilted. He looked straight through me with those raw majestic eyes. I forgot who I was and what I was doing. Unfortunately for him, I was pouring coffee at that moment and missed the cup completely. I'd never seen anyone move that fast. Needless to say, I was mortified and Mark almost decapitated me. Kayne was a huge whale to land, and I nearly fucked it all up. Luckily for me, he had a sense of humor.

"You dropped to your knees and told me to take my pants off." Kayne is full-blown laughing now. I'm glad it's such an amusing memory for him. I tried to scrub my brain of it for months.

"I was sort of disappointed you didn't." I lift my head slightly and eye him lasciviously.

"If there wasn't a room full of people, I would have. Then I would have taken yours off too, and laid you out on the conference room table." Kayne threads his fingers into my hair and tugs lightly. He licks my lower lip like he's trying to memorize the taste. "Do you know how many times I fantasized about fucking you on that table?"

"I had no idea you fantasized about me at all." I dart my tongue out to touch his.

"Every time I walked into Expo and sat down for a meeting, I was half listening to Mark, half imagining you kneeling at my feet." He grabs hold of my hair a little harder, taking control of my head. "Imagining you spreading your legs for me and letting me lick you senseless, then driving myself so deep inside you, we'd both forget we were ever two separate people." I moan as he bites my neck and grabs my ass.

"I would have let you." I run my hands up his chest and over his shoulders, digging my nails into his skin in response to the grip he has on my hair.

"Ellie?" Kayne rasps. Sliding his hand along my side. "Can I ask you something?"

"Yes, Kayne," I respond robotically. He spanks my ass lightly. I jolt. Even the littlest bit of pain feels volcanic.

"I said don't be a wise ass."

"I wasn't being a wise ass, I was answering you like you expect me to."

"Not right now. Right now I'm invoking Cupcake."

I crack a smile. "What do you want to know?"

He swipes his thumb across my cheek and I can't help but turn into his touch. "Do you think if the circumstances were different? If we did things the normal way, you could have accepted who I am? My way of life?"

I contemplate his question while searching his eyes. Why does he want to know? What does it matter?

"I'm not sure. What aspects are you talking about?"

Surely not the kidnapping.

"My domineering side. You would have never known about my 'other' business."

I ponder his question some more then shrug. "I don't know how you build a relationship on lies. But you never gave me a chance to find out on my own, so I guess we'll never know." It's an honest answer. He nods, with a small frown.

"How did you end up like this? End up here?" I ask curiously. I have so many questions. There are so many things I want to know. Kayne rolls on top of me, my body crying out from his weight. He rubs his nose softly against mine, as if conflicted. "That story is for another time. Another lifetime. But I promise one day I'll tell you."

"Why can't you tell me now?"

He shakes his head. "Now's not the time."

"When will be the time?" I question him.

"I'm not sure exactly. But soon. Just try to keep an open mind, and remember things aren't always as they appear. It's all I can say about it."

If I wasn't so emotionally exhausted and physically drained, I'd try to coerce more information out of him. I like him like this, open and affectionate. I like the Dom too. I'm beginning to realize I'm fond of all of Kayne's sides, which I know is a dangerous thing. He kidnapped me; he keeps me on a leash and collared like a puppy. I'm his to control and more and more, I'm acclimating to this lifestyle.

"Okay," I acquiesce.

"Good. Can you get up and take a shower?"

"Jett usually puts me in the bath after one of your punishings."

Kayne shoots me a twisted look. "One of my punishings? Is that how you see sex with me?"

"Sometimes." I shrug demurely.

All the time.

Kayne smiles boldly. "Good. Because no one will ever give it to you as good as me."

On some deep elemental level, I know it's the truth.

Kayne gets up and walks into the bathroom butt naked, and I hear him run the tub. A few minutes later the smell of eucalyptus drifts into the bedroom.

He comes back once the water stops running.

"Can you get up?" He holds out a hand.

I sit up, and every fiber of my being protests, especially the ones between my knees.

Kayne must see the agony on my face, because he scoops me up without a word and carries me into the bathroom. He steps into the tub and submerges both of us into the steaming hot water.

"Ah." It feels like I'm being pelted with stones as the water works to relax my exploited muscles. Kayne leans me against his chest, wrapping me up in his strong arms. I liquefy.

"Who do you belong to, Ellie?" He kisses my temple, the two of us immersed in overflowing bubbles.

"You, Kayne."

AYNE

ALL I CAN THINK ABOUT is Ellie's ass.

And how she felt in my arms this morning. I pick at my bottom lip mindlessly as I fantasize about her. Her toned body, her sultry green eyes, her sexy smirk, her wet fucking ...

"Kayne." Jett waves his hand in front of my face. "Hello, Kayne. Can you please stop daydreaming?"

I'm trying, but Ellie seems to be all I can think about. She's invaded my life like a force I never saw coming. I want to keep her more than anything. But after all this? After everything I've put her through? A life without her is a fate worse than death. Which is a strong possibility, too, if everything gets fucked up.

"Javier is up to something. We should have heard from El Rey by now. There should be meetings set up. A drop point. Accounts established. None of that has happened. It's been a month." Jett paces in front of my desk.

"It hasn't gone unnoticed," I inform him.

El Rey, *The King,* is one of largest drug kingpins in the world. He is notorious for being a ghost and responsible for over fifty percent of the cocaine and heroin smuggled into the US. Javier is his right-hand man and our only line to meeting him face to face.

"Well what the fuck should we do? Endeavor is breathing down my neck. They know El Rey is within reach."

"Tell Endeavor to cool their jets. There's nothing we can do but wait. If we make the wrong move our cover will be blown and years of hard work will be worth shit." Jett huffs. He knows I'm right. Situations like these are dangerous and deadly and need to be handled with delicate care.

"How is Spice?" I ask.

"Healing." Jett clenches his fist. He takes looking after the women in the house as a serious task. He dotes over them like prize-winning orchids. They provide an invaluable service of their own free will. They are rare, exquisite creatures, according to him, and seeing one of them hurt nearly sent him on a murderous rampage. Javier seems to have that effect on people.

Jett may look more like a laidback surfer than cold-blooded killer, but he has a dark side just like the rest of us. He wanted to kill Javier. Like, take a rusty kitchen knife and slit his throat. I would have held the spineless worm down while he did it, but we need the Mexican motherfucker alive. "She's recuperating, but she still wants to go."

I groan, annoyed. The girls who work for me come from all walks of life. Some are ex-prostitutes from the slums of the streets looking for a safe environment. Some are from upper class communities, looking to fulfill the piece of them that's missing. Sex fiends with insatiable appetites. No matter where they come from, they're treated all the same. Trained and educated in all sexual aspects to provide my clientele the erotic experience they pay top dollar for.

I don't want to see her go, but I won't force her to stay.

"If she leaves, make sure she's compensated accordingly," I tell him, rocking back in my black leather office chair.

Jett nods with a frown. He doesn't want her to go either.

"I'll have a word with Javier. See if I can grease the wheels." I crack my knuckles irked.

"I think that's smart." He glances at his watch. "I need to check on Ellie."

"Dress her. I want to take her for a walk," I tell him pointedly.

Jett just stares, those fucking aqua eyes probing me.

"What?" I insist.

"You know you can't keep her," he reminds me.

I growl at him. *She's mine.*

"What's going to happen when she finds out the truth?" He treads lightly.

My world will end.

"It will be over." I shrug, trying to play off the inevitable apocalypse.

"Are you going to be able to live with that?" he asks delicately.

"I'll have no other choice," I respond indifferently, while my heart secretly granulates in my chest.

If I'm even alive at all.

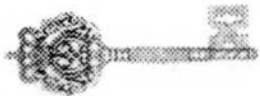

I FIND JAVIER EATING IN the grand dining room. Its walls are a light yellow, with an extravagant baroque mural on the recessed ceiling overhead.

"Kayne." He smiles smugly with a mouth full of food.

I sit across the expansive mahogany table from him. I keep my expression cool and my demeanor even colder.

"Javier." I address him.

"Are you here to share a meal with me?" he asks with his thick accent.

"No."

"A woman then?"

"Definitely not," I scowl.

"Then what can I do for you, amigo?"

"You can tell me what the fuck is going on. You have been under my roof for a month. Eaten my food and fucked my women. But made no mention of El Rey."

"That's not a very nice tone for a house guest." He fiddles with the silver knife in his left hand. I track his every movement.

"Have you ever heard the expression constant company is never welcome?" I ask short tempered.

"No. In Mexico, it's mi casa es su casa."

I glare at the complacent bastard.

Six months ago an associate of mine contacted me. A real stand up hell of a guy. He informed me El Rey had caught wind of my tequila empire. He looked into me and liked what he found. An American who exports alcohol out of Mexico and runs an elite brothel. My less than perfect morals intrigued him. He saw an opportunity to do business with me, because what goes better with drugs than alcohol? It's as natural as peanut butter and jelly. That's when I first met Javier. We exchanged correspondences, and as El Rey's right hand, he was responsible for informing me of The King's interests and coordinating the details. They wanted to utilize my exportation of tequila to move drugs into the US. I have plenty of customs agents in my pocket, which El Rey was already aware of. He definitely does his homework. He wouldn't be the man he is if he didn't. Yes couldn't come out of my mouth fast enough.

Three months ago I was invited to Mexico for a sit down with

Javier. Me, being an American, had both El Rey and Javier taking extra precautions. You never know who you're dealing with in this business. Friend or foe, ally or enemy. Law enforcement or not. Javier flew me down in a private jet, and then had me amicably escorted by gunpoint to his home. It was the most terrifying car ride of my life. Once there, I realized the true depth of evil I was dealing with. Besides being a main player for one of Mexico's largest drug cartels, he was also a slave trader. He had dozens of girls broken beyond repair. They crawled around his house on all fours like cats and were never permitted to stand. Naked and starved, some were so thin you could see their spine and ribcage. He kept them in tiny metal crates so small they were forced to crouch in a ball. And every night he tortured one of them. For the three days I was there, I heard their screams. And there wasn't one fucking thing I could do about it. I had a mission. That was my focus, as unbearable as it was. The last night the wails were the worst. They were bloodcurdling, echoing through the entire house. The disturbing shrieks still haunt me. I don't think they'll ever stop. I nearly cracked, damning it all to hell. My hero complex flared, but just as I got out of bed to end the madness, the screams stopped. Sometime later I heard digging in the backyard. I peeked out the window to see one of Javier's thugs kicking a body into a shallow grave under the moonlight. He killed her. While I was in his fucking house. No shame, no concern.

I nearly puked at the sight of her bloodied, abused state. After that night, I swore that girl's death wouldn't be in vain. I would destroy Javier, El Rey, and anyone else associated with them.

That time is coming soon. I'm walking a tightrope that keeps getting narrower and narrower, and I just have to keep my balance for a little while longer.

That's why I took Ellie. I knew what Javier was capable of. I flashed back to that moment and saw her lifeless form the moment he said he wanted her.

And as I've said before, like fucking hell I was going to let that happen. If anyone was going to torture her, it was going to be me. So I took her before he had the chance to pursue her. And he would have. Once Javier wants something, he doesn't stop until he gets it.

"What the fuck is going on, Javier? Has there been any word from El Rey? Is he interested or not? I don't have the time or patience to fuck around. I gave him my price and my conditions. They are more than reasonable."

"Yes, he's agreed." He wipes his mouth with the white cloth napkin, and then tosses it on the table. A stupid smile on his face. This prick is always smiling. I wish I knew what was so fucking amusing.

"So what's the hold up?"

"How's your whore, Kayne? Does she miss me?" he diverts.

"She's got nothing to fucking do with this conversation."

"I hear the two of you, you know. I listen at the door while you make her scream. She's very impressive." My blood boils in my veins. That motherfucker is never getting near Ellie again. "What if I wanted her to be part of the deal?" he asks darkly.

"I'd tell you to fuck off," I snarl.

"You'd pass on millions of dollars because of some whore?" He raises his eyebrows intrigued.

"She's mine. I'm prideful, what can I say." I keep my voice firm, desperately suppressing the dread clawing up my throat.

"I'd love to dip my dick and see what's makes her so special." He licks his lips. I want to pull his tongue right out of his mouth and wrap it around his head.

"She a delicacy you'll never indulge in." I glare.

"Again," he taunts me.

"Ever. Again," I threaten. "Talk to your boss. Make the deal. I have everything prepared. If he's not interested, get the fuck out. I don't need his money or your aggravation. I do just fine by myself." I stand up, sending the chair screeching across the hardwood floor.

"Arrogante Americano," Javier spats.

Arrogant American.

"Maybe so, but The King came to me, remember?"

"I didn't forget," he sneers.

"Tiene cuartena y ocho horas," I order directly.

You have forty-eight hours.

Then I stalk out of the room and up the staircase with my heart ricocheting all around my chest. By the time I make it to Ellie's door, I'm a shitstorm of rage, lust, anger, and wrath. I need to bury myself as deep as I can inside of her while she's chained to the bed and fuck her until my murderous thoughts eradicate. She's quickly become the solace in my tumultuous life. With her, I'm the best part of all my sides. All my faces. With her they blend into one cohesive man. She's the glue.

I press my thumb to the fingerprint recognition screen. I had a state-of-the-art lock installed the morning after Javier assaulted her. No way was I going to allow that cocksucker a second chance at picking the lock. He'll have to slice off my fucking fingers before he gets in her room again. I open the door and find Ellie exactly where she should be. Kneeling on the bed, mostly naked, with her tag dangling from her collar. My dick swells to almost painful. She's so beautiful, so perfect. All mine. I don't say a word as I stomp over to her.

I push her onto her back, possess her mouth, and drag her legs apart. I grind the missile my cock has become against her, and she moans. But it's not in pleasure, it's an anguished sound. She's in pain, and it's because of me. It's all because of me. She would never be in this dangerous predicament if it wasn't for *me.* It takes everything I have to beat back the beast and pull my lips away from hers. They're swollen and red from my forceful kiss. She's looking up at me curiously. Always curious, always lively, always playful. That's Ellie. Intense and bewitching. I've been drawn to her since the moment we met. Somewhere deep down I have always felt something proprietary when it came to her.

I run my fingers along her face, soaking in her beauty. Her acute green eyes rimmed in black, her high cheek bones dusted in pink, her full mouth stained a dark blush.

"I would kill for you." I speak the words that can never be taken back. I speak the truth.

She sucks in a breath, her breasts swell, and her eyes widen. I kiss her again, darting my tongue between her lips. I don't want a response. I just want her to know in a roundabout way how I feel.

After a few minutes of indulging myself in Ellie's mouth, I pull away.

"Are you ready for your walk?" I skim her neck with my teeth softly, wanting nothing more than to rip her panties off and live inside her.

"Are you?" she pants.

"Wrong answer, Ellie." I tweak her nipple, and she jolts.

"Yes, Kayne," she corrects herself immediately.

"Good girl."

I reluctantly remove myself from her and my cock curses me. But she's already in pain, and I'm not in the mood to punish her body more than I already have.

I unlock her chain from the headboard and urge her up. Once on her feet, I begin to lead her out of the room, but her leash jerks in my hand. I turn to find her standing there, gazing up at me through her lashes.

"Come on, kitten." I jingle her leash.

She takes two steps forward then drops to her knees.

She looks up at me with her hands on her thighs and lust in her eyes. She's asking something. Permission?

I pet her head. "Is there something you'd like, Ellie?

"Yes, Kayne." She licks her bottom lip seductively. My already throbbing cock is now kicking. My little kitten wants to play.

"Go ahead then." I press my pelvis forward.

She lifts her hands to my belt and unbuckles it. She then unclasps the waist of my slacks and lowers my zipper. She hooks her fingers into my underwear and drags both my boxer briefs and pants down, springing me free directly in front of her face. Does she know how much I need this? Need her?

Ellie darts her tongue out, licking the tip of my erection. It feels like an electrical shock through my system.

I slide my hands into her light brown hair. Jett left it down, and it's sexy as hell. Just like Ellie. She works my cock into her mouth. Sliding it in and out, taking it a little deeper each time. I groan freely, loving the feel of the way she takes me. Possesses me. Of her initiating the blow job in general. My grip tightens in her hair as she swallows all of me, the head of my pulsating erection touching the back of her throat. I try to stay still and let her suck me to an orgasm, but it feels too damn good, too damn tempting. I hold her head and thrust into her mouth. She absorbs each jab, never moving; the goddess that she is on her knees. My orgasm moves quick, snaking its way down my spine and tingling my tailbone. I come so fucking hard I roar like a wild animal. Ellie swallows every drop of my release, sucking me until I run dry.

I can barely stand as the remnants of my climax vaporizes. Ellie just stays on her knees with her head bowed, waiting for my direction. I run my hands through her hair reverently.

"You little minx." She looks up with blazing green eyes. I scratch her under her chin.

She smirks impishly.

I barely recognize the woman in front of me. She's a seductress. A temptress.

And I realize now, she's not the only one who's owned in this room.

JAVIER'S FORTY-EIGHT HOURS ARE ALMOST up. I can't wait to throw that Mexican piece of shit out with the trash. There are going to be some very unhappy people if this deal doesn't go through. A lot of wasted hours and money spent, but that's the nature of this fucked-up business. Everyone is a snake. Everyone is out for blood.

There's a knock on my office door. I look up with just my eyes.

"Come in."

Javier appears in front of me. I'm shocked he actually used his manners. He saunters haughtily into the room and takes a seat in the wing-back chair across from my desk.

"Coming to say goodbye?" I ask snidely.

"Quite the contrary. El Rey will be arriving in two days. The arrangements will be made prior, all accounts approved. He will stay for one night for a face-to-face meeting. Then I will stay behind to make sure the shipments arrive effortlessly."

"I have full faith in the company I use," I tell him arrogantly.

"I'm sure you do, but what's the saying, better safe than sorry. Don't you agree, amigo?"

"Let's get something straight." I lean forward menacingly. "I am not your amigo. We do business. I tolerate you in my house. That's it." I tap the pencil I'm holding against the desk repeatedly. Riled, agitated, and on the brink of committing a homicide.

"Yo comprende," he responds with dark eyes.

"Good. Now get out," I bite.

Javier stands but moves slowly. "I'd like to throw a party. El Rey hasn't stepped foot on American soil in over a decade. Let's make his one and only night a memorable one."

"You want to throw him a party?" I raise my eyebrows.

Javier nods.

"Okay." I smirk deviously. "I'll throw him a party he'll never forget."

"Excellente." Javier smiles wily, then walks out of the room.

I snap the pencil in two, wishing it was his neck.

ELLIE

SOMETHING RAPTUROUS TOOK HOLD WHEN Kayne professed that he'd kill for me. He meant every syllable. I could feel the verity vibrate through my bones. Then, insanely, I dropped to my knees, and for the first time since the night he took me, I craved to please him. To sate him. I don't know when things changed, or how they changed, but making Kayne fall apart had my adrenaline pumping and my pussy throbbing. For a split second I contemplated lying on my back and splaying my legs so he could have me, but when he grinded himself against me moments before, I knew my body couldn't handle another punishing. My mouth was the next best thing, and it seemed to work just fine. I was especially proud of myself when his eyes rolled into the back of his head.

My time with Kayne has been enlightening, to say the least. It's blossomed a desire inside me that I never dreamed existed. He pushes all my limits, all my boundaries, all the confines of my mind. He's making me into someone new. Someone strong and sexual and barely recognizable. Someone who's learning she loves to serve him.

Presently, Kayne is feeding me dinner. I'm on my knees between his legs, taking pieces of beef bourguignon straight from his hand. It's sweet and tangy and sinfully delectable.

"Ellie?"

"Mmmm hmmm?" I suck his fingers into my mouth a little further than necessary. His breathing accelerates.

"Behave," he chastises with just the slightest hint of menace. I quake with need.

"Yes, Kayne," I purr.

His eyes dilate as he zeroes in on my lips and then my naked chest. He didn't touch me last night. He gave my body some reprieve, but I fear whatever he has planned tonight will make up for the lost time.

"Tomorrow night I'm throwing a party. A very special guest is arriving," he says. "You need to be on your best behavior. Can you be a good kitten for me?" He feeds me another piece of meat. I nod while I chew.

"Yes, Kayne," I say after I swallow.

"Good girl. I want to show you off. I want everyone to see what's mine. And be green with envy." He jingles the tag on my collar, and then glides his thumb and middle finger down my delicate diamond body jewelry until he reaches the middle of my breasts. He touches one nipple so softly I barely feel it, and yet it still somehow manages to make me tingle between my thighs.

"This is going to be a party unlike any you've ever been to. It may be a little shocking. I want to warn you now. You know the business I run."

I blink at him inquisitively as heat creeps over my skin. I know exactly the type of business he runs. I've seen it, I've experienced it. I fucked one of his employees because of it.

"Yes, Kayne."

"And no one will touch you but me. Regardless of what they perceive." His tone is resolute.

"Yes, Kayne." My voice wavers.

"Mine, Ellie. Only mine." He yanks my collar, bringing my lips to meet his. The kiss is gentle. Emotion filled. It floods me with confusion. What's happening here?

"You have been such a good girl." He gropes me. "But I'm dying to spank you." He palms my ass and my heart rate accelerates.

"Yes, Kayne," I respond immediately, remembering what happened last time he told me he wanted to spank me.

"I told you that lesson would stick," he says haughtily.

He definitely remembers, too.

Kayne pulls me to my feet by my new leash. A thick chain with delicate pink ribbon threaded through the links. My legs are wobbly. My body hasn't fully recovered from the other night, and I'm not particularly inclined to pain. It's moments like these that bring blaring clarity to my situation. I can't say no. There is no, *no.* Or stop. No amount of begging will change his mind. He's only given me the choice once, with Sugar.

"On the bed. Get on all fours. Facing the headboard."

I immediately do as I'm told. I walk over robotically with my heart jack-hammering in my chest, crawl onto the mattress, and position myself on my hands and knees.

I watch as Kayne picks up the shackled cuffs lying on the table of torture, and then another chain from one of the drawers. I try to breathe steadily, but my body instinctively reacts to what's on the horizon. Kayne walks over to the bed and places the items next to me. He kisses my back, starting from the middle of my shoulder blades, down my spine until he reaches my tailbone. Then he sheds his clothes, shrugging his collared shirt off first, then his pants. Naked, he's a god—tall, toned, the standard of excellence.

"Get up and grab the top of the headboard." He kisses my neck, right above my studded collar.

I scurry up the gargantuan bed and reach as high as I can, my fingers not quite making it to the top. Kayne crawls up behind me and presses his hard body flush against mine, pinning me against the vining iron. He loops the cuffs through an opening then secures both of my wrists. If it weren't for the pillows, I would be dangling by just my arms. Then he fastens the end of my leash to a high curve forcing me to look up. I'm panting now, in yet another unyielding position.

"Mmmm," he moans as he takes advantage of my overstretched body. Touching me wherever he wants. Massaging my breasts, my ass, my thighs, my clit, jutting my hips out a little farther after he's finished copping his feel.

"Ready?" he growls primitively in my ear and I hear the clink of the other chain. I panic. I don't want the pain. At least not that much.

"Kayne, please don't." My voice strains from the pool of tears welling in my eyes. "Please don't hurt me." I tremble in my restraints as I await the first blow. But nothing comes. Except soft kisses across my skin.

"Shhhh, Ellie. I'll never hurt you again." I feel him fasten the other chain to the back loop of my collar, a second leash. "Unless you make me." He says it flippantly, but there is still an undercurrent of menace in his voice. A warning. A message: don't fuck with me.

He massages me gently, lulling me into submission, then tightens his grip on the chain. The collar strains in two directions and I can no longer move my head.

"Fuck, you look so hot like this."

I whimper as he rubs his cock against me, then lands the first blow. A sharp smack right to my ass cheek that stings like a son of a bitch. My body tenses all over. He hits me again and I grit my teeth, absorbing the pain, unable to move. He rubs my heated skin, tempering the sting.

He hits the same spot again—the fleshiest part of my buttocks—and I cry out.

Oh, God what did I ever do to deserve this?

"You're doing so good baby," he coos, licking my neck. "Let's see if you're wet." Kayne slips his finger between my legs and slides it through my folds. "Fuck, Ellie. You're soaked." He withdraws his finger and lines the head of his cock right at my entrance. I brace myself, for what I don't know. Another hit? For him to take me hard and fast, like he usually does?

He rocks against me, entering me slow and controlled, the movement foreign to me. "God. Ellie you feel so fucking right." His voice is thick with lust as he pushes himself all the way in. A drawn out moan escapes my lips. He's so big for my little body. Every time, stretching me wide, and filling me to the point of almost bursting. I'm helpless under his strict command; my wrists tethered over my head, my body dangling, my neck strained. He fucks me leisurely, sliding all the way out, then driving his cock directly back in. I'm losing my mind, the pace is perfect. It's sending me to another planet. Then he whacks me again and I jolt back to the here and now. My relaxed muscles clench hard causing him to groan.

"One more baby. Then that will be five. You've been such a good little kitten, it spared you from ten." The last hit is the hardest of all. I scream his name in protest.

He drops the leash—it smacks my backside—and grips my hips with both hands. Digging his fingers into my flesh, he still continues to move slowly. Like he's savoring me. He never savors. He always just takes. Takes from my body, takes from my mind. This is different. The way he touches me, the way he moves.

"You have no idea how much you mean to me, Ellie. How much I want to keep you." He removes one of his hands and begins to rub my clit, circling it lightly. Mind-bendingly good.

"Kaaaayne," I moan, as everything aches; my arms, my ass, my pussy.

"Do you like that, Ellie?"

"Yes, Kayne."

"Tell me the truth."

My brain is on autopilot as he twists all of my senses. "I love it. I don't ever want you to stop."

My orgasm is arresting me, the same way my wrists are tied. It's coming on strong, full force. But I need more of him to explode.

"I don't ever want to stop."

"Please, please," I whimper.

"Please what?" He presses harder against my clit with his finger.

"You know." I'm shaking, unable to push myself over the edge.

"Say the words," he demands. "I want you to tell me to fuck you."

I'm so desperate to come, I'd say just about anything to him right now.

"Fuck me, Kayne. Please fuck me, make me come," I nearly sob.

"Anything for you." He sucks on my neck right above my collar as he begins to pound into me, feeding my body exactly what it needs. Exactly want it's starved for, even though it's fed every night. My climax pressurizes then explodes, unleashing a hailstorm of ecstasy. I come unashamed, while screaming his name.

"Fuck, give it to me," he grinds out, thrusting harder. "Give it all to me. I want every fucking ounce."

He wrings me out. My body going slack in my restraints as he ruptures, stilling forcefully, buried deep inside me. He drops his head against my back and breathes heavily, as he recovers from the euphoric high.

After he comes around, Kayne hoists me up, so I'm straddling his thighs. It takes the pressure off my arms and neck. He massages my shoulders while dusting soft kisses across my fevered skin.

"You are so sexy. I can't tear my hands or my lips or my eyes off you. You're my most prized possession," he growls in my ear. "I meant it when I said I would kill for you, Ellie. I'd do anything for you."

A rash of goose bumps erupts all over my body. I feel safe. I feel wanted. I feel desired. In this new life, my goals and ambitions are vapor. And as much as that saddens me, my existence has morphed into something else entirely. I secretly enjoy the things he says, and the way he makes me feel. I believe him when he tells me I'm important. It gives me a sense of purpose to please another. To please him.

"Tired baby?" he asks as he continues to rub me down.

"Yes, Kayne." I'm physically depleted and emotionally spent. Every interaction with Kayne drains me completely.

He removes the second chain, unbinds my hands, and hooks my leash back in its usual spot. My arms and back feel stretched, sore. He forces me to lie down on the cool satin, all while watching my naked movements with his mesmerizing eyes. I feel like they're peeling away every layer of my existence. I want to know what he's thinking. Why he's looking at me like this might be last time he ever sees me.

"Sleep baby." He kisses my forehead lightly and moves off the bed.

"Aren't you staying?" I ask timidly.

"Not tonight." He slips on his pants. "A lot of things are going to change very fast. I have to make sure everything is ready.

"Changes?" I ask, my voice small.

Kayne chastises me with a harsh facial expression. "Shhhh. No more talking. No questions." Then his eyes soften as he runs a finger lovingly along my jawline. So mercurial. "Sleep, Ellie."

"Yes, Kayne," I reply forlornly.

I don't want him to leave.

KAYNE

TWELVE HOURS.

The countdown has begun. Tonight is what I have lived the last six years for. El Rey will be on American soil. He will be in my home. The deal will be made. Shit will implode. My mission will be complete. And I have no idea where it will leave me and Ellie in the aftermath. My stomach actually rolls thinking about what we have coming to an end. Whatever that may be. Having her in my life on a daily basis has made a mundane existence shine with brilliance. She invaded my heart like a sneak attack and now she's a permanent fixture.

"Everything is set." Jett has been rambling for the last half hour and I don't think I've heard one word he's said. "Kayne." He snaps his fingers in front of my face. "Are you listening? This is the most important night of our lives. Let's not fuck it up, okay?"

I curl my lip at him. If he were anyone else I would snap his skinny ass like the twig he is.

"Do they hurt?" I ask randomly.

"Does what hurt?" he asks lost.

"Your balls. Do they hurt being strangled in those fucking pants all day?"

"Hate on my style all you want." He grabs his junk. "My shit shoots just fine."

"Good to know. Because if it didn't I'd have to hire a new trainer."

"You won't need one after tonight." He smiles coyly.

I involuntarily grimace. Jett's eyes soften.

"Don't fucking look at me like that," I snap.

"Like what?" His eyes widen. Like he doesn't know.

"Like you feel sorry for me or something."

"False accusation. You're an asshole scumbag who doesn't deserve an ounce of pity."

Man, ain't that the truth. I glance at the security feed. The mansion is quiet. No one is around. All the girls are preparing, Ellie is sleeping, and Javier is lurking.

It's the calm before the storm.

"Since we're on the subject," Jett probes. "Are you going to be able to handle whatever happens after the shit goes down?"

Probably not.

"I'll have to, won't I?" I look over at him. He's dressed in a light blue V-neck shirt and tight white pants. His normal attire.

"She may forgive you." Jett slips that in there.

"Would you forgive me?" I counter.

"Well, that's not a fair question, is it? No one knows you better than me. And knowing what I do, I would say hell no. And tell you to fucking die."

I glare at him. "Is this supposed to be a pep talk? Because it sucks. "

"Ellie doesn't know all your dark corners. She may take pity on you." He paces in front of my desk. "After a shitload of spoiling and groveling on your part of course. Are you man enough to handle that? You prideful jackass?"

"I don't know. Maybe. Probably. If it means I get to keep her." I cross my arms and brood.

"We both knew this life wasn't going to last forever."

"Yes we did," I sigh.

"Maybe she'll forgive you." He reiterates.

"Maybe pigs will fly and your dick will breathe in those pants."

"Hater."

"Dream on. Speaking of Ellie"

"Already covered." Jett raises his hand to halt my sentence. "Your jaw is going to drop."

"Oh really?" I cock an eyebrow.

"Yup. It's your last night together. Thought I'd make it special."

"Well aren't you just my fairy fucking godfather in heinously ugly skinny jeans."

"You're just jealous you can't pull them off."

"Insanely." I roll my eyes. "Go see to my kitten. Make sure she's happy." I dismiss him.

"I think the only time she's happy is when she's with you," he says over his shoulder as he walks out the door.

I really fucking hope that's true.

ELLIE

JETT HAS SPENT THE LAST two hours primping me. I have never been dolled-up this much in my life. He has straightened my hair and pinned half of it back. Smoked my eyes out with purple shadow and black eye liner. Put on false eyelashes and stained my lips a bright pink. Presently he is slipping me into some sheer intricate lingerie number that's nude-colored, floor length, and has a plunging neckline. There's a butterfly pattern on the front made out of white lace that barely covers my breasts and wraps around my ribcage. With a skimpy thong to match, I think it's the most clothing I've worn since I've been here.

Jett crosses his arms and stares at me, admiring his handy work.

"Bellemiso." He makes that gesture where he kisses the tips of his fingers.

I eye him entertained. "You are a very odd individual."

"I know. One of a kind."

"How did you come to be this way? If you were gay, I'd understand."

Jett smiles his oh-so-pretty smile while running a hand through his blond hair. "One day I'll tell you the whole story. But the cliff notes version? I grew up around a lot of women."

"Sisters?" I ask.

He laughs like it's some kind of private joke. "No, not exactly, but my mom did take in a lot of strays. Me and a house full of females, I learned a few things."

"Like how they think and what they like?"

"Yes, that, among other *things.*" He emphasizes the word things.

"What things?" I probe.

He clams up.

As close as I feel to Jett, I know very little about him. Besides his favorite color being blue, his favorite ice cream mint chocolate chip, and his weapon of choice, wax.

"Jett, since I've been here, you have bathed me, dressed me, and groomed me. Made me laugh and consoled me. It's sort of unfair. You know more than most about me, and I know nothing about you."

"You know that I care about you," he counters.

"Jett." I put my hands on my hips and glare playfully at him.

"Those eyes are killer." He sighs as his resolve crumbles. "My mother was a Madame, Ellie."

"What?" I respond bemused.

"Yup. I grew up in a very affluent whore house. While other boys were playing football in high school, I was learning the family trade."

I'm rendered speechless.

"It's how Mansion came to be," he informs me.

"Mansion?" I question.

"Yes, that is what we call the business. I train all the women who work for us."

"Train? Like how Kayne trained me?"

"Yes. Very much like that."

"And they just let you?" The concept is foreign to me.

"Yes, Ellie. Some women crave to be controlled. It's a lifestyle that isn't always understood. But in this house it's done in a safe environment with likeminded people. Happy you asked now?"

"I guess," I reply blankly, trying to digest this new information.

"Not what you were expecting to hear?" he asks casually, as he fiddles with my hair.

"No," I divulge truthfully.

"It never is." He laughs. "I'll tell you more about my upbringing and Mansion one day. But for now," he claps his hands like it's back to business, "we need to get going. Kayne is going to flip. Like lose his shit completely when he sees you."

"You think?" I bite my lip, glancing down at my … outfit? No, ensemble.

"I know," he says confidently. "I've known Kayne a long time. And I know what he likes."

I frown, now knowing what I do about Jett, Mansion, and Kayne, I suddenly feel a little inadequate. "Has he been with many women?"

Jett's mouth falls open. "Umm?"

"That many, huh?" I respond insecurely.

"No, not exactly. It's just this lifestyle allows for an open tap of unadulterated pleasure. He's never hurt for company."

"Then why did he take me?" That is the question I feel I will never find out the answer to. Jett rests his hands on my arms. "You're going to know soon enough, sweet thing. And it's something Kayne has to explain."

"I don't like the way that sounds, Jett."

"And you shouldn't."

I swallow hard, a sudden upshot of fear grabbing me. "He keeps telling me things are going to change. Is he going to sell me?"

Jett's pretty aqua eyes bulge. "Where did you get a ridiculous idea like that?"

I shrug. "I'm a slave. Slaves get sold."

Jett shakes his blond head. "No more erotic suspense novels for you. And I can say with absolute certainty he would never sell you. But he is afraid he won't be able to keep you."

"I don't understand."

"You don't have to. All will be revealed after time. "Jett walks over to my bed and picks up my collar. "Final accessories." He fastens it around my neck then goes to the armoire and opens one side of the double doors. He returns with rhinestone wrist cuffs attached to several strings of thick crystals. One string he fastens to the D-ring on the front of my collar, then he clamps each of my wrists. I'm a dolled-up pet. A kitten on an ultra-extravagant leash.

"Perfect. It's time, sweet thing."

"Time for what?"

"You're unveiling. This party is important. Be on your best behavior. Listen to Kayne. Stay by his side no matter what."

"He has me on a leash, where do you think I'm going to go?"

Jett snickers. "I've become quite fond of you, little one. And that snarky mouth."

"It's all I have left. My snark."

Jett looks at me with a melancholy expression. His acute eyes sad. They remind me of a puppy in the pound. I wish I understood what he was feeling. I want to ask, but I think I've exhausted my allotment of questions for the day. I'm meant to live in the dark. And Jett and Kayne are experts at keeping me there.

Jett leads me toward the door by my shiny new jewelry.

"Where are we going?" I ask curiously. Kayne is the only one who takes me for walks.

"Kayne's room."

"Why?"

"Because you're his birthday surprise."

"It's his birthday? Is that what the party is for?"

"Not really. He'll probably decapitate me for telling you. But I don't give a fuck." He looks back and winks at me. I follow Jett through the dark hallway with the deep purple carpet and hand-blown chandeliers toward the sweeping staircase. I can hear music playing faintly from the first floor as we walk down one flight of stairs to the second level.

"Wait till you see this party. It's my best yet. Going to be a real *bang.*"

Something in my gut jolts from way he says *bang.* I don't like it one bit.

We stop at a huge wooden door where two very large men are exiting.

"Everything set up?" Jett asks them.

"Done," the tall blond responds. He reminds me of Thor with his brawn and long wavy hair.

"Excellent."

Jett ushers me inside Kayne's room and it strikes me as strange being here. The only environment I know him in is my room and our walks around the mansion. I observe my surroundings, noting it's very much a man's space. Understated, with dark cherry furniture and glossy wood floors. Against the back wall is an impressive canopy bed with maroon bedding. Very majestic, very commanding, very magisterial. Just like my owner. What I find most peculiar is the giant birdcage in the middle of the room.

"We have to hurry. Kayne takes a long shower, but I don't want to run the risk of him walking out and ruining the surprise."

"What surprise?"

"Why you, of course." Jett leads me inside the enormous cage with shackles hanging in the center. He removes one pair of cuffs from my wrists and replaces them with another. My heart races as I dangle dead center in the middle of the cage.

I feel like a virgin sacrifice.

"These cages are decorations for the party. I thought it would be a fun birthday present for Kayne to have his own captive angel. That's the theme." He smiles. The irony of his statement is not lost on me.

"I'm already his captive," I remind him dryly.

"True. But I think deep down, you like it. You like serving him. And obeying him. And being dominated by him."

I don't respond. Partly because I don't want to admit he's right, and partly because I think my affections go way deeper than like.

"You look entrancing, sweet thing." He pulls a red ribbon out of his pocket and ties it in a bow around my chest. He then pulls a thin chain out of his other pocket. He's like a walking vending machine tonight. He takes the delicate cord and weaves it through my fingers suspended above my head.

"What's that?" I look up.

"Kayne will know." He smirks devilishly, and right then I know I'm in trouble.

"My work here is done. I'll see you at the party, gorgeous girl. Behave." He taps my nose playfully with his index finger.

"I don't know how much trouble I can get in just hanging around." I pull on the restraints. If it wasn't for my heels, I'd be stretched and struggling on my toes.

"Well, just in case you get any ideas." He winks, closing the cage door. Then leaves the room. All I can do is wait. Now that it's just me, I can hear the hushed sound of the shower running. I jingle the chain around my fingers trying to figure out what it is. But all I see is silver metal. The wait for Kayne becomes suspenseful. I wonder what he'll think of Jett's present? What he'll think when he finds me in his room. He's never brought me here. Never even suggested it. So I wonder idly if he'll feel like I'm encroaching on his personal space. I'd rather like to avoid him taking out his displeasure with Jett on my behind. I tell myself he won't do that. Please don't. Please don't. I hear the shower turn off, and I tense in my chains. I drop my head submissively as I wait for Kayne to find me.

"Well, what do we have here?" I hear his voice and look up through my eyelashes. He's walking toward me slowly. The hunter stalking his prey. His eyes are wide and there's a mischievous grin on his face. "A sexy little kitten in a cage, just for me?"

"Jett said I was your birthday surprise."

"My birthday? He spilled the beans?"

"Yes, Kayne."

"Look at me, kitten."

I raise my head. He's standing in front of me in just a towel and tempting smile.

"This may be the best birthday present I ever received."

My cheeks heat. He looks like a hungry cat about to devour a helpless canary.

"Watch me get dressed." My eyes follow him as he moves through his room, pulling out clothes from his dresser and closet. He lays everything on the bed, and then discards his towel. He's standing in front of me stark naked, moving gradually so I get a good look at every inch of his hard sculpted body and the tattoos on his chest, arm, and side. He's freakin' drool worthy. I'll never deny it.

"Like what you see, kitten?" Kayne asks flirtatiously.

"Yes, Kayne," I reply with a raspy voice. Just looking at him has my mouth dry and body responding.

"Good." He smiles, then proceeds to get dressed. This feels so intimate. Watching him in the privacy of his room. Seeing him in a completely different light than I've ever seen him before. Once he's dressed in a plain white dress shirt and white pants, he joins me in the cage; his shirt partially unbuttoned.

I stare up silently, while he stares down.

"I guess I should unwrap you now." Kayne tugs lightly on the ribbon and the bow falls apart.

He drinks me in from head to toe, scanning his luminous eyes over my face, my chest, my torso, my legs, licking his lips as he goes. It's all at once nerve-racking, stimulating, and sexy as hell.

"I need to give Jett a raise," he tells me as he leans in and kisses me. There's no warning or asking of permission as his tongue invades my mouth. Jabbing and rolling, he asserts his dominance. His control. Reminding me I'm his. Like I could ever forget.

When we break apart I can barely breathe, my lungs working double time to suck in oxygen.

He runs his hands over my body, taking advantage of my powerless state.

"God, you're beautiful," he moans as he squeezes my breasts, fondling both of them at the same time. Kayne rests his head against mine, inhaling deeply like he's memorizing my scent. "Everything is going to change tonight, kitten." I look up into his majestic eyes. The brown lightning bolt more pronounced, ominous almost.

"You keep saying that, but what do you mean?"

"It means all will be revealed," he sighs forlornly.

"What will be revealed?" I urge.

"You'll see. Then it will all make sense."

"Is something going to happen to us?" I ask warily.

"Maybe."

"What?" I press, needing to know.

"I'm not sure. Possibly everything."

"I'm scared," I admit abruptly.

"Of what?"

"The unknown."

Kayne runs his thumb across my cheek. It's such a consoling caress.

"Do you trust me, Ellie?"

I pause, drinking in the earnest expression on his handsome face. Do I?

"Yes. I trust you," I tell him truthfully. When did everything between us shift? I don't really know. What I do know, and what I can say with certainty is, when I look at Kayne, there's more than just lust or need or want in his eyes. There's devotion and admiration.

"Good. Because I'll never let anything bad happen to you. I'll never let anyone hurt you again," he says pained. "I don't want to lose you, Ellie. Ever."

"I don't want to lose you either," I reply, unable to stop the words even if I wanted to. I am truly owned by him.

"You won't. Even if you push me away," he assures me resolutely. He then kisses me, causing my body to sway in the restraints. I tighten my fists and stiffen my limbs in an attempt to not lose my footing. The little chain Jett wrapped around my fingers clinks, spurring Kayne to glance up. He reaches for it, unraveling it from my hand.

"Fucking, Jett." He plays with the shiny string.

"What is it? Another present for you?"

"It's more a present for us." His blue eyes flash with venturesome lust as he dangles the strand in front of my face. It's long with a tiny clamp on the end.

"What's that for?" I ask cautiously.

"I can't wait to show you. Open your legs."

I do as I'm told. Kayne threads one end of the chain through the loop on my collar, the other end he slips into my dainty panties, then, using his fingers, spreads my folds wide. There's a sudden bite of pain as he pinches my clit with the clamp. "Oh God!" I gasp. Then he pulls on the chain and my knees go weak as a bolt of stinging ecstasy spirals through me.

"So you behave." He kisses my cheek lightly.

A ravenous urge builds within me as he repeatedly yanks on the chain commanding the clamp.

"Kayne, please."

"Please what, baby? Stop or go on?" he taunts me.

"I don't know." I drop my head back as my body depletes of energy. The sensations are much too much.

"You have no idea how sexy you look," Kayne breathes against my neck. "You have no idea what your body does to me." He grabs my ass and grinds his erection against my aching clit. I groan as the clamp pokes and prods at me, making me dizzy with desire. "You have no idea what I would do to keep you." He nips at my skin.

"Fuck, Ellie," he says tortured, grabbing my face in his hands. "I ... I ..." He searches my eyes, desperate and afraid.

Afraid of what, I can't begin to imagine. "... I want to watch you come." He cops out.

Reaching down, he slides my thong over to the side, and then inserts one finger into my throbbing core.

I moan uncontrollably as he strikes the right spot over and over.

"Shit, you're wet baby."

"You're going to make me come." I pull on the restraints as my body seizes, the clamp working the sensations double time. I buck in the shackles with my climax just out of reach.

"Kayne, please!" My voice is hoarse and my body is trembling.

"Not yet, kitten." He slows his rhythm, and I nearly combust into tears.

"Why?" I plead.

"Because I want you to remember who controls your pleasure. No matter where you go or who you're with. You'll always be mine." He leans into my neck, and I realize too late that he has the chain to the clit clamp between his teeth. Before I know what's happening, he slips another finger inside me and jerks his head. The dual sensations cause me to spark, splintering my existence into a thousand tiny pieces as Kayne commands my pleasure. His words echo like the threat they are. And the promise. My body gives way as every muscle strains, leaving me demolished in the restraints. My arms feel like they are going to dislocate, but I can't bring myself to stand. I'm destroyed once again. My mind, my body, my soul, my heart. They all feel like they're bleeding.

"Remember my words, Ellie." He hoists me up.

"Yes, Kayne," I reply, like I'm doped up on something. Like I'm doped up on him.

"My kitten." He smoothes his hand over my hair. "Recuperate and I'll clean you up."

He leaves me hanging, literally, and disappears into the bathroom. Kayne returns with two folded hand towels and a small bowl of water. He drops to his knees in front of me and removes my lacy thong. With the first towel, he wipes between my legs. With the second, he dips it into the bowl and proceeds to wash me. The water is warm and fragrant with something I can't place. It feels incredible as he moves up the inside of one thigh and down the other. His touch is so skilled and wonderfully tender. When he's through, he pats me dry; remaining on his knees he gazes up at me with an idolizing expression. The moment is surreal and also oppressive. The weight of his stare is almost too much to endure, but no matter how hard I try, I can't bring myself to turn away.

"Can I ask one thing of you?" Kayne places his hands gently on my hips.

"What?"

"Forgive me." He drops his head. "Forgive me for every wrong I have ever done to you."

The request sidelines me. Forgive him? Forgive him for kidnapping me? Forgive him for forcing me into sexual slavery? For beating me and humiliating me? For not protecting me and letting some scumbag accost me?

Forgive him for penetrating my heart, because even after everything, I want to remain his?

"I forgive you," I say delicately.

He heaves a sigh of relief. Then places a soft chaste kiss right below my belly button. It feels almost reverent. This man is so complicated and intriguing and frustrating and exciting. One minute he's an ice cold Dom, the next his affection could warm Antarctica. I'll never understand.

Kayne suddenly drops, his entire body falling to the floor at my feet. He places a light kiss on my ankle, then on the inside of my calf, my thigh, my stomach, both of my breasts, my neck then finally my mouth. He kisses me firmly, but affectionately, like he's trying to communicate something.

"You own me as much as I own you," he sighs against my lips. His eyes closed, his voice woeful. There are a million conflicting emotions spiraling through me. I should hate him, but I don't. I should want to run, but I won't.

"Kayne ..."

"Shhhh, baby. No more talking. There's been enough said."

And before I can make any leeway, he puts me right back in my place.

KAYNE

I FINISH GETTING DRESSED WITH my kitten watching me in her cage. She's tethered, clamped, and collared. I don't think anything is hotter. I button my shirt and slide my belt through the loops. Dressed solely in white, per Jett's request.

Tonight everything changes.

My life as I've known it for the last six years.

I never take my eyes off Ellie. As much as I want to stick a plug in her ass and fuck her delirious in that cage, I'm refraining.

I almost told her everything.

I almost told her I love her.

I almost told her she was free.

I don't know how I'm going to handle it if she walks away.

If?

When.

She says she's forgiven me. But I know once the curtain falls, the past will be our biggest obstacle. The truth will derail everything, and I'm dreading that unavoidable moment.

My phone beeps and I check the message.

Jett: Go time. It's been a pleasure serving with you.

I chew the inside of my cheek. Sentimental motherfucker.

"Time to go, kitten." I turn to Ellie with the most sorrow I have ever felt in my life. I keep my expression stoic, but the emotion reaches all the way from the tips of my fingers to the bottom of my soles.

I unclasp Ellie from her binds and rub her wrists. Then kiss her lightly on the lips. She's regarding me quizzically. I know I'm acting all kinds of weird, but I feel like a short-circuiting television. Cutting in and out between protection, duty, obligation, and love.

"Best behavior tonight, kitten." I buckle each of her crystal wrist cuffs. Then I grab both her leash and the newly added chain dangling through her collar's ring and yank lightly. She groans as the clamp tugs on her clit. My dick stirs. The clamp will keep her in line and aroused until I'm ready for her. "Head down, walk behind me, and only speak when spoken to."

"Yes, Kayne," she pants, and it revs my sex drive like a turbo engine. I will never get tired of hearing Ellie say those words. I will dream about them when I'm asleep and long to hear them when I'm awake.

I lead Ellie out of my room, loving the fact she was in my space. I fantasized about her sleeping in my bed, with a secret hope she'd become a permanent fixture one day. I have a foreboding feeling though, 'permanent' will never be an option with Ellie.

As we approach the staircase, the distinct sound of dance music floats up around us. Jett went balls to the wall for this party. Go big or go home, right?

We're going for a sonic boom.

Ellie and I walk down the extravagant stairs; the foyer already filled with people dressed solely in white. As we descend, I scan the crowd. Many people I recognize—most on my client list—and many I don't. I hope everyone has fun while they can, because it all ends tonight. I walk Ellie through the foyer and into the great room. I feel all eyes on me and my tempting little kitten. I have never owned a slave before, willing or otherwise. I like control, I like to fuck, and this lifestyle affords me that, with no strings attached. I never had to worry about conventional Dominant/submissive roles.

I was never interested in being responsible for someone else, until I experienced what it was like to break down another human being and truly be in control of them. To literally rule their life. Watching Ellie crawl on the floor and lay at my feet while she wore my collar was a rush unlike any I've ever known before, and probably unlike any I'll ever know again. For the first time, I not only wanted to take care of another person, I wanted them to take care of me. I want *her* to take care of me. That's probably the most terrifying admission of my pathetic existence. I've never depended on anyone; I was never given the chance. Ellie opened up a part of me I didn't even know was there. I want to keep her my kitten forever. Not an option, I know. Doesn't mean a man can't dream.

I shake hands with a few associates in passing as I stride into the room with Ellie in tow. It's dark, with black lights illuminating the walls and everyone's white attire. Even Ellie's dainty white lace glows. It looks like she's wearing only a skimpy bikini. I travel deeper into the room, snaking my way through the crowd with a tight grip on Ellie's leash. She's a fraction of a centimeter behind me, but I feel her everywhere; brushing up against my body, highlighting my heart, sweeping over my soul. She makes it hard to concentrate.

Everything looks as it should. People drinking, dancing, and partaking in immoral self-indulgence. Women, half naked on chains, are being felt up by anyone their Master will allow, while lewd acts are being performed on the white wing-back chairs and tufted flatbed couches. If Ellie is in shock, her outward appearance isn't showing it.

We make our way to the very back of the room where there's a roped-off section. This, right here, is what makes Mansion's parties legendary. We dubbed it the playroom. An open space set up with tables, crosses, and swings. Basically everything your average kinky fucker could desire. What makes the playroom so special is that it comes complete with women, ready and willing. Take your pick of apparatus and have at it with the girl who's already there or one of your own choosing. I told you, my girls provide an invaluable service. The medieval stocks are always a favorite. At least that's what our clients tell us. Women confined, with their hands and head trapped between wooden boards, bent over, accessible for the taking.

The playroom serves a dual purpose; entertainment for those who want to watch and entertainment for those who want to partake. We feed all appetites here.

I pull Ellie in front of me and rest my hands on her hips. "Look, kitten," I murmur in her ear.

She looks up and directly in front of us is one of my girls — Pepper — strapped to a table, exactly like the one in Ellie's room. Her hands are tied above her head and her legs are secured to the stirrups, spread wide.

"Do you remember that day, kitten? When I strapped you to the table in your room?" I ask seductively. "I fucked you right after I gave you this." I run my nose against her neck and tickle her tag. "You came so hard. You like being mine."

"I could never forget," she responds, breathing strenuously. I can feel her heartbeat knock against my chest, as clear as *Seven Nation Army's* bass pumping through the room.

We observe Pepper lying on the table like a lamb waiting for the slaughter. She doesn't lie there long. Soon she's taken; her indefensible state an open invitation to anyone who wants her.

"Watch, kitten." I hold Ellie's face, as Pepper is fucked by a dark-haired man dressed solely in white.

"Do you wish that was us? Do you want me to tie you down and satisfy your ache?" I tug at the delicate chain attached to the clit clamp. She drops her head back against me and groans.

"Answer me." I jerk a little harder, my erection digging into her back.

"Yes, Kayne!" Her body stiffens and I release the chain.

"Soon, baby. But not yet. I want you frustrated." She moans like she's already there.

"You're mean," she murmurs with her head rolling all over my shoulder.

"I know." I kiss her cheek.

I force Ellie to watch Pepper come. It's a spectacle of a scene. Screaming and writhing and deep penetration. Either that guy's really good, or she really needs a promotion. Whichever, it is a good show.

Ellie is nearly falling apart in my arms by the time they're done. Rubbing herself against my erect cock with panting little breaths.

"You like to watch, kitten," I remark smugly. "I approve. Do you want me to take you in there and fuck you? Maybe pin you to the cross or secure you to the stock?"

She leans her head back and looks me in the eyes. Her eyelashes are huge tonight. "No."

"Why not?" I challenge, dipping my face closer just so I can inhale her scent. She smells like lemons.

"Because I don't want to share you with the public."

Okay. Time out. I wasn't expecting that answer.

I tighten my arms around her. My spirit flying high. "I don't want to share you either. Unless it's with Sugar," I leer.

Ellie chuckles. "Only behind closed doors." She flutters her long eyelashes. I nearly fragment. My frisky little kitten.

I grab her boob. "We have to go." I can be frisky too. I turn her around and give her a quick kiss on the lips, then snatch up her leash. I need to get back to prowling the floor and stop getting distracted by my sultry little pleasure kitten, with her gorgeous eyes, tempting mouth, and smokin' hot body.

All in good time, baby. All in good time.

I spot Jett a few minutes later. Just the person I am looking for. He's standing next to one of the many cages scattered all over the room containing captive angels. Girls dressed in barely there lingerie and huge white wings, dancing provocatively. It sort of reminds me of a Victoria's Secret runway show. As I get closer, I realize it's Sugar in the cage. It doesn't surprise me. She's his favorite girl.

"He's here," Jett informs me as I stand casually beside him.

I spy the room and spot Javier standing next to an older, light skinned man with silver hair.

"El Rey is American?" I've never seen a picture of him. He prides himself on being a ghost. The simple fact he's here is exceedingly rare. And it's a rarity that needs to be exploited.

"Half. Actually," Jett informs me. "The genes must run strong on his father's side."

"Clearly. What time is it?" I ask as the music thumps and strobe lights flicker on the ceiling.

Jett glances at his watch as I continue to survey the room. "Nine fifteen. Eleven thirty-seven is execution."

"Got it." I squeeze my grip on Ellie's leash and glance back at her. She's pressed against me, her cheeks are flushed and her eyes are down. The clamp and our little peep show must be weighing on her. Two and a half hours, kitten. Two and a half hours left. I look back at Jett and zero in on Javier and El Rey walking our way. Here we go. As the two men approach, I look both of them in the eye.

"Senor Roberts," El Rey addresses me, shaking my hand. He's a tall, well-groomed man with viciousness in his dark brown eyes. "I thank you for welcoming me and celebrating me in your home."

"Mi placer. Es un gesto para expresar mi entusiasmo para las actividades futuras."

My pleasure. It's a gesture to express my enthusiasm for future endeavors. I respond in his native tongue to show respect.

Piece of shit.

He smiles brightly. "Yes, I look forward to it. Javier has confirmed everything is in place and the first transaction should happen next week. I'm very pleased."

I glance at Javier. He hasn't taken his evil stare off Ellie since he reached us. It makes me want to stab his soulless black eyes right out of his head.

I feel the tension rippling off of her. She recognizes him, and she's scared.

"As am I," I respond evenly, even though a reel of murderous images are playing through my mind.

He nods with approval, and the deal is done. Funny how such a simple exchange can fortify a multimillion dollar business partnership. A very illegal, dangerous, clandestine agreement.

I smile insincerely. "Now that the formalities are out of the way. Please enjoy. Indulge. Jett went above and beyond for the guest of honor."

"Yes, I'm interested to see where this night goes. White attire?" He looks at Jett.

Jett shrugs, holding on to one of the bars of Sugar's cage. "All I can say is be prepared for a bang."

El Rey cocks an eyebrow. Javier glares. I keep smiling. Javier then turns his attention to Ellie. She's been perfect this whole time. If I wasn't holding on to her leash for dear life, she'd be a figment of my imagination.

"How's your whore, Kayne?" he asks, and Ellie stiffens.

I want to slit his throat open and remove his vocal cords with tweezers.

"Still mine," I growl.

El Rey glances behind me, and then very lightly tugs on her chain drawing her out from behind my back. I hear her expel a little gasp, the clamp continuously doing its job. Which pleases me and pisses me off all at the same time. I'm the only one who's supposed to pull her strings.

"She's quite stunning." El Rey drinks her in with a greedy stare. Ellie stands perfectly still, with her head down and hands cuffed in rhinestones by her side. "Look up, my dear."

She doesn't move. He frowns. "Not trained?"

"She's trained. This is her first outing." I jingle her chain, knowing she feels it right between her legs. "Look up, kitten."

Ellie sweeps her head up, breathing hard. Her eyes are glassy and her cheeks are bright red.

"Exquisite." He regards her, stepping closer. "Is she for sale?"

"No," I immediately reply.

"Borrow, then?"

"No."

"No price at all?" he questions.

El Rey could pay, I have no doubt. But Ellie is invaluable.

"No. This one is mine." I glare at Javier. *Got that Mexican scum of the earth?*

"I don't blame you for keeping her all to yourself." He runs his thumb down her chest and over the delicate chain attached to the clamp. Then he tugs and Ellie nearly falls over. I need to count to a thousand so I don't flip my shit on the spot and go on a shooting spree. But this is part of my cover. Having him believe I'm as big of a douchebag as he is.

"We have plenty of pets to play with," Jett chimes in, gaining both Javier and El Rey's attention.

"Yes. I'd hate to miss out on the festivities." El Rey steps away from Ellie, but Javier lingers a second longer. Then he squeezes her breast. Ellie whimpers and retreats behind me. I will cut his hand off for that.

"Your whore still needs work," he sneers.

I glare at him, throwing daggers with my eyes. Soon motherfucker. Soon.

Jett leads Javier and El Rey toward the back of the room, and I know exactly where he's taking them. The playroom. Mansion's VIP area for public sex and women for the gorging. That should keep them occupied for the rest of the night.

I wait until the three of them are out of sight, then turn to Ellie. She's shaking. I take her face in my hands and force her to look at me. "You did so good." I kiss her lips as a tear escapes down her cheek. I lick it off.

"How about we relax and have a little fun?"

"Fun?" she repeats curiously. She probably thinks I want to fuck, given the environment and porno being projected on the wall. But I have something else in mind.

"Mmmm hmmm." I grab her hands and start to sway my hips to Flo Rida's *Wild Ones* pumping through the room. People are dancing all around us, and I think it's time we join in. Ellie smiles brightly as we begin to move. I swear it's the most genuine smile she's donned since the night of Mark's party. The night everything went so terribly wrong. I pledge after this is all over, I'll keep that expression on her face for the rest of her life. I will do anything to keep her safe, keep her smiling, keep her mine. I'll walk over jagged glass, run through a blazing fire, crawl on my hands and knees through the desert, wear a collar and lie at her feet.

Anything.

Cannons suddenly blast, pelting everyone in the room with liquid color. There's Jett's bang. They ring in succession, one after the other, turning a sea of white into waves of splotchy color. My shirt, my pants, my face, even my hair, is splattered with a vibrant rainbow. The same with Ellie. We kiss passionately and laugh foolhardily as we smear color all over each other while dancing to the music. In my entire life, I have never been so happy. This single moment will live infinitely.

I grab her ass and grind my hips against her. She moans in agony. The clamp is torturing her.

"Uncomfortable baby?" I murmur in her ear.

"Yes," she pants, and I'm sure if she could sweat through her tongue she would.

"Need me to take care of you?" I rest my cheek against hers and trap her face with my hand.

"Yes, Kayne." It's a desperate plea.

That's all I have to hear.

I drag my multihued kitten off the dance floor and through the first door I see, making sure to lock it behind us. We're in one of the mansion's zillion bathrooms. I think this is the first time I've ever been in this one. It's decorated in several different shades of blue.

"Bend over," I order.

Without delay she braces herself on the speckled cobalt vanity right between the double sinks. My cock throbs. There's nothing more tantalizing than Ellie wide open and prime for the taking. I lift the long sheer material of her lingerie up her back and then glance at her in the mirror. There's paint all over her face and in her hair, across her chest and down her stomach. It looks like we've been rolling around in colorful mud. I grind my erection against her ass and she lets out an injured moan.

"Need me baby?" I taunt her.

"Yes," she heaves.

I slowly unbuckle my belt and unzip my fly, all the while watching Ellie watch me. She looks like a starved animal, and the son of a bitch in me loves it.

I press the head of my cock against her entrance and she juts her hips back begging for it. "Stay," I order, and she stops moving.

I reach over her shoulder and grab the thin chain attached to the clamp, drawing it behind her. Then I tie it to the loop on the back of her collar, making sure there's no slack. She's breathing savagely with wild eyes.

This is going to be intense.

I lace my hands behind my head and stand steadily with my legs spread apart. Ellie watching me idly through the mirror.

"Go on, kitten. Move. Take your pleasure. I want to watch you make yourself come."

She stares at me silently. I've never given her control before and by the look on her face, she has no idea what to do with it.

"Fuck me, Ellie." I nudge my hips infinitesimally.

She trembles, steeling herself on her hands. And after an elongated beat, she impales herself onto my cock and cries out, her head snapping back as her body ingests all of me. She's soaking wet and fucking on fire.

I watch, entrapped, as she begins moving urgently, pumping her pussy hard against me. I don't budge, even though the need to grab her hips and pound into her is suffocating me. She doesn't last long, a few heated seconds, before the orgasm eating her alive grabs hold. Ellie claws at the blue granite as she screams through her soul-sucking climax, the physical exertion visible on her pretty face as she saturates me with her arousal. My little kitten, in the throes of ecstasy—nothing is more powerful or stimulating.

My cock twitches and my heart hammers as the urge to fuck her senseless takes over.

She collapses forward after the tremors pass. Damn, that clamp is no joke.

I lean over her and kiss her behind the ear.

"My turn."

"Kayne," she cries, with her cheek pressed against the cool stone. Soft sobs wracking her body. "Cupcake."

Instantly, everything inside me feels like it's freefalling. All at once I withdraw from Ellie, spin her around, and plop her on the counter in front of me. I wrap her legs around my waist and slide back into her delicately. She shudders. She's still sensitive and hot as a fever.

"What happened, Ellie?" I hold her face in my hands, dropping soft kisses on her cheeks, her nose, her eyes, anywhere and everywhere I can get my lips. She looks up at me with a harrowing expression.

"I just need to touch you." The anguish in her voice rocks me. It's the first time she's ever invoked cupcake, and I know exactly what she needs.

Me.

A connection.

Sometimes I forget Ellie isn't accustomed to this life. She endures everything I throw at her, no matter how taxing. Her strength seduces me, constantly spurring me to push both our limits.

I rip my shirt open, sending the buttons flying everywhere. She places her hands on my chest, her right one landing directly on top of the intricate compass tattooed on my pec. She explores my body, touching my face, my arms, and my stomach all while I'm nestled snugly inside of her.

"I'm yours, Ellie. Every single inch." I want to assure her. I want her to know she can have me if she wants.

She eyes my torso, brushing her fingertips over words inscribed on my ribs. *It takes a certain kind of darkness for the stars to shine.*

"What does it mean?" she asks.

I swipe my thumb across her cheek. "It's a reminder that sometimes you have to do bad things for good reasons."

Ellie creases her brow as I feather soft kisses against her lips. "I hope one day you'll be able to understand."

"Understand what?" she asks a little dazed.

"Me." I shift inside her and she sucks in a sharp breath.

"Take it off," she pleads, rocking her hips. I instantly remove the clamp and she winces, breathing through the pain as blood rushes to her clit.

"Better?"

"Yes." She looks worn out, but the lust in her eyes is evident. She's not sated yet.

"What do you need?" I ask, dotting kisses on her lips.

"You." She tightens her legs and wraps her arms around my neck.

I'm hers for the taking, the devouring, the destroying.

I lean forward, with Ellie latched onto me for dear life, and brace myself with one hand on the countertop, aligning us at the perfect angle. I thrust slowly, in and out, savoring her soft sighs and indulging in her pleasured moans. God, she feels good. Tight, wet, warm, euphoric.

"You're perfect." I punch deep inside her. "Perfectly made, just for me."

She groans, sliding her hands into my hair. Her muscles contracting, squeezing me tight, driving the orgasm I'm fighting to control right up the fucking wall.

"Make me forget," she pleads, undulating against me. "Make me forget everything but you."

I grab her ass and slam into her. What my kitten wants, she gets.

"Oh, God yes!" She lifts her legs higher, giving me deeper access. I slam into her again, and again and again until she's flooding with desire.

"More," she demands, so more I give. Striking my hips over and over, our skin slapping together as her starving little pussy eats up every inch of my cock it can.

Wet, hot, branding arousal, that's what she damns me with. Because I know no one will ever make me feel the things she does. No one will ever wield my emotions or satisfy the beast that hungers only for her. I need to keep her.

The relentless pounding and asphyxiating contractions of Ellie's core causes my orgasm to spark at my tailbone. There's no controlling it as it ignites up my spine.

"I'm going to fucking come," I warn her.

"So am I!" she cries out, a rush of warm heat drenching my cock, spurring my orgasm to catch fire all over my body. We freefall together. A symphony of untamed, feral sounds echo around the room, bounce off the walls, and ricochet straight through my soul.

Holy fuck.

Did she feel it? Our connection, our link. *You're mine.*

With ragged breaths I open my eyes and hold her tight. "Will you stay with me, Ellie?" I ask in desperation. "Would you wear my collar not because I forced you to, but because you wanted to?"

She pops her eyes open, her gaze the darkest I have ever seen, like I'm staring straight into an evergreen forest.

She searches my face with confliction on her own. I never find out her answer because someone starts pounding on the door.

"Fuck off!" I snarl, still staring right at Ellie. I need to know, *will you stay?*

"Amigo," Javier's voice penetrates through the door like a buzzsaw. Ellie stiffens in my arms.

"You're safe," I whisper.

She nods silently, with wide frightened eyes.

"Que?" I answer.

"Your presence is requested." I don't like his slimy tone one bit.

Fucker.

"Coming," I snap, withdrawing from Ellie, beyond irritated. I was hoping to still be in the bathroom when the shit went down. I glance at my watch, ten after eleven.

We put ourselves back together in a hurry. We're still covered in color and now smell like sex. The scent I've come to live for.

I grab Ellie's leash once she's done cleaning herself up, kiss her on the lips, and then wind the chain around my hand. "Behave. I'm right here; I won't let anything happen to you." I kiss her again. I never want to stop.

"Amigo!" Javier pounds on the door wildly. Yup. Definitely cutting off that motherfucker's hands.

"Fuck you!" I bark, and then look over my shoulder at Ellie. "It will be over very soon." I try to reassure her as I grab the door knob and turn.

She nods, panicked and confused. I think her ability to speak is gone.

I swing open the door to Javier, two of his thugs, and three semi-automatic weapons pointed right at me.

"That was quite an earful," Javier says lewdly with that evil smirk.

"WHAT THE FUCK IS THIS?" I spit.

"Armed escort. Move." Javier motions with the pistol in his hand.

With no other option at the moment, I do as he says; walking down the hall surrounded by muscle and machine guns. I keep Ellie close. This shit isn't good.

We're forced into my study at the front of the house. It's away from the party and very secluded.

"I think El Rey would have something to say about you treating your host like his." I sneer.

"I'm sure he will." Javier smiles brightly. A moment later The King is strong-armed into the room at gunpoint.

Definitely not good.

"What's the meaning of this?!?" he demands outraged, looking between me and Javier.

"Hostile takeover." Javier lifts his gun and shoots El Rey right in the head. Ellie screams as The King's body falls to the floor and bleeds out all over the hardwood. I stare Javier down as Ellie quickly crumbles.

"Shut your bitch up!" He motions with the gun. "I'd shoot her too, but I have plans for you both."

I try to calm a trembling, pleading Ellie down, but she's in shock. It's no wonder, she's been traumatized over and over ever since she stepped foot in this house.

"Shhhh. Ellie. Calm." I yank on her chain, trying to command her. I'd rather wrap her in my arms and console her, but the moment calls for dictative actions. She looks at me with the most distressed eyes I have ever seen on a living human being.

"Kneel," I order, my voice firm, cold, and calculating. Nothing like the man she was with moments ago. I'd much rather be that man, but he has flaws and feelings. And those two things can get you killed.

"Do it," I hiss through my teeth and spank her so hard my hand stings. She drops to my feet so fast her knees slam against the floor.

If we survive this, the penance I will pay.

"I'll teach her better." Javier snatches her leash out of my hand and drags her across the room. I bolt forward but am met with several guns shoved into my chest.

"Not yours anymore," he heckles with a grip so tight on Ellie's collar he's restricting her airway. She's gasping and clawing at the leather begging for oxygen.

I'm quaking with rage from the inside out. I am going to kill him. Fuck cutting off his hands, I'm just going to put my fist through his chest and rip out his heart. I watch helplessly as he ties the leash to a thick gold sconce high on the wall.

"Kneel," he orders her.

Ellie doesn't move quickly enough and he shoves her down, the collar nearly hanging her. "Move and I'll rape you in front of everyone with that letter opener on the desk." My steel-plated letter opener that looks like a mini sword. Ellie kneels with barely enough chain to reach the ground. That cocksucker has turned her collar into a noose. She stares at me with pleading eyes as she slowly starts to suffocate.

I weigh my options. There aren't many. I have no gun, I'm outnumbered, and I don't want to go all Rambo and end up getting her killed.

As I formulate a strategy, Javier drops another bomb. He pulls something out of his pocket and throws it at my feet.

"Recognize that?"

I stare down, studying the scrap of something on the floor. I nudge it with my toe and then realize what it is. My head snaps up. "Where is he?"

"Gone," Javier sings. Terrorizing me.

All rational thought evaporates. That scrap on the floor in front of me is skin. Jett's nautical star tattooed on his left arm, Javier sliced it off. In a moment of unbridled rage, I go after him.

He lifts his gun without hesitation and shoots me in the shoulder; pain rings through my whole body as I grab my arm and fall to my knees. Son of a bitch.

Javier stands over me and presses the barrel of the gun to my forehead.

"What's yours is now mine, amigo."

He presses harder and I steady myself with my heartbeat echoing in my ears and my blood whooshing through my veins like white water rapids. I glance at Ellie fighting for her life and fearing for mine. Then I look at the clock on the wall and erupt in a fit of laughter.

Javier looks at me like I've lost my mind. Maybe I have.

Eleven thirty-seven.

"Jett's death won't be in vain." I glare at him manically. *"BANG."*

Moments later, a dozen men dressed in black and armed for war flood the room. They break through the bay windows and kick down the door. When shots ring out, I hurl myself at Ellie, shielding her with my body. I yank on the chain, pulling the sconce right out of the wall. The gunfire lasts only a few seconds, but I'm sure it feels like years to her.

When the commotion ceases, I lift my head with Ellie trembling uncontrollably in my arms.

"It's okay. It's over now." I smooth her hair and kiss her head repeatedly while she latches onto me like it's the end of the world.

I'm sure for her it is.

I glance around. Javier, El Rey, and all their thugs lay dead on the floor. The room is destroyed, bullet holes in all my books, the walls, and my desk. The cherry wood looks like it's been chewed on by wild animals.

"Can you stand?" I ask Ellie delicately.

She looks up at me, drained of life.

I lift her to her feet and secure her in my arms. I'm never letting go. "It's okay. It's over. It's all over."

"Agent Rivers."

I stand at attention at the call of my name. "Commander."

Ellie looks at me funny. *Yeah, kitten, we have a lot to talk about.*

"You alright?"

I nod. "Affirmative, sir."

"Nice work." He puts his hand out. Commander Adams is the A-typical Army commando. Short buzz cut, thick mustache, and no nonsense. He's one of the best people I know. Next to Jett.

My heart sinks. I hug Ellie tighter with the arm I still have around her. She's the only thing grounding me at the moment. The only thing holding me together. I try not to think of Jett and the terrible end he faced. Images upon horrific images infiltrate my mind.

"Thank you, sir." My response is strained.

"Debrief at 0800. The house will be wiped."

"Sir," I answer mechanically.

Ellie watches our exchange. I know she thinks she's in the twilight zone.

One of the Special Forces soldiers wraps her in a blanket as I converse with Commander Adams. Then he tries to remove her collar. I want to growl, but I don't. *Mine.* When he finds he can't because of the padlock, he disappears. Good riddance.

"Get that wound taken care of, Rivers. See you in the AM."

I nod compliantly.

"Sir?"

"Yes, Solider?"

"Did the team I requested deploy?"

"An hour ago."

I nod again. I sent a fleet to diffuse and disband Javier's slave operation. The team was instructed to evacuate the estate and then burn the house to the ground. I vowed I wouldn't let that girl's death be in vain and I always stand by my word. Now I'm freeing them all.

Commander Adams gives Ellie a once-over, then cocks an eyebrow at me. He leaves without another word after that. Ask me no questions, and I'll tell you no lies. That's how this operation works. Execute the mission. End of story.

"Please tell me what's going on before I fall to pieces." Ellie finally speaks once we're alone.

"I'll tell you everything, but I want to get you out of here first." I put my arm around her to lead her out of the room, but she backs away.

"No, Kayne, now. Here. Tell me." There are so many emotions laced in her voice. She's scared, confused, upset, and rightfully so. I've kept her captive for a month, told her nothing about anything, and then just dropped it all in her lap.

A room full of dead people is not exactly where I wanted to have this conversation, but Ellie seems adamant and my time as her proprietor is over. I owe her answers, and it's time to fess up. Heaven help me.

"What's going on is it's over. Everything."

"What's over?"

"My mission."

"Mission?" she repeats, trying to understand.

"Ellie." I drop my forehead to hers. Where do I start? I guess from the beginning. "I spent my entire life in and out of foster homes, and to say my upbringing was rough is putting it mildly. When I was eighteen, I joined the Army. It was either enlist or live on the street." Ellie frowns, her eyes compassionate but hard at the same time. "I scored particularly high on certain parts of the aptitude test and was recruited for a pilot program called Black Dawn. It's where I met Jett."

"Jett was in the Army?" Ellie interrupts.

"Hard to picture, I know." My lip quirks solemnly. Every inch of me hurts, inside and out. And the mere mention of Jett's name magnifies the pain twenty-fold.

"Mutual friends," she muses.

"Excuse me?" I question trying to understand her statement.

Ellie's eyes water. "He said the two of you met through mutual friends. I understand now. Sorry, go on." She wipes a stray tear away from her cheek. I want to lick it off of her finger, but I don't. Instead I continue.

"We were trained for three years in covert ops."

"What, like spy school?" She tightens the blanket around her.

"That's one way to put it. After the training was complete, they let us out into the world. Leaving us to our own devices." She looks at me puzzled. Explaining this is harder than I initially thought. "They gave us free license to break the law, with hopes of aligning and infiltrating ourselves with drug dealers, arms traders, terrorists. Really anyone who is a threat to national security." Ellie looks around the room at the covered bodies and blood oozing all over the floor.

"So that makes you what exactly?"

"An undercover special ops agent for a covert operation called Endeavor. For six years I have lived and worked under the alias Kayne Roberts. I have assumed the identity of an entrepreneur, liquor distributor, and proprietor of an elite sex club called Mansion," I spew. It feels like an act of confession. "It was a cover. A government trap used to lure the enemy. And it lured one of most notorious drug lords on Earth. That was my mission, bring down the bad guy."

"So Kayne Roberts isn't your real name?" she asks.

"No, Kayne Roberts doesn't exist. Kayne Rivers does."

I can see the wheels grinding as she digests this information. I'm no one she's ever known me to be. Not since day one.

"Is Jett really dead?" Her voice cracks, it's like she's coming out of a coma.

"Yes." I put my hands on her arms, heartsick. Death is a harsh reality in this business. Jett and I both know that. We willingly chose this life, fully aware of the consequences. It still doesn't make losing my best friend, my brother, any easier. I take a cleansing breath—my shoulder is fucking killing me—as I grab onto Ellie. She has no idea she's my support. My rock. My everything. And I have to tell her.

More tears spill out of her eyes.

"No need to cry, sweet thing. Those fuckers had it coming."

I whip my head over to find a ghost standing next to us. I don't think I've ever been so elated in my life.

"Jett!" Ellie throws herself at him before I can move. Apparently I'm not the only elated one.

"Easy, killer." He winces as he catches her in his arms. He looks like shit, all bloodied and bruised.

"You're alive," she weeps.

"Barely." He smiles weakly, his left eye swollen shut. "It's going to take more than three goons and a paring knife to take me down." He lifts up his sleeve and shows me his arm. There's a thick white bandage around his bicep. "That was unpleasant."

"So was this." I point to my bleeding shoulder. "The fucking thing went straight through."

"I'm glad you're alright." He grins, dried blood caked on his mouth.

"You too."

Jett looks uneasily between me and Ellie. He knows we need our time. And it's now. "Well, I just wanted to find you and let you know I was alive before you started planning a funeral." He smiles at me with sad eyes.

"The night's not over yet. A funeral might not be taken out of the equation." I glance down at Ellie.

She frowns.

That moment the solider chooses to return.

"Ma'am." He holds up bolt cutters. Motherfucker. Then he snaps Ellie's collar in two. The leather falls to the floor, landing right at my feet. It feels like a bomb just went off. Ellie looks up at me with wide eyes as she grabs her neck.

"Am I free?"

Jett takes that as his cue to leave.

"I'll just be over there." He backs up, thumbing in the direction of the door.

Traitor. I shoot him a death glare.

"You've always been free," I reluctantly admit, snapping the delicate strings of crystals off her wrist cuffs.

"I don't understand." Her voice wavers.

"I did it to protect you," I blurt out. Cause really how do you tell someone that you kidnapped them and turned them into your sex slave so some other pervert didn't get to them first?

"Protect me from what?" Ellie spits.

"Not what, who. Javier, he wanted you. The night of Mark's party, he wanted to take you. So I took you first." I start to ramble. "I did it to protect you. You saw how he is. What he was capable of. I couldn't let him get near you."

"He did get near me." She starts to tremble.

"It was a drop in the bucket compared to what he could have done."

I see the storm brewing in her eyes. "It wasn't a drop in the bucket to me. Why didn't you just tell me? Why put me through all ... *that?* All those *things?*" The agony in her voice destroys me. I know she's recounting every second of the last month. Everything I forced her to do, the brutal fuckings, the spankings, the chains, the collars, the beatings, the humiliation.

"I couldn't. I had to make you believe. I had to make everyone believe." I take a step forward and she takes a step back. It guts me.

"Ellie, I'm sorry. I'm sorry for lying to you, I'm sorry for hurting you, I'm sorry for falling in love with you."

The words that have been stinging the tip of my tongue finally spill out. She looks at me dejectedly. I fly into a panic.

"Ellie, please." I feel her slipping away. "I love you. Forgive me."

She shakes her head, recoiling. "Get away from me," she hisses, taking another step back. I take another step forward.

"Ellie, stay." It comes out more like a command than the desperate plea I meant it to be.

She glares at me, disgusted.

"Ellie, *please* stay with me," I beg. The tables have finally been turned. Tears pour out of her eyes as she looks anywhere but at me.

"Jett!" she suddenly calls out frantically. I watch, helplessly, as she flies across the room and into Jett's welcoming arms. She sobs against his chest as he wraps her in an embrace. My jealousy flares.

I have never wanted to hurt Jett so badly before, but at the moment I want to break every bone in his upper body just so he can't lift his arms. I'm the one who's supposed to be hugging her, consoling her. Loving her. *Mine.*

All I can do is watch numbly as Jett leads a broken Ellie out of the room. He throws me a sympathetic look over his shoulder just before they disappear.

My existence has just been eradicated. Everything is gone; my life, my soul, my beating heart. My eyes water as I stare into the void. I blink rapidly as something trickles down my cheek. I wipe my face. Tears. I lick my hand, they taste just like hers.

ELLIE

IT FEELS LIKE I JUST woke up from a hundred-year dream.

The air is cool, but my skin is on fire. It's the first time I've been outside in I don't know how long. The sky is clear and dotted with thousands of stars and the moon is a thin crescent above our heads. Jett is talking to me, but I can't decipher a word he's saying. My thoughts are just a mess.

"Ellie!" I hear Kayne's distraught voice echo behind me as Jett tries to usher me into the back seat of a blacked-out SUV. "Ellie, wait, please, just listen to me!" When I feel him grab my arm, something inside me snaps.

"Get your hands off me!" I screech, batting him away. "I don't want to hear anything you have to say! I hate you, you asshole!" I start throwing punches. Kayne deflects my fists with his forearms in an attempt to shield himself from my physical explosion. I do manage to get one good shot in. My open hand connects with his face; the loud slap rings out and my palm stings just before Jett encircles his arm around my waist and tosses me into the back of the Suburban. I breathe erratically as I crash against the leather seat.

"Jett, get out of my way." Kayne tries to climb in after me, but Jett blocks him with his body.

"Kayne, back the fuck up." He shoves him hard and Kayne is forced to take a step back. Jett uses the split-second separation to hop into the car and slam the door. "Drive!" he barks at the man behind the wheel. Less than a moment later we peel out, tires screeching as we pull away from the house. I glance back to see Kayne's shrinking figure crouched on the driveway with his hands laced behind his head.

Ellie, I'm sorry. I'm sorry for lying to you, I'm sorry for hurting you, I'm sorry for falling in love with you. I take one look at Jett and unstoppable tears start to fall. He pulls me into his arms as I begin to sob. For God's sake, it feels like I have been crying for an eternity. It's a wonder my body doesn't just give out from dehydration.

As we drive, my life comes into sharp clarity. Like a fog has lifted. *You've always been free.* I cry harder and I don't understand why. I'm free, but I have the heaviest feeling of loss crushing my chest. It's almost suffocating me.

"Shhhh, Ellie." Jett comforts me. "Everything is okay. You're okay."

"I'm far from okay, Jett!" I explode. "I was just held captive for I don't know how long and forced to do unspeakable things with a man I once worshiped. I feel betrayed. I feel humiliated. I feel …" *Alone.*

"He did it to protect you." Jett defends Kayne.

"There had to be another way!" I demand, my emotions overflowing everywhere. There's no containing them.

"There wasn't. It was a split-second decision and we ran with it. Kayne couldn't allow you to be tortured at the hands of a monster. It was the only way to keep you safe. We both agreed."

"You both agreed to what? *Him* becoming the monster?!" I shout. The man driving the car never turns his head to look at us. He just steers the car, keeping his attention on the road. I'm grateful for his disinterest. Or his feign of disinterest. I'm sure I look and sound like a raving lunatic right now.

Jett scowls at me. Like he has any right. "Let me paint you a picture, Ellie. Say Kayne did tell you exactly who he was and exactly what was going on. And Javier came into your room that night and found you munching on popcorn and watching a movie instead of chained to the bed. Do you know what he would have done?"

I shake my head slowly.

"He would have tortured you until you talked. Until you divulged every one of Kayne's secrets. Do you think you could have handled him yanking out your teeth one by one? Or carving you up one tiny slice at a time? Because that's the kind of fucking animal he was."

I swallow hard, my throat sore from trying not to cry, my eyes wet with residual tears. "And after he finished with you, he would have gone after everyone else in the house. There was more than just your life at stake. So yes, we mutually agreed it was the best way. It wasn't premeditated. If you belonged to Kayne, theoretically Javier should have stayed away."

"Well he didn't stay away!" I wipe away the tears that are now escaping down my cheeks, reliving the aggressive, inhumane way he orally raped me.

"Evil is unpredictable. But he got what he deserved. Javier's death will ripple through the trafficking community. Countless lives will be saved."

"At what expense?" My voice is an agonizing whisper.

"Ellie, the world is at war, and sometimes innocent bystanders get caught in the crossfire. What happened to you was unfortunate, but you can't tell me you honestly believe Kayne is a monster."

"I don't know what to believe."

"Yes, you do. Believe what's in your heart. Over the last month I watched the two of you fall in love and now he's falling apart because you left him."

"He doesn't love me," I reply desolately. He can't. None of it was real.

"No, you're right. He doesn't love you. His feelings run so much deeper than that. He's obsessed with you. He always has been. Since the moment he met you, you're all he's ever wanted," Jett informs me directly. "And for Kayne to feel that way is huge. Beyond Mt. Kilimanjaro huge."

I shake my head furiously. "No." I don't want to believe it. I want to believe Kayne is a monster who doesn't deserve me. *No matter where you go or who you're with. You'll always be mine.*

"Javier wanted you." Jett clutches my arms and shakes me. "He would have stopped at nothing to get you, and once that happened, Kayne wouldn't have been able to intervene. Javier would have killed you. Do you understand? It was the only way." Jett's phone rings in his pocket and we both pause. He pulls it out and glances at the screen then looks up at me; his aqua eyes illuminating from the oncoming headlights on the opposite side of the road. "Kayne."

"Don't!" I frantically smack the cell phone out of his hand before he can answer it.

"Ellie!?" Jett chastises me.

"I don't want you to talk to him!" I don't even want to hear a susurration of his voice.

"I never want to see him again."

The End

PLAYLIST

Out of The Black ~ Royal Blood

Wild Ones ~ Flo Rida

Control ~ Puddle of Mudd

Sing ~ Ed Sheeran

Seven Nation Army ~ White Stripes

What You Wanted ~ One Republic

Stay With Me ~ Sam Smith

M. NEVER

Your naked body should only belong to those who fall in love with your naked soul. ~ unknown

PROLOGUE

I KNOW WHO IT IS before I even answer the phone.

"What's up, Jimmy?"

"Your boy is at it again. Gettin' belligerent and disrupting my customers."

"Awesome," I groan under my breath. "I'll be there in ten minutes."

"Five minutes. This is my last courtesy call. Next time, I'm calling the cops."

"I hear ya loud and clear."

"Good." Click.

Fuck. I shrug on a pair of jeans and run my fingers through my hair. The first time I can sleep through the night in six years and this jackass repeatedly picks three a.m. to self-destruct. If it were anyone else, I'd have told Jimmy to toss him in the gutter and let him sleep off his load. But I can't do that, not to Kayne. At least not this time, but possibly the next. This shit is getting old.

It takes me exactly seven minutes to drive to the hole Kayne has taken up residence in the last three months. Transition into the civilian world has been significantly harder for him than myself. Losing Ellie destroyed him, more so than even I could have predicted. He was fucked up when it came to women to begin with, and getting wrapped up with her only magnified his issues twentyfold. Sometimes I worry he's reached a point of no return.

I walk into the dark little bar with a rainbow of shady characters. No, Kayne couldn't just pick any bar to get drunk in; he had to pick the one where the baddest motherfuckers in town hang out. A place where the wrong look can get you stabbed or the wrong word will earn you a bottle smashed over your head.

I spot him in the corner being corralled by two linebackers in motorcycle jackets. *Just fucking great.* He's swaying on his feet with his bottom lip busted wide open. But it's the look in his eyes that has me worried. His stare is dark and removed like his soul has disappeared.

"You're late," Jimmy sneers from behind the bar.

"Keep your shirt on. I'm here, aren't I? What happened?" I ask as we walk the length of the room side by side toward Kayne.

"What happened is your friend came, got shitfaced, and started a fight. Again," he snarls. "I've had it. He's out, and if he shows his face in here one more time, I'm not going to intervene when he gets what's coming to him. Got me?" the burly man asks with his arms crossed and a glare that can make the average person piss themselves.

"I got it." I wave my hand. I'm sure if I was anyone else, I'd be intimidated. But I don't have time for hard-asses who think they're tough shit. If Kayne wasn't fucked up, we could wipe the floor with every douchebag in this entire place.

I squeeze through the two mountains blocking him. "Excuse me, fellas. I got it from here." I grab Kayne's arm, and he growls at me. "Easy, killer. Just taking you to get some air." I pull him through the bar, stumbling drunk, and cursing like a sailor. To be honest, I'm impressed he has the ability to speak given the condition he's in.

Once outside, I haul off and punch him in the gut. Why? Because the last thing I need is a ticking time bomb. Which is exactly what Kayne is at the moment—what he's been since the moment Ellie walked out of his life. And the only way for him to come to terms with what he's feeling is to face it head on. I have learned this about him the hard way.

Kayne hunches over, caught off guard for a second, and then retaliates by tackling me against the car. "Come on, cocksucker, get it all out." I continue with the kidney shots as he crushes me against the driver's side door. "She's gone! She's gone! And you have to fucking accept that!" I scream at him.

"I can't!" Kayne howls like a wounded animal then slumps to the ground, trying—and failing miserably—to hide the emotion leaking out of his eyes. Ughhhh, messed-up motherfucker. I prop him up on the sidewalk. He hits my soft spot every time.

"You can't keep doing this to yourself." I clasp his shoulder as he clumsily sits on the curb, pulling his legs up to steady himself. "You're going to wind up getting hurt, or worse, getting dead. Is that what you worked so hard for? Sacrificed so much of your life for?" I shake him. "To be buried six feet under?"

"I'd be better off dead." He wipes his cheeks roughly with the palms of his hands, his elbows resting on his knees.

"That's the alcohol talking."

"No, it's not. What's the point of living if you have nothing to live for?" He looks up at me with bloodshot eyes.

My flesh actually heats.

"You selfish scumbag. You have nothing to live for? What the fuck am I? I don't count just because you can't fuck me?"

"What?" His expression falls. "No . . . That's not . . . You're my best friend. My brother . . . The only family I have." He stumbles over his words.

"Well, how do you think your brother would feel if you end up dead?" I get in his face.

Kayne shrugs. "Shitty?"

"Yeah. Pretty. Fucking. Shitty," I snap.

Kayne stares at me blankly. I know he's in there *somewhere.* Then he drops his head in his hands pathetically. "I just miss her so damn much."

"I know."

"Is there ever going to be a woman in my life who doesn't break my heart?"

Aww shit, he's going there. "You can't blame Ellie for breaking your heart. We both knew the possible outcome when we took her."

"I just can't stand her being gone. It's killing me." His voice cracks as he buries his face in the crook of his arm and recoils into a ball.

"For now," I assert. "She's gone for now. That doesn't mean she'll be gone forever."

"How can you possibly know that?" He raises his head and sniffs.

I roll my eyes. "Haven't you learned yet? I know everything."

Kayne actually chuckles. It's a deranged sound, but at least he's connecting with me on some coherent level.

We stare at each other for some time before I concede. It's late, I'm tired, and he's smashed.

"Come on, big man. Let's get you home and cleaned up. You bled all over yourself." Splattered red stains are covering his white shirt.

"Not my blood." He grins up at me. "It's the fucker's who was stupid enough to fight me. He never got a shot in."

"Then what happened to your lip?"

"Fell off the barstool."

"You what?" Oh, for Christ's sake, he can throw down in a bar fight, but he can't take a damn leak.

"Let's go." I hold out my hand exasperated.

Kayne teeters a bit before his palm finally connects with mine. I haul him to his feet, and it feels like I'm pulling on a steel anchor. Once standing, I rest him against the car and manually unlock the doors. My 1966 Chevelle didn't exactly come equipped with keyless entry. After I dump him in the front seat, I slide behind the wheel and start the engine. My red devil purrs to life, and I can't help but think there's only one other kind of hum that's better than this car's.

I glance over at Kayne; he looks green and is barely conscious. "Listen man, you puke in here, and I'm tossing you out while we're still moving."

Kayne smirks, his head bobbing all over the place as I pull away. In no time at all, he's passed out and breathing loudly.

What am I going to do with his dumbass? He's a wreck.

I can't fault the guy completely for all his fuckedupness; he's had a rough life. Abused, neglected, and cast aside; not to mention abandoned by the one person who was supposed to love him the most. It's tragic, really. And then, when he finally gets one tiny flicker of happiness, what happens? It's corrupted by evil and shrouded in darkness. Sometimes, you just can't win for trying.

"Ellie," Kayne moans miserably beside me while grabbing his crotch in his drunken sleep.

All I can do is shake my head.

Oy, what a fucking hot mess.

ELLIE

"NO MATTER WHERE YOU GO or who you're with, you'll always be mine." His voice echoes in the darkness. *"Mine, Ellie."* I hurl myself up out of a dead sleep, panting. My hair is sticking to my forehead from sweat, and my tank top is clinging to my chest. I catch my breath and remind myself it was only a dream.

Only a dream. Only a dream.

The tropical nighttime breeze flutters through the half-open window and cools my burning skin. I fall back down onto my pillow and try to banish the vision of majestic blue eyes haunting my mind. Not only his eyes—his voice, his scent, his words. *"I'd much rather shower you with pleasure than torture you with pain . . . but I'll do what I have to do to make you submit."*

It's been a year since I left him—the man who abducted me, trained me, used me, owned me, *deceived* me. A whole year since I found out I was free.

Immediately after I left Mansion, I was held in a safe house for three days. Jett stayed with me the whole time. He laid with me while I slept, held my hand while I was debriefed by a very shady man in a black suit threatening me with jail time if I divulged one word about the classified operation, and held me when I fell to pieces night after night. He was my sanity. Which is crazy, when you think about it. He was one-half of the duo who held me captive, forced me to submit, and conformed me into a slave. A sex slave. But no matter how low I felt, it was Jett who lifted me up. When the curtain fell, he was the only one I could trust. Warped as it may have been.

I look up at my apartment building. It looks exactly the same. Red brick and concrete stairs.

"Last stop on the crazy train," Jett says grinning.

I feel the anxiety stampede through me as I gaze out the tinted window of the truck. Do I look different? I definitely feel different. I wonder if everyone will be able to see the scars of my experiences sliced all over my skin. I guess I'm about to find out.

I barely allowed myself to miss anyone while I was gone, and all that suppressed emotion is threatening to break through the surface of my facade. I'm finally home. My eyes burn as I fight back tears.

"Remember what we talked about. Only recount very vague details. You were kidnapped, drugged, and you don't remember much of your time in captivity."

I frown and nod.

"It's important you keep the accounts of what happened to yourself."

I nod some more. I understand. I really do.

"Am I ever going to see you again?" I ask Jett with a shaky voice.

"Maybe. It's up to you."

"If I forgive Kayne?" I narrow my eyes.

He shrugs. "We're a package deal."

The tears I'm trying to contain fall. I sadly realize that I'm never going to see Jett again. It feels like my soul has been ripped from my body, and now I'm losing my best friend in the process.

"No tears, sweet thing." He wipes my cheek with his thumb. "Time to be the strong girl I know you are. This is your decision."

And I stand by it.

"Where are you going now that this is all over?"

"I have some unfinished business of my own to take care of." He fiddles with the cuff of his sleeve. "But don't miss me too much; I might not be as far as you think." He winks.

"What does that mean?"

"It means just because I'm leaving now it doesn't mean I'll be gone forever."

I look at him like the crazy man he is. I'm too tired for riddles.

"Go on." he nudges me. "Time to go home."

I hug him one last time and step out of the car.

Time to go home.

After my very teary return, I spent months trying to acclimate back into some semblance of a 'normal' life. I quit Expo (despite Mark's protests), started seeing a psychiatrist, and spent most of the summer down the shore—away from the city and the reminders of the past. Reminders of *him.*

I meant it when I said I never wanted to see him again, and when I finally felt like I was moving on, a package arrived on August twenty-eighth, my twenty-third birthday. It was a large, rectangular, white box with a plain white card and a simple white bow. When I opened the card, I nearly fell apart. One word was inscribed on the inside:

CUPCAKE

I ripped open the box with overflowing tears to find two dozen miniature red velvet cupcakes. I cried even harder. I didn't even know why. I vowed to put Kayne Roberts behind me, and up until that moment, I thought I had. But one look at that word and a whole world of emotion let loose. I tore up the card and chucked the cupcakes in the dumpster on the side of my building. I just couldn't. I was leaving for school, and that's where my focus had to stay. I would never again let someone take my hopes and dreams and future away. Never. I had no idea who Kayne was. He deceived me from the very moment I met him. How do you care about someone you don't know at all? On a basic human level, maybe. But to love someone, expose yourself to them, and trust them with your entire heart?

Hell no.

I left for Hawaii the very next day.

If I had ever wished to see paradise, I had finally arrived. Oahu is beyond beautiful—the landscape, the flowers, the ocean. Being five thousand miles away from New York, I could breathe. It was a new beginning, and I took complete advantage. I learned to surf on the beaches of Waikiki, hiked to the top of Diamond Head, and snorkeled with tropical fish and sea turtles in Hanauma Bay.

The dark clouds had finally separated. Or so I thought.

I didn't even realize it was happening. It was like a tiny tear in your favorite shirt that you never even notice until there is a gaping hole in the seam. I tried to ignore it, tried to keep myself busy with classes and extracurricular activities, but it was always there. The heaviness in my chest weighing me down. Thoughts of him fogging my mind. And once I acknowledged the feelings sprouting inside me, they grew rapidly, like radioactive flowers.

You can't love him, I kept telling myself. He kidnapped you, held you captive, forced you to wear a collar and be his slave. And he did it all under false pretenses. None of it was real. I pounded that mantra into my head. None of it was real. *"I would kill for you."*

Was it?

That brings me to present day.

My freshman year of college is almost over. I'm living the life I thought I wanted and second-guessing myself every day.

I close my eyes and try not to think, try to ignore the heat my body is missing, and the way a certain pair of hands used to touch me, hold me, subdue me until I was coming undone at his command. Nights like these are the worst because nothing can satisfy the need. Trust me, I've tried relentlessly to fulfill it—but my desire only wants one thing. Or only one person, I should say. My body is still a lecherous traitor even after all this time. I slip my hands into my underwear and massage the ungodly ache.

"Every morsel of food you eat, every breath of air you take is because of me. Because I allow it . . . You live because of me. You live for me. Remember that when you fall asleep with my come inside you."

IT'S A BEAUTIFUL, CLEAR MORNING.

I have a cup of Starbucks in my hand and the roof off my Jeep. I bought it the first week I was here. An obnoxious yellow Wrangler I am absolutely in love with. With the money I saved over the years, some grants, and a very large severance package from Mark, my finances are sitting pretty for the foreseeable future. I don't need much, a one-bedroom apartment, my car, and some groceries keep me living modestly, but happy. The fact that all those things are located in the middle of paradise doesn't hurt, either.

I take a seat in my English class, prepared to ace my last final.

"Morning, good looking." Michael slips into the seat next to me.

"Morning yourself," I reply as I take a sip of my blonde roast.

"Ready to crush this test?" he asks with a cute grin and huge dimples. He's adorable. I met Michael in this very seat at the beginning of the semester. He's in the same boat I am; he started college late, and is immersed in a sea of barely legal adults. Being a twenty-three-year-old freshman can have its downfalls. Like cradle robbing.

Michael wasn't shy; he sat right next to me, struck up a conversation, and we haven't stopped talking since. We started hanging out after class, then on the weekends, and what started out as an innocent friendship snowballed into something more. Something fun and physical and completely carefree. At least for me. I know Michael wants more, but there's just no way I'm ready for that. I'm perfectly happy getting drunk, having sex, and leaving it at that.

"Up for a little surfing after this?" Michael asks with his big brown eyes as the tests are handed out.

I shrug. “The rest of the day looks pretty wide open.”

“That’s what I like to hear.” He grins, picks up his pen, and starts writing.

I WATCH FROM THE BEACH as Michael rides in his last wave of the day. He’s quite the hottie—all tan skin, dark hair, and flat stomach. Michael was a military brat and lived all over the world, but he says Hawaii is home. When he was seventeen, his mother relocated to California, but Michael refused to leave. So, family friends took him in until he was able to support himself on his own. We’re kindreds like that. He put off school until he had enough money stashed away to work part time and still live comfortably. By the looks of him, his plan is working out just fine.

He runs up the beach with his surfboard under his arm and his body dotted with water droplets. As I watch him approach, I can’t stop myself from imagining another face grinning at me from the shoreline—one with crystal-blue eyes, a seductive mouth, and tattoos on his skin. A face that haunts me when I sleep, and is impossible to find when I’m awake.

“Ellie? El? Where’d you go?” Michael asks pulling me out of my daydream. I smile, hiding the embarrassment of being caught.

“Nowhere, I’m right here.”

“Sure about that, gorgeous? You looked like you were visiting la-la land.”

“The ocean must have put me in a trance.”

“The ocean, huh?” he pokes fun.

I smack his stomach. “Okay, maybe it was a totally hot surfer. But he’s gone now.” I pout.

“You think you’re funny?” Michael raises his eyebrows devilishly.

“I think I’m hilarious.” I start to giggle nervously.

“Let’s see how funny you are after I throw you in.” He lunges at me.

“Michael!” I screech as he hauls me over his shoulder and jogs toward the water’s edge.

He then tosses me in and wrestles with me under the water. I come up for air, gasping and laughing all at the same time.

“You’re a jerk.” I splash him.

“And you’re hilarious, remember?”

“Yes. And now very wet.” I wade back to the shore.

"Is there a better way to be?" he asks salaciously.

I roll my eyes and splash him again. Men.

Once dry, Michael picks up both boards. "I'm going to the North Shore to surf tomorrow," he tells me as we walk to our cars. "Want to come? There's supposed to be a kickass party on the beach, too."

"That sounds like fun," I tell him as he slides my surfboard into the backseat of my Jeep.

"Perfect. I'll pick you up around noon. I have to work in the morning."

"I'll be ready." I smile. I am nowhere near skilled enough to surf North Shore waves, but I like hanging out on the beach and watching everyone else. Especially Michael.

"You know, I can come over later tonight if you want." He steps closer to me and puts his hands on my hips, smelling of salt and sand. "That way I don't have to wait a whole twenty-four hours to see you again."

"Is that such a torturous amount of time?" I flirt.

"For me, yes. You, I wonder sometimes."

"What is that supposed to mean?" I question him.

Michael doesn't answer; instead, he leans in and presses his lips firmly against mine. I kiss him back, but the fire doesn't burn as brightly on my end. I'm trying, I really am, but the past and all these crazy feelings I have are holding me back.

Michael sighs when I pull away, pressing his forehead against mine. "One day, whatever demons are inside of you are going to have to come out. And when they do, I'll be right next to you."

I stare into Michael's big brown eyes. They're so sweet and kind. I almost feel guilty for keeping all my secrets from him. But what would he think if he found out about my past? That I was owned? Or that there's an hysteria of conflicting desires inside me that I can't make heads or tails of? I don't respond because what can I possibly say? I can't make him any promises or give him any guarantees.

"I'll see you tomorrow." I kiss him chastely on the lips.

"I'm counting on it." He spanks me playfully on the ass, and I'm flooded with a million emotions, and way too many memories to even count. My breathing speeds up and my head feels light as I climb into my Jeep. "*You've been such a good kitten; it spared you from ten.*" I try to hide everything I'm feeling as I turn on the car, unsure if Michael senses anything is off. I say one last goodbye, and then speed away with the ghost of Kayne's hands stinging my ass.

I drive around until it's dark, just letting my idle thoughts wonder. "*You are so sexy. I can't tear my hands or my lips or my eyes off of you.*

You're my most prized possession. I meant it when I said I would kill for you, Ellie. I'd do anything for you."

I pull into my little apartment complex a few hours later, park, and then just sit in the car under the cover of night. I clutch the steering wheel and rest my forehead on my hands. How would I even begin to look for him? Someone who doesn't exist, at least on paper. Maybe I should put an ad on Craigslist. Desperately seeking slave owner.

It's official. I've completely lost my mind.

I think what I really need is a big glass of wine, a bath, and a sleeping pill. Maybe a dozen of them.

As I get out and walk to the front door of my duplex, I resolve to put Kayne Roberts behind me. Right now, this second. My life is good, I'm living out my dreams, and I have an amazingly sweet guy who is trying his damnedest to be everything I need. What more can one person ask for? *"No matter where you go or who you're with. You'll always be mine."*

I walk up the steps to the second floor landing like I'm dragging rocks. I've been bugging the super for weeks to fix the porch light. I hate coming home late and not being able to see my front door.

"You know, Ellie," a male voice says from behind me, and I nearly jump out of my skin. "The first rule of protection is self-awareness. And a young, beautiful girl like yourself, sitting in her open Jeep all alone in the dark, just begs for some sick pervert to pounce." Jett emerges from the shadows, the small light from his phone illuminating his features. I freeze in place for a split second before I tackle him. "Jett!" It's an involuntary reaction.

"I missed you, too, sweet thing." He chuckles, squeezing me hard. I'm overwhelmed with emotion as Jett holds me in his arms. And in Jett fashion, he hugs me for as long as I need.

"Do you make a habit of lurking around dark porches?" I ask shakily, "Or just mine?"

"Depends," he answers flippantly, releasing me. I can't see much of his face, but I can make out the shadow of his smile.

"What are you doing here?" I gain my wits while wiping away the stray happy tear from the corner of my eye.

"Do you want me to tell you while we're standing in the dark, or shall we go inside and talk?"

"Inside." I quickly unlock the door and flick on the lights with Jett right behind me. My apartment isn't anything extravagant, it's nothing like the opulent room Kayne kept me in. My most expensive piece of furniture is a Pottery Barn couch. I figured I was going to be doing a lot of studying in my little living room, so I might as well be comfortable. I haven't regretted my purchase for one minute.

"Do you want something to drink?" I ask nervously. Why am I suddenly nervous?

Jett watches me with entertained eyes as I fidget around my apartment, opening and closing the refrigerator door like I have OCD.

"I'm good, Ellie, but maybe you should have one?" He raises his eyebrows suggestively. I grab a water from the fridge and sit down on the couch. Jett follows, plopping down beside me. "Hmmm." He bounces a few times. "Comfy."

I nearly burst out laughing.

"It's good to see you smile," Jett says.

"It feels good to smile," I tell him. There's a few seconds' pause.

"Why are you here, Jett? Not that I'm not happy to see you, it's just so out of the blue." I'm not complaining, trust me.

"I've come to deliver a message."

"A message?"

"From Kayne." He pulls an envelope out of the back pocket of his jeans and hands it to me.

I take it, inspecting it curiously.

"Open it," he urges.

My hands start to tremble, and my heart starts to pound as I rip it open. *You wanted this,* I remind myself—repeatedly. I pull out the contents of the envelope, and am now thoroughly confused. "A plane ticket?"

"There's something else," Jett informs me. I look inside the envelope again, and pull out the thin piece of paper that was hiding under the ticket. I unfold it to read its contents, and just like before, only one word is scribbled:

CUPCAKE

I can't explain what seeing that word does to me. It unleashes so many sparring emotions, it feels like they're trying to kill me.

"Ellie?" Jett's voice sounds far away. I look up at him not even realizing I started to cry.

Jett takes my hand. "I know you went through a lot. We all did. But if there is any chance you can forgive him, get on that plane tomorrow."

"Tomorrow?" I study the ticket. Yup, tomorrow's date, to "Bora Bora?"

Jett shrugs.

"How is he?" I ask guardedly.

Jett shoots me a sad smile. "Better, now that he stopped drinking and started showering again."

"Did he really take me leaving that hard?"

"You have no idea, Ellie." His tone is bleak.

"Why didn't he come himself?"

"He didn't want you to feel pressured or uncomfortable. Although, personally, I think he's just afraid of your right hook." Jett winks.

I roll my eyes. "It probably didn't even hurt."

"Ellie, you slapped him so hard, *I* felt it."

"He deserved it." I defend my actions.

"I suppose on some level he did. But what he really deserves now is your forgiveness," Jett implores me. "Not just what he deserves, but what he needs."

I crush the envelope, ticket, and piece of paper to my chest conflicted. This is what I wanted, so why am I having such a hard time coming to terms?

"I can't make any promises I'll be on that plane." It's the truth. It's time to pull the trigger, and I'm hesitating. I'm pretty sure instances like that can get you killed.

Jett just nods. "It's your choice. A car will be here to pick you up at noon. Think about it, Ellie." He puts his hand on my knee and then stands up.

"Are you leaving?" I follow his movements worried.

Jett nods. He looks the same—A shock of blond hair, turquoise eyes, and a quiet air of authority.

"But you just got here."

"I did what I came to do. Now it's time to go."

I frown.

"If you make the right decision, you'll see me again," he says with one finger under my chin.

I look away. I have a lot of thinking to do, and not a whole lot of time to do it. I stand up and reluctantly walk Jett to the door.

He stops just before he leaves, looking at me with those with penetrating eyes. "This is his last attempt, Ellie. If you don't show up, he's disappearing, and this time it will be for good."

I respond silently with a confused expression. He kisses me on the cheek then vanishes into the darkness.

Disappearing for good?

KAYNE

I WAIT IMPATIENTLY IN THE car while Jett and Ellie's silhouettes move slowly around her apartment. I can't stop my leg from shaking or my heart from hammering. As soon as I saw her pull up, I wanted to rip her out of the car and crush her body against mine. I wanted to feel her lips and smell her skin and taste her sweetness. I want what we had back, every single thread of it.

It feels like hours have passed by the time Jett leaves Ellie's apartment. He slips into the driver's seat and turns on the engine without a word. I wait for a report, but he just throws the car into drive and pulls away. I burn a hole through the side of his head as he rolls the window down and plays with the radio.

"Are you fucking serious right now?"

"What?" Jett asks aloofly as his hair flutters in the wind.

"Are you going to tell me what she said, or do I have to beat it out of you?" I ask crazily.

"First of all, you wish you could kick my ass. Secondly, all you had to do was ask me nicely."

"Jett," I growl. "This is not the time for fucking around. Is she coming or not?"

"I don't know," he answers directly, and my heart drops out of my chest.

"She still doesn't want to see me?"

"I don't know that, either."

"Well, what the fuck do you know?" I erupt.

"Jesus, chill out. I know if you keep acting like this you're going to be minus one girl and one friend."

I put my hand over my face and let out a frustrated sigh. I don't think I can survive living one more day without Ellie.

"Please, Jett," I say as calmly as possible. "Tell me what you do know."

"Much better, cocksucker."

I glare at him out of the corner of my eye.

"I think she wants to see you. She still seems conflicted. But she did ask about you."

"What did she ask?" I'm starving for any morsel of information I can get.

"She asked if you were okay. And why didn't you come yourself."

"That's good, right?"

"It's anyone's guess."

"For fuck's sake, you read women like tarot cards, and you can't tell if she wants to see me or not?"

"I think she does. I also think she's scared."

"Of what?"

"Oh, I don't know, maybe you slapping a collar on her and locking her in a dark room?"

"That isn't fucking funny." I can't stop myself from smirking. "I did love her in that collar, though."

"Didn't we all."

Jett pulls up to our destination. I stare idly at the plane. "Let's do this." He slaps me on the arm.

I nod with a knot the size of Texas in my throat. I'm half considering driving back to Ellie's house and throwing her over my shoulder so she has no choice but to come with me, but I don't think that scenario will fly. I don't want her to feel forced or like she's being backed into a corner. I want her to come because she wants to. I want her to see for herself that I'm not the tyrant she believes me to be. Yes, I love dominance and submission, but I also love Ellie in any way I can have her. She controls the playing field, and I'll abide by her rules. Even if that means changing who I am. For her, I would do it. For her, I'd do anything.

"Clock's ticking, Kayne." Jett slams on the hood of his Chevelle.

I take a deep breath and get out of the car, carrying with me the most lethal arsenal on the planet.

Hope.

I LAY AWAKE STARING OUT the window at yet another clear blue Hawaiian morning.

After Jett left last night, I skipped the bath, and went straight for the wine and sleeping pills. They helped me relax, but in no way provided the restful night's sleep I was hoping for. I tossed and turned, dreaming about majestic blue eyes, a firm hand, and clashing feelings. Throwing the covers off, I get out of bed. In the kitchen, I pick up the envelope that has the plane ticket and note stuffed inside. I pull out the white folded piece of paper and stare at the word written in his handwriting: Cupcake. That one single word holds so much power it could be deemed a deadly weapon. *"I'll use it so you know you mean more to me than just sex.*

"Do I?"

"Yes, baby. So much more."

It's amazing how you can get handed exactly what you want and not feel anything like you thought you would. I thought this would make me happy, make me excited, but all it makes me is anxious. I stare at the word for what feels like forever, finally deciding I have to see him. I need to figure out if what I'm feeling is real or just a psychotic episode. And if I'm going to do this, I need to go shopping! A girl can't reconnect with her ex-slave owner wearing the tattered old rags she calls clothes hanging in her closet.

In record time, I change into a denim miniskirt and tank top, throw my hair into a ponytail, and grab my keys off the kitchen counter. I've given myself exactly four hours to shop, shower, and pack, leaving one hour to hyperventilate before the car picks me up.

I DUMP MY HAUL OF sexy little sundresses, underwear, and bikinis onto my bed. Not bad for a few hours' work. I pack in a hurry, leaving out the white tube dress with hot pink embroidery on the hem and the strappy wedge heels I fell in love with at first sight. I shower and blow-dry my hair then attempt to apply some makeup. Where is Jett when I really need him? Luckily, I received a crash course at the MAC counter after one of the makeup artists witnessed me trying to apply eyeliner. After she had rubbed the crooked lines off my eyelids, she informed me that all I really needed was a little eye shadow and a few thick coats of mascara. Then she applied a shimmery brown powder all over my face and stained my lips a bright pink. She said the secret to makeup is using just enough to enhance my natural beauty. I believed her, because when I looked in the mirror, I still felt like myself only sexed up a bit. It really is amazing what a little makeup can do.

I've come pretty damn close to recreating her masterpiece.

I'm barely finished getting ready when there's a knock at my door. My heart freefalls into my stomach. It's time to go. I open the door to a tall, nice looking man dressed in black with a driver's hat on. "Miss Stevens," he addresses me professionally.

"Yes." My voice is small.

"All set to go, ma'am? Can I carry your bags?"

I can't see his eyes behind the dark glasses he's wearing, but his wavy brown hair is tousled at the nape of his neck and his grin is relaxed, mischievous almost.

He seems harmless enough.

"Yes, please." I step aside and allow him to retrieve my one and only suitcase. Steeling my nerves, I lock the door behind me, and follow the driver to the black Town Car parked in the visitor's space outside my building. Just as he places my suitcase in the trunk, a familiar pickup pulls up behind us.

Shit. I completely forgot.

Michael steps out of his truck with a confused expression. Shit. Shit. Shit. Jett's visit completely scrambled my brain.

"Going somewhere?" He eyes the car and the driver, who is suddenly standing uncomfortably close to me.

"Bora Bora," I reply nervously.

"Tahiti?" His eyebrows shoot up.

"Yes."

"Why?"

What do I tell him? I'm going to see the man who abducted me, chained me to a bed for over a month, and used me as a living, breathing sex toy? The man who—though ruthless, intense and merciless at times—somehow penetrated my soul, and may now be irreversibly connected to?

"Exorcise some demons," is my response. It's the God's honest truth.

Michael stares at me with multiple expressions playing across his face, and for the first time since we met, I'm having trouble reading him.

"Ma'am." The driver interrupts our silent exchange.

"I have to go," I say softly.

Michael nods, and then unexpectedly grabs my arm. He yanks me to him, then forcefully crushes his lips against mine. *Whoa.* I barely kiss him back as my emotions wage war. Michael is the one I should want. He's sweet and kind and generous—not to mention gorgeous—but the spark between us pales in comparison to what just thinking about Kayne does to me. It lights my entire world on fire, burning everything around me to ash.

"Stay," he presses. "I know you've been harboring something bad. Stay with me and we can work it out together."

I look at Michael sadly. I should want to stay, but I don't. What I want, deep down, is to see Kayne.

It's an incurable urge.

"I can't." I kiss him on the cheek and free myself from his death grip.

"Ellie," he protests my leaving with some bite.

"Sorry." I slip into the backseat of the sedan with Michael's dark-brown eyes searing into me the whole time. Once the door shuts, I exhale the breath I didn't even realize I was holding.

The ride to the airport was silent and the flight uneventful, minus the hour delay. Kayne didn't spare one expense; I flew first class, pampered with hot towels and bubbly champagne the whole four-hour trip. Some girls might feel guilty that a man is spending ridiculous amounts of money on them. Not me—at least not in this scenario. After everything he put me through, I deserve to be spoiled. And by the looks of it so far, he agrees.

The airport is ultra-bright from the sunlight pouring in through the windows. If living on an island has taught me anything, it's come prepared with dark sunglasses. After I retrieve my suitcase, I follow the crowd outside where I am struck by the most beautiful turquoise-blue water I have ever seen. I then find Jett holding a little sign that says 'Stevens.'

I can't stop the grin from spreading across my face as I approach him. I don't know what it is, but Jett always feels comfortable. Like Southern cooking and fresh-squeezed lemonade. Just standing next to him puts me at ease and assures me everything is going to be okay, even when I doubt all my decisions.

"You look delicious," he whispers in my ear as he hugs me.

"Thank you?" I giggle. He has such an odd way with compliments.

"You're welcome." Jett releases me and picks up my suitcase. "You smell delicious, too. This way," he motions with his head.

Jett leads me up the dock until we get to a small speedboat tied up near the end.

"Your chariot." He hops in first, then grabs my suitcase and motions to the bag on my arm. Once all my items are in the boat, he extends his hands to me. I'm definitely not wearing the right shoes for this; I carefully place my hands in his and hold my breath as I step down. Before I realize it, Jett has one arm hooked around me and is gingerly placing me on my feet. He winks. "Think I would let you break an ankle?"

"I'd hope not."

"Never. Kayne would castrate me for even a scratch."

My stomach flips from just the mere mention of his name. Fuck, I'm really doing this.

"Ellie, are you okay? You just went pale," Jett asks with concerned eyes.

"I'm fine. Just a little nervous, I guess." I put on my bravest smile.

"Sweet thing, just a word to the wise." Jett places his hands on my shoulders. "This can be as easy or as hard as you make it. When I told you that you held all the power, I wasn't lying. It's still true. The ball is in your court. What you choose to do with it will determine the outcome. Okay?"

"Okay," I reply, although I'm not exactly sure I understand. At the moment, I'm not sure I understand anything; my thoughts and emotions are just a great big jumbled mess. There are so many interconnecting wires, my insides feel like one big knot.

Jett motions for me to sit, unties the ropes, and then starts the engine. The little boat purrs to life, and a few seconds later, we take off. I concentrate on the scenery to distract me from my nerves—the crystal-blue lagoon, the lush greenery of Mount Otemanu, and the rainbow beaming through the clouds over the volcano. I'll never deny

Hawaii is magnificent, but Bora Bora's beauty is indescribable. The landscape almost gleams like a fairy tale.

The boat ride is short and silent which, in all honesty, I'm grateful for. I'm not sure how engaging my small talk would be. All my thoughts are gravitating to *him.* My heart is beating and my palms are sweating. I keep asking myself if this is the right thing. Do I still have time to change my mind? What would happen if I did? I know the answer to that question. The nagging regret would eventually eat me alive. I have to see him. I have to know. *Was it real?* And if it was, do we just start over? I can get past the whips and chains and fuckings, but the lying? The deceiving? Even if it was for the right reason, I still question his sincerity. Not to mention my sanity.

Jett cuts the engine, and I snap out of my wandering thoughts. We've arrived at a resort. A very posh, exclusive resort from the looks of it.

"Showtime," Jett says as he lifts me out of the boat and onto dry land. There's a tall man standing in front of the lobby doors watching us intently. It sort of makes me uncomfortable. I move a little closer to Jett once he's grabbed my luggage and secured the boat. The man then approaches us with a kind smile.

"Monsieur." He addresses Jett with a pleasant French accent.

"Matias." He and Jett shake hands then Matias immediately turns his attention to me. "Mademoiselle." He kisses my hand. I think I actually blush.

"Ellie, Matias," Jett formally introduces us. "He'll escort you from here."

"Oui." Matias grabs my suitcase dutifully. "Monsieur Andrews is quite anxious for your arrival."

"Andrews?" I repeat as Matias places my bag in the backseat of a golf cart parked off to the side.

"Alias," Jett leans in discreetly and whispers in my ear. "Just go with it."

I nod silently, fortifying my nerves. He needs an alias?

"Kayne will explain. Now go."

I frown. "Why aren't you taking me?"

Jett flashes me a smile. "This is my stop, sweet thing."

I eye Matias standing next to the golf cart waiting expectantly.

"You're in good hands. And you'll be in even better ones once you see Kayne. Now go." He slaps me on the ass.

"Jett!" I scold him. He just winks at me. "If you need me, I'm in bungalow forty-six. Scoot."

"Fine," I huff, rubbing my backside. I'm going! Holy shit! I walk to Matias, and he helps me into the cart. He hops in next to me and turns on the engine. A moment later, a soft breeze is flipping my light-brown hair as we drive down a little pathway, away from the lobby and toward the beach.

"Your first time in Tahiti?" Matias asks casually with one hand draped over the steering wheel.

"Yes," I answer as we pull onto a boarded pathway stretching out over the aquamarine water. Oversized tiki huts are situated on both sides of us, each with straw-covered roofs and unobstructed views.

"And what do you think so far?"

"Well, considering I've only seen the airport and lagoon, I'd say it's amazing."

Matias laughs lightly. I'm glad someone is relaxed. Every overwater bungalow we pass jacks my unease up another level. I'm going to be a string ready to snap by the time we reach our destination.

We travel as far as we can on the boardwalk path until we reach the very end. Three very large two-story bungalows hug the round boardwalk.

Matias parks in front of the one in the middle.

"Arrived." He smiles brightly and my heart actually stops beating. I'm nervous, excited, anxious, and terrified. I feel like I'm strapped into a rollercoaster fearfully awaiting the ride.

And that's exactly what Kayne is, the Kingda Ka—a man who can launch your body and mind one hundred, twenty-eight miles per hour in three point five seconds.

Once Matias helps me out of the cart, I nervously smooth my dress and fidget with my hair. He rolls my suitcase behind him, and opens the front door; that's when I freefall from four hundred, fifty feet in the air. Matias stands at the entrance of the villa naive to my hesitation. He has no idea; no idea what I've been through, or what the person inside subjected me to.

"Miss?" He raises his eyebrows concerned.

I smile weakly and command my feet to move, one foot in front of the other until I cross the threshold. My basic motor functions cease to exist as the man who has haunted my dreams and consumed my thoughts stands across the room looking like the demonic perfection I remember him to be. The two of us just stare, the tension so thick it feels like we're trapped in the middle of an Amazon rainforest, and need a machete to hack through the brush. Matias emerges from a room to my left, minus my bags. I didn't even notice him disappear; I'm so engrossed by the human being standing in front of me.

Matias stands between us, glancing from me to Kayne and then back again. He has to feel it, the unstable energy smothering the elegantly decorated room.

"Let me show you around," Matias says. Following him in a haze, he shows me the living area with a couch, television, wet bar, and small working desk. The bedroom he placed my things in and the sundeck with private pool. Upstairs is the 'well-being room' with twin massage tables, balcony, and sauna. This freaking place is bigger than my apartment and my parents' combined. Matias chatters nonstop as we make our way back downstairs.

" . . . And as Mr. Andrews knows, I am here for whatever you need, whenever you need it." He smiles, the skin wrinkling around his kind eyes.

"Thank you."

"*Monsieur?* Will there be anything else?" He turns to Kayne, who hasn't moved from his spot.

"No, that will be all," he answers, and his voice feels like an oversized tuning fork vibrating against my body.

"Ring me when you are ready to leave for dinner," Matias responds in a hurry.

Kayne nods, never taking his eyes off me—those majestic blue eyes with the brown lightning bolt that have the ability to cut me right in half. Once Matias is gone, it's just me, Kayne, and a whole shitload of awkward silence.

"How was your flight?" Kayne finally asks, breaking the ice.

"Fine," I answer flatly.

"The boat ride?"

"Fine."

"What do you think of the island?"

"It's fine."

"Is there anything that isn't fine?"

"No."

Kayne smirks, and I wonder what the fuck is so amusing.

Awkward silence regains control of the room.

"Ellie, I—" Kayne takes a few steps forward, and I take a few steps back. He freezes with a frown.

"I've arranged dinner for us," he informs me, and then continues to approach me.

I nod, persistently backing up as he stalks across the room. I bump into a wall, and can only watch with wide eyes as he closes the distance between us. He crowds me, coming so close that I can feel the heat of his body and inhale the fresh scent of his cologne. He can still make me weak, even after all this time. *After everything.*

Kayne lifts his hand to my face and skims his thumb across my cheek. I stand paralyzed, caught by his touch and the hypnotic look in his eyes.

"I'm glad you're here, Ellie." He leans in, inching closer and closer to my mouth. My heartbeat speeds up, and my brain function slows down as he brushes his lips against mine. Then he does it again, this time adding more pressure and swiping his tongue between my lips. I nearly fall apart. The third time, he full-blown kisses me with no hesitation or second thought. He takes full possession of my mouth, trapping my face in his hands, and pinning my body flat against the wall. I kiss him back with even more force than I knew I was capable of. Our tongues twist together as we both fight for air. The longer we kiss, the more aware I become of heightening sensations and overflowing feelings. I start to spin out of control, trying frantically to untangle the strings of my emotions.

"Kayne—" I pull away.

"Ellie." He returns with so much need it nearly cripples me. I have to think, and that's not going to happen while he detains me with his oppressive presence.

"Please stop." I grab onto his linen shirt for dear life.

He takes a deep breath, fighting the urge I know we're both feeling. But I'm not just going to fall into his bed, or get tangled up in his seductive web. There are issues that need to be worked out, and questions that need to be answered.

"I'd like to freshen up." I try to move away from him, but he cages me in by planting both hands on the wall.

"I have missed you every single second of every single day that we have been apart."

And it's quite clear his words are true. His sharp stare and rock hard erection digging into my stomach convey as much.

"Kayne, please." Cocksucker has me begging already.

He hesitates for a beat then pushes off the wall, giving me the room I so desperately need.

"Whatever you want, Ellie." His words send both a chill and a tingle down my spine. They're as menacing as they are promising.

Kayne watches me with a guarded expression as I escape into the bedroom and slam the door behind me.

Once inside, I sink to the floor, breathing for the very first time since I stepped foot on this island.

KAYNE

THE DOOR SLAMS, AND I think I actually jump.

My dick is hard, my heart is hammering, and lips are tingling. That kiss was nothing but a fucking cock tease. Ellie and her monosyllables. I forgot how much I missed them—although, I'll admit, I much prefer them when we're having sex. I couldn't control myself with her standing there all sexy and doe-eyed and completely irresistible. I wasn't lying when I said I missed her every single second of every single day. It's been excruciating living without her. And now that she's here, under the same roof, she still feels just as unattainable as when we were apart. For now.

I hope.

Pray?

Okay, beg.

I rest my forehead against her door, silently pleading for her to come out. I contemplate going in, but I'll give her space. I know that's what she needs. Jett has been preaching it to me for almost a year. That's why I didn't pursue her sooner, even though I wanted to.

Every single second of every single day.

I sent the cupcakes to test the water, to see where her head was. Which, to my great disappointment, was nowhere near forgiving me, since she trashed them a nanosecond after she opened the box. How do I know that? I'm a black operative—spying is what I do. And I've been spying on Ellie since the day she left me. I know everything there is to know about her, right down to her little boy toy.

I pace the bungalow so many times I think I wear through the hardwood floor. I have a drink, and then another. I take a piss, and then wait some more. I'm about to go mad, so I finally say fuck it and knock on her door.

"Ellie?"

No answer.

"Ellie?" I jiggle the door handle.

"I'll be out in a sec," she yells. I wonder how long that is in girl time. I decide to call Matias and arrange for our ride. Here's hoping, right?

After I hang up with the butler, Ellie finally emerges. She's changed. No longer wearing the white little dress she arrived in. She's transformed into a dark angel. Her light-brown hair is pulled back into a low ponytail and her eye makeup is heavy, but it's her dress that makes my jaw drop. It's a loose fitting, shiny material that drapes over her body. It almost reminds me of a piece of lingerie, something Jett would dress her in just to entice me. The black strings curving over her shoulders so thin I could floss my freakin' teeth with them. I think she's trying to kill me.

"You look . . . amazing." Yes, I sound just like a love-struck fool because that's exactly what I am; a man stupidly in love with a sultry little kitten who holds his beating heart in the palm of her hand.

"Thank you." She fidgets slightly.

There's a knock at the door a moment later.

"Our ride is here." I smile as genuinely as possible. Ellie exits first, brushing against me in the doorway. Her sweet smell is heady, and her contact makes me horny. Holy hell. This may just be the most trying night of my life. As Matias assists Ellie into the golf cart, I catch the hem of her dress riding up so far it makes my cock kick.

Damn.

I climb in next to her, and my big body crowds her small frame in the backseat. Our legs touch and shoulders bump. Ellie folds her arms over her chest and crosses her legs, withdrawing into herself. Typical body language for someone who is clearly uncomfortable. I hate that I make her feel that way. I hate that she recoils and is anxious around me. But I'm not exactly sure how to fix it. Fix us. I'm sure if I were Jett, I would think of something clever to say, get her talking, have her laughing and be completely open by the time we sat down to dinner. But here is where I lack finesse. I know how to speak with my body, but words are more difficult.

"Where are we going anyway?" she asks as we pass bungalow after bungalow.

"I set up a private dinner. So we can talk."

Ironic, I know.

"Private?" The word dances warily on her tongue.

"Yes."

"Will there be a seat for me at this dinner or will I be dining between your knees?" she asks caustically.

I can't stop my lip from twitching with amusement. God, I didn't realize how much I loved her fire until it was taken away from me. I glance at Matias. He is happily driving through the resort, not giving away if he heard Ellie's statement or not. If he did, he is smart not to acknowledge it. In response, I dip my head, bringing my mouth as close to her ear as possible. Ellie stiffens as I inhale her scent. "Tonight, you have a chair, but I'll never object to you dining between my knees."

I may be a desperate man, but I am still me, and the image of Ellie naked, kneeling, and taking food from my hand is enough to send me right into sexual orbit.

She glares at me with my face an inch away from hers. "Keep dreaming," she spits. "I'll never kneel for you again." There's so much fight in in her voice, but there's also doubt, too. People often rebel against the things that make them vulnerable, while at the same time tempting them like sin. Maybe Ellie will never kneel for me again, and that's okay. I've made peace with that fact. Changing my ways is a sacrifice I'm willing to make. A year apart has altered so many things; it's given me perspective and time to think. I have never wanted a woman the way I want Ellie. Never wanted to pursue a relationship or take that scary step of caring for another human being. I had no example to learn from so what good would I have been at it? That's what I thought my whole life until I met Ellie—until I was forced to care, to protect, to feel. And I don't want to give that up because I as much as I believed I could live without love, in a second flat she proved me wrong. The moment she was put in danger, the moment there was a chance I could lose her forever. That single moment I knew I could be more. Give more. To her.

We pull up to a secluded part of the resort with a sandy pathway leading to the beach.

"When you said dinner, I was expecting a restaurant," she says as she slips out of the golf cart. She stops short just before we step onto the sand.

"Ellie?"

"One sec." She puts her hand on my arm then pulls off the black stiletto heels from her feet. The ones that are as deadly as they are sexy.

My mind explodes with images of what I could do to her while wearing those shoes.

Behave.

We walk toward the water, around some palm trees, and through some light brush until we come to a clearing. There, tucked away, is our own private table lit with white candles, and pink paper lanterns dangling overhead. I can't take credit for the romantic setting, that's all Jett. I just told him to create something Ellie would love. I watch her out of the corner of my eye as we slowly approach the table. Her arms are still wrapped defensively around her upper body, the hem of her dress is rippling slightly in the wind.

"This is very nice," she says once we're standing next to the table, and for the life of me I can't figure out what her melancholy tone is about.

"Shall we?" I pull out her chair, and Ellie sits. Then I take my seat adjacent to hers. The table is dressed with a white tablecloth, porcelain plates, and shiny silverware. The centerpiece is three multitiered cylinder vases with submerged orchids and candles floating on top. There are more orchids situated on the mirrored base, and even some wrapped around our napkins, like holders. Ellie fiddles with hers, inspecting the delicate white flower that is just as beautiful as she is.

"Wine, mademoiselle?" Matias appears with two bottles in his hands, pulling Ellie out of her wandering thoughts.

"Oh, yes. Red, please." She smiles. He pours her glass and then turns to me.

"The same." Before Matias is even done pouring my glass, Ellie has guzzled down half of her own.

"Easy there, killer. This night is going to be over for you before it even begins if you keep up that pace."

"Are you always going to be in the business of telling me what to do?"

I put my hands up in surrender. "I wasn't trying to tell you what to do. I was merely making an observation. If you want to get shitfaced, by all means do so. I'll hold your hair back while you puke."

"Would you?" she asks sharply.

"Of course, I would. If you needed me, I'd be there."

She breathes heavily as she stares at me like she's trying to stab me to death with just her pupils. Did I say something wrong?

I wait for her to speak, but it seems she has nothing to say. That unnerves me. "Ellie, what are you thinking?" I ask delicately. It feels like I'm suddenly walking over a field of landmines.

"I'm wondering why you brought me here."

"To dinner? We're both humans. We need to eat."

"That's not what I meant. Why did you beckon me to Tahiti?"

"You said you wanted to see paradise," I answer honestly.

"I live in Hawaii," she responds flatly, placing her wine down and crossing her arms.

"Neutral ground?" I try again.

Ellie shakes her head sternly, completely unconvinced.

I huff. "Fine." She wants to do this, then we'll do this. "I brought you here to reclaim what's mine," I tell her straight out.

Her jaw drops. "You still think I'm yours?"

"Not think," I correct her. "Know."

Ellie looks at me beyond irritated. Her mossy-green eyes flashing with disbelief.

"I was never yours."

"Now, we both know that's not true." I take a sip of the Pinot noir arrogantly.

Ellie's irritated expression morphs into anger.

"What do you want from me?"

I laugh, more to myself than at her. "What do I want?" I muse. "Probably too much."

"And what exactly is too much?"

"What did I want before?"

Ellie frowns. "My obedience, my submission, and my body."

"And your love," I stipulate. "What I want most is your love. But what I want is irrelevant. It's what you're willing to give me that's important."

"Why should I give you anything?" The question sounds more sad and hurtful than anything else.

I shrug. "Maybe you shouldn't. But I'm holding out hope that one day you might consider forgiving me and let what was happening between us continue into something more."

"More?" she says exasperated. This conversation is going beautifully. Exactly where I hoped. Right down the fucking toilet.

"Yes, more," I continue.

"And what exactly would be more?"

"I already told you. Love." I add ardently.

"You use that word quite freely."

"It's because I know what I feel. And even though I'm terrified of it, I'm not going to run from it."

"You have no idea what fear is," she replies bitterly.

"Of course, I do. I've lived in fear my whole life, and I've caused it. I know *exactly* what fear is."

"No wonder you were so good at dishing it out."

"Do what you know," I respond sharply, echoing a conversation we once had forever ago.

I can actually feel the rage radiating off Ellie. I don't mean to be so petulant, but when I feel threatened, my defenses go up, especially when it comes to a woman; and Ellie is definitely gunning for me tonight.

I have to keep reminding myself that she's different from all the rest, that her anger is warranted, but I'm afraid it will consume her. Consume us.

"Ellie, I don't want to fight. I want to talk."

"About love?" she fumes. It's like that word is acid to her.

"That can be the first topic of conversation, and once we get that squared away, we can move on to a more titillating subject." I smile impishly, attempting to cut away from the disastrous turn our talk has taken.

"And what subject would that be?"

"Your body." I gulp down another mouthful of wine as Ellie shakes her head incredulously. I'm sure there are a boatload of other topics I could have picked, but I panicked.

"My body?" she repeats, gazing at me shrewdly.

"Mmm hmm."

"And what exactly would you do to my body if you had it?"

"So many wonderful things." I lick my bottom lip.

"Oh really?" She stands seductively and takes a sip of wine like she's trying to entice me. Which, she is.

"Would you pleasure it?" she asks holding the glass to her chest.

"Yes," I answer looking up at her with only my eyes.

"How?" She places the wineglass down on the table and inches toward me.

"However you would let me."

"Would you lick me?" She crosses her ankles all sultry like. I know what she's doing; I'm not an idiot. I know when I'm being goaded. But at the moment, I just don't care.

"Yes." I drink her in—every sexy, dangerous inch of her.

"Suck me?"

"Yes." I sweep my eyes over her five-foot-four frame.

"Finger me?"

"Yes."

"Fuck me?" she taunts, coming closer until our bodies are touching.

"Hell, yes." I look up, breathing heavy. "There isn't anything I want more."

"Would you spank me?" Her voice suddenly turns hard. "Would you spank me until I cried? Beat me while I begged you to stop? Chain me to the bed and use me as you saw fit all while you lied to me? Make me think I actually mean something when all I really am is a plaything?" she lashes out.

I freeze. Hold up. She may be pissed, but I'm not going to let her believe things that just aren't true.

"You were never just a plaything," I growl, standing up so I tower over her. "You don't put your life on the line for a *plaything.* You don't risk six years of work, an entire household full of people, and your own fucking heart for a *plaything.* You may be angry with me, Ellie, but I did what I did for a reason, and I would do it again without blinking an eye. Not only because I loved dominating you, but because you are here, standing in front of me, alive and mentally sound."

Something sparks in her eyes. Hatred maybe?

"Says you!" She picks up a glass of wine and throws it in my face, staining the front of my white shirt red. Then she runs off.

"Ellie!" Goddamn it, I wipe my face with my hand. This is definitely not how I saw dinner going. I start to go after her, determined to toss her over my shoulder and spank some sense into her, but Jett's words ring in my ears, stopping me from moving. *She needs space.*

Ughhhh! I punch the table, rattling the entire thing.

Can I just tell you how fucking over space I am.

ELLIE

I RUN BAREFOOT THROUGH THE resort with my emotions in a stir.

"You don't put your life on the line for a plaything. You don't risk six years of work, a house full of people, and your own heart for a plaything." His words echo resoundingly.

Before I know it, I'm standing in front of bungalow number forty-six, knocking—more like pounding—on the door. *Jett, please be here.* I urgently wipe away the tears from under my eyes, black streaks staining my fingers from my watery mascara.

"Hang on!" I hear him shout from behind the door. Thank God! A moment later, it swings open to a half-naked Jett. I nearly choke on my tears. "Ellie?" He looks at me with a perplexed expression. It's half-confused, half-concerned.

Holy shit. I can't respond because my jaw has unhinged from my face. Jett is ripped, like completely shredded.

"Ellie?" he repeats again, but I can't draw my eyes away from his body, his glinting nipple ring, or the brightly colored tattoos running over his collarbone and down his chest like a wave crashing over the shoreline. All the time Jett and I spent together, I never so much as saw him without a shirt, and now I sort of feel shortchanged. He saw me naked every day and deprived me of the view in return.

"See something you like, sweet thing?" Jett asks flirtatiously, grabbing onto the doorframe above his head. The cuts of his muscles rippling, becoming more defined.

Um, hell yes.

"Ahhhh . . ." I finally look up into his eyes and they are dancing with humor, and possibly something else. Something hot and completely forbidden.

"What are you doing here, Ellie? Shouldn't you be trying to reconcile with Kayne?" he asks suggestively. Oh, how little does he know. Kayne and I are nowhere near reconciling. Like not even a little.

"We got into a fight." I bite my lip.

"A fight?"

"I threw wine in his face."

Jett frowns. "I see."

"I'm so confused."

"About what?" he asks concerned.

"Everything," I answer exasperated.

"Oh boy." Jett releases the doorframe and steps outside. "Let's talk."

I nod.

Jett and I sit on the side of the wooden walkway, our feet dangling over the edge. I fiddle with my fingers silently not knowing where to start.

"Ellie." Jett takes one of my hands in his, and I tighten my grip. I feel grounded when I'm with him. "Tell me what's going on."

I heave a sigh, looking over at him. You know it's really not fair to the rest of the men in this world. Jett is too pretty and nice and intuitive for his own good. He has me gawking like a fool at his cut muscles and light eyes accentuated in the moonlight.

"What's going on?" I repeat. "Great question."

I gnaw on my lip, hard, nearly drawing blood as I try to figure out where to start.

"Um?" I struggle, trying to pinpoint exactly where everything went wrong. Probably when I got on the plane.

"Okay," Jett senses my dilemma, "let's start at the very beginning. How did you feel when you saw him again?"

"Confused."

"Confused how?"

"I didn't know how to act," I admit ridiculously. "I wasn't sure if I should kneel at his feet or spit in his face. I don't know who to be around him."

"Ellie," Jett's voice pitches. "You don't need to be anyone but yourself. That's who Kayne wants."

"Myself?" I scoff. "I barely know who that is. I'm nothing but a twenty-three-year-old college freshman trying to figure out her life. That's who he wants?"

"Sweet thing," Jett squeezes my hand, "I'll let you in on a little secret, we are all just twenty-three-year-old college freshman trying to figure out our lives. Kayne especially."

I give him a skeptical look.

"I wouldn't lie to you, Ellie. Kayne is in the same place you are. He's just as confused, and borderline desperate."

"Desperate?"

"Mmm hmm. Desperate to get you back."

"What if I can't . . ."

"Forgive him?"

"Trust him."

Jett studies me like a science experiment, those turquoise-blue eyes poking me like probes.

"Trust him not to lie to you?"

I look up at the stars and take a deep breath. "In a way. I'm afraid he's always going to see me as an object. I'm afraid his feelings aren't real, and I'm afraid if I open myself up I'm just going to get hurt again."

Jett puts his arm around my shoulders comforting me. "I get it, Ellie. I do. You and Kayne have a very sordid past. Your fears are justified, but I can tell you with absolute certainty that Kayne's feelings are real." He lifts my chin so I'm looking at him in the eyes. I'm convinced they are the most genuine eyes on the planet. "Let me tell you something about Kayne. Trusting women is a hard limit for him."

I sit up straight, surprised. "Why?"

"It stems from his upbringing. I'll let him give you the gory details. You should hear it from him anyway. It's his story to tell. But I can say confidently, with you, he's shattering all his insecurities. And it's making him vulnerable."

"Vulnerable?" I question skeptically. Are we talking about the same alpha male who stripped me naked, forced me to submit, and controlled my entire existence without one bat of an eyelash?

"Yes," Jett confirms, "and that's a very dangerous place for Kayne."

"Why?"

"Because it makes him lose control."

"Control of what?"

"His life."

"Oh." I frown.

"Ellie, let me paint you a picture to try and help you understand.

Imagine what it would be like to live your entire life in the dark, and then one day suddenly experience the sun. To feel its warmth and bask in its light, to feed off it and become dependent on it. And then in a flash have it ripped away leaving you in the cold dark place you once were.

"Kayne lived in the dark. And then you came. You were his sun, and his light, and his warmth. The moment you left, he was thrust back into the darkness. An abysmal place where he drowns in the demons of his past. He needs the light now more than ever. He needs you. Don't doubt the sincerity of his feelings. They're more real than you and me, and the air that we breathe. Trust me, I would never lie to you about something as delicate as Kayne's feelings.

"He'll never intentionally hurt you. Of that, I'm sure. The man is more loyal than a dog. But I'll be honest, Kayne is intense and sometimes hard to handle, especially when his emotions get involved. That's why he was so over the top when it came to you, in all aspects," he insinuates, and I nod, understanding. "He wanted you to feel what he was feeling. And it was the only way he knew how to show it."

My cheeks suddenly heat. The man does know what he's doing between the sheets. I can still feel every orgasm like they were branded between my legs.

"Ellie?" Jett wiggles my hand.

"Hmmm?"

"Where did you go?"

I feel my cheeks burn brighter.

Jett eyes me knowingly. "Oh, I know. Taking a little trip down memory lane?"

"There is nothing little about it," I smile.

Jett rolls his eyes playfully. "Incorrigible."

"Definitely," I confirm with a shameless smile, and we both laugh.

"It's good to see you smile."

"It feels good to smile." I sigh, relaxed for the first time since I stepped foot on this island.

"How about you go give Kayne one of those smiles, and put him out of his misery."

"Maybe I should let him suffer just a little while longer," I joke.

"Ellie, Kayne has been suffering his whole life. He needs some peace, and you're it."

"You really know how to work a girl over." I elbow him.

"And proud of it." Jett kisses me on the cheek then hauls me to my feet. "Where do you think Kayne learned it from? I taught him everything he knows," Jett whispers in my ear, sending chills down my spine.

"Everything?" I question.

Jett nods sternly. His aqua eyes so bright they're crackling like live wires.

Holy shit. I'm suddenly overheating from just the mere thought of what Kayne and Jett are capable of.

"Now, go get your man." Jett smacks me on the ass. "I know he's waiting for you. Probably has a search party out right now."

"Jett, you're so dramatic."

He shoots me a deadpan look.

"Oh, no."

"Oh, yes."

Oh, shit. My nerves re-emerge with a vengeance.

"Think he'll forgive me for throwing wine in his face?" It's a rhetorical question.

"Probably, but you can always make it up to him."

"How?"

"Do you remember the conversation we had when I told you I know what all men like? And you so colorfully answered a blowjob?"

"Yes."

He pops his eyebrows at me.

"Ugh, guys are such cavemen."

"Perhaps, but it works every time," he smiles widely, "do you want me to walk you back to your bungalow?"

"No, I think I can manage," I smirk.

"Okay. Good. Now, if we're finished, I have to go club a beautiful redhead and drag her to bed."

I roll my eyes.

Cavemen. Definitely cavemen.

KAYNE

I AM WALLOWING IN MY misery. Yes, wallowing, because I see now Ellie will never be able to forgive me. I took it too far and ruined any small chance I had with her.

I won't beg her to stay when she walks into this room and demands to go home. I won't crack or crumble until she's gone. I did this. And I'll face the consequences. My heart sinks a little further. Tomorrow, I'll disappear. Go so deep undercover that I'll forget this life, and any other life ever existed, and hopefully one day forget Ellie exists, too. Because the memory of her will slowly destroy me. Like it is now. She'll never understand the effect of those few precious weeks. How she changed me. How I loved her. *Love* her.

I hear the front door creak open, and my insides petrify. I can't allow myself to feel anything or I'll never survive her leaving again. I'm on the brink of a meltdown already.

"Hi," she says unsurely as she stands in the darkness on the edge of the room.

"Hi," I respond desolately.

The silence stretches for a long time before Ellie takes a deep breath and crosses the living room to where I'm sitting on the couch, the moonlight spilling through the windows highlighting her slim body and bare feet.

"Can I sit?" she asks, fiddling with her fingers nervously.

I gaze up at her with just my eyes, hoping she sees a steely look instead of a dying man.

"Of course."

Ellie climbs onto the couch, tucking her legs underneath her, sitting much closer than I expect.

"Kayne, I'm sorry."

"For what?" I ask floored. The last thing I expected from Ellie was an apology.

"For getting upset and throwing wine at you. I think I was harboring some residual anger."

I actually laugh. "Ellie, you have nothing to be sorry for. I deserved it. That, and so much more. I just wish . . ." I swallow the emotion that's trying to choke me. " . . . I just wish you could find a way to forgive me."

"Forgive you? I forgave you a long time ago. Trust is the problem. I trusted you." Her voice strains and my heart twists. "After everything you put me through, I still trusted you, and then you betrayed me. I didn't know what to believe anymore. First, you were one person, then you were another, and then you were someone entirely different. I felt so used. So humiliated. So stupid." Angry tears start to well in her eyes. It's clear she had already been crying from her smudged mascara, and here she is about to do it again. I wonder if I'll ever be able to make her smile as much as I've made her cry.

"Ellie, I'm sorry." I try to reach for her, but she pushes me away.

"Please let me finish. You were right when you said I liked being yours." It sounds like that was very hard to admit. "And after you pulled the rug out from under me, I hated myself for it. I hated you. I was ready to give up everything for you. I was content," she says tormented.

I have no idea how to respond to that, so I just apologize again. "I'm sorry."

"Don't be sorry," she snaps frustrated. "Just tell me why. Why did you feel the need to take it to such an extreme?"

"Why did I need to take it to such an extreme?" I repeat her question, running through the thousands of answers I had come up with over the last year because I knew this conversation was inevitable. "Part necessity, part appearance, part selfish desire," I answer truthfully. Because right now, the truth is all I have to give.

Ellie looks at me confounded.

"I didn't know you'd become so important in such a short amount of time." Now I'm the one who sounds tormented.

"What?" She shakes her head not understanding.

"Those few hours sitting together on the couch during Mark's party." I start to recount. "Talking, laughing, flirting. I didn't want the night to end, and I never wanted to let you go. But my life was so complicated, I wasn't sure how much I could give. Then Javier showed up and everything spun out of control. I knew what he was capable of, I'd seen it firsthand."

I tighten my fists from the traumatic memories.

"Women, so many women . . ." I get a headache just thinking about it. "Crawling around the floor like animals. Stuffed into cages so small they were hunched in a ball, all of them starved and abused."

"What? Why?" Ellie asks horrified.

"Money. Some of them were for his personal use. Most were to be sold off as sex slaves." Ellie turns pale. The light may be dim in the room, but the color of her skin unmistakable. "But that's not the worst part," I continue, on a mission to make her understand. "I visited his home once. Three months before he came to the States. While I was there, he made a habit of abusing one of them nightly. Screams . . . all night I heard them scream, like he wanted to make a point. He wanted me to know exactly who I was dealing with, and unfortunately, he made an impression. I'll never deny it. The sounds still haunt me.

"But the last night was the worst. God, what he put that poor girl through." I still get sick thinking about it. "She screamed for hours until I finally couldn't take it anymore. If there was ever a time I was going to chuck it all, it was that moment. But just as I was about to leave my room and go on a murderous rampage slash suicide mission, it all stopped. A little while later, I heard digging in the backyard. That's when I saw her, lying dead on the ground, mutilated beyond recognition. Her bloody and contorted body looked like a prop in a horror movie. She almost didn't even seem real. I watched sickly while one of his thugs dug her shallow grave."

Ellie turns from white to green. That's the right reaction; I nearly puked just retelling the story myself.

"That night I vowed that girl's death wouldn't be in vain. Her blood will always be on my hands because I did nothing to stop him. I will have to live with that until the day I die. It's also why I was so hell-bent on not blowing my cover. Why I went to such an extreme. There was so much riding on that operation, so many lives at stake. Including yours.

"When Javier said he wanted you, all I could see was your face next to that grave. He had to believe that you were mine. He had to believe that I was taking a page from his book. It was the only way to keep him away."

"He didn't stay away." Angry tears fall.

"I know." I cup her cheek in my hand. "And I'm sorry. I did my best to protect you. But he got what he deserved. He's dead. And I swear to God, Ellie, I would have killed him right there in front of you that night if it were under any other circumstances. *I swear.* Everything would have been different." I wipe away the wetness on her face. "I didn't know how serious he was when he said he wanted you. If I made you disappear, it might have looked suspicious, and possibly blown my cover. If I did nothing, I ran the risk of Javier pursuing you. The only thing I was truly sure of is that somehow you'd become more important to me than my own life. I'd fallen in love with you and didn't even know it. Or maybe I did and just didn't know how to recognize it. Either way, I made a split-second decision and claimed you before he could."

She clutches my wrist as she listens to me speak, like it's anchoring her to the ground. I know it's anchoring me.

"I just wanted to do what I thought was right for everyone. It may have been deceitful, and felt like I misled you, but it delivered the outcome I was hoping for. So, please tell me, Ellie, now that you know everything, which is the bigger betrayal? Handing you over to the monster so you could die, or becoming the monster so you could live?"

Not a peep leaves Ellie's mouth, not even a flow of air.

"What happened to the other girls? Did you save them?" She finally blinks, causing more tears to fall.

"Yes. Seventeen of them. And Javier's house was burned to the ground."

"Good." She wipes her eyes roughly with the tips of her fingers. When she's finished, I take her hand and lick up every last drop of her tears. She watches me thoughtfully, as if being reminded of a memory. They taste the same now as they did then, salty and sad.

"Did you like doing all those things to me?" She sniffs. "Hurting me? Making me cry?"

I pause, breathing heavily. "That's a complicated answer."

"Why?" She looks at me so intensely, like she wants to pick me apart.

"Because . . . I did." I lower her hand and tangle her fingers with mine. "But I wish we did those things under different circumstances."

"What kind of different circumstances?" She's enthralled now.

"Ellie, the only women I have ever been with have been submissive. They expected certain treatment, and I expected certain behavior. Spanking, whipping, and punishment is what we were both accustomed to. You, as far as I was aware, knew nothing of the sort so I had to teach you. If you were going to truly be my slave, you needed to act a certain way, portray a certain persona. And you did. You surprised everyone, especially me. You endured everything I threw at you, facing it head on. I never forced a woman before. To be honest, I didn't even know if I had it in me. But being with you was like a drug, I couldn't stop myself from pushing you, wanting to find out just how far I could go. How far you would go."

"You pushed me pretty far." She admits.

"You pushed me pretty far, too."

"I did?"

"Yes. You're the strongest person I've ever met."

"And you would want that with me again? To be submissive?" Her tone tells me she doesn't like that idea, but the question opens all kinds of promise.

"I told you that I'll take whatever you're willing to give me. I've made peace with giving up that lifestyle. You're what's important."

"What happened to kink being king in your world?"

"That world doesn't exist anymore."

"You expect me to believe you're okay with walking away from everything you know just so we can be together?"

I nod, confidently.

I can see the indecisiveness in her smoky-green eyes. The ones I've gotten lost in so many times. "I've never had love in my life, Ellie. Never thought I wanted it or needed it, or even deserved it. Then I met you, and everything changed. I don't know how or why, I just knew you were different.

"I know I can't force you to love me. I just thought if I could make you see *me,* see that I'm not the monster you think I am, maybe there could still be a chance." I pull her closer so her body is pressed up against mine. She feels so good and so perfect, I pray to God I'm saying the right things to convince her to say. "I want you in my life," I plead with her. "You just need to be brave enough to want me back."

She takes a long deep breath, clearly battling with the demons inside her.

"I don't want to go," she expels softly. "But it's going to be hard to trust you again."

Hope swells inside of me. "We'll take it slow. We have this place for two weeks. We can spend it getting to know each other. No pressure."

Ellie just flicks the collar of my shirt thoughtfully, not agreeing to anything. That tiny bit of hope rising inside me suddenly becomes a violent cyclone of water escaping down a drain.

"I ruined your shirt," she says.

"I don't give two shits about my shirt." I grab her, straddling her legs over my lap, serious now. "You can get mad, scream, hit me, beat me, torture me if you want. I'll endure it all if it means you'll stay." I hold onto her hips tightly, vulnerability seeping out of every pore in my body. "I don't think I can survive another day without you in my life."

She stares deeply into my eyes with her hands resting on my chest, so wrackingly quiet.

"Please," I beg. Yes, me. I beg.

"Okay." Her response is so soft I barely hear it.

"Okay?" I repeat just to make sure I didn't dream it.

"Okay. I'll stay."

"Really?"

Ellie cracks a smile. "Yes, really. But we go slowly."

"I can do slow." *Yeah, right.* But I'll try.

Ellie brushes her hands over my chest, separating my shirt. I unbuttoned it with the intention of changing, but I never made it past the couch or the last two buttons. I struggle to sit still while she reacquaints herself with my body, running her palms over my skin and stopping at my tattoo. She always was fascinated by the large colorful compass over my heart.

"Look hard," I tell her.

"At what?"

"The ink."

She stares at the tattoo, then gasps. Written in very tiny script is her name on the needle pointing North.

"You're crazy."

"Without a doubt," I chuckle.

Her expression softens as she rubs the tip of her finger over her name. I have no control over what happens next. She feels so fucking good straddled on top of me, touching me the way she is. I tuck a piece of hair that's come loose from her ponytail behind her ear and the contact is magnetic. I lean forward, starving for just one tiny taste. She allows me to brush my lips against hers, never closing her eyes. I do it again, our gazes still locked. The third time, I apply more pressure, wrapping my arm around her waist. She kisses me back with just as much ferocity as this afternoon, and soon our slow, simple act becomes passionately charged.

I slide my hands eagerly under her dress and palm her ass while I swipe my tongue between her lips. She opens her mouth, allowing me in while simultaneously wrapping her arms around my neck. I crush her down against my erection, the two of us moaning as our hips clash together. With my heart starting to race, I slip my thumb under the silky material of her thong desperate to play with her, tickle her, lick her, fuck her. All the things she dangled in front of my face earlier tonight. Just as I begin to massage small circles over her folds, eager to sink my finger into the wet heat I've been dreaming about for the last twelve months, Ellie grabs my wrist.

"Kayne, no."

"No?" I halt. "Why no?" I test the waters by trying to move my hand.

Ellie pants. "Because I need to know that no is an option." She rests her forehead against mine.

"Of course, it is. I never want to take anything away from you. Ever again. I want to give you everything. Make you happy any way I can." I look up at her. "I would lie, cheat, steal, *kill* to keep you happy, Ellie. I would kill for you." I grab her neck. "I meant it then, and I mean it even more now. I would kill for you." I stress the words, caught up in her penetrating stare.

With a small smile, she drops a kiss on my lips. "Tonight," she breathes, "I need you to just lay with me."

I WAKE UP WITH KAYNE'S arm locked around my waist. His hold is so tight it's nearly suffocating me.

Last night was one of the longest of my life. So much information shared, so many questions answered, and an abundance of emotion soaring to the surface. Jett was right; Kayne has some deep-seated insecurities and has been severely deprived. But he also showed me how passionate and strong his convictions lie. Yes, what he did was monumentally fucked up, but there's no denying it bonded us. The pull is so strong it feels unbreakable. And that's scary as hell.

I don't know where I found the strength to deny him last night, but I needed to do it. I needed to know that he would never force me again. And he didn't, despite his raging hard on and the unbridled lust in his eyes. He just carried me to bed, wrapped me in his arms, and fell asleep. Almost too easily. Too naturally.

He feels so good pressed up against me. So right and wrong.

I'm in such a dangerous place. I know all too well what he's capable of, and yet at the same time, I barely know him at all. I'm certain exploring this path will lead to one of two things. An epic love, or my calamitous self-destruction.

Kayne stirs in his sleep as the early-morning sun brightens the room and the glorious view on display before us. He couldn't have picked a dreamier destination. I could lay here all day and just admire the tranquil turquoise-blue of the water.

"Mmmm." Kayne stirs again, this time sliding his hand over my stomach, pulling the hem of my dress up as he goes. "You stayed."

"Why wouldn't I?"

"Don't know. I guess I expect the worst."

I put my hand over his, lacing his fingers with mine. He hugs me tighter, digging his erection into my back, making my blood flow increase in speed.

"What would help ease your mind?" I ask softly.

"Knowing last night made a difference." He skims our entwined fingers down my bare thigh, and kisses me behind my ear.

"It did." I tilt my head, giving him better access to my neck.

"Good." He sucks hard on my skin, spurring my whole body to come alive. I let go of his hand as it explores my body, sliding from my hip to my torso then straight up to my breast. He squeezes it roughly over the fabric, pinching my nipple until it pebbles.

"Ellie," Kayne utters my name painfully, and I know there's no turning back now. Not that I want to. "I need you so much."

"I need you, too." I turn in his arms, desperate for him just to kiss me. And kiss me he does. Like a starving man who's never tasted sugar before, he invades my mouth, sucking my tongue, forcefully pushing my head into the pillow.

I'm drowning already, and he's barely even touched me. Kayne breaks our kiss just long enough to rip the lacey panties off my body then reclaims my mouth. I meet him roll for roll and thrust for thrust as our tongues tangle together. "I want to show you," he says between kisses. "I want to show you how much I missed you."

Before I even have a chance to respond, he's repositioning us, sliding off the bed and onto the floor, dragging my lower body with him until my legs are dangling over the side of the mattress. He pulls me up into a sitting position and situates himself between my knees. This is a first, Kayne kneeling before me.

Kayne sucks on his lower lip as he gazes at me, his eyes hungry and his body ready. He takes both thin straps of my dress between his fingers and slowly lowers them down my arms, exposing my breasts. The hunger in his eyes quickly morphs into famine as he drinks in my naked chest, my nipples hardening just from his stare. He leans forward, and I brace myself for his touch, for his lips to find my skin, his mouth to find my aching points. But he only grazes his teeth against my neck and runs his hands up the outside of my thighs. "Can I touch you, Ellie?"

"Yes." I drop my head back and moan as he kisses my neck and massages my breasts.

"Can I taste you, baby? Can I put my mouth on your pussy and lick you until you come?" Kayne swirls his tongue against my skin mimicking exactly what he would do if I say yes. I'm panting before I know it, his words as illicit as his actions. "Can I?"

"Yes." I force out the word as he rolls my rock hard nipples between his fingers. God, the effect this man has on me. It's inhuman and maddening and utterly blissful. Kayne kisses his way down my body, sucking on each of my breasts and stopping short just below my navel. I'm so tuned up I can barely stand it. I almost beg, but I refrain. Anticipating his next move, I watch engrossed as he hooks his arms around my thighs and spreads me wide, locking my legs in place.

"Lean back, Ellie." He pulls my lower body closer to the edge of the bed just so a bit of my ass is hovering off the side. Resting back on my hands, I grab onto the sheet for support, the two of us breathing raggedly as we stare into each other's eyes. "I want you to watch. I want you to see how much I missed you." Kayne tightens his arms and drops his head, and all I can do is hold my breath as his tongue darts out to take its first taste. The contact feels electric as Kayne launches a full-on assault, making sure I see every circle and every thrust. Pink flesh meeting pink flesh, both glistening with my arousal.

Kayne moans against me as he sucks vigorously on my clit.

"You really do taste like cupcakes." He laps me up like sugary frosting, and all I can do is quiver uncontrollably. He isn't wasting a moment pushing me to the brink.

"Kayne." I moan his name, close my eyes, and drop my head back as the sensations completely take over.

"Don't take your eyes off me, Ellie." He halts all movement, and I snap my head up. "I want you to see. I want you to watch me make you come." His stare is sharp as a knife and dark with desire. I know that look. It's his unyielding need for control—his dominant side waking from a yearlong slumber. It makes me shiver in all the right ways. It's such a fucking turn on that I almost hate myself for loving it. But it's his dominance that made me realize what we were both capable of. I drop my gaze as Kayne leans back down, trapping my swollen clit between his teeth and gently bites. I try to buck my hips as a zap of pleasure courses through my body, but his hold has my lower half restrained.

Oh God, I'm so close—watching him, feeling him, succumbing to him.

"Kayne, please," I cry out as he brushes his tongue over the entire length of my slit, driving me mad.

I've had just about all I can take when he finally decides to take pity on me and apply the pressure I need. Forced to watch as he fucks me with his mouth, stabbing my entrance repeatedly with his masterful tongue, everything south tightens and tingles. "Oh God, please."

I gasp. "Please, Kayne, may I come?"

As soon as the words leave my lips, the energy in the room changes. He looks up at me as I stare down, my heart pounding in my ears as he slows his strokes.

"Ellie, you just made me hard as fuck, but you don't have to ask my permission anymore," he says gruffly, between licks. "You're free to come whenever you want."

Embarrassment washes over me like I have never known, deflating my orgasm like a vented hot air balloon, and suddenly all I want to do is escape.

"Come for me, baby." He continues to lick me, but I grab his hair.

"No. Stop. Let go. Stop." I fight to jerk my legs out of his iron tight hold.

Kayne releases me, thankfully, with a worried expression.

"Ellie?" He tries to touch me, but all I want to do is disappear. I bolt up and retreat into the bathroom, locking the door behind me. Such a fucking idiot! I asked his permission!

I kick away my dress that is now pooling at my feet and turn on the shower, wanting to scrub the last five minutes away. I step into the freezing cold spray and bury my face in my hands.

"Ellie?" Kayne bangs on the door as I slowly die of mortification. "Ellie, please let me in." I can't tell the frame of mind he's in over the running water. On some level, I'm afraid he's mad and will want to punish me. On another, I know that's ludicrous given the conversation we had last night. My head is just too screwed up to think straight, and it's all thanks to Kayne.

"Ellie!" He bangs on the door harder, and I jump.

"Can you just give me a minute?" I snap.

This reunion is going spectacularly. For the first time, I strongly believe I made the wrong decision coming here. Maybe I wasn't ready. Maybe I'll never be ready. Maybe I'll always believe I'm nothing more than just a slave.

Just as I turn under the showerhead to wet my hair, I catch Kayne climbing through the window.

"What the fuck are you doing?" I ask as he drops his pants, shrugs out of his stained shirt and steps into the shower with me.

"Your minute is up." He stalks forward and pins me against the tiled wall.

"Kayne," I protest not meeting his eyes.

"Ellie." He grabs my chin and forces me to look at him. "Let's get a few things straight. First, no more running from me. That shit's over. You've had over a year to come to terms with everything. I'm done waiting. You run, and I'll come after you."

I stare into his eyes silently, my chest heaving, water dotting my face as the stream ricochets off his body. Part of me wants to fight him, to tell him to fuck off, and the other wants to melt into his arms and submit. It's a constant tug-of-war battling inside me.

"Second," his voice turns velvety soft, "if you want to ask my permission to come, be my guest. It makes me fucking hard as a rock." He pushes his erection against my belly.

"I don't want to ask your permission. I never want you to control me again." But even as I say the words, I know they're only partly true. Kayne's dominance is what makes him so seductive, what draws me to him like a dancing flame, and that's exactly the problem—one tiny touch and I get burned.

"I'll never do anything you don't want me to do, but I'm not going to let you walk all over me, either. I want to be with you, Ellie, however I can have you," he repeats his words from last night. The same ones that won me over. One simple sentence that sealed my fate.

I take a deep breath and pull myself together. I want to be here, with him.

"I just hate that I'm conditioned," I tell him honestly.

Kayne smirks and cups my face in his hand. "Well, we'll just have to recondition you." He closes his mouth over mine, flicking his tongue against my teeth. "Starting now." He embraces me more urgently, pressing his big body flush against mine. There are so many promises in that kiss; it's like a swear, an oath, an affirmation.

"How do you want me to make you come? Do you want me to lick or fuck an orgasm out of you?"

My worried thoughts become nothing but a haze as he manipulates my mind with his profane words.

"Ellie, tell me," he urges gently, sucking my earlobe into his mouth.

I search for my voice, finding it behind the searing need shooting through my system. "Both?" I struggle to answer.

I feel Kayne smirk against my cheek. "That's my girl." He doesn't waste a second kissing his way down my body until he's settled on his knees. "Hang on, baby." That's my only warning as he hooks his arms under my thighs and hoists me right off the ground.

"Oh!" I steady myself with one hand against the wall as Kayne buries his face between my legs and licks until I'm writhing and moaning, fisting his hair, and squaring off with the orgasm that eluded me just a short while ago. "Oh God, oh God." My voice pitches as I slump in his arms, my climax grabbing hold and yanking me down into a spiraling black abyss.

I come around cocooned in Kayne's arms, the warm spray of the shower tickling my skin and the even hotter caress of his lips traveling down my neck.

"Welcome back."

"Mmm."

"How was your trip?"

"Too short."

"We can go again." He squeezes me in his arms, his erection digging into my thigh. "I need you so bad, Ellie," he says strained.

"You can have me," I reply without even opening my eyes. At this very moment, he could do anything he wanted to me and I wouldn't protest.

Kayne growls in my ear. "Turn around. Put your hands over your head."

I do as he says, placing my hands against the wall. A moment later, he's pinning my wrists together with his fingers, like a zip tie. He splays his free hand on my lower abdomen and juts my hips out. I'm stretched and tethered and in seemingly familiar territory.

Kayne teases my pussy with the length of his erection, skimming through my wet folds before he fully penetrates me. I know what he's doing, drawing out my desire until I'm desperate again. He plays that game so well.

I moan as he grazes my sensitive slit, winding me up.

"I thought you said you needed me?" I rock against his steel-hard erection.

"I do, I just want to make sure you need me back." He keeps up the leisurely pace between my legs.

"Do you? Do you need me, baby?" he rasps in my ear, and as much as it pains me to admit it, I do.

"Yes, I need you," I whisper.

"I need you, too." With that, he thrusts into me, filling me to the brim. His fingers tighten around my wrists as my muscles clench around his cock. Kayne groans, burying his face in my neck while stalling inside me for a few heat-induced seconds. "Fuck," he spits as he starts to move, pulling all the way out then driving back in, each thrust a little more urgent than the last. "God, I missed you." He picks up the pace, keeping me positioned exactly how he wants me, hands pinned, hips out. Hitting my sweet spot over and over until everything inside me gravitates to the pulsing sensation between my legs. The ache is unbearable, but at the same time so deliciously good.

"Ellie, come with me," he grinds out as he slams into me so hard he lifts me right off the ground. "Come."

"Oh God!" I'm almost there, barreling down the last lengths, as Kayne clouds my mind the same way the steam is clouding the shower. When he drops his hand from my abdomen and circles my swollen clit with his finger, I detonate, crying out and coming hard all over his cock.

Kayne pulls out at the tail end of my orgasm and jerks off all over my ass, warm semen coating my skin as he groans like a dying man. He drops his head onto my shoulder and breathes the word 'mine' so softly I don't think I was meant to hear; but I did, and the declaration sends chills down my spine and hot lava through my veins.

Kayne releases my wrists and grabs onto my waist. I rest my hands on the shower wall, thankful for the reprieve, and peek at him over my shoulder. I'm still slightly bent over, and he's still slightly lust drunk. He rubs his come into my skin, making small circles down my behind until he's cupping one of my ass cheeks in his hand. I tense as he squeezes it, not hard enough to hurt, but in a way that tells me he's tempted to spank me. I brace myself for the blow, but it never comes. Instead, he just looks up into my eyes. "I needed that," he says sedately, right before the corners of his mouth curve up into a devilish smile.

"So you said," I mock, and the heavy energy between us cracks as we both start laughing.

Kayne hauls me into his arms with happiness radiating from his body.

"I also need you." He kisses me sweetly as he positions me under the spray washing away his sticky remnants from my backside.

"So you said." I sigh, kissing him back.

"I'll say it as many times as I have to until you believe it."

KAYNE'S PHONE BUZZES ON THE nightstand. I ignore it the first time, but it persistently vibrates for several minutes while I lay in bed—Kayne's bed—recuperating and processing the events of the morning. I glance around our vacation bungalow. The one with a view of Bora Bora to die for, expensive furnishings, and glass floors where fish swim beneath us. This is definitely paradise, and he's spared no expense.

His phone goes off again, and now I think it might be important. I grab the towel off the floor, wrap it around my naked self, and then pick up the phone. I walk into the bathroom to find him standing in front of the sink brushing his teeth. I pause in the doorway and just watch. Kayne catches me staring through the mirror. He spits, wipes his mouth, and then asks, "What's up, Ellie?"

"Oh, um." I snap out of my suspended state and walk over to him. "Your phone kept buzzing. I thought it might be important."

Kayne pulls me against him while he takes the phone. "Why were you looking at me funny before?" He glances at his screen with his arm securely around my waist.

"I've never seen you brush your teeth before," I admit. "It's so . . . normal."

Kayne laughs. "I'm not an alien, Ellie," he says as he types something with his free hand.

"To me you are," I giggle. "Ever since I met you, you've always had this persona that felt way bigger than me. First wealthy businessman, and then . . . well . . . you know," I fidget and blush. *The controlling Dom.* "Then undercover super spy."

Kayne laughs dropping his face closer to mine. "I'm just a man, Ellie. I put my pants on one leg at a time just like everyone else."

Yeah, right! Kayne is way more than just a man. He can try to convince me, and himself, and the world that he's just like everyone else, but that's so far from the truth it's actually comical. He's a force, half angel, half demon, wrapped up in a package of male perfection. No, he's no alien; he's a predator. He entices you with his charm, lures you with his appeal, traps you with his will, then pounces on you when you least expect it, ready to kill.

Just a man, my ass.

Kayne's phone buzzes in his hand again.

"You're popular," I comment.

"Not really." He looks down at the screen and frowns.

"Everything okay?"

"Fine." He pastes on a fake smile. "Just work."

"Just work?" I repeat. He refers to his job so nonchalantly, like he's a computer programmer instead of an international man of mystery.

"Yes, work. And it's fine."

"So fine you have to use an alias?"

He looks at me slyly. "The alias is just for precaution. You don't take down one of the most dangerous drug lords in the world and not take necessary steps to protect yourself."

"Are you in danger?" I ask concerned.

"No, at least none that we know of."

"We?"

"Yes, I have a twenty-four-hour surveillance team scanning for threats. And there aren't any that we're aware of at the moment."

"But there could be?"

"There's always a possibility of retribution."

"Kayne—"

"Ellie," he interrupts me, "I will tell you this. You have nothing to worry about. I would die before I let something bad happen to you."

"I don't think it's me I'm worried about."

Kayne smiles. His facial expression is endearing, but his eyes tell a completely different story. They're deadly and cold, and actually scare me. "Baby," he says almost threateningly. "If someone is stupid enough to come after me, they better have their funeral arrangements made. Got me?"

"Yes."

"Good." He drops a kiss on my lips, but doesn't let go of me.

"Do you have to go back undercover?" I ask.

"There's a possibility I could be activated again, but the probability of me running an operation is slim to none. I'm too high profile now, so I would most likely be backup support."

I blink rapidly; it's so strange to hear him talk like this. It's just one more layer of this complicated man.

"I'm not sure what means exactly."

"Different operatives have different responsibilities." He finally let's go of me. "I was a field operative, so my face was out there on the front lines. There are cyber, communications, linguists, and administrative operatives who work behind the scenes."

"For the government?"

"Yes and no. I was trained by the government, but work for an independent contractor."

"You're losing me," I say clearly confused.

"That's probably a good thing. The less you know about my occupation, the better."

"So, you're not a government spook?"

Kayne chuckles. "I'm not even sure what that means. What I am is a former U.S. soldier who was recruited for a special operations program because I possessed certain personality traits."

"And those traits are?" I'm engrossed by every ounce of information he feeds me.

"Low morality and no identity. I didn't mind killing people, and I didn't care if I got killed. That's the most lethal kind of agent. It's also the kind of agent the government doesn't like to associate themselves with directly, which is why I'm employed by a privately funded contractor. It gives us, and them, flexibility to go around the law so to speak."

"Do you still feel that way?" I frown.

"What way?"

"That you don't care if you get killed?"

Kayne's face softens. "I'll let you know at the end of our vacation." He runs his thumb down my cheek. "Enough shop talk. Let me worry about protecting the free world and you not worry at all. How does getting out of here for a little while sound? We can go check out the white sand beaches and down a dozen fruity drinks with those stupid little umbrellas in them."

"Sounds like a plan," I laugh, "and the recipe for a really bad hangover."

I DECIDE ON ONE OF my new bathing suits for the beach. The strapless stringy two-piece that barely covers my ass. I was going to save this one, but the idea of seeing Kayne's face when I wear it is too tempting to pass up. He's either going to love it, hate it, or—and my money's on this one—hate the fact that he loves me wearing it. Either way, I win on all accounts.

I walk out into the living room where Kayne is waiting for me, and his expression falls. "Ellie, what are you wearing?"

I look down at my body. "A bathing suit?" I reply innocently.

Kayne raises his eyebrows. "Ellie, that isn't a bathing suit; that is a string wrapped around your body." He clearly disapproves. I smile to myself. "I have a cover-up." I show him the sheer white shirt that's practically see-through.

He grimaces. Too bad.

"Are we going?" I walk past him toward the front door. "I want to see the island."

Just as I turn the knob and crack the door open, it slams shut. I glance behind me.

"You can't go out like that."

"Why not?"

"Why not?" he asks exasperated. "Because you're indecent!"

"It's a bathing suit," I argue.

"That is not a bathing suit," he reiterates. "It's something Jett would dress you in to entice me."

"Who says that's not what I'm trying to do?" I bat my eyelashes at him.

"Baby, I'm already enticed. Now, please go change."

"No."

"Ellie." His patience is wearing thin. Good.

"Kayne," I mimic his tone, "my father doesn't even tell me how to dress, so don't think you're going to."

"I think if your father saw you wearing that he might have something to say."

"Well, he's not here. And you don't own me," I remind him. "I can do what I want. So move your hand, and let's go." I stare him down, just daring him to challenge me.

Kayne glares back at me with an ice-cold expression, the blue in his eyes as vibrant as a winter sky. He can try to intimidate me all he wants. I'm not backing down. It's my body and my life. After a few long heated beats, he gives in. "Fine."

Victory, I sing to myself. He really is a smart man. He knows if he argues with me it's going to get him nowhere fast. I was curious to see just how serious he was when he said he wasn't interested in controlling me. I will admit his jealousy kind of turns me on. I love how protective he is.

Although I won't tell him that.

Yet.

Kayne removes his hand from the door. "Can you please wear your cover-up at least?" he asks, straining for composure.

"Okay." I slip the loose fitting shirt over my head and cover myself.

"Happy?" I ask.

"No," he replies sourly.

I giggle uncontrollably. This is gonna be fun.

We climb into the golf cart where Matias is already waiting behind the wheel. I snuggle up next to Kayne in the tiny seat. I don't want him to be upset, but I do want him to know that I'm through taking orders and following commands. He immediately puts his arm around me and nuzzles his nose into my hair. It makes me tingle. Matias glances at us and smirks as he drives off. We're a far cry from the couple who first climbed into his cart nearly twenty-four hours ago.

"Kayne?" I whisper in his ear.

"Mmm hmm?" he answers, holding me tightly.

"What happened to your house and the business?"

He looks quickly at Matias before he answers me. Maybe I should have waited until we were in private to ask, but our conversation this morning has me wondering.

Kayne drops his head, pressing his lips to my ear. "Gone," he murmurs so only I can hear. "Everything was liquidated."

"Oh," I reply surprised, and he shakes his head sternly. I take the hint. This conversation is over.

"Later," he whispers while skimming my neck with his teeth.

"Sorry."

"Don't be." He drops a kiss on my lips just as Matias pulls up to our destination. The resort's private beach—complete with crystal-blue lagoon, cushioned lounge chairs, and tiki bar.

"Ring when you need me, sir," Matias says to Kayne as they shake hands.

"Will do."

Kayne and I walk the short distance to the bar when I suddenly spot a familiar face dressed in board shorts and a smile heading our way.

"Jett!" I nearly jump into his arms. "I didn't think we were going to see you."

"I'm always around." He hugs me.

"Thank you for last night," I whisper in his ear right before he releases me.

"Anytime. You know that," he whispers back.

"Ellie, do you want something to drink?" Kayne asks from behind me. It's such a simple question, but his flat tone implies something so much more. Is he jealous of Jett? I couldn't fathom it. He was the one who took care of me all that time. The only one he trusted me with.

"Yes, please." I turn and walk over to him. I can't see his eyes behind those brown aviator sunglasses he always wears, but I can see the curve of his lips, and the way they're turned down.

"Downing a dozen, remember?" I slide up against him.

"I didn't forget." He puts his arm around me and kisses the top of my head.

"One for me, too." Jett casually leans against the bar beside us, arms folded, eyes bright, the color almost a perfect match to the turquoise water.

"Three Mai Tais," Kayne orders as I steal glimpses of the two hottest men I have ever met.

Jett cocks his eyebrow at me, acknowledging how perfectly content I am with Kayne's protective arm around me. I pull down my sunglasses and exaggerate an eye roll at him.

He chuckles, his nipple ring glinting in the sun.

"What's so funny?" Kayne asks Jett over my head.

"The image of you holding a girlie drink with a pink umbrella."

"I'm channeling my inner bitch just for you."

I glance up at Kayne.

"Sorry. Was that offensive?"

I smile. "Maybe if I was anyone else. But my sense of humor is pretty liberal."

"Perfect, you'll fit right in with the perverts," Jett jokes.

"Speak for yourself." Kayne scoffs.

"Hmmm, I don't think Jett is too far out of line. Birds of a feather . . ." I point out. I know firsthand just how perverted Kayne can be.

"I love her," Jett laughs.

Kayne leers at me, sucking his bottom lip between his teeth. His eyes just barely visible behind the brown lenses.

"Ellie, why don't you go grab us a seat. I need to talk to Jett for a minute," he says, running his hand down my back and over my behind. "I'll bring your drink when it's ready."

"Okay," I frown. "Sure." Why does it feel like I'm suddenly being dismissed?

Kayne drops a kiss on my lips and spanks my ass lightly, sending me on my way.

Fine, then.

I saunter down to where the sand meets the water. It's a glorious day. The beach itself is quiet, but there are people snorkeling several yards away and jet skiing in the distance.

I discard my cover-up, and then glance behind me. Jett and Kayne look like they're talking casually, but I can feel both of their heated stares searing into my skin.

KAYNE

I WATCH ELLIE SHIMMY AWAY wearing nothing more than an R-rated bikini and a sorry excuse for a cover-up. It took everything I had to let her walk out of the bungalow like that without leaving handprints on her ass. I have to keep reminding myself our dynamic has changed. She is no longer my slave, and I am no longer her Master, which really fucking sucks sometimes. Like now. I have a feeling she is going to test me at every turn.

"You got laid." Jett shifts his eyes to me.

"How could you possibly know that?" I respond flatly.

"Because, for the first time in almost twelve months, your energy isn't hostile and Ellie is the perfect shade of post-coital peach."

"You need to lay off the Zen. And yes, we had sex."

"So you two are working things out?"

"Looks like it. She's still here. Although she is hell-bent on making sure I understand she is independent and won't take any shit from me."

Jett grins, and then immediately frowns. "Is that bathing suit part of her independence?" he asks as Ellie disrobes, catching every single eye on the beach. Including ours.

"Yup."

"You let her out in that?"

"She didn't give me much of a choice. Tough little thing." I smile to myself.

"That she is."

The bartender serves us our drinks. Finally. Paradise service takes forever. It's annoying.

"You read that text this morning?" I ask Jett as I take a sip of my drink. Looks like we were both wrong. No pink umbrellas, just red hibiscus garnishing our Mai Tais. Much more manly.

"Yup."

"Were you able to get any more information?"

"Yeah. I figured you'd be busy, so I checked in."

"And?"

"It was confirmed the Jackal landed in Honolulu this morning via private jet."

"Do we know what he wants?" I ask softly, standing as casually as possible, watching Ellie dip her toes in the water.

"Negative. Could be nothing. Could be one of Javier's most dangerous American allies' just wants to listen to some authentic Hawaiian music and dine on kalua pig."

"Right, with me doing the hula in a grass skirt," I retort cynically, tracking Ellie's every move.

"You have the abs for it."

"Yeah, well, the only way he's going to get close enough to see my abs is if I have him in a headlock."

"No need for violence if it isn't necessary."

"Violence is always necessary," I contest.

Jett snickers. We have always butted heads on this subject. He believes in avoiding a mess. I always take the bloody way out. I believe it leaves more of an impression.

"Juice has eyes on him. We'll know soon enough if he's up to something."

"Good." My pulse beats double time in my neck. "The last thing I want to do is upset Ellie with reminders of Javier."

"Amen, brother." Jett taps his cup against mine. "Um, Kayne, speaking of reminders, did you happen to tell Ellie about Sugar?"

"You haven't called her that since Mansion."

"I know, but it's the only name Ellie knows her by," Jett says as Sugar approaches Ellie on the beach. All we can do is watch the train wreck happen as we walk quickly down to the girls.

They speak briefly, like for a split second, before Ellie starts walking backward, then bumps into a lounge chair, and ends up falling flat on her ass.

"Ooo," Jett and I both collectively respond.

"Oh! Are you okay?" we hear Sugar ask, reaching for her.

Ellie just nods stunned. She looks embarrassed, uneasy, and disoriented all at the same time.

"Ellie." Jett slips his arms around Sugar's—or I should say London's—waist. That's her real name. "I see you two are getting reacquainted."

She glances silently between Jett, London, and me.

"You look confused, Ellie," I comment offhandedly. It's clear she's been blindsided and doesn't know how to react. I probably should have warned her about the two of them. But, to be honest, it was the last thing on my mind.

"I am." She eyes me irately.

"London is here with me," Jett clarifies. "We're together."

"Together?"

"Yeah, you know, like dating," I chime in.

"I know dating." Her answer is short.

"I figured. Mai Tai?" I shove a drink in her face.

"Just the one? I think I need all twelve."

"YOU DIDN'T THINK TO WARN me that Jett was dating a ghost from our sordid past?" Ellie fumes, half a mile down the beach, away from where London and Jett can hear.

"Didn't seem like such a big deal," I shrug.

"Maybe to you."

"Are you ashamed of what happened between the three of us?"

"No, yes, no . . . ugh." Ellie turns red. "It's just . . . Just."

"Just?"

"I just didn't think I was ever going to see her again," she finally admits, frustrated.

"Well, she was excited to see you if that makes you feel any better."

"I don't know how that makes me feel." She crosses her arms and looks up at me with just her gorgeous green eyes.

"It really isn't a big deal." I try to reassure her.

"To you, maybe."

"Can you just give it a chance? I know the dynamic is different. It's something we all have to get used to. But she's a great girl, and Jett is head over heels, stupidly in love with her." *Sort of the exact same way I feel about you.*

"Were they together when we were together?" she asks uncomfortably, plucking the string on her bikini bottom.

"I'm not sure, honestly. Something was going on, I think, but they didn't hook up officially until after everything cooled down."

Ellie frowns, wringing her fingers together. "Did you sleep with her?"

"Ah . . ." Oh, shit. I wasn't expecting her to ask that.

"I'll take that as a yes. Of course you did. She was one of your 'girls.'" She makes air quotes.

"It's not what you think."

"Then please tell me what to think."

Fuck, I wasn't ready for this conversation so early in the day.

"Yes, I slept with her," I admit. "A few times, but only when Jett wanted to share her."

"Excuse me?" Her head tilts as she looks up at me puzzled.

"Jett and I had a threesome with London," I speak slowly, clarifying my sentence.

"Oh." Her eyes widen.

"Really, we're all even if you think about it. Jett and I have been with London, and you and I have been with London, so it's all good." I try to rationalize.

"That's not how I see it at all. If I sleep with Jett, then we'd be all good." She counters with her own rationale. It ain't flying.

"Over my fucking dead body. Jett may get off on sharing his women, but I don't. Unless it's with another woman." I slip that in there.

Ellie folds her arms and smirks. "Yes, I remember how much you enjoyed seeing me with another woman."

"If I recall, you enjoyed it, too." I cautiously slide my arm around her waist.

"I did." She embraces my subtle surrender, running her nails down my biceps, over my barbed-wire tattoo, giving me the chills. "But you still could have warned me."

"I'm sorry. Please forgive my oversight. Only one woman has been on my mind."

"Oh, yeah? Who's that?" she asks seductively, skimming the tip of her tongue up my neck.

"Like you don't know." I grab her ass and crush her body against mine. "If you don't quit that I'm going to have to drag you into the lagoon and tear that tiny bikini off you."

She giggles, "No way, I'm still mad at you. You'll have to suffer." She sucks on my skin.

"Would it have really made that much a difference if you knew or not?" Her mouth feels so good I'm starting to unravel.

"Possibly. I could have avoided looking like a blindsided idiot."

"It was cute."

"It definitely wasn't."

"It definitely was. And what I say goes."

"Mmm hmm. Keep thinking that."

"I will." I squeeze Ellie's ass cheek and nearly lift her off the ground. She lets out a little half scream, and I can't help but think that's not the only way I'm going to make her scream. "Can we go try and make nice?" I set her down and take her hand. I need to walk off my waking arousal, and walk it off right now.

"I guess I don't really have a choice," she resigns.

Once back, Ellie and I snuggle up in the lounge chair next to Jett and London. Jett throws me a look as Ellie situates herself between my legs and lays back on my chest.

I return a head nod indicating things are all good, even though Ellie still feels a little tense. I rub her shoulders in an attempt to relax her, and after a few minutes, she inhales deeply and melts against me. I smile to myself, feeding off her energy. She'll never understand the effect she has on me.

For the next hour, the four of us just lounge like fat cats, soaking up the sun and sucking down drinks.

I can't remember the last time I sat around and did nothing, and actually enjoyed myself.

"Oh!" Ellie sits up as two people standing on surfboards float by. "Do you want to go paddleboarding? I learned how to do it in Hawaii. It's fun!"

I curl my lip. "Fun? No engine, no pedal, no throttle. How much fun could it be?"

Ellie's eyebrows shoot up. "Oh, well, excuse me, Mr. Adrenaline Junkie." She pushes me playfully. "You can just watch me then."

"It would be my pleasure," I answer as she gets up haughtily, and walks down the beach to the man sitting under a straw umbrella signing out water sports equipment.

"How much fun could it be?" Jett punches me in the arm out of the blue.

"Hey! What the fuck was that for?" I rub my arm.

"You are an idiot," he snaps.

"What? Why?"

"Do *you* know how much fun it could be?" he gets in my face. "*I'll* show you how much fun it can be."

I gape at him silently. "What's got your nuts in a twist?"

"You, you moron." With that, he takes off in the same direction as Ellie.

I glance over at London cluelessly. She just shrugs.

I watch as Jett and Ellie walk their boards out into the water, then quickly and effortlessly mount them by kneeling first then standing. Ellie impresses me by how comfortably she can move in that skimpy little bikini I plan on burning once we get back to the bungalow.

Jett and Ellie push off with their sticks, sending them gliding over the crystal-blue lagoon, both keeping pace with each other. I still don't see how this is supposed to be fun. I want to yawn just watching them. I place my hands behind head, close my eyes, and relax. That's when I hear Ellie scream. My heart nearly jumps out of my throat. I pop up to find Jett on Ellie's surfboard. They're play fighting, Jett attempting to push her off the board and then catching her just before she falls into the water. Ellie is laughing hysterically trying her damnedest to fend him off. I glare, my blood heating, as he puts his hands all over her mostly exposed body.

Okay, he's made his point. Repeatedly. Especially over Ellie's back, sides, and thighs.

"The man sure knows how to send a message," London comments behind her large black sunglasses.

"That he fucking does," I gripe just as he grabs her ass with both hands and presses her against him.

"Jett!" Ellie cries out laughing even harder wiggling in his arms.

That's it. Jett may be my best friend and all, but he is crossing the line. My girl, my body, and only my hands touch it.

I toss my aviators down and storm off into the water, wading out to Jett and Ellie. She doesn't see me coming because her back is turned, but Jett and I lock eyes. Just as I get a foot away, Jett pushes Ellie with some force, knocking her back right into my arms.

"Oh!" she startles when I catch her. "Where did you come from?" she asks laughing.

"I'm always around," I tell her, tightening my grip.

"Good to know."

"You're having too much fun with Jett." I hiss.

"Jett was the only one who wanted to have any fun."

"That's not true. We had fun this morning," I whisper in her ear.

"Yes, we did." Ellie's cheeks burn bright pink.

Jett clears his throat. "My work here is done." He jumps off the board and into the water.

"Work?" Ellie repeats.

"Ignore him, he has Tourette's. Bogus shit just flies out of his mouth."

"Keep telling yourself that, bro," Jett digs.

"Get fucking lost." I turn my full attention to Ellie.

"With pleasure, cranky pants," Jett says as he swims off.

Ellie just looks at me with a strange expression.

"What?"

"I think that was the first conversation I've ever heard the two of you have."

"And?"

"Enlightening."

"Yeah, well, you almost lose your life with a person a few times, you come to appreciate them."

"Oh? That's how you talk to someone you appreciate? And how many times have you almost lost your life?" she says, sidetracked.

"A few." I press my forehead against hers. "That's all you need to know. I'm here, and that's what's important."

"Yes, it is." She kisses me softly on the lips.

I return the kiss, adding a little more pressure before I pull away.

"I'm sorry," I apologize earnestly.

"For what?"

"Blowing you off."

"You didn't blow me off."

"I should have come paddleboarding with you."

"Why? I don't expect us to like all the same things. That's unrealistic."

"Are you a realist, Ellie?" I tease her.

"No, I just have common sense."

"Glad one of us does."

"You admit to your flaws?" she jests.

"My honesty is all I have left."

"Says the black operative."

"You got me there." I curl her in my arms.

"Kayne?"

"Yeah?"

"Did Jett make you jealous?"

"Baby, when it comes to you, everyone makes me jealous."

"You don't have anything to worry about with Jett. We're just friends."

"Yes," I reflect. "I know all about Jett and his *friends.*"

I place Ellie on the board. "Enough talk about Jett. Show me." I climb on after her. She smiles brightly. Happily. It makes my chest hurt. All I've wanted was to see that expression, and I'm such an idiot I didn't realize it'd take something as simple as paddleboarding to put it there.

Once we stand, she positions the stick in the water steadying herself. I firmly place both my hands on her abdomen, pressing her back against my front. “Let’s see your skills, beach bunny.”

ELLIE

I WASN'T EXACTLY UPSET THAT Kayne didn't want to paddleboard, but it was nice to spend time with him doing something other than having sex.

After an hour of quality time, we spent the rest of the day on the beach consuming copious amounts of alcohol and talking about a variety of subjects. School, my family, Mark. Such mundane things to the average person, but so critical to our fragile relationship.

"Why don't we all have dinner?" London asks as Kayne and I stand to leave.

Both Kayne and Jett look at me. No pressure or anything.

"Um, sure." I smile as genuinely as possible. "That sounds fun."

I think.

"Good!" London responds excitedly. "The sushi restaurant here is supposed to be amazing."

"Sushi it is, then." I pull on my cover-up.

"You eat sushi?" Kayne asks me.

"Of course, I do. I'm from New York. It's one of my five food groups."

"Perfect! Mine, too." London's big blue eyes sparkle. I stole glances at her and Jett all throughout the day. They make one beautiful couple. "She could live off the stuff," Jett chimes in.

"Eight o'clock?" I ask.

London nods zealously.

"See you then," I say as Kayne laces our fingers together and leads me away from the beach. I tighten my grip, still getting used to him holding my hand. Still getting used to him holding me period—not ashamed to admit that I like the way it feels.

"Do you eat sushi?" I ask him, realizing I have no idea if he likes raw fish or not. Or if he has any allergies or likes to sleep on the right or left side of the bed. Besides how he takes his coffee and his sexual preferences, I really don't know much about him.

"Yes. If I'm forced to." He grins down at me.

"Oh, no." I stop walking.

"It's fine, Ellie." He tugs me along. "There will be something on the menu that I'll eat. I'm not picky. Trust me. It's a meal, I'll never pass it up."

"Okay. Well, what do you like to eat?"

"Simple stuff. I'm a meat and potatoes guy. I could live off rare steak and cold beer."

"I'll keep that in mind. Is there a preferred dessert I should know about?"

"Cupcakes, of course. And before you ask, my favorite flavor is between your legs." He informs me lewdly.

"Kayne." I smack him playfully right on his washboard abs.

"It's the truth." He hugs me against him as we walk toward the long line of bungalows stretching out over the water. Ours is far off in the distance.

"Where did you grow up?" I ask.

"Detroit."

"Tough city."

"You have no idea."

"Tigers fan?"

"Not in the least."

"Yankees fan?"

"I'm not much into baseball. More a hockey guy. I like confrontation."

"Why does that not surprise me?"

He shrugs, "You've seen my aggressive side?"

"I don't think I even scratched the surface."

"Let's hope you never have to, either."

We stroll a few minutes in comfortable silence, taking in the scenery. It's crazy, but Mount Otemanu almost looks blue this time of day.

"So, now that you have whisked me away, whatever shall you do with me?" I toy as our bungalow comes into view.

"I have dozens of ideas," his voice vibrates with desire. "The question is what do you want to do?"

I bite my lip before I speak. "I want to rent a Jeep and explore. And go snorkeling and learn to kite surf," I say excitedly. "I read about this awesome tour guide who takes you on a private excursion around the island on his boat then makes you dinner on a secluded beach from the fish he catches that day."

"Had some time to do some research, have we?" Kayne asks highly amused.

"Yes! I was googling on the plane. I get excited going to new places!" I say enthusiastically.

"Do you always bounce?" Kayne laughs as I pop up and down on my toes.

"No, not usually," I giggle, planting my feet back on the ground. I'm probably making the biggest ass of myself. I am a severely deprived world traveler. "I only get hyper when you feed me too many sugary drinks."

"Good to know. I'll make sure you stick to vodka and tonics with a lemon from now on."

"You remember?" I stop walking.

"I remember everything, Ellie."

I can't stop myself from smiling.

"Maybe I should just stick to wine. Too many vodka and tonics make me horny."

"And we have a winner." Kayne makes a fist over his head.

I pepper Kayne with more questions as we get closer and closer to the bungalow.

"Favorite color?"

"Green."

"Favorite city?"

"Amsterdam."

"You've been to Holland?"

"I've been all over the world."

"All over?"

"All over," he confirms.

"The Middle East?" I ask cautiously.

"Yes."

"For business or pleasure?"

"Both. Dubai is nice, but I wouldn't recommend Bagram nowadays."

It's sobering to hear him say that.

"Ellie? Did I say something to upset you?" Kayne's face drops.

"Why were you there? Can you tell me?"

"Training exercises mostly. We were dropped in the baddest of the bad and left to find our way back to home station."

"But you don't have to go back, right?"

"No, not at the moment. But there's always a possibility. Does that worry you?"

"Maybe." I chew the inside of my cheek. It makes me think long and hard about what it's like caring for a man who puts himself in danger as his day job.

"Hey. Whatever you're thinking about, please stop. I don't like that look."

"I'm sorry." I blink rapidly out of my silent thoughts. "I'm not thinking about anything."

"Ellie, please. Let's get something straight. You'll never be able to lie to me. No matter how hard you try. So if something is on your mind, just say it."

I'm not sure I'm ready to tell him that putting his life in danger terrifies me. That after only spending one day together, I'm already getting attached. Or that old feelings are resurfacing faster than I expected. No, I'm not ready to tell him any of that yet, because I'm just coming to terms with it myself.

"It's just scary, that's all."

"What's scary?"

"The thought of you being in a place that's so dangerous."

"You get used to it after a while." He starts ushering me along.

"How about we sit down with Matias and set up some excursions. This vacation is all about fun, and I think we can both use a huge dose of that." He does a good job of spinning the topic of conversation.

"Agreed," I relent, wrapping my arms around his waist and squeezing tightly. A healthy dose of fun is exactly what I need. We walk arm in arm until we reach our butler's office, then spend over an hour plotting out activities for the next week.

"I AM SO READY FOR a shower." I head straight for the bathroom once we get back to the bungalow.

"Sounds like a plan to me." Kayne rips off his shirt and follows close behind me.

"I don't remember inviting you." I coquettishly look over my shoulder at him.

"I didn't think I needed an invitation." Kayne wraps his arms around me and kisses my cheek. It's a sexy, lust-fueled gesture.

"What if I said no?"

"I would respect that, and then just stand here and watch you lather up all my favorite parts of your body. I enjoy watching you touch yourself just as much as I enjoy touching you." He slides my bathing suit top over my head.

"Oh, really?"

"Yup." My bottoms are gone a second later.

He drops my bikini into the sink.

"I'm never going to see that again, am I?" I ask him.

"Nope. Now get in the shower." He taps me lightly on the ass.

I step into the cream-colored stone stall with Kayne right behind me.

"Stay there," he orders. Mr. Bossy is never far away.

With my back to him, I'm suddenly very aware of what can happen in situations like these. I brace myself for his hands. Not in a bad way, but in a domineering, I'm going to take you right here right now and you have nothing to say about it way. But Kayne surprises me. Instead of going straight for the kill like I'm expecting, he starts to wash my hair. Massaging my scalp in such a way it almost doesn't feel like him. Or does it? I remember those times. Those faint moments when he touched me with such tenderness it actually felt like he loved me. Back then, I couldn't decipher, but now his intentions are very clear.

"How does that feel?"

"So good." I close my eyes and get lost in the ministrations of his fingers.

"It's longer."

"What's longer?"

"Your hair. It's lighter and longer. I like it."

"More of it for you to pull," I tease.

"That's not what I was getting at." He tugs gently.

"You couldn't resist."

"You planted the seed. I was trying to be nice."

"And you are," I moan as he presses harder.

"Good to know I can elicit sounds from you the *nice* way."

"It's a pleasant surprise for me, too."

"I'm hoping to surprise you a lot during this vacation." He spins me around and tips my head back to rinse out the soap.

"I'm keeping an open mind," I speak with my eyes closed.

"I'm very thankful for that." He drops a kiss on my lips, and then starts to lather my body, making sure he covers every curve.

I glance up at him through my wet eyelashes, darting my eyes away shyly once they meet his.

"Ask, Ellie." Kayne brushes over my breasts, his hands sliding easily from the soap.

"How did you know?"

"I'm trained to read people, and I've made it my business to read you like a book."

"What's my tell?" I put my hand on my hip. I didn't think I was that easy to pick apart.

"It's your eyes. They're too inquisitive, especially when something is on your mind. So ask me whatever you want to know. I'll answer as honestly as I can."

"Your honest side is refreshing." I run my fingertips over his stomach, tracing the words etched on his ribs. *A certain kind of darkness is needed to see the stars.*

"I told you, I don't want to keep anything from you. I only kept secrets for a reason. A very important reason," he stipulates.

"I know."

"Do you?" He lifts my chin with his finger.

"Yes. Now, I do."

"Good. So ask already."

I chew on my lip, then fire away. "What happened to the women who worked for you?"

"They were compensated for their services and sent on their way."

"Sent where?"

"Wherever they wanted to go," he says breezily. "Some stayed in the life. Some started fresh. I'm not exactly sure what happened to each and every one of them, but I do know they're safe and doing what they want."

"Did you sleep with all of them?"

Kayne freezes with his hands on my backside.

"No, Ellie, I didn't."

"How many then?"

"Does it really matter?" he questions stiffly. "You're the only one I want to sleep with now."

"I want to know. How many women have you been with?"

Kayne huffs, staring at me intensely. "Seven women."

"Seven? That's it?" I can't hide the surprise in my voice.

"You were expecting a higher number?"

"Honestly, yes."

"Why?"

"Because . . ."

"Because why?" he presses

"Because . . . you're you."

"What does that mean?" He's clearly uncomfortable now.

"You know exactly what that means."

"No, I don't." His eyes narrow.

"Yes, you do. Don't play dumb."

"Are you saying you like the way I touch you?" His mood morphs from touchy to feely. He can still give me whiplash.

"I'm saying you are very skilled with your body. That's all."

"So, you do like the way I touch you?" he asks again with a shameless grin, and I come to realize he hides behind sex when he feels insecure.

"I liked it when you were massaging my scalp."

"Are you dancing around my question on purpose?" He squeezes my ass.

"Maybe."

"Maybe I'll show you what my body can really do."

"I think I already have an idea." I grab the bottle of soap and squirt some into my hands. "My turn."

"Be my guest."

I rub Kayne's chest, working a thick lather over his skin, and then moving my hands down his stomach.

"You can go lower if you want." He releases my waist and takes a small step back.

"I'm happy right where I am." I circle my hands over his rock-hard abs, which incidentally aren't the only thing that's rock-hard on him at the moment.

"Don't you want to know how many men I've been with?" I ask as I wash him.

"No," he scoffs. "As far as I'm concerned, I'm the only man you've ever been with."

That makes me laugh.

"Why so few?" I keep probing.

Kayne's muscles tense under my fingertips. I look up into his eyes and see hesitation there.

"Is there something I should know?" I query.

"No."

"You sure?"

"Yes. Now who's trying to read who?" His voice is firm. Not threatening, just cautious. There is definitely a side of him he doesn't want to show.

"Jett told me that trusting women is a hard limit for you," I state with sensitivity.

"And when did he tell you that?" His eyes smolder.

"Last night."

"Oh, really?"

"Yes. I was upset and confused. He was just trying to help."

"Right," he sneers.

"You once said that you wanted me to understand you."

Kayne sighs, then runs his hands down my face and kisses me lightly. "I know," he replies pained. It nearly breaks my heart. "And I really want you to."

"So tell me why so few women."

Steam clouds around us as Kayne stares down at me. He wavers before answering.

"I need to feel comfortable with a woman in order to have sex with her."

"Comfortable? Like in a relationship?"

"No. No relationships. That was the last thing I wanted. I had a few girls on retainer who I slept with. Sex with no strings. Simpler that way."

"And no emotion," I frown.

"Emotion was expendable at the time."

"And now?"

"Now it's essential." He swipes his thumb across my cheek. It feels like it leaves a trail of fire in its wake.

"Did you keep those women on retainer while we were apart?" I ask without looking at him, circling my hands over his chest.

"No. I haven't been with anyone since you."

My eyes fly to his. I know they're as wide as saucers. It's been a year.

"It's true. I could break a steel plate with my forearm. You were, and are, the only person I want," he says resolutely. The statement makes my heart flutter.

"Why me?" I ask the burning question.

Kayne shrugs, pulling me into his body. "I don't know why exactly. You never intimidated me. You were always happy and smiling, and when you looked at me, it wasn't anything but warm."

"Oh, I was warm all right," I laugh. "I overheated every time I saw you."

"I guess I liked it." He leans in to kiss me.

"How old were you when you lost your virginity?" I ask right before his lips touch mine.

"What does it matter?"

"Just another piece of the puzzle." I rub up against his erection in an attempt to relax him.

Kayne closes his eyes and moans softly.

"Nineteen. I was nineteen when I lost it," he answers

absentmindedly, getting lost in the friction of our bodies.

"Did you love her?"

"No. I have never been interested in love until I met you. If it wasn't for Jett, I might still be a virgin."

"Did he introduce the two of you or something?"

Kayne grabs hold of my waist and stops all movements. He's breathing hard, his eyes are dilated, and water is spilling down his face.

"It's not like that. Jett was there with me, Ellie. We were on leave, and since I didn't have any place to go, I went home to California with him. I don't know if Jett ever told you the business his family runs or who his mother is—"

"He told me," I interrupt him.

That last night at Mansion I pried Jett for information and he gave it to me, divulging his mother is a Madame, and why he grew up around a lot of women.

"So you know what I'm talking about?" Kayne asks, and I nod. "It's not like I got there, and he threw me into a bedroom with a random girl. It's like he handpicked her specifically for me. She spent a few days warming up to me, getting to know me, and then one night we all went out and got drunk. Jett instigated the whole thing. Like he knew I wouldn't go through with it unless I had moral support. He was probably right. So we did it. All three of us. Together."

"She became my first submissive, but I never loved her. And she never loved me, either. But you I love, whether you're submissive or not."

"You sure about that?" I test him.

"Absolutely, one-hundred-percent." With that, he pins me against the wall and crushes his lips against mine. The kiss nearly steals the air right out of my lungs.

"I want things to be different with you." He rubs his nose against my cheek.

"Different how?" I press my chest against his as my core becomes as hot as the running water.

"I'll show you." He closes the distance between our mouths, and I brace for another soul shattering connection, but Kayne switches gears and kisses me unlike any way he has ever kissed me before—passionately, affectionately, devotedly, reverently—every word that could possibly describe an all-consuming, unstoppable love. And I know it's too fast, too soon, but the weight of his affection overwhelms me to the point I can no longer think, or see, or even breathe. So I just kiss him back, pouring whatever amount of emotion I'm capable of giving him at the moment into the embrace.

Kayne lifts me off the floor, forcing my legs around his hips as he steps under the steaming spray of water, rinsing off whatever suds are left on us. Then he turns the shower off. We never break our kiss as he steps out of the stall and walks into the bedroom, the two of us dripping wet.

Not even bothering with a towel, he lays me down on the bed, trapping my body beneath his.

"Hold onto me. Whatever you do, don't let go." He positions his erection between my legs, the head pushing at my entrance gently. He's not even inside me, and I'm already responding, flooding with desire as the tip of his cock slides easily between my wet folds.

Then, in one fluid motion, he sinks into me so perfectly slow that I nearly split in two.

"Oh, God." I dig my face into his neck as my arms and legs and pussy all tighten painfully around him.

"Ellie," he moans, nudging my cheek with his nose coaxing me to look up at him. He drops kisses on my lips over and over as he rocks in and out of me.

"You feel so good." Kayne dips his tongue into my mouth, pressing his body harder against mine, his pelvis repeatedly brushing over my throbbing clit as our wet bodies slide easily against each other from the thin residue of soap still left on our skin.

"So do you." I get lost in the feel of him, the way his long, measured thrusts stretch and fill me, producing not only a physical response but an emotional one. My heart and pussy constrict at the same time as the orgasm inside me grows fast and furiously, threatening to unleash.

"You're going to make me come." I squirm breathless underneath him, unable to control it.

"Not yet, Ellie. Hold onto it." He hugs me tighter and thrusts deeper. My body spasms. "You feel too fucking good."

But I can't hold on, because he feels the exact same way, so thick and hard and overpowering.

"Oh God, oh God, oh God." I chant against his neck without a prayer. "Kayne!" My orgasm steamrolls me, and I tumble over the edge, my clit aching and muscles contracting violently.

A few moments later, at the tail end of my internal frenzy, Kayne grabs my thigh with one hand and slams into me, groaning in what sounds like unbearable pleasure.

He collapses on top of me once his orgasm subsides, wrapping me in his arms and breathing heavily.

"I love you." The words flow out in a whisper as he hugs me tightly. I flutter my eyes open and stare up at the thin white fabric covering the canopy bed, a whirlwind of emotions running through me.

"I know," I kiss the side of his face. It's the only response I have. I'm not ready to go there. He's so sure about how he feels. And although I want to be here, with him, I'm still coming to terms with what I want and how much I can give.

"Good, always remember that." He kisses my forehead and then rolls off me, pulling me into his side so I am snuggled in the crook of his arm. I lay my head on his chest and listen to his heartbeat. It's such a strong, soothing sound, almost hypnotic. I put my hand next to my ear to feel it.

"It beats because of you."

"What?"

"It never beat until I met you." He puts his hand over mine.

"I find that hard to believe."

"It's true. I never had a reason to live until you, Ellie."

I blush and hide my face. How can he be so open? I thought men were supposed to be closed off and devoid of all emotion?

"Did I say something to upset you?"

"No," I snuggle closer to him, "you're just making it very hard to resist you."

"Baby, that's the idea." He kisses my head and laughs.

I doze off warm and content in Kayne's arms as the last bit of light fades away from the day.

"HEY, SLEEPYHEAD," KAYNE SHAKES ME lightly. "We're going to be late for dinner."

I crack open my eyes to find him showered and dressed. He smells good, like shaving cream. "I let you sleep as long as I could."

"Do we have to go?" I stretch sleepily.

"Yes. We promised." It sounds like there's no getting out of it.

"Fine." If my stomach wasn't rumbling, I would throw the covers over my head and protest.

"Up you go, sleeping beauty." Kayne picks me up off the bed and I go limp in his arms. "Funny," he mocks. "Are you always such a lazy riser?"

"No. Only when I'm interrupted from such a comfortable sleep." He carries me into the bathroom.

"A hot bath should help wake you up." I look down to see the tub full of water and overflowing with bubbles.

I look up and smile at him. "Now you're just sucking up."

"Maybe a little." He grins, his blue eyes shining.

I kiss him on the cheek, his skin smooth against my lips. He presses his face into the kiss and moans softly. Not a 'you're making me hot' kind of moan. An 'I love that gesture' kind of moan. It makes me all warm and tingly inside.

"We have to hurry." Kayne places me on my feet in the tub. "Ten minutes enough time to soak?"

"Yes." I drop down into the water, the bubbles covering up my body. "I'm surprised you're letting me bathe alone."

"I figured you might want some time to yourself. Am I wrong?"

"Yes and no," I answer, leaving it at that. "I'll be out in a few."

Kayne nods then walks out, closing the door behind him. I lean against the edge of tub and gaze out the picture window into the dark. I daydream about this afternoon. The way Kayne touched me, the things he said. *"I love you."* It's never been like that between us before. It felt like he was trying to give me everything. Every part of him. It's overwhelming in a good and bad way. I don't want to rush into anything, and I don't want to feel too much, but Kayne is a force to be reckoned with; especially when it comes to sex, love, even emotion.

"Ellie?" Kayne knocks.

"Times up?" I answer.

"For now."

I climb out of the tub and dry off. I walk out of the bathroom and head for my bedroom, thinking about what I should wear.

"Where are you going?" Kayne asks from the chair in the corner of the room. He's holding his phone, regarding me smugly.

"To get dressed. My clothes are in the other room."

"Not anymore." He nods his head toward the door behind him.

I walk cautiously by him and through the doorway. I'll be damned, he moved me in. Everything I stuffed into my suitcase is now hanging on one side of the closet, opposite his clothes, which are situated just as neatly.

"Been busy have you?" I ask as he stands behind me.

"I didn't think you'd mind." He kisses my bare shoulder.

"I don't, but only because I hate unpacking."

"See? I'm good for something."

"You're good for a few things. Like telling me where you hid my underwear." I walk into the closet. It's as big as the bathroom in my apartment.

Kayne follows me in and pulls open a drawer.

"Underwear and bras." He opens the next one down. "Shirts." And then the last, grazing my arm with his lips as he goes. "Bathing suits."

"Are you always so organized?" I sigh from the heat of his mouth.

"Yes. Repercussion of military life. I'm always on time, too. So get dressed," he hisses in my ear playfully then leaves.

Fine then.

I dress quickly in a black miniskirt and midriff top with a flowy sheer overlay stitched with a funky black, white, and peach pattern. It was an impulse buy, but I like it. Kayne will hate it. I don't regret the rash purchase one bit. I throw my damp hair into a high bun and attempt some makeup. Lastly, I rub some shimmery lotion on my arms and legs to moisturize and highlight my tanned skin.

I walk out of the bedroom exactly twenty minutes later and Kayne's jaw drops.

"Like my outfit?" I spin.

"No."

I laugh. Didn't think so.

"Not a patterns guy?" I curl my lip.

He growls. "No, I'm not a 'my girlfriend's skirt is so short she's flashing the world her ass' kind of guy."

"Hmm," I muse. "I must have missed the conversation where we established labels."

He glares at me.

"Are we going? I know how much you hate to be late." I walk out of the bedroom.

"Brat," he snaps from behind me.

I smirk devilishly and saunter out the front door. I can actually feel the frustration radiating from Kayne's body. It's increasing the island's already tropical temperature. I love it.

After a silent ride with a brooding Kayne, we make it to the restaurant right on time. He steps out first then escorts me. Matias smiles at us. I smile back, Kayne just grimaces.

"Have a nice evening," he says jovially and drives away. Apparently, I'm not the only one amused by Kayne's annoyance.

I grab his hand and bat my eyelashes at him. "Are you going to be pissy all night?"

"Maybe," he answers flatly.

This evening should be fun, sitting across from my bisexual one-night stand trying to make nice, while my ex-slave owner acts like a petulant child beside me. Awesome.

I heave a breath and start walking for the door, but am stopped abruptly by Kayne's statue-like stance. He yanks me into his chest and locks me against him with one arm.

"I hate that outfit," he growls. "I hate that I have to figure out a way to walk in front of you and behind you all at the same time while resisting the urge to stab out every single eye that ogles you. How's that for honesty?"

"You did say you didn't want to keep anything from me." I inhale sharply as he tightens his hold.

"You look so hot my cock is on fire," he whispers in my ear while people pass by us. "I don't want you making any other man feel that way." He slips his finger between my legs and strokes my clit.

"Kayne!" I gasp, grabbing his wrist. "We're in public."

"I know." He grabs my ass. "Mine."

I look up at him with flushed cheeks and a racing heart. For a fleeting second, he holds my stare.

"Yours or not, you still don't get to tell me what to wear."

"We'll see." He releases me, and I stumble a little. Jerk still has the power to immobilize me. "You're missing something."

"I'm wearing underwear," I huff.

He smiles, trying desperately to contain his composure. "That's not what I meant."

"Oh. What did you mean?" I pull down the hem of my skirt. Kayne reaches into his pocket and pulls something out. He opens his hand and inside are a small pair of stud earrings.

I look up at him. "For me?"

"Well, I don't have my ears pierced, and I think they might clash with this shirt."

"You sound like Jett now." I take the earrings after he offers them to me. They're so different. Not a common pair of studs. These look like tiny balls of tangled platinum yarn. Sort of appropriate considering that's how my insides felt when I got here.

"The jeweler called them love knots," he says aloof, almost as if he's embarrassed. "I took a chance. Jett suggested diamonds."

"I love them," I say as I put them on. "How do they look?"

"Perfect."

"Thank you. They're a very thoughtful gift," I say, touching my earlobe.

"You're welcome." He kisses me softly on the lips and my emotions soar. It's one thing for a man to buy you jewelry; it's something entirely different when he puts thought and effort into the meaning. It makes me love them even more.

I catch a quick glimpse of my new earrings in the reflection of the door. They shine brightly in the light.

Kayne pushes me slightly in front of him as we walk through the restaurant, his arm placed firmly around my waist. I think he's attempting to protect his assets. Or what he thinks are his assets.

That's still to be determined.

Jett and London are already at the bar waiting for us. The room is dimly lit with amber up-lighting and gold accents. Very posh. Feels like New York, and I love it.

Jett stands and hugs me as soon as I'm in arm's reach.

"Nice earrings," he murmurs in my ear.

"How did you know? Kayne show you?"

"Nope. A girl only smiles the way you are when she receives something extra special. Looks good on you."

"What? The earrings or the smile?"

"Both."

"Alright," Kayne nearly rips me out of Jett's arms. "What are you two going for, the world record for longest hug?"

I roll my eyes at him. Dramatic much?

"Just being friendly," Jett responds.

"Uh-huh," Kayne returns flippantly.

"Hey, Ellie." London chirps from her chair while she sips on a red drink in a martini glass. She's dressed very similar to me, short skirt, high heels, and skimpy light pink top made of a satiny material. The most notable difference is she's gorgeous on a whole other level with her long red hair, big breasts, and sparkling blue eyes. It's official. She and Jett make one seriously intimidating couple.

"Hey, London." I try to smile naturally, but I'm still a little uncomfortable around her. I keep picturing her naked, wearing a collar, and feeling me up. I glance at Kayne; I wonder if that's what he sees when he looks at us.

Is it suddenly hot in here?

"Ellie?" Kayne gives me a strange look. I blush.

"I need to use the restroom," I announce spontaneously.

"Everything okay?" he asks worried.

"Fine."

"Well, our table is ready," Jett tells me. "Do you want us to wait for you?"

"No. I'll find you. The place isn't very big." I begin to step away.

"You sure?" Kayne presses.

"Positive."

"You know what?" London puts her drink down. "I'll come with you." She hops off her seat and smiles. "We can use some girl time." She hooks her arm into mine, and both Jett and Kayne's eyes glaze over. Maybe she should have used a different term.

London leads me away from the two drooling men. If they weren't picturing us together before, they definitely are now.

We walk into the bathroom still arm and arm just as an older woman exits. She eyes us judgmentally as she passes by. Is it that obvious something conspired between us? Or am I just being paranoid. It feels like there is a huge flashing sign hovering over our heads that reads 'We Had Sex.'

The bathroom is small with only two stalls, wooden doors, and a marble vanity with double sinks. London lets go of my arm and settles her hip on the sink, standing closer to me than a normal girlfriend would.

"I'm glad we have a second alone. I've really wanted to talk to you," she begins.

"About what?"

"Look, Ellie," she sighs. "I don't want things to be weird between us because of what happened. I was only doing my job." London bites down on her bottom lip.

I frown. Am I the only one who finds this conversation totally fucked up?

"Oh, no, please don't think I didn't enjoy it." She puts her hand on my arm reassuringly. "That night was one of the hottest of my life."

I can't lie—mine, too.

"Jett still gets upset that he missed it."

"What?"

"Yeah, he wishes he was there," she smirks.

"Were you two together when . . . *we were together?*" I clear my throat.

"No, not exactly. It was complicated. After everything happened, I didn't think I was ever going to see him again. Boy, was I wrong."

"I didn't think I was ever going to see either of them again. Or you." I laugh.

"Well, I'm glad you're here. Kayne was so miserable for such a long time. I think if you didn't show up, it would have destroyed him. Like, literally killed him."

"Well, I'm here, and we're working on things."

"Good. He really is a good man."

"Did you know who Kayne and Jett really were?"

"Nope, no idea. Not until after. Until Jett explained everything to me."

"Nice to know I wasn't the only one in the dark."

London shakes her head. "Kayne and Jett are good at keeping secrets."

"That's part of what scares me."

"It shouldn't. I've never felt safer than I do with Jett. I really love him, Ellie. And Kayne really loves you. They're a package deal. So please can we try and be friends?" she implores me.

"I say go for it," a voice echoes through the small bathroom, and then a toilet flushes. London and I look at each other with wide eyes as an elderly woman emerges from one of the privacy stalls.

"I don't know which one of you was talking, but very sincere." A short, gray-haired woman in a printed dress walks out and nonchalantly washes her hands. "I didn't mean to eavesdrop, but you were entertaining me." She smiles kindly.

London and I just stare at her dumbfounded.

"Have a good evening." She grins, thoroughly amused, and then leaves.

Once she's gone, London and I look at each other and immediately burst out laughing.

"We would be terrible spies!" I double over as the sound of our cackles fills the room.

I LOST MY VIRGINITY TODAY.

Yes, I may have slept with other women, but for the first time, I didn't bind one or spank one or bring one to tears. Instead, I just poured my entire heart and soul into loving another human being. So, as far as I'm concerned, today is the day I officially lost my virginity.

I'll never regret it was with Ellie, either; even if this thing between us doesn't work out, which I pray to God that it does. She is the only one who deserves to own that part of me. She's the only one I want to own it.

"Have you heard anything else from our friend visiting the Aloha State?" I ask Jett as casually as if asking for the time.

"Quiet as a mouse. Juice has ears to the ground. If he's up to something, we'll know."

"Shit." My jaw ticks. Twelve months without an inkling of retribution and suddenly this guy surfaces out of the blue. "It doesn't feel right."

"Well, there's no sense making waves if we don't have to."

"The last thing I want is to be caught off guard." I glare at Jett sternly. "Like last time."

"No one wants that." Jett pulls on the collar of his light-blue dress shirt, scanning the restaurant. "Just let Juice and Endeavor handle it for now. You have more important things to worry about," he says as Ellie and London approach, arm in arm, falling all over each other, laughing. I shoot Jett a questioning look. He just shrugs. "That bathroom must have magic toilet paper or something," he mutters under his breath.

"Apparently." Considering Ellie was as stiff as a board when she left with London a few minutes ago, and now they look like best friends. We both stand when the girls reach the table.

"Is there an inside joke you want to let us in on?" Jett asks London, which seems to make her and Ellie giggle harder.

"Nope." She tries to compose herself by turning away. Ellie just looks up at me smiling brightly, her cheeks pink and eyes soft.

"What's that smile for?" I ask.

"No reason. Just because," she says sweetly.

I glance at Jett once more. He just smirks. Alrighty then, magic toilet paper it is.

"What do you like, Ellie? London asks fanning herself with the menu. She's finally pulled herself together.

"Everything. I eat everything," she informs her.

"Except sesame seeds," I chime in.

Ellie whips her head up at me. "How did you know I was allergic to sesame seeds?"

I shrug. "I know everything I need to know about you."

"Oh really?"

"Mmm hmm." I lean in close to her, getting a whiff of her sweet smelling perfume. "Elizabeth Anne Stevens, born August twenty-eighth to Alec and Monica Stevens. Sister Tara, three years younger. You attended Long Island City High School in Queens. You ran track, which explains why you're so damn fast." I smile from the memory of chasing Ellie down the hall at Mansion, and being surprised at how quick she was. "You also graduated with honors. Shortly after that, you were hired at Expo, a small but thriving import/export company owned and operated by Mark J. Atkins, where you quickly moved up the ranks from secretary to personal assistant. Your favorite color is purple, your blood type is O, and your favorite cupcake flavor is a toss-up between red velvet and lemon drop." I flash her a haughty grin.

Ellie's eyes are as wide as green soda bottles by the time I finish speaking.

"Kayne, that's creepy."

"It's my job to know things, Ellie."

"Still. Creepy."

"Creepy enough to scare you away?"

"No, although I am curious, Super Stalker Extraordinaire. You know I'm allergic to sesame seeds, but do you know how I found out?" Ellie asks loud enough for everyone at the table to hear.

"Um . . ."

"Yeah, do ya?" Jett repeats annoyingly.

"No," I snap at him.

Ellie giggles. "Mark."

"Mark?" London asks.

"My old boss in New York."

"And what does Mark have to do with it?" I ask.

"Well, when I started working for him, I was eighteen, right out of high school, and pretty green when it came to, well, mostly everything. Especially fancy dinners. So Mark, being Mark, wanted to broaden my horizons, starting with sushi." Ellie chuckles to herself.

"So what happened?" Jett inquires.

"He ordered some seared ahi tuna, and did nothing but rave about how much I was going to love it. I took about three bites before my face started to blow up." She uses her hands to emulate the swelling. "Mark did nothing but freak out while I went into anaphylactic shock. My throat closed, and I came close to passing out. That's when he pulled out his EpiPen from his man purse and stabbed me with it." She mocks her story by pretending to stab herself in the neck and laugh. "He even screamed like a woman when he did it."

"What kind of man screams like a woman?" London says, giggling along with Ellie's infectious energy.

This makes Ellie laugh harder. "A flaming gay one with drama written all over him," she explains. "He had a full-on panic attack right afterward because he thought he almost killed me. The waiters had to bring him a brown bag to breathe into."

The story has the table chuckling so long we don't even notice the waiter standing over us until he clears his throat. Loudly.

After we order enough sushi to feed a small army, Ellie continues to captivate everyone at the table with her charm and spirited personality. She tells us all about her sister and parents, and what it was like growing up in New York. She recounts the story of when we first met and how she spilled hot coffee in my lap. Also, how she attended the prom with two black eyes because her track coach made her run hurdles, even though she begged him not to because she always fell.

By time we get the check, my love for Ellie has grown leaps and bounds. As if that was even possible. I memorize the way her green eyes sparkle and face lights up when she laughs. How she talks with her hands when she gets into a story and how attentive she is to everyone at the table, London included. The tension between them seems to have completely dissipated as they whisper to each other and gang up on Jett and me to do more Saki bombs.

All I keep thinking about is that picture pinned up on Ellie's old desk of her and Mark on St. Patrick's Day, and how much I wanted to know that girl. Well, tonight I think I'm finally getting my first glimpse. What did Mark call her once? Oh yeah, magic glitter in high heels. I'm starting to see why. She's enchanting.

After a memorable meal and way too many shots, Jett, London, Ellie and I end up closing down the restaurant. They were nearly kicking out our rowdy bunch.

After some quick goodbyes and promises to meet up tomorrow, we each go our separate ways. I hail a ride for us back to our bungalow as Jett and London walk off to theirs. I'm assuming. You never know with Jett, though.

"Did you have fun tonight?" I run my nose up Ellie's neck once we're in the golf cart.

"Yes." She sighs as she wraps her arms around my neck and pulls me close. We have a hard time keeping our hands and lips off each other as we're chauffeured through the resort. I hear the driver chuckle to himself as we nearly give him a show.

"Have a good evening," the young man says, highly entertained, as we climb out of the cart a hot, drunken mess.

"We will." I grin roguishly at him as Ellie and I stumble to the front door. Once inside, we nearly take a tumble as Ellie rips off her shoes and tries to kiss me all at the same time.

"Let's go skinny dipping." She pulls me through the living room, driving her tongue into my mouth.

Now what stupid man would say no to that?

By the time we make it out to the deck, we're nothing but hungry mouths, hot bodies, and frenzied hands. I turn Ellie in my arms and press her back to my front, devouring her neck and groping her breasts. I may have just had dinner, but I am still a starving man. I pull the straps of her shirt down her arms to expose her chest, clutching and massaging and stroking her nipples until they are hard little pebbles beneath my fingertips. She moans freely, rubbing herself against my now throbbing cock. It makes me crazy, makes me need her, makes me delirious with lust.

"Bend over," I order her, as we stand a few feet away from the pool. She bends, grabbing onto the metal railing that rings around the entire sundeck.

I can hardly breathe as I run my palms along the back of her smooth thighs and up over her ass. Her clingy skirt bunches around her waist as I work my hands over her two perfect little round cheeks.

God, how I love Ellie's ass. The beast swings his spiked tail against the door of its cage, demanding to be set free as I press and knead her behind over the delicate lace underwear that barely covers her bottom. I ignore the snarling monster, and the overwhelming urge to spank her as I peel her panties down to her thighs.

Ellie glances back at me, her eyes hooded and lips parted, like she's just daring me to touch her. But I have other ideas. I lean over and trap her face, covering her mouth with mine. I thrust my tongue and my hips at the same time, as I subdue her against my body. Ellie kisses me back with such intensity it takes me by surprise and eggs me on all at the same time.

"Touch yourself, Ellie."

I don't know if it's the alcohol or the need or just my kinky desires that spurs the request, but I run with it, hoping I'm not pushing her too far too fast. "Touch yourself, baby, and get wet for me," I rasp in her ear. Ellie pants loudly as she slowly removes one of her hands from the railing and places it between her legs. "That's it."

She closes her eyes and nuzzles her nose against my jaw as she starts to massage herself. I hold onto her tight, digging my cock into her ass as tiny pleasured sounds begin escaping from her throat.

"Feel good?"

"Yes."

"Did you ever touch yourself when we were apart? Did you ever finger your sweet little pussy and think of me?" I ask, tightening my grip on her face.

She inhales and exhales hard.

"Did you?" I urge.

"Yes," she expels the word with a huff, still rubbing herself. "I thought about you all the time. I couldn't get you out of my head."

"Me, too." I graze my nose against hers. "I pictured you every time. I thought about the first time I made you touch yourself. How fucking hot you looked with my cock inside you rubbing your clit. Remember that?

"I could never forget," she chokes out, stroking herself harder, pressing up against my pulsing erection.

"You came so fucking hard; I can still feel how tight you squeezed me."

"You tortured me," she moans.

"You liked it," I counter. "I loved it. Will you show me again? Will you let me watch you make yourself come?"

Ellie is nearly falling apart by the time she forces out her answer. "Yes."

"Good girl." I release her and spin her around, stripping her of all her clothes in a second flat. "Show me." I pin her hips against the railing.

With deep breaths, Ellie runs her hand down her stomach until she reaches her wet folds. She spreads herself wide, exposing the engorged pink flesh of her clit, and begins to rub in slow circles as if she knows just how it's going to affect me.

"Feel good?" I can barely speak; she looks so fucking hot completely naked, touching herself under the moonlight.

"Yes, but I'm missing something." She looks up into my eyes, the blazing lust evident.

"Need me, baby?" I lift one corner of my mouth wickedly.

"Need and want." She slips one finger inside her pussy, and I become an unhinged man.

"Fuck, Ellie." I crush my lips against hers as I tear off my pants.

Once out of the way, I grab one of her thighs and hook it around mine, so her legs are wide and my view is unobstructed.

"Keep touching yourself." I sink inside her half way and am bathed in her scorching wet heat. "So good."

Ellie moans as she strokes and massages herself into a frantic state with me partly buried inside her.

"Kayne, more," she pleads, her voice elevating, her hips jerking.

"No, baby that's all of me you get. You have to make yourself come first."

She groans in agony. "Please."

"No," I deny her as her face contorts, tormented with pleasure, just tempting me to slam inside her and shatter on the spot. "Keep going."

"Oh God!" She moans loudly as her sweltering little pussy sucks on the tip of my cock vigorously. "I'm going to come." She fists her free hand in my shirt just as the tremors begin and fluid drips down my shaft.

I thrust inside her at that exact moment and fuck her straight through her orgasm as she screams out into the dark night.

"Fuck, fuck!" I fight off my own orgasm until she's depleted and limp, then I lift her right off the ground and impale her onto my throbbing cock, once, twice, three times, until I explode inside the tightest, wettest, most heavenly pussy on the face of the Earth.

Still shaky from the aftershocks, I sink to the floor with Ellie wrapped around me, the both of us sucking in air like it's going out of style.

I hold Ellie in my arms as she snuggles against me with a million stars twinkling over our heads.

"Too much too fast?" I exhale breathless, suddenly worried.

She shakes her head. "If I didn't want to, I would have said no."

I tilt her head up so I can look at her.

"You can always say no."

She kisses me lightly, "I know."

"Good."

"Can we still go skinny dipping?"

"Sure," I chuckle.

"Good." She nestles herself back up against me. "It will be nice to see you naked and wet for a change."

"Ellie." I laugh, hugging her tight.

I may never, ever let go.

I'M COLD. IT FEELS LIKE my heart has stopped pumping blood through my body. I roll over to reach for Ellie, but she's not there. I snap open my eyes and sit up. It's still dark out. I get out of bed and search the bungalow, tearing through the living room, bathroom, and sundeck like a madman. I check upstairs as well before my craziness gets the best of me, and I open the front door.

She's gone.

A streak of dread runs through me. Did she just leave? I check the closet. All her things are still exactly where I put them.

Did someone take her? Paranoia flares.

I storm into the bedroom and swipe my phone off the end table. Just as I'm about to dial Jett, I hear the front door open and shut. It feels like all the organs inside me sag in relief when Ellie walks into the bedroom.

"You're up," she says surprised, wearing tight black shorts and one of my white wife beaters.

"Yeah. Apparently, so are you," I snap sharply. "Where were you?" I don't mean to bite her head off, but she just fucking left. In the middle of the night. Without telling me. Does she have any idea how neurotic I can be?

Of course she doesn't. You haven't shown her your self-deprecating, mistrusting, shithead side yet that's wracked with mommy issues.

"I went for a walk," she wraps her arms around herself.

"In the dark?"

Ellie nods.

"By yourself?"

Ellie bites her lip. "I wasn't exactly alone."

"You were with someone?" I raise my eyebrows about to blow.

She nods again.

"London?"

She shakes her head.

"Jett?" I try again.

"Yes."

"Why?"

"I needed to talk." Her smoky-green eyes cut through me in the darkness.

"To Jett?"

"*With* Jett," she corrects.

"About what?"

Ellie shrugs. She's being difficult, and I don't like it.

"Stuff."

"Stuff?"

"Stuff," she repeats. Her and her fucking monosyllables.

"Wanna tell me what kind of stuff?"

"No." She fidgets with her fingers.

What!?!

"Is everything okay?" I ask, on the brink of a nervous breakdown.

"Yes."

"Did I do something to upset you?" I ask, trying not to snap the thin strand of composure keeping me together. I'm sure losing my shit won't encourage her to talk.

"No." Her face drops. "Why would you think that?"

"Because you snuck out of bed in the middle of the night to go see my best friend!"

"He's my friend, too," she asserts.

"And you needed to talk to him?"

"Yes."

"Why can't you talk to me?" I have always had this issue with Jett and Ellie. I want to be the one she talks to and confides in. The one she trusts. It's apparent I still have a lot of work to do before that happens.

Ellie takes a cautious step closer to me. "I didn't want to wake you. And I didn't mean to upset you." She takes another step, then another.

"Well, you did wake me. It's like my body knew you weren't there. I didn't like that feeling, Ellie, and I didn't like not knowing where you were."

"I'm sorry." She's standing in front of me now looking apologetic, and sexy and utterly irresistible in my ribbed undershirt.

"You're forgiven." I pull her against me, and she fastens her arms around my neck. *Sucker.*

"You can talk to me, Ellie. You can tell me anything. I'll listen."

She hugs me tighter. "I know."

Then why did you have to turn to Jett?

"I know I'm not perfect and I'm going to make mistakes. I've never done this before," I babble nervously, as I hug her. "But I'm learning."

"We're both learning, okay?" Her words console me.

I nod silently. Crushing her to me.

"Can we go back to bed?" she asks seductively, nuzzling my neck.

"Can I feel you up once we lay down?"

"You're actually asking permission?"

"For now." I smile against her temple.

"I think there are a few places on my body that could use a good rub."

"Well, if there's one thing I know how to do, it's rub." I kiss her roughly, tangling our tongues together. She moans into mouth, jump-starting my blood flow, sending an excess straight to the head of my cock.

When we break apart, I trap Ellie's chin between my thumb and forefinger, forcing her to look up at me.

"I love you," I whisper sternly.

"I know," she responds softly.

"Good," I reply, hoping beyond hope one day she'll love me back.

ELLIE

HOW AM I SUPPOSED TO talk to Kayne when he's the one we're talking about?

Tonight overwhelmed me to the point the aftermath woke me up out a dead sleep.

It's all coming at me so hard and so fast. I'm scared, excited, hopeful, and doubtful all at the same time. It's a dizzying state. Kayne keeps telling me he loves me. Drilling it into my head the same way he drilled his perversions into my body. I just needed to talk to someone, hear a voice of reason, and Jett has always been that for me when it comes to Kayne. I was in such disarray, I didn't know up from down or right from left. I needed to purge everything I was feeling, and I knew Jett would listen.

When I called Kayne the Kingda Ka, I meant it. He's a sharply winding trestle built for speed, and I'm not sure if I want the ride to stop or make it go faster.

KAYNE

I WAKE TO MY PHONE vibrating on the nightstand. I snatch it up then glance over at Ellie's naked form. She's fast asleep on her stomach breathing softly. The sun is just starting to rise, casting a bright orangey glow over the horizon.

I keep the phone close to my body as I read the text:

FYSA. Second insurgent identified. Threat level elevated.

What the fuck? I hit delete and slip out of bed, careful not to disturb Ellie. Tucking myself into the shadows, I dial the secure number I have memorized.

"Yo," a man answers.

"Juice." I keep my voice low.

"Loverboy. Didn't think I was going to hear from you." He sounds way too awake and chipper for my liking. But that's Juice.

"Yeah, well, when you send text messages like that, I'm inclined to call in. What second insurgent?"

"Nicky Cruz."

"Holy shit. He's one of the biggest drug runners on the West Coast."

"Yup. We don't believe it's a coincidence that two of the most high-powered drug traffickers in the U.S. are both visiting the Rainbow State at the same time just for a holiday."

My blood pressure spikes.

"A commission meeting?" I ask.

"Could be. Or maybe they're both looking for the same person." I immediately glance at Ellie. She hasn't budged an inch.

"You need to fucking find out what they're doing there," I growl menacingly.

"On it, killer," he says aloofly, unfazed by my tone. "Probably a good thing you're vapor. Watch your back."

Click.

I crush the phone against my forehead and groan. Shit. Shit. Shit. Never a dull moment.

I drop my cell back on the nightstand just as Ellie shifts with a small sigh as if searching for me while she dreams. I crawl into bed and pull her against me, locking her in my arms. Locked. That's exactly how I intend to keep her—safe, secure, and completely protected. Except for once, it's not her I'm worried about. No, that conversation meant something else entirely. It meant someone might be looking for *me*, or, even worse, coming for me.

I've expected this, even anticipated it. I wasn't lying when I told Ellie you don't bring down one of the world's most notorious drug lords without repercussions. I messed up a lot of powerful people's businesses, and criminals don't usually take kindly to people screwing with their income. But I'm ready and waiting. So, let them come.

"You're awake?" Ellie stirs.

I glance down at her. Her eyes are still closed and her face is still pressed firmly against my chest.

"How did you know?"

"I heard you thinking."

I chuckle distantly. "I'm sorry if my thoughts woke you."

"It's fine." She smiles sweetly, and I melt. Jesus, the woman can cut my balls off with one twitch of her lips. "Is something wrong?" she asks, her eyebrows furrowed.

"Nope. Not a thing." I kiss her head.

"I'll take your word at face value, but I know you're full of shit."

I exhale profoundly, half amused by Ellie, and half worried about the rest of the world. "It's just—"

"Work. I know. I get it. You have to keep different kinds of secrets now." She cracks her eyes open, and the green is so deep her irises almost look brown.

"I don't want to keep anything from you." Even though, I am.

"Then don't."

"Some things I don't have a choice about."

"I can accept that. Just don't lie to me about who you are. I want to know the real you, not who you have to be for work or who you think you have to be for me."

"I wish I knew who the real me is." I've been someone else for so long, it's hard going back to who you were. Not that I really want to be that person, either.

"We can figure it out together." She snuggles up against me, and I nearly fall apart. I think that's most comforting thing anyone has ever said to me. Maybe with Ellie in my life, the person I am isn't so bad.

"There is something I do have to tell you."

"Oh yeah, what's that?"

I brace myself for the confession. "You're not the only one living in Hawaii."

"What?" She lifts her head and pierces me with her now very awake green eyes.

"I've been living in Waikiki with Jett."

"For how long?" She sits up hastily using the sheet to cover her naked form.

"Ten months."

"What!?"

"I needed to make sure you were all right," I say quickly.

"You needed to stalk me." Ellie expresses her own interpretation.

"I prefer to call it twenty-four-hour surveillance."

"So you've been watching everything I do?"

"Not everything. I respected your privacy," I inform her. "I was just making sure there were no intrusions to your life."

"Was there anything that threatened to intrude?"

"No. Nothing that I was aware of. And I intend to keep it that way."

"So you really do know everything about me?" I nod. "Even about—"

"Your boy toy? Yes," I interrupt her.

"He's not a boy toy," she responds affronted.

"He can't be very important if you're here naked with me."

"He's a friend," she specifies. "And I can be naked with anyone I want. I'm unattached," she reminds me harshly. I cringe inside.

"I'm hoping to change that."

"I know you are," she says sternly, but her expression is soft.

Good sign.

"Forgive me?"

"For stalking me?" she asks drily.

"For watching over you," I correct her.

"No."

"Come on. Wrong thing for the right reasons." I try to argue my side.

"So, you admit it was wrong."

"Nope," I contradict myself. Us spies are good at that. "Protecting you will never be wrong, no matter how I do it."

"You're going to be a very busy man then, because I don't like to sit still."

"Don't I know it." I trap her head in my hand and graze my teeth along her neck. "You're a very busy little bee."

"There's a lot to see in this world."

"I'll show you everything if you let me."

"That could take a long time." She closes her eyes and sighs as I skim the tip of my tongue under her jaw.

"Ellie, I've got nothing but time."

"Why didn't you let me know you were there?" she asks almost sadly.

"Truthfully?" I quit caressing her with my mouth. "To give you space. Plus, I saw what you did to those cupcakes."

"You saw?"

"Baby, I have never been far away," I divulge. "If you want to get mad at me for staying close, go ahead. I told you, I'll endure it just as long as I get you in the end."

"Get me how exactly?"

"Mind, body, and soul," I tell her simply.

Ellie looks at me skeptically. What I wouldn't give to be telepathic right now.

"What are you thinking?" I ask.

"What kind of stipulations come with those things."

"None. No strings, no expectations, no demands. I told you that before. I will take whatever you're willing to give me. And I mean it. I never go back on my word. You may not believe it now, but someday you will."

"Are you always so sure of yourself?"

"Yes. When I want something, I get it. First rule of survival, identify your surroundings, accept them, and then try to improve them. I've identified, accepted, and now I'm trying to improve."

"Sounds like a lengthy process."

"Depends on the crisis."

"Are we in a crisis?" she creases her eyebrows.

"At the moment, no. But if your boy toy becomes a problem, maybe."

Ellie stares at me silently as the sun creeps up over the water brightening the room. Then she smiles impishly. "What boy toy . . ."

Now that's what I'm talking about.

I FLOP ONTO THE BED, beat.

The last five days have been the very best of my life, hands down, undisputed. Every day with Ellie I learn something new about her and myself. Her energy and love for life is infectious. She laughs more than I thought possible for a single person; she's always smiling, always frisky, always playful. I never thought I'd say this, but she's freaking wearing me out.

"Tired, old man?" she yells from the sundeck. Ever since she found out I was a whole five years older, she has teased me about my age.

"Not a lick," I lie, waiting for my second wind. I've always been energetic, but Ellie takes stamina to the next level. She never stops, whether we're out somewhere or in between the sheets. Not only have I met my match, I've met my competition.

I check my phone. No new messages. I haven't heard from Juice in three days, so I'm taking that as a good sign. Although in the spy game, no news isn't necessarily good news.

I shoot a quick text to Jett.

Me: Hear any good gossip?

Jett: No. Stop being a busybody. Only worry about that hot little piece of ass you're hell-bent on keeping all to yourself.

Me: I was never taught to share. Fuck off.

And you wonder why I'm a possessive lunatic when it comes to Ellie. Everyone wants her, even my best friend. Not that he's stupid enough to touch her, but he'll let it be known the interest is there.

"Kayne, what are you doing!?" Ellie shouts from the sundeck. "Come outside, and let's go swimming!"

I lift my head to look at her with wide eyes as she dips her foot into the pool. "We just spent the whole day snorkeling."

"So?" She shrugs.

I can't stop the smile from cracking my face. Energizer Bunny!

We have literally done everything from off-roading to jet skiing to kiteboarding. Today we took that private tour of the island Ellie was so excited about. It's been nonstop days and marathon nights. I've never been so sleep deprived in my life, even when I was on a twenty-four-hour surveillance mission in Afghanistan.

"How about instead you come inside and sit on my cock and let me watch those hot little tits bounce in the air."

Crickets.

I drop back down and close my eyes. Guess not.

"Such the romantic," Ellie chides playfully a few moments later, crawling onto the bed like a hungry cat stalking a mouse. "Is there at least going to be a little foreplay to get me wet, or should I just get right to it and fuck you?"

My cock twitches from just her words; she's definitely not shy about being verbal anymore.

I lift my head and look straight in her smoldering emerald eyes. "You want foreplay? Sit on my face."

I grab her hand and drag her upward until I can reach her waist.

"Kayne, I'm still wearing my bathing suit!" she says as I pull her body over my chest and bury my head between her legs.

"So what? I'll chew right through them to get to your clit if I have to." I bite and suck over the material.

"Oh!" She throws her head back. "You don't need to destroy my clothes. I'll take them off." She squirms, rubbing her pussy against my mouth.

"Off." I nip at her as she quickly unties each side of the pink bikini bottoms, fumbling with the strings as I tease her with the tip of my finger, slipping it just under the clingy material and stroking her lightly.

"Oh, God." She rips off her bottoms exposing her inflamed, pink pussy an inch away from my mouth. I don't waste one second diving back between her legs and licking up the sweet taste of her arousal. It has my need roaring. Relentlessly, I swipe my tongue through her wet folds, every so often sinking it deeply into her entrance until she is writhing and shuddering and soaking my face.

"Oh fuck, you're going to make me come." She grips my hair with both hands and tugs as hard as she can, fusing her pussy directly against my lips. I stiffen my tongue as she rides my mouth, bucking, moaning, and gasping for air.

Like a shattered dam, Ellie floods when she comes, her arousal as sugary as a mouthful of candy. I lap her up and suck on her clit as she lazily comes around.

"Adequate foreplay?" I ask as I wipe my mouth against her inner thigh.

"Yes," she answers sluggishly.

"Good. Now sit that wet pussy on my cock. It feels best right after you come."

"You really need to stop with the hearts and flowers. You're going to spoil me."

"I definitely wouldn't want to do that, now would I?" I answer as Ellie slinks down my body. Hurriedly, she rips off my board shorts, moving quickly to next discard the white Ginny-t clinging to my chest. As she pulls it over my head, it snags on my arms and tangles around my wrists. I try to pull free, but she stops me, tightening the stretchy shirt around my hands as if caught in some kind of trance. Silently she gazes down at me as if asking permission and me staring back—holy fuck—grants it. I've never let a woman take control before, at least not like this. Ellie binds my wrists, tying a secure knot with the fabric. Like a perfect storm of anticipation and fear, my heart hammers, my cock throbs, and my head feels light. Ellie has no idea how much trust it's taking for me to submit. To hand myself over and give her control.

"Kayne?" she speaks softly, kissing my neck, my cheek, my lips. "Tell me if this isn't okay."

"It's fine." I grip onto the underside of the headboard and respond robotically. I understand so much at this moment. So much of what I put Ellie through. How I restrained her mind and her body. For a split second, I can't even believe this woman is with me. I can't believe she is giving me a second chance. She is, without a doubt, stronger than I will ever be.

I lift my head to kiss her, trusting her with all my insecurities and all my fears.

"I love your body." She skims her fingernails from the top of my chest, over my abdomen, all the way down to the sensitive skin right above my cock. I break out in goose bumps as she does it a second time. "I also love the way you feel when you're inside me." I watch engrossed as she straddles my hips and teases my cock with her slippery little pussy. My stomach muscles tense involuntarily as she slides her slit over my pounding erection, but denies me penetration. I moan helplessly.

"Ellie," I groan, lifting my pelvis, begging to just thrust up inside her once.

"Need me, baby?" She throws my own words back at me as she glides over my length a second, a third, and a fourth time.

"You know I do." I yank on the headboard dying to get my hands on her.

"Tell me what you want." She leans over and swirls her tongue against my neck. "Do you want me to suck you? Stroke you? Fuck you?" she whispers lasciviously in my ear.

Little temptress, she knows just what she's doing. Driving me mad.

"I want you to take your top off so I can suck on your tits while you fuck me."

You can never say I'm not a man who doesn't know what he wants. Ellie gazes down at me hotly as she slowly unties the back of her bikini top. It loosens but doesn't expose any skin until she slips it over her head and her breasts hang free. Gradually, teasingly, she leans forward and skims one nipple over my lips. I latch onto it and suck hard, causing us both to moan. As I lick and nibble and bite the little stone her nipple has become, Ellie eagerly lines up the head of my erection with the entrance of her pussy. I can't wait; I'm beyond desperate so I thrust upward, obtaining the penetration I so desperately need. Her head snaps back and her body bows as my entire length is submerged in her completely.

"Do I feel good?" Ellie asks as she takes me, engulfing my cock entirely in her tight, wet channel.

"You know you do. Nothing feels as good as you," I groan against her breast, sucking the skin until it turns purple.

"Nothing?" She starts to rock her hips in an elongated movement, stroking my entire dick from base to tip.

"Nothing. Not one thing on the face of this Earth feels better than you," I hiss as we fuck leisurely, Ellie in complete control.

"I could say the same." She sits up straight and arches her back, giving me a bird's-eye view of her naked body. I'm close to ripping the shirt around my wrists in two. If she doesn't start moving quickly and feed my body more, my arousal is going to spark into an unstoppable fury.

"Ellie." I grind my teeth and pull on the headboard until the wood strains, "move."

"Beg me." She plants her hands on my chest and digs her nails into my skin. "Beg me to make you come."

Fuck! Little brat, she's using my own tactics against me, spurring my need to soar and the beast to howl as she purposely torments me.

"Please." I clench my jaw as she tortures me with pleasure. "Please, baby, make me come."

"Let me come," she corrects me.

I inhale hard. "*Let* me come." I stare into her eyes. I can't imagine what I look like—inside I'm a shitstorm of raging hormones, on the outside, I'm trying frantically to keep my cool. I wonder if Ellie knows which side is winning out? "Ellie, goddamn it, please," I growl as I buck beneath her, her muscles clenching my cock brutally. This submissive bullshit is for the birds. I just want to grab her hips, flip her over, and fuck her until she screams, but Ellie seems to have her own agenda. Not to mention, her own frustratingly slow pace.

She leans down and kisses me hard, driving her tongue between my lips, assailing my mouth. "Good boy," she rasps as she begins to move, riding me fast, digging her nails even deeper into my chest until she's close to drawing blood.

Watching Ellie does something to me. It affects me in ways that I never believed imaginable. Letting her take control, feeling her body move, and seeing her cheeks heat with arousal physically destroys me. "Fuck! I'm going to come." My cock sharpens and my tendons threaten to tear as my orgasm speeds through my system.

"Me, too," Ellie hisses, her face tight as she keeps up the mind-bending rhythm. A few seconds later, she moans above me as I explode beneath her. Her throbbing pussy milking my climax for everything it's worth. Once the two of us are depleted, she collapses on top of me.

"God," I tear my shirt to shreds in order to release my hands and secure Ellie in my arms with this overwhelming need to hold her.

There are so many emotions escalating through me, I can barely get my thoughts straight.

"You okay?" Ellie asks, as if she can see my instability dancing like a shadow on the wall.

I don't answer.

"Kayne?" Ellie lifts her head worried.

"I'm fine," I finally answer. "That was just . . . Was just . . . way more than watching your tits bounce in the air."

We stare at each other for a beat then erupt into laughter. For me, it's a cathartic laugh. Being with Ellie is just so goddamn easy. Every stressful moment of my life seems to fade away.

Seems to never have existed.

"You scared me for a second." She lies back down.

"You scare me every second," I admit, threading my fingers into her hair.

"Why?"

"You do things to me, Ellie."

"Like tie you up with your undershirt?"

"That would be one thing," I chuckle. "But not exactly what I mean. I've never been able to relax. I've always been anxious and on edge. But with you, I feel calm. It's new."

Ellie smiles shyly at me then kisses my chest right where her name is tattooed. She doesn't say a word because nothing needs to be said.

We just lay there lazily as she nestles her face against my side while I brush my hand along her back.

"Kayne?"

"Mmmm?"

"What do you think would have happened that night if things hadn't gotten all messed up?"

I smile to myself with my eyes closed. "Exactly what I planned. I would've taken you back to my penthouse and fucked you."

"Would you have tried to tie me up?" I feel her look up at me.

"Probably. Would you have let me?" I glance down at her.

"Probably."

"Interesting to know."

ELLIE

SEVEN DAYS. I HAVE SPENT six nights and seven days with Kayne, and he has me flying high. Like, literally, ten thousand feet in the air. At the moment, I'm being strapped to his body with a skintight harness. To say I'm not shitting myself would be a lie. Skydiving was the one activity Kayne pushed for. When he saw the brochure on Matias' desk, his eyes lit up so brightly they nearly blinded us. I immediately protested, arguing that if God wanted humans to fly, he would have given us wings. Kayne contested, saying God improvised and gave us parachutes. Only after a lengthy, one-sided conversation of Kayne explaining how he's probably more experienced than a skydiving instructor, having jumped over fifty times, did he finally persuade me to give in. Which brings us to now, the two of us standing in an open doorway of a tiny plane looking down at turquoise-blue water and the small circular-shaped island of Bora Bora. I think I'm going to throw up.

Kayne is nothing like I dreamed about, but everything I could have ever wanted. Every day together just gets better and better. It's almost surreal, but definitely not perfect. There's something missing. Something he's holding back, which in turn makes me hold back. I know my late-night conversations with Jett don't help, but what he doesn't understand is that by me talking to someone else, I allow myself to open up to him. It helps me process and helps me accept. Letting go of the anger and the feeling of betrayal wasn't easy. But Jett helped me work through it.

I swear he's a shrink, a sexual connoisseur, and a fashionista all rolled into one.

And as to why we talk in the middle of the night? At first, it was because I couldn't sleep, but it quickly became because I didn't want to miss one second with Kayne while he is awake.

"Ready?" Kayne asks with his mouth close to my ear.

"No." I dig my fingernails into his thighs.

"Relax," he purrs. "I would never let anything happen to you. Trust me?"

I flash back to the last time he asked me that. I was tied up then, too. The answer is still the same; I just hope the outcome is different. A few short hours after he asked me if I trusted him the last time, the sky fell on me. Now, I'm about to fall through the sky.

"Yes," I answer faintly with my heart beating so hard it's leaving an indentation on my chest.

"On three." Kayne cradles my face against his shoulder and then criss-crosses our arms in front of my chest so I'm pressed snugly against him. "Count with me." He raises his voice over the hum of the engine.

I take a deep breath and nod with my eyes closed, hoping I find the courage to actually make it to three.

"One!" Kayne yells as we inch closer to the edge. It feels like a vacuum is trying to suck us up.

"Two!" we say together, and then suddenly we're falling nose first into a wind tunnel. A piercing scream rips from my throat as we plummet downward, cool air whipping right through our clothes. *What the fuck happened to three!?!*

I know it's only supposed to last two minutes, but the seconds suddenly feel like hours as the adrenaline pumps triple time through my body. I don't know at what altitude I finally allow myself to breathe and take it all in, but once I do, the feeling is euphoric; an entrancing split of body and mind.

"Hang on!" Kayne yells as he pulls the ripcord and the parachute deploys, jerking us back only to release us a moment later into a soft glide.

"Holy shit!" I exclaim as my pounding heart echoes in my ears.

"Not too many people can say they saw the island from this angle."

"I'm sure that's true," I reply in awe as we fall slowly, drinking in the indescribable view. From here, you can see everything—the reefs at the bottom of the turquoise lagoon, the dark-green landscape, and the top of Mt. Otemanu surrounded by a ring of white puffy clouds.

"Ellie, I'm releasing the parachute. We're going to land in shallow water. Be ready for the impact," Kayne tells me all too soon as he pulls another cord a foot or two over the water. We drop, but land easily as the water cushions our fall. Once Kayne unhooks my harness, I turn instantly and jump into his arms. The adrenaline coursing through my veins like a fast moving stream.

"That was amazing!"

"You liked it?" He laughs lifting me up.

"I loved it!" I kiss him. "Let's do it again!"

"Now?"

"Yes!"

"Like the rush, huh?"

"Yes. And it's all your fault." I plunge my tongue into his mouth and kiss him fiercely.

"I created a monster?"

"You have no idea," I growl trying to kiss him again as something dark and primitive bubbles deep down inside me.

Kayne pulls away and looks at me funny. I feel high. It's the same feeling I used to get when he would control me, when he would command me. I want to tell him I want that again, but the words fall flat and insecurity takes over. What I'm scared of, I don't know. Him taking it too far? Me letting him? I know what he's capable of and how much he gets off on pushing my limits. I also know it's his dominant side he's holding back. It's the part of him that still terrifies me and thrills me all the same; I don't think any amount of time is going to change that, but it doesn't intimidate me the way it used to. I know I have a choice now, and I choose to want it. To want him. Every side and every angle.

"Ellie?"

"Yeah?" Kayne catches me staring at his mouth. That mouth that is so spectacular and mind-blowing it could be the eighth wonder of the world.

"You seriously want to go again?"

I look up into his eyes. They're bright blue from the glare of the sun; the brown patch a stark contrast to the light color.

"Yes," I answer confidently.

He gazes at me inquisitively. "We are still talking about skydiving, right?"

"For now," I answer darkly.

"HUNGRY?" KAYNE ASKS AS HE deposits me onto the bed. I'm beat. Skydiving takes a lot out of you, or at least a lot out of me. I nodded off in the golf cart on the way back to the bungalow. I'm pretty sure my lack of sleep isn't helping either. I've barely gotten four hours a night since I arrived.

"Starving," I tell him while he is hovering over me.

"Dine in or eat out?"

"Eat out?" I can't help it; I burst out laughing right in his face.

"You're a pervert," he chuckles.

"Says the man who loves whips and chains and butt plugs!" I roll over holding my side.

"And spanking," he smacks me on the ass, and I jerk. "Don't forget spanking."

"Oh!" I moan loudly and all laughter dies. It suddenly feels like a thick cloud of tension has blanketed the room.

Kayne's eyes smolder, the look so hot it could burn coal. My thighs actually clench from need. But as quickly as the excitement surfaces, it disappears. Why is he holding back? Kayne straightens and clears his throat, but his arousal is still evident. It's pitching a tent in his shorts.

"Go out or eat in?" he rephrases, adjusting himself.

"Eat in," I answer softly.

He nods pensively. "What would you like?"

"Cheeseburger and French fries."

Kayne smirks. "Done."

"What's so amusing?"

"Nothing. I just like that you like what I like."

I don't think he realizes how true his statement is.

"I'll order." He heads over to the nightstand.

"Oh and—" I roll onto my stomach to follow him.

"A bottle of champagne and a glass of mango juice." He picks up the receiver. "I know."

I smile. I had the mango Bellini the other night at dinner and now I'm addicted. While Kayne orders dinner, I get up and go outside. A few more minutes of lying around and I will be out for the count. Besides, I don't want to miss the sunset. It's my favorite time of day. I shrug out of my cover-up and slip into the pool, making myself comfortable on the seat built into the side. I bask in the warm water as the sky illuminates in a medley of blues and purples and oranges and reds. I feel Kayne swim up behind me and pull me into his arms.

"Enjoying the view?"

"It never gets old." I spin around and gaze at the angelic face capable of so many demonic things, all of which he seems to keep hidden away under lock and key. I straddle his thighs and dot kisses on his lips to distract myself from my esoteric desires. I don't know how to tell him what I want because I'm still trying to figure it out myself. How do you tell your former owner that you want him to own you all over again? It sounds crazy even to me.

"Why did you join the Army?" I ask curiously. Kayne has been forthcoming about most things, but he does dance around some subjects, like his childhood, expertly. Kayne clams up for a beat before he answers robotically. "It was three hot meals a day and a roof over my head. Not very patriotic, I know, but the truth. I didn't have many choices then, it was either keep living on the street or enlist."

"You were homeless?" This is new information.

"For a little while, yeah. Not my proudest moment, but it was better than another shitty foster home."

"Was foster care that bad?" I ask.

Kayne shudders. "Let's put it this way, I won the lottery every time for crappiest foster parents."

I frown. "What was it like?"

He looks away, and I'm convinced he's shutting down.

"When I wasn't starving to death or being used as a human punching bag?" he answers bitterly, "Hell."

"How long did you live on the street?" I scan over his beautiful face, the lines angular, his jaw clean shaven and clenched tight.

He looks back at me, his eyes devoid of all emotion, like he has to put up a wall just to talk about it.

"Six months. That last home did me in."

"How?" I frown.

Kayne expels a deep breath and closes his eyes. This is clearly difficult for him.

"We don't have to talk about it if you don't want."

It looks like he's considering my out, but he surprises me and continues talking.

"I had just turned seventeen when I went to live with the Millers. My social worker raved about them," he says detached. "Said they were the best of the best. I didn't believe a word she said. By that time, I was so broken, so raw, I didn't believe anything anyone said to me. I was always on the defensive because it was all I knew how to be. They were a pretty young couple, maybe early forties. I remember them being very welcoming. Their house was big and clean, and for the first time in my life, I had a room of my own. I pretty much holed up in it for the first month I was there. Mrs. Miller would bring me all my meals and gave me the space they told her that I needed. Both she and Mr. Miller would try to talk to me, but they quickly realized how far gone I was. It took a few long months to finally believe they weren't out to hurt me. I was always waiting for them to punish me somehow, hit me, starve me, do something I was used to. But neither of them ever laid a hand on me. They just waited patiently for me to come around. After about three months, I started eating dinner at the table with the two of them and then helping around the house after school. Mr. Miller let me hang out in the garage while he worked on his old car listening to eighties' music. Mrs. Miller taught me how to do laundry and make scrambled eggs. She was the closest thing to a mother-figure I ever had. And after about six months, I finally relaxed and believed I had found two people I could trust. That's when everything went wrong."

"Wrong how?"

"Mr. Miller would go away on business trips periodically. Not for very long, a few days at the most. Mrs. Miller, or Kim by that time, and I were cooking dinner. It had become sort of a thing for us. It was our time to talk. She was really nice, funny, and easygoing. But that night she was acting weird. Usually, she dressed pretty conservatively in sweaters and dress pants, but she had on tight jeans and a button up that wasn't exactly buttoned up. She was drinking wine and being really flirty. It was odd. And then, while I was cutting peppers, she brushed up against me and it definitely wasn't by accident. I nearly sliced my finger open. I didn't like women to begin with, and I *really* didn't like it when they invaded my personal space. I tried to move away, but she ended up stalking me into a corner, telling me how attractive she thought I was, and how much she wanted me, and how Mr. Miller, Rob, would never have to know. Ellie, I was horrified. I wanted to escape down the kitchen sink. And then she kissed me and I completely freaked. I pushed her away as hard as I could and then just ran. It was my breaking point." Kayne laughs crazily. "My first real kiss and it was with a forty-year-old woman trying to take advantage of me." He looks at me so dejectedly that my heart disintegrates right on the spot. "My trust had been shattered, again. By *another* woman. I was done. So I chose one hellhole over another."

"What was living on the street like?" I search his hollow eyes.

"Fucking cold. And lonely, and hard. But it was safe because I depended on myself, and I was the only person I could trust."

I am incapable of speaking. So many things are starting to make sense.

"I spent eight hours in the recruiter's office the eve of my eighteenth birthday just waiting until the minute I could sign. It was the best decision I ever made."

"Why?"

"Being in the Army gave me structure and stability. It redefined me. I was ready to be someone new. Then I met Jett, and my life changed in a whole other set of ways. I was a wild animal before the two; I had no discipline, no self-respect, no integrity. They built me up into more. Not that I'm saying I'm perfect. We both know that I'm not, but I'm way better off than I was. And with you in my life, I'm even better." He tangles our fingers and holds on tightly.

"Are you sure about that?"

"I've never been more sure about anything. I don't think you understand how much power you have."

"I don't think I do, either."

Kayne clenches my hand, our palms smashing together. "Ellie, you're the one person who can destroy me. You're my sin and my absolution, my indulgence and my starvation, and every right to all my wrongs."

Oh Jesus, I think I just dissolved. This man can govern me with just his words. There's no controlling the onslaught of emotion that overcomes me. Compulsively, I crush my lips against his and fight back the tears as I suck and lick and plunge my tongue deeply into his mouth.

He kisses me back with matched force until we need to come up for air. "What did you mean when you said your trust had been shattered by another woman?" I press my forehead against his, winded, with my heart beating rapidly.

Kayne looks up into my eyes and his anguished expression almost destroys me. He grabs onto my neck and closes his eyes like he's holding onto me for dear life.

"Kayne?"

"Ellie," he says my name so wounded. "I'm not sure I can."

I have no idea how to keep him talking or even if I should, but I blurt out, "In high school, my prom date tried to rape me." Kayne's eyes fly open. "He was drunk and we were at an after party at a hotel. We were in the bathroom fooling around, and when we went as far as I was comfortable with, I told him to stop and he wouldn't."

Kayne looks at me disturbed. "Ellie, are you trying to kick me while I'm down?"

"What? No. Why would you say that?" Then I realize. "Kayne, you never raped me."

"I might as well have." He drops his head back and knocks it against the pool's edge.

I force his face back up so I can look at him.

"I never told anyone about it."

"Then why are you telling me now?" His voice is guarded.

"Because you said I could talk to you about anything. And I want to be able to do that. I just don't want it to be one-sided."

"I don't want that, either, but I don't know if I can . . . about this."

"We all have things that tear us up inside, and I can tell you from experience that talking about it helps."

Kayne sighs heavily. "You've been spending way too much time with Jett."

"I'm not going to force you to tell me. But I'll listen whenever you're ready." I kiss him on the lips with an abundance of *love*. Yes, exactly that. Love.

"I'm going to go dry off for dinner." I go to pull myself up so I can get out of the pool, but Kayne latches on to my thighs and stops me dead with just his impenetrable stare. The wall just got two feet thicker and twenty feet higher.

"I only met my mother once," he says, his voice so cold it freezes the pool. "I was seven and having a really rough time with the foster family I was with. They were especially abusive." I settle back down onto Kayne's lap. "They would lock me in a dark, tiny closet and leave me there for days. I still don't know why, maybe so they didn't have to deal with me." He swallows a very large lump in his throat, and I'm suddenly having second thoughts about him taking this trip down memory lane. "They made me pee in a bowl and eat scraps of food they threw at me like a dog." He clears his throat. "One morning my social worker shows up with this woman. She was really pretty." He says it like a child as his eyes tear up. "She even sort of looked like me. Same face and eyes, even hair color. And she was sweet. Really sweet. The two of them took me out, we went to the park, and for pizza, and even got ice cream. It was probably the best day of my life." His voice cracks and so does my heart. "When they took me back to my foster home, the woman, her name was Sarah, took my hand and sat me on the curb. That's when she told me who she was."

"Your mom."

He nods. "She said she had been sick and wasn't able to take care of me for a long time, but she was better now and wanted us to be a family again. I remember asking her if she would take me to the park if we were a family. She said yes, often. That's your biggest concern as a seven-year-old, you know, if you get to play." He laughs sadly. "I hugged her so hard before she left, pleading with her to take me with her. She was my mom, I belonged with her. But she said that there were things that needed to be worked out, so I needed to stay where I was a little while longer. She promised she would be back. She looked me straight in the eyes and promised. And I believed her. I fucking believed her and I *loved* her." Kayne splashes his face with the pool water, as if trying to wash away the surge of emotion. "She never came back, Ellie. I waited for days, weeks, months, years—sometimes I think I'm still waiting." He breaks, tears spilling out of his eyes. Unable to stop myself, I throw my arms around his neck and hug him as tightly as my arms will allow. "She destroyed me with hope, the same way Mrs. Miller destroyed me with trust." He hugs me back, digging his face into the curve of my neck. "You're the first woman I have ever entrusted with those two things."

I pull back and look at him. I think I finally understand the power that I hold. His tears continue to fall, trickles of heart wrenching sadness running down his face. They compel me as much as they destroy me. With no hesitation I lick his cheek tasting the salty anguish on my own tongue.

He jerks back, stunned. "Why did you do that?"

"You always lick away my tears," I respond simply. Looking back, every tear I ever shed in his presence was never done in vain. It was his strange way of connecting, showing me he cared.

The doorbell rings, causing us both to jump.

"Room service," Kayne mutters.

"I'll get it." I kiss him firmly before hurrying out of the pool. I grab a towel to wrap around me, and let the young man in, directing him to set the food on the table outside on the deck. I follow him through the bungalow, and when we get outside, Kayne is already out of the pool and drying off. His mannerisms are stiff and his face is blank.

The young, tan waiter quickly sets up our plates and leaves unobtrusively. Kayne and I both stare down at the food, but I don't think either of us is hungry at the moment.

"I'm going to go shower," he tells me withdrawn, walking toward the sliding doors leading to our bedroom. I grab his wrist as he passes by me. "We can take one together later if you want." I look up at him naked of all reservations. This man's emotional deprivation runs deeper than I could have ever imagined.

"Of course, I want that." His voice is gruff. "Do you still want it, that's the question?"

"Why wouldn't I?"

"Because I was just acting like the biggest pussy on the face of the Earth."

He's hiding again.

"No, you weren't. You were acting human, and that's the sexiest thing on the face of the Earth." I cuddle up to him, encouraging him to take me in his arms.

"You can hurt me, Ellie," he says, stripped bare.

"I know, but that's the last thing I want to do."

"I hope so," he breathes.

"Just keep trusting me, the way I've learned to trust you."

KAYNE

ELLIE IS HOLDING ONTO MY wrist with a death grip telling me to trust her. What she doesn't realize is that I do. Completely, wholeheartedly. I'm all in—one-hundred-percent. I'm just not sure if she is. Hearing her tell me that she trusts me gives me faith in whatever it is we have, but she hasn't even hinted to me about how she really feels. It makes me wonder if she can ever really love me. If she can let go of who I was in the past and accept me for who I am now. Whomever that may be. My biggest fear is that Ellie will wake up one day and realize I'm not what she wants, that I'm too intense or controlling or broken to truly love. I know it's only been a week, but Ellie has become an unshakable part of me, my nucleus.

I can only hope that she feels it, the truth of my love, and someday gives me the truth of hers in return.

ELLIE

I KNOCK SOFTLY ON JETT'S door.

I know he's expecting me.

The door creaks open exposing a dim light and a shirtless Jett.

"Evening," he says flippantly.

"Hey."

"You know, this ritual is starting to bug London. She thinks there's something going on with us, and she's jealous she can't join in."

"I highly doubt talking about all my jumbled feelings is going to excite her."

"Sexually, no. But she likes you, Ellie. She wants things to work out with you and Kayne. I do, too. I didn't realize how much I missed having you around. I even miss dressing you up." He grins.

"And by dressing me up, you mean seeing me naked."

"Exactly." He shoots a finger and winks.

I roll my eyes.

"So? What are we chatting about tonight?" He walks outside, and we take our usual seat on the ledge of the wooden walkway right outside his bungalow.

I shrug as I gaze up at the sky. It's the middle of the night and the stars look like a blanket woven together by streaks of silver clouds.

"We went skydiving today."

"I heard. Twice. Someone is a closet adrenaline junkie." I don't think Jett realizes how true that statement is. I bite my lip nervously. "Ellie? Can I be frank?"

"Are you ever not frank?"

"You've got me there. So here I go. I feel like there is something you want to talk about. Something very deep-seated and dark. But you're holding back. Am I right?"

I stare at Jett. How the fuck does he do that?

"Kayne told me about his mother," I divert.

Jett nods. "I figured he would. He told you way sooner than he told me. Took him years."

"She really just abandoned him like that?"

"Apparently. I've tried to talk him into looking for her. See what happened and get some closure, but he doesn't want anything to with it. That wound is just too deep."

"It nearly killed me when he told me. To see him hurt that much." My heart is still stinging.

"Yeah, but being with you is definitely filling a void in him."

"You think?"

"Definitely. He actually smiles now. Like genuinely smiles. And he isn't so uptight either. I swear there were times he was so tense, I worried he was going to trigger a natural disaster."

"That sounds pretty extreme."

"Yeah, well, Kayne is pretty extreme." He swings his bare feet.

"Then I guess I haven't experienced the eye of the storm yet."

"What do you mean?"

I fiddle with my hair, running my fingers through my low ponytail manically. "You weren't wrong when you said there was something deep-seated and dark that I wanted to talk about."

"Go on." Jett is now tremendously invested in our conversation.

"I just feel like Kayne is holding back."

"Holding back? His feelings?" Jett raises his eyebrows.

"No, he's very clear about how he feels, but physically he treats me very *delicately*. That's the best way I can describe it."

"Delicately," Jett ponders. "Like, makes sweet love to you?"

"Like he's suddenly taken a liking to vanilla."

"Oh."

"And your tastes have evolved beyond vanilla."

"Way beyond." I turn red.

"You want him to dominate you?"

"I want him to *own* me. The way he used to," I admit. Is there a hole I can crawl into and die?

"Oh, you are far gone."

"I'm crazy." I put my face on my hands.

"No, you're not. You were exposed to the lifestyle, and you liked it. It's perfectly normal, and it speaks volumes about how you feel about Kayne and the bond the two of you share."

"But everything is so different now. I don't think he wants that with me anymore."

"I disagree. He's afraid he's going to scare you off."

"That's funny, because I'm scared of the same thing."

"Impossible. Short of you sprouting a dick, that man isn't going anywhere. And trust me when I tell you, even if he isn't showing it, he wants to own you just as much as you want him to."

"What do I do?" I ask anxiously.

"Sweet thing, the best advice I can give you is to put on your big girl panties and tell your man what you want. Communication is important in any relationship, but it is vital in the one you're after."

"Why is communication such a scary thing?" I bite my nail.

"I don't know. You seem to have no problem communicating with me."

"I don't sleep with you." I elbow him.

"I know, it's such a shame." Jett shakes his blond head.

"Jett," I chastise him.

"What? Kayne is stingy. I share."

"Maybe if our communicating goes well, I can persuade him."

"Sweets, if your communicating goes well, I'll never see that cute little pussy again."

"I didn't realize you wanted me." I bat my eyelashes flirtatiously. It's an empty gesture, but it's still fun to play around.

Jett leans in close to me. "Do you remember the first time we met and you asked me if Kayne and I both owned you?"

"Yes." My eyes widen.

"If it had been up to me, we would have."

"Seriously?"

"Mmm hmm." He moves in a little closer and inhales me. It actually makes me tingle. Don't get me wrong, Jett is, well, Jett. He's smooth and seductive and drop dead gorgeous, but I never considered he actually wanted me like that. Up until this moment, we've always just exchanged flirtatious banter. It was innocent at best, but at the moment he's stirring something very deep inside me. Something surprising. Don't misunderstand, I'd never be unfaithful to Kayne—unless he gave me his permission. "I think it's time for you to go, Ellie," Jett says like I'm in danger. Like he's a vampire catching a whiff of forbidden blood.

"I think you're right." We both stand up hastily.

"I also think this is our last late-night conversation. You know what you want and how you feel. You don't need me anymore. Just be the strong girl we all know you are and take it slow." He tucks a strand of hair behind my ear and smiles. "You need a haircut."

"I know," I laugh. "Kayne likes it long."

"You're beautiful either way."

"Thanks."

"Now go make my best friend a happy man." Jett spanks me. "He deserves it, and so do you," he whispers then kisses me on the cheek. It feels like he just cut the last string of the past, and I'm perfectly okay with that.

More okay than I have been in twelve months.

I CLOSE THE DOOR TO the bedroom as quietly as I can. The room is darker than usual, the shades to the sliding glass doors are pulled, and all the window treatments are drawn. Strange.

"You and Jett have a nice chat?" Kayne's voice startles the hell out of me in the darkness.

"Jesus." I jump as he flicks on a small light. I turn to find him standing behind me, leaning against the wall, shirtless, with his arms and legs crossed and his eyes a harrowing black. "What are you doing up?"

"I could ask the same, but I already know." His voice is as cold as his stare.

"Why is it so dark in here?"

"Complements my mood."

"What's wrong?"

"Oh, I don't know." He stalks across the room toward me. "Maybe it's the fact you sneak out of bed every night to see my best friend."

"Just to talk," I respond automatically.

"Yeah, talk. Talking is important. I talk to you, Ellie. I tell you my deepest darkest secrets. I slice myself open and let my emotions pour out and what do you do? You leave. Not one night do you have the decency to stay with me. So tell me, little girl, is there something going on between you and Jett?" He crowds me, forcing me to step backward. "Do you want him, Ellie? Do you want him now that you know all about poor, pathetic Kayne and his fucked-up issues?"

"No." I bump up against the wall. "It isn't like that."

"Then what is it like? Tell me."

"We're just friends," I scramble. Pissed off Kayne is a scary thing. "He was there; he's the only one who knows what happened between us. Who else am I supposed to talk to?" Tears cloud my vision.

"Who else?" Kayne seethes. *"Me!"*

I jump. "How am I supposed to talk to you about you?"

"You can talk to me about anything. I have been trying, Ellie, really trying to be everything you want, everything you need. But it's just not enough. I will never ever be enough." He hits his chest with a closed fist.

"That's not true. You're everything."

"Then why run to Jett?"

"Because I was confused!"

"About what?"

"How I felt."

"About me?"

"Yes, at first and then . . . then . . ."

"Then?" He hangs on my last word.

"What I wanted."

"Wanted!? You don't want me, Ellie?"

"No . . ." I shake my head flustered. "Yes! Of course I want you. It's just . . ." My lip quivers, this is not how I pictured this conversation going.

"Just? Dammit, Ellie, tell me!" Kayne erupts.

I start to breathe heavily as the tears roll down my cheeks. I hate that I'm being such a girl, but this hard for me, wanting something so taboo. More than wanting . . . dying for.

"I want you," I profess.

"You have me."

"Only part of you," I contest.

Kayne looks at me like he's staring at one of those crazy 3D pictures.

"What are you trying to tell me?" He steps forward and takes my face in his hands, wiping away my tears with his thumbs.

"Being with you changed me." I look up at him. Now that he's a little calmer, it's easier for me to talk. "You made me want things. Things I could never want with anyone else."

"Things?" There's surprise in his voice.

I nod, pressing my cheek into his palm.

He stares silently for several long moments. "Are you telling me what I think you're telling me?" Fire ignites in his eyes and burns straight through to my core.

I nod again.

"Ellie," he breathes my name, and it sounds excruciating. "I don't know."

"Please."

"If I open Pandora's Box, I don't think I'll be able to close it again."

"You won't have to."

"I'm not sure I want to take that chance. I swore to myself I wouldn't hurt you. I wouldn't give you another reason to leave me. I don't know if I could survive losing you again. You mean too much."

"You won't lose me. I want it as much as you do."

He shakes his head, clearly torn.

"Guarantee me," he demands. "Guarantee me that if we do this you will still be here, you'll still want me."

"I promise. I need you." I swallow the lump in my throat. "I need you to own me."

"Why?" He searches my face intensely. I shrug.

"Maybe you're not the only one with a beast inside you."

"Shit, baby, that could be a dangerous thing."

"I know, and I don't care."

I'm being reckless, I'm fully aware, but Kayne is my drug of choice and I can't wait to get high. He looks me in the eye, hesitant to act.

"I told you, I want all of you. All your sides." I try to reassure him. Coax him. I thought he would jump at this opportunity, but his reluctance only makes me want him more, care about him more. It tells me how precious I really am to him. How he really meant those words he spoke back in that room, my luxury prison.

"Beg me."

I smile. "Please, please." I lean in and try to kiss him, but he stops me, trapping my head with his hands that are still clutching my face.

"I didn't give you permission to move," he growls, and I shiver. That voice. That stern, commanding, all-encompassing voice that makes my insides flip-flop.

"Yes, Kayne," I reply obediently, and that seems to stir something inside him.

"Fuck," he mutters to himself like he knows he's in trouble. Like he just gave in. "Kneel. Now."

I drop in front of him, surrendering complete control, pressing my forehead to the wood floor attempting to get as low as possible.

"Good kitten." At the use of my pet name, I literally liquefy. My panties drench with want and my pussy pulsates with need.

"Stay," he orders, and then I hear his heavy footsteps move around the room. I'm shaking; I'm so anxious, nervous, and excited.

A few moments later, he returns to me. "Ellie, look up."

I raise the upper half of my body but remain on my knees. Kayne lovingly runs one finger under my jawbone while he stares down. There are so many emotions playing across his face—worry, elation, fascination, and fear. I'm so entrapped by him; I don't notice what he's holding in his left hand until he moves to wrap it around my neck. The light in the room is dim, but I can still make out the leather belt with the double holes along its entire length. Kayne fastens it, leaving just enough room for me to breathe, yet tight enough to keep me in line. He yanks on the end forcing me to my feet.

He's panting as hard as I am as he backs me up against the wall. "Ellie, what's your safe word?"

Safe word? He's never let me have one of those before. Things really are different.

"Cupcake," I exhale.

"Good." He places his thumb on my lower lip and drags it down. "I want you to know what's going to happen next. I'm going to beat you, then fuck you, and I expect you to thank me when it's all over. Understand?"

I nod, dry mouthed.

"I'm very upset with you, kitten. You left me. You walked away and didn't look back and now you need to be punished. To be reminded of who owns you." He tugs hard on the belt, jerking my head. "What do you say?"

"Yes, Kayne," I reply immediately, surprised I can even use my voice.

"Good girl." He steps back with an hysterical look in his eyes. I know that look—it's manic, lust-fueled desire. It's Kayne's point of no return. "I want you to run, Ellie. I want you to run so I can remind you what happens when even the thought of leaving me crosses your mind." He snaps another leather belt in front of my face making me jump sky high. Holy shit.

The last time I ran from Kayne, my ass hurt for days, and I definitely remembered who I belonged to. He steps back, giving me some much-needed space.

"Go!" He snaps the belt again, and I take off, tearing out of the bedroom into the living room with Kayne right behind me. I dart and dash, jumping over the couch and knocking over a lamp in an attempt to get away. I scream as Kayne grabs one of my ankles and takes me down. My knees hit the floor hard, but I dig my nails into the wood and attempt crawl away from him. That's when he hits me the first time. Crack! Right across my backside. I see stars and shriek at the top of my lungs. I'm suddenly caught up in fight or flight, not wanting to suffer another hit. I kick and flail until Kayne loses his grip on my ankle. I hear him chuckle a little; he loves this game. Me, I'm not so sure. I run through the bungalow heaving for air with Kayne still hot on my tail.

"All around the mulberry bush the monkey chased the weasel," he taunts as he chases me. It's disturbing. I catch sight of the stairs. We haven't been up there before, but in a rash decision, I think now is as good a time as any to explore. With my heart jackhammering in my chest, I book it two stairs at a time while Kayne sings behind me, "A penny for a spool of thread. A penny for a needle." I make it to the top step, and he catches my ankle again. "That's the way the monkey goes." He pulls my leg out from underneath me causing me to fall face down on my stomach. "Pop goes the weasel." Crack! He hits me once more, and I let out a scream.

"Kayne," I cry as I crawl across the floor away from him. The second floor is an all open space. There is a massage table in front of us, wide-open windows, and a large sundeck with Jacuzzi and lounge chairs. The door to the sauna is all the way in the back.

"Am I making an impression, kitten? Is this what you wanted?" He hauls me up by my shirt, the spandex material ripping slightly. I don't answer. I just suck in the oxygen my lungs so desperately need.

"I asked you a question, Ellie." He slams me face first onto the massage table and pins me there with his forearm. Then he hits me again. Whack! Harder than the two times before. Oh shit, my poor ass.

"Is this what you wanted?!" he asks again.

"No, maybe. I don't know!" Tears stream down my face.

"Do you want me to stop?" he pants.

"Do you want to stop?"

"No, I want to peel your pants down to your thighs, spank you until your ass turns red, then fuck you until you beg me to stop."

"Then do it! You never gave me the choice before!" I'm not sure what's driving me here. Residual anger? Overpowering lust? I'm goading him for a reason. I need to know if this is what I truly want. I've dreamed about it, obsessed about it, and now I'm facing the moment of truth.

Kayne doesn't respond. Not verbally anyway, I feel him rip my yoga shorts down to my knees, exposing my bare behind. Oh shit, oh shit, the belt really hurts!

Whack! The first bare blow knocks the wind right out of me. I try to push myself up, but Kayne's strength overpowers mine.

"You're not going anywhere."

Whack!

"Understand?"

Whack!

"Answer!"

Whack!

"Yes, Kayne!" I sob.

"Ever, Ellie. I'm never going to let you go. Ever!"

Whack!

"Ah!" I screech.

"I'll kill you before I let that happen again."

WHACK! He hits me again, and I wail like I never have before. My body is strung so tight it feels like my muscles may rip. I whine feebly as I hear the creak of the leather and prepare for another blow, but it doesn't come. Only the feel of his erection pressing into my ass. The contact is brutal; my backside feels like he lit my skin on fire.

"I'm going to fuck you now. Are you wet for me, baby?" He slides one finger easily into my pussy. Shamefully, I am. I want this man so badly I endured brutality just so he'd fuck me freely, with no reservations, and nothing holding him back.

I nod zealously.

He grabs hold of the end of the belt around my neck and pulls it tautly, forcing my head to snap back. He's going to ride me like an animal. Like his pet. I grab onto the edge of the table for dear life and brace myself. Good thing, too, because he slams into me violently, the dual sensation of his stabbing cock and stiff hips colliding with my abused ass makes everything inside me constrict to the point of almost painful. *"Ohh,"* I grate. Kayne said he was going to fuck me and that's exactly what he does, beating into me over and over, pulling on the belt hard while my body bucks forward. I'm completely helpless, rendered his.

I claw at the table as his cock thickens inside me. Hitting me harder and deeper each time. My body tenses, as an all-consuming orgasm booms like thunder in my core.

When I moan, Kayne moans, when I gasp, Kayne gasps—like we're in sync. He feels what I feel.

"Come, Ellie," he grits out as his thrusts become erratic. "Come all over my cock and show me how much you need me."

My head is twisting with conflicting thoughts, but my body, my body is reveling in the tyrannical way he takes me, the way he commands me. He feels so fucking good, I freely give into the sensations storming inside me, give into Kayne and to my fucked-up desires. I push my throbbing ass back against him and let go, screaming, crying, and moaning as my orgasm unleashes. Then, without any warning, Kayne snaps the belt against my ass cheek just at the height of my pleasure, and I let out a hoarse howl as my climax ratchets up several more notches, sending me flying. The world vaporizes as I get lost in the elongated seconds of extreme ecstasy; Kayne hammering away at me as I drench both of us with my uncontainable arousal.

"So good," he chants, "so fucking good." He slams into me one last time, his fingertips piercing into my hips as a sound so powerful and male escapes from him it shakes just a few more drops of pleasure out of me.

The two of us collapse forward, moaning feebly in the aftermath. Kayne's large, hard body covering mine. After a few long wit-collecting moments, he begins kissing my shoulders; sweet, soft kisses that tickle my skin.

"Ellie?"

"Mmm?" I answer absently, still reveling in the lingering bliss.

"You know I would never kill you right?"

"I hoped you weren't being serious." I smirk.

"No." He tightens his arms around me. "If you decide to leave, I'll kill myself."

My eyes pop open. "Kayne, don't talk like that. No one is killing anyone, and I'm not going anywhere." I crane my neck to look at him. His eyes are so raw. "I promise."

We stare vehemently at each other before he wraps his hand around my throat and pulls me against him, crushing his mouth to mine. The kiss is awkward yet passion-filled all at the same time. Kayne is still buried inside me, and I feel him growing hard again. I moan freely, so ready for round two.

"I love you." He pulls away and digs his face into my neck. "I love you, I love you."

I smile. "I know. I lo—"

We're suddenly interrupted by someone banging on the front door.

"Monsieur! Monsieur!"

Kayne and I both freeze. "The night concierge," he tells me. "I'll handle it."

Kayne withdraws from me, and my body frowns. It misses him already. I watch over my shoulder as he pulls on his shorts and hurries down the stairs. I suppose I should do the same, but my body is so sore, and the thought of pulling my pants over my battered ass is distressing. I'm not going to be able to sit down tomorrow, I'm sure of it. Probably not the next day, either, so I just lie there spent.

I listen to the faint voices of Kayne and a very upset concierge. Then I hear something that shocks me. Kayne speaking French. Like fluent, beautiful French. It's totally arousing. He's full of so many surprises. And I love surprises.

"Ellie?" I hear Kayne jog up the stairs.

"Mmm hmm?" I answer still draped over the massage table.

Kayne chuckles as he pulls me up. I groan miserably.

"Everything okay?" I ask him.

"Yes, crisis averted." He kneels in front of me and removes my pants so I'm left standing in just my ripped pink tank top and belt around my neck.

Scratch that, he just pulled off my top. "We scared the neighbors."

"Us? Preposterous," I snort.

Kayne laughs, tugging me by the makeshift collar into a quick kiss. "Yes, I had to assure him it was just a bout of rough sex."

"In French?" I look up at him.

"Yes, speaking his native tongue helped." He smiles.

"I didn't know you spoke French."

"Yup." Kayne nods. "And Spanish and Arabic and Mandarin."

"No Italian?" I joke. "Such an underachiever."

"Tell me about it," he jokes. "Maybe I can learn a few choice words just for you."

"Mmm. Maybe." I lean against him seductively and kiss him right where my name is tattooed on his skin. His chest is warm and smells so good, like sex and sweat and body wash.

"Come on, siren," he moans. "Let's take care of that bottom before we go another round."

"I'm all for another round."

"In bed," he promises darkly, then takes the end of the belt and leads me back downstairs. It's so hot, him toting me around the bungalow, I almost want to purr.

"Lay down," Kayne commands once we're back in the bedroom. I slide forward on the bed and stretch my body out like a lazy cat. Kayne's lazy kitten. He groans appreciatively behind me.

"Relax." He rubs my back starting from the tip of my tailbone and circling upward. I just sigh, sated, until I feel the tickle of his warm breath against my cheek.

"I'll be right back."

"Where are you going?" I protest.

"To get something to rub on your ass. I didn't exactly come prepared for this."

"For what?" I question.

"Kink."

"I think you're doing a bang-up job so far."

He glances at me fiendishly then walks out of the room.

"The only thing I could find was Vaseline," he says as he climbs onto the bed and straddles my thighs. "This might hurt a little." He rubs the sticky substance over my welts.

I whimper in return. It does hurt. Like a son of a bitch.

"Kitten, are you okay?" Kayne almost sounds worried. I crack my eyes open and look at him over my shoulder. "I'm fine." I smile. "Better than fine." I blush.

"I wasn't expecting that," he confesses as he wipes his hands with the towel he also brought from the bathroom.

"Neither was I."

Kayne stares at me quizzically. "I don't understand."

"What's to understand? Being with you changed me. Or awoke something in me." I try to rationalize.

"You like it when I dominate you?"

I shrug demurely. "Apparently. I like it when you're rough."

Kayne palms my sore ass, and I hiss. "You like getting punished?"

I nod silently.

"You like being reminded who you belong to?" He grins like the Cheshire cat.

"Yes. To a point." I wince as he rubs.

"What happened to you hating being conditioned?"

I touch my chin to my shoulder flirtatiously. "I guess it's not so bad when it's my choice."

"Ellie." Kayne breathes my name like I'm a deity he worships, burying his face into my neck. "You are so mine."

Agreed.

KAYNE

I RUB MY TEMPLES AS I stare out over the water. My head feels like it's going to explode.

I unleashed myself last night. I let the beast out of its cage and handed over control. To say I didn't like it would be lying. I loved it, every second of it. From the moment I wrapped that belt around Ellie's neck, I was a goner. I keep playing it over and over, the way she ran from me, the way she fought me, the tears she shed, the reddening of her smooth white ass and the plush feel of her soaking wet pussy. All reason and rationale flew out the window as soon as she knelt at my feet. She was so turned on. It was more than I could have ever asked for—to have my kitten back for just one night—but it is also the one thing that feeds my fear. It's a serpent-like creature that burrows itself into the recesses of my subconscious. A gnawing worry that makes me regret last night ever happened. Because, in that dark black cavity, my one true terror lives—that Ellie is going to wake up and realize it was all a mistake. That she's going to wash her hands of whatever it is we have and leave. I keep telling myself she isn't my mother, but the nagging little voice in the background keeps reminding me that she left me once, she could do it again.

The thought nearly demolishes me. She really is the one person who can destroy me. She may kneel at my feet, but she holds all the power. I'm the slave. I always have been. I stare out into the blue-green abyss trying to picture my life without Ellie. It's nearly impossible. I wasn't living before her, and I could never live after her. My chest feels like it's going to cave in. Why do I do this to myself? I let the worry and anxiety win. *"I'm not going anywhere."* I replay her words over and over trying to reassure myself.

"I'm not going anywhere."

"I'm not going anywhere."

She's not going anywhere.

I suddenly feel a nudge against my leg, and it yanks me away from my worrisome thoughts. When I look down, I nearly fall back in my chair because Ellie is kneeling on the ground, wearing nothing but a collar and one of my white Ginny-tees.

"ELLIE, WHAT-WHAT ARE YOU DOING?" I can barely speak.

She looks up at me with just her eyes, the green extra vibrant from the bright island sun.

"I wasn't snooping, I swear." She crawls up my legs to sit on my lap. "I wanted to wear one of your shirts, and I accidentally kicked over your suitcase. When it fell open, the tag caught my eye," she says coiling into herself, a little insecure and a whole lot sexy.

"I didn't bring it with any expectations," I blurt out. "It just made me feel close to you." I run my finger over the leather. It's not exactly the same collar she wore when she was with me at Mansion—that one was snapped in two—but this one is close. Thick black leather with large rhinestones adjacent to three D-rings and a light pink satin interior. Just feminine enough with a bit of bondage edge.

"It makes me feel close to you, too."

"You don't have to wear it." Although, now that she has it on, I never want her to take it off.

"I want to wear it."

"Why?"

She shrugs shyly. "Do you really have to ask?"

I search Ellie's face for any kind of reluctance or inkling of uncertainty. But there's none, only sincere eyes and a sultry expression.

"Say it." *Say the words I have been dying to hear.*

Ellie leans forward and slides her hands up the back of my neck and into my hair. "I love you. I have always loved you. Even when I hated you, I loved you. And I love you even more now."

My chest feels like it's going to explode. Those three words unlock something deep inside me.

"Say it again." I grab onto Ellie's bare ass. She's naked under my shirt.

"I love you," she says again, and I slam my lips against hers. Of all the emotions Ellie's made me feel—this moment, right now, is the most potent. I'm aerating with so much happiness I almost feel stoned, like I smoked straight elation.

"Don't stop saying it," I mumble against her mouth as I shoot up, Ellie wrapping her legs around my waist for support. "I want to hear you say it while I make you come." I walk straight into the bedroom while driving my tongue deep into her mouth. She moans loudly and my erection hardens into a stiff peak. I flip Ellie onto the mattress, and she lands on her back with a firm bounce. I shrug off my basketball shorts and climb onto the bed. "Lift your shirt up," I order as I crawl over her. With wide eyes, she immediately pulls the soft white material up to her chin exposing her completely naked form to me. My cock pulses with anticipation. It already knows how good she feels, how soft, warm and wet, and all for me.

"Open your legs, wide," I direct as I grab her wrists and pin her down. Panting heavily, she obeys, dropping her knees as far as they can go.

Good girl.

"Say it, Ellie." I rub my throbbing cock against her entrance.

"I love you," she breathes, her eyes fixated on mine.

"Again."

"I love you."

I thrust into her as deeply as I can. *"Oh!"* She closes her eyes and strains.

"That's not what I want to hear." I pull back and drive in deeply again.

"Look at me, Ellie. Look at me and say it," I snap.

Ellie's eyes fly open, and then with clipped breaths, she repeats the words. "I love you, I love you, I love you, I love you." Her voice elevates, and her face tightens as I keep a painfully slow tempo with my hips, brushing my pelvis over her swollen clit until she's struggling beneath me.

"Kayne, please," she begs as her pussy clamps down around me. "Faster, harder. Please," she expels.

Ellie begging does it to me every time.

"Tell me again, baby. Tell me while I make you come." My voice is unrecognizable as my body unleashes. I no longer have control as I pound into her, her breasts bouncing and tag jingling on her collar. Fuck, she really is completely mine.

"Oh God, I love you!" she cries out trying to fight against me, trying to find an outlet for her orgasm, only to realize it's being forced between her legs. Her fists clench in my hands and her body quakes as her climax rockets through her.

The hot rush of her arousal washes over me like lava and I come without any warning and absolutely no control. It's pure instinct, primal and primitive. Our hips fasten together as I bury my cock as deep inside her as it can possibly go, as if my body wants to become one with hers.

Once the sensations subside, the only thing that's left of us is labored breathing and warm fluids.

I look down at Ellie and for the first time, I see my life with clarity, in bright shining color. "Marry me." The words just fall straight from my lips, and I mean them with everything I am, everything I have.

"What?" Ellie's eyes pop open.

With a quick tug, I pull her up and place her on my lap. "Marry me," I say again. I never planned to propose, at least not this soon, so her shock is as genuine as mine. "Stay with me, Ellie. Wear my ring and my collar. Become my family, make me whole."

Ellie stares at me speechless, and I wonder if I've pushed her too far. Her silence is deafening. I prepare for a 'no,' for 'it's too soon' or 'I need to think about it.' My manhood shrivels. Stupid idiot.

"Yes," she finally speaks.

"What?" My eyes widen to the point my eyelids nearly rip off.

"Yes, I'll marry you," she repeats, for my sake I'm sure. "I'll wear your ring and your collar. I'll make you whole."

It may not have been a perfect proposal, but that was definitely the perfect response.

I lay Ellie on the bed and nestle myself between her legs. "It's my turn to tell you how much I love you." I nudge my semierect cock against her slick entrance.

She smiles up at me. "You can tell me as many times as you want." She rocks her hips, inviting me inside her.

"That could take a lifetime." I slide easily into her.

Ellie wraps her arms and legs around me. "We have an entire one to share."

I love the sound of that.

ELLIE

"ELLIE, WAKE UP." I FEEL something cold run over my lips, and I flinch. "Kitten, wake up, I can't watch you sleep anymore." The cold wetness drips over one of my nipples, and my eyes fly open.

"Morning," Kayne smiles hedonistically as he massages the ice cube against my clit. I suck in a sharp breath from the freezing sensation.

"How long have I been sleeping?" I rub my legs together and glance out the door. The sun is already setting.

"A while." Kayne pops the ice cube into his mouth and stares down at me with ravenous blue eyes. It's a gaze I recognize immediately.

"You're wearing me out." I smirk.

"I haven't even begun to wear you out. Up." He pulls me by my hands, and my body willingly goes. "Go to the bathroom and then come right back." There's authority in his voice. The kind that reduces me to just sensitive nerve endings.

I hurry up and do my business—my butt still so sore from last night—and immediately return to the bedroom. Once standing in front of him, Kayne runs his fingers reverently up my neck, over my collar, and then threads them into my hair. Controlling my head with a firm grip, he tilts my face up and spears his tongue into my mouth. I melt against him as the kiss consumes me.

"Kitten," he says once he pulls away. It isn't a question; it's a statement, a fact. Part of our foundation. "Do you still want to marry me?" he asks so vulnerably.

"Of course, I do. Nothing will ever change that. I'm yours," I reassure him.

"Good." He drops a chaste kiss on my lips. "Because I'm dying to play." His eyes burn bright and so does my core. This is what I've been missing, what I've been craving. Kayne in complete control—control of my mind, control of my body, control of my pain, and my pleasure. Am I crazy? Maybe. But isn't that what love is? Insane. I wasn't lying when I said I wasn't snooping. I found the collar exactly the way I said I did, by accident. As soon as I saw that little silver heart, I knew it was mine. The first time Kayne fastened a collar around my neck, I hated it—I hated him. But after a while, things changed. I changed. And once I held it in my hand again, felt the leather under my fingertips and read the inscriptions on the tag—one side Kayne's Kitten, the other side, Loved, Collared, and Owned by Him—I couldn't resist. It was like I found a missing part of me.

I never knew that second inscription existed. Maybe if I had, things might have ended differently. Regardless of past outcomes, it's the truth of the present that's important now.

And the truth is Kayne has always owned me, since day one. I'm pretty sure I would have done anything he asked whether I was wearing a collar or not. That's the claim he has on me—the power, the authority, the domination. And I wouldn't want it any other way. I love every part of him—the Dom, the thrill-seeker, and even the broken man—I couldn't stop myself even if I tried.

I breathe heavily with anticipation. He hasn't even touched me yet and I'm already coming undone. Kayne pushes me back until I'm crushed between his hard body and one of the bedposts. "Put your hands up and hold on."

I raise my arms and grasp the square post with both hands. Kayne steps back and looks greedily at my scantily covered form. I'm dressed in only his soft white undershirt and black collar, my nipples sharp as nails under the cotton material.

"Stay," he commands, and then leaves the room. I wait anxiously as I grip the bedpost trying not to combust.

Kayne returns with a small bundle of zip ties of various sizes and a silk tie. I look at him curiously, but don't say a word.

"Some things you just don't leave home without," he says haughtily as he pulls out several plastic ties. My heart rate speeds up as I watch Kayne fasten one zip tie around the top beam of the canopy bed directly above me. Then he connects another to that, and so on, until he's constructed a plastic chain link. Finally, he takes the maroon silk tie and wraps it around my wrists. "So it won't leave any marks." He winks as he binds my hands with a zip tie, tightening it so my wrists crush together. Once secure, he pulls my arms up until I'm forced to stand on my toes, and attaches my bound wrists to the hanging zip ties.

"Perfect." He admires his handiwork. Me, hung like a fish on a hook, helpless and gasping for air.

Kayne takes advantage of my defenseless state, cupping my pussy and groping my breasts until he has me moaning.

"Don't get too wound up, kitten. No more orgasms for you."

I frown.

"At least for a little while." I swallow hard, trying to keep my balance on my tippy toes. "Baby, I want you to understand. I'm going to punish you, tease you, and fuck you so hard . . ." Kayne outlines my lips with the tip of his thumb. "But I'm going to love you even harder." He then shoves his thumb into my mouth forcing me to suck on it energetically. I moan, unhinged.

"Good girl." He removes his finger from my mouth then grabs my chin. "Now hang out and think about what it means to be a good little kitten. I'll be back."

With that, he leaves the room and me dangling.

Anticipation is always what gets me. The waiting, the solitude, and the fear of the unknown are the worst kind of mind games and the most powerful kind of arousal. Kayne playing me perfectly each time.

After way too much time alone with my thoughts, Kayne returns wearing only a pair of white linen pants that hang loosely on his hips. No shirt, no shoes, but definitely ready to be serviced. I can't help but stare at my demonic angel who's capable of being as bad as he is good. I shiver from just the thought of what he can do.

"Still hanging around, kitten?" He stands in front of me holding a rocks glass with bourbon in it. I know this because I recognize the smell. It's Kayne's drink of choice.

"You haven't given me much of an option," I respond.

Kayne arches his eyebrow at me with the glass close to his lips. "Getting sassy are we?"

"No. Just stating a fact." I wriggle in my restraints. My body is starting to ache from its overstretched position.

"How disappointing." Kayne takes a sip of his drink then places it on the end table next to the bed. He then opens the drawer and pulls out what looks like a pocketknife. I jump as he flips it open and holds the blade up in front of my face. "Something else I never leave home without," he says as he runs the tip of the knife down my neck. Holy shit. I know Kayne likes pain, but I'm not sure I'm prepared for this. I hold my breath as he continues to run the tip over my collarbone and down to the center of my chest right above the line of my shirt. He presses lightly, digging the blade into my skin until it pinches. I whimper as my heart completely stops.

"Trust me?" he asks.

I nod unsurely because, up till this moment, I have trusted him, but now I'm not so sure.

"Good." With a quick flick of his wrist, he slices my shirt open, the fabric ripping right down the middle. I nearly pass out.

"Relax, Ellie. I'm not really into knife play unless I'm stabbing it into the heart of someone who deserves it."

"Good to know," I swallow hard, breathing heavily.

"I do, however, like to inflict a little pain." Kayne reaches into his pocket and pulls out three little black *things*. It takes me a second to realize what they are.

"Binder clips?"

"Second rule of survival. Utilize your surroundings. I told you I didn't come prepared for kink so I had to use my imagination." He pinches one of the clips with his fingers. I think I go pale. "I found these in the workstation desk. I'm getting my money's worth at this resort." He smiles. I don't see the humor, only little chomping metal clips with a death grip.

"You look worried, Ellie. Don't think you can handle it?"

I shake my head.

"I think you can." Kayne begins stretching the clips, testing them on the tip of his finger several times before he's satisfied. "That should do. Now be a good kitten and stand still."

Like I have any other choice!

Kayne leans down and sucks my left nipple into his mouth, pulling on it hard with his teeth until it stiffens into a firm pebble. I can't contain the moan from the feel of his mouth and how he can make my insides spiral. Then, without warning, he clamps my engorged nipple. "Oh, God!" My whole body goes rigid.

Kayne tsks me. "Didn't we have this conversation? Oh, Kayne," he reminds me. "I'm your maker now, Ellie."

I'll never forget that conversation or that situation. Strapped to a table while Kayne clamped my nipples, very much like he's doing now. I'll also never forget the orgasm he gave me. I still feel it in my dreams. Even sometimes when I'm awake. "I think we need a refresher course." He sucks my other nipple into his mouth, repeating the process. The second clamp is just as severe as the first. I'm panting heavily trying to channel the pulsating pain.

"Kayne," I protest.

"I love that sound." He leans in close to my ear. "That tortured plea."

I look down to see him adjust himself, the head of his erection peeking out the top of his pants. "I've barely touched you, and I already want to fuck your brains out." He circles my clit with the tip of his finger.

"Yes, please," I mewl feebly, my head dropping back.

"Much better, kitten. You're starting to remember your manners." Kayne drops to his knees. "But this isn't about pleasure. At least not yours. Not yet anyway." He runs his tongue between my folds, lashing at my clit before he sucks it into his mouth. I groan noisily as my body tightens and a knot begins to grow in my stomach.

"Kayne, please." My nipples throb, my arms strain, and my pussy clenches.

"Sorry, kitten," he says as he clamps my inflamed clit, and I cry out. Holy shit!

"Perfect." He tugs on the binder clip, and I nearly see stars. By the time he stands, I'm gasping for air, my whole body is on fire, and there is an ache growing inside me faster than the speed of sound. "Now let's review.

Who owns you, Ellie?" He yanks on one clamped nipple.

"You do," I draw in a sharp breath.

"When I tell you to kneel, what do you say?"

"Yes, Kayne," I grate as he pulls on the other binder clip. The sensation shooting through my breast like a bolt of lightning.

"When I tell you to lie down and open your legs, what do you say?"

"Yes, Kayne." I sag in my restraints.

"When I tell you go bend over so I can spank you, what do you say?"

"Yes, Kayne."

"What do I want from you, Ellie?"

I look straight into his eyes. "My obedience."

"And?" He lightly twists the clamp on my clit.

"My submission," my voice pitches.

"And?" He does it again and every one of my muscle fibers constrict.

"My body."

"Do I have those things?"

"Yes," I pant.

"What about your heart? Do I have your heart?"

"Yes, Kayne. It's yours," I say exhausted.

"Good. No one will ever protect it better than me."

"I know." I smile weakly as he steps back and takes a long sip of his drink sitting on the nightstand.

He swirls the brown liquid while he gazes at me with piercing eyes, starving with desire and glowing like bright-blue orbs.

"I never had the chance to appreciate you, Ellie. To really take you in like I would have if things had been different." He finishes the last bit of his bourbon, and places the glass aside. He then proceeds to just stare, absorbing every single clamped, tethered inch of me. It's oppressive, uncomfortable, and highly erotic as he begins to stroke himself while looking at me.

"Fuck, Ellie." He steps closer so our bodies are touching. I can feel the stroke of his hand against my abdomen as he jerks himself off. "See what your body does to me? All I need to do is look and you make me want to come." He yanks himself harder, grabbing one of my tender breasts forcing a loud, torturous moan out of me as the clamp bites my nipple. True to his word, he loves my agonizing sounds, squeezing my breast again and again, using my strain, struggle and torment to get himself off.

"I'm going to come," he heaves in my ear. "You're going to make me fucking come." A moment later, a warm blast of semen coats my stomach as Kayne lets go. I can't do anything but hang there as he marks me, my arousal turning up a notch as I watch him explode.

With a few deep breaths, he composes himself, wiping off the ejaculation on his palm across my thigh like I'm a hand towel as he nuzzles my neck right above my collar.

"Time to get clean, kitten. But first."

He leans in and kisses me, swiping his tongue roughly against mine as he simultaneously unclamps my nipples. I whimper and kiss him harder as all the blood rushes to the surface causing the sensitive skin to thump with returned feeling. He then unclamps my clit, and I bite down on his lip as it pounds and throbs with a dull pain.

"Easy." He rubs between my legs gently, easing away the discomfort.

"Please don't stop," I sigh desperately as I drop my forehead to his chest, an orgasm so achingly close.

"Sorry, Ellie." He removes his hand, and I nearly weep. "Only when I say."

I slump in my restraints. Kayne gives me a few minutes to decompress—or so he thinks, my orgasm nowhere near tapering off—before he picks up the switchblade from the bed and cuts me loose, catching me before I hit the floor. My body is completely limp from dangling so long. He unties my wrists, then lifts my dead weight into his arms and carries me into the bathroom. He doesn't put me in the shower or run a bath; he merely places me in the tub and turns on the water.

"Hands and knees," he says as he sits on the edge. I frown at him.

"Aren't you going to take a bath with me?" I ask.

"Nope. I'm cleaning my dirty kitten. That's all. Now get on your hands and knees."

I do as he says with a sulk. Kayne chuckles. He knows exactly what he's doing. I do, too. He's re-establishing roles. Master and slave. I suppose it has to be done for the order of things. It doesn't mean I have to like it any more now than I did then, but he's the only one who can give me what I want, what I need. And he's making damn sure it's clear I understand that.

Kayne lathers me up, not missing one single spot on my quivering body. His touch feels good and so does the warm water. He washes my back and my front as I stay situated on my hands and knees like I'm a dog at the groomer.

Kayne works his sudsy hands over my ass and I tense. Not because it's still sore, which it is, but because he presses the tip of his thumb against my back entrance.

"I can't wait to fuck you here, Ellie." He pushes in and penetrates the tight ring of muscle.

"Oh," I moan over the running water. It doesn't exactly hurt, but it doesn't exactly feel good, either. Not until he fingers my ass several times do my muscles relax and then tense up again in a completely different way.

"Mmm." I push back into his hand as my orgasm starts to rapidly grow.

"You like that?" he asks as he slides his middle finger into my pussy and simultaneously fucks both holes. "It feel good?"

"God yes, please don't stop." I'm so fucking close to the explosion I desperately need I can practically taste it.

"That's all you get, kitten." He withdraws his fingers, and my body deflates.

"Kayne!" I whine. I need to fucking come!

He slaps me hard on the ass, and I yelp.

"Are you complaining, kitten?" he chastises me. I don't have a chance to respond because he goes on. "You're wearing my collar. And that means you do as I say. And I say when you come, understand?"

I shrink, "Yes, Kayne."

"Good girl." He spanks me again, and I clench my jaw. My backside is still overly tender. "Next time you talk back, I'm using the belt. And my dick won't be in you when I'm done."

"Yes, Kayne," I answer softly as he rinses me off. I know I should feel embarrassed or put off that he scolded me, but it just makes me want him more. Want to please him more. I don't understand it, and I don't think I ever will. All I know is that I have an erotic compulsion to obey him. To make him happy.

Kayne rinses me, then turns off the water. The ends of my hair are wet and so is the rest of my body, except for my face and neck. He didn't wash me there because he never removed my collar.

He helps me to stand, and once I'm out of the tub, Kayne dries me off, still feeling like a windup toy ready to race.

"There. All clean." He drops the towel into the hamper. "But I'm not sure for how long." He smiles wickedly.

I stare up at him, trying not to give away how needy I am. It's his fault, by the way. He created the insatiable monster.

"Now stay." He grabs my chin and lifts my face, dropping a small kiss on my lips, then walks out of the bathroom, with me completely naked and a soft breeze from the wide-open window caressing my skin. I have a feeling clothes are a thing of the past, at least for the time being. Kayne returns holding a leash, a thin chain with a light pink satin ribbon braided through it that matches the color on the inside of my collar.

"I told you I had no premeditated intention when I bought these, but since we're embracing the moment, I figure I'll use it." He hooks the leash to the front ring of my collar. "No locks, okay? No locks ever again." He runs his hand down the chain and I nod.

"You always have a choice, Ellie," he reminds me.

"Always?" My lip twitches.

"Yes."

"Then I choose for you to fuck me."

Kayne laughs. "I love when you talk dirty, but that's not how it works. You chose to wear that collar, you choose to obey me. House rules. I tell you what to do, you say, yes, Kayne. You will please me. End of story."

I just had a bout of déjà vu.

"So, are we doing this?" He yanks the chain.

"Yes, Kayne," I answer taunting him. Bring it on.

"Good girl. Now get on your knees and crawl. No standing unless I give you permission."

I sink to the floor, never taking my eyes off Kayne's. His gaze morphs into a perverse approval. My arousal spikes as my hands touch the smooth wood. Jesus, this man makes me so hot my insides just sizzled to dust.

"Come, kitten. I want to pet you." He jingles my leash, and then leads me out of the bathroom and into the living room. He picks up the back cushion of the chair and drops it onto the floor in front of the couch.

"Kneel there." I climb onto the light cream pillow and kneel as I remember, with my feet tucked underneath me and my head bowed.

"Your refresher course in obedience training seems to be working well."

I don't know why, but I smile to myself. I like the praise in his voice.

I hear Kayne pour a drink, but I never lift my eyes to look at him. I just wait. Once he's finished, he sits on the couch, making sure I'm situated right between his knees.

"Closer, Ellie." He motions with his hand, and I immediately scoot closer, placing my head on his lap. Kayne smirks as he runs his fingers through my hair, massaging my scalp as he sips on his drink. In some weird way, I feel closer to him like this than I do when we're kissing or fucking or even making love.

"My kitten?" he asks as the sun sets, casting shadows around the room.

I nod as he lulls me. "You're the only one who can make me purr."

"HUNGRY, KITTEN?" KAYNE ASKS AS I crawl behind him out onto the sundeck.

"Yes," I answer, but not for food.

"I figured. You had a long night," he says with some amusement. Long is an understatement. I've been playing consensual sex slave for over thirty-six hours, and in that time, Kayne has licked, fingered, and fucked me, chained me to the bed and spanked me, and used my body as a canvas to paint with his cum, all the while denying me an orgasm. I'm about as fragile as a thin piece of blown glass. I need release so badly, I could shatter with slightest kiss of an island breeze.

And Kayne fucking knows it.

The table outside is set up with breakfast; room service is a miraculous thing. It's how we've sustained nutrition the last day and a half.

I kneel, naked except for my collar and chain, on the pillow he put down for me next to his chair. It's another perfect morning, the sun shining brightly, the temperature warm, and the water sparkling. But it's Kayne's eyes that have my full attention. They've been on fire ever since I slipped my neck jewelry back on. It's that look—that acute, heated gaze that's so hot it could set the Society Islands on fire. That's the look I live for, lust for, endure for. Because I know for as much punishment he inflicts, he'll match it with an equal amount of pleasure, possibly even more. What this man makes me feel is above and beyond just physical. He reaches further inside me than anyone else, stroking my mind and caressing my soul; consuming me to the point that all I'm aware of is him. The outside world ceases to exist; I've become his willing captive, and I love every second of it.

I watch transfixed as Kayne picks up a piece of fruit from his plate, an orange cube of cantaloupe. He brings it to my mouth and rims it around my lips. I go to bite it, but he pulls it away.

He shakes his head, moving his hand down my naked breast to massage my nipple with the cold piece of fruit; it hardens to a painful point. I'm over-stimulated, moaning inwardly as I try to control the ravenous need flaring inside me.

Kayne pops the melon into his mouth then feeds me a piece. He repeats the teasing and massaging on each of my breasts until all of the cantaloupe is gone, and I am a panting mess.

"Please," I beg. I've had enough. I've reached my breaking point; I don't even care what I sound like, what I look like. I just need to come. "Kayne, please." The tone of my voice is pathetic, broken down and desperate. He smiles because he has me exactly where he wants me. Which is dependent on him. And I am. His reconditional training worked. I'm enslaved, his bonded servant, trained to obey.

"Okay, kitten. You've been a very good girl, time for a treat." He picks up a large strawberry from his plate. I stare half mentally removed as he brings it to his mouth and licks it with his tongue the exact same way he licked cream cheese frosting off a red velvet cupcake. *Holy fucking shit.* "Hmm, sweet," he muses then reaches down between my legs. I gasp as the chilled strawberry tip grazes my sensitive clit.

"I want you to come, kitten." He rubs the strawberry firmly against me and my need ruptures.

"Oh, God." I sink my nails into my thighs as everything below my navel tightens. "Kayne," I whimper as he rubs in a circular motion, making me crazy. I start to rock my hips as my orgasm takes on a life of its own, commanding me to climax.

"Who owns your pleasure, Ellie?"

"You do." I suck in a ragged breath.

"Who owns your body?" he asks as he slips the strawberry into my pussy and fucks me with it.

"You do," I moan deep in my throat.

"Who owns your heart?"

"You do!" I come so fucking hard and loud I'm pretty sure the neighbors hear as every ounce of pent-up frustration gushes out of me onto the strawberry and Kayne's hand. Oh God, I'm destroyed. My body feels like Jell-O and I can't hold up my head, but I stay kneeling until Kayne instructs me to move.

"Mmm," I hear Kayne moan. I crack open my eyes just as he bites the last bit of the dark-red fruit. "You're sweeter than whipped cream." He licks his fingers, then plucks me up from the ground and straddles me on his lap. "Feel better?" He nudges my cheek with his nose and grinds his erection between my legs.

"Honestly? No," I laugh. "I could use ten more of those."

"Good." Kayne slams both of his hands on my bare ass and I jump like a spooked cat. I'm still unbearably sensitive. "Because I'm not done with you yet." He kisses me hard, spearing his tongue into my mouth and my arousal begins a countdown to launch.

"Go—" He starts to order me, but we're interrupted by someone banging on the front door. Oh no, not again.

"Kayne!" We hear Jett's voice. "Kayne, come on, man! Open up!"

"Shit," Kayne mutters. "Next time, I'm taking you to a private island with no neighbors, no doors, and no interruptions."

I giggle. "I'm in."

"You don't have a choice." He yanks on my chain.

"Kayne!" Jett bangs again.

"Coming!" he barks so loud, I jolt. Jeez, he can be scary in so many different ways.

"Sorry." He kisses me softly. "Go inside and clean up, then wait for me bent over the side of the bed." He threads his fingers into the underside of my hair and grips tightly. "I want your ass, Ellie." Then he kisses me again, deep and hard, and my body responds without delay.

"KAYNE!" Jett's voice breaks us from our kiss.

"Go." He spanks me with blatant irritation. I slide off him quickly and scurry into the bedroom. "Jett, this better be important or I'm going to rearrange your face." I hear Kayne yell from somewhere inside the bungalow.

I quickly wipe off the cum dripping down the inside of my leg with a damp washcloth, then position myself exactly the way Kayne wants me—bent over with my ass in the air and my hands placed firmly on the mattress. I shake, still wanton with need and slightly distressed. I know what's coming, and it's going to hurt just as much as it's going to be pleasurable.

"Fine," I hear Kayne say loudly, and Jett laughs.

I can't imagine what they're talking about. A minute later, Kayne walks into the bedroom. I'm facing the headboard so I have to look slightly over my shoulder to see him.

"Damn." He slows his pace as he walks over to me.

"Everything okay?" I ask.

"Fine," Kayne answers oblivious, solely fixated on my bare, wide open ass.

"What did he want?"

"Nothing." He caresses my left butt cheek. "We can talk about it later." He squeezes, and I wince.

"Jesus, Ellie. You don't know how many times I dreamed about you just like this." He runs his finger along my ass crack, putting slight pressure against my hole. I hold my breath.

"Ellie, I love you." It's a statement, like a reassurance.

"I know." I peer at him.

"Good. Because this is going to be intense. It's going to hurt, and I'm going to like it." He stares at me with manic lust.

Oh, shit.

"What's your safe word?"

"Cupcake," I automatically answer.

"Good girl. Stay." He walks into the bathroom, and a few seconds later, returns with what I recognize as a very tiny bottle of lubricant. In that small fraction of time my anxiety has spiked through the roof.

"Another thing you never leave home without?" I ask shakily.

I hear the top pop. "When you're in a committed relationship with your hand for a year, yes." He drizzles the sticky substance over my tiny little hole. I glance back to see Kayne naked and fully erect, rubbing his length down with the lube as well.

"I'm going to stretch you with only my cock, Ellie. No fingers. We'll go slow."

He lines up behind me, and I feel the head of his erection poking against my tight little rose bud. I haven't had anal sex in over a year, and it's only ever been with Kayne. He penetrates me with the tip of his cock, the lube helping to ease it in, and the pain is immediate. I lunge forward, but he grips my hips and pulls me back.

"Don't. Take it." He pushes harder, and I whimper as he slowly rips me open. I claw at crumpled sheets, the bed a messy sea of white from last night.

Kayne relentlessly works himself into my behind, every inch a battle, every tear a victory. I heave air as he rocks in and out, the pain gripping me like a vice. I moan in agony as my body tries to reject the foreign object plunging its way into me.

"Let it out," he grunts with a firm thrust, and my eyes spill over with tears. I press my face into the mattress and sob with his cock halfway inside me. When he pulls out, it only gives me one second of relief before he's pushing back in, deeper than before. When he bends over me and grabs my collar, I know I'm done for. There's no more reprieve, no more withdrawing, only a straight shot of hard cock directly into my ass. Kayne yanks at my collar as he thrusts, using it almost as leverage to bury himself to the hilt, reducing me to nothing but saggy bones and uncontrollable sobs. He takes over my body exactly the way he wanted—he invaded, enslaved, and then conquered it.

"I love your tears, Ellie." His voice is rough, and his hips are relentless as I cry helplessly on the bed, letting the tears fall freely because I know that's what he likes, what gets him off. I remember all too well, Kayne's favorite things are pleasure, pain, and pushing me to my limit. Seeing how far he can take me before I finally crack.

"Fuck, I missed this," he strains. "I missed getting strangled by your tight little ass." His thrusts become jerky and erratic. "Touch yourself, Ellie. Touch yourself now." He slams into me, and I cry out. With my face still planted on the mattress, I slide my shaky hands between my legs and do as he says, massaging my clit until my pussy relaxes.

"That's it, baby." He moves freely now, my burning ass completely stretched to accommodate his long length and wide girth.

"I wish you could see it," he groans as he fluidly slides all the way in and then pulls all the way out like he was always made to fit me. "How you swallow me whole." He sinks himself inside me again. "And fuck, it's so good." He slaps my ass so that my muscles clench around him. "Finger yourself. I want you to come. I want you to come with me." He starts to pump fast, and I have to bite my lip to absorb the discomfort, the tears a steady, constant flow. But even with all he's put me through, the need for release is still as strong as ever. I need him to fuck me; I want him to fuck me. I sink my middle and ring fingers inside my now soaking wet pussy and press my palm to my clit. I rub and finger myself all while Kayne uses my body for his wicked pleasure, the three acts swirling together to become the perfect storm of desire. My orgasm comes on like a high-speed turbine, all pressure and velocity, intensely working its way through my system until I can't contain it anymore.

"Please, may I come?" I scream out at the very last second before I seize, my muscles grinding like steel brakes as my insides splinter.

Kayne doesn't respond, he just repeats 'mine, mine, mine, mine' like a broken record as he's sucked down with me, stabbing into my ass so deep I swear I can feel my heart beating against the head of his cock.

He pins me against the mattress as we both collapse to our knees, breathing harder than I think we've ever breathed before. When he withdraws, I feel like an overused rag doll who has been taken off her stick. I am sore, battered, and I think half dead. I cry some more. I'm not even sure why, I think just for some cathartic relief. The past day and a half has been the most taxing of my life. Being denied orgasm after orgasm and then broken open like a coconut has depleted my mind and my body.

Kayne wraps his arms around me and licks my face the same way he has all the other times I've cried in his presence.

"Your body and your tears are the closest to heaven I will ever get." He burrows his face between my shoulder blades. "You're the purest thing in my life."

"There's nothing pure about me, anymore," I giggle and sniffle all at the same time.

"Your love is pure."

I glance at Kayne out of the corner of my eye. The ferocity of his gaze is what makes me love him so much. It's always drawn me to him. His presence is all empowering. That stare tells me I'm his entire fucking world, and he would do anything to protect it. To protect me.

How do you walk away from something like that?

Someone like that?

The answer is simple. You don't.

KAYNE PLACES ME IN A steaming hot tub, and my muscles whistle like a kettle. Oh, that feels so good.

He climbs in right after me, situating himself underneath me. The tub is quite large and looks out over the lagoon. There isn't one lousy view from any room. Kayne massages my back, rubbing firm, hard circles over my spine as our bodies slip and slide together from the bubbles.

"You feeling okay?" he asks as he kisses my neck and holds me close.

"There's a pain in my ass," I reply drily.

"And I bet you love it." He nips at me.

"Maybe just a little." I rub up against him, the water sloshing, and slip my tongue between his lips. I suddenly break our kiss. "Oh! What did Jett want?"

Kayne frowns. "You're kissing me passionately and thinking about Jett?"

That does kind of look bad.

"Not in the sexual, *I want you to own me, rule over me, spank me kind of way.*" I flutter my eyelashes at him.

"Well, thank God for that." Kayne rolls his eyes, the brown lightning bolt prominent in bright sunlight.

I kiss him again. Hard, but playfully. He tickles me, sending more water over the edge of the tub.

"Hey!" I squeak.

"That's what you get."

"For asking about Jett?" I laugh and squirm as his fingers dig into my side.

"For asking about Jett while you're naked and wet!"

"I'm sorry!" I screech. "It just happened! Kayne!" I try to claw my way out of the tub, but he pulls me back and kisses me, wrapping one leg around mine.

"Forgiven. Don't do it again." He spanks me, but the hit is broken by the water so I barely feel it."

"Yes, Kayne," I purr anyway.

"Good kitten," he patronizes.

"So really, what did he want?" I ask again.

Kayne sinks deeper into the tub, locking his arm around my lower back crushing me to him. "He wanted to make sure we were both alive."

"What?"

Kayne nods. "Since he couldn't get ahold of me all day yesterday, he wanted to check in. I think he was more concerned about you than me."

"Me? Why?"

Kayne shrugs. "You were one of his girls once. For Jett, that doesn't just go away. You were as important as any of them. Even more so."

"Oh. Does that bother you?"

"No. I'm glad he cares. He's the only other man I would ever trust you with."

"I sort of got that impression." I smile and hook my arm around his neck. The man did wax me, bathe me, and dress me up like his doll. "Kayne? Speaking of being someone's girl." I bite my lip. "How come you never made me call you Master?"

"What?" He eyes me surprised.

"Well, in the books I read and the research I did, most submissives call their Dom Master or Sir. You never made me do that. Not even now."

"You did research?" He raises his eyebrows.

"I was curious. Being with you made me curious." I blush.

"I guess that's understandable. I did expose you to a lot of things in a short amount of time." That's putting it mildly. "Why didn't I make you call me Master?" he considers. "To be honest, it felt too impersonal. I wanted us to have a connection, even if I couldn't tell you that. I thought letting you call me by my name would somehow humanize me, even if I wasn't acting very human." He brushes his hand lovingly down my back. "And as for why I don't make you do it now? It still feels too impersonal. I like hearing you say my name. It's reassuring, and I need that," he says apprehensively.

If there's one thing I've learned in the very short time I've been with Kayne, it's that he hates his vulnerability as much as he realizes it's what makes him human. "I understand."

"Does it bother you that I call you kitten?"

"No," I answer honestly. "I like it. It makes me feel sexy."

"You are sexy. And smart and funny and loved. You are so fucking loved, Ellie." Kayne kisses me feverishly as if trying to personify his affection, but he doesn't need to bring it to life, I can already feel its warmth and fluttering heartbeat.

AFTER A VERY LONG SOAK in the tub, until our fingers pruned and our muscles unfurled, Kayne and I lounged around the bungalow. It was a nice afternoon. Relaxing and stress-free.

Now, I'm just about finished with my makeup, swiping blackest black mascara over my eyelashes. I'm starting to get the hang of this, I think, as I inspect myself in the mirror.

Apparently, Kayne's word wasn't good enough for Jett because he insisted that he produce me at dinner tonight. If you ask me, I just think he and London miss us.

I catch Kayne leaning against the doorway staring at me through the mirror. He's wearing a light-brown button-up shirt, tan dress pants, and a scorching hot expression, like he wants to devour me right where I stand.

"See something you like?" I ask him as I close the mascara and place it back in my makeup bag.

"Maybe." He strolls up behind me. "These are a bit short." He tugs on the hem of my white shorts.

"So?"

"You know how I feel about you showing your body off to anyone but me."

I turn to look at him, placing my hands on his chest. The material of his shirt so incredibly soft.

"I think we need to establish something," I flirt. "The only place you get to tell me what I can and cannot wear is in the bedroom. Outside those doors, I'm my own woman."

Kayne's eyes flash with something I've never seen before, nothing angry, but excited, perverted almost. "Oh, yeah? That's good to know because I do want to dress you up. I want you to really be my kitten. I want to slide a pair of ears on your head and plug a tail in your ass and fuck you while you purr," he says groping my behind. My jaw drops from the vivid image.

"I didn't realize you were into fetish," I reply breathlessly as he kisses and tickles my neck with his warm breath.

"I never really was, but being with you makes me want to . . . *explore.*" He looks at me with ravenous lust in his striking blue eyes.

I'm trapped in place, my knees about to buckle. This man is going to be the death of me.

"So, is that a yes, Ellie?" He rasps in my ear while unbuttoning my pants and dropping them to the floor.

"Yes," I gasp as he slips his hand into my panties and starts to finger me. "Oh God, yes." My eyes roll into the back of my head. "If it will turn you on, I'll do it." He caresses me slowly, allowing me to feel every microscopic touch as he massages the walls of my pussy.

"Good girl. Shit, you're wet. Looks like I'm not the only one the idea of fetish excites." He presses his rock solid erection against my thigh.

"No," I answer mindlessly, flinching as my orgasm flares like a wildfire. "Are you trying to make me come?" I breathe harshly.

"Maybe." He fingers me faster. "Maybe not." He withdraws from me completely, and I nearly topple over.

"Kayne," I whine miserably.

"Sorry, kitten." He slides his middle finger into his mouth and sucks off my remnants. I just watch with wide, transfixed eyes.

"Definitely sweeter than whipped cream." He hums then fishes his hand into his pocket. He retrieves his switchblade and pops it open right next to my head. I jump.

"I would also like to establish something." He runs the switchblade all the way down my body stopping at my hips. "I will always have some kind of say in what you wear." There's a loud tear as he slices through the spandex and lace of my underwear. "No panties tonight." He repeats the motion on the other side, leaving me stunned. He picks up my mutilated underwear and discards it in the trash.

"Now what do you have to say about that?"

"Yes, Kayne," I answer automatically like I'm conditioned to do.

"Good, kitten. Now hurry up and fix yourself, I don't want to be late." He makes for the door, his erection uncensored in his pants.

"God forbid," I snark.

He leers at me while he adjusts then disappears into the bedroom.

Tease!

Pulling myself together like instructed, I blot between my legs with some toilet paper and pull up my shorts. I look in the mirror. I'm flushed and feel achy, and it's all Kayne's fault. I huff, throwing some of my hair over one shoulder as I leave the bathroom. He really is going to be the death of me.

Kayne opens the front door for me once I emerge from the bedroom.

"Our ride will be here any second." We walk outside into the pleasant evening air fragrant with something sweet. Island flowers, maybe.

We see Matias driving a six-seater golf cart down the boardwalk, his white shirt and dark hair rippling in the wind.

He stops in front of us with a wide smile, and we climb onto the cart. I'm starting to get spoiled being chauffeured around like this. He takes off and stops at the large bungalow right next to ours where another couple is waiting. They're a bit older and very well dressed, late forties I would say. When they see us, their looks are ones of curiosity, and I think disdain. I cuddle next to Kayne as they sit behind us, suddenly uncomfortable. He puts his arm around me and glances back at them. I'm certain he also feels the quiet hostility. The ride up to the main part of the resort is silent and quite uncomfortable, even with Matias' best attempt at casual conversation. I've never been so happy to see a lobby in my life.

Kayne gets off the golf cart hastily, extending his hand to help. As he does, the woman comments offhandedly, "Women deserve to be treated with respect."

Kayne and I both freeze as she pins us with her cold blue stare. If I was suspicious before, I'm confident now that these are the neighbors who called the concierge on us the other night.

Kayne smiles, without showing any teeth, but it's contradictory to the vicious look in his eyes.

"I couldn't agree more," he responds evenly. "They also deserve to be fucked. Maybe you should let your husband try it sometime. Right in your opinionated mouth."

The woman gasps in horror.

"Kayne!" I chastise as I jump out of the cart.

"Young man!" The woman's husband stands up outraged.

"Let's go." I push him away before there is a brawl right before my very eyes. He steps backward, unable to remove his crazed stare from the couple.

"What the hell was that about? You should have just ignored her," I say once we're safely inside the lobby.

"I'm not going to let anyone accuse me of not respecting you. I respect you more than any other man ever will. What we do in our bedroom is our business. I won't let anyone ruin that."

"It's going to take more than one ignorant comment to ruin what we have." I try to placate him, realizing something very important. Kayne will become aggressive when he feels threatened despite where we are or who we're with.

"I'm not going to let anyone take you away from me, Ellie." Determination dripping from his tone.

"No one is going to take me away, and I know you respect me."

"Good. You're the most resilient person I have ever met." He swipes his thumb across my cheek.

"And you're the scariest." I laugh.

"It's part of my conditioning. I don't take shit."

"Clearly. But you can't just pop off on people like that."

"I can and I will," he argues with me.

"Kayne," I sigh.

"Ellie. This one you'll never win. I'll never roll over and play dead where you or we are concerned," he says with an unyielding look in his eye.

"You're crazy."

"Yup. Mostly about you." He presses a kiss on my lips. "Now come on." He takes my hand. "We have to make a stop before we go to the restaurant."

"Stop?" I repeat confused as he drags me down a white marbled hallway clustered with stores and enters the jewelry store.

"What are we doing in here?" I ask.

"Good evening." A bright-eyed salesman in a dark gray suit greets us.

"Engagement rings?" Kayne asks, and I nearly fall over my feet.

"What?"

"Last case in the back." The man motions fluidly with his hand.

"Thank you." We reach the case with Kayne still clutching my hand. "I asked you to marry me, and you said yes. You need a ring. I may not know much, but I do know that. So, go ahead. Pick whichever one you like. I want you to be happy."

"What?" I repeat again an octave higher than before.

"Ellie." Kayne laughs at me as the salesman steps in front of us. His name is James, according to his tag.

"What can I show you?"

I look down into the glass at the shimmering diamonds and truly feel like a cat mesmerized by the light.

"Let's see a variety," Kayne answers for me, and the nice looking man with salt and pepper hair immediately pulls out several different rings. Some with round diamonds, some with square, one with an emerald cut. If someone told me when I got on that plane a week and a half ago that I'd be shopping for an engagement ring, I'd have laughed in their face—like cackled loudly. Yet here I am, staring down at some of the most beautiful jewelry I have ever seen, and it becomes a sobering reality.

"Hmm." Kayne doesn't seem impressed with any of them. "See anything you like?"

I'm overwhelmed. "Maybe you should just pick for me."

"You deserve an opinion. You're the one who has to wear it."

"If I may," James cuts in politely. "Not to offend you, but can you tell me your price cap?"

"We don't have one," Kayne tells him matter-of-factly. The salesman's eyes glitter just as brightly as the diamonds in front of us.

"In that case," he pulls out a ring from the far side of the case and places it in front of me, "you two seem unique. I can tell these things. I see many couples walk through that door, and I can usually read them pretty well."

I glance at Kayne and blush scarlet. Are we that obvious?

"You should wear a ring that reflects your personality. Two-carat cushion-cut diamond with a half carat of pink sapphires haloing around the center stone," he explains.

I immediately fall in love.

"What do you think, Ellie?" Kayne inquires.

I'm speechless.

He chuckles, taking the ring from the James's hand, "I think she likes it," and places it on my ring finger. "Will you marry me?" he asks softly, and my breath catches. I look at the perfect ring and then at the perfect man with tears forming in my eyes. *Is this really happening?* I reflect. First, Kayne was the man of my dreams, then he was a monster, and now he's . . . *everything.*

"Yes," I answer and know beyond a shadow of a doubt that regardless of what happened in the past, it's the future that's important now.

"We'll take it," he tells the salesman, then bends down to kiss me on the cheek, whispering, "Cupcake," in my ear.

"There is also a matching wedding band. It's a set if you're interested?"

"Fine, yes, we'll take that, too," Kayne says still looking at me.

"And what about you, sir?"

"Me?" Kayne looks over at him confused.

"Yes. You'll need a ring eventually. Would you like to take a look while you're here?"

I cock an eyebrow. This guy has balls. He's going to squeeze every dime out of Kayne he can, and Kayne totally knows it, too.

"I'll take a look," he says shrewdly.

"You look like a titanium man." James pulls out a flat velvet board with a number of rings impressed in it.

Kayne looks them over and then shrugs at me.

"That one." I point to a silver band with an extremely thin row of black diamonds.

"Ah. Very nice choice," James comments with dollar signs in his eyes as Kayne slips the ring on and makes a fist several times, trying to get used to the feel.

"Make you anxious?" I tease him.

"Makes me excited." His eyes flash with something sinful.

I bite my lip, knowing full well that look means trouble. A delicious kind of trouble.

"Done." He slips the ring off and hands it back to the deliriously happy man in the gray suit. I can't even imagine how much money he just spent, and frankly, I don't want to know. Kayne is wealthy. That's obviously no secret. He has been since I met him. I'm just not exactly used to him spending large amounts of money on me. I guess that's something I'm going to have to get used to.

"I can have the two rings wrapped up and sent to your room if you'd like," James says. "It looks like you're going out."

"That's fine." Kayne starts to peruse some other glass cases while I admire my new ring. This *is* really happening.

A few moments later, I hear Kayne ask James to see something at the far end of the store, near the front.

"Ellie," he calls me over. "Stand here," he says once I reach him, both of us positioned in front of a mirror. "Pull your hair back, please."

I move my long, sun-kissed hair to the side. I blew it out straight and braided the front like a headband. Kayne drops something in front of my face, a necklace, and fastens it around my neck.

"Now you can always be collared," he murmurs in my ear as the salesman watches us.

"The heart is Tiffany," James informs us as I admire the sparkly pave charm attached to a black silk choker in the mirror. "We can change it up if you like. Maybe put the heart on a platinum chain?"

"No," Kayne snaps mildly. "It's perfect."

I keep my mouth shut. This purchase is much more for him than it is for me. I secretly love it, and I'll show him how much later.

"Very good, sir. I'll add it to the bill."

"Thank you."

I glare at him over my shoulder. "This was your diabolical plan the whole time," I accuse him playfully.

He shrugs. "A man always has to have a plan." He tickles the heart on my 'necklace.' A prideful gleam of ownership shining in his eyes.

I barely remember the walk to the restaurant, and I'm pretty sure if Kayne wasn't leading me by the hand, I would have walked straight into a wall.

This *is* really happening.

"Ellie? Earth to Ellie?" Jett waves his hand in front of my face.

"Huh?" I blink.

"I said congratulations." His big aqua eyes sparkle.

Where the heck did I go?

I think the enormity of the last week and a half—hell, the last year of jumbled feelings, the love, the hate, and the confusion—is finally hitting me like a ton of bricks.

"Thank you," I smile brightly because, for the first time in so long, I am truly happy.

Kayne pulls out my chair at the table and the four of us sit.

"You okay?" he asks quietly, concerned.

"Yes," I reply in my most confident voice, because I am.

"A bottle of your best Prosecco, please." I hear Jett order and see the waiter hurry off.

"Let me see again!" London grabs my hand and moves it so my engagement ring catches the light. "I love the pink! It's perfect for you, Ellie." She leans over and kisses my cheek.

"Thank you." I feel like that's all I've been saying for the last ten minutes.

The waiter returns with four champagne glasses and the chilled bottle of Prosecco. I suppose if you're going to drink Italian champagne, the best place to do it is at a high-end Italian restaurant.

When our glasses are full, we raise them for a toast.

"I'd like to say something," Jett announces.

"Oh shit," I hear Kayne mutter.

"Shut up, idiot," Jett snaps. "I just wanted to say that I'm elated this story has a happy ending. God knows we all needed it, not just you two."

"Cheers," Kayne says hastily.

"No," Jett pulls his glass back. "Quit ruining my moment," he spits.

"Fine." Kayne drops his head and huffs.

"I want to relay something someone very wise once told me. A man's most precious possession is the woman who walks by his side. And I don't think you could have found a more perfect woman." Jett clinks Kayne's glass. Kayne stares at him idly with a glint in his eye and ghost of a smile playing on his lips.

"I couldn't have said it better myself."

"You couldn't have said it at all. You suck at heartfelt speeches." Jett gulps his Prosecco.

"I'm not so sure about that," I grin behind my glass right before I take a sip. The champagne is delectably sweet, clean, and crisp. Delicious.

Dinner moves swiftly as we dine on flaky bread, fennel and aged pecorino salad, filet mignon with a balsamic glaze, and indulge in several more bottles of expensive Prosecco. By the time dessert rolls around, not only am I stuffed, but feeling no pain as well.

"You know what I think you guys should do," London says as she drains the last drops of champagne from her glass, "and it may sound crazy, but I think you two should do it while you're here."

All three of us look at her strangely.

"Not that. I know you do that." She sticks her tongue out and laughs. "I mean get married. You should totally find a deserted beach at sunset and get married."

"I'm sure Ellie would want her family there," Jett says.

I nod, glancing at Kayne. He's staring at London stoically. A little tingle of worry runs down my spine. Did she just spook him? Is he coming to realize we're moving too fast? Is he suddenly having second thoughts?

"Probably." London drops her head into her hand dreamily. "It would be romantic, though."

"We can always have a sunset ceremony. On Maui maybe?" I look at Kayne apprehensively.

"We can have anything you want." He smiles, but it's a distant expression.

I internally panic, but I'm not going to dwell. If there's something to be worried about, I'll find out soon enough.

Once the bill is paid, we move outside to the patio where oversized couches surround a large brick fireplace; dark-red lanterns hang overhead and sweet smelling cigar smoke lingers in the air. London and I park on a couch while Kayne and Jett stand by the bar and cut new cigars. I never found it appealing—a man smoking a cigar—until now. Until I watch Kayne wrap his lips around the thick brown Churchill and elegantly puff one O out after another.

"You happy, Ellie?" London asks as she lazily twirls a piece of my hair around her finger.

"Yes. Are you?" I ask surprised.

She smiles, her eyes glassy from all the alcohol. "Deliriously. Even if Jett and I never get married, he could make me happy for the rest of my life."

"Well, that's good to know. I'd hate for you to spend it with a man who makes you miserable," I laugh.

She laughs, too, her head resting comfortably against the thick maroon cushion. "You're funny," she says as she gazes at me, the fire illuminating her dark-red hair and crystal-blue eyes. "And really beautiful, you know that?"

"You think?" I tuck some hair behind my ear shyly. It's one thing to get compliments from a man, but a woman, a woman who you've had sexual relations with, is a whole other story.

"Can I tell you a secret?" She sits up and scoots closer to me so our bare legs are touching. I nod, having to keep my knees together to keep from being tickled by the nighttime breeze as it brushes up under my shorts and pets my unclad privates.

"Sure," I shift.

She leans over to whisper in my ear. "Sometimes, when Jett makes me touch myself, I think about you."

"What?" My eyes fly to hers.

"I've had a lot of sexual experiences, but that night with you was one of the best." She looks down at my lips, and my heart skips like a scratched record.

"Do you think . . ." She runs one soft finger up the inside of my thigh, "you'd want to give Kayne an engagement present?"

I'm momentarily stunned. One, because she's hitting on me; two, because the memories of that night are uncontrollably flooding my mind, and three, because suddenly I really want her to kiss me.

"Same sex is an acquired taste," I hear Jett say, and he's right. That night was one of the hottest, if not the hottest, of my life. I glance over at Jett and Kayne as my mouth and London's hover closely together. Vance Joy singing about riptides and dark sides softly in the background. They're both watching us closely, like two lions spying on a gazelle.

"I think he'd like that," I tell her summoning my courage and stroking my excitement all at the same time. London brushes her lips against mine, and I inhale a sharp breath. She smells good, like some kind of spicy perfume, but feels even better. When our tongues graze, a million little tingles race all over my skin. For a second, I forget where I am, solely concentrating on the feel of London's mouth and the smooth caress of her hand on my naked thigh.

Someone suddenly clears their throat very loudly, breaking the spell the two of us are under.

I look up to see Jett standing over us, with Kayne behind him, arms crossed.

"Time to go," Jett informs us. "You two are drawing a little too much attention," he says with a wicked gleam.

I glance around to see most, if not everyone, on the patio staring at us. Oops. Jett extends his hand to London and pulls her to her feet. Then Kayne does the same to me. I look up at him a little guilty. Should we have asked permission first? How does this work?

"Yes. You're in trouble." Fire dances in his unique, spellbinding eyes. I gulp.

"You told me I could fuck as many women as I want."

His gaze darkens. I don't think I'm helping myself here.

"I remember. I also told you I would be the only man who ever touches you. So don't get any ideas."

"Ideas?" I say as he pulls me in the direction of London and Jett. In no time at all, the four of us are crunched in the back of a golf cart.

"Bungalow forty-six," Jett tells the driver, and he steps on the pedal. "Please." He then turns to London and me. We're practically sitting on top of each other. "Feel free to pick up where you left off."

London doesn't miss a beat, she dives her tongue back into my mouth and kisses me without any hesitation. I'm suddenly trapped, my back pinned to Kayne while she freely explores my body, her hand brushing down my neck, over my breasts, and around to my ass.

The golf cart suddenly jolts to a stop and I realize we have reached bungalow forty-six.

The four of us pile out, London yanking me eagerly behind her. I see Jett pull out a wad of cash and smack some into the driver's hand. "Bet you don't get tips like that every day," he says to the wide-eyed boy. I giggle to myself; he so wasn't talking about money.

The inside of London and Jett's bungalow doesn't look much different from ours; it's just on a smaller scale.

"How come you aren't staying in a big bungalow like ours?" I ask Jett as he turns on a light.

"I'm not ostentatious. Besides, this is enough."

"All we really need is a beach and bedroom," London says impishly. "The bedroom is this way," she tugs me. I glance back at Kayne as I follow her. He's been threateningly quiet, despite his howling presence. Images of him from the first night London and I spent together turn over in my thoughts, the way he touched himself as he watched us, the way he instructed us, the way he fucked me while I made her come. It was barely human.

Once inside the bedroom I stop, slipping my hand out of London's. What was I saying about their bungalow not being much different than ours?

I was dead wrong.

There are shackles attached to each post of the canopy bed and a thick black collar dangling by a chain on the headboard. The nightstand is covered with an array of sex toys, a ball gag, lubricants, and wax candles. But it's the long rope on the floor that has me looking at Jett strangely. He just shrugs. "I'm into Kinbaku."

I draw in my eyebrows. "What?"

"Rope bondage."

"Oh." I stare at him blankly.

"It's a very beautiful art form," he tries to explain, almost like he's defending it.

"Okay." He doesn't need to sell me. I willingly walked through the looking glass. *This time.*

"I'm a kinky bastard. What can I say?"

He brushes past me to the opposite side of the room, opens the sliding glass door and pulls in two chairs from the sundeck.

"It takes one to know one?" I jest.

Jett smiles entertained as he sits in one chair and Kayne sits in the other, suddenly making me feel like the main attraction in a private XXX show.

"London, come," Jett says, and she immediately drops to all fours and crawls to him. Once she reaches him, she kneels submissively between his legs. I automatically look at Kayne.

He just lifts his hand off his knee slightly as if signaling me to stay.

Jett lifts London's face so she's looking directly into his incandescent eyes.

"You're a bad girl," he admonishes her, "and I love it. Now stand up and take your clothes off."

"Yes, Jett," she hums, and for some reason I shiver with excitement.

London rises to her feet and slowly starts peeling off her navy tube dress that's clinging to her body. I can only see her back from my angle, but Kayne and Jett seem quite invested in her little strip show. Once she's left standing in just a black thong and high heels, Kayne looks over at me and smiles like the demon he is.

"Good robin. Now take Ellie's off," Jett instructs her.

"Hold it." Kayne suddenly stops her in her tracks, and all three of us pause to look at him. I'm suddenly nervous. God only knows what's going to flow out of his mouth. With all the apparatuses in the room, I could end up being fucked upside down while hanging from the ceiling. "Ground rules." He glares at Jett. "London can touch Ellie all she wants, but you keep your hands off my fiancée."

Jett grimaces, "You're such a party pooper."

"Tough shit, I don't share."

"I'm calling sexism. You're discriminating against me just because I have a cock."

"Exactly, and it's not getting anywhere near *her*. Call it whatever you want. Accuse me of being prejudice, of being a chauvinist, whatever. You still can't touch her or I'll break your hands."

Jett bristles. "I'll still be able to use my cock." He sticks his tongue out at Kayne.

"I could always break that, too," Kayne informs him menacingly.

I know I probably shouldn't, but I laugh.

"Do you find my jealous, overbearing side funny, Ellie?" Kayne asks, without looking at me.

"No. Kayne." I clear my throat and find my composure. That's his 'do not fuck with me' tone. London and I may have started it, but it's clear Kayne and Jett are going to finish it.

"Good. Now, London, go undress my kitten."

"Slow your roll," Jett interjects. "I'm giving the orders. You've already driven one of these."

Kayne rolls his eyes. "Fine. Be my guest."

"London, go undress Kayne's kitten," he instructs with mirth.

These two.

London turns to me, displaying her mostly naked body. I almost forgot how perfect she is—tall, toned, and curvaceous. I felt a little inadequate then with my petite frame and small breasts, and I still feel inadequate now. But it's a little too late for insecurities because London drops to the floor and crawls across the room to me. I feel, rather than hear, the collective intake of breath as she approaches me swathed in seductiveness, servile and obedient. I nearly come on the spot. I now understand the appeal, the feeling of power and domination, as one person freely hands themselves over to another. I also understand that in this position I would never want to hurt or take advantage of that person's trust or safekeeping. It makes me see the relationship I have with Kayne from a completely different angle.

Once London reaches me, she rises to her knees. I gaze down at her and run my hands earnestly through her thick red hair, hoping she understands my subtle gesture of respect. I find it amazing that I can be just as sexually attracted to a woman as I can to a man.

London kisses my navel as she unbuttons my shorts, taking her time with her mouth as she lowers the zipper. She pulls the white material down my thighs and follows the path with her tongue until she realizes I'm not wearing any underwear. She moans softly, eagerly, but stops kissing me as she slides my pants the rest of the way off. She pushes up my shirt but can't reach past my breasts, so I end up yanking the top over my head for her. I'm not wearing a bra, either, because of the tunic's open back. As soon as my nipples hit the air, they harden, sending a ripple of excitement straight through to my core.

With her cheek pressed against my abdomen, London and I look over at Jett and Kayne now that we're just as they want us. Both men appear composed, but if you look hard, you can see the quick compressions of their chests and the tightening of their forearms. Not to mention the carnivorous lust in their light eyes.

"Do you want to touch Ellie, London?" Jett asks.

"Yes, Jett," she hums.

"Where?"

"Everywhere."

"With what?"

"My tongue."

"You've wanted to do that for a long time, huh?"

"Yes." She glances up at me.

"Ellie, do you want her to lick you?"

"Yes."

"Where?"

"Everywhere."

"So go ahead, bird. Show Ellie how much you want to taste her."

London wets her lips before she presses her mouth to my pussy and tongues my clit.

"Oh." The pleasure is immediate as she applies pressure and explores my slit, stroking and sucking rhythmically until my legs start to shake.

"She feel good, Ellie?" Kayne asks.

"Yes," I strain, trying to absorb the dizzying sensation of London lapping me up.

"She making you want to come?"

"Yes." My voice is engulfed by a panting whisper. My body feels so heavy, and I want so much more of London's mouth, so without even thinking I sit on the edge of the bed, lean back and spread my legs wider.

Both men groan as London buries her head between my thighs, sinking her tongue deeply into my entrance. I gasp loudly, grabbing her head as she nearly eats me alive. Just as I begin to undulate against her mouth, Jett snaps, "Enough." Within half a second London pulls away, leaving me a winded mess on the bed. "No one is coming yet."

I grumble silently, my body feels like it's being put through a wringer.

"Come. Both of you," he commands.

London crawls over to Jett and I follow suit to Kayne. Sitting on our knees, we wait for one of them to instruct us.

"You like my little bird eating you up, Ellie?" Jett asks as he pets her reverently. I glance up at Kayne before I answer. It feels like his stare is going to drill a hole right through my chest.

"Yes," I tell him truthfully.

"She is one of a kind." He tilts London's face up with one finger. It's clear how much he adores her. I've seen many expressions on Jett's face, but it's the first time I've seen this one. It's a mix of what looks like admiration, loyalty, and possibly a hint of fear, as if he's terrified of losing her.

"Will you make her feel good, Ellie? I know how much she wants you to make her come," he says.

I nod, stumbling into the intensity of Jett's aqua eyes once he turns his head to look at me. I have no idea how London and Jett came to be, but something tells me it wasn't just some casual thing. I recognize that gaze, that desperate love, because Kayne looks at me exactly the same way.

"Go sit on the bed," Kayne finally speaks. I restrain myself from running my hands over his thighs and climbing into his lap. As much as I want London to touch me, I want Kayne to touch me, too. "Go."

He tickles the heart dangling from my throat, one of his new symbols of ownership over me.

I sit on the end of the bed like directed.

"Stand in front of her, London," Jett orders as both he and Kayne get up and walk to each side of the four-poster bed. London positions herself between my legs. "Take her panties off," he says from behind me. I move to slide the dainty lace thong off London's hips and down her long legs. Once removed, I sit back further on the mattress. That's when I feel it dip behind me and Kayne swiftly fasten a blindfold over my eyes. I inhale harshly from surprise.

"Relax, Ellie. Trust me." He kisses my neck and whispers in my ear.

"You've never blindfolded me before." I touch the lace-like material.

"First time for everything," I hear Jett comment.

"It won't be the last time. There are so many things I'm going to do to you, Ellie." It's a promise. "Now lay back." He pushes me down. "Enough playing around. London, sit on her face."

I nearly combust with need as I feel London crawl up my body and straddle my head, the fragrance of her arousal potent and heady.

"Lick her, Ellie. Slowly. London, don't come," Kayne instructs.

I flatten my tongue against London's pussy, eager to please. The sound that escapes from her is pure delight. Although I can't see, my sense of smell, hearing, taste, and touch amplifies, making me hyper-aware of everything around me.

As I lick between London's folds leisurely, I feel someone grab one of my ankles. I flinch, but the hand grips me tighter.

"Easy." Kayne placates me like he's talking to a spooked horse. I relax momentarily until I feel him strap a restraint around my ankle.

"Don't stop, Ellie," Jett encourages me as the mattress dips above my head. I try to breathe steadily, concentrating on London, as Kayne fastens my other ankle.

"Does she feel good?" I hear Jett ask London between kisses, the bed teetering slightly from their entwining bodies.

"Yes," she whimpers. "Oh God, yes."

I reflexively stab my tongue into her entrance when Kayne tickles the inside of my thighs.

"Ellie!" she gasps, grabbing my hair.

I pull my tongue back and take a breath, giving us both a second's reprieve. I squirm in the restraints, my knees slightly bent and my legs spread wide open.

Then I hear the distinct sound of a zipper and the rustling of clothes.

A moment later, I feel a light touch trace my lips. Jett? Then a finger is slipped into my mouth. "I want you to make my little bird come." He pumps his finger in and out, coercing me to suck. It's the most erotic gesture Jett and I have ever shared. I hold onto the moment as long as I can, picturing his face as I swallow his finger, wishing secretly that for just one second Kayne would share.

Jett grunts as he withdraws his hand, leaving me wanton.

"Put your mouth on me," I hear him say, and London leans forward, situating her clit at an even more accessible angle to my face. "I want to feel everything she makes you feel." There's more shifting over my head, and then a loud moan from Jett. Just listening to him is arousing as hell. "Make her come, Ellie."

The room almost feels like a pressure cooker of elicit desire as I begin to lick London, sliding my tongue in and out of her slick folds and circling it around her clit. I'm completely lost in her soft feel and the carnal sounds of Jett's panting breaths when Kayne brushes something up the inside of my leg. His fingers? His nose, maybe his lips, I'm not sure. But the added sensation makes me jerk on my restraints and apply more pressure to London's pussy. When Kayne sinks his tongue deep inside me, I spasm, spurring a chain reaction—me to lick faster, London to suck harder, Jett to moan louder.

"Shit! London!" Jett hisses as she lets out a jagged, muffled cry, suddenly coming uncontrollably. I writhe beneath her, yanking at the leg restraints as she floods my mouth, while Kayne at the same time dangles me right over a razor-sharp edge. I fruitlessly kick and squirm as my own orgasm converges in the dead center of my thighs.

"Fuck. I'm coming," Jett groans while the sweet taste of London's arousal stains my lips, the bed dipping rapidly over my head, as he fucks her mouth.

"Please, please, please!" I hear myself beg as London is suddenly pulled off me and replaced by the brute force of Kayne on top of me. I recognize the fresh smell of his cologne and feel of his skin as he breathes wildly in my ear, slams into me savagely, pulls my hair, and sinks his teeth into my neck like a blood-starved vampire.

There's no time for even a sound as I follow Kayne into the light. My clit aches and my pussy throbs as my orgasm tears me apart, limb from quivering limb.

The last thing I remember is hearing Kayne's jagged lungful of air, seeing shadows move on the ceiling, and then darkness sucking me under.

I WAKE UP IN A tangle of bodies.

"Ellie," Kayne whispers, nudging me with his nose.

"Hmm?" I respond lazily, realizing I'm sandwiched between him and London.

"Come on, baby. Let's go," he speaks softly.

"Go where?" I open one eye.

Early dawn is just peeking over the horizon. It's still mostly dark, but a crack of light is allowing me to see.

Kayne slides out of bed first and shrugs on his pants. I reluctantly follow, as he moves me away from London and drags me up into a sitting position. I then follow suit by sleepily searching for my shorts and top as London and Jett lay soundlessly in bed. Her hair is a mess of red against the white sheets, his hand over her stomach almost protectively.

"Oh." I put my hand on my head once I stand up straight. "I think I'm hung over."

Kayne laughs quietly. "That's what happens when you drink three bottles of Prosecco yourself," Kayne whispers.

"We were celebrating."

"That we were," he says happily, picking up my shoes.

"Did you like your engagement present?" I ask, knowing I look like a hot mess.

He nearly burns a hole straight through me with a blistering glaze. "What do you think?"

"I think I need medical attention because someone tried to gnaw through my neck." I touch the sore spot right above my necklace, where I'm sure I have a bruise.

"It was a love bite." He takes my hand and leads me out of the bedroom, through the living room, and into the warm morning air.

"A love bite by a crazed man with a loaded erection."

"That's what happens when you feed my addiction." He puts his arm around me and draws me tightly into his side as we walk back to our bungalow.

"I like to feed the beast," I tell him lasciviously.

"So I've noticed." He kisses the top of my head firmly and cuddles me tightly. "Brat."

"It's all your fault." I giggle accusingly.

We continue to walk while the sun comes up. It's a showy display of golden rays over the aquamarine water and clouds colored different shades of orange and blue.

"Ellie?" Kayne says tentatively. "I've sort of been thinking."

"Yeah, about what?" I reply dreamily, a mixture of exhaustion and happiness.

"What if we did it?"

"Did what?"

"Got married while we're here. Just the two of us."

I stop walking. "What?" I stare up at him, and he stares back. I open my mouth to say something then close it again.

"You're being serious?" I finally muster.

He nods like he's holding his breath.

"Kayne," I sigh.

"That's a no, I take it." He sounds disappointed and starts walking again.

"No, it's not a no," I scramble, grabbing his arm. "It's an '*I don't know.*' I mean, it's one thing to get engaged, but it's a whole other thing to rush into an actual marriage."

"You think we're rushing?"

"You don't?" I actually laugh.

"No. I want to be with you, you want to be with me. I don't see what's so complicated."

"It's not complicated, it's just—"

"Just what?" he asks anxiously.

"We haven't really talked about anything."

"What's there to talk about?"

"I don't know? Kids," I blurt out.

"Kids?" he replies incredulously.

"Yes, like, do you want them?"

"I don't know." At least he's being honest. "I never really thought about it. I never thought I would get married. Do you want them?"

"Yes, I think. Eventually."

Kayne ponders this. "Okay, so we'll have them. Eventually."

"Just like that?"

"If it's what you want, Ellie. If it will make you happy."

"Will it make *you* happy?" I counter. "It'll never work if it's all give and no take."

He looks at me strangely. Like he's seriously considering my words. "I think I take plenty." He grins.

I snort. "I don't mean take like that."

"I know. I think kids would make me happy, especially if they're half of you. I sort of like the idea of giving someone a childhood I never had."

I frown immediately. I never took into consideration Kayne's past when I brought up the subject of kids.

"Oh . . . I'm sorry . . . I wasn't thinking," I stumble over my sentences.

"It's fine." He smiles. "You've got me looking forward to first words and bedtime stories." Although those are two very happy thoughts, the sound of his voice tells me he thinks differently.

"Did anyone ever read you bedtime stories?" I ask carefully.

His expression turns grim. "Yes. Once. I was about nine. There was this older girl in one of my foster homes, she was about fifteen or sixteen. She would read *Peter Pan* to me and the two other boys who lived there. She read it mostly every night before our foster father would come home drunk and rape her."

I look at him horrified, and suddenly can't help but wonder if all his childhood memories are laced with such atrocities.

"Kayne – "

"It's all right, Ellie. It's in the past."

My heart literally breaks for him.

"Okay, let's do it," I announce hastily.

"Excuse me?"

"Let's do it. We can get married under one condition."

"What's that?" The corners of his mouth curve up.

"We can have another wedding when we get home. One with our friends and family."

My parents and sister have to attend at least one ceremony. Even if it is a second one.

Will they be upset when I tell them I ran off and got married to a man they never met? Probably, but not surprised. If anything they would expect it. I have always been somewhat impulsive.

"That's fair. And I kind of like that idea," he agrees.

"Okay, good." I nestle up against him and stand on my tippy toes for a kiss.

Kayne's face feels warm and soft, despite the little bit of stubble growing on his cheeks.

"Sealed with a kiss," he says.

"I have a feeling we're going to be doing a lot of kissing Mr . . . *Rivers?* Is that your real last name? Would we have to use an alias?"

"Ellie. Shhh." He pulls me close. "Yes, it's Rivers," he whispers, "and I don't know. We can use that for now."

Ellie Rivers. I can live with that.

"Okay." I yawn. "Good talk."

"Tired, kitten?" Kayne chuckles.

"Yes. I've had a very trying night. Prosecco, foursomes, weddings. I'm pooped."

"So let's go get some sleep. We have a few more days before I have to share with you with the rest of the world. I plan to take full advantage."

"I bet you do," I purr as our two-story bungalow comes into view. Looking at it now, it does seem a bit ostentatious compared to all the rest.

I fall back and melt into the mattress once inside. I lift my hand in front of my face and inspect my engagement ring, noticing how the white and pink stones glimmer even in dim light. I've barely had a chance to admire it with everything that went on last night.

"It's perfect." Kayne lies down next to me. "It's just like you—unique, brilliant, and strong enough to cut glass."

I snuggle up next to him, realizing I will be sharing a bed with this man for the rest of my life.

Crazy.

Our original bond was one built with bricks of deception and lies. The bond we share now is fused by love. A single strand of twine, woven together with trust, and stronger than steel.

"I love you," I sigh sleepily.

Kayne moans in appreciation. "You have no idea what those words do to me. No idea how much I need to hear them. How much I need you." He tickles kisses across my cheek.

"You have me. Till death do us part."

Kayne clutches me protectively, and for a split second I think I've said something wrong.

"Go to sleep, Ellie. We can talk nuptials later." He embraces me firmly, yet tenderly, banishing everything else in my life except him.

"Yes, Kayne," I murmur against his lips and let slumber have me.

I DON'T THINK ELLIE AND I have been laying down for more than five minutes when I hear my cell phone beep. Three distinct chimes that communicate a problem.

"Kayne? What is that?" Ellie stirs.

The chimes sound again as I grab my pants off the floor and fish my phone out of the pocket.

"Nothing. Go to back to sleep," I say urgently, but when I turn to look at her, she's sitting up, bright-eyed and bushy-tailed. Sleep doesn't seem like much of an option at the moment.

I stand up and dial a secure number, waiting impatiently to be connected. "Sundial enterprises," a woman's robotic voice answers.

"Seven AM on the eastern shore," I reply.

"Pin, please."

"007263."

"Codename."

"Havok with a K."

"Password?"

I glance back at Ellie. "Elizabeth Ann."

"Confirmed. Hold for patch."

"Kayne?" Juice's voice comes through.

"What's up?"

"We have a security breach."

"What kind?"

"Someone's hacked Endeavor's classified server."

"What does that mean?"

"The identities of all operatives, handlers, informants, and analysts have been compromised."

"Jesus."

"Yeah. The bosses are on a rampage. They're calling in everyone that they can. They want them secure, which means your fun in the sun is over."

"Shit." My heart beats riotously.

"Sorry, man."

"Yeah, me too."

"Be in the air within an hour. I'll check back then."

"Roger."

The call ends.

"Everything okay?" The voice that can cut through my darkest nightmares fills the room.

"No. Get up. We have to go."

"Now?" She clutches the sheet to her chest.

"Yes. Grab only what you need. Everything else will be packed and shipped later."

A moment later my phone rings again.

"Yeah," I snap.

"I've called ahead. The plane will be ready," Jett informs me. There are no formalities now, only protocol and procedure.

"We'll meet you at the boat. Ten."

"Roger."

Click.

I rush Ellie around the room. She changes into a sundress and comfortable shoes. I throw on shorts, a hat, and a t-shirt and set up a ride to the lobby with Matias.

Making sure we both have all the essentials, we vacate the bungalow and our private escape.

"Kayne?" Ellie asks worried as we walk outside. I know she's scared and confused and wants answers, but I just can't give her any at the moment.

"Not now, okay?" I squeeze her hand. "We'll talk about everything later."

She nods as we climb into the golf cart.

"Book it. We have a plane to catch," I tell Matias, and he takes off, flooring the cart as fast as it can go. I think the thing only tops out at fifteen miles per hour.

Almost exactly ten minutes later to the second, we pull up to the lobby and the long dock housing multiple white boats. I spot Jett readying one near the end.

"I'm sorry your stay had to end so abruptly," Matias says to us once we're out of the cart.

"Yes. It is disappointing." I quickly pull out a wad of cash. "Your service was impeccable." I hand it to him.

"Thank you, Monsieur."

"De rien."

You're welcome.

I glance around us as I lead Ellie to the boat. She hasn't stopped crushing my hand since we left.

The speedboat looks to be a thirty-footer with a dark-blue canopy. It's nothing flashy but will fit the four of us comfortably.

I help Ellie onto the boat then jump in after her, still keeping a sharp eye on our surroundings.

"Ready?" Jett turns on the ignition and the engine purrs.

"Yup." I untie the two ropes anchoring us to the dock and push off.

"Hang on. This is going to be a quick ride," Jett says as we get out into open water. Then he pulls the throttle and the boat speeds through the glassy water, throwing Ellie and London back in their chairs and jolting me on my feet.

I hear a groan and look over to see London with her head on Ellie's lap.

"What's wrong with you?" I ask as Ellie strokes her hair.

"She's hung over. Hasn't stopped puking all morning," Jett informs me.

That sucks.

"There's ginger ale on the plane," I tell her, like that's supposed to help.

She makes a face. "I don't think I can even keep liquids down. I am never drinking again."

"I think I've heard you say that three times on this trip." Jett laughs behind the wheel. He's wearing a baseball cap, mirrored sunglasses and looks like he's a born captain in boat shoes and chino shorts.

"That's because I've been sick almost every morning that I've been here. You're trying to kill me," she accuses him.

"Oh, that's right, blame me." Jett laughs. "I was the one pouring martinis down your throat."

"I hate you sometimes." She snuggles closer to Ellie.

"I love you all the time," he replies.

Ellie and I smirk at each other during London and Jett's little exchange. Of all the women I've seen Jett with—and it's been *a lot*—he's never had a rapport with any of them like he does with London.

We dock the boat and hurry the girls along.

"Ellie, this way," I tug on her hand when she veers toward the main entrance of Motu Mute airport. We enter through a side service door in order to lay low, and then walk straight out onto the runway.

"Don't we need tickets?" she asks confused.

"Not this time, baby." Our private jet is already waiting with the doors open.

"This yours?"

"Mine and Jett's. It's smaller than our old one but it gets the job done."

"Old one?" She raises her eyebrows.

I nod. "Liquidated."

"Oh." She then understands. We had to get rid of everything that tied us to our undercover op, including the G600 I loved.

"Mr. Andrews. Mr. Collins," the captain greets us once were safely inside.

"Henry." He's an older man with gray hair and a crisp white uniform. He's also an ex-fighter pilot and employed by Endeavor.

"Please sit down and buckle up. The runway is clear, I plan to have us in the air in ten minutes."

"Sounds good." Jett and I both shake his hand.

"Also, comms are set up in the back."

"Very good." We take our seats. I strap Ellie in next to me. Jett does the same to a sickly looking London. I wonder idly if she's going to throw up during takeoff.

I watch a curious Ellie inspect the interior of the plane decorated in a cool beige and glossy wooden accents.

Without delay, the jet roars to life and the interior lights flash.

"Stand by for taxi." Henry's voice comes on over the loudspeaker.

Ellie grabs my hand. "Are you afraid of flying?" I ask her.

"Only when under duress."

"It'll be fine." I try to assure her. "The safest place is in the air."

"If you say so." The plane begins to roll.

After we are at thirty thousand feet, Jett and I leave the girls up front and head to the back of the plane where a laptop is all set up for use.

With one hit of a button, we're connected to Juice.

"Yo." His face pops up on the screen.

"Yo, yourself. Any updates?" Jett asks him.

"Nada. Endeavor is working to find out who the hacker is, but nothing yet."

"Do you think this has any connection with our visitors on Oahu?"

I question.

"There has been no identifiable connection." He swivels in his chair, "But I don't think they're ruling anything out."

"Fuckin' great." I run my hand through my hair. I glance up and see Ellie and London sitting together. London's head resting on Ellie's shoulder; it seems they've become quite comfortable with each other.

"I'll check in if anything changes. For now, just sit back, relax, and enjoy the friendly skies," Juice says, tossing a small basketball up over his head like he's pretending to shoot.

"Roger that." I snap the laptop closed and suck in a breath. *Relax?* Yeah, right. It feels like the universe is out to get me. Not one hiccup in twelve months, then BAM—this happens. Just when my life feels like it's finally coming together.

"I'm going to check on London. I'll send Ellie back." Jett taps my shoulder as he stands.

I nod, sliding down a black hole of despair.

"Kayne?" I hear Ellie's concerned voice and look up. "Where were you?"

I just shake my head. "Someplace you don't need to worry about." I put my hand out to her. She takes it and slips onto my lap, curling up like the kitten she is.

"You're tense," she says concerned.

"I call it more alert," I clarify.

"Do you know what's going on?"

"No, not entirely. Not yet."

"Will you have to go away once you do?" She looks up at me with troubled green eyes.

I want to tell her no, that I'll never leave her side, but I can't guarantee that. At the moment, I can't guarantee anything, and it sucks.

"I don't know, Ellie."

She hugs me securely. "All that time I was with you, do you know when I was most scared?"

"No."

"When Javier had that gun to your head. I just remember thinking this man is going to take you away and destroy me right on the spot."

"Ellie, stop—"

"I know this is your job," she keeps speaking despite my protest, "and that you're proud of what you do. I just want you to know I'm proud of you, too. No matter what happens. I'm proud to love you."

"Ellie," my voice wavers, and my chest aches.

"I just wanted you to know." She rubs her nose against my chin. "I wouldn't change one second of our past. It helped shape who we are. And I really love *us.*"

"I really love *us,* too." I bury my face in her neck and crush her against me.

I hold Ellie in my arms until her eyes close and she's breathing heavily. It's no wonder she crashed hard. The last forty-eight hours have been *demanding,* so to speak. Yet, in true Ellie fashion, she surprises me with her fearlessness, her resilience, and her buoyancy. Now more than ever, I'm convinced this woman was made specifically for me.

She's my sanity, and my reason, and my glue. I'm seven broken pieces of a fucked up man, held together solely because of her.

"Sleep, baby." I kiss her forehead, preparing for whatever danger may come my way.

"WHERE ARE WE GOING?" ELLIE asks as we drive down Kalakaua Avenue in Waikiki. The day, like always, is perfect. Tourists fill the streets, the beach is crowded with sunbathers, and the water active with surfers.

"Home. As soon as possible." A disgusted—not to mention shirtless—Jett answers.

"I said I was sorry," London grumbles in the fetal position next to him. "The landing was bumpy."

"The landing wasn't that bumpy. And I know you're sorry. It's not your fault." Jett pets her head.

I feel sorry for London; she's miserable. But I wish I had a camera when she threw up on Jett. His face was priceless. I would have blown it up and stuck it on a billboard.

"Where is home, anyway?" Ellie asks with a raised eyebrow.

I lean over her and point out the window to a high rise. "The tallest one."

"Why does that not surprise me?" she quips.

I grin duplicitously. "Part appearance, part necessity, part selfish desire."

Ellie rolls her eyes at me. "Is that your excuse for everything?"

"I find it covers all bases," I reply as we pull onto a side road, and then into an underground garage.

"Good thing we live someplace tropical," Jett comments as he helps London out of the limousine.

The air is cooler in the garage, but still comfortable enough to get away with limited clothing.

The four of us step into the marble elevator, and I hit the code for PH36. We're then whooshed up thirty-six floors to the penthouse Jett and I share.

The doors open to a large foyer with colored orchids etched on the mirrors and a light wooden floor. Jett exits with London first and unlocks the front door.

Ellie and I follow close behind.

"Oh." Ellie does a slow pirouette as we walk through the apartment. "This is . . ." she seems to be at a loss for words.

"Nice?" I answer for her.

"Very."

The condominium is a split-level with an open floor plan and one hundred, eighty-degree views of Diamond Head, Koolau Mountains, and the Pacific Ocean. Cherry wood frames the two-story French windows encasing the ultra-modern decor. Clean lines and dark accents make it a vast contradiction to the mansion we lived in on the East Coast.

"Come on. I'll show you the rest of the house later. We need to check in first." I take her hand and lead her through the kitchen.

"Bye, Ellie," London croaks behind us.

"Feel better," Ellie replies as Jett helps London climb miserably up the stairs.

"I'll be right there," Jett tells me.

"I really feel bad for her," Ellie pouts. "Maybe she has food poisoning?"

"Maybe? I'm sure if she doesn't start feeling better, Jett will take her to the doctor. He isn't one to make a woman suffer. At least not in the sickly way." I wink.

"Seriously, the two of you."

"The two of us, what?" I ask defensively.

"Are terrible."

"So terrible both you and London are madly in love with us?"

"Brainwashed is more like it." She teases.

I shrug. "Whatever works." I drop a kiss on her lips then place all five of my fingertips on a mirror hanging on the back wall of the condo. A moment later a pair of pocket doors slide open.

Ellie's gasp is all I need to hear to know I've made an impression.

"You have an arsenal in your apartment," she says as we walk into the secret room. Every wall is decorated with some kind of specialized firearm—submachine guns, assault rifles, breaching shotguns, sniper rifles.

"We like to call it the Toy Box." Juice spins in his chair and stands up. "Welcome home," he shakes my hand.

"Thanks. Wish it was under different circumstances."

"You? I know you." Ellie interrupts us, examining Juice closely.

"Ma'am," he says with a smile, which sparks her recognition.

"The driver?" She looks up at me.

"Well, I couldn't just send anyone to pick up my precious cargo."

"You work for him?" she asks Juice.

He laughs boastfully. "I work *with* him," he corrects her. "And I'm CJ, by the way." He puts his hand out.

Ellie takes it graciously. "It's nice to formally meet you."

"You, too."

A moment later the door opens and Jett appears. "Did I miss anything?" He walks in donning a new shirt.

"Just introductions," I tell him.

"How is London feeling?" Ellie asks him.

"Still not great, but she's resting."

"Good."

"Maybe you can go keep her company," I suggest, glancing at Jett, "while we work."

Ellie catches on immediately. "Oh. Yes. Of course. I need to charge my phone anyway. I have a bunch of calls to make." She starts backing up.

"Who do you have to call?" I follow her, opening the door so she can get back into the apartment.

"My mom. My sister. Mark. Michael."

"Michael?" I step out after her, possessiveness flaring.

"Yeah. I just picked up and left. I sort of owe him an explanation."

"You don't owe him jack shit, Ellie," I snap.

"Kayne. Don't be ridiculous. He's my friend."

"He's a guy you were fucking," I snarl.

"Keep your voice down!" she hisses, her stare glacial. "We had a relationship, yes. But that's over now. I at least have to tell him why."

"And what exactly are you going to tell him?" I ask warily.

"As much of the truth as possible."

"Which is?"

"You want me to recite what I'm going to say?" she asks confounded.

"Yes."

"Fine. I haven't really thought about it, but it will probably go something like this. I dated this guy. He was a total douchebag. I thought it was over, but apparently it's not."

Douchebag?

"Does he know anything about said douchebag?" I ask irritably, my hand twitching. She's going to get so punished for calling me that.

"No. I never said anything. I never even uttered your name. I was told I could land in jail if anyone found out about you or the operation," she says bitterly.

As much as it kills me to hear her say that, I'm relieved.

"Now if you'll excuse me, I have to go break up with my boy toy." She starts to storm off and then stops. "Where the fuck am I going?" she huffs annoyed.

"My room is upstairs. Last door on the left."

She doesn't even turn to look at me, just stomps away.

Shit.

I walk back into the Toy Box nearly pulling out my hair.

"Trouble in paradise?" Jett asks. I want to punch him in his sarcastic mouth.

"Just a hiccup." I plop down in one of the black leather rolling chairs.

"Women, like cheap wine, can give you a headache," Jett offers his two cents.

"They also, like cheap wine, can make you drunk and horny," Juice adds.

I rub my temples. These two are not helping.

The thought of Ellie even talking to that guy has me wanting to put my fist through a window.

"Relax. Ellie isn't doing anything to hurt you. If anything, she's cutting ties so nothing is stopping the two of you from being together. She's a very well brought up girl. She has morals and family values. You're going to have to step up your game," Jett says entertained. He's eating this up; me and my domestic issues.

I just glare at him. "How would you feel if London was conversing with one of her exes?"

"Me? I'd gut him with a fishhook. But we're not talking about me."

"Five minutes in your presence and I'm reminded why I elect to stay single." Juice laughs, tossing that stupid basketball in the air. I stand up and grab it, then squash it with my bare hands. It screams while it dies. I feel much better.

Juice gasps. "You just killed Wilson. He was my only friend."

"You need to get out more." I toss the flat basketball back at him.

He catches it. "I would, but the two of you keep me chained to this desk like a slave."

I freeze, and Jett blanches. "Don't ever fucking say that around Ellie," I bark, about to rip his throat out. "Even if it is a joke."

"Okay." Juice puts his hands up. "I think we need to take a step back. Everyone's tensions are running a little high."

I take a deep breath. I haven't kicked the crap out of anything or anyone in nearly two weeks. I thought sex would sate me, but apparently that's not the case. I need to make someone bleed.

I didn't realize how difficult it was going to be sharing Ellie with the people in her life. I think I might be totally screwed.

Like I've said before, I've never really been good at sharing.

"Why don't you brief us on any updates," Jett suggests.

Juice shakes his head. "There aren't any. It's been nothing but radio silence. We just have to lay low and wait for word."

Wonderful.

"I'm going to check on Ellie then." I push out my chair.

"Go smooth things over?" Juice digs.

"Shut up or I'm going to smooth cement over your face while you're still breathing."

"So hostile." He heckles me.

"Isn't he?" Jett agrees.

"Fuck you both." I storm out of the room. I need to either fuck, run, or slam the shit out of a punching bag real soon.

I climb the stairs quickly and quietly, silently making my way down the hall. The door to my room is slightly ajar and when I peek in, I see Ellie sitting on the floor, looking out the wall of windows with the phone to her ear.

"The Starbucks on the corner in an hour? . . . Yes, I'll explain everything. That's why I want to see you . . . I know, I'm sorry I up and left like that, but I needed to . . . Okay . . . yeah, okay, bye."

I watch her for several long seconds before I push the door open. "Going somewhere?" My voice vibrates and Ellie jumps.

"Were you listening to my conversation?" she asks annoyed.

"Yes." I lean against the doorframe and cross my arms.

"That's rude."

"I was never taught manners."

"I find that hard to believe." She stands up. "You just pick and choose when to use them."

I try, but fail miserably, to stop an evil smile from spreading across my lips. "You're mad at me."

"You're acting like a jealous asshole."

"I am a jealous asshole." I walk into the room.

"There's nothing to be jealous of," she responds steadfastly as she watches me approach her. "You're the one I want. You're the one I'm marrying." She holds up her hand and shows me the ring.

"I know." I take her hand in mine. "That doesn't mean I don't feel threatened. It doesn't mean I won't always worry about some guy trying to steal you away. Or you getting tired or frustrated or fed up with me. I told you I wasn't perfect, that I'd make mistakes. I always knew I'd have to share you at some point, I just wasn't prepared for it to happen so fast."

"You don't have to share me. I'm yours."

"That's not true. You have a life and friends and goals and dreams. I have four walls, a dangerous job, and you. That's it. That's my entire world. Three entities."

"What about Jett? He's part of your life."

"For how long? He has London. He wants to get out. I can't lean on him forever."

"You don't have to, you have me." She grabs my shirt and looks up at me.

"Prove that's true and don't go. Blow him off."

She shakes her head. "I have to go. I have to do this. For my peace of mind. I won't be able to live with the guilt. Michael has been a good friend to me. He was there when I needed someone."

"I would have been there for you."

"I know. But I was so mad at you, it wouldn't have helped."

"I could always lock you in my room and force you to stay."

"You could, but I don't think that would be very healthy for our new relationship, do you?"

"No. But it would be fun." I slide my hands down her back and grab both of her butt cheeks. "Mine."

"Yes, yours, and nothing's going to change that. I'm ruined."

I snap my head back and look at her. "Ruined?"

"Yes. You ruined me."

"Ruined you how?" I ask in a panic.

"You ruined me for all other men. So you can scratch someone stealing me away off your list."

I breathe a sigh of relief. I've always worried that Ellie's time as my captive did ruin her somehow. That *I* ruined her somehow. But if the worst side effect was ruining her for other men, I can definitely live with that.

"Don't go," I press her again.

"I'll be two blocks away and gone for an hour."

I bite my tongue and refrain from demanding her to stay. Refrain from tying her up and gagging her while she's locked up tight behind closed doors.

"You know I have other ways to persuade you to stay." I press her up against the window and slip my hand under her dress.

"Yes." She goes up on her toes as I caress her clit over her soft cotton underwear. *"Kayne."*

"What?" I rasp.

"Don't." She grabs my wrist.

"Are you saying no to me, Ellie?"

I slide my middle finger under the fabric and straight into her pussy.

"Yes," she moans, "I'm saying no."

"You can't."

"What?" she gasps as I finger her.

"As long as that necklace is wrapped around your throat, I own you. Wherever, whenever. You're mine. And I want you right here, right now."

"No."

"Are you disobeying me, Ellie?"

"Yes."

"Do I have to show you what happens to bad kittens who disobey?"

"Yes." Her eyes smolder with defiance.

"Tell me to stop," I dare her.

"Stop," she says sternly.

As soon as the word leaves her lips I pull her across the room and slam her on top of the red wooden dresser.

"Beg me. Beg me to stop."

She squirms beneath me, trying to kick and punch, but I force her legs open and grind my erection right between her thighs. "That's going to be inside of you in two seconds whether you want it or not," I snarl in her ear as all the pent-up aggression of the morning brews like a hurricane inside me.

"No!" she screams, but I can smell her arousal like perfume in the air. She wants it.

"Fight me all you want. I'm still going to fuck you." I wrap one hand around her neck and pin her against the large square mirror behind her. A small, scared whimper escapes from her, doing nothing but urging me on. I swiftly pull down my shorts, springing my throbbing erection free with Ellie still flailing, but her fight is diminishing. She wants me. Wants this. Wants me to take her, possess her, rule over her. I can see the carnal desire flashing in her bright green eyes. With my free hand, I slide her panties over and thrust into her in one rapid blow. She nearly climbs the wall as she cries out.

"I know that's good, baby. I know you love it." I push her skirt up and pull the top of her dress down so she's as exposed as possible. "Watch me fuck you. Watch me fuck you so you never forget who owns this pussy," I slam into her again, jerking her back, "or this mouth," I swipe my thumb across her lower lip then place it back over her jugular. "Or this body." I grab her breast until she moans in pain.

"Watch." I clasp her neck a little tighter. Gasping, she lowers her eyes as I feed my cock into her starving little cunt, over and over.

"I know you like that. I know you love to watch. I remember how wet it makes you."

She whimpers as I relentlessly slide in and out of her, making sure she feels the entire length of my erection. From this angle, I can see how much bigger I truly am compared to her. From my height to my muscle mass to the way my cock stretches her to the max. She has to strain just to take me all in.

"Kayne," she mewls as her pussy tightens, begging for it. I have her exactly where I want her. Legs high and wide, upper body subdued, airway compressed. She's fundamentally the twisted little sex toy she agreed to be.

Ellie's breathing quickens and her knuckles turn white from gripping the edge of the dresser as she frenziedly saturates my cock with her arousal.

"Please," she fights to speak.

"Please what?" I continue my assault on her body, the dresser shaking violently.

"Please may I come?"

"Why the fuck are you asking me? You clearly do whatever you want."

I thrust into her again, finally shattering her to pieces. She expels a strangled scream as she comes, my cock glistening, greased by her arousal.

"Fuck," I grind out as my dick swells to the point the buildup is almost unbearable. Right before I blow a load, I lean over and hiss in her ear, "I may not have you locked away, but you're still my slave, still my possession, and one thing will never change. Everywhere I touch you, inside and out, will always be mine." I pound into her one last time still clutching her neck and fucking explode, a river of ecstasy flowing over my bones.

The moments after are fuzzy as I float down from the ceiling like a piece of burning ember. I open my eyes to find Ellie limp and wheezing beneath me.

I have no words or explanation for what just happened. So I just haul her up and take her into my arms. Languidly, she hugs me back.

"Ellie?" I whisper worriedly.

"Yup," she answers drily. "Definitely ruined."

I actually chuckle and then steal a glance at her face. Her eyes are closed and her cheek is resting on my shoulder.

"You okay?" My heart is beating uncontrollably in my chest from a mix of physical exertion and fear. I'll never stop worrying that one day I'll take it too far. Push her over the edge and drive her away.

She nods. "Yes. And I'm still going."

Now I full-out laugh. "I know."

"Good. That was fucking amazing," she says lethargically.

"I was worried I was pushing too hard."

"No such thing," she giggles.

"I love you." I can't help but say the words.

"I love you, too." She squeezes me. "Too much for my own good."

"No such thing," I repeat.

She nestles herself against me. "I need a shower."

"Not a chance in hell. You're going with my scent and sweat and cum inside of you."

"Fine," she relents. I really just think she's too spent to argue. "See, we can compromise."

"I have a feeling we're going to be doing a lot of *compromising.*" I shift so I can look down at her.

Ellie nods eagerly in agreement. "And I can't wait."

"You're a little minx, you know that?" I kiss her nose.

"I'd be boring if I wasn't."

"True. I also have a feeling you're going to make me go prematurely gray."

"Ooo. I love older men."

I pick her up and whack her ass as she wraps her legs around my waist. "I'm not that much older."

"Says you. You're in your *late* twenties."

"Ugh." I groan as I lay us on the bed and cuddle Ellie in my arms. "I'm going to spank the shit out of you later for saying that. And for calling me a douchebag."

"I'll make sure to be extra bad, then," she purrs.

I have created a monster.

"When I get back, I think we should go shopping online," she says.

"For what?"

"Ears and a tail." She looks up at me with just her eyes like she's a little embarrassed and a lot excited by the idea. "So I can prove to you how much I love you and how much you own me."

"Fuck, baby, you better be careful about what you say." I grab my now rapidly growing cock. "There might be round two."

The picture of Ellie naked, wearing ears, a tail, and a collar has just relaunched my arousal.

"Save it for later."

"Are you telling me what to do?" I challenge her.

"No, Kayne," she hums.

"I didn't think so." I smack her ass.

ELLIE AND I DON'T GET much downtime. Before I know it, she's out of bed, fixing her clothes and re-braiding her hair.

"Do you have a toothbrush I can use?" she asks.

"Why? Plan on kissing someone?" I ask petulantly.

"Eventually," she taunts. I know she's talking about me, but still, she's spending the next hour with another man. It's bothering me. "I'm going out in public. I care about my personal hygiene."

"Bathroom." I point behind me to the door.

Ellie skips past me and my annoyance grows. Does she have to be so damn cheerful?

I drag myself out of bed and change my clothes as Ellie attends to her personal hygiene concerns. At least she agreed not to shower. I'll bathe her later, and spank her, and fuck her, all over again.

I walk out of my closet to find Ellie checking herself in the mirror one last time. I step behind her and put one hand on her hip. In the reflection, we look like any ordinary, run of the mill couple. She, dressed casually in a light-blue sundress and sneakers, me in my favorite pair of worn jeans and black t-shirt. But appearances can be deceiving. I know that better than anyone.

We aren't ordinary, and we aren't run of the mill. We're . . . *us.* Just like Ellie said. I never thought I'd be part of an *us.* I now understand why I was so easily provoked. The thought of losing *us* strangles me with fear.

Ellie and I walk hand in hand down the stairs. I don't know if it's my paranoia or my possessive side, but something in me just doesn't want her to go.

I try to ignore it. I tell myself I'm being overprotective and irrational. Ellie is a big girl, and big girls do what they want. Unfortunately for me.

"Can you give me the key to your apartment? I want to start having some of your things brought over," I ask her as we reach the last stair.

"Things?"

"Yeah, things. Like clothes and whatever."

"Am I moving in?" she asks.

"Yes."

"Really?"

"Yes, Ellie. You're my fiancée, and I'm not going to spend another night without you for as long as I live." I put my hand out for the key.

"Don't you think you should ask Jett if it's okay? He lives here, too, right?" She digs through her purse and pulls out a key ring.

I look at her *like don't be ridiculous.* "Jett would never say no. He'll probably want to have a pajama party tonight."

Ellie laughs. "You mean there'd actually be pajamas?"

"Yes, and I'm sure they'd be highly inappropriate." Ellie hands me the key. "Is there anything in particular you want?" I place it in my pocket.

"My toothbrush." She smiles.

"I'll buy you a case so you never run out."

"You spoil me." She lifts onto her toes to kiss me.

"You have no idea." I back her up against the wall. I *really* don't want her to go.

"I'll be back in an hour," she breathes heavily.

"Exactly sixty minutes," I stipulate, "or I'm coming down there and dragging you home myself."

"I might like that."

"Ellie." I bite her lip. "Behave."

"Yes, Kayne."

The way she says that sends tingles down my spine and blood pumping straight to my cock. I once dreamed of hearing Ellie say that of her own free will. Of belonging to me—not because she was forced, but because she wanted me. It was the first time I ever let myself wish for anything. She was the first thing I ever wanted in my entire life, and I finally have her. I imagine this feeling is similar to winning the lottery. Amazement, bewilderment, joy. Joy. Such a foreign concept for me, yet so easily accepted when I'm with her.

"I'll see you in an hour." She kisses me one last time, but before she turns the knob, I stop her.

"Wait," I put my hand on the door. "Just wait right here."

I leave her standing in the foyer and head back into the Toy Box where Jett and Juice are still hanging out.

"Do we have any Jimmies?" I ask Juice. "Like really small ones?"

"In the cabinet," he points to the right, "second drawer."

"What do you need that for?" Jett asks as I pull out what looks like a dark slate business card.

"You'll see." I hand it to Juice. "Activate it. I'll tell you when to turn it on."

Juice takes the card, punches a few numbers and letters into his computer, and hands it back. I pop out the tiny little chip from the cardboard and peel off the paper from the back. It's so small you can barely decipher what it is on the tip of my finger.

I walk back out to Ellie, who is pacing the foyer. "Is everything okay?" she asks restlessly.

"As okay as it can be." I tickle the heart dangling from her throat.

"Did I hurt you upstairs?"

"No. It was intense. A little scary. But fucking amazing. I know you'd never intentionally hurt me." She smiles coyly. "No matter how mad I make you."

"I warned you I was going to fuck you hard. But baby, I meant it when I said I would love you harder." I trap her face with one hand.

"I know." She melts against me as I lean down and kiss her. Her lips are warm and her breath is minty.

"Now go." I land a hard blow on her behind. "When you get back, I'm chaining you to the bed and eating you for dinner."

"Oh God," she says, flustered with desire. "I'm going."

"Just give the doorman your name when you get back," I tell Ellie as she steps on the elevator. "You'll be on the list."

She grins and does a little sexy wave to acknowledge me just as the doors close. Then she's gone.

And I'm completely miserable.

I head back into the Toy Box and plop down into a seat. Both Jett and Juice stare at me.

"What?" I ask defensively.

"Whatcha doing?" Jett asks.

"What does it look like I'm doing? Sitting down."

"Where's Ellie?"

"She went out."

"To do what?" His eyebrows crease.

"Break up with her boy toy."

"And you let her?" His tone elevates.

"Yeah. What do you think the jimmy was for?"

"You bugged your fiancée?"

"Well, I had to keep an eye, or ear, in this case, on her somehow. I know I couldn't force her to stay." *Unfortunately.*

"Don't you think that's a little . . . stalkerish?" Juice asks.

I glare at both of them. "There is an unidentified threat out there, and although it doesn't seem to involve Ellie, I decided to play it safe anyway."

"Translation," Jett arbitrates, "I am insecure about my fiancée hanging out with another man, so I took it upon myself to eavesdrop."

"Fuck you," I spit. "If the two of you have such a problem with my moral turpitude, you can leave."

Jett and Juice glance at each other decisively.

"I'll get the popcorn." Juice jumps up.

That's what I thought.

Once gone, Jett swivels his chair so he's looking directly at me. "You've come far, Grasshopper."

I raise my eyebrows at him. Condescending cocksucker. "You do know I'm going to throw knives at your head while you're sleeping tonight, right?"

"Good." He runs his hand through his blond hair. "Take a little off the top. I'm due for a trim."

"Ass—" Loud popping noises like gunshots suddenly echo from inside the apartment.

"Juice!?" We both yell as we jump up and grab the closest firearm in reaching distance. We hear more pops and then the smell of popcorn fills the air.

We glance at each other hesitantly, waiting a few moments before Juice reappears with a big bowl in one hand a bottle of soda in the other.

"Should I put my hands up?" he asks as he stares down the barrel of two semi-automatic handguns.

Jett and I both exhale.

"When you said popcorn, I thought you meant you were going to rip open a bag."

"No way." He sits back down in his captain's chair. "This is first-class entertainment. It warrants the real stuff." He pops a kernel into his mouth.

"Just turn the fucking thing on." I uncock the gun, and then grab a handful of popcorn for myself.

A few seconds later, the sound of cars passing and Ellie humming plays through the room.

"Good acoustics," Juice mouths.

I roll my eyes; idiot loves his gadgets.

She has to be close to the coffee house by now, if not there already.

There's a low ringing noise, and then a muffled voice I recognize.

"You've reached Mark at Expo Shipping and Receiving. I'm sorry I missed your call but please leave a message and I'll get back to you as soon as possible."

Beep!

"Mark, you going to be really sorry you missed this call! I'll only forgive you if you're doing something really important, like Pretty Pete. Call me! I have to ask you something. Bye."

Ask him something?

"Pretty Pete?" Juice asks with wide brown eyes.

I shrug. "He's gay. It's her old boss."

"Ah." He acknowledges, then goes back to munching on his popcorn.

A few moments after she hangs up, tires screech, there's a sharp intake of breath, and then what sounds like a scuffle. I fly out of my seat when I hear Ellie scream *'no!'* and a car door slam.

"Ellie!"

The sound of tires peeling out tears through the room, and then there's just silence.

I barely remember making it down to the street—there's just a faint recollection of Jett ordering me into the elevator because the stairs would take too long. We retrace Ellie's steps with my mind in a panic. Someone took her. Someone took her *again.* I can't think, I can't see, as pedestrians and tourists knock me around. I feel like I'm caught in a wind tunnel.

"Kayne!" Jett calls a few yards away from me. He's crouching by the curb on the corner. I walk over to him dazed. He stands up, holding Ellie's necklace. "They grabbed her here."

Those words slice through me like I've just been cut with a burning blade.

"And look." He points to several spots. "Traffic cameras and ATM machines. Maybe they caught something."

"They better fucking have."

I'm shaking with rage by the time we get back to the Toy Box. Juice's fingers are already flying as he hacks into every camera in the area.

"Anything?" I growl.

"Not yet. Give me a second."

"Juice, fucking find something," I snap.

"You yelling at me isn't going to make the process go faster, so back the fuck off." He concentrates on the screen.

"Kayne." Jett pulls me back and I begin pacing like a lunatic. Who am I kidding, I am a lunatic. SOMEONE TOOK ELLIE! This is all my fault. I knew I shouldn't have let her leave. I should have listened to my fucking gut. It's the one thing that's kept me alive the past twenty-eight years. I just gambled with, and lost, the most important thing in my life and these two want me stay fucking calm.

"Okay." There are lots of different things popping up on Juice's screen. "Look there," he points to a few mismatched images lined up in a row. "Here she's walking." He points to her back. "Then here." A car pulls up right in front of her just as she reaches the corner. It only takes a second, the picture is blurry, but there's definitely two of them—one driving an old model sedan and the one who grabbed her. It literally took a split second to get her in the car and drive away.

My brain feels like it's expanding in my skull from stress.

"Can we get a better picture of the car? Maybe a shot of the license plate?" Jett asks.

"Yup, found that." Juice bangs on the keys. "It's only a partial, but you can see the make, too. That's huge."

The letters FHK and MALIBU display across the big screen on the wall.

"I'm cross-referencing both identifiers in the DMV database and searching to see if there are any police reports about a stolen Malibu."

The whole process feels like it takes forever. I know every second that ticks by is one more second our chance of finding Ellie diminishes.

"Okay," Juice finally announces. "There are three potential hits on the car with that make and license plate letters. No reports of stolen vehicles."

"Three?"

"Yeah, two in Honolulu and one in Ma'ili. I would try that one first." He scribbles on a piece of paper and hands it to Jett.

"Why do you say that?" he asks.

"Ms. Kalani has a brother who was released from prison three months ago. Drug trafficking." He cocks an eyebrow. "Her address is listed as his last known."

I look at Jett. "Let's go."

THE ADDRESS JUICE GAVE US is a small farmhouse in the middle of nowhere. I think you can literally only fit a couch and a television in the rundown structure.

There are chickens and goats roaming the property, and the grounds are completely overgrown. If I was a douchebag drug smuggler, this is exactly where I would live.

I yank on the black leather gloves covering my hands, the ones with the brass knuckles sewn right into them.

"Ready?" Jett asks as he opens the car door.

"To break someone's face? Hell yeah."

"Hey," he puts a hand on my chest. "Don't kill him before he talks."

"I wouldn't dream of it."

"We're going to get her back." I know what Jett is trying to do. He's trying to appease me so I can focus, but I've never been more focused in my life.

"In what condition?" I mutter rhetorically. I've run through every horrific scenario possible. Beaten, raped, drugged, sold, killed. There isn't one thing I've left out.

"You knock on the front door. I'll go around back. Maybe we can snuff him out."

"I know the drill."

"Glad to hear. Now get the fuck out of the car."

I walk up the front path overgrown with weeds as Jett makes his way to the side of the house. He clucks to get my attention right before I knock on the door.

"Car," he mouths. It must be hidden in the back.

I nod, then bang on the door. "Anyone home?" I yell. "I seem to be lost. And my GPS isn't working out here." I try to sound like a tourist. "Hello?" I bang again.

A second later the door jerks open to a very large Hawaiian woman in a Muu Muu dress and flower in her hair. She takes one look at me in my skintight black shirt, cargo pants, and gun holster and knows I'm no tourist. She tries to slam the door in my face, but I stop her with my hand.

"Where's Pilipo?"

"Never heard of him."

"Bullshit."

"Kayne!" I hear Jett yell. "Coming around!"

I turn my head just in time to see someone disappearing into the woods. Perfect, a chase. It's exactly what I need. My heart starts to punch through my chest as I book it across the front lawn and into the thick greenery. I can see his shaved head and tattooed arms fighting against the dense branches as I track him like an animal. *I'm going to tear you apart* is all I can think as adrenaline courses through my veins.

Just as I come up behind Pilipo, Jett barrels into him from the left side. They both hit the ground hard, rolling down a small hill. The medium-sized man ends up on top giving him the upper hand. He lands a hard blow across Jett's face, causing him to spit blood.

A second later, I yank the piece of shit up and return the favor, smashing his nose.

"Where is she?" I bark.

"Who?" he screams back wiping blood from his face.

"The girl you took this morning." I knee him in the stomach.

He keels over. "I don't know nothing about any girl." He looks up at me, and I immediately know he's lying.

"Wanna try that answer again?" I kick him in the face, and he hits the ground hard.

"I don't know shit." He splutters, his mouth foaming with saliva and blood.

I glance at Jett. He's standing on the opposite side of Pilipo. "I think he needs some incentive to talk."

He looks up at me with blood stained teeth. "I couldn't agree more." Jett hauls Pilipo up and locks him in a full nelson. Arms subdued over his head.

Pilipo is sucking in air, and although he isn't acting scared, I'm about to make him shit.

"I'm going to make this easy. I ask, you answer. Nod if you understand."

He spits on me. I wipe my shirt. This job is so glamorous sometimes. "Okay, then. I'll take that as a yes." I pull a picture out of the side pocket on my leg. "Recognize her?"

Pilipo turns white as a ghost.

"That's your daughter, yeah?"

He doesn't say a word.

"She's cute. Just turned four?" I taunt him.

He glares at me.

"Want someone to take her away?" I ask waving the picture of the little dark-haired girl blowing out her birthday candles.

His breathing becomes more erratic and his stare hostile.

"Tell me where you took her," I lean in closer, "or I'm going to take *her*. We know a lot of the same people, brother, and what they're capable of."

He doesn't utter a word, just snarls at me. I wait him out, but he doesn't budge.

"Fine. Let him go," I instruct Jett. "You just signed your daughter's death sentence." Jett drops him to the ground. "And I'll make sure you never find her body."

"Wait!" Pilipo punches the dirt. "Fuck. Swear you won't touch her!"

"Give me the information I want and I'll think about it," I sneer.

He glowers at me on all fours. "An estate. In Kailua."

"Who hired you to take her?" I grab his face.

"I don't know his name! All I know is he calls himself Protégé and is trying to take over the cartel I used to run for."

"Who's cartel?" I demand.

"El Rey's."

I look at Jett.

Shit.

WE LEFT PILIPO LYING IN a pool of his own blood.

I'm just ripping off my bloody glove when my phone rings. It's Juice.

I put it on speaker as Jett drives down a muddy road back to the highway.

"What's up?"

"Got news. We know who hacked Endeavor."

"Who?" we ask.

"Simon."

"Simon? Like the Gatekeeper, Simon?" Jett questions.

"One and the same." Juice confirms.

"Isn't he supposed be the one protecting our classified information?"

"Yes, but he also doubles as a hacker. Turns out he's been working an undercover mission of his own."

"And no one knew about it?"

"Adams did."

"Of course, he did," I state aggravated. Commander Adams knows everything that goes on with Endeavor, he's the fucking man behind the curtain. "He didn't think to clue anyone else in?"

"Too dangerous. They wanted this guy. Bad."

"Bad enough to let him think he was hacking one of the most powerful security agencies in the world?" Jett asks.

"So it seems. Simon had to lay low until all the information was transferred. Well, all the wrong information anyway."

"So, no identities have been compromised?" I ask.

"None but the guy who hired Simon to hack us."

"And that would be who exactly?" I inquire on the edge of my seat.

"That's what I'm calling about. Kayne, you're not going to like this. I'm sending a pic."

A new message pops up on my screen.

"His name is Eduardo Sanchez or, as he's known on the street, Protégé."

"Protégé?" Jett and I repeat in unison as I open the text.

"Holy fucking shit."

"What?" Jett glances tensely between me and the road as he drives. "What is it?"

I hold up my phone so he can see, all the blood draining from my body.

"It's Michael."

"I CAN'T BREATHE!" I SCREAM as I kick and flail, being hauled around with a hood over my head.

I'm suddenly dropped on the floor, hard.

Ouch!

I don't know what happened. One minute I was walking down the street minding my own business, and the next I was being forced into the backseat of a car where I was tied up, gagged, and then shrouded in darkness. I'm now lying helplessly on my side with my hands bound behind my back and my heart on the verge of giving out. It's been beating triple time since I was grabbed.

"Well, look who finally decided to come home," a male voice says. The hood is removed, and I look up into a pair of dark chocolate-brown eyes. Michael's eyes. I glance around erratically. I'm in a bedroom. A very fancy bedroom that has a beautiful view of the Pacific, white décor, and a polished wood floor. The smell of fresh flowers is as potent as air freshener.

"You look hot as hell like that, Ellie," he says as I stare at him angry, confused, and unable to speak.

He props me up so I'm sitting on my butt and removes the gag. I work my jaw quickly, trying to get the feeling back.

"Is this some kind of joke?" I demand.

Michael laughs at me. "Have fun on your trip?" He lifts my chin and regards the large bite mark on my neck.

I refuse to answer.

"Looks to me like you did. You never let me give you hickeys."

"You never tried."

"I was holding back."

"Why?"

"So I didn't kill you," he says matter-of-factly.

"What?"

"Ellie, Ellie, Ellie. Little gullible Ellie," he recites.

I stare at him like he's deranged. "What the fuck is going on?"

"Let me tell you a story." Michael diverts, avoiding my question. "There was this boy who had a father whom he loved dearly. A man he looked up to and idolized. A man who wanted him to go to college and live a straight-laced life. But the boy wanted to be just like his father. Wanted money and power and women. So the father took the boy under his wing and groomed him. And when the boy was just old enough, and had proven himself just enough," his voice elevates, "his father is killed in cold blood and his kingdom is destroyed. Do you know what that does to a child?"

I shake my head.

"It makes him want revenge." His eyes widen rabidly.

"Revenge on who?"

"The man who killed my father. The man who is your Master."

"I don't have a Master," I contest.

"Don't lie to me, Ellie. I saw it with my own eyes. I was there that night. I watched as he toted you around like he owned you and the world. I fucked right in front of the two of you."

My eyes widen as images of that night, the night of the party, flash in front of my eyes. Jett dressing me up. Kayne leading me around. The roped off section of the room where we watched one of his girls get taken on the same kind of table that was in my room. Taken by Michael?

"Why were you there?" I ask dubiously.

"It was a party. I was invited." He shrugs.

"I don't understand." I shake my head.

Michael sighs and crouches down so we're eye level.

"You know, I was actually jealous of him. You were so beautiful and raw and intoxicating. I wanted what he had. I wanted you."

He leans forward and for a second I think he's going to kiss me. I pull away.

"Skittish all of a sudden?" He unties my hands, and I rub my wrists once they're free. "You always used to like it when I kissed you."

"Tell me what the hell is going on."

"I'm getting my revenge on the man who killed my father and the organization who destroyed my birthright."

"Who is your father?" I erupt.

Michael grabs my hair and yanks my head back. My scalp stings. He looks down directly into my eyes, and any warmth or feeling is completely gone. Just void. It's like I don't even know this person in front of me.

"EL REY!" he screams, and I flinch, his grip still tight on my hair.

"I don't know who that is!" I cry from the pain.

Michael looks at me like I'm insane. "I would honestly believe he has you brainwashed. You are an excellent actress." I still don't understand. "I saw him speak to you that night, Ellie. He yanked on your slave chain."

Recognition suddenly sparks. The man with Javier. The one who wanted to buy me. I see the resemblance now, straight nose, prominent cheekbones, and dark-brown eyes. They look much more like his father's at the moment. Cold and calculating, capable of anything.

"Kayne didn't kill your father!" I blurt out.

"Of course, you would say that. You're protecting him." He painfully shakes my head around with his firm hold.

I wince helplessly. "I'm not lying, I was there." I grab his hand like that's somehow going to loosen his grip. "Javier killed him. He shot him in the head right in front of us!"

"Liar!" he snaps. "Javier was my father's most loyal disciple. He would never turn on him."

"He did," I scream as Michael pulls harder. My scalp feels like it's going to rip right off my skull. "I remember his words right before he shot him. He said," I pant loudly, "'hostile takeover.'"

Michael breathes raggedly as he searches my eyes. I almost think he believes me. I pray silently that he believes me.

"You would say anything to protect him."

I have no response for that because it's the truth.

"He didn't kill him. I swear," I whisper desperately.

"Even if he didn't kill him, which he did, the organization he works for took everything from me. It's reason enough to destroy them both."

"Michael, no," I beg.

I can't believe this is the same person I've spent the last three months with. The man who would buy me shaved ice as we walked along the beach, who would listen to me ramble about nonsense and make me laugh with stupid jokes. A man who was so warm and sweet and caring.

"I don't understand. You cozied up to me all that time for what?"

"To get to Kayne, of course. I figured find you, find him. But it didn't exactly work that way." He lets go of my hair and climbs on top of me, forcing me back onto my elbows. "He was nowhere to be found. Not even a whisper in your life. I began to think that maybe you weren't as important to him as I originally thought." He's directly on top of me now. "It was your pussy that kept me coming back. You gave it up so easily. You really are a whore."

Tears well in my eyes. "I thought you were nice."

"I think you were just looking for someone to buy time with until your Master came for you." He presses his body flush against mine. An erection growing in his pants. My stomach turns. I try to wriggle away, but he wraps his hand around my throat and squeezes tightly. "I knew the minute I pulled up to your house that day it was him you were going to see. The minute I saw the car and the driver." He unbuttons his jeans and slides down his fly as I frantically squirm beneath him, clawing at his forearm.

"I love it when you fight, Ellie. This might be the most exciting sex we've ever had."

"Michael, no!" I strain, as he crushes my windpipe with one hand and rips my panties off with the other.

"Michael!" Tears flow like a river down my cheeks as I try to fight him.

"Did you miss saying my name?" He thrusts into me, and it feels like someone just sliced me open with a serrated knife.

"Stop!" My voice is barely audible as he chokes me, while at the same time violating me over and over again.

I cry harder with every passing second he wrecks me, the pain becoming unbearable, my legs spasming, my fingernails wet with blood from stabbing them into his skin.

"Michael!" I whimper one last time before my vision fades and my spirit breaks.

"Your pussy saves you every time."

It's the last thing I hear before I pass out.

I SWEAR I WAS DEAD.

I come around to Michael zipping his pants while I lay ruined on the floor. Every inch of my body is throbbing.

"I missed you, Ellie. Never thought I'd say that."

I glare at him. "You're a monster. Just like your father."

Michael's eyes flash as he crouches down and clutches my face painfully. "Don't speak unkindly of the dead. Now go clean yourself up." He says it like he loathes me. "We have a plane to catch."

"We?"

"Yes, Ellie. You're mine now."

I look at him dismayed. "What else could you possibly want from me?"

"My cock in your mouth next time." He lifts me off the floor. "Once a whore always a whore."

Tears threaten once more. I can't live as someone's slave again. Especially Michael's. I'd rather kill myself.

"What about Kayne? You going to kill him?"

"Yes, eventually. A very long time from now. My father taught me if you really want to destroy a man, destroy what's most important to him. First, I'm going to destroy his organization, then I'm going to destroy you. And when I'm finished, I'll return you to your owner a shell of a human being."

I nearly throw up from his words. I now explicitly understand. I understand why Kayne did what he did—why he went to such extreme measures to protect me. To save from heinous creatures like this.

"You really are a monster." I seethe.

Michael's lips curl cruelly. "We're all monsters in our own way. You have ten minutes." He turns and then stops.

"One more thing," he snaps, spinning to face me again. "You won't need this anymore." He lifts my hand and pulls off my engagement ring, tossing it over his head. I gasp as I hear it ding on the wooden floor, and then watch as it rolls and bounces into a corner. "While you two were off picking out china patterns, I was assembling my army and appointing new captains. My father ruled a kingdom, I'm going to rule an empire." He glances at the ring. "Pick it up and I'll cut off your hand. Understand?"

I look at him with tear-soaked eyes. I despise this man.

"Ellie?" he grabs my chin.

I nod.

"If you want to be mad at someone, be mad at Kayne."

With that, he leaves, and all I can think about is how wrong he is. The person I should be mad at is myself.

My concentration is hazy as I clean the blood from between my legs. It literally feels like I have been hacked wide open with a meat cleaver. I cry silently, not wanting anyone to hear. What are the odds a person is kidnapped twice in their lifetime to be used as a sex slave? I must be one fucking lucky woman, I think bitterly as I throw away the white towel stained with red.

I have ten minutes to figure a way out of this. I pace the bedroom.

I have a feeling this is going to be the last bit of luxury I see if Michael forces me to leave with him.

I hurry and pull on the French doors that lead to the lani. Locked. Shit. I try some windows, but they're built right into the wall, like an all-natural picture frame. I search them all, hoping beyond hope that just one has a latch. The last ones I try are at the back of the room on either side of the bed. It opens! I look down to see a slanted roof below me and a trellis just adjacent to it. There's nothing but green land all around the house, and the ocean and mountains in the distance. I remember telling Kayne that I'd rather be lost in the wilderness than be his slave. Those words were never truer. Just as I'm about to push open the window, I hear the door unlock and see Michael walk in.

"Let's go." He orders.

I just stand there.

"Didn't hear me the first time? It's time to go," he says annoyed.

I say something quietly in response.

"What?"

I say it again, no louder.

"What are you saying?" He stomps over to me enraged and grabs my arm.

"I said," I look him dead in the eye, "I'd rather die than live as someone's slave again." With that, I swiftly knee him in the balls as hard as I can. As he falls to the floor, I escape out the window with my heart battering the inside of my chest.

"Bitch!" I hear him yell as I shuffle sideways across the slanted roof until I reach the trellis and swing down. Then I run like hell, past the pool and soft lit gazebo, toward the setting sun and lush green mountains.

JUST FOR THE RECORD, I did not enjoy using Pilipo's daughter as a bargaining chip. I just did what had to be done. I did what I had to do to protect my own.

"Are you speaking to me yet?" Juice asks from the front seat of the Suburban.

"No," I growl. "You're lucky I haven't killed you yet."

"That would look bad in your personnel file. Killing a fellow employee."

I shoot him the most deadly look I'm capable of.

"I ran the background check like you asked me to."

"If you don't stop talking, I'm going to wire your jaw shut."

Juice huffs. It's mostly his fault we are in this situation. I told him to run a background check on Michael the second Ellie had a conversation with him. It came back clean. Not even a parking ticket. But there should have been something to tip us off as to who he was or what he was involved in. There's always something, and Juice missed it.

"The guy was tight. Clean as a whistle. Nothing to even suggest criminal activity."

"Or that fact he was a drug lord's son," I add vindictively.

"Come on. That identity was buried so deep, it took a hacker much more skilled than me to uncover it. We all know El Rey was a master at concealing his identity. So how far-fetched is it that he did the same with his offspring?"

"Just save it." I clench my jaw so tightly, I may just crack a molar.

I know it's not all Juice's fault. It's just easier to blame someone else at the moment. Maybe if I wasn't shitfaced half the time wallowing in my own misery, I would have done the background check myself and dug until I found something on the conniving little piece of shit whose head I'm going to gladly rip off with my bare hands.

"Is everything ready?" Jett asks, collected—always in control no matter the circumstance.

"As ready as it will ever be." Juice fiddles with the laptop on his dashboard. We are currently parked in the woods three miles away from Michael's compound. Satellite images confirmed this is where they're holding Ellie and surveillance shows there are nine guards heavily armed.

We were able to assemble a twenty-man team in under three hours with the help of Honolulu S.W.A.T.

"HSWAT come in, over." Juice talks into a walkie-talkie.

"Copy HSWAT," the commander answers.

"In position?" Juice asks.

"Roger. Falcon One. Diversion set for nineteen hundred hours," which is seven PM civilian time and in twelve minutes. "Men positioned on foot."

"Copy," Juice replies and the walkie hisses. "You two ready?" He turns to Jett and me in the backseat.

I pull on my brass-knuckled gloves, and the leather creaks. "Can't wait." I tighten my fist and curl my biceps ready to pound Michael's face in.

"Good. It should be fully dark by the time you emerge from the woods and reach the edge of the property. Don't breach the perimeter until you hear the explosion. That should divert all shitheads to the front of the house, leaving Ellie light on muscle." Juice tips the laptops so we can see the schematics of the immense structure in infrared. "It looks like they're keeping her in this back bedroom, which boasts well for you, since there's a trellis and slanted roof right underneath it. Easy in, easy out." Jett and I nod, memorizing the layout.

"Got it," Jett confirms.

"I'll be on comms the whole time," he puts in an ear piece, "so no pillow talk you two. I want to keep my lunch in my stomach."

"You're just jealous no one loves you that much." I grin callously.

"Insanely." Juice rolls his eyes. As much as we bust his chops, the man can run an operation like no other. He was mine and Jett's handler the six years we were undercover. He knew the ins and outs of everything, advised us in sticky situations, and basically saved mine and Ellie's lives by knowing where in the mansion we were and exactly how to infiltrate.

"See you on the flip side." The three of us bump fists, and then Jett and I are gone.

We jog straight toward the sunset, pushing brush out of our way as we go.

"Comms check, Alpha Green," I hear Juice say in my ear.

"Loud and clear, Falcon one. Roger."

"Test, test," he says again. "Come in, Charlie Blue."

"Copy," Jett responds. "You have such a lovely speaking voice, Falcon One."

"Can it," Juice responds.

"Just wanted to make you feel loved."

"Stay the course," he says seriously.

"I don't think you could divert Alpha Green if you launched a missile."

"Roger," Juice repeats, some amusement in his voice.

Jett and I cover ground quickly, keeping to the strict timeline and markers. We're two hundred yards out when Juice chatters in my ear. "Alpha Green we have movement on the south side, over."

"Identify, over?"

"Switching to satellite."

Seconds tick.

"Shit. It's Ellie. She made a break for it," Juice informs me.

"What?" Jett and I both pick up the pace.

"She's heading straight for you. Man, she's quick."

I can't help but smirk as I push my body to the max, flying through the woods.

"There's someone tailing her. Coming up fast." The hiss of the walkie-talkie echoes in my ear.

"HSWAT, we are a go," he yells. "Push the panic button."

"Shit. Shit." I run faster, branches catching me in the face and whipping my arms.

Moments later, we hear a blast as the car bomb is detonated.

"Check in, Falcon One," I huff.

Silence.

"Juice!"

"Motherfucker, he caught her." My chest explodes. "They're fighting. Damn, your girl has one hell of a right hook."

"Don't I know it." I can still feel the sting from when she hit me outside Mansion.

I see a clearing, the perimeter of the property. I burst through the trees onto a manicured lawn with Jett by my side. It's nearly dark, only a sliver of light left. I break out into full-blown sprint as my lungs burn and my leg muscles tear.

"Oh, man." It sounds like Juice winces.

"What!"

"He's beating her. Kill that cocksucker, Kayne."

"With immense pleasure," I pant.

Just as the last shreds of light disappear, Ellie comes into view.

With each breath, a montage of images flash in front of me one after the other.

Ellie on the ground, Michael standing over her. A gun pointed at her head.

"ELLIE!" Her name rips from my throat, and then a gunshot rings out.

"NO!" I tackle Michael to the ground, knocking the gun out of his hand. We roll over the thick lush grass, struggling for control. I pull a power move, grabbing under one of his legs and hooking an arm around his neck. He punches me in the head and kicks out of my hold. We both get to our feet and I don't waste a second going back at his body, grabbing hold of his chest and landing a kidney shot. He knees me in the stomach, but I barely register it. There's so much adrenaline pumping through my system it feels like I have wings.

"I'm going to let you be the first to see what happens when someone fucks with what's mine." I smash Michael right in the face and his nose explodes with blood.

"Fuck!" He stumbles back making a go for his gun. He grabs it and points it at me, but I kick it out of his hand then punch him again. He drops to the ground, and I continue to pound on his face. Soon, it's barely recognizable. His cheeks are swollen, his lips are split, and his eyebrows are ripped open. I pull my fist back about to slam him again when he speaks.

"Do it! Kill me, you motherfucker! Just like you killed my father!" I pause to look at him mid punch. He thinks I killed El Rey? Everything begins to make sense now. Ellie, Endeavor, he was trying to get to me.

I lower my fist and respond harshly. "You're wrong about one thing. I didn't kill your father." He sputters blood as I speak. "But you're right about the other. I am going to kill *you.*" I jerk a Glock out of my back holster and pull the trigger, shooting him square between the eyes. Then I pull it again—and again and again. I pull it until the chamber clicks.

Then I reload and repeat.

"Kayne!" I hear Juice's sharpened voice cut through my murderous rampage. "I think he's dead!"

"Not enough for me." I squeeze the trigger one last time.

"Heel man. Jett needs you. *Ellie* needs you."

"Ellie!?" I snap out of my lethal haze and turn to see Jett leaning over her body under the bright moonlight.

"Ellie? Ellie?" I crawl over to them. "Ellie?" I examine her face. Her eye is swollen, and her lip is bleeding.

"Give me your shirt!" Jett roars. It takes a second for my mind to catch up with my body as I process the scene in front of me. Jett's hands covered in blood. Ellie lying still as a statue, a pool of red staining the grass underneath her, growing larger by the second.

"Kayne now! She's going to bleed out!"

Without thinking, I rip off my holster and tear off my shirt. "I need you to hold here." He takes my hand and places it on his already soaked T-shirt pressed against her abdomen.

"I think it went straight through. I need to compress the exit wound." He tilts her body, assesses her back, and then applies pressure with my shirt.

"There's a medivac already on its way. The house is secured." He talks to me, but all I see is Ellie, dying right before my eyes.

We hear the chopper in the distance. "Two minutes max," he says.

It's going to be the longest two minutes of my life.

"Kayne," Ellie's faint voice calls my name.

"Ellie, I'm right here. Hold on." I wish I could scoop her up in my arms and hold her, but I know my hands need to stay where they are.

"You were right," she murmurs.

"About what, baby?" I try to keep her talking.

She doesn't open her eyes as she speaks. "I am a terrible judge of character." I nearly lose it. That's what I said to her when she was locked in the dungeon. *"I won't hold it against you for being a bad judge of character."*

"I don't know shit. I was talking out of my ass," I choke.

"It's so cold in the city." She shivers. I glance at Jett.

"She's hallucinating. She thinks she's in New York," I say, shaking.

"She's going into shock," he tells me as her eyes flutter and chest compresses just as the air ambulance hovers overhead.

"Shit! Come on, Ellie!" Jett yells over the propellers. "Be the strong girl we all know you are!"

The spotlight shines on us as the EMS helicopter lands. The door flies open and two flight paramedics dressed in all white exit with a gurney and oxygen.

They check her vitals as soon as they reach us and instruct Jett and me not to move.

"Ellie?" one of the medics asks. "Ellie, can you hear me?"

She doesn't respond.

I watch withdrawn as the two men work rapidly to bandage the bleeding, place her on the gurney, and cover her face with an oxygen mask. Right before they lift her, I whisper in her ear. "Ellie, if your hearts stop beating so will mine. Third rule of survival, fight like hell. Stay with me." Tears escape down my cheeks as she's carried away, leaving me helpless, hopeless, and in utter despair.

"Come on, come on." Jett pulls on my arm, lifting me to my feet as the helicopter takes off. My entire existence is in that aircraft. Everything I have to live for.

He hauls me into the back of a Suburban I didn't even see pull up, and we speed off in the same direction as the transport.

"It's going to be okay. It's going to be okay." Juice's voice is distant compared to Ellie's in my head. *"Till death do us part."* She only said that yesterday. Yesterday was the start of our tomorrow and now tomorrow might not even exist.

"Put this on," Jett whips a shirt in my face while Juice drives like a maniac. "And here," he hands me a pack of wipes. Black op survival kit, a change of clothes and baby wipes. "We gotta clean up, they'll never let us in the hospital looking like we just left the scene of a massacre."

"Didn't we?" I tighten my fists and draw them into my chest. I don't want to clean Ellie's blood off my hands. It's the only piece of her I have to hold on to.

"Kayne." Jett chastises me as we speed through Honolulu. "Come on." He grabs my hands and starts wiping frantically in the dark. I look up at him, removed. I feel like I'm six years old again. Helpless, alone, and scared out of my mind. "If she dies, you're going to have to bury me with her."

Jett pulls his lips into a tight line. "She's not going to die."

"How do you know?"

"Because I know everything," he says, not sounding very confident of knowing anything at all.

Juice pulls up in front of the hospital, and Jett and I jump out. We're somewhat put together, but still look like we just walked through hell. Or maybe that's just me.

"Ellie Stevens," Jett asks the front desk guard. "She was brought in by medivac. Gunshot wound."

The elderly man in a security uniform punches something into his computer.

"Steven or Stevens?" he asks.

"Stevens," Jett answers. I pace.

"Ellie with a Y or i.e.?"

"I.e."

The man shakes his head.

"Female?"

I fume. What the fuck is wrong with this guy? I slam my fist onto the desk. "Elizabeth Anne Stevens. Female, with a fucking F!"

The man jumps.

"Kayne!" Jett yanks me back. "Re-fucking-lax. We're all worried about her, but giving the security guard a heart attack won't help."

"Fine!' I throw my hands up and walk away, leaving Jett to deal with the incompetent man.

"Down the hall, second set of double doors. Emergency medicine."

Finally.

At Emergency medicine, we don't find out much more except Ellie is in surgery, and all we can do is wait—which feels like a set of red-hot butter knives are slicing me open one long, slow slit at a time.

"I think we should contact Ellie's parents," Jett tells me. "If something happens, they should be here." There's a grave tone in his voice. I just nod. What else can I fucking do? I've done everything. Everything wrong. I drop my head into my hands. I should have never gone that night. I should have stayed away like my gut told me to. She wouldn't be here right now fighting for her life. She'd be out having fun, living the way she so desperately wanted to. And I took that all away.

"Hey," Jett puts his hand on my shoulder, "don't do it."

"Do what?" I look up at him.

"Blame yourself."

"Too late. Too. Fucking. Late."

He frowns. "I'm going to go arrange to have Ellie's family flown out."

I just nod despairingly.

Three hours. I have watched every second on the clock tick by for three agonizing hours.

"I'm looking for the family of Elizabeth Stevens," a man in light-blue scrubs and a mask hanging off his face announces in the waiting room. Jett and I immediately stand up.

"I'm Dr. Holiday. I worked on Ms. Stevens." He shakes both our hands.

"Jett Fox." "Kayne Rivers." We both reply.

"How are you related?" he inquires.

"I'm her fiancé," I answer with a thread of composure. "How is she?"

The doctor sighs. "Ms. Stevens wound was severe. She lost a lot of blood and coded on the way to the OR."

My knees nearly give out. Jett catches my arm and holds me up. "She—"

"No," Dr. Holiday continues. "We were able to revive her, but she was deprived of oxygen for nearly five minutes. She's stable, but in a coma," he says gently.

"So, that's good? Right?" I grasp at any tiny reassurance Ellie is going to be okay.

"It's promising, but there is a chance, Mr. Rivers, that she'll never wake up.

"Never?" my voice nearly disappears.

"The next forty-eight hours are critical."

I nod, barely holding it together.

"There was something else," the doctor frowns.

"What?"

"Our examination showed severe trauma to the vaginal region."

I blink rapidly at the doctor. "She was raped?"

He nods. "If she does wake up, a social worker will be visiting."

I don't hear the last part as rage explodes inside me like a nuclear bomb. I punch a hole right through the wall to relieve the pressure in my chest.

"Mr. Rivers!" the doctor shouts. "I understand this is distressing news, but please compose yourself, or I'll be forced to call security."

I breathe savagely in his face. "You don't understand jack shit."

"Kayne!" Jett yells at me for the umpteenth time tonight. "I apologize for my friend." He steps between me and the doctor. "He's had a very rough night."

Dr. Holiday acknowledges with a head nod. "Hearing someone you love was hurt is never easy."

"No, it's not," Jett agrees as I seethe behind him, wishing I could kill Michael all over again.

"Can we see her?" Jett asks.

"When *he* calms down." With that, Dr. Holiday turns and leaves.

NOT ONLY DID JETT ARRANGE for Ellie's parents to be flown in from New York, but he also arranged for her to have a private room with extra care.

Sometimes I don't know how I would function without him.

My first look at Ellie lying in a hospital bed, unconscious with tubes sticking out of her, was almost too much to bear. Knowing what Michael did to her was the grain of sand that tipped the scale. Alone with Ellie, as still as silence, I finally broke down. Her suffering will always be my fault.

"I'm sorry," I sob exhausted. "I'm so sorry. I wish I could take it away. I'd carry it all. It should have been me."

"Kayne?" I feel a hand on my back. I pick my head up off Ellie's mattress and wipe my face hastily.

"Hey. What's up, man?" I ask Juice, trying, but failing miserably, to pretend to pull it together.

"They found this when they swept the house." I turn to see he's holding Ellie's engagement ring. "I thought you'd want it."

"Thank you." I take the ring and slip it back on Ellie's finger and nearly start crying all over again. I'm really not sure I'm going to survive this. I lived through a lot of fucked-up shit in my life, but this? It's the worst of the worst.

"I'll be back in the morning. Ellie's parents are due in at ten. I'm picking them up and bringing them straight here."

"Okay. Thanks." I hide my face. "Have you seen Jett?"

"He's in the emergency room with London."

I snap my head back to look at him. "For what?"

"She was still sick. Couldn't stop throwing up, so he made her come in. They're giving her IV fluids."

"Why didn't he tell me?"

"Figured you have enough on your plate," Juice states the obvious. "Get some rest, man." He taps the doorframe then leaves.

Yeah, right.

I WATCH THE SUN COME up through the window. Bright yellow rays breaking through the dark sky.

Ellie hasn't moved a muscle, or fluttered an eyelash, or twitched a lip.

The nurses come and go—readjusting pillows, checking vitals, and taking blood. I never move from her side. I just hold her hand and imagine all the things I want to do with her when she wakes up. The wedding I'm going to give her, the honeymoon I'll surprise her with.

"Ellie, you have to wake up. There are so many things I have to tell you." My heart pinches in my chest. "All the ways you've changed my life. I want to tell you all my secrets. I want you to be the one to know." I caress her hand with my thumb. Always so soft. "I've been thinking. You know how you asked which last name we should use? Well, since I've never really had a family of my own, I thought maybe we could use yours? You're the closest thing to family I have besides Jett. What do you think? Kayne Stevens doesn't sound bad, right?" I'm just fucking rambling now, slowly unraveling.

"I want to know who's responsible!" a man's voice bellows from the hallway. I immediately stand up as the door to Ellie's room swings open. "I want to know why my little girl is laying in a hospital bed fighting for her life!" I stand there frozen as Juice walks in with three people I only know from pictures. Ellie's family.

"Alec, please stop shouting."

"Stop shouting! How can I stop shouting? Look at her!" There's obvious emotion in the man's green eyes. The same eyes as Ellie's.

"Kayne. Alec, Monica, and Tara Stevens," Juice introduces us.

"Kayne?" Her mother repeats my name as if she recognizes it. Tara eyes me suspiciously.

"Who the hell are you?" Alec snaps at me.

"Kayne Rivers, sir." I put out my hand over Ellie. He doesn't take it. The tension in the room intensifies. He hates me already. Can't say that I blame him.

"I see it's a party," Jett walks in a moment later whiter than a ghost.

"How's London?" I ask worriedly. I think this is the worst I've ever seen him.

"Pregnant." Every head in the room swings toward him.

"What?" My jaw hits the floor.

Jett just shrugs, dumbfounded.

"Mazel tov," Alec spits. "Now is someone going to tell me what happened here?" He motions to Ellie.

The room becomes deadly silent.

"I believe Mazel tov is used for a wedding." Jett breaks the ice.

"Whatever. I'm very happy for you, son. Your life just got a hell of a lot more complicated, but right now I'd like to know what the hell happened to my daughter."

"A very unfortunate accident," I answer. "She was in the wrong place at the wrong time," I lie. Lie upon lie upon lie. It's what my life is built upon. Ellie is my only truth.

"Has there been an arrest?"

"No arrest," I tell him.

"Why the hell not?" he barks.

"The perpetrator has been taken care of," Jett informs him.

"I thought you said he hasn't been arrested?" Alec looks crazily between Jett and me.

"He hasn't," I tell him menacingly calm.

"Then how—"

"He's dead."

"Who killed him?" Alec's face contorts.

"Me," I say evenly, staring straight into his eyes.

Alec glares at me for what seems like a lifetime before he nods, almost satisfied, then sits down next to Ellie. I look around the room; it's suddenly very crowded and very uncomfortable. Tara makes her way next to me and picks up Ellie's hand.

"Why is she wearing an engagement ring?"

All attention falls on me.

I clear my throat. I suddenly feel like I'm suffocating. "I asked Ellie to marry me, and she said yes."

"What?" Alec scowls at me, Monica gasps, and Tara scoffs.

"That is *so* Ellie." Tara laughs.

"What's so Ellie?" I ask her.

Tara tosses her long platinum hair over her shoulder and looks over at me. She's a cute girl. Big blue eyes and a nice smile. "Getting engaged to a man she didn't even tell us she was dating. I'm surprised you two didn't already elope."

I glance at Jett. "We didn't get the chance."

Alec looks like he's about to go into cardiac arrest, he's turning so many shades of red.

"Why don't we give Ellie and her family some time alone?" Jett suggests to me. I want to throw daggers at him. There's no way in hell I'm leaving her side. He gestures with his head. I shake him off. "Get the fuck out," he mouths strictly. I bare my teeth at him, but do as he says, begrudgingly.

"If you need anything, I'll be outside," I tell her family.

"Thank you." Monica grabs my arm and I flinch. She smiles up at me, but I don't understand why. I don't really appreciate her touching me either, even if she is Ellie's mother and my potential mother-in-law.

"Big daddy Jett." Juice clasps his shoulders once we're outside in the hallway.

"Yeah." He looks like he's in shock.

"You happy?" I ask him, keeping an eye on Ellie's room.

"Yeah." I think that's the only word he's capable of at the moment.

"You going to make an honest woman out of her?" Juice asks.

"I was planning to propose when we got back from Tahiti."

"Why not while you were on vacation?"

"Too cliché." he laughs, regarding me.

I flip him the finger. "That wasn't planned."

But I'm happy as hell that it happened.

ELLIE HAS BEEN UNCONSCIOUS FOR three days.

I haven't left her side for one minute. I've basically moved into her hospital room. I eat, sleep, and shower here. I'll live here for the rest of my life if I have to.

We put Alec, Monica, and Tara up in a hotel nearby so they can come and go as they please. Presently, Alec is pacing the hallway. The man doesn't sit still. I now know where Ellie gets it. Monica is sitting beside me watching Ellie, and Tara is having lunch with Juice. Not sure how I feel about that. He says it's innocent, but we'll see. We call him Juice for a reason.

I've spent the most time with Monica. Despite my issues with women, matriarchal figures in particular, she quickly grew on me. She's nurturing and mellow and very non-threatening. All the same traits that drew me to Ellie.

"I remember that night," Monica says randomly, staring at Ellie.

"What night?"

"The night she was going to meet you. She was so excited, on another level even for Ellie." Monica smiles. Her dark-brown hair is pulled back in a low ponytail and her bangs are falling into her eyes. I don't think she's slept since she arrived. "Tara kept teasing her, and she and Alec were fighting over her dress," she reminisces.

"He didn't approve?"

"The man has died seven times over from the girl's wardrobe alone." She glances over at me amused.

"Really?" I say intrigued.

"Yes. Those girls drive him nuts. But Ellie is Ellie, and she does what she wants. She kissed us goodbye," Monica's eyes water, "then she disappeared."

Oh, shit.

"She went through a lot," I say softly, a mix of guilt and impenitence battling inside me.

Monica nods, wiping away a stray tear. "She did. I don't know how you two crossed paths again, but I'm glad. I could see how much she liked you."

"I sought her out," I tell her truthfully. "I really liked her, too.

Now I love her."

"That's very clear."

"What was Ellie like as a child?" I ask, wanting to know as much about her past as possible. If I can't ask Ellie, I can ask the next best person.

" A pain in the ass," Monica laughs.

"What?"

"She was. She never stopped moving, she got into everything and was independent to a fault. We used to call her Hurricane Elizabeth."

I chuckle. "That is surprisingly a very accurate nickname." Considering the way she turned my world upside down.

"She was also very loving and so, so adorable. Like a living doll. She could knock you over with just one dimpled smile. I think that's how she survived childhood. She had us all wrapped around her little finger." Monica is now laughing and crying all at the same time. I'm not sure how to interpret that.

"It's how I survive adulthood, too," Ellie murmurs, and both Monica and I jump up. "How did you two end up in the same room?" she asks as she cracks her eyes open. I think *I'm* about to start laughing and crying.

"Were you eavesdropping on us?" I ask, as my heart starts beating again with short shallow pumps.

"Yes. You're not the only one who can spy," she responds groggy.

Monica shoots me a funny look. I grin uncomfortably. "Inside joke."

"Oh, well I guess that's a good sign that she's making jokes."

"Why does it feel like I was shot?" Ellie groans in pain.

"Because you were," Monica tells her kissing her forehead. "I have to go get the doctor and your father," she announces overjoyed. "I'm so glad you're awake."

Once she's out of the room, Ellie looks up at me confused. I want to smother her with kisses, but I brush my lips lightly all over her face instead.

"How long have I been out?" she strains.

"Three days." I kiss her lips, reacquainting myself with the feel of them. "I'm sorry, baby," I nearly weep, the guilt eating me alive.

"Sorry for what?"

"Everything. Every single second of suffering I've ever caused you."

"It wasn't your fault," she grimaces as she tries to move.

"That's a fucking lie, and we both know it."

"Kayne, don't. Just tell me it's over." She says exhausted.

"It is. He's dead."

Ellie's eyes start to cloud with tears. She's been up for five seconds, and she's upset already.

"Do you know?" Her lip quivers.

I nod solemnly.

"Do my parents know?" Her voice tapers off.

I shake my head.

"Good," she sighs with relief.

"Do you remember everything that happened?" I ask delicately.

"Yes," tears drip down her face.

I grab her cheeks in my hands and wipe away the wetness with my thumbs. My heart cracks in nine different directions. It's amazing how many times that muscle can be destroyed and still keep working.

"I killed him, Ellie," I tell her with conviction. Like somehow that's supposed to make everything better.

"Good. I hope it hurt."

"I can assure you it did."

"Can I please have some water?" She tries to sit up.

"Lie down," I order. "I'll get it." I dutifully pour her a glass and press the straw to her lips, allowing her take several long sips.

"Thank you," she smiles weakly.

"You're welcome." I skim my knuckles across her face. God, I can't believe how much I missed touching her. "I'm not going to leave your side. We're going to get better together."

"We?" she asks concerned. "Are you hurt?"

I nod, rubbing my chest. "Funny thing about pain," I laugh, not finding anything funny about it at all. "It's a hell of a lot easier to deal with the physical than it is to deal with the emotional. I could run twelve miles and ignore the burning in my legs or take a bullet and withstand the throbbing in my arm. But try to take away someone I love? There's no escaping that agony. I may not be lying in a hospital bed, but I'm still injured."

Ellie sighs trying to hold back the overload of emotion that is so clearly evident on her face. "What now?"

I smile. "We move forward. We can get married, have children, travel. Whatever you want to do."

"No children," she fires back at me spontaneously.

I look at her funny. "Why no children?"

Her dark-green eyes widen and completely well with tears. "Kayne, my mother needed more therapy than I did after I came home. And after going through what I went through—" she wipes her cheeks as large the reflective droplets fall, "there's so much evil in this world. I don't think I could handle it." She starts to cry so hard she can't breathe. "I don't think I could handle—" I wrap her snugly in my arms. "Okay, Ellie. It's okay. We don't have to talk about any of that right now." I let her sob on my shoulder, worried someone is going to walk through the door any second. I don't want her family to see her like this. "Shhhh . . ."

"You still want to marry me even though I don't want kids?" She sniffles, eyes puffy and face red.

"Of course I do," I assure her. "You are the only person I need in this world. Whatever makes you happy will make me happy. Okay?"

She nods sternly, burying her face in the crook of my arm.

"Please don't cry," I beg her. "Everything will be okay."

I hear the door swing open as Monica, Alec, Tara, Juice, and the doctor on rounds appears in the room.

"Where's my little girl?" Alec announces. I reluctantly let go of Ellie, and I have to give it to her, she puts on her bravest face. She really is the most resilient person I have ever met.

"Right here, Daddy." She rubs her eyes and smiles.

I step back and watch as she's showered with love, hoping like hell everything really is going to be okay.

IT HAS BEEN ONE VERY long, tiring, trying week. Ellie spent the last seven days recuperating in the hospital, and today she finally gets to go home. I watch as she signs the discharge papers the nurse hands to her and listens as the sweet older woman explains how to change her dressings and which medications she should take when. She's been prescribed so many antibiotics, pain killers and anti-depressants, she could start her own cartel.

"I'm going to get the car." I kiss her head once she sitting in the wheelchair.

She nods silently. Silent. That's Ellie these days. Her superficial wounds may be healing, but more often than not she's lost inside her head.

It's making me a lunatic. I worry nonstop. I don't eat, I barely sleep, terrified that Michael may have succeeded in taking her away from me. He might not have killed her, but her spirit is definitely broken, and I'm scrambling to figure out how to fix it.

I pull up to the front of the hospital just as Ellie is wheeled outside. It's another perfect day in paradise. Blue skies, white puffy clouds and rainbows in the distance. Ellie's parents went home yesterday, leaving her in my care. We may all be screwed. To say I'm not nervous would be lying. We've had this discussion—I've never looked after another person in my life. Never had anyone have to depend on me, or commit myself to caring for another person. But I'm going to do my damndest with Ellie.

I just hope it's enough.

I help her gingerly climb into the car, and then hop in the driver's seat.

She looks around the interior strangely.

"Whose car is this?" she asks mildly confused.

"Mine."

"You drive?" I almost think she's trying to be funny.

I snicker. "Of course I drive. Why'd you say that?" I punch on the engine and the Jag rumbles to life.

"Because I've never seen you drive a car before." She grabs her seat, surprised by the vibrations. "You always showed up in a limo when you came to Expo and we were carted all over the place in Bora Bora. Jett even drove the boat to and from the airport."

I laugh to myself as I put on my sunglasses. Oh, how little does she know. I can drive all sorts of thing.

"Well, I guess I'm full of surprises." I press a button and the roof retracts, Ellie squints as the sun shine hits her face. I open the glove compartment. "Sunglasses?" I hand her a brand new pair that Jett picked out especially for her.

"Thank you." She takes them, smiling shyly. "What kind of car is this anyway?" she asks, gliding her hand over the door handle.

"Jaguar F-Type." I hit the gas in my black V8 and take off.

"One of your toys?" Ellie inquires, as her hair blows in the wind.

"One of the many." I grin carefree, placing my hand over hers, and just drive.

I notice Ellie start to look around curiously as we drive through and then out of Waikiki.

"Where are we going?" she asks confused.

"Home," I tell her, not taking my eyes off the road.

I feel her staring at me peculiarly. I just smirk and continue to drive.

Ten minutes later we are rolling through the Diamond Head section of Honolulu.

"Seriously, where are you taking me?" she asks again, and I can't stop myself from smiling widely.

"I told you," I pull into a driveway. "Home." I throw the car in park.

Ellie freezes as she takes in the two-story stucco house.

"Exactly whose home are we going to?"

"Ours." I hop out of the car.

"Ours?" she repeats perplexed as I walk around the convertible, open her door and carefully help her stand up.

I think it's a record. That's the most she's spoken in a week.

"Yup." I take her hand and lead her to the front door. The walkway is landscaped with lots of bright island flowers and tall green trees. Once inside, Ellie gasps. Yeah, it's pretty insane. I fell in love with the house as soon as I saw it online. It was so different and modern, yet homey as well. The website boasted it was an award-winning design, inspired by the shape of a sundial, the back of the house curved with one hundred, eighty degree views of the ocean and mountains. Between you and me, I had already put an offer in prior to leaving for Bora Bora. It was some serious wishful thinking on my part, but I couldn't help myself. Every time I looked at it, I could see Ellie and me living here.

I walk her through the kitchen decorated with light cabinets and dark granite. I grab a small remote off the counter and continue straight back into the living room. I glance at Ellie taking it all in. Then I hit a button and the electric curtains rise. The entire room is made of windows, and as they lift, an unobstructed view of the Pacific blinds us, as if we're sitting right on top of it.

"Oh my God." Ellie puts her hand over her mouth as she looks out over the lani, curved swimming pool hugging the house, and vast blue water.

"Like it?" I ask nervously.

She doesn't answer, just stares straight ahead.

"Ellie?" I put my hand on nape of her neck and rub my thumb back and forth over her skin. "You don't like it?" I frown disappointed.

Like she snaps out of a trance she looks up at me, her eyes shining with unshed tears. I can't tell if they're happy or sad, but by the looks of it, it may be the latter.

"Oh no," she sniffles. "I love it. It's perfect. You're perfect."

"Then what's wrong?" I hear the distress in my own voice.

"Nothing. Everything," she contradicts herself.

"Well, which is it?" I search her face. "Baby, you can talk to me."

"I'm sorry," she blurts out.

"For what?" My heart stops.

"I keep trying to convince myself I'm stronger than what happened, but I just keep getting sucked down. It's like I can't breathe and

I can't fight." She starts to cry. I pull her against me and let her sob into my chest. "I don't want to be broken, but I think that I am."

Thank god, finally she speaks!

I stroke her hair and hold her close.

"Ellie, if there's one thing I've learned being with you, things that are broken can always be fixed. They can be made stronger. You make me stronger, and I'm the most broken person I know."

She lifts her head and looks at me with soaking wet eyes.

"How am I going to get stronger?"

I smile down at her. "You're going to fight. And I'm going to help you. If there's one thing I know how to do, it's fight."

I hug her and she squeaks in pain, but she holds on to me, inhaling me like I'm air, like I'm the oxygen she needs to breathe." Use me, Ellie. I told you before—get mad, scream, hit me, beat me, torture me if you want. I'll endure it all if it will help you get better."

She sighs heavily, "I think all I really need is for you to lay with me."

I chuckle. That's exactly what she said to me the first night in Bora Bora. The same words that opened the doorway for our relationship to heal. I'm hopeful for the first time in over a week.

"Whatever you need, Ellie." I reassure her.

"I have exactly what I need." She draws in a small shaky breath and gazes up at me. "You."

EPILOGUE

One year later

"TIME TO WAKE UP, SLEEPYHEAD!" Tara jumps on me.

"Umph." I jolt awake.

"Someone has to get beautiful for her wedding day," she sings, her blue eyes bright, platinum-blonde hair even brighter. She used to wake me up the same way when we were kids.

"Nice to see nothing has changed." I try to push her off me.

"You missed me, admit."

"I'll admit I missed pulling your hair when you annoyed me." I yank on her long strands.

"Ouch!" she laughs.

"Serves you right! Disturbing the bride's beauty sleep."

"You're going to need way more than eight hours to help you with your beauty."

"Bitch!" We both laugh as I hit her with a pillow. "And I can't believe you pierced your nose!" I grab her face and examine the tiny stud. It actually looks good on her.

"It's not the only thing I pierced." She pops her eyebrows at me.

"You didn't!"

"I did! Want to see?" She bounces around the bed overflowing with white Egyptian sheets.

"No!" I smack her with a pillow again. "Please keep your panties in their place."

"Who says I'm wearing any?" Tara laughs.

"Slut."

"Call me whatever you want. The orgasms are worth it! You should totally do it."

I pause, thinking of all the ways Kayne could possibly torture me if I had a clit ring.

My blood heats. I might consider it.

"This came for you, by the way." She hands me a box wrapped in silver paper with a white bow.

"When?" I sit up and take it from her.

"Just now. CJ dropped it off." She grins wickedly.

Oh no, I know that look.

"He's yummy." She sucks on her bottom lip like she can already taste him.

"Tara," I chide.

"What?"

"I noticed the two of you flirting last night."

"So?" She bats her eyelashes innocently.

"He's ten years older than you," I point out.

"So?" she repeats.

"I'm not sure Kayne would approve." Actually, I know he wouldn't approve since I overheard him threatening Juice's life if he touched her.

"Well, Kayne isn't my father," she argues.

"I'm not sure our father would approve, either."

"He doesn't approve of anything we do." She rolls her eyes dismissively.

She has me there.

"Look, this day isn't about me." She changes the subject artfully, clearly done with this conversation. "So open your present already so we can drink some mimosas and start getting ready!"

"Fine." I appease her. Besides, I think her and Juice sort of make a cute couple, even if it would be short lived—like four days long since they live on opposite sides of the country.

I open the card first. It's plain white with perforated edges and reads:

Your naked body should only belong to those who fall in love with your naked soul. ~ unknown
And I own both.
Kayne

That he does, I think to myself as I grin like an idiot.

I rip off the paper and flip open the flat box. Tara curls her lip. "It looks just like the one you already wear, except with a white ribbon."

I touch the necklace with the little diamond heart. "It has a special meaning."

"It looks like a freakin' expensive collar if you ask me." I flick my eyes up at her and try to hide my smile.

"I said it has special meaning."

"Seriously, Ellie. I don't want to know what freaky shit you and Kayne are into. He's so possessive, I wouldn't be surprised if he made you wear a collar." I nearly lose it. If she only knew!

"I'm ready to start celebrating." Tara slinks off the bed.

God, me too. I fall back onto the pillow and stare up at the ceiling, balancing the box on my stomach. The last twelve months have not been easy. Kayne and I adjusting as roommates was the least of our problems. Not only did my body need to heal, but so did my mind. When Jett told me Kayne was more loyal than a dog, he meant it. He never left my side. He came to every physical therapy session and therapist appointment. He sat beside me as I recounted every horrific minute with Michael, held me as I cried every tear, and comforted me after every single nightmare. Sex was a challenge. Not because I didn't want it, but because intimacy was difficult. I was disconnected from my emotions and had somehow lost my sense of security. There was a time I thought I was never going to get out from under the depression and fear. It had taken a while before things started to get easier, before I started to feel more like myself. After about six months, my therapist suggested I find something positive to concentrate on. That's when Kayne and I decided to set a date. May sixteenth, to be exact. Some may think wedding planning is stressful, and I guess that's true in some cases. Not in ours. If anything, it was therapeutic. It gave us something to look forward to, it helped fortify our very new and fragile relationship, and sparked hope. So here I lay, in a penthouse suite on Maui, about to become someone's wife.

I've never looked more forward to a sunset in my life.

"Ellie!" Tara yells. "Get up!"

"I'm up!" I yell back.

After a morning massage, a nice long hot shower, and several mimosas courtesy of Tara, I'm ready to start the beautification process. Hair, nails, makeup, dress—in that order, apparently.

By midafternoon, my hotel room—and future honeymoon suite—is buzzing with people. My mother and sister, of course, the hair stylist and manicurist and Mark. Yes, Mark. Like he would be left out of all the girlie fun. Plus, he wanted a manicure. How could I say no?

"You know, it's because of me that Kayne and Ellie met." He grins at the older woman with long, jet-black hair filing his nails. She just nods and smiles. I roll my eyes. He's been telling everyone that. Like he hooked us up or something. In reality, he was just responsible for letting two strangers' paths meet, but we won't burst his bubble and tell him that.

There's a knock at the door.

"I'll get it!" Tara announces, hopping off her stool, hair half curled.

"Oh, hi." She sounds almost disappointed as Jett walks in. My mother and I glance knowingly at each other.

"Hey, sweet thing." Jett walks over and kisses me hello just as the stylist finishes pinning a white orchid into my hair. "Very nice." He looks at the masterpiece she's been working on for the last hour. After about a million trials, I decided to wear it down in loosely textured curls accented with the flower.

"Jealous you didn't do it?" I jest.

"Maybe." He laughs, his aqua eyes sparkling back at me in the mirror. "You finally got that haircut."

"Just a trim," I joke. "What are you doing here?"

"I come bearing gifts." He holds up a small wrapped box and a large card.

I look at him confused. "Juice already dropped off my wedding present from Kayne."

"He got you two." Jett takes my hand and helps me up. "And he asked that you open it in private."

I glare at Jett. I don't like the sound of this.

"Just need to borrow her for a sec," he announces as he pulls me into the bedroom.

"If you think I'm going to let you clamp any part of me, you have another thing coming." I cross my arms. "It's my wedding day, and I'm not going to walk around like a cat in freakin' heat!"

Jett looks at me like he's out to bust a gut. His golden hair is styled back, and he's wearing a white T-shirt and dress pants. "I don't know what's in the box," his lips twitch fitfully, "but I'm pretty sure it isn't a clit clamp. He wants you to open the card first."

"Okay." I take them from him. "If it's nothing kinky then why the privacy?"

"I never said it wasn't anything kinky, he just didn't tell me what it was."

I roll my eyes as I slide my finger under the flap. My eyes water immediately. The card has one simple picture on the front. A little boy holding a cupcake. I flip it open to a long, handwritten note inside.

Ellie,

I'm not very good with words. I'll probably never be able to express fully the way I feel, but I've wanted to tell you something I've never told anyone before. Not even Jett. It's not something I'm proud of and not something I talk about. Ever. But when I was seventeen, I tried to commit suicide. It was the darkest time in my life. I was alone, homeless, and just wanted it all to end. I don't mean to upset you by telling you this. It's just ever since that day, a small part of me has always wished my attempt was successful. I'm sure you're wondering why I picked today of all days to tell you this. It's because, for the first time since that day, I woke up and was thankful to be alive. Thankful I failed because the happiness I feel outweighs every bad moment in my life. Every. Single. One. And it's all because of you. You ll a piece of me I never knew existed, never thought I deserved. You're the best part of all my sides, all my faces. You're the glue. Thank you for being everything. My strength, my light, my hope, my warmth.

I love you always,
Kayne

By the time I finish reading the letter, I'm a blubbering mess and Jett is consoling me.

"What the hell was in that letter?"

I just shake my head and wipe my eyes. "The truth." I smile.

"Are you okay?" Jett slides his hands up and down my arms and examines me closely.

"Yes. Fine, actually."

He stares for a few seconds more. "Do I need to beat him up for making you cry?" He sounds like an overprotective older brother.

"No." I laugh, glad my makeup isn't done yet. "A black eye would look terrible in pictures.

"True. Why don't you open your present?" he suggests.

"Yeah, good idea." I sniff as I rip off the silver paper and pop open the small gift box. "Oh!" I gasp as a pair of diamond earrings stare back at me—ones that look exactly like my engagement ring. Two cushion-cut stones with a halo of pink diamonds around them.

"Perfect. Just like the girl who is going to wear them." Jett smiles.

"You just always know what to say," I quip.

"It's a curse." He sighs dramatically.

"I'm sure," I respond drily as he kisses me firmly on the cheek.

"My work here is done."

I grab his arm. "Not quite yet."

I walk over to the closet and retrieve a large, white flat box and hand it over. "Make sure he opens it in private."

Jett frowns. "Oh, no. Is it going to make him cry?"

I shrug playfully. "It might bring him to tears."

I FIGHT WITH MY VEIL as it blows around in the wind. My stomach is in knots and my heart is pounding in my ears. I have been hidden in a small alcove for the last twenty minutes as the guests arrive and take their seats. I'm so nervous, I'm bouncing in my barefoot sandals.

"You still have time to run, kid," my father jokes.

"Kayne would find me." I laugh nervously. It's completely true. Besides, I may be nervous, but I know I could never live without him. Now more than ever.

I check myself one last time in the reflective wall of the 'bride's staging area.' At least that's what the wedding coordinator called it. My hair is falling in perfect waves around my face, my makeup is flawless, and my dress is hugging and pinching in all the right places. I went for something simple and romantic—a diamond white, backless A-line with double spaghetti straps and an empire waist. My favorite part—it has pockets.

"Time!" the wedding coordinator pokes her head in and announces just as the procession music starts to play.

Here goes everything.

Clutching my bouquet made of white roses and blue orchids, my father begins to lead me toward the aisle. We turn the corner to an expansive view of the Pacific Ocean, several small rows of chairs, and an arbor draped with white fabric, strings of crystals, and two small chandeliers. But as magnificent as the setup is, it's only Kayne I see. Once our eyes lock, it's like I gravitate toward him, float almost. He's dressed in a white buttoned-down shirt and dress pants, the blue of his irises ablaze in the sunlight. His expression is composed, yet full of emotion all at the same time.

My father lifts my veil and kisses my cheek like we practiced at the rehearsal the night before and then gives me away. I take Kayne's hand with a shaky breath as I step under the arbor with him. The smile that suddenly beams from his face nearly knocks me over, and I can't help but laugh nervously, tears stinging my eyes.

"You look *so* beautiful," he breathes right before the officiant begins.

"Dearly beloved . . ."

"HAPPY, MRS. STEVENS?" KAYNE ASKS as we sway steadily to the encore of our wedding song.

"Deliriously, Mr. Stevens." When Kayne suggested taking my last name, I was a little stunned at first. But when he explained *why*, there was no way could I refuse. He finally has a home and the family he's deserved all along.

"You almost ready to sneak out of here?" he asks, his breath tickling my ear.

"Yes." I nestle up against him as David Cook sings about fading and colors bleeding into one.

"Me, too," he growls, pulling me closer.

I grasp onto the last seconds of the song, trying to memorize what's left of the night. Pink candle holders hanging from fishing wire over the round tables on the beach. The devoured red velvet cupcake tower, my parents talking and laughing, Jett holding his infant daughter, Layla, and Tara and Juice dancing way too close for comfort a few feet away.

When the song ends, Kayne still holds me close, kissing my temple lovingly.

We didn't accept any gifts for the wedding. Instead, we asked for donations to our foundation. To Catch a Falling Star. Kayne, Jett, London, and I started it a few months ago. It was my second positive thing to concentrate on. It gives victims of sexual abuse and human trafficking a chance to see paradise. We've already sent over twenty families on the vacation of their dreams. I plan to expand the organization once I finish college.

"Let's go." Kayne tugs on my hand to start our hurried goodbyes.

As we walk to the elevator, we catch sight of Juice and Tara huddled in a corner, kissing. Kayne tries to let go of my hand, no doubt to interrupt them, but I pull him back.

"Leave them alone. They're consenting adults."

Kayne frowns just as the elevator doors open. "That's what I'm afraid of."

I giggle and haul him inside. "I'm the only consenting adult you have to worry about at the moment." I pull his face to mine and kiss him passionately, dying for the feel of his tongue against mine.

"Mmm." He pushes me up against the wall, easily distracted as he devours me, running his hands all over my body, causing my nipples to harden instantly.

The doors ding open, and we break apart restlessly. Before we exit the elevator, Kayne lifts me into his arms.

"What are you doing?!" I throw my arms around his neck.

"Carrying you over the threshold. Duh." He steps out, and then walks down the hall to our suite.

I laugh freely as we walk through the living room toward the bedroom, then inhale sharply when he opens the door and we are engulfed in candlelight. There must be one hundred white pillar candles lit all around the room.

"Someone was busy," I muse.

"Who?" He responds sarcastically.

"Did we take a funny pill tonight?" I ask as he sets me down.

Kayne shakes his head. "A happy pill."

"Same differen—" The last syllable of the word is cut off as he smothers me with a kiss so deep, he actually forces me to lean back.

"As much as I love you in this dress, it's time for it to come off," he pants as he pulls at the straps, yanking the top straight down. I barely have time to unzip before he rips it completely off. Animal. He then starts pushing me toward the bed, our mouths fused together, his hands kneading my naked breasts.

"Did you like my wedding present?" I ask as he forces me down.

He pauses, ogling me wickedly. "I loved it. I had to go jerk off in the bathroom while I looked at it."

I smile. I wracked my brain trying to figure out what to give Kayne as a wedding present. The logical answer was me. So I had an ultra-sexy boudoir album made. Lots of lacy underwear, pearls, and bows. It was one step above a porno magazine.

"By the way, who took those pictures?" His eyes storm.

I bite my lip. "London."

"Oh, really?" his irritation turns to curiosity.

"She's really good with a camera," I responded apprehensively.

"I saw that. Several times." He bites my neck. "You two didn't do anything you weren't supposed to?"

I swallow thickly. "Can I plead the fifth?"

"You bad girls." He manhandles me, smacks my ass, and then

pinches it hard. "Next time Jett and I will be the ones with the camera."

"Yes, Kayne," I purr.

"Damn straight." He caresses my behind and grinds his erection between my legs. "Did you like my present?"

"Which one?" I lift my hips and press my pussy right up against him.

"Both of them," he groans.

"Yes." I kiss him gently. "The second one made me cry."

"I didn't mean to upset you." He tells me earnestly.

"It's okay. I'm glad you told me. I'm glad you're not carrying around those feelings anymore." I touch his cheek.

"Me, too." He chokes out the words, and my heart splits.

"I have a second present for you," I tell him. No unhappiness tonight.

"Oh really? I'm starting to enjoy getting presents."

I nearly gnaw through my lip this time. "Want it now?"

"If you want to give it to me."

"I do."

"Why do you sound nervous?"

"Because I am." I push him lightly so he rolls off me and retrieve another large white box from the closest. This one with a red ribbon around it.

I place it next to him. "Go ahead. Open it."

He pulls the box toward him inquisitively and unties the ribbon while I wring my hands together like a lunatic. Once he removes the top, his face falls. Oh, shit. He cocks his head as if studying the contents of the box.

"You don't like it?" I ask, feeling foolish. Maybe he thinks it's too soon.

"I . . ." He starts pulling out everything that's inside. White ears and a long bushy tail, a new white collar with my tag, matching wrist cuffs, and a studded leash.

He looks up at me silently, candlelight flickering on his face.

"We don't have to . . . I just thought . . ." I scramble, trying to stuff everything back in the box. How ridiculous do I feel?

"Ellie, stop." Kayne stands up and grabs my wrist, pulling me into his body. His erection like a stone slab against my thigh. "Are *you* ready?"

I glance up at him timidly through my eyelashes. "Yes. I'm ready. I'm ready to get back to *us*." And it's the truth.

"I don't want to do anything to upset you. To trigger anything."

"You won't. I want this."

He runs the pad of his thumb along my cheek, staring deeply into my eyes as if trying to read my soul. Ever since Michael, Kayne has been overly cautious with our sex life, fearful his dominance might spark a flashback or deter my progress in some way. It's not illogical—my therapist said it could happen. But it never has. If anything, I feel most safe when I submit, and I need that security. The same way Kayne needs to hear me say his name. I've been slowly hinting that I'm ready to move things to the next level; that I really am ready to get back to *us*.

"Please," I implore him.

"Please, what?"

"Unleash the beast. I need both our monsters to come out."

Kayne breathes heavily, no doubt at war with himself. He never has been able to deny me when I press him to take control.

"On one condition."

"What's that?"

"No begging or pleading tonight. I want you to come freely, like a waterfall. I want this night to be as pleasurable for you as it is for me."

"Okay," I agree, ready to attack him.

"Good. I love you." He kisses me tenderly.

"I love you, too."

"Now sit on the edge of the bed," he instructs.

I sit immediately. He pulls the flower from my hair then picks up the ears and places them on my head. His eyes dilate and something in my stomach jolts. "Stay." He runs a finger under my chin. I'm molten inside already.

He then steps back and pops open the bottle of champagne sitting in the ice bucket on the small table adjacent from the bed. He comes to stand in front of me holding it with one hand.

"Take my clothes off."

I scoot forward in just my white satin bikini briefs and garters adorned with a bow on the back of each thigh. I quickly unbutton his shirt and push it off his shoulders. It falls to the ground exposing his perfectly formed tattooed body. Yes, Kayne is human perfection. And why shouldn't he be? He works out like an animal. Ripped abs, strong chest, and chiseled arms—I can't wait to run my tongue over every pristine inch of him. I take off his pants next, bringing me face to face with the tip of his cock. I want to dart my tongue out and lick it, but I'll behave and wait to do as I'm told.

"You know, you missed something in the box," I tell him wetting my lips.

"Oh?" Kayne takes a swig of the champagne right from the bottle.

I reach in and pull out a tiny pill bottle. Kayne's eyes widen.

"Is that what I think it is?"

I nod. "I told you I want you to unleash the beast."

I open the top and shake out a little circular pill.

"You know there's only one way to satisfy the beast?" He takes it and swallows it.

"Yes."

"How?"

"Give it what it wants. Hours and hours submerged in my wet pussy and tight little ass."

Kayne nearly fries me with a scorching hot look. "That's right, kitten. Are you ready for that?"

"Yes," I answer, my voice thick with desire.

"Good girl." He drops to his knees in front of me, placing the bottle on the ground. He hasn't even touched me yet, and my pussy is already throbbing.

He skims his hands up my thighs and slips his one finger beneath each garter. "These are sexy as hell. They stay on. But these go." He slides my panties off in one fluid motion. He licks his bottom lip and moans gutturally as he stares at my bare folds. Kayne then reaches into the box beside me and pulls out the collar. My arousal spikes as he fastens it around my neck, right over my new white necklace. He tickles the tag once it's secure with a bold blatant look of propriety.

"Mine," he says as he claims my mouth, stretching it wide as he rolls his tongue languidly against mine.

"Yours," I reply breathless once he pulls away. I watch engrossed as he picks up the bottle of champagne and pours it down the middle of my naked body. I jump from the cold and moan loudly from the abrupt heat of his mouth. Kayne rests his head on my thigh as he continues to pour the champagne, soaking the bed and my pussy. He licks up the wetness all while watching me get off on the feel of his tongue. That wicked evil tongue that's capable of so many perverse things.

"Kayne." I grab his head and lift my leg begging for more—deeper, harder, rougher. He pours another shot of champagne on me and licks a slow hot drag up my slit, his wide flat tongue covering every single inch of me.

"Oh God, please." I don't mean to beg, but it's my go-to response. He takes pity on me, burying his head between my legs and fucks me with his mouth until I fall apart, an avalanche giving way inside me as I grip his hair and scream out loud.

He makes sure to lap up every drop of my orgasm and the champagne before he flips my limp body over and pulls me up on all fours.

Breathing like a mad man, I see him reach into the box and retrieve my tail. My excitement cranks. I'm nervous and aroused and scared all at the same time. Then I feel him sink one finger inside me. I'm still sensitive from my orgasm so it tickles. "Oh."

He doesn't waste any time smearing my wetness up away from my pussy and into my ass, pushing the same finger into me, and after a few seconds, adds another. I don't even have time to prepare for the bite as he scissors me open. My muscles spasm.

Then I feel him withdraw, his fingers replaced by the tip of the butt plug attached to the tail. I grab onto the comforter as Kayne works the spade-shaped plug past the tight ring of muscle. My stretched little hole tenses around the metal once all the way in.

"Holy shit." He strokes the tail now nestled in my ass. I turn to look at him, both sets of cheeks on fire.

He stares at the tail like he's starving with lust, then his eyes lift to meet mine.

"Hold still." His chest is expanding and contracting, his lips are pressed tight and his cock is the hardest I think I've ever seen it. The skin is pulled so taut his veins are visible even in soft candlelight.

"This is going to be hard and fast, kitten," Kayne says, shaking with need as he lines up behind me, nudging the tip of his unearthly erection against my wet entrance several times over. "You look so fucking hot." His voice is gravelly. I brace myself as he digs his fingers into my hips and thrusts brutally into me. We both cry out as his cock slices through my pussy like a hot knife through melted butter.

"Kitten, kitten, kitten, kitten," he chants as he fucks me exactly the way he said he was going to, fast and hard. Like he's using me. I expel a breath with every clash of our hips, the butt plug playing on my need, forcing me to the edge faster and faster.

"Don't come. Don't come." It's not a demand, it's a request as Kayne beats into me from behind. I fight to control the sensations battling to take over as Kayne's cock twitches right before he comes.

"Fuck!" he yells as he traps my hips and pushes his pelvis forward as if trying to cram another half inch of himself inside me.

"Shit." He leans forward and hugs me, his chest to my back, breathing erratically.

"I guess you like the tail," I tease breathless, still on all fours.

"I fucking love it," he snarls, withdrawing from me and yanking my collar. "Turn."

I turn around. He's still panting heavily, a sheen of sweat on his chest.

Kayne picks up the bottle of champagne again as I kneel on all fours by the edge of the bed.

"Do you know what little kittens are good at?" He pours some

champagne over his still erect cock. "Using their tongues to lick things clean." He takes me by the collar and shoves his dripping wet dick in my face. I purr as I dart my tongue out and proceed to lick every drop of champagne off his shaft. "That's it, baby." He grips my collar tighter as I take him into my mouth and swallow him whole, the taste of crisp dry bubbles mixing with my saliva. I suck repeatedly, so turned on my gag reflex has completely disappeared.

"Enough." Kayne pulls his hips away, his cock popping out of my mouth. "Good kitten."

I eye him hungrily.

"Stay." He touches the tip of my nose.

I watch as he moves around the room, sliding the small loveseat near the window in front of the bed. Then he removes one of the large mirrors from the wall and places it against the footboard, directly beneath me. I look at him strangely, just like the curious little kitten I am. He sits on the loveseat directly across from me and strokes his cock.

"Come," he calls me.

I slide off the bed and onto the floor, crawling provocatively across the room until I am directly between his legs.

"Sexy little girl," he jingles my tag then slips his thumb into my mouth. I suck on it deliberately, swirling my tongue around it just to tease him.

"I know how fucking good that mouth is, but I want to be inside you." He withdraws his hand and pats his lap. "Sit on my cock, Ellie. I want to watch you fuck me."

With that, he pulls me off the floor, forces me to straddle him and impales me onto his erection. *"Oh!"* From this angle he digs in deep, reaching all the way to my navel.

"Ride me, baby. I feel how bad you have to come." He's right, I'm strung so tight I could snap in a second. The tail never giving my arousal any reprieve. He straightens so he can peek over my shoulder as I move up and down.

"Oh, God." I drop my head back as I use Kayne to chase my orgasm.

"That's it, kitten," he sounds distracted, "make yourself come."

I look down at him in a fog of lust and realize his attention is engrossed in the mirror behind me. I turn my head to see what he sees, and the image is erotic as all hell. My naked body straddled over his, the bows of my garters, the tail in my ass, my hair falling down my back and ears on top of my head.

I bob faster and harder as I watch us in the mirror, my orgasm coming at me like a heat-seeking missile.

"Kayne," I cry, I pant, I moan. "Kayne," I clench, everything inside me constricting.

"Let go, Ellie," he strains as he caresses every part of my body.

"Oh, God," my voice elevates several octaves, as the buildup pressurizes. "I'm going to come. You're going to make me come." I slam down onto his cock and the sensations give way, lighting every single one of my nerve endings on fire.

I ride out my orgasm, literally, until there's nothing left of me. Until I'm bare bones draped over a heaving man.

Kayne's feathery kisses on my shoulders, neck and cheeks bring me back.

"Did you enjoy the show?" I ask him lethargically.

"Immensely," he laughs. "You?"

"Yes. You know I love to watch."

"I love that about you." He gropes me gently.

"I love everything about you." I kiss him in return.

"Good 'cause you're stuck with me for a lifetime."

"I'm pretty okay with that. Did you have a good birthday?" I ask desirously, rubbing my entire body against his.

"The best one yet." He rocks his erection between my legs. "There is only one thing that could make it better." He puts both hands on my stomach.

I immediately snatch his wrist. "That is still up for discussion."

"I know." He skims his nose under my jawline. "I just don't want you to have any regrets down the line."

"You're starting to sound like Jett, you know that?"

"He was bound to rub off on me eventually." Kayne yanks on my tail and I jerk on his lap.

"Mmm. You better be careful." I warn.

"Is that a threat?"

"Maybe," I slide my arms back around his neck.

"What are you going to do?" he challenges me.

"So many naughty things," I nip at him.

"I can't wait." He claims my mouth, slipping his tongue fervently between my lips.

"I love you," I exhale, showering his face with kisses.

"I love you, too." He strokes my tail affectionately. "Good kitten . . . *Cupcake.*"

The End

PLAYLIST

Lights Go Out ~ Fozzy

Beast Within ~ Blood

Take Me to Church ~ Hozier

Control ~Puddle of Mudd

Gravity ~ Sara Bareilles

If You Only Knew ~ Shinedown

Fade Into Me ~ David Cook

Don't Tell Em' ~ Jeremiah

Freak On a Leash ~ Korn

Riptide ~ Vance Joy

M. NEVER

DEDICATION

For the readers . . .

PROLOGUE

C.S. LEWIS ONCE SAID, "LIFE is too deep for words, so don't try to describe it, just live it."

ELLIE

"ELLIE! BREAKFAST!" KAYNE'S VOICE BOOMS through the house. "You can come down now, kitten!"

I stretch atop the cluster of pillows laid out for me on the floor. Kayne and I have been playing, and I've been bad—*again.* I smile to myself as my muscles elongate. I like being bad.

"Ellie!" he calls again.

All right, I'm coming. Hopefully, several times this morning. I pull myself up onto my hands and knees and stretch once more, like the lazy, spoiled kitten I am. The bushy white tail inserted in my behind shifts, sending a frizzle of pleasure up my spine. I take a quick glance around the brightly lit room; the sunlight is pouring through every window, highlighting the abundance of metal as I crawl past it. Similar to my living quarters in Mansion, Kayne and I have converted the sitting room off our bedroom into our own personal play space. Three hundred square feet decorated with crops and whips on the wall, a bondage horse, a swing suspended from the ceiling, a leather chest full of sex toys, and one table of torture. Oh, and my bed made up of fluffy white pillows on the floor. He loves watching me sit there, sleep there, beg there. I won't lie; I love it, too.

I crawl out of the bedroom and down the stairs of our magnificent home, migrating toward the kitchen. Sometimes I still can't believe it's ours. I never imagined I'd live somewhere so beautiful, spacious, and warm. Truth be told, I never imagined I'd be involved in a BDSM marriage where I crawled around on the floor half the time either. But hey, c'est la vie, right?

The tag on my collar jingles as I reach the first floor and make my way to where Kayne is standing by the stove. I may be the one on my hands and knees, but he's the one doing the cooking. Don't be fooled,

I'm not the only one who's trained. I kneel right beside him.

"'Bout time, kitten." He pets my head and continues to cook. It smells like pancakes, but I can't be sure. It might be waffles. I can't exactly see from my vantage point on the floor.

"Did you think about what a bad little kitten you are?" he asks without looking at me.

"Maybe," I answer.

"Maybe?" He glances down with a raised eyebrow.

"I thought about how maybe I like being bad," I inform him.

"There's no 'maybe' about it." He chuckles, shirtless and completely drool worthy. Cut abs, defined chest, and chiseled arms. A barbed wire tattoo circling one flexing bicep, writing scribbled across his rib cage, and my personal favorite, a colorful compass with my name on it over his heart. If I were wearing panties, they'd be drenched.

"Go outside. I'll be there in a minute," he orders, grabbing a plate from the cabinet.

I sit for a second, not obeying immediately as he expects. I'm going to get in so much trouble.

"Is there a problem, kitten?" Kayne asks with a hint of menace. I may not call him Master but, for all intents and purposes, he is. And 'Master' does not like it when I'm disobedient. I, however, love to push his buttons.

"No, Kayne," I drawl, still kneeling beside him.

"Then get." His blue eyes flash and my stomach muscles clench.

"Yes, Kayne." I place my hands on the cool tile floor and begin to crawl out of the kitchen and into the living room where the doors to the lanai are wide open. There's a breeze coming off the ocean and the sky is a deep cobalt blue. I have never once regretted moving to paradise. Even after . . . well, I don't want to ruin the mood by thinking about that.

I kneel on the pillow next to the table. Most mornings, I sit in a chair like a civilized human being, but today, we're playing. And it's so much fun when we play. I, however, always wear neck jewelry, whether it's my inconspicuous slave collar or my real one. This morning, I woke up with Kayne's head between my legs and the thick white leather one around my throat. He had that look in his eyes—the starving beast wanted to feed.

I notice the table already has cut fruit, orange juice, and one place setting right before Kayne appears with a plate of pancakes and a bottle of syrup. I can almost guarantee this is going to get messy. He loves to get me dirty and then clean me up—*with his tongue.* I shiver internally at just the thought.

Kayne places the plate and syrup down then sits in the chair directly in front of me. He's angled it so he can access both the table and me.

"Closer." He yanks on my collar wedging me between his legs. "Much better." He slides his hand down my chest and massages one of my breasts. I close my eyes and inhale as sensations start to brew from the rough way he kneads and pulls on my nipple. We haven't had sex in over a week, and I am seriously frustrated. I'm fairly certain he's been planning this little escapade.

My frustration is a large part of the reason I got into trouble. I touched when I wasn't supposed to. (More like put my mouth where I wasn't supposed to.)

"Are you going to behave while I feed you?" he asks as he pulls away and begins to put food on his plate. Some fresh mango, a pancake, and a drizzle of syrup.

"I can't make any promises," I purr.

He pauses as he cuts the pancake. "You know the more you misbehave the more severe the punishment?"

"I know." *This isn't my first rodeo.*

"But you're willing to push me anyway?" He picks up a small triangle from his plate and feeds it to me.

I nod as I chew, my heated gaze mirroring his.

"You made me come when you weren't supposed to." He feeds me another piece of pancake. I take it from his hand, sucking the syrup off his fingers as seductively as I can.

"I know." I watch as he picks up a piece of mango and places it in front of me. I open my mouth, but he pulls it back. Shaking his head, he rings the orange-colored fruit around my lips like he's applying lip gloss.

"Lick," he orders me. I run my tongue over the sweet juice coating my lips. "I wanted to take this slow. I wanted to savor you in the fresh air. Build you up and break you down until you were begging . . ."

"I'll still beg," I hastily interrupt him.

"You just love being naughty." He grabs my chin. "I never gave you permission to speak."

I smile wickedly. "I don't need your permission to speak."

"Oh, no? What do you need permission for?"

"To come."

"And is that what you want?"

"Yes."

"Naughty kittens don't get to come." His voice vibrates with authority.

"Yes, they do," I argue with him.

"Not by my hand."

"I have my own hands."

"You're not supposed to touch yourself unless I say so."

"You said it yourself . . . I'm naughty."

"Yes, you are." He leans in and kisses me, a ravishing assault that warns me about what's to come. By the time Kayne pulls away, my lips are throbbing and so is my clit. I need him to touch me, sate me, but I know that's not in the plans for a very long while.

Breathing heavily, he hauls me off the floor and lays me out on the tabletop.

"Open," he orders, lifting my legs so my ass is hanging just off the edge of the table. My thighs are wide, and I'm on display. I know I'm glistening in the sunlight; I've never been good at controlling my arousal, especially when my husband's tongue is mere inches away from me.

"Kayne," I whimper, wanting to clench my thighs as my pussy tingles.

"Yes?" He hovers over my slit as close as humanly possible but never touches it. The only thing I can feel is the warm caress of his breath mingled with the morning breeze.

"You want my tongue on you?" he asks, a hair away from my wide-open folds.

"Yes," I rasp.

"Yes, what?"

"Yes, please." I twitch.

"I don't think that's the right answer."

"Yes, Kayne," I correct myself. My excitement is getting the better of me as he strokes my tail, teasing me with the plug lodged deeply in my ass.

Kayne drapes my legs over his shoulders then reaches for the syrup. *I knew this was going to get messy.*

"You had your breakfast. Now, it's time for mine." He squeezes the bottle and coats my pussy with the sticky substance. It's lukewarm and tickles as it drips down my heated pink flesh. "Come and I'll spank you."

"Promise?" I ask just as he puts his mouth on me and begins to lick. My muscles immediately spasm.

"Oh, shit!" I cry out as he laps up every last drop of syrup while simultaneously fucking me with the plug. My tiny little rosebud expands and contracts as Kayne mercilessly eats me alive. I know I shouldn't come, but his threat is just too enticing. I want it rough. I want him to punish me. I want him to fuck me so hard that we're both launched far, far away.

"Kayne!" I scream as I let go, pulling his hair as my orgasm cripples me. He licks harder and pumps the plug faster until he squeezes out every possible drop of my arousal. *Oh god, I needed that. Desperately.* He then lifts his head and looks up at me over my heaving chest, his eyes a sharp, piercing blue in the sunlight, the brown patch bold and dominant. Just like my 'Master.'

"You are a very bad little girl," he says as he shifts, pulling me down the table and placing me on my feet.

"I know," I respond with satisfaction.

"How many lessons do I have to teach you before one sticks?"

"Many. I'm a slow study."

"I've noticed. Clean up breakfast then come upstairs," he orders resolutely.

"Yes, Kayne," I answer obediently.

With that he steps away—his erection standing tall and proud—and disappears inside. I know I'm in trouble. A delicious kind of earth-shattering trouble that's going to both push my limits and send me soaring.

I clean up quickly, placing the dishes in the sink and covering the fruit and pancakes; I know Kayne will house them later. The man eats like he's a growing teenage boy.

I hurry up the stairs and into our bedroom. It's cleanly decorated in creams and whites with bold pops of color. It has a tranquil, airy feel, like an island escape.

I drop to all fours before I enter the playroom. Kayne is already waiting for me, leaning up against the bondage horse wielding his weapon of choice—a riding crop.

He hits it against the palm of his hand, watching me intently as I crawl across the room and kneel right at his feet.

"So here we are," he states. "Is this what you wanted, kitten?" He uses the end of the crop to lift my face.

"Yes," I squeak, then clear my throat and answer again more confidently. "Yes."

"Kitten, kitten, kitten. You love to be punished as much as I love to punish you. What a pair we make."

I smile up at him. "Is there anything wrong with being made for each other?"

"No, baby. Not a damn thing." He holds my face in place.

"What's your safe word, Ellie?"

"Cupcake."

Kayne nods. We go through this ritual every time. In the four years we've been married, I have never used my safe word, no matter how far he's pushed me. And there were times it was pretty far. But every experience has brought us closer together. I don't think today will be any different.

"On." He smacks the horse with the crop and the crack echoes throughout the room.

What makes Kayne so skilled at enlivening my emotions is the element of surprise. I never know what he's going to do or what direction he's going to turn. We don't use the horse very often. Truth be told, I don't get punished a whole lot. The last time was a few months ago. We've shifted more toward kinky sex than anything else, but every so often, our beasts demand to be let out.

I climb onto the black padded contraption with restraints on all four legs. Straddling it, I rest on my stomach as Kayne fastens my wrists first and then my ankles. The cuffs are tight and barely leave any wiggle room. He did that on purpose. In this position, my ass and back are completely vulnerable. The leather is cool against my cheek, but my skin is on fire. My breathing quickens.

"Comfortable, kitten?" Kayne runs the crop over my bare back. "Or are you beginning to regret ever being bad?"

I always have a little bit of anxiety when I'm strapped down about to be punished. It's what makes this experience so illicit. "No. I don't regret it," I force out.

He leans over and rasps in my ear, "Such a brave little kitten even when she's scared." I shake with anticipation, excitement, and a small amount of fear. Then I hear the crop cut through the air and connect on my ass cheek. "Kayne!" I jump, but the ankle and wrist cuffs restrain me; I'm not budging an inch.

"You wanted this, kitten," he reminds me as he lands another blow.

"Ouch!" My behind stings.

Kayne rubs the inflamed skin until it tempers. He doesn't utter a sound, knowing the silence is killer. Then, without warning, he whacks me on the opposite cheek. My body tenses all over again, my muscles gripping at the butt plug while my clit rubs against the unforgiving leather.

"Those were just warm-up shots." Kayne walks around the horse until he's standing in front of me. His blinding erection right in my face.

"Pick your head up. Open your mouth," he directs. I do as he says; my head the only part of my body I can move. As I open my mouth, he pulls his shorts down, springing himself free. He then grabs the back of my head, gripping a handful of hair, and slides his cock in until it feels like it's touching my tonsils. "Good girl. Now swallow me." He pumps shallowly, keeping eighty percent of his erect length in my mouth. I fight to keep my jaw open and not choke on my spit as he pummels me. My eyes start to water and I pull against the restraints as he purposely gags me. He was never going to spank me. This was always going to be my punishment. I went down on him this morning when he told me not to, and he ended up coming rampantly in my mouth. Then I added fuel to the fire at the table outside by deliberately disobeying him.

He buries his cock all the way down my throat and we both have our own reaction. He shivers with lust, and I whimper helplessly. He then pulls out spontaneously, breathing erratically. "Going to think twice before putting your mouth where it's not allowed?"

I sputter then grin deviously. "Maybe," I pant.

"Maybe, your ass," he mocks, repositioning himself behind me and landing another blow with the crop. *Oh, shit.*

The kinetic energy in the room electrifies as I feel Kayne move about. I hear one of the drawers to the chest open and close before I feel the warmth of his body behind me once again. A second later, the distinct sound of the lubrication top pops.

"I'm going to fuck you hard, Ellie." The distance is blatant in his voice, the overpowering arousal taking over, making him blind with need.

"Kayne." My response is timid, hesitant.

"You asked for this, kitten."

He's right, I did. I want it. Doesn't mean I'm not scared.

I hear his inconsistent breaths as he inserts one finger into my entrance.

"Get wet for me, baby." He pumps his hand fast then adds a second finger and then a third. Before I know it, I'm grinding my clit against the hard leather, sprinting after an orgasm I didn't even see coming.

"Keep rubbing, kitten." Kayne continues to finger me as he yanks the tail from my ass. My body locks up because I know what's coming. He spanks me, and I let out a shrill cry. He hits me again and again, with all three fingers buried inside me. I don't know which is torturing me more, the pleasure or the sting of pain. I reach the precipice fast and hard.

"Kayne, please may I come?!" I wail, my pussy clenching and my clit aching.

"Come, kitten. Come." There's turmoil in his voice. Just as I let go and begin to freefall, Kayne withdraws his fingers and smears my arousal up into my pulsating buttonhole. He then plunges every inch of his concrete cock into my ass at once. I yelp like a wounded dog as his erection and my orgasm tear me right in two. The pain as shocking as the pleasure.

I cling to the wave of my climax for as long as possible while Kayne fucks me with reckless abandonment until he reaches his own peak.

"Fuck, I'm going to come." He grunts, pulling on my hair. "Baby, you feel so good, you're going to make me come." He slams into me and I jerk forward in the restraints, my ankles and wrists straining, the tears flowing freely.

"Kayne!"

With one more deafening blow, he unleashes, coming deep inside my exploited ass and limp body.

In the aftermath, there's nothing but static, sunlight, and the sound of our tattered breathing in the now stormless room.

"Hey." Kayne kisses me softly, licking up the tears that are still flowing steadily down my cheeks.

"Hey." I sniffle, looking up at him in my peripheral vision.

"You okay?"

"Yeah." I smile, and I am.

"I love you," he whispers, still licking and kissing my face.

"I know." I close my eyes serenely. "And no one loves you more than I do."

"Only by the grace of God."

He's trying to be funny, but Kayne's funny always has a bit of truth behind it. In this case, anyway. He still feels like he doesn't deserve me, and I came to terms a long time ago that it's just a character flaw we both have to live with. Doesn't mean I won't keep trying to drill it into his head that he is loved and more deserving than he believes.

Kayne kisses me one last time before he withdraws himself from my body. My taut little butthole relaxes for the first time today. I breathe more easily as all the tension uncurls itself from my limbs.

"Hang tight, kitten. I'll clean you up." *Like I have any other option.* Kayne returns from the bathroom with a damp washcloth and caringly wipes away the sticky remnants before he unfastens each restraint; rubbing my wrists and ankles as he goes. When I'm finally free, he urges me to sit up then lifts me into his arms.

Lethargically, I mold myself to him, resting my head on his chest.

He tightens his hold, keeping me close.

I'm nearly asleep by the time he places me in bed and curls up beside me.

I snuggle up next to him, placing my ear over his heart, letting the strong, steady sound soothe me like it always does.

"Did I hurt you, Ellie?" he asks with a hint of worry as he runs one finger through my hair.

"You utterly ruined me." That's always my response after a bout of rough sex. It's my way of telling him no one will ever compare to the way he loves me, physically or emotionally.

"Good." There's contentment in his voice. "You're such a naughty little kitten."

"I know. You made me that way." I look up at him.

"I know. Do you hate me for it?"

"Does it seem like I hate you?"

"No."

"Then there's your answer."

Kayne hugs me tighter as I stare up at him, and then glance away immediately once our eyes meet.

I feel his energy shift. "Ask me, Ellie."

Shit. Kayne has told me repeatedly that I can't hide anything from him, and as hard as I try to conceal what I'm thinking, one evasive glance always gives me away.

I nibble on my lip, hesitant to go down this road.

"Ellie . . ." Kayne nudges me, urging me to talk. He gets agitated when he knows that I'm deliberately keeping something from him. I chew on my lip harder.

"I want to be more naughty," I state timidly.

"More naughty?" His eyebrows shoot up.

I nod cautiously, knowing this conversation could be world war three in the making. "I want to know what it's like to be with two men."

There, I said it, and should now probably take cover.

The severity of Kayne's silence tells me everything I need to know. I just pissed him off big time. It doesn't happen often, but when it does, it's frightening. I think I just pierced my tongue with my incisor. I never should have said a damn thing.

Kayne suddenly expels a heated breath. "Do you really want to be with Jett that badly?"

"I really want to be with both of you that badly," I clarify. "It isn't just about Jett."

He stares up at the ceiling. I know he's at war with himself. He wants to give me what I want without losing himself in the process. The last time Jett, London, Kayne, and I fooled around, we took it further than we ever have before. For the first time, I was sexually intimate with Jett. I don't even know how it happened, natural progression maybe, but my lips ended up around his dick. I sucked him off, while Kayne fucked me from behind, and London sat on his face. That was only a few weeks ago, but I haven't stopped thinking about it since. Haven't stopped thinking about Jett and Kayne sandwiching me together and taking me at the same time.

"I know you didn't hate watching me with him. You fucked me the exact same way you do when I'm with London."

"How's that?" he questions.

"Recklessly."

His lips twitch. "It wasn't so bad watching you suck another man's dick."

"You liked it?"

Kayne maintains his silence.

"Did you like having threesomes with Jett?"

"I like threesomes, period. But I always used to lean toward me being the minority. Jett used to like sharing his woman. Engulfing their senses, he used to say."

That doesn't sound so bad to me.

"You wouldn't want to engulf my senses?"

"I thought I already did." He frowns.

"You do . . . I mean . . ." Oh shit, I think I just insulted him.

Kayne smiles down at me, clearly amused by my stupidity. "It's okay, kitten." He yanks me by the collar, forcing my face close to his. "You can have both of us under one condition."

"What's that?" I swallow roughly, caught up in the power of his gaze.

"You remember who you belong to when it's over."

"Like I could ever forget. Your palm print is permanently stamped on my ass."

"Damn straight." He spanks me hard, causing me to jerk. "Now lie on your stomach." He flips me over, still keeping a firm grip on my collar. "All this talk about threesomes and head and engulfing your senses has made me hard." He keeps my face planted on the pillow with one hand on my collar and pulls up my hips with the other. I instantly liquefy.

"Now fucking scream my name, kitten. So I know you'll never forget." With that, he slams into me, bucking me forward. *"Oh!"* I grab onto the edge of the mattress as his cock hits me square in my center, causing my muscles to coil around him like a snake.

"Who owns you, Ellie?" he asks as he beats into me from behind, my body completely subdued by his hold on my collar and hand clamped on my hip.

"You!" I exclaim as my pussy floods with forced arousal.

"And who am I?" he demands as our skin slaps together.

"My life, my love, my happiness!" I spout as he ruins me in the most delicious kind of way.

Kayne halts, buried deep inside me. "That's right, kitten." He leans over and murmurs in my ear, "Who else am I?"

I look up at him through the corner of my eye. "My owner. You own me." I speak the words he wants to hear.

"That's right, baby. Till death do us part."

I nod.

"Now tell me you love me."

"I love you," I proclaim with no hesitation. "Only you."

Kayne kisses my cheek affectionately then pulls out and repositions me on my back. "I love you, too." He slides into me sweetly. "Only you." He looks directly into my eyes as I spread my legs, inviting him inside. "That's right, kitten, let me in." He sinks deeply into my channel, penetrating all the way to my core.

"Kayne," I moan, as he splits me open.

"Ellie." He exhales my name, the same need evident in his tone.

"Make me come," I implore, as he fucks me leisurely.

"You know I'll give you anything you want. I can never say no to you."

And that's the truth. Kayne would deny me very few things. An orgasm when I'm bad is one thing on that very short list, but right now, I could ask for the moon on a silver platter and he would find a way to bring it to me.

"Mmm." He closes his eyes and rests his forehead against mine as his cock thickens.

I run my hands through his dark brown hair as he rocks in and out of me, both of us on a razor sharp edge about to topple over.

"Kayne." I whimper and shake as his body commands mine. *"Kayne!"* He thrusts in deep, shattering us both, the two of us moaning and panting and gyrating until the tumultuous ache subsides and all that's left in the climatic aftermath is two stripped bodies and a pile of bare bones.

Ruined . . .

I'm most definitely ruined.

ELLIE

IT'S DARK IN MY ROOM. The shadows on the wall look like blobs of moving ink as the clouds cover the moon and its white reflective light. Like every night, I wait anxiously for my owner. I sit on my knees chained to the bed, apprehensively expecting his arrival. I've fought him for so long, but tonight I will finally give in. Give in to him and the darkness. It will be my descent. The door creaks open and my body tenses. I keep my head down and listen to his footsteps. They sound different tonight. Lighter, but more ominous. When I look up, it isn't my owner standing in front of me, but it is a man I recognize. A man with a cold, calculating stare and unrepentant desires. A man who craves pain and delivers it explicitly. As soon as our eyes meet, I cower away, attempting to escape the impending doom. I know it's a vain effort, as he overtakes me every time.

"No!" I scream as he snatches my chain like lightning and yanks me toward him.

"That word doesn't exist in my world," he sneers. It's the same words every time. *"Bite me and I'll beat you unconscious."* Then I'm choking and crying and gagging all at the same time as he rams his cock mercilessly down my throat. Michael stands behind him laughing as I fruitlessly fight, knowing the torture is just beginning. Before I know it, I'm forced to my back, my throat raw and my voice hoarse from screaming. It just echoes around me, trapping me in. No one can hear me; no one can save me.

The first thrust feels like a serrated hot poker stabbing between my legs. The second scars me permanently. I kick and flail, but no amount of resistance will stop him. I know this. I have lived through this horror many times before.

"Stop!" I sob. "Stop! Stop!"

He laughs maniacally, reveling in my pain.

"Your pussy saves you every time." Michael's voice evaporates.

"ELLIE!" Kayne shakes me.

"Ellie, wake up!"

I gasp as I open my eyes to meet Kayne's worried blue ones. My stomach rolls. "Oh god, get off!" I push him then fly out of bed and into the bathroom, reaching the toilet bowl just in time. I throw up violently, purging the sickening feelings until my stomach is empty.

Kayne kneels on the floor beside me, holding my hair and rubbing my back as I dry heave uncontrollably.

When there's absolutely nothing left, I slump next to the toilet.

Kayne pulls me into his chest and presses my face against his warm skin.

"Shhhh." He pets my head and rocks me until I'm calm. I cling to him while the leftover bile burns my throat. "That hasn't happened to you in a long time."

"I know," I answer feebly as my body begins to relax.

"Was it me? Did I trigger it?" he asks worried, no doubt believing it was our bout of rough sex that brought on the dream.

"No," I say truthfully. I haven't had a violent nightmare about Javier and Michael in almost six months. But that doesn't mean what they did to me has vanished from my subconscious. I used to have that same dream all the time. Sometimes five nights in a row. When the hospital discharged me, I lost a considerable amount of weight because I puked every time I startled awake. The exact same way I did tonight.

"I'm fine." I wipe the tears from my face. "I just need some water." I try to smile, try to placate him, because the last thing I want is Kayne worrying that he's the cause of my recurring nightmares.

"C'mon." He lifts me to my feet and helps to steady me. Our bathroom is enormous so it takes several steps to get from the toilet bowl to the sink. The whole room is white marble with copper fixtures. It's a spa-like oasis with the shower and soaking tub overlooking the picturesque landscape.

I turn on the faucet and rinse my mouth with some cold water then swish some Scope around to kill the nasty vomit taste. Kayne stands by my side, his worried stare searing through the side of my head the whole time.

Once I dry my mouth, he pulls me next to him, so my side is touching his. We gaze at each other in the mirror as he raises the hem of my shirt—one of his white clingy undershirts that I've made a habit of living in. He only lifts it as far as my ribcage, exposing the circular tattoo that matches his. Around the scar where Michael shot me are the words *That which does not destroy us* written in fancy cursive. The same words circle Kayne's scar where Javier shot him in the shoulder. I know what he's trying to tell me. Fight. And I am. I have been for the last four years, and I'll continue to fight for the rest of my life. If I didn't, I wouldn't survive. And that's just not an option.

The tattoos were Kayne's idea. We got them on our first wedding anniversary. As a reminder, a symbol, a signification of strength. I've come to learn my husband loves philosophy, theology, and metaphysical poetry. He's filled our home office with works of Richard Crashaw, Friedrich Nietzsche, John Donne, and John Wesley. Apparently, Jett was the influence for Kayne's educational interests. When they first met, Kayne was a bit "rough around the edges." That's how Jett put it anyway, attempting to be sarcastic and empathetic all at the same time. Before Kayne met Jett, his reading material consisted of comic books and car magazines. The first book Jett ever gave him was the *Canterbury Tales,* and I quote, said, "Read it, Neanderthal." Kayne wasn't a fan at first, but somehow, Jett instilled a love for literature and philosophy in him.

"Are you sure you're okay?" Kayne asks, cutting through the severe silence.

I nod, resting my head against his arm. "I'm fine."

"I didn't trigger it?" Insecurity peeks through his stoic façade.

I stare at him in the mirror.

Well . . . not in the way he thinks. Kayne's dominant behavior didn't bring on the nightmare. I think his mention of kids did. He asked about starting a family a few days ago. No pressure, he was just poking around to see how I felt about it. I can tell you that I feel the same way as I did four years ago—resistant to the idea.

I'm not sure I want to disrupt the perfect little life we've carved out. And starting a family would definitely do that. Am I being selfish? Maybe. Do I have justification to feel that way? I think I do, given everything I've been through.

"No," I assure him once more. It's half the truth. "I'm ready to go back to bed."

"Okay." He kisses my head tentatively then walks me back into our bedroom with a death grip on my hand. Once under the covers, I cuddle up next to him, my body drawing calmness from his warmth. He's always warm and eager to hold me. I drift off listening to the sound of Kayne's breathing and the soft laps of the ocean just outside. I don't dream of Michael or Javier again. Instead, I dream of a young, dark-haired, green-eyed boy playing in the sand, calling out Mom.

ELLIE

"YOU ALMOST READY, KITTEN?" KAYNE asks, leaning against the doorframe of our office looking good enough to eat.

"I'm responding to my last email." I flick my eyes up at him.

And also responding to the way you look in those wind pants and tight t-shirt. Whoa.

Our foundation, and my current baby, has taken off tremendously. Over the last three years, we have sent nearly four hundred survivors and their families to all seven continents. I personally coordinate all the arrangements with the help of a local travel agent on Oahu. So many stories and so many survivors. I correspond with each and every one of them. My soul just floods with joy knowing that I'm providing someone with something they could only dream about. I dreamed of paradise for so long, and at one point even believed my hopes and aspirations were stolen away from me. Luckily, that wasn't the case, and I came away with more than I could have anticipated.

A husband who once told me he would kill for me, and then made good on his promise. A husband who gives me everything and asks only that I love him honestly in return, flaws and all. Which I do.

I'm compelled to share some of my good fortune, and through To Catch a Falling Star, I do. The foundation got its name from the tattoo scribbled on Kayne's rib cage, *It takes a certain kind of darkness for the stars to shine* and the knowledge of all those girls he saved from Javier's home. I think about them often, even though I never personally met any of them. I wonder if maybe one or two of them were part of the four hundred we've sent away thus far. A tiny piece of me hopes so.

I hit send, then push away from the desk. I've been plugging away at the computer since six a.m.

"Do you have everything you need?" I ask Kayne as we walk

hand in hand down the curved staircase.

"Yup. Bottled water, snacks, and a hat."

"What about a compass?" I ask.

Kayne smiles. "Have that, too." He taps his chest, right where the brightly colored tattoo is inked over his heart. "It always brings me home. I just follow North."

He makes me grin like an idiot sometimes. On the needle pointing North is my name permanently written in small lettering. That's right. *I'm* home. Signed, sealed, and delivered.

Six months after Kayne and I got married, he and Jett left on one last mission; when they returned home, they both resigned from Endeavor. Although he was only gone a few days and in little to no danger, (his words though I'm still skeptical), it was trying. Very, very trying. Not knowing where he was or what he was doing. My imagination had a field day at my expense. I don't know how spouses of duty men and women do it. I was a nervous wreck until the minute he came home.

And as thrilled as I was that he decided to retire from the super-secret black op spy business, I sort of had a feeling his retirement would be short lived. And I was right because six months later, a knock came at the door. It was the commander of Honolulu SWAT. The same SWAT team Jett and Kayne worked with to save me. A few openings had 'materialized.' I use quotes because two positions were basically created specifically for them. Both Kayne and Jett said yes, and my husband went from nonexistent undercover operative to specialized service provider. AKA full-time, gun-toting, Kevlar-wearing badass.

Which, of course, he loves.

I sort of do, too. Especially when he walks around the house dressed in black fatigues with firearms holstered all over his body. *Hot.*

We climb into my Jeep. Not the one I used to drive, no. Kayne felt I needed an upgrade, so he purchased a new white Rubicon complete with body armor—a steel cage looking thing over the roof and front grille—for me. Boys and their toys. I end up driving the Jag half the time because he's always hogging the Wrangler.

We drive several blocks in the perfect October weather before we pull up to our destination. A large two-story house with a Chevelle parked in the driveway. We don't even bother knocking as we walk into Jett and London's home. They moved into the neighborhood shortly after Kayne and I did. It was sort of a whirlwind. Baby, house, marriage, in that order, but it was clear they couldn't be happier, despite London's horrific morning sickness.

"Peanut butter!" a high-pitched voice squeaks as soon as Kayne walks into the living room. Jett and London's house may be as large and spacious as ours is with the same panoramic view, but it feels much different with baby gates and toys tossed all around.

"Jelly!" Kayne lifts Layla as she runs and jumps into his arms. I don't exactly know where the nicknames came from, but they've been calling each other that since Layla could talk. "Pretty girl, what's all over your face?" he asks as he examines her.

"Makeup." She chortles like she knows she's not supposed to be wearing it but doesn't care.

"Yup, Jett caught her red handed playing in our bathroom," London says as she bounces six-month-old Beckett around on her hip, the newest member of the Fox household. "After he scolded her, he taught her how to apply blush. He's stealing all my thunder." She laughs.

"We were just having some daddy-daughter time," Jett announces as he comes down the stairs. He's dressed similar to Kayne in a white T-shirt, form-fitting hiking pants, and a pair of Ray Bans sitting on his blond head.

"Yeah, London, he needs his girl time or he'll lose all his estrogen," Kayne digs.

"What's esprjin?" Layla asks cheerfully.

We all erupt.

"It's your daddy's super power," Kayne tells her, highly amused.

"That's right." Jett tries to grab the gorgeous little blonde with her daddy's coloring and mommy's stunning face, but she latches onto Kayne's neck. Jett should know by now those two really are stuck together like peanut butter and jelly.

"Fine, then," he says to Layla, sticking out his tongue. She just laughs at him while holding Kayne tight.

"You're going to have to let go sooner or later." London delivers her the bad news as she puts Becks in his playpen. "Daddy and Uncle Kayne are going hiking."

"I wanna go!" She bops in Kayne's arms. "Please, please, please!"

Kayne and Jett throw a communicative look at each other.

"I don't have a problem with it." Kayne shrugs, more than happy to take her.

Jett huffs. "You really want to go?" he asks Layla directly.

"Yes, *pleassse,* Daddy?" Her turquoise eyes sparkle just like his.

"What do you think?" Jett consults London.

"It's fine with me. I just need to grab a hat and some sunscreen for her."

Let me tell you something. Kayne and Jett may think they run things, but this little girl rules the roost.

"I'll grab the carrier," Jett sighs, pretending to be annoyed. He pinches Layla's calf right before he walks out of the room. She giggles loudly in triumph.

As we wait for Jett to return, London grabs sunscreen from the bathroom and lathers Layla up. She then retrieves some snacks and a juice box from the kitchen just as Jett returns with a blue book bag looking thing.

"I want to go on Uncle Kayne's back!" Layla demands in a whiney tone.

"Fine with me," Jett agrees all too willingly.

"Of course, you can," Kayne placates her sweetly, resting his forehead against hers. "Your daddy couldn't carry a butterfly up a hill."

"I like butterflies."

"I know you do, pretty girl." He chuckles.

Jett leers at Kayne, "Aww, ffff . . . *Fudgesicle.*"

"I want a Fudgesicle!" Layla exclaims.

London and I can barely hold it together. The interaction between the three of them is just too cute.

"Okay. Time to go." London starts ushering the two men and a little lady out.

Layla becomes excited. "I want to see fish! And a waterfall and a rainbow!"

"Whatever you want, jelly," Kayne appeases her as he carries her out the front door. "You can put in your full order in the car."

Yes, my heart actually skips a beat watching the two of them together.

"Have fun!" London yells. "Be careful! Jett, stay on the trail!"

I don't hear Jett's response clearly, but I think it was along the lines of "Yeah, yeah, woman, I know!"

Once gone, London shuts the door, turns around, and gives me a look. *That look.* Oh no, here it comes.

"That man needs a child." The words fly out of her mouth as if on cue.

"Please don't start," I implore her, instantly annoyed.

"I am just making an observation," she defends her statement.

"You've been making that observation a lot lately."

"I can't help what I see."

I lean on the kitchen island and stare at London. "I'm just not sure."

She dispenses a sympathetic look. "I know the subject of family is between you and Kayne, but Ellie, just tell me what you're afraid of."

It takes me a few moments to answer her, as I try to put my feelings into words. "Everything."

"Everything?" She crosses her arms confounded. "Do you think you're going to be a bad mother?"

"Compared to you, maybe," I joke.

"Ellie."

"No, it's not that." I wrap my arms around myself. "I just know what's out there. I don't want what happened to me to happen to my children."

London's face drops. "Oh, Ellie."

I wipe my eye, a rebel tear forming in the corner.

"I didn't mean to upset you."

"I know." I try to smile. "I just don't know how you do it."

London moves closer to me until our bodies are touching. She plays with the ends my hair and looks at me sympathetically. "I wish I could give you a guarantee. I wish I could tell you that everything will always be perfect, but I think you're smart enough to know that's not true."

"You could lie to me."

"I could, but I won't. What I will tell you is that you have an advantage."

"Advantage?"

"Yup. You know what's out there. You can recognize the danger and teach your children the signs. If you ever decide to have any." She winks. "We've all been through our own traumatic shit. But the way I see it, if you let it get in the way of your happiness, you're letting it win."

She does have a point. And London has lived through her own personal hell, one that was way longer and way worse than mine, and she's not letting it hold her back.

Are my negative experiences holding me back? Am I making excuses because of my fear? Maybe. Or maybe I've already committed myself to someone and I'm not ready to share him yet. Maybe, I'm scared it will change what we have. And like I've said before, I really love *us.*

"Whatever you decide, I'll support you. I just don't want you look back and have regrets."

"I don't want that, either." I also don't want to deprive my husband of something he really wants.

"Good." London walks out of the kitchen to check on Becks, who's been extremely quiet.

"God, I love this child," I hear her say.

"Why?" I peek into the living room to see Becks cuddled up in the corner of his playpen fast asleep.

"Because he's such a man. Eat, sleep, poop. That's his life."

"At six months old, what more do you need?"

"Nothing." She smiles down at the little towhead. He, too, got his father's coloring, but his mommy's dark blue eyes.

"So . . . speaking of men, do you think you can get Malia to babysit overnight next weekend?" I decide now is as good a time as any to change the subject.

London snaps her head up. "I'm sure I can, why?"

I smile, unable to hide my excitement. "Kayne said yes."

Her eyes widen to the size of satellites. "You got him to agree?"

"Yes!" The rock in the pit of my stomach does a summersault. "Do you suddenly have a problem with me sleeping with your husband?"

London and I have talked about this. Extensively. She knows how much I want to be with both Kayne and Jett and has been nothing but supportive.

"No." She tiptoes away from Beckett quietly and directs me back to the kitchen. "I slept with your husband. It's only fair. Just be prepared. I've been the filling in that alpha sandwich."

"I know." I pout. "And I'm tired of living vicariously through you."

"Apparently, you won't have to much longer."

ELLIE

WE WATCH AS THE LAST bits of daylight fade away, casting a grayish-blue hue on the ocean and mountainous landscape. Jett, London, Kayne, and I have just finished a dinner on the lanai of grilled steak, mashed potatoes, and sautéed asparagus. I swallow the last of my wine before I start clearing the table.

"Do you want some help, Ellie?" London asks, moving to stand.

"I'm fine." I motion for her to sit. "You clean up twenty-four hours a day."

"That isn't a lie." She smiles as she sinks back into her chair. I pile the plates and bring them into the kitchen as Kayne scrubs the grill and Jett irritates him by pointing out all the spots he missed. I laugh to myself while rinsing the dishes, highly amused by the three people I love in each their own way. After loading the dishwasher, I jump when I feel Jett standing behind me.

"Jesus!"

"Nope, just Jett." He grins. I swear he and Kayne can be silent as shadows when they want to be. "Silverware?" He holds up a handful of forks and knives.

"Just stick them in the sink," I instruct as I head to the refrigerator. I hear the metal clink behind me.

"Any dessert?" Jett asks, curiously. When he and London come over, I always know to have dessert. He has one wicked sweet tooth.

"Of course." I pull out a cake from the fridge. "Red velvet."

I place it on the counter in front of him and remove the Saran Wrap. I then swipe my finger in the icing and hold it up to him. "The cream cheese frosting is even homemade, especially for you."

Jett stares down at my finger, a small little smirk playing on his lips. "You know it's not nice to tease me, Ellie."

I step closer to him. "Who's teasing?"

Jett's mouth falls slightly open. It's not often he's surprised, but when he is, it's a classic moment. I watch closely as he glances outside to see Kayne's reaction. He's just standing casually next to London, the two of them voyeurs to our little show. He nods at Jett, as if giving him the okay.

"You sure about this?" Jett asks, bringing his attention back to me, his turquoise eyes now wild and alight.

"Yes," I answer confidently.

"You know once we start, there's no stopping." Jett wraps one of his hands around mine, bringing my frosting covered finger to his lips. "Are you ready for that?"

I swallow thickly, staring directly into Jett's eyes. I nod, the heat coming on faster than I anticipated.

"You're blushing, sweet thing." Jett slips my finger into his mouth and swirls his tongue around the tip. My knees go weak. "Answer me, Ellie," Jett urges. "Are you ready?"

"Yes," I breathe out. "I know exactly who I belong to."

Jett smirks fiendishly. "After tonight, you may reconsider that."

"Don't make me kill you." Kayne's voice cuts through the sexual tension smothering the room. I glance over to see him and London on the other side of the breakfast bar and wonder idly how long they've been standing there. "I don't feel like looking for a new best friend."

"In situations like these, you know I have no control over the outcome," Jett taunts him.

They share a silent exchange before Jett asks outright, "Are you okay with this?"

Kayne sighs, relenting, "What my kitten wants, she gets."

"And your kitten wants me?" Jett responds, gratified, almost triumphant.

"I want both of you," I clarify.

"Then both of us you shall have." With that, he swiftly scoops me up and throws me over his shoulder.

I squeal instinctively.

Jett makes it upstairs in record time, Kayne and London hot on his heels. Once in the master bedroom, he tosses me onto the bed. "Stay," he orders as Kayne pins me with a heated stare.

I glance over at London, worried and disheveled on the bed. She communicates silently, *you asked for this, be prepared.* She did warn me numerous times that taking on Kayne and Jett is like trying to tame two wild animals. But the warning always excited me more than scared me. Except now, about to be in the thick of it, I wonder if I'm biting off more than I can chew.

I guess I'll soon find out.

"London, undress Ellie." The command comes swiftly from Jett, like a hard slap. She moves quickly, pulling my jean skirt down. She then pulls me up and rips off my tank top. In five seconds flat, I'm naked in front of the three of them.

"Thank you," Jett kisses her promptly on the cheek as she steps back between the four starving eyes raking over my bare body.

"Up." Jett crooks a finger at me.

I crawl to the edge of the bed and sit on my knees. I'm suddenly shaking. Tonight is going to be completely different. Different than any other time the four of us have shared. There are no boundaries tonight, no invisible line forbidden to cross. No more imagining . . . only experiencing. I steal a look at Kayne. He's cool and collected on the outside, but I wonder what he's feeling on the inside. His majestic blue gaze gives nothing away except fanatical lust.

"Be a good kitten and sit still," Jett instructs as he reaches over and grabs my collar, which is peeking out from under our pillows. Kayne likes to keep it chained to the vining iron headboard, right along with me. Jett fastens the white leather around my neck as I regard him curiously. He's never referred to me as kitten before, directly or indirectly. Kayne is the only one who has ever used my pet name. It feels strange and completely unlawful. But that is the whole point of tonight, breaking the rules of attraction. Jett smirks as if registering my silent thought. Once finished with my collar, he slides his hand into my hair and yanks firmly, tipping my face up. "Kayne may own you," he murmurs, his warm breath tickling the shell of my ear, "but a little piece of you has always belonged to me."

I sit like a statue processing his bold statement, agreeing with him beyond reason. Jett always has been an exotic spice in mine and Kayne's mix. "Tonight, you're our pet," he announces, jerking on my chain. The word *our* is not lost on me; it refers to all three people in this room. "I want to watch you pleasure my little bird, and if she isn't satisfied, you're going to get punished." Jett's lips curve up as mine turn down. He's never threatened to punish me before. I look at Kayne. He just shrugs a shoulder, as if agreeing with Jett. This is an odd, new dynamic. I don't know what I was expecting going into this, but being a shared pet with the threat of punishment definitely wasn't it.

"How do you answer, kitten?" Kayne's voice is hard, rough, dusted with desire.

"Yes, Jett," I answer obediently.

"Good girl." There's an air about Jett that I've never experienced before. It's commanding and authoritative, but not like the Jett I know. This person in front of me is someone else completely; this person is a huntsman, a skilled, cunning individual who appreciates the chase as much as the kill. I see it reflecting in his turquoise eyes. Eyes that have only shown flickers of the man who lurks beneath the surface.

London crawls onto the bed and kneels right in front of me. Even she is different tonight. There is not a blip of submissive energy radiating from her. Tonight, she's an equal to Kayne and Jett. It's sexy and intimidating all at the same time. She stares at my mouth, knowing full well what it's capable of, and eager for me to put it to good use.

"Undress me, kitten." Being called by my pet name by others sends a chill right down my spine. I never knew it could affect me in such a way, making me feel totally bound while at the same time so completely free.

I grab the hem of her loose fitting sundress and run my fingers along her skin as I pull it up. She's not wearing anything underneath, except a skimpy, bright orange thong. Once off, she tugs on my collar, bringing our faces close together. She's controlling the show, kissing me how she wants and where she wants. My lips, my cheeks, my neck, moving down until she reaches my breasts, biting and licking my nipples while Kayne and Jett watch fixated.

"I want your tongue all over me," London hisses in my ear, as she leans backward, pulling me along with a firm grip on my collar. She lies on her back, situating me directly on top of her. With an iron-clad grasp, she leads my face to her neck. Like instructed, I begin to lick. I run my tongue over her collarbone, down the center of her chest, until I reach her naked breasts, I tease each nipple with a slash of my tongue and suck hard, nipping her the way she did to me not moments ago. She moans audibly as she yanks on my collar, drawing me further down her body. She wants my mouth on her pussy; there's no disputing it. London is always greedy when it comes to me. She likes me one place, and that's with my head right between her thighs. I yank off her panties, nearly ripping them from excitement. Just as I take my first lick of her slit, I feel the bed dip both in front of me and behind me. My defenses instantly fly up. Shit's about to get real. I flick my eyes up to see Jett in front of me, leaning over London's outstretched body and feel Kayne's hands caressing the small of my back.

"Don't stop," Jett instructs as he presses his lips to London's arched chest. I keep up a fluid rhythm with my tongue as he moves down her body, following the same path I took seconds ago. I watch engrossed as he pulls each of her nipples into his mouth, stretching skin then moving down to her torso. He never takes his sharp turquoise stare off me as he comes closer, closer until his mouth is a breath away from mine. London squirms and moans beneath us, as I continually skim over her clit. Then it happens, Jett lashes out his tongue, simultaneously French kissing us both. The contact sends a heat wave through my whole body, blowing the doors of exhilaration wide open, desire and want running rampant through my entire nervous system.

London expels a low, throaty moan as the two of us begin to pleasure her, dueling tongues brushing over her fiery flesh and against each other. It's impossible not to lose myself at the moment, not to let the arousal take over and become my ruler. All at once, London rushes to her peak, Jett grabs a fistful of my hair, and Kayne sinks a finger into my entrance. With a controlling grip, Jett secures my face against London's pussy as Kayne smears my wetness up away from my folds, and teases the tight ring of muscle over and over with his thumb.

"Make her come, Ellie," Jett demands between licks, his long flat tongue lapping up my saliva and the juices of London's excitement. Subdued in place, I suck and circle and stab at London's pussy as Kayne penetrates both my holes, priming and stretching, driving me completely insane.

"Oh, god!" London squirms like a fish. "I'm going to come! I'm going to come!" she exclaims in distress. "Fuck, you're both going to make me come!" She rocks her pussy against my face as a sudden rush of heat saturates my lips.

"Lick it up, Ellie. Suck up every single drop." Jett's voice is stern, commanding. His hold on my hair unyielding as I do as I'm told, consuming every droplet of desire that's threatening to drown me. Once her tremors subside and she's moaning languidly, Jett jerks my head up and smothers me with a kiss, his tongue aggressively claiming my mouth, the urgency nearly stealing my breath away.

"Good, kitten," he patronizes once we break apart. I look up at him winded as Kayne continues to finger me, scissoring open my rosebud as wide as my muscles will allow. I groan as he pushes past the point of pleasure. "We need you loose, baby," I hear Jett say as he lifts a limp and sated London off the bed and deposits her on the curved chaise on the opposite side of the room. "Be a good little bird and watch." He kisses her, sucking her bottom lip between his teeth.

"Yes, Jett," she purrs euphorically.

With that, he returns to the bed, shedding his clothes on the way. First, he tears off his T-shirt exposing his chiseled chest, nipple ring, and bright wavelike tattoos. Second, he unbuckles his belt like a man who knows exactly how to wield it, then drops his pants. Jett's nipple isn't the only part of his body that's pierced. Through his foreskin, a metal barbell with two large balls protrudes right under the head of his penis. It's one of the hottest things I have ever seen and when my tongue grazed it for the first time, I nearly expired. Since then, I've been aching to know what it feels like inside me. My mouth goes dry as he climbs onto the mattress, the hunter finally cornering his prey.

Kayne lifts me from all fours by my collar, the chain attached to the headboard straining as far as it can go. In a blink, I'm sandwiched between two solid bodies, four hands touching me, two mouths devouring me, and two pulsing cocks gunning for my pleasure. I don't know where or who to touch first, so I just try and keep up as Kayne twists my head to kiss me while Jett fondles my breasts and bites my neck. The sensations come on like a tornado—angst, lust, desire, need—all engulf me as I'm pushed and pulled, grabbed, fingered, and squeezed.

"It's your turn, little girl," Jett growls as he holds his hand over mine and jerks on his cock, showing me exactly how he likes it. Before I know it, I'm being positioned back on all fours, Kayne detaining my hips and Jett holding my chin.

"Open. Wide." He pokes the head of his erection against my lips and I open like instructed. He slowly slides his cock into the recesses of my mouth; the odd sensation of metal scraping against my tongue from his piercing again tickles my gag reflex.

"That mouth of yours is so good, Ellie." He pumps several greedy times before pulling out. "But that's not where I'm coming tonight," he tells me as he moves aside, allowing Kayne to push me forward onto my stomach.

"Over," Kayne orders with a slap on my ass. I roll onto my back, catching sight of him shedding his clothes. He moves differently than Jett, more rugged and rough. One a skilled hunter; the other a savage predator. Once his shirt and pants are gone, he covers my naked body with his, pressing me into the mattress, kissing my mouth rapturously and touching my body gluttonously. He twists one of my nipples and I release a muffled whimper.

"One of my favorite sounds," Kayne remarks as he pushes himself up, then manhandles me so I am lying directly on top of him, my back against his front. It's crystal clear that I have no say in what goes on here. My body belongs to them, and they will use it and abuse it exactly how they see fit.

Jett grabs my hands and pins them over my head. "This is our body tonight." He articulates my silent thoughts.

My anxiety spikes as he secures my wrists with the chain in an iron-clad binding. My heart pounds and my thighs tremble as Jett spreads my legs and Kayne nestles his rock-solid cock in the crack of my ass. "You ready, kitten?" Kayne asks as he nips on my earlobe and massages my breasts.

I can't even respond; the anticipation and fear have swallowed my voice. I'll be lucky to force a moan out. "I think she is." Jett ogles my naked, outstretched body, currently being served up specifically for him. "Just know, Ellie . . ." Jett slips his tongue into my ear and I shiver. "I have fantasized about tasting you here." He licks between my lips. "And here." He skims his finger over my soaking wet slit as he moves his tongue in slow circles around my mouth. "And when I take you," his voice is drenched with desire, "I'm not going to hold back."

There's something about Jett's tone—it's a hundred-proof cocktail made up of a warning, a threat, and a promise. Like all the delicious and frightening things he's capable of are about to rain down directly on top of me.

Jett swiftly kisses his way along my body, wasting no time tasting all the places he's fantasized about. When buries his face between my legs, it has a galvanic effect and I nearly convulse.

His tongue, oh Jesus, his tongue and the way he bends and curves it. The way he sucks and strikes and skims has me writhing, has me pulling on my restraints and moaning out loud.

"You like that, kitten?" Kayne rasps in my ear as he holds me still. "You like the way Jett eats *my* pussy?"

Again, I can't respond because I am caught in this alternate universe of pleasure. I merely mewl, detached as Jett licks me senseless.

"Answer him, kitten." Jett flicks my clit with his fingers, electrocuting my nerve endings. "Do you like the way I eat *his* pussy?"

I huff and puff, not answering fast enough, and Jett flicks my clit harder this time, causing me to cry out.

"Yes!" I pant, "Yes, I like the way you eat my pussy."

"Whose pussy?" Kayne bites my shoulder so hard I know I'm going to have a mark. "Your pussy!" I correct myself.

"That's right, kitten. Never forget it." He runs his tongue over my broken skin, lapping up the dewy drops of blood.

"No," I whimper illogically as Jett uses his fingertip to caress my throbbing clit. This whole situation is making me so crazy and so wet my arousal is literally dripping down my slit, and I haven't even climaxed yet.

"Something else belongs to me, too," Kayne says as he lifts my hips and pokes the head of his cock against my little puckered hole. "Stay still." He holds onto me firmly as he works his erection into my ass. Despite my evenly split moans of protest and pleasure, he continues his backdoor assault, sliding four inches in and two inches out over and over until he fully penetrates me. A small sheen of sweat covers my body as I breathe through the initial bites of discomfort. In this position, I am overly stretched, overly subdued, and overly vulnerable.

"My turn." Jett climbs on top of me and I become a bundle of nerves, so turned on and so unsure of what to expect. "Look at me, Ellie." The way he says my name, the way he grabs my chin and forces me to look him in the eyes, I nearly disintegrate. It's too exposing, too intense. I don't think I can handle it. I shut my eyes, but he grips me tighter and shakes my face. "Look. At. Me." He doesn't say it with anger; he says it with authority. He says it like he wants me to experience exactly what he's experiencing. I open my eyes when I feel his cock swimming through my soaked folds. My breath catches and then completely evaporates when he slides into me—slowly, leisurely, indulgingly—his gaze bestial as he fills me completely, the barbell through his foreskin stroking the walls of my channel, making the sensations that much more powerful. I've never felt anything like it. So filled, so stretched, so aroused, so desperate.

"Oh, god." I drop my head and tense in my restraints as they start to move, start to use me exactly how they want to, as a vessel for inconceivable pleasure.

Almost instantly, my body responds, begging to come. I try to contain it, but being engulfed in the heat of their bodies is enough to make me melt.

"Come," I distantly hear Kayne order me. "Come all over Jett's cock so he knows just how good you feel." He thrusts up into my ass just as Jett pulls out of my pussy. I nearly see stars, my insides crackling like live wires.

"Come, kitten." I hear the strain in his voice as he pulls on my collar.

"Yeah, come, kitten," Jett mimics Kayne's words and actions, thrusting into me while gripping my collar. I'm already trembling under a constellation of sensations when Kayne reaches around and rubs my clit. It feels like he hit a panic button as all of my senses go haywire. My vision blinks in and out as an unstoppable orgasm hits me like a wrecking ball. There's no stopping the shudders or the wracking or the coiling of my muscles around the two cocks buried deep inside me, reaping every single ounce of my pleasure. Demanding it. Sucking it straight from my core until there's nothing left to give. Until I'm only a languid mass sandwiched between two of the most intoxicating men I have ever met.

Mentally removed, I hear Jett and Kayne moan in my ear as they put their hands all over me, massaging my stressed limbs and taking advantage of my tethered state.

One, I'm not sure which, unbinds my wrists. My eyes are closed and I'm zapped of energy so I just let them do what they want, pulling out of me and flipping me over so I am now chest to chest with Kayne.

"Hi, kitten." He traps my head and kisses me. "Feeling okay?" he asks haughtily. He's enjoying this, I think, more than either of us expected.

I just grunt in response, attempting to cuddle up and fall asleep in his arms.

"We're not through yet," he informs me as he runs his hands down my sides and grabs both of ass cheeks.

"I told you there was a certain place I wanted to come," Jett murmurs behind me. His heated skin pressing against my own. "Let me in." He rubs his still erect cock between my cheeks as Kayne spreads them open.

"Let us both in." They simultaneously move to enter me. Kayne first, sliding into my pussy easily, while Jett works his way into my already exploited buttonhole. My womb knots like a twisted rope as I'm filled again, my body bowed in the new position.

"Come with us, Ellie." Kayne threads his fingers in my hair and grabs hold, keeping my face an inch away from his. He licks and bites on my bottom lip as the two of them let loose, fucking me hard, pursuing their own pleasure. "Come on, baby, come." Kayne thrusts at the same time as Jett and my body locks up.

"No," I plead. I don't think I can survive another earth-shattering quake like the one before.

"Yes."

"I can't." I strain as their cocks swell inside me, close to the brink.

"You can, and you will, because we say so."

"No." I nearly cry as one of them rubs my clit, adamantly, unforgivingly.

"Yes." Jett pulls my head back and kisses me, plunging his tongue into my mouth the same way he's plunging his cock into my ass.

"Come." My clit is rubbed harder, my nipples are teased and I'm filled to the brim as I dance the darkest rhythm of my life. Then it happens, an orgasm snowballs inside me, growing larger and larger with every strike and stroke and pinch until there's no stopping it. Until the demands on my body win out and my core catches fire and burns me alive.

I scream into Jett's mouth as I'm thoroughly fucked. Fucked until I go slack and the two men controlling me come. Come in my bruised, sore, supremely satisfied body.

Holy mother of God.

The last thing I remember is being cocooned in a blanket of warmth, heavy breathing, and soft lingering kisses, right before I pass out cold.

I WAKE UP TO THE sound of laughter echoing faintly through the house and the smell of coffee. I sit up in bed, my aching body protesting as I stretch my arms and legs. I'm still chained to the headboard; there are bruises on my hips and a bite mark on my shoulder. I look like a wreck, but I feel completely blissful. I unbuckle my collar and slink out of bed. Holy shit, I'm sore from tip to tip between my legs. I hobble into the bathroom to brush my teeth then throw on a pair of shorts and a tank top. I'm just at the top of the stairs when Kayne comes bounding up. When my eyes meet his, I suddenly blush, unexpectedly self-conscious.

"Hey." He cups my face and gives me a kiss.

"Hey," I respond shyly. Why am I uncomfortable? This is my husband.

"Why are you so red?" he asks curiously.

Because you shared me with your best friend last night and I'm not sure how I feel about it.

Or how you feel about it.

I shrug in response. "Do you still love me?" I wonder out loud.

"Ellie?" Kayne is thoroughly amused. "Why would you ask something so ridiculous?"

"Because of last night?"

"You think I'm mad?"

I shrug again, attempting to be cute and, well, tempting.

"Do I sound mad?"

I shake my head.

"Do I look mad?"

I shake my head once more. He actually looks refreshed and very happy.

"Then there's your answer."

"Did you enjoy it?" I can't help but ask. I have to know.

Kayne looks at me impishly. "Let's just say I was hoping you were still sleeping so I could wake you up with my tongue." He takes my hand and puts it between his legs so I feel his stiff erection.

"You liked it that much?"

Kayne nods, his eyes on fire. "I think the four of us have turned a corner in our sexual relationship."

My jaw drops. "Are you being serious? You'd do it again?"

"Again and so much more."

"More?" I repeat.

"Mmm hmm." He drops a kiss on my lips. "We can talk about *more,* later. London and Jett are getting ready to leave. Come say good-bye." He leads me down the stairs into the kitchen. That same sense of self-consciousness resurfaces when I come face to face with Jett. What the hell is wrong with me?

"Well, Sleeping Beauty finally decided to wake up," he comments as he takes a sip of coffee.

I regard him silently as heat creeps up over my cheeks. All I can picture is him naked, tattooed, and pierced. *Not good.* I need to get a grip.

I grab a coffee mug and pour myself a cup, finally mustering enough nerve to answer him.

"A girl needs her caffeine fix."

"That's not the only fix a girl needs." Jett pokes fun at me. I could smack him.

I roll my eyes in response instead. "And she got it."

I throw a glance at London, and she winks. Yes, the four of us have a weird dynamic, but it works.

London's phone chirps on the counter, and she hurries to check it. "Layla is asking for us, *again.*"

Jett takes one more large gulp of coffee. "That's our cue." He and London stand up. Adult swim is over for them.

Jett and London walk around the breakfast bar to say their good-byes. London breezily kisses me on the cheek, like nothing unusual occurred at all. Like, I didn't just sleep with her husband last night.

"Watching you with Jett was one of the hottest things I have ever seen," she whispers in my ear. "And you know I have seen a lot."

That she has. Probably more than any one person should see in a lifetime.

"Really?" I respond quietly, almost timid.

She nods, her dark-blue eyes sparkling perversely. London is always the picture of perfection outside the bedroom door. But behind it, her multifaceted persona peeks through. Her fiendish, fearless, provocative side.

When Jett hugs me, several emotions stir simultaneously—excitement, embarrassment, and a calming affection. It's obvious I wasn't prepared for the impact of last night, although it seems like I'm the only one who's rattled.

"You know what, Ellie?" Jett speaks softly as he embraces me.

"What?"

"You really do taste like cupcakes," he whispers in amusement.

I reply with a small gasp. Kayne must be sharing our secrets. He always tells me I taste like cupcakes.

Jett kisses me on the cheek, a firm, wet, sloppy gesture before he takes London by the hand and leaves.

ELLIE

LONDON AND I HAVE ALTERNATED hosting Thanksgiving for the last four years, and this year it's my turn. The house smells amazing. I made my mother's sweet potato pie, my grandmother's stuffing, and cooked a turkey big enough to feed twelve.

"Kayne!" I yell into the living room. "Can you come in here and help me with this monstrosity of a bird you made me buy!" Yes, the turkey was all him. He wanted leftovers . . . for a month. I swear the man eats like a racehorse. I always joke that I need a part-time job just to pay the grocery bill.

"Coming!" He walks into the kitchen holding Layla under his arm like a football.

"Now how are you supposed to help me when your arms are full?" I joke, tapping Layla's little nose. She giggles.

"Only one arm is full." He squeezes her and she squeaks. "I still have this one." He grabs one of the oven mitts off the counter. "If I can bench press you with one hand, I can pull a thirty-pound turkey out the oven."

I don't have a second to respond before London swoops in and slips Layla out from under Kayne's arm. "I'll take her. We'll just stand over here and watch." She steps back behind the island.

"Fair enough." Kayne grabs the other oven mitt and pulls the turkey from the oven. It looks so perfect I almost squeal. I don't know when I became so domestic, but seeing that beautiful brown bird come out of the oven gives me chills.

Kayne carves it and I place it on the set table. Not two seconds after he sits down, Layla is off her chair and climbing onto his lap. London scolds her but she insists, refusing to eat unless she stays put.

"It's fine," Kayne smoothes his hand over Layla's blonde hair.

"She can eat wherever she wants."

Sucker.

"You spoil her," London scolds *him* now.

Kayne just shrugs. "My house, my rules."

I just shake my head, laughing internally. How many times have I heard that?

Everyone begins to make their plates while talking and passing and sampling. This is Becks' first Thanksgiving, so we all get to experience his first taste of turkey. He doesn't seem like a fan; he just keeps throwing it on the floor.

Just as we all begin to eat, Jett raises his wine glass. "A toast."

With the fork a few inches from his mouth, Kayne groans. "Really? Every time?"

I nudge him with my foot under the table, reminding him of his manners. Sometimes he forgets. As much as he looks like a well-groomed adult, he can sometimes act like a surly teenager.

"Go ahead," I encourage Jett.

"I'll make this short and sweet." He glares at Kayne. If there weren't children at the table, I know what Kayne's choice response to that look would be. "I just wanted to thank Ellie for this wonderful meal and say I am grateful for all the past holidays we have spent at this table and am looking forward to many more. Cheers."

"Cheers," the rest of us respond.

"See? Short."

"And very sweet," I add.

Kayne snorts. "Wonderful. Can we eat now?"

"By all means, savage." Jett facetiously grants permission.

Kayne scoops an oversized forkful of mashed potatoes into his mouth then smiles condescendingly at Jett. *Boys.*

The rest of dinner sails by with an abundance of laughter and energy. Both children, the stars of the show. Layla sings and plays with her food on Kayne's lap while Becks keeps London busy with smeared mashed potatoes and squished turkey.

"You know what you're eating?" Kayne asks Layla as she pops her peas into her mouth, one by one.

"A pea!" she enthusiastically answers, holding up the little green ball.

"Nuh-uh."

"Uh-huh!" She's adamant.

"Lizard poop," he tells her.

"Ewww!"

"Kayne!" Jett admonishes. "Do you have any idea how long it

took us to get her to eat peas? They're the only vegetable she'll eat!"

"Not anymore." Kayne laughs as Layla pushes her peas around on her plate like they're contaminated with something.

"Are they really lizard poop, Daddy?"

"No, honey. They come out of the pod, remember? Mommy and I showed you. Uncle Kayne is just teasing."

"Oh, yeah! I remember!" Her turquoise eyes shine brightly.

I won't lie and say my heart doesn't melt seeing Kayne with Layla, watching her happily feed him lizard poop and him happily eating it.

London's words haven't stopped ringing in my ears all night. *That man needs a child.*

Deep down—very far down—I know that she's right. I know he wants one desperately. I also know my reservations and fears shouldn't stop us from having a family, but they are.

After dessert is served, the table is cleared, and the children have fallen asleep, London and Jett call it a night. Layla passed out in Kayne's arms while he and Jett watched football on the couch.

I've already started on the dishes when Kayne comes back inside from walking London and Jett out. He wraps his arms around my waist and hugs me affectionately with his chin resting on my shoulder. We stand like that for several minutes as I continually rinse each plate.

"It's quiet now," he states.

"What's quiet?" I ask.

"The house. It's quiet now with everyone gone."

I stop and listen. It definitely is.

"Maybe it's time we fill it up," I say delicately, drying my hands with a dishtowel. I feel Kayne's arms tighten before he spins me around.

"Fill it up?"

"Yeah," I answer coyly. "Maybe it's time we start a family of our own." It's an impulsive decision because that's how I do things, but it feels like the right one.

My heart beats erratically as Kayne just stands there and stares at me. I think I just shocked him. Actually, I know I did.

"Are you being serious?"

"Yes," I answer pointedly. "And a lot of things are going to have to change around here if we have a baby. Our lifestyle, namely."

Kayne grins deviously. "We can cross that bridge when we come to it. Jett and London make it work. We can, too."

They definitely do. If I have learned anything from the two of them, it's that you don't stop being who you are just because you start a family. If anything, you hold on tighter to the person you were, somehow incorporating your old life with your new one.

"How soon can you stop your birth control?" Kayne asks excitedly.

"I'm supposed to go for a shot next month. I can skip it."

"A month, huh?" I can see the wheels turning. "That gives us time to practice."

"Practice for what?"

"Making babies." He grabs my neck and crushes his mouth against mine. The kiss consumes me, stealing my essence right out of me. We kiss and kiss, our tongues tangling as our hands roam all over each other.

"I say we start practicing right now." He grazes his teeth along my neck then bites my earlobe.

"No time like the present." I moan as he caresses me between my legs, over the fabric of my jeans.

"Let's go." He hauls me off the ground, encouraging me to lock my legs around his waist. I grind on his cock the whole way to our room, expecting him to toss me on the bed, but he apparently has other ideas as he walks us into our playroom.

"Take your clothes off," he orders as he drops me in front of the swing. My arousal skyrockets. His dominance will always be my undoing. Kayne watches as I pull each piece of clothing off. My white gauzy shirt, my Capri jeans, and boy short underwear. The ones made entirely of hot pink lace. Almost immediately, I'm completely naked while he is still fully dressed.

He sighs appreciatively as he gropes my breasts, teases my nipples, and consumes my mouth, stretching it wide as he forcefully circles his tongue. I can't help but whimper, knowing full well the assault he's about to launch on my body.

He lifts me into the harness, two thick nylon straps supporting me, one under my butt the other behind my back. On each of the four straps hanging from the ceiling are wrist and ankle cuffs, which Kayne wastes no time buckling me into. Once tethered, he stalks around me, the spider inspecting his spun-up prey. I see the lust illuminating in his eyes as he runs one finger along the inside of my outstretched thighs.

I have no idea what he's planning; the only thing I can be sure of is that this isn't going to be a straight-up fuck. He wants to play. And I'm the toy.

"Comfortable?" He strums my clit.

"I'd be more comfortable with you inside me," I tell him point blank. I want him to fuck me and fuck me right now. Those soft, light caresses are eliciting a slow burn from the inside out.

"Soon enough." He walks away, out of sight. Kayne purposely keeps our treasure chest in a corner of the room I can't see. He likes to surprise me. He likes to be in complete control. And I don't just mean control of my body. He likes to mess with my mind and trifle with my desire. While I hang here helpless, the room suddenly goes black as Kayne ties a silk blindfold around my head. After he tightens it, he murmurs in my ear, "Beautifully bound, exactly how I like you." I feel him tickle the diamond heart hanging on my choker. One of his many symbols of ownership over me. Maybe the most significant.

I then feel him nudge something against my entrance. It's hard and thick and penetrates me fully. With a click, the vibrator hums to life, waking up every single one of my nerve endings. "Oh." I shudder with need, but the soft buzz only teases me. There's not nearly enough vibration to bring me close to the edge.

"Hang around, kitten. I'll be back." There's amusement and excitement in Kayne's voice as I catch the sound of strange clicks in the darkness.

Strapped in the swing, I have no choice but to do as he says while my arousal slowly stifles me like smoke. The light buzz kindling my excitement while suppressing it all at the same time. I fuss helplessly, knowing Kayne will only return when *he's* ready. I try to concentrate on the shower running when I begin to smell a spicy blend of cinnamon, vanilla, and nutmeg in the room. I don't know how long I'm alone, but the wait is excruciating as my need curls around my limbs and weighs me down.

"Miss me, kitten?" Kayne says suddenly.

"Yes," I answer, wanting.

"Yes, what?" He snaps something against my nipple and I flinch.

"Yes, Kayne." I grit my teeth.

"Good girl. Just because we are preparing for things to change doesn't mean they have yet." He flicks my nipple again with what I think is the towel, and it bites me harder this time. "Yes, Kayne!" My voice pitches from the pain.

"Mmm . . . those word from your lips." I feel the straps by my hands strain and the weight of my husband against me. "I'll never get tired of hearing you say them. I'll never get tired of hearing you beg. You will always be mine." He nips at my bottom lip, but that's all I get of him. "I'll never, ever let you go."

"I don't ever want you to let me go," I rasp, feeding off his energy.

"Good." With that, I feel the first burn against my skin, a fiery line across my lower abdomen. I squeal in surprise. Wax, hot wax. That's what the spicy smell was, a burning candle. It cools quickly, hardening on my torso. I only have a second of reprieve before I feel it again. This time the fiery trail moves upwards on my stomach, some drips are bigger than others, but they all light my body on fire the same way. I squirm when he covers one of my nipples, the little nub baking under the heat.

"Oh, god." He does the same to the other breast, the wax dripping down my side, reaching all the way to my back. I'm caught between a constant state of kindle and flame. The vibrator tortures the inside of my body while the hot wax does a number on the outside. I drop my head back as I feel him make his way up my chest and stop just below my necklace.

"Hold still."

I do as he says, on the brink of disarray. A shutter sound, like a camera clicking, flutters through the room. He's documenting this.

"Perfect. You've been a very good girl. Are you ready for me to fuck you?"

"Yes." I pant, my skin inflamed, my body desperate, my pussy aching and soaking wet.

"Yes, what, baby?" Kayne massages my inner thigh.

"Yes, please fuck me. Make me come."

"Oh, I plan to." He spreads my folds wide and pours some wax right onto my swollen, throbbing clit.

"Holy shit!" My head spins and I buck in the swing as the burn of the wax does something inexplicable, makes my arousal magnify and my adrenaline spike almost like a runner's high.

"Shit. Please. Please, I need you," I beg as my climax teeters on a sharpened point.

"Say it again." Kayne rips the vibrator out of my pussy.

"I need you! I need you!" I chant.

"Again!" He slams into me, quelling the ache, feeding the flame.

"I need you!" I shout as our hips clash together over and over, until my muscles tighten and milk his erection for everything it's worth.

"Oh fuck, baby, come," he growls as I soak us both, my climax making a mess on his cock and my inner thighs.

"Fuck!" he hisses as he plows into my pussy, steady and hard, like he's cleaving through a turbulent sea. He doesn't stop thrusting until he's buried so deep, it feels like our orgasms become one.

"Kitten," he rumbles disoriented as he pumps in and out, emptying himself inside me.

Left slack in the swing, Kayne grabs my face and kisses me lethargically until we both come back around.

"How do you feel?" he asks between flicks of his tongue.

"Exceedingly used," I reply honestly, still unable to see him.

Kayne chuckles. "Exactly how you should feel. This is my body and I'll use it however I see fit."

"You never disappoint in that aspect," I say, as he removes my blindfold.

"Did I hurt you?" He searches my eyes.

"Yes."

Kayne frowns. "You didn't use your safe word."

"I didn't want to use my safe word. You like hurting me and I like being hurt."

It's the ugly truth. I am the masochist to his sadist. I crave his pleasure at the same time demanding his pain. We are two misplaced pieces of a puzzle that fit perfectly together. And I wouldn't have it any other way.

Kayne unstraps me from the swing and helps me to stand. My wrists are sore from straining against the restraints, my pussy is tender from the rough fuck, and my skin is prickly from the hot wax.

"Take a shower with me?" I ask Kayne as I nuzzle up against his toned, naked body.

"Do you really need to ask?" He tilts my chin up.

"I wasn't sure if you wanted another one."

"If it's with you, I'd never say no. You should know that by now."

A smile is my only reply. In the bathroom, I inspect his masterpiece in the brighter light. The playroom was dim. I look closely at the way the wax runs along my body, the pattern almost looks like letters. Wait. It *is* letters. K-A-Y-N-E

"Are you serious?" I turn to him.

"What?" He grins, proudly.

"You wrote your name on my body in hot wax?"

He shrugs nonchalantly. "You're mine. Signed, sealed, and delivered."

Hmm . . . where have I heard that before?

All I can do is shake my head and laugh.

Crazy man.

ELLIE

I SPACE OUT AS MY mother chatters away on the other end of the phone. "Tara bought me this adorable pair of earrings. I loved them so much I made her get a pair for you. They're in the mail."

"Thanks, Mom," I half-heartedly respond.

"How's the weather?" She changes the subject for the fourth time, trying to engage me. "It's May and still cold here," she says frustrated.

"Sunny and eighty-five degrees," I inform her.

"I'm so jealous. I'm ready for some tropical climate. I keep trying to convince your father it's time to move."

I scoff to myself. "You know that man will never leave New York."

"I know." I can almost see her pout. "At least we get to visit soon. I can't wait to see you."

My parents make a trip out to Hawaii at least twice a year. I love it when they visit. My family is the one piece of my nearly perfect life that's missing.

"I can't wait to see you, too," I respond sullenly.

"Oh, honey. Try not to think about so much." Her voice softens. "It will happen when it's supposed to."

"If you say so."

"I do." She's resolute. "Dad wants to say hi. I love you."

"Love you too, Mom."

"How's my girl?" My father asks the same question in the same parental tone every time I speak to him.

"Fine, Dad."

"Mmm hmm. How's that husband of yours treating you?"

"Like a princess."

"He better be. Don't want to have to come out there and crack any skulls."

"Dad . . ." I actually chuckle. You know that old saying girls marry their fathers? I think it's true. A possessive, overprotective man raised me, and then I went and married one. Thankfully, as much as they are alike, my father and Kayne have a wonderful relationship.

"Miss you, sweetheart. I can't wait to see you."

"Me, too," I reply, trying to mask my blue mood.

I hang up with my parents and go back to staring at the picture on my computer screen. I've been looking at it most of the morning. A survivor and her five-year-old son standing on the Great Wall of China smiling brightly. It was accompanied by a thank-you letter I received in my inbox.

Dear Mrs. Stevens,

I can never say thank you enough for the generosity of your organization. I never dreamed I would leave the country, let alone get to experience another culture in such an unbelievable way. Hope and happiness are sometimes hard to come by, but you have given me both.

Sincerely,

Stacy

I usually love receiving letters like this. Hope and happiness, that's exactly what I want to provide. I receive so many requests, so many stories of pain and brutality, of people looking for an escape or distraction from their experiences, even if just temporarily. But seeing her hold her child in her arms does nothing but make me sad.

Kayne and I have been trying to conceive for over six months and nothing; not even a late period.

I inspect every feature of the little boy's face—shaggy brown hair, big blue eyes, and olive skin. But it's his smile that destroys me the most. He isn't looking at the camera; he's looking at his mother. Sometimes I wonder if I am being punished for not wanting to have children in the first place, and now that I do, more than anything, I feel like a failure as a woman. Like I'm incapable of doing the one thing a female is meant to do. Give her husband a child.

"Ellie?" I hear Kayne before I see him and discreetly wipe away the moisture in my eyes.

"Yeah?" I attempt to sound upbeat as he leans on the doorframe of my office.

"You ready to go?"

"I see you are." He's dressed in his black fatigues and gun holster, looking undeniably hot. My stomach flutters as I think back to the other night and how he arrested me for indecent exposure. What that man can do with handcuffs and a nightstick should be illegal.

I close my laptop and stand up, knowing I need either a cold shower or a firm fucking. Both of which will have to wait. Kayne is leaving on an overnight training exercise and dropping me off to stay with London while he and Jett are gone.

Grabbing my packed bag by the front door, I hop into our souped-up Jeep as Kayne locks up the house.

My mind wanders as we drive past all the beautifully manicured homes in the neighborhood. All pristine and vibrantly green.

"Are you and London going to behave tonight?" Kayne asks, squeezing my knee playfully.

"I can't promise anything. We get lonely when you and Jett are gone."

"I bet." He smiles salaciously, no doubt picturing us together.

"Still, you better behave."

"I don't think you have anything to worry about. I foresee a G-rated evening of nail painting, *Frozen,* and pizza."

Kayne shakes his head, his dark sunglasses concealing his eyes. "Poor Becks."

"He's a man, he'll sleep through most of it," I assure him.

Jett, London, and both children are outside on the expansive front lawn when we arrive. On cue, Layla darts across the grass to Kayne while London and Jett sit with a sleeping Beckett on a blanket.

"See, I told you." I nudge Kayne as we walk up. "Sleeping already."

He chuckles while throwing Layla around. "Higher, peanut butter!" she squeals, and Kayne obliges.

"What did you do?" I sit down next to London and grab a strand of her hair. She makes a face like she's not sure how she feels about the chop job.

"You like it?" she asks unsurely.

"I love it." Her long purplish red hair is now a shoulder-length bob.

"I feel like I needed to simplify my life."

"So you cut off all your hair?"

"It was a start. You'll understand when you have kids."

I drop my eyes. "If I ever I have kids," I mutter to myself.

London puts her hand over mine. It's her discreet understanding gesture.

"Okay! Time to go!" Jett stands up at a breakneck speed and snatches Layla right out of the air before she drops back into Kayne's hands.

"Daddy!" She giggles happily, and it tickles all of our hearts.

"Do you have to go?" She hugs him.

"It's only for one night," he assures her, their blond hair the exact same color in the sun. "And when I get back, we can go swimming in the ocean," Jett promises her.

"With swimmies," Layla says seriously. No messing around.

"Maybe without swimmies?" he tests the waters.

"Definitely swimmies. Mommy says I need swimmies until I can hold my breath under the water."

"You hold your breath under water when you're in the tub. Why can't you do it in the ocean?"

"There are no waves or fish in the tub!"

"Oh, is that the difference?"

"Yes!" Layla confirms, like *duh!*

"Okay then." He chuckles, placing Layla on the ground. "Be good for Mommy and Aunt Ellie."

"And be a good big sister to Beckett," she adds cheerfully.

"Yes," Jett agrees while kissing her little forehead. I dissolve.

London and I both stand up and say good-bye to our men.

Once out of ear shot, London purrs so only I can hear. "I hate it when they leave, but god I love to watch them walk away," she says as Kayne and Jett stride to the Jeep, muscled backs and tight asses on display.

I elbow her lightheartedly but can't dispute her claim; their butts do look great in those pants.

LONDON AND I BOTH COLLAPSE on the bed.

"Where do you and Jett find the energy to do anything else besides run after those kids?"

"The part-time nanny is our lifesaver. She'll be here bright and early tomorrow morning so I can actually sleep."

We had one crazy night keeping those children occupied, out of trouble, clean, and fed. Now that Beckett is running around, he never stops moving and gets into everything. I turned my back for one second and he had unraveled an entire roll of toilet paper into the toilet. Luckily, we caught him before he flushed. I left London to clean up the aftermath of that one.

"Are you sure you like my hair?" London asks self-consciously.

"Of course, I do." I twirl a strand around my finger. "You could shave your head and still look like a supermodel. I hate you for that."

"Stop." She taps me lightly. "I do not look like a supermodel."

"Sure." I close my eyes and smile. "Keep telling yourself that."

"Whatever." She brushes me off. "Wanna send a picture of us sleeping together to Kayne and Jett?"

I grin. "Yes."

London grabs her phone off the nightstand and shimmies up next to me.

"Okay, close your eyes." She positions the lens above us, rests her head on mine and then clicks away.

"Perfect." She picks out the best picture and then hits send with the caption:

London: Bedtime is no fun without you.

Her phone dings a few seconds later.

Jett: We'll bring the fun tomorrow night. Behave.

London: Behave? Now there's definitely no fun in that.

Jett: Send me a pic of your tits.

London and I both crack up. Men and their one-track minds. We pull our shirts up and send the boys more sinful selfies. Us kissing, touching, fingering, coming. That should hold all four of us over until tomorrow.

When we finally do go to sleep, I realize this has been the first night in a long while I haven't pined over what I don't have and appreciate what I do.

I WAKE UP WITH A sharp pain in my abdomen. "Oh." I roll over and try to breathe.

"London?" I shake her awake. "London."

"Mmm?"

"Ouch!"

"Ellie?" She opens her eyes.

"Something's happening."

"Something like what?" She sits up and throws the covers off us then gasps. "Ellie, did you get your period?"

"I just had it." I look down at the blood staining my inner thighs and the sheets. "Oh!" Another stabbing pain immobilizes me.

"Okay. Come on, up." She scoots out of bed. "We're going to the hospital."

"Hospital?"

"Yes." She rushes around her bedroom, putting on clothes and pulling her hair into a low ponytail. "Go wash off. Where's your over-night bag?"

"Downstairs," I tell her as I slide carefully off the bed.

"I'll grab you a change a clothes and check on the kids. Then straight to the ER."

"Do you think that's necessary?" I ask and she creases her eyebrows.

"Absolutely. I'm not letting anything happen to you on my watch. Better safe than having to deal with the wrath of Kayne."

She has a point there.

"Okay." I walk slowly into the bathroom and turn on the shower. My stomach constantly tortured with cramps. As I wash away the blood, I worry what besides my period would make me feel this way. Vaginal cancer is the only thing that comes to mind. The thought terrifies me. My mother's sister was diagnosed at the ripe old age of thirty-five. The disease runs in my family. I dry off frantically and find my clothes on the stripped bed in London and Jett's room. Thankfully, the blood didn't stain the mattress. By the time I make it downstairs, London has the car keys in her hand and is kissing Layla and Beckett good-bye.

The ride to the hospital is tense and quiet. London holds my hand the whole way, while every bump jolts my fragile insides.

The ER is relatively quiet for a Saturday morning. Only one other person is in the waiting room.

"Please fill this out." The nurse behind the counter hands me a clipboard. I sit with London and fill out the paperwork in a fog.

"Do you want me to call Kayne?" London asks as I return to the clipboard to the receptionist.

"No." I curl into a ball next to her. "Let's just see what the doctor has to say." Although I'm pretty sure I might already know the answer. Maybe that's why I can't get pregnant? I'm sick.

"Ellie Stevens." A male nurse calls my name. London and I follow him through the door, past several pulled curtains, until we come to an empty alcove with a bed and strange machines. It reminds me of when I was in the hospital after I was shot. I shiver. I haven't been back to one in almost five years, and I was hoping the next time I did visit, it would be under happier circumstances.

"Okay." The young male nurse with light-brown hair and eyes looks over my information. "I see you've had some cramping and bleeding?"

"Yes."

"Any chance you could be pregnant?"

"No. I just had my period last week."

"Okay. And I see you have a family history of vaginal cancer."

I nod, close to bursting into tears.

"Well, I'm going to check your vitals, take some blood, and then the doctor will be in to see you."

I nod again, incapable of speaking.

"I'm John, by the way," he says kindly as he checks my pulse and takes my blood pressure.

"Nice to meet you," I reply softly, sinking into myself.

When he draws my blood, I wince and look away, concentrating on the small television in the upper left-hand corner of the room.

"All right." He picks up a tray with several vials of my blood. "I'll go get these to the lab and the doctor should be here shortly. It's not too busy this morning. For once." He smiles then walks off.

I once again curl up into a ball on the thin mattress and stare off into space. The cramps haven't subsided and there is a constant throbbing in my lower abdomen.

"How about some trashy TV?" London turns up the volume and scoots her chair closer to the bed. "I never got to watch television growing up. It was always piano lessons or French tutors or studying. It was such a sheltered existence," she reminisces.

She has told me this before, but it doesn't sound like she was sheltered; it sounds more like she's cultured and worldly.

"The only words I know in French are ménage à trois." I try to joke, but when I giggle, my sensitive muscles contract painfully.

"Those are really the only important ones," she jests.

London strokes my hair as I lay on my side miserably, watching trashy reality TV. I don't know how long we wait, but another episode of the same show comes on.

"Ellie Stevens?" An older man in a white coat announces my name.

"Yes, that me." I turn onto my back. He looks at me as if he recognizes me.

"I'm Doctor Holiday." He introduces himself as John rolls in a machine behind him. "We never formally met, but I'm the doctor who performed your surgery the night you were shot."

"Oh, yes. I remember hearing your name." I struggle to sit up.

"It's good to see you doing well." He smiles as he pulls up a chair next to me.

"I think that is yet to be determined."

Doctor Holiday grins slightly as he pulls up my shirt. "How's your fiancé?"

I look at him thrown. "He's my husband now. You know him?"

"We met briefly. Quite the intense individual."

London snickers. "That's one way to describe him."

Doctor Holiday pushes on my abdomen. "Any pain?"

"A little." I wince.

"Still bleeding?"

"No, I don't think so."

"Good." He takes a seat in the chair and plays with the knobs on the machine John rolled in. "When was the last time you had your period?"

"Last week."

"And everything seemed normal? Normal blood flow?"

I take a moment to think back. "Actually, it was lighter than usual, and it only lasted two days."

"Mmm hmm. A little warm." He squirts some jelly on my lower stomach. My heart starts to palpitate.

A few seconds later, a new nurse comes in with a folder. "Labs," she announces as she hands it to John.

"I think I already know what it's going to say." Doctor Holiday puts the wand of the machine against my belly and swirls it around. There's nothing at first, but then we hear it. A strange, underwater thumping sound.

"Oh, my god!" London slaps her hand over her mouth.

"Just as I suspected. John, can you confirm?"

John flips open the folder. "Yup. Positive."

"Positive for what?" I ask, behind the curve.

"Congratulations, Mrs. Stevens, you're pregnant. That's your baby's heartbeat you're hearing."

"What?" I repeat again in utter shock.

"Ellie, you're pregnant!" London erupts.

"But what about the bleeding? And my period?"

"That wasn't your period," Dr. Holiday explains. "You were

spotting. It's normal, and the cramping is probably just from the implantation of the fertilized egg in the lining of your uterus. My advice is make an appointment with your OB as soon as possible and try to eliminate stress during your first trimester."

The information is a little slow to sink in.

"I'm really pregnant?"

"You heard it here first," the mild-mannered doctor beams.

"Can I hear it one more time? Just for a second?"

The doctor glances back and forth between John and London. "Sure. Why not."

"Give me my purse." I motion to London. She hands it to me and I pull out my phone.

"Okay."

Dr. Holiday puts the wand back on my stomach and the fast-paced underwater sound fills the tiny room once again, and I cry.

ELLIE

"HOW ARE YOU GOING TO tell Kayne?" London asks ecstatically as I wipe the jelly off my stomach and pull down my shirt.

"I have no idea." My voice is shaky from the shock. I'm not sure I even believe it yet.

I'm actually pregnant.

"I want another one," London abruptly discloses.

"Another one?"

"Yes, just one more."

"Think Jett will go for it?"

She nods. "I've always wanted a big family. He knows that. And maybe if we hurry we can be pregnant together."

"Oh, Jesus," I laugh loudly. "Could you imagine the hormones?"

"I can imagine holding two little ones at the same time." She's practically burning up with baby fever.

"You better be careful what you wish for. You might end up with twins."

London shrugs. "So be it."

"You're cra-" the chiming on the television catches my attention.

"WE INTERRUPT THIS PROGRAM WITH A SPECIAL REPORT," the newscaster announces. "EARLIER TODAY, OFFICIALS RECEIVED A TIP THAT TWO MISSING BOYS, JAMES ANTHONY AND RODNEY O'CONNELL, WERE BEING HELD IN A REMOTE HOME ON THE NORTH SIDE OF OAHU. THE TWO BOYS WERE REPORTED MISSING LAST THURSDAY AFTER NOT RETURNING HOME FROM A LATE SOCCER PRACTICE. THE OWNER OF THE HOME AND SUSPECTED CAPTOR IS CHARLES TINLEY. TINLEY, A REGISTERED SEX OFFENDER, WAS THE PRIME SUSPECT IN THE DISAPPEARANCE OF THIRTEEN-YEAR-OLD JUSTIN COPELAND SEVERAL YEARS AGO, BUT NO CHARGES WERE EVER FILED. TINLEY ALSO HAS A HISTORY OF MENTAL ILLNESS AND HAS BEEN CALLED 'A THREAT TO HIMSELF AND TO OTHERS WHEN NOT TAKING HIS

MEDICATION.'"

London turns up the volume as we listen more intently to the young, pretty newscaster speak. She's one of the anchors on the morning news show Kayne and I sometimes watch.

"Early this morning, a hiker heard screaming in the woods close to his campsite. Richard Price followed the sounds until he came upon Tinley's residence. There, he saw Tinley torturing one of the boys with a lit cigarette while tied to a tree. Price immediately called authorities. When he confronted Tinley, Tinley pulled out a knife and retreated into the house. Price managed to get Rodney O'Connell free, but was informed that James Anthony was still inside the residence. Once officials arrived on the scene, Tinley fired several warning shots at the officers with a shotgun. When officials gave Tinley the option to surrender, he informed the officers he was 'in possession of explosives and would blow him and the boy up if they didn't leave.'

Due to the nature and severity of the situation, Honolulu SWAT was dispatched and has now taken control of the scene."

That's when my stomach drops. The camera flashes to a live feed of the house, surrounded by a dozen and a half men dressed in black body armor. Some holding machine guns; some holding protective shields. The image is too far away to see any facial features, but both London and I know Kayne and Jett are somewhere in the mix of the Special Weapons and Tactics Team. All we can do is watch as the men carry out what they were trained to do—defuse violent situations. We sit in a frozen state as the team surrounds the tiny rundown house while too many antagonistic words play on repeat in my mind—*a history of mental illness, a threat to him and others, explosives.*

The men just hold their ground, while London and I hold our breath. What are they waiting for? I lived through the raid at Mansion, and Kayne had told me the story of my attempted extraction when Michael kidnapped me, but I have never really seen him in action, so to speak. Never witnessed firsthand how he puts his life on the line until now—*a history of mental illness, a threat to him and others, explosives.*

My lungs cycle oxygen sluggishly as the men descend on the house, kicking the door down and crashing through windows. But nothing prepares me for what happens next.

BOOM.

"IT IS REPORTED SEVERAL OFFICERS HAVE SUSTAINED LIFE-THREATENING INJURIES."

It feels like that sentence is stuck on repeat.

"It is reported several officers have sustained life-threatening injuries."

"It is reported several officers have sustained life-threatening injuries."

But they don't say which officers. We can't even see their faces as they're dragged from the wreckage. What remains of the house is nothing more than a pile of destroyed wood. It's been almost seventeen minutes since the bomb exploded.

"CHARLES TINLEY IS REPORTED DEAD."

Is it wrong to be thankful of that and still be resentful because he hurt people in the process? Possibly hurt my husband or one of my best friends?

I feel sick. Like I want to throw up. Neither Kayne nor Jett are answering their cell phones, which only makes my rampant thoughts run wilder.

I compulsively twist my wedding ring around my finger. A white gold band with pink diamonds and the words, 'Ruined By Him' etched on the inside.

Kayne has a similar engraving on his, 'Owned By Her.'

He surprised me with the inscriptions during the ceremony. I could barely hold it together as it was—then he showed me his little surprise, and it sent me right over the edge. That moment was perfect and beautiful and magical, and I know it can never be emulated again. Our wedding was a one-of-a-kind day; the same way my husband is a one-of-a-kind man. Anomalous. Unique. Irreplaceable.

The one person I could never live without.

"It is reported several officers have sustained life-threatening injuries."

The emergency room is in an uproar, no doubt preparing for the mass injuries about to barrel through the door. One of them possibly my husband. I clutch my stomach instinctively. This is supposed to be a happy day.

When the first gurney carrying a hurt officer rolls by my patient room, I lose the battle with my nausea and puke in the biohazard bag. My nerves just can't take this.

"Ellie." London holds my hair until the contents of my stomach are empty.

"I feel the same way," she tells me as I dry heave.

"Ugh. Yuck." I wipe my mouth.

"I know." She moves me back to the bed and digs around in her purse.

"Here." She pulls out a juice box.

I just stare at it. "Seriously?"

"Yes, seriously. I'm a mom. I come prepared. You'll be the same way, carrying around a bag of tricks." She rips off the little plastic straw, unwraps it, then stabs it in the hole.

"Thank you." I accept the purple and red box from her, take a sip, and swish the apple-flavored liquid around in an attempt to get rid of the nasty taste in my mouth.

That's when I hear a very distinct voice barking outside the little room. Both London and I barrel out of the alcove to find Kayne towering over my nurse, John. There's soot smeared on his face and dirt covering his clothes, but that seems to be the extent of his injuries. Unless you count self-induced hypertension. He's pissed.

"Kayne?" He glances over when he hears his name.

"Ellie?" I nearly knock him over when he looks directly at me.

"Where's Jett?" London asks frantically.

"In there." He tries to point to a room similar to mine, while I climb all over him.

"Baby, what are you doing here?"

I ignore his question. "Are you okay?" And instead ask my own. "I saw everything, the news report, the explosion . . ." My voice quivers. "They kept saying officers had life-threatening injuries but didn't say which ones."

My eyes tear as I cling to his shirt. If you think being married to a Dom is difficult, try being married to an ex black operative who is now part of an elite SWAT unit.

I would take the Dom any day.

"Shh, Ellie, I'm okay. Everything is okay." He runs his hand through my hair. That should soothe me, make me feel comforted, but it somehow has the opposite effect.

"You scared the shit out of me!" I lash out, slamming both fists on his chest. "I thought you were hurt!" I hit him again, crying. "Or worse!" The third time he grabs my wrists before impact.

"Whoa, killer. I'm fine. There's no need to beat me up," he says humorously, before his facial expression changes. "How did you know I would be here? Did someone call you?"

"No."

"London, then?"

"No. We were actually already here," I confess, sniffling.

"What?" His grasp tightens. "Why?"

Oh shit, this is not the way I envisioned telling Kayne he's going to be a daddy. Right after an explosion with a death grip around my wrists.

"I woke up bleeding this morning," I divulge.

"What? Where?" There's a mix of fear and anger in his eyes.

"Between my legs," I admit softly, so only he can hear.

"And you didn't think to call and tell me?"

"London rushed me to the hospital. I didn't want to worry you while you were away." Although, selfishly, in hindsight, I wish I had. That way he wouldn't have been anywhere near a crazy man with explosives.

"So what's wrong?" he asks concerned.

"Nothing," I tell him truthfully.

"Ellie," he says strictly. Like, *don't fuck around with me* strict.

"I'm pregnant." I rush the words out. They're amazing to say.

"What?" It looks like I just slapped him.

I nod. My angry tears turning into joyful ones.

"Honest to god?"

I nod more fervently, unable to speak from the overwhelming happiness.

"Holy shit!" He hauls me into his arms and plants an exaggerated kiss right on my lips. I wrap my legs around him and squeeze with every ounce of strength I have.

"But wait." He pulls away. "Why were you bleeding? Is something wrong?"

"No. The doctor says it's normal in the first trimester. I just have to keep my stress level low. Which has been a bit difficult this morning."

"I'm sorry. I didn't mean to scare you. I should have called and told you I was all right, except Jett got hit with some shrapnel and I needed to make sure he was okay."

"Is he?"

"As far as I know, it grazed under his eye. That part of the skin bleeds profusely. I think it looks worse than it is."

"Is that why you were yelling at the nurse? To get someone to check on him?"

"Of course."

"Were you inside the house when the bomb went off?" I ask meekly, unsure if I want to know the answer.

"No. Several of us had gone around back to extract the other boy. He was in bad shape. Beaten up, starved, and severely dehydrated. Once he was out, that's when the other team went in. Jett wasn't wearing his protective eyewear and caught some flying debris."

"Are the boys going to be okay?"

"I think so, but from what I understand, they were abused in more ways than one. We might want to send them a business card sometime down the line."

"Oh, no." I frown, a mash up of emotions hitting me.

"Tinley has a rap sheet a mile long, and most of it is child abuse."

"Disgusting monster."

"I couldn't have said it better myself."

"I'm just glad you're okay." I rest my head on his shoulder.

"I'm fine." He hugs me. "It's going to take more than a pipe bomb to get rid of me."

"I don't want to get rid of you. Ever."

"You say that now." He chuckles.

"I'll say that always." I close my eyes, suddenly exhausted. "Can we go home?

"Sure, kitten. We can take a nap right after you lick me clean." He nuzzles my neck.

I giggle. "Insatiable."

"It's who I am. *Love me or leave me.*"

"I choose *love you.*"

"I can only hope."

I roll my eyes, faithless man. "I need to grab my purse before we leave. Do you need to say good-bye to Jett?"

"Nah." Kayne starts walking in the direction London and I bombarded him from. "London is with him. I'll check in on him later."

I direct Kayne into the small space I spent most of the morning in. He sets me on the ground and I grab my bag.

"Wait." I stop him as he takes my hand to leave. "I didn't exactly tell you I was pregnant the way I wanted to. Or hoped to. Can we sit for a second?"

"Sure." Kayne looks confused but takes a seat on the bed anyway. I yank the curtain closed for privacy then crawl onto the mattress next to him. I pull out my phone and hand it to him.

"Am I supposed to call the baby?" he asks, even more perplexed.

"No." I laugh as I swipe the screen and hit an app. "Just press play."

He does, and a second later, that quickly pounding underwater sound pulsates through the air.

His eyebrows crease before understanding hits.

"Is that . . . ?" He brings the phone closer to his ear.

"The baby's heartbeat. I wanted you to hear it when I told you."

Kayne just sits there spellbound, listening to the rhythmic sound. "It's the most amazing thing I have ever heard." His voice is breathy and his eyes are glassy.

I snuggle up against him. "I think so, too."

ELLIE

KAYNE STARES SILENTLY OUT THE living room window.

That's his position of choice these days. Leaning against the glass, ominously quiet, lost in his own head.

I'm six months today; my belly has finally popped and I have given up trying to squeeze into any of my pre-pregnancy pants. Maternity it is from here on out. I wish not fitting into my clothes was my biggest problem. Kayne had been over the moon about being a father up until about a month ago; when we went for my twenty-week ultrasound and found out we were having a boy. When, for the first time, we were able to see our baby's little feet and hands and face in a 3D picture. Everything changed after that. He retreated into himself. I know my husband, and beneath that cocky, *I'll break you in half* exterior is a high-strung, excitable man who needs to exercise restraint when it comes to his emotions. They can become a Molotov cocktail if he's not careful. Believe me, I know; I've been in the direct line of fire when he flies out of control.

Kayne walks a fine line every day, and lately that line seems to be getting narrower and narrower. It doesn't take a rocket scientist to know what he's thinking about. *Her,* his mother, his childhood, and all the shitty things that happened to him while growing up. I'm beginning to worry that starting a family is going to have a negative effect on him. That instead of completing us, it's going to tear us apart. I know I had reservations in the beginning, and I know I'll always worry, but what really scares me is the thought of raising this child alone.

"Hey." I speak to Kayne's back.

"What's up, kitten?" His reply is flat.

"I think we need to talk."

"Oh yeah, 'bout what?"

"What's bothering you."

"Nothing is bothering me," he fires back.

"We both know that's not true."

"I'm fine, Ellie."

"No, you're not. You barely sleep, you barely eat, and you haven't touched me in almost a month."

"Is that what this is about? You're horny?"

"No. That's not what this is about. It's about you and your issues."

"I have issues?"

"Lately, you do."

"The only issue I have is you accusing me of having issues." He's being obtuse and pissing me off.

"Kayne. In three months, we are bringing a child into this world. I want him to know his real father, not this watered-down version who can't even look at me."

"Are you saying I'm not the real father?"

I sigh exaggeratedly. "I'm saying you're an asshole who won't face what's bothering him."

Kayne finally turns around, anger burning in his eyes. Good. Finally, a reaction other than just aloof.

"Did you just call me an asshole?"

"I did. Do want me to repeat myself so you can hear it again?"

"That isn't a very nice thing to say."

"Well, I had to get your attention somehow."

"You have it. What do you want to talk about, Ellie?" His tone is menacing.

"What's bothering you."

"I told you, nothing is bothering me."

"I call bullshit. Your mother is bothering you. Your past is bothering you. Becoming a father is bothering you."

"Becoming a father isn't bothering me."

"But thoughts of your mother are?"

Kayne remains quiet.

"Maybe it's time you found out what happened to her," I suggest.

"Maybe not," he seethes. I know this is a gaping wound for Kayne, a painful buckshot right to the gut. But he has to face it and now is the time.

"I can't keep living like this. I need my husband back. I feel alone and scared and I don't want to do this by myself."

His expression softens but not enough to give me hope.

"I can't, Ellie."

"You have to," I push.

"I don't have to do anything," he argues.

"Yes, you do! For me! For our child!"

"Let me remind you of something, kitten," he snaps and I jump. "*I* own *you,* so that means *I* tell *you* what to do, not the other way around. And if I say no, it's no!"

"Kayne!"

"Enough!" he shouts at me. "Go find a corner to curl up in and leave me alone!"

"You condescending cocksucker!" I hiss. Outraged, I pick up the remote control off the coffee table and hurl it at him as hard as I can, missing his head by a half inch. It smashes into the window behind him, creating a starburst crack.

"What the fuck, Ellie!"

"I'll do better than find a corner. I'll find a new place to live!" I storm out of the living room crying, snatch my keys off the kitchen counter, and slam the front door behind me.

I DROVE AROUND FOR HOURS, knowing without fail I would end up here.

I ring the doorbell and London answers moments later.

"Hey." She hugs me.

"Expecting me?"

She nods. "Kayne was here a little while ago looking for you. He said you had an argument."

"Argument is an understatement. I cracked one of the windows in the living room."

"One of the big ones?" Her eyes widen.

"Yup," I confirm.

"Did you try and put his head through it?"

I laugh. It feels cathartic. "I threw the remote at him and missed. Let's hope this baby doesn't inherit my accuracy." I put my hands on my protruding stomach. "Is Jett around? I need to talk to him."

"Upstairs. He just finished giving Becks a bath. Somehow, he got into the pantry, climbed on the shelf, and opened the peanut butter jar. The kicker, instead of eating it, he decided to rub it all over his body and the kitchen walls."

"No." I gasp.

"Yes." She sighs exasperated.

"And you want another one?"

"If I change my mind, it's too late now."

I stare at her funny. "Are you . . . ?"

London nods precariously.

"Oh!" I hug her. "You're insane and a little bit my hero."

"Mommy?" Becks calls for London from the top of the stairs.

"Here, baby." He walks down all clean. Blond hair blow-dried and blue eyes mischievous.

London lifts him into her arms. "Mommy has a baby in her belly," he tells me in his sweet little raspy voice.

"I heard." I smile at the gorgeous little boy.

"And let's hope he or she only looks like you." London touches her forehead to his. Becks chortles spiritedly, like he understands his mother's joke. "Go on upstairs, Ellie. I need to give this little rascal some dinner."

"Okay." I walk up the stairs while London carries Becks into the kitchen. I love London and Jett's house. It is so warm and full of love with pictures of them and the children everywhere. My favorites are the artistic shots in black and white. London loves photography and is extremely talented with a camera. I've already recruited her to take the baby's first newborn shots.

Upstairs, I find Jett rinsing out the tub.

"A father's work is never done," I quip as I lean against the doorframe.

"Nope. And I wouldn't have it any other way." He flashes a smile at me, the front of his shirt soaking wet.

"I hear congratulations are in order, *again,*" I say cheerfully.

He grins brightly, confirming the news. "Yes, they are."

"You're going to have a baseball team by the time London is done with you."

"If that's what she wants." He dries his hands off and comes to stand in front of me. "How are you doing, sweet thing?"

"I want to kill my husband," I reply half-serious, half-sardonically. "You have some peanut butter . . ." I point to his hair.

"Yeah, we've all been there." He rakes his fingers through the front of his blond strands, removing the clump of peanut butter. "Little bugger," he muses.

"Who? Kayne or Beckett?

"Both," he shoots back.

I can't stop myself from laughing.

Jett washes off his hands, tickled. He is the most laid-back father.

Nothing seems to rattle him, even Becks' most outlandish antics. When he's finished drying them, he puts his arm around me and walks me down the hall to his office. "Let's talk."

I take a seat on the cozy loveseat across from his desk. He always jokes he bought the piece of furniture for his therapy sessions. Right now, it's coming in handy.

"I heard Kayne was here," I say.

"Yup. Looking for his lost kitten."

"Not lost, runaway. There's a difference."

"Yes, there is," Jett agrees. "What was the fight about? Had to be pretty bad if you left."

I groan. I'm irritable, frustrated, and utterly exhausted. "He's been distant. Barely talks or eats or sleeps."

"How long has this been going on?"

"About a month. Ever since we went for my twenty-week exam."

"I see," Jett ponders.

"When I finally confronted him today, everything just blew up." I make an explosion gesture with my hands.

"He was pretty upset you left. Probably has half the SWAT team out looking for you right now."

"Good, let them look. Serves him right for dismissing me into a corner like I really am a naughty cat."

"He didn't." Jett's eyes widen.

"Oh, he did. That's when I threw the remote at him and stormed out."

"Did you hit him?" Jett asks overly interested.

I shake my head.

"Too bad. I would have loved to see your throwing arm." He chuckles.

"It's not as impressive as you may think."

"So what do you think his issue is?"

"The same issue that has been bothering him his whole life."

"His mom." Jett provides the obvious answer.

I nod, sadly. "I just think he needs to face it. And he won't listen to me. He just pushes me away. I know the baby is affecting him. He was so excited to be a father, and now, he's just completely different. He's shutting us out, and it's terrifying me."

"Ellie, listen." Jett takes a seat on the couch and wraps one arm around me. "First, I want to be clear. Kayne will never abandon you. And if the thought even crosses his mind, I'll kill him, and I'll make sure it hurts. Second, you'll never be alone. No matter what happens, you have me and London and we love you like family."

"Thank you." I rest my head on his shoulder. "That's very reassuring, but I'm not worried about me. I want our child to know his father. Know the person I know. I really think you need to talk to him. Convince him that he needs to find out what happened and put the past to rest. It's the only way he's going to move on."

Jett stiffens before he lets out a huge sigh. "Ellie, I think there's something I need to tell you, and I think now is definitely the time."

I look up at him warily. "What?"

Jett gets up from the couch and walks around his desk. He opens a drawer, pulls out a folder, and drops it on the desktop.

"What's that?"

"The smoking gun."

"Huh?"

"It's a copy of Kayne's caseworker's file. The one who was assigned to him when his mother was trying to regain custody."

"What?!" I fly to my feet.

"How long have you had this?" I snatch the folder up and open it. The contents contain a bunch of papers and a picture of a seven-year-old Kayne sad enough to break your heart into a million pieces.

"Since right before we went undercover together."

"What." You could knock me over with a feather right now. "That's like . . ." if my math is right, "over ten years."

Jett confirms with a reluctant nod. "I had to be prepared in case of any surprises. So I looked into what happened to her."

"And . . . ? What happened?" I flip through the file looking for answers. "Where is she?"

Jett's expression just gets bleaker. "She's dead, Ellie. She died shortly after Kayne met her for the first time."

"No." My chest tightens.

"I'm sorry."

"How?"

"A car accident."

"No, I mean how does Kayne not know this? He was in the system. He had a caseworker. Wasn't it their responsibility to tell him?" I ask irate.

"I have a theory about that."

"A theory?" I huff.

"Yes. At the same time Kayne's mom was working to gain back custody from the state, Kayne was living with two of the most abhorrent foster parents in Motor City. It doesn't say this in the file, but I believe what happened was when the social worker showed up unannounced to deliver the news, she caught the couple abusing Kayne. It says she 'found him locked in a small broom closet, dirty and naked and smelling like urine.'"

"Oh, god." My stomach turns. Animals.

"I believe, since it doesn't say much after that account, the social worker didn't want to traumatize Kayne further. So when she removed him from the home, she didn't tell him about his mother."

"Okay, well, she should have told him eventually, no?"

"Yes, I'm sure, but researching further, I came across the elderly woman's death certificate. In an unforeseen twist of fate, she apparently died of a heart attack three days after she removed Kayne from the household."

"You're shitting me."

"I could not make this stuff up."

"So your theory?"

"She never got a chance to tell Kayne that his mother didn't up and abandon him, and his next caseworker was unaware he didn't know or didn't bother to tell him. Either way, the information slipped through the cracks."

"That's almost too impossible to believe."

"Crazier things have happened. A woman once gave the man who kidnapped her, lied to her, and forced her to submit a second chance, and now she's having his baby."

I squint petulantly at Jett. We are not talking about me and my questionable decisions.

"We need to tell him. We need to just bite the bullet, tell him, and hope we survive the wrath of Kayne." I pace the room.

"Hold that thought." Jett pulls his phone out from his back pocket and glances at the screen. "That wrath may come sooner than you think," he informs me before he answers it. "Hey, man. Yeah," he looks directly at me, "she's here."

Oh, shit.

"Okay . . . see you in a few." He hangs up. "You're done blowing in the wind."

"Apparently. You just gave me up."

"We have like seven seconds before he gets here."

"Should we take cover?"

The doorbell rings.

Too late.

"At least he's using his manners and didn't break down the door," Jett points out.

"He probably just doesn't want to pay for another home repair."

"Ellie!" Kayne's voice blasts through the house.

"Up here!" Jett yells back.

Moments later, Kayne appears in the doorway. He's wearing loose jeans and a fitted blue t-shirt. His hair is a mess—my guess from trying to pull it out—and there's a hollow look in his eyes.

"Let's go." He tries to grab my arm, but I step back.

"No." I see the devastation on his face, but we have to do this. We have to address the albatross in Kayne's life.

"Ellie, now." His tone becomes stricter, desperate almost.

"We need to talk." I hold my ground.

"No, we don't."

"Yes. We do." I'm adamant.

"Maybe you should listen to her," Jett interjects.

"Maybe you should mind your own fucking business. She's *my* wife—"

"Yes, I know," Jett cuts him off sharply. "You love to remind everyone of that. Maybe you should remind yourself why you married her. Wait. I'll do it for you. Because she has your best interests at heart and only wants what's best for you. *For you* and *your* child."

Kayne immediately clams up. I know he wants to argue with Jett, wants to tell him to fuck off and drag me out of the house, but he's exercising his restraint. He may be excitable, but he's not stupid.

"Sit." I gesture with my head to the couch. "Jett has something he needs to tell you."

"I'd rather stand."

"For fuck's sake! Can you not be difficult for one minute today!?" I erupt and the baby kicks me. "Oh!" I double over.

"Ellie?" Kayne grabs me. "Are you okay?"

"Yes, I'm fine, but you're pissing the baby off. Now can you please just sit?" I grimace. "I think he has your front kick." I rub my sore stomach.

"Fine," Kayne grumbles, dragging me to the couch with him. "But if I sit, you sit."

"Fine," I spit back. Such a loving couple, aren't we?

"What do you have to tell me?" He directs his question at Jett, tension emanating from his pores. He may be trying to play it cool, but he is a bundle of nerves.

Jett takes a deep breath and leans on the edge of the desk directly across from us. With compassionate eyes, the eyes that are the most genuine on the planet, he recites almost verbatim what he told me only minutes ago. About Kayne's mother, the social worker, and his 'theory.' Kayne remains silent the whole time . . . barely blinking, barely breathing. Once Jett finishes, you could hear a pin drop.

Kayne is intimidating to begin with, but menacingly-silent Kayne is downright scary.

"Kayne." I lace my fingers with his and rub my thumb across the back of his hand. He doesn't utter a word, not one, single word. After a few moments, he spontaneously stands up, hauling me with him with a death grip on my hand. He stalks over to Jett, who straightens, pushing out his chest, almost defensively. Kayne glowers as he reaches for the folder, never breaking eye contact with Jett. The tension in the room could suffocate a tyrannosaurus rex. Once he has it, he drags me away, quieter than a mime. Outside the house, he opens the door to his Jag and motions for me to get in.

"Can you drive right now?" I ask as he walks around the front end.

No answer. He just slips into the front seat and hands me the folder. He punches the ignition and takes off in the direction of our home. Peeling through the quiet neighborhood, we make it there in record time.

"Kayne." I try to engage him, but he shuts me out, not even acknowledging my attempt. After we're inside, he drags me upstairs to our bedroom. Taking the folder from my hand, he drops it on the dresser then proceeds to strip me of all my clothes. Every single article until I'm completely naked and he is still fully dressed.

"Lay down," he orders, his tone downright daunting. Guardedly, I crawl onto the mattress and rest my head on the pillow. Kayne kicks off his shoes then follows right behind me. To say I'm not a little apprehensive would be a lie. I don't think my husband would ever intentionally hurt me, but when his emotions become too much for him to handle, he tends to get rough. And with me being pregnant, I'm not sure how that will fair.

Kayne slides his hand over my naked body, feeling every microscopic inch of my skin, before he lies down next to me. Practically wrapping me up like a mummy with his limbs, he places his head on my bare chest and begins to cry. Hard, deep sobs that shake us both. I'm completely thrown, but at the same time, completely sympathetic and a little destroyed. He finally knows the truth and now has to deal with it.

"Shhh . . ." I kiss his head and run my fingers through his hair, encouraging him to purge all the feelings out.

"Shhh . . ."

I WAKE UP ALONE AND to the smell of breakfast. My stomach growls. Someone is hungry.

I slide out of bed, grab a cotton sundress from my closet to slip on, brush my teeth, and use the bathroom. Once downstairs, I find Kayne working away in front of the stove. Whatever he's making smells delicious. I walk quietly up behind him, not to scare him, but because I'm not sure what frame of mind he's in. Yesterday, he confronted his darkest demons; who knows how that's affecting him today.

"Hey," I say softly as I stand next to him.

"Morning." He kisses me on the head while he continues beating—"Eggs? You're making eggs?" Now that I'm close, I see a host of different ingredients spread out on the counter—pancake batter, butter, milk, chopped green peppers, and shredded cheddar cheese. I also notice his caseworker's file laying open off to the side. I have no doubt that he's been reading it. If I know him, dissecting it would be a better word. "You hate eggs. They remind you—"

"Not today," he cuts me off. "Today, I love eggs. Today is a new day." He scoops up the chopped peppers with his hands and drops them into the bowl then pours the half cup of shredded cheddar in afterward.

I feel like I'm in the twilight zone. *"Today, I love eggs. Today is a new day." What?* For the past five years, just looking at a carton of eggs made Kayne shudder because it reminded him of Kim, the foster mother who tried to seduce him when he was seventeen. Making eggs was apparently their "thing".

"How long have you been up?" I glance at the clock. It's only seven forty-five in the morning.

"A while. I couldn't sleep, so I worked out. We need a new punching bag, by the way. Then I went for a run with Jett around six. I showered, and now here I am." He dumps the eggs into the heated frying pan and they sizzle.

"And how are you doing?" I ask delicately.

He pulls in a deep breath and then exhales, pushing the eggs around with a wooden spoon. "I think I'm okay."

"You're *okay?* Some serious information was dropped in your lap yesterday and you're *okay?"*

I don't mean to sound skeptical, but this is my husband we're talking about. Usually, he reacts quite passionately when railroaded with information.

"Ellie," he huffs, putting down the spoon and turning to face me. "I have spent damn near my entire life obsessing. Wondering what, why, how. I don't want to do it anymore. I'm finally going to take Jett's advice and just put the past behind me. I have more important things to worry about now." He puts his hand on my stomach. It's such a sweet gesture, I almost tear up. Damn hormones.

"I have one memory of my mother, and it's a happy one. She wanted me, and that's what I'm going to remember."

"Really?"

"Yes."

Okay, I won't lie. I'm flabbergasted. I didn't expect this when I woke up. I thought I was going to be putting him back together one tiny piece at a time, but it seems Kayne had some revelations while I was sleeping.

"You're the most important thing in my life. I'm sorry if I've disappointed you lately." He kisses the inside of my wrist.

"You didn't disappoint me. You scared me."

"I know." He pulls me closer and drops his forehead to mine then kisses me again before stirring the eggs around. "And I'm sorry for being a condescending cocksucker."

"It's okay. You can't help who you are," I tease him.

Kayne smirks. "Brat."

"And proud of it." I grab a little piece of green pepper and pop it into my mouth.

"Clearly." He snakes his arm around my waist and secures me against him. "You're the only one who can tame me, Ellie."

"I'm not interested in taming you." I run the tip of my nose up his neck. "I like you just the way you are."

Kayne tightens his hold, his eyes flashing with excitement. I quiver.

"Are you hungry?" he purrs.

"Starved." My mouth waters for more than just eggs.

"I bet."

My stomach interrupts us, growling loudly, and we both laugh. "Someone is impatient."

"You missed dinner last night. Can't blame him."

"He eats just like you."

"If that's the case, let's go feed our boy." Kayne sucks and licks my lips before he lets me go.

I grab some plates and silverware, while Kayne finishes cooking the eggs and pulls out a stack of pancakes warming in the oven. Once everything is set up on the patio outside, we sit down to eat. Well, Kayne sits. I kneel between his legs, but not as a submissive, instead just a woman who is madly in love with her man.

"My mother's name was Sarah," Kayne proceeds to tell me as I take pieces of pancake from his fingers. "Sarah Rivers. She had me when she was fourteen. There was no mention of my father on my birth certificate." I chew slowly, listening attentively. "She was hooked on drugs and in no condition to raise a child, so the state took me away from her when I was thirteen months old. She eventually got clean and pulled her life together. She was twenty-one when she died." I run my hands over his thighs as he speaks. "She wanted me."

"Of course she did." My composure nearly shatters. "She was your mother. Of course she wanted you." I take his face in my hands and kiss him. A deep, emotive kiss that screams I want him, too.

"When we have another baby—"

"Another one? We haven't even had this one." I laugh.

"Well, when, if, we have another baby, and it's a girl, I want to name her Sarah."

"That's fine. Done deal," I agree immediately.

"Good." It's almost like he sighs with relief. Did he think I would say no to such a heartfelt request like that? He then attacks my mouth, smothering it with passion-fueled kisses.

"Aren't you hungry?" I ask when we break for air.

"Starved. But I want dessert first."

It doesn't take long before our hands are roaming all over each other and breakfast is a distant memory. I guess I wasn't the only one starving in more than one way.

"Touch me, Ellie." My name vibrates low and deep in his throat as I pull on the waistband of his basketball shorts and jerk his rock-hard cock with both hands. He kisses me more aggressively, his fingers tangled securely in my hair. After a few pulsating seconds, Kayne lifts me to my feet and pushes me back so I am leaning against the edge of the table. Forcefully, he spreads my thighs then buries his head between my legs. I hold on to the table for dear life as he licks through my folds incessantly, my knees nearly giving way.

"*Ohhhh . . .*" I moan insufferably as the sweet ache of pleasure spreads through my whole body. "Yes," I pant rapidly as my climax electrifies.

"Oh no," Kayne removes his mouth from my ravished pussy. "Not this time." He pulls down his shorts just low enough so his cock pops free. "This time, you're coming all over me." He hauls me up into his arms and impales me onto his straining length. My muscles immediately tighten, shocking my arousal.

"Oh, shit," I mutter helplessly as Kayne hooks his arms under my thighs.

"Already, baby?" He impales me onto his thick rigid cock over and over, like he's doing bicep curls with my body. Drawing me all the way up then dropping me all the way back down.

"I can't help it," I wince as he slices through me, my muscles painfully contracting and my clit tingling. "It's the hormones, all you have to do is look at me and I pop. *Oh, god!*" I practically screech when I come, my control crumbling to pieces.

Kayne growls against my neck as he fucks out every last drop of my orgasm, demanding my demise like he always does. I barely have the strength to hold onto his neck as he walks us inside and lays me down on the dining room table.

"This is exactly how I want you." He thrusts deeply into my depleted body, pushing up my dress. "Destroyed, shattered, ruined, demolished."

I moan incapacitated, exactly all those things and more. He ravages me repeatedly, plundering my pussy with no apologies, taking exactly what belongs to him. My pleasure.

"I love you like this, Ellie." He places both hands on my stomach and slows his pace. "I love that a piece of me is inside you." He caresses my little bump.

"I love it, too," I respond in a state of ecstasy.

"Come with me, kitten?" Kayne rubs my clit and I arch my back.

"Yes, please. Please make me come." He knows just how to touch me; he knows all my secret spots.

"Hurry." He rubs harder, circling his hips, punching his swelling cock into my dripping wet channel.

"Don't stop." I exhale sharply as another orgasm forms like a cyclone. "Kayne! Kayne!" All I can do is cry his name as he calls forth my arousal, my addiction. The sensations that bind me to him.

"Kitten." He slams into me once, twice, three severe times, right before we fuse as one.

"Fuck, Ellie." Kayne stills as I shudder around him, stretched and filled to the point of breaking.

Lost in our own little post-coital world, my husband worships me with his mouth like he loves to do, covering my entire body with lingering kisses. My favorite—the one he plants right in the center of my stomach.

"That's how it's done," I hear him whisper.

"Kayne!" I scold him, teasingly.

"What?" Gotta teach him early." He laughs.

I am only capable of responding with an eye roll.

Men.

ELLIE

"THIS KID NEEDS TO COME out, now!" I complain miserably, sprawled out on the bed. The baby is a week late and showing no signs of wanting to grace the world with his presence.

"He's comfortable in there. He knows how good it is." Kayne makes an off-color joke.

I smack him with a pillow. "Well, Mommy is ready to have her body back." I'm hot, swollen, and convinced my bladder has disappeared with how much I pee.

"We can go for another walk?" Kayne suggests.

"No. If I walk around the block one more time, I may scream."

"Have sex?"

"Definitely not."

"Thai for dinner? Maybe some spicy food will light a fire under him."

"No."

"Just want to lay here and be miserable?"

"Yes," I whine.

"Can I go work out while you're parked on the bed?"

"Abandoning me when the going gets tough already?"

It's Kayne's turn to hit me with a pillow.

"I'd never abandon you."

"I know. Sure, go ahead." I sigh. "I'll be here . . . fat, miserable, and immobile."

"Miserable?"

"Miserable."

"I promise I'll bring you up some ice cream when I'm done." He gets up off the bed.

"I won't get too excited. Your workouts are like four hours long."

"I'll make this one fast." He chuckles and leans down to kiss me.

"Oh!" I sit up suddenly and end up colliding with Kayne's face.

"Ouch, Ellie you just head-butted me," he rubs his nose.

"I'm sorry. I got a pain." I stroke my huge stomach.

"Are you okay?" He sits back down on the bed then immediately shoots up. "Did you pee?"

"What? No! Oh shit! I think my water just broke!"

Kayne looks at me stunned. "He heard you."

"Good! At least I know he listens." I push myself up and swing my legs over the side of the mattress. This is gross. "We have to go."

"Ya, think? Good thing I'm trained for emergency situations." He helps me stand.

"You are not delivering this baby in the backseat of our car."

"If we don't get you to the hospital soon, I might."

"Shit!" I nearly keel over as another contraction hits.

"Quick, we gotta change your clothes and get out of here."

"I need to take a shower first."

"What?"

"I'm all sticky. I need to shower."

"Ellie, we don't have time."

"It will only take a second. I can't show up at the hospital with amniotic fluid dripping down my thighs. Just please get me something to wear while I wash off."

Kayne grumbles. "You better not be cursing me when I tell you to push in the backseat of the Jeep."

"You're not delivering this baby in the car! Now go!" I waddle into the bathroom and hop in the shower.

"I'll remind you of that when you have your legs spread wide open and dangling over the roll bar!" he yells over the shower.

If he were close, I would punch him. This kid makes me very aggressive.

I clean up in record time and change into the shorts and T-shirt Kayne grabbed for me.

"Ready?" Kayne has both of our hospital bags slung over each shoulder.

"What about the bed?" I ask. "We should clean it up."

"It's going. I'll order a new mattress and have it express delivered."

I won't argue with that.

As I walk down the stairs, another contraction hits. "Oh!" The pain shoots up and around my stomach and lands right in my lower back.

"Ellie? Are you okay?"' Kayne holds me up by my arm. I swear I could just sit right here and never get up.

"I'm not sure." I breathe heavily in and out.

"Come on, we have to go. Now."

My contractions come on hard and fast, and by the time we get to the hospital, Kayne is clocking them at three minutes apart.

I can tell you, the maternity ward is no-nonsense and efficient. The minute we got here, I was put in a delivery room, hooked up to a fetal monitor, and examined thoroughly.

"Do I have time for an epidural?" I ask the nurse after she checks my cervix.

"Unfortunately, no. You're at eight centimeters with contractions less than three minutes apart. This baby is coming soon."

"Shit. Shit!" Another contraction begins, making me see stars. The pain is in my back and utterly excruciating.

"Fuck, this hurts." I crush Kayne's hand. "I don't know if I can do this without drugs."

"Ellie, you have to. You heard the nurse. He's coming soon." There are so many emotions in my husband's voice.

"I can't."

"You can, just breathe. You're strong enough."

"You're going to have to keep reminding me of that."

"Till death do us part, you know that."

I can only nod frantically as another contraction pummels me.

"They're getting closer." Kayne looks at his watch while he holds my hand. There is ungodly pressure between my legs, like I'm about to rip in two. I almost hate him for being so calm.

The nurse comes in to check on my progress again. "How's Mom doing?"

"Dying," I whine.

"Ellie," Kayne snaps at me. "Not even funny when it's a joke."

"I'm not joking!" I scream as another wave of pain hits.

"Hopefully, it will be over soon." She measures my cervix again. "Oh!" Her face perks up. "It looks like we need to page the doctor. You're fully dilated." She smiles, removing her latex gloves. "As soon as he gets here, you can start pushing. Hang on for a few more minutes."

That seems like an unbearable amount of time.

The pain is constant now, just a steady stream of agony.

"Ellie." My doctor walks into the room smiling brightly. I'm glad someone is in a good mood.

The OB practice I go to has several doctors, all of whom I met and could potentially deliver the baby depending who was on the floor.

Luckily, my main doctor is at the hospital today.

"So, looks like we're ready." He pulls up a chair and sits right in front of my wide-open legs. I have been told childbirth is beautiful and wondrous, but up until now, I've felt more like a lab rat, poked and prodded with my lady bits on display than an excited mother-to-be.

"Okay, Ellie. We're going to push," Dr. Hanini tells me. "On three."

"Okay."

"One. Two. Three." I push with all my might, hoping the baby comes out on the first try.

"Good. Relax." Dr. Hanini is in his late forties, has golden brown skin, and is native to Hawaii. I connected with him the minute he walked into the room. He just has this wonderful calm energy and the nicest bedside manner. Even Kayne likes him, which is saying a lot since he's seen my vagina just as much as my husband has over the last nine months.

"Again, Ellie." I push once more, squeezing Kayne's hand for dear life.

"Come on, baby, you can do this." Kayne is peering down over my legs to see what's going on.

"Can you see anything yet?" I ask, drained already.

"Nothing, not yet," he tells me.

"Gotta keep pushing," the doctor encourages me.

And I do, for over two excruciating hours.

"WHY WON'T HE COME OUT!" I'm crying by this point, exhausted and ready to pass out.

"A little more, Ellie. You need to hold on a little more," Dr. Hanini urges me to keep going.

"I can't. I'm so tired," I protest, nearly delirious.

"Ellie, come on. Strong enough, remember?" Kayne wipes some sweat away from my brow and feeds me some ice chips. "You've been through worse than this."

"Okay," I pant, determined to push this kid out.

With a deep breath, I summon the little bit of energy I have left and push again. It feels like something gives way and suddenly there is a little less pressure.

"Good, Ellie. His head is out!" Dr. Hanini exclaims, and then his expression turns grim. "Stop. Stop pushing."

"What? I can't stop!" Now that the baby has momentum it feels like I no longer have control. My body is on autopilot.

"Fetal heart rate is dropping."

"What?" I look back and forth between Kayne and the doctor. Both their faces are expressionless, but Kayne's eyes are wild.

"What's happening? What's going on?"

"Ellie, try to relax. The cord is wrapped around the baby's neck," one of the nurses informs me in a palliative tone.

"One second." Dr. Hanini works quickly, doing something I can't see.

"Please hurry! I have to push!"

"Okay, now!" The doctor gives me the green light. I barely even push before I see a still, silent, little blue infant being lifted into the air. I nearly pass out.

"Let me see him! I need to see him!" He's not crying and all the nurses are crowded around the doctor and my baby.

"Kayne!" I grab his wrist, but he's still as stone as he watches the hospital staff work on our child.

My emotions spin further out of control every second there's no sound.

I don't know how long time lingers before we hear it.

The first wail of our newborn son.

It breaks me out of my petrified state of panic.

"Is he okay? Please tell me he's okay."

"He's perfect." One of the nurses places him on my chest, and I burst out into tears.

"We just needed to suction him."

I hold him close as he squirms, instantly bonding with the helpless little angel. I fall in love for the second time in my life. I look up at Kayne. He's stiller than a glassy lake. I think he's in shock. Actually, I know he is.

"Say hi to your son."

Only his blue eyes move. From me to the baby and back again.

Definitely in shock.

"Okay. Time to clean up this little fella." One of the nurses lifts him off of me.

"Already! I just got him."

"It will only be for a few minutes, and then I'll give him right back." She's a sweet woman, very smiley, but I still give him up reluctantly.

Kayne tails the nurse, putting his super stalking skills to good use and hovering already.

"What's his name, Mom?" One of the other nurses in the room asks.

"Alec. Alec Jett Stevens. AJ for short." I wipe away my happy tears as they fall one by one.

"Jett? Oh, I like that." She smiles coyly.

If you knew him, you'd like it even more.

Kayne and I both wanted to name him after someone important in our lives. Who's more important than my father and Jett?

I watch as Kayne's towering figure spies on everything the nurses do to AJ, while at the same time battling with fatigue. The adrenaline that was keeping me awake is now fading fast, exhaustion settling in its place.

"I HAVE SEEN A LOT of nasty shit, oops, I mean stuff. Daddy needs to learn to watch his language, but that black tar in your diaper takes the cake." I hear Kayne before I even open my eyes.

When I crack them open, I watch silently as he wraps AJ up in a little blue blanket and lifts him from the hospital's bassinet.

"I know you've only been here a few hours, but I think now is a good time to have our first talk."

Kayne sits down in the rocking chair in the corner of the room and proceeds to talk to the tiny bundle nestled in his arms. AJ looks even smaller when he holds him, like an oversized peanut.

"First, and this is extremely important, always keep your head down and hands up in a fight." He lifts one of AJ's little hands to his face. It doesn't surprise me in the least that that's the first piece of advice he shares with his son.

"Second, ketchup is delicious on eggs. Don't let anyone tell you different. Especially Mommy.

Third, don't be afraid to talk to girls. Uncle Jett may need to help you with this in the future. Daddy isn't very good at it. It's the only thing Daddy isn't good at." The arrogance is blatant in his voice. Heaven help me.

"Lastly, and this is the most important, it takes courage to love. Mommy taught me that. She's the strongest, most resilient person I know. She was brave enough to love me, and it changed my entire life. So try to be a good boy for her. I already give her enough grief." Kayne's tone gets softer as he kisses AJ's forehead. He's so sweet with him I could melt.

"When did you learn to swaddle?" I ask, interrupting the love fest.

Kayne looks up at me and smiles the most brilliant smile I have ever seen.

"While you were sleeping. The little man and I were having some quality father-son time."

"And how is that going for the two of you?" As if I didn't already know.

"Amazing." Kayne glances down lovingly at AJ. "How do you feel?"

"Better." I sigh. "I want to see him."

Kayne walks AJ over to me. He handles him like a natural. When I take my first good look at his little face, my heart nearly explodes with joy. His eyes are open and alert, and he's trying to fit his entire fist into his mouth. I think someone's hungry.

"He's so perfect, Ellie," Kayne breathes.

"He is," I agree.

Ten tiny fingers and toes, a little mouth shaped like a heart, and vibrant blue eyes just like his daddy.

Kayne sits down on the edge of the bed, reluctant to give AJ up. "For nine months, I felt like a spectator, and now that he's here and I can actually hold him, it all suddenly feels real." Kayne draws his gaze away from the infant. "How did this happen?" he asks in awe. "How did this become my life?"

I laugh softly. "Evolution?"

"No." He shakes his head resolutely. "A miracle."

"Knock knock," a soft voice rasps just before Jett, Layla, Beckett and a very pregnant London walk into the room. She's having a girl, and they're naming her Shia.

Kayne turns his head, and clears the emotion from his throat before he faces our extended family.

"I want to see!" Layla rushes to Kayne, and stands on her tippy toes. He leans in slightly to show the children AJ.

"Baby." Beckett giggles trying to touch him.

"There's going to be one of these in your house soon," Kayne tells him.

"They can't wait," London informs us, putting a loving hand on Becks' blond head. He returns a little chicklet-toothed smile.

Kayne hands me AJ and steps back so Jett and London can get a better look. I cannot put into words what it feels like to hold my child. It's surreal. A manifestation of two people who's more beautiful and more perfect than I ever dared to imagine.

London caresses AJ's sweet little cheek with the tip of her finger. "I love him already, Ellie."

"I do, too," I reply, brimming with emotions I never knew I had.

Kayne and Jett just look on like two proud lions protective of their pride.

"You've done good, grasshopper." Jett elbows Kayne.

Kayne clenches his jaw and flares his nostrils. "*Please* don't make me kill you. I don't want to shed blood on such a happy day."

Jett laughs melodramatically. "Like *you* could ever kill *me*."

London and I just roll our eyes in response to our husbands' ceaseless banter.

No matter how crazy or life-altering the moment, some things will just never change. . . .

KAYNE

C.S. LEWIS ONCE SAID, "LIFE is too deep for words, so don't try to describe it, just live it."

That quote simplifies my whole existence. It reminds me to let the past be the past, let the present be the present, and let the future be the future. For a man who loves control, I've learned sometimes you just have to let go. I'm not afraid to do that anymore, because I know if I fall (which I do a lot) there is always someone there to catch me. And she catches me every single time.

I watch Ellie playing with AJ in the backyard from the kitchen. He wants her to pick him up, but she's doing everything in her power to keep him on the ground. She's eight months pregnant with our second child, and I know she's exhausted. AJ demands most of her attention. The two-and-a-half-year-old is as aggressive as his father and as loving as his mother. He's the perfect split, right down to his looks. My face with Ellie's green eyes and light-brown hair.

"Okay, time for some juice and a rest." She carries AJ into the house.

"Dwink! Dwink!" he demands.

"Bossy little thing," Ellie comments as she grabs a juice box from the refrigerator and then sits AJ on the countertop next to me. "Wonder where you get that from?" she jokes with him, and he smiles from her playful tone.

I smile, too. What can I say? Like father, like son.

"How's my girl?" I put my arm around Ellie as AJ sucks down his apple juice.

"Busy." She grabs my hand and puts it on her stomach so I can feel the flutters. "She always knows when you're close. She's a daddy's girl already. I'm going to get replaced pretty soon."

"No one could ever replace you." I lift her chin with one finger. "When I asked how my girl was, I meant you."

"Oh, well, in that case, I feel fat, bloated, and completely unattractive."

"Nonsense. I see sexy, alluring, and completely gorgeous."

"Daddy needs his eyes examined," she says flippantly to AJ, once again causing him to giggle.

As much as she complains about being fat and tired and pregnant, to me she really is the sexiest thing in the world. No amount of chains or collars or restraints can compare to the way she looks in a sundress with a baby growing in her belly.

Being a father changed me profoundly. I always thought I saw Ellie, but I didn't. Not really, not the way I see her now. I'm completely consumed with love—love for her, love for our children, and love for this life I was miraculously blessed with. Love that envelops me, sustains me, and grounds me. Before Ellie, I thought I knew my fate—a faceless man living a life undercover, just drifting along. But that's the funny thing about life. You never know what direction it's going to shove you in. I never thought I would fall in love, never dreamed of getting married or having a family, yet here I am with an amazing wife, a beautiful son, and a daughter on the way. I don't think words can express the depth of my happiness. The monumental gratitude I feel every time I look at my family. *My* family. The idea was such a foreign concept, but now that I have everything I never knew I wanted, I would do anything to keep us together. Keep my children safe and my wife happy. *Anything*. I killed for Ellie once; I wouldn't hesitate to do it again.

"Cupcake!" AJ squeals. "Mommy, pwease! Pwease! Cupcake!" He points to the miniature, chocolate frosted cupcakes sitting on the counter.

"Okay, just one." Ellie picks him up and places him in his high chair.

"Sugar before sleep? Always works for me," I tease her.

"Good because you'll be the one putting him down."

"Oh?" I laugh at her as she peels off the wrapper and hands AJ his fudgy treat.

"Yup." She licks some frosting off her finger.

As I watch my son devour his snack, I can't help but think how one simple lick of a cupcake tilted my world on its axis and spun it in a completely different direction. Yes, life definitely is too deep to be described, it can only be lived.

"Kayne, what are you thinking about?" Ellie asks intuitively.

I possessively slip my arm around her waist and pull her against me. "Just how much I love cupcakes."

The End

PLAYLIST

Angels ~ The xx

Animals ~ Maroon 5

Sex and Candy ~ Maroon 5

Heartbeat Song ~ Kelly Clarkson

Lights Go Out ~ Fozzy

Bonus Material

Owned Alternate POV

I SEE HER COMING BEFORE she sees me.

She's squeezing through the traffic jam of people in front of the door to her office building. She looks perfectly sexy like always, long brownish blonde hair flipping in the breeze, tight skirt hugging all the right curves, and white button-up top leaving everything to the imagination. I walk slowly up the sidewalk, taking my time so I can watch her. I always watch her. And right now I'm watching as her heel gets caught in a crack in the sidewalk. Watching as she flies forward and lands on her hands and knees mere feet in front of me. I hurry to help her as people pass by, either ignoring her or snickering at her as she tries to pull her wits together.

"Okay down there?" I put my hand out to help her. She looks up at me with large green eyes and rosy red cheeks. I feel my blood flow speed up. Ellie on her knees, all doe-eyed and humiliated. I'd take her in that position any day. She doesn't respond, and I frown. Did I say something wrong? Maybe she's really hurt. "Ellie, are you okay? Do you need me to carry you?"

Her lips finally move. "No, I'm okay." She fumbles as I pluck her up and help her to stand. She stares at me, looking a little lost. I smile down at her, and then drop my gaze lower, unable to stop myself, with her cleavage on full display; if I thought that shirt left everything to the imagination, I was just proven wrong. Her perky, smooth breasts cupped in white lace has my arousal running wild.

"Nice," I quip before I can stop myself.

She grabs her shirt and yanks it closed, her cheeks glowing brighter. Not wanting to embarrass her any further, I open the door as she rights her shirt and re-fastens the buttons. To say I'm not disappointed would be a lie, I would much rather have her take her clothes off then put them back on.

We walk silently to the elevator, and once on, Ellie pulls the hem of her skirt up just a bit to check the scrape on her knee. I try not to gawk, but she's giving me all types of views I have only fantasized about. I maintain my distance and professionalism when I visit Expo, the shipping company that handles the exportation of my company goods out of Mexico. Tequila and limes have been extraordinarily lucrative for me, and so has Mark, Expo's owner. Although eccentric, he is extremely brilliant at what he does. Which is exactly why I hired him. If there is a way to save a dime, Mark will find it.

The elevator doors ding open, and mine and Ellie's private time is over all too soon.

"Kayne," Mark greets me with a handshake while also blinding me with a bright purple dress shirt.

"Mark," I return.

"Everything is set up," he informs me. "Ellie, please escort Mr. Roberts to the conference room. And tend to whatever he needs."

"Yes, Mark," she answers dutifully, and I swear to god hearing those words leave her lips makes me instantly hard. I take a deep breath to calm myself. I have way too many erotic images of Ellie running through my mind already, her succumbing to my darkest desires may just be the temptation of all temptations to step over the line of self-control. I don't know what is it about this girl, but from the moment I laid eyes on her, I have wanted to possess her like the sun owns the light. It's very unlike me.

I follow Ellie to the conference room. I don't really need an escort, I've been here enough times to find it on my own, but I'm not complaining. I get to watch Ellie shimmy down the hallway in that tight skirt, hugging all the right curves of her hips and ass. As nice as Ellie's tits are, it's her ass that has my full attention.

I make myself comfortable in one of the leather office chairs once inside the immense room with large picture windows overlooking New York City. It's not the greatest view in the world, but for Mark's budding company, it's impressive enough.

"Coffee?" Ellie asks me.

"Yes, please." I smooth my tie, trying to feign disinterest, "Milk-"

"No sugar," she finishes my sentence. I can't help but smile.

"You remembered." I don't know why this surprises me, but it does. And not only does it surprise me, but pleasantly so. I like the idea of her knowing what I like. Call it my selfish desire to be served, or even better, serviced, by her.

"It's my job not to forget," she responds.

"Rare quality. Attentiveness," I muse, suddenly picturing Ellie's mouth attentively around my cock.

"I guess." She shrugs, seeming uncomfortable. I wonder if she can read my mind, or if my professional exterior is just wavering. "I'll be right back." She leaves the room in a hurry.

I wonder if my stiff demeanor scared her off. Playing professional is much more of a challenge today.

Disappointingly, Ellie doesn't return before the meeting gets started. Mark was quick to rush in right after she left with his entourage of personnel. Maybe it's for the best. My erotic little fantasies are probably better off being just that, fantasies. Ellie is off limits, untouchable. She doesn't belong in my world, and I certainly don't belong in hers. Our differences are just too wide spread. Even if she was open to my self-indulgent ideals, would I really want to corrupt something so adorable? So frisky and warm? Turn a cuddly little kitten into a lecherous house cat? As she hands me my coffee and our fingers brush, I consider the answer to maybe be yes. Definitely yes. Hell fucking yes. I want her to be my kitten. My naked, submissive, lascivious little sex kitten, who comes in a multitude of ways when I call her.

I need to stop. Put the idea of Ellie being mine completely out of my head. *It can't happen,* I tell myself as I stare blatantly at her ass while she bends over and places a plate of baked goods in the center of the table. I can still look even if I can't touch. It's a disappointing sentiment, but one I have to stick by, no matter how much my cock curses me.

I force myself to concentrate on Mark as Ellie leaves the room. I'm here for business and that's what I need to focus on. Too bad my mind has other plans and wanders off to an image of Ellie splayed out on the conference room table, her shirt ripped open, her breasts exposed, her skirt hiked up to her hips with my head buried between her legs-licking, sucking, savoring her sweet spot as I make her come. I'd relish in her screams right before I buried myself balls deep in her wet pussy and fucked her until I forgot where she began and I ended.

"Kayne?" I faintly hear my name. "Kayne?" Mark's voice cuts through my vivid fantasy.

"Mmm?" I answer, mindlessly.

"What do you think?" The new route? It's a huge cost savings in the end."

"It's good." I try to sound self-assured, even though I heard little to nothing of what Mark said.

"So I can start the charters next week?" he asks eagerly.

"Absolutely." I'm going to have to study this plan later on today. That's what I get for daydreaming. I glance out one of the windows into the office and see Ellie. My fantasizing was totally worth it.

"Wonderful." Mark closes his leather folder and zips it up. The meeting is adjourned.

"Do you mind if I stay and send a few emails before I go?" I ask Mark as everyone else files out.

"Of course, by all means." He smiles.

Good, because I need a minute. If I stand up, it will be clear the very last thing I was concentrating on was work. I start to doodle on the paper in front of me, attempting to distract myself from my raging hormones.

"Ellie. Can you clean up in there?" I hear Mark yell. Oh shit. "I'm heading to lunch."

"Yes, Mark", is her obedient response once again, and yet another trigger for my arousal. I'm never going to get out of here. I'm screwed.

"How was the meeting?" she asks sweetly as she collects the information folders left behind.

"Excellent. Mark is a genius at logistics. He found an alternate route out of Mexico that will save a few hundred thousand over the next year. I'm pleased." See? I was sort of paying attention.

"That's good." She smiles, and the sentiment shines in her eyes. There's no false pretenses with Ellie—what you see is what you get. Maybe that's what draws me to her, she's genuine. I haven't had much honest-to-goodness in my life. It's refreshing.

"No lunch for you?" she asks, as she makes her way around the table.

"I have another meeting in an hour. Mark said I can utilize the conference room to do some work and kill time."

Bullshit.

"I see." She picks up the last file folder and is now standing quite close to me.

"What about you?" I ask as I eye her.

"My lunch is sitting right in front of you. I'll be dining on miniature cupcakes."

"Healthy," I mock.

"I know, but they're little. So . . . less calories." She shrugs playfully.

"I guess that's one way to spin it," I respond, pulling the silver tray toward me. "Which flavor is your favorite?" I pin my stare on her.

She swallows thickly, "It's a toss-up between red velvet and lemon drop."

"Well, I'm a red velvet man myself." I pick up the last red velvet cupcake on the plate. "Would you mind sharing your lunch with me, Ellie?"

"Of course not, it's only polite to share," she says, fiddling with the collar of her shirt. I think I'm getting to her. I know I shouldn't toy with her, but it's just too easy, and I want her so much. I wonder if I pull the blinds so no one in the office can see us, could I seduce her right here on the spot, live out my fantasy just once, then never look back again? Instant gratification and selfish desire all wrapped up in sunny afternoon.

I pull the wrapper off the red cake and then split it in two. "Sit." I order her.

Ellie immediately sits, clutching the file folders tightly to her chest. I offer her one half of the cupcake, and she takes it with shaky fingers.

"Do I make you nervous, Ellie?" I ask as I lightly lick the cream cheese frosting.

"No. Just too much coffee." She tries to play it cool, but I can see right through her. Reading people is what I do. And I definitely intimidate Ellie.

"I see." I stare at her intently, licking off the icing exactly how I would lick her clit given the change; slowly, in a circular motion, covering every single inch. "Aren't you going to eat?" I ask enticingly, right before I stuff the naked cupcake into my mouth. *Yum.*

I raise my eyebrows expectantly as Ellie just sits there unable to move. That's when she shoves her half of the cupcake into her mouth. I can't help but smirk and brush a crumb off her bottom lip. This is the most unintimidating woman I have ever met, and hands down the sexiest.

If I were ever going to break my own rules, it would definitely be for her.

Character Interview

Alpha Book Club

Do we have a treat for you today! Recently I caught up with Kayne Stevens and Jett Fox and they agreed to sit down with me in an impromptu interview of sorts—and boy did I ask them some questions! If you are not familiar with who Kayne and Jett are, they are the stars of M. Never's very erotic series "Decadence after Dark" The titles include Owned, Claimed and Ruined.

So without further ado, here is their live interview—uncut.

Warning: this may be disturbing for some readers, discretion is advised

Jaime: Hello, gentlemen and thank you for stopping by—We know you are very busy!

Kayne: We are happy to be here. Anything for our number one fan *Kayne flashes a smile, Jaime's panties melt*

Jaime: So as M. has told you both the readers have questions, and some of these questions are pretty personal, but we know neither of you are shy!

Jett: We're not afraid to bare it all.

Jaime: *Fans self* Thanks Jett and Kayne . . . Ok guys Here is the rules, I know you love rules Kayne, so I will ask a question and if it's not directed to one of you, then either one or both of you can answer—but one of you has to answer *picks up wooden paddle with heart cut out* and just in case you boys get shy . . . I brought some motivation . . .

Kayne: *Looks at paddle* Ellie was wondering where that was.

smirks

Jaime: Yes, I am sure it was Ellie who was looking for it. .ok time for questions -

Jaime: Kayne—Tell us your favorite thing about Ellie?

Kayne: Really? You have to ask? *grins*

Jett: Don't be an ass

Kayne: ass being the operative word

Jaime: Ah yes, that's right you're an ass man. *snickers* Ok Jett this is for you, Do you feel bad about your part in Ellie's abduction in Owned? Why or why Not?

Jett: yes and no, I hated lying to her, but it was necessary. Life and death situations often result in taking the wrong road for the right reasons. I luckily received a close friend out of it. If I was put in the position again, I wouldn't hesitate to repeat my actions.

Jaime: Alright, so tell us guys—what is your favorite sex position?

Kayne: trick question. There is no answer.

Jett *rolls eyes* woman on top, hands tied to the headboard preferably.

Jaime: Wow! *Imagines Jett's description* ok, so Kayne, since you are being evasive tell us something that nobody knows about you?

Kayne: If I told you, then everyone would know.

Jett: for god's sake, can you just give the woman a straight answer!

Kayne: I don't give my secrets away for free *smiles suggestively*

Jaime: *Fans self while squirming in seat* Ok, moving on . . . throughout Owned and Claimed there is talk about how both of you

frequently shared women—what is it about sharing a woman that turns you both on so much?

Jett: The power. Two against one. The forbidden act, and chasing after an indescribable high.

Kayne: Everything he said.

Jaime: Tell me guys, what's your preference: spanking, bondage, wax play, orgasm denial?

Kayne: Orgasm denial. Nothing like seeing Ellie pant.

Jett: All of the above. I like seeing Ellie pant, too.

Jaime: *smirks* Alright, so you both have unique sexual tastes. How do you feel about male/male interaction, have you ever had any male/male sexual experiences? Some men don't mind this in 3 or 4somes . . . where do you both draw the line?

Kayne: Hell no, that's where I draw the line.

Jett: Not my forte, but I won't say I never tried it.

Jaime: Ok, well how about each of yours most embarrassing sexual moment?

Kayne: Got caught by Ellie's parents having sex. We were visiting for Christmas and they caught us in the bathroom. It was the middle of night. They thought someone was trying to break down the front door. I should have tied her up. *shrugs*

Jett: My mom giving me pointers when I was fourteen. It wouldn't have been so bad if I wasn't right in the middle of the act.

Jaime: *laughing* Oh, Kayne that sounds just like something you and Ellie would do and Poor Jett—but hey at least she wasn't afraid to talk to you about sex. Well, that leads to our next question—your fans want to know how you are both always so raring to go—If ya know what I mean—ever have any trouble performing? Need any little blue pills?

Kayne: no 'required' enhancements as of yet. Just recreational use.

Jett: Same here.

Jaime: Well that is fortunate for both Ellie and London *fans self once again* Ok, this question is for Jett, your fans want to know what made you fall in love with London? What is it about her that stands out from everyone else?—(yes! I know that is sorta personal but give us something Jett as we don't know your story yet!)

Jett: I will say you will find out in Elicit.

Kayne: Who's being vague now?

Jett: *huffs* She was the most sexually adventurous woman I had ever met and the most closed off. The confliction drove me batshit crazy.

Jaime: Thank you Jett for telling us what you can—I surely don't want to get you into any trouble. So Jett—you are a Dad now, congrats! How have you adjusted to fatherhood?

Jett: I love being a father. There was no adjustment just natural fruition.

Jaime: That is just so great! And from what we see you are a great dad. Kayne, tell us what it is that drew you to Ellie, the moment you knew you had to have her?

Kayne: In all honesty? Ellie never intimidated me. If you read Owned and Claimed you know about my hang ups. I never felt a connection like that to anyone in my life. I couldn't let it go. I couldn't let *her* go. Next question.

Jaime: Alright then. So boys, tell me what is your preference: SHOWER, BED, OR TABLE? (yes, where do you prefer to have sex out of those three.)

Kayne: First the table, then the bed, then the shower. Wash, rinse, repeat.

Jett: That order works for me.

Jaime: Works for me too. Kayne some readers think you are a little twisted and sexist making Ellie crawl around like an animal and kneeling at your feet . . . How would you explain your relationship to those who don't understand. To those who are curious but just don't fully understand. Before you spout off . . . please give us an answer that explains the Dom/sub relationship or Owner/slave . . . And Jett if you would like to please feel free to chime in.

Kayne: It's really all about trust and pushing yourself to the limit. It's about handing yourself over to another person and finding euphoria as they control you completely. I guess there's no way to really explain it unless you've experienced it. It takes special people to live the lifestyle we do. You have to want it.

Jett: *nodding* That sums it up pretty well.

Jaime: Well, we know Kayne's sexual preferences. Tell us Jett—do you identify yourself as a Dominant as well? A Master?

Jett: I don't like to classify myself. I like control, but I also like participation. A walk a fine line and go with how I'm feeling. My partner needs to be open and flexible. Which London is . . .

Kayne: In more ways than one. *snickers*

Jaime: Have either of you ever participated in sex clubs or live Dom/sub play? If so, did you enjoy? If not . . . would you?

Kayne: Participated in sex clubs? We owned one. So yes we've participated, but live Dom/ sub play? Not so much. We're more about sexual gratification. As in the act of sex. So, no sex, not interested.

Jaime: Yes, Kayne—sex is so much better when the man is aiming for mutual sexual gratification *squirms in seat & fans self* Ok, Jett—When we finally get to your story . . . tell us will we think Kayne is calm after we get to know you?

Jett: Calm? I guess that depends on your definition. I would say different.

Jaime: Well, I know you are both very busy so I won't keep you much longer. But I do have to ask is there anything about Ruined

that you can tell us? I know you cannot give specifics—we don't want M. to gag you both *snickers* but tell the readers something you think you can get away with!

Kayne: I know M is always aiming for three things when she writes, strong characterization, a good story (she likes plot twists) and hot sex.

Jett: *chimes in* Which I think she pulls off.

Kayne: I have no complaints. *grins shamelessly* neither does Ellie. So I think you can always expect that from her.

Jaime: Alright, thank you for that—I know we are all very much looking forward to Ruined. Before you leave we are going to do a lightning round of sorts. I will ask you a question and you will answer as your significant other (Kayne that means you're answering as Ellie & Jett you are going to answer as London) ;-)

Just Answer as fast as you can and honestly—we will compare your answers to their answers next week. . . .

Jaime: Ready?!

Kayne: I am always ready *winks*

Jett: Will you stop fucking around, she'll never want to talk to us again!

Kayne: Oh I think she'll *WANT* us again—*chuckles darkly*

Jaime: *blushes* ok—FAVORITE THING ABOUT YOUR HUSBAND.

Kayne: His cock *sarcastic tone*

Jett: Same *completely serious*

Jaime: REASON YOUR SEX IS SO HOT?

Kayne: The man knows how to surprise me

Jett: The man knows how to get into my head

Jaime: SECRET FANTASY?

Kayne: Hmmm . . . I don't think she has any left.

Jett: Sex beneath a cherry blossom tree

Jaime: Ok, Thank you both again for taking the time to talk to me and answer these questions!

Kayne: Anytime, anywhere.

Jaime: *waves bye* Until next time—We Love You!

CJ

FOUR DAYS.

That's all we had. Four precious days that rattled my world. We told each other it wasn't anything more than Type I fun and great sex. Great. Fucking. Sex. The best of my life.

I keep trying to tell myself that's all it was—easy fun and casual sex. *Convince myself.* Because she is five thousand miles away in New York, and I am here confined in a room surrounded by semi-automatic weapons in Hawaii.

All I see are her eyes.

They're the only thing I've been able to think about for the last six months.

Well, that's not entirely true . . . I think about her lips and her tongue and her body and her smile. But her dark blue eyes are the most prevalent. Just the way they used to suck me in, read me, devour me, seduce me. Shine when they looked at me, even if it was all too briefly.

Four days.

Four, simple, carefree days is what I had with Tara Stevens. I knew I was a dead man walking during that last dance at Kayne and Ellie's wedding as our bodies swayed and touched and caressed to David Cook's *Fade into Me*. That's exactly what it felt like, too, like we were fading into each other, the world disappearing right before our very eyes as the spark of attraction became so hot it felt as if it was fueled by kerosene. I had to have her despite the fact Kayne threatened my life not twenty-four hours before. He's as protective of Tara as he is of Ellie, but nothing could stop the lust converging between us like two electrically charged particles—not even a six-foot-three, two-hundred-pound killing machine.

I fiddle with the little plastic plumeria flower Tara wore in her hair. You can find them all over the island in an array of colors. I squeeze the clip between my fingers and watch as the light pink flower teeters up and down. I can still picture it pinned in her platinum blonde hair. Hair so long and thick, I would wrap it around my wrist and pull while I fucked her. One notable time on the hood of my car parked on a secluded cliff overlooking a waterfall and a green, mountainous landscape.

My cock stiffens painfully from just the memory.

I have to stop fucking doing this to myself. It's torture. What we had is over. It was never anything to begin with. Type I fun—fun in the purest sense—and great sex.

I clip the flower back on the top edge of my monitor and try to ignore the memory of Tara naked, spread across the black hood of my Charger, while I took her hard from behind. How she loved it, how she encouraged it; a façade of innocence with the flower in her hair.

I learned quickly that Tara is anything but innocent. She's the most sexually adventurous woman I have ever met. A live wire, up for anything. I've tried that submissive stuff Kayne and Jett are into, but it just wasn't for me. I prefer a more active participant, and Tara definitely fit that bill. Giving me head on the H3 while we drove to the North Shore, sex in the ocean with a beach full of people, letting me fuck her any and every possible way in my hotel room the night of the wedding. And don't get me started on her little clit ring; I can still feel it clinking against my teeth as I made her come. Still taste her sweetness as she exploded on my tongue.

I grab my cock with desperate need. Desperate need for Tara.

I know I have to stop thinking about her, fantasizing about her, but she seems to be woven into my every thought. It's been six months; I should have moved on by now, but I feel like I'm stuck. Stuck on a vivacious blonde I can't get out of my head.

"Hey, man." I hear Jett suddenly behind me.

"Hey." I clear my throat and straighten hastily in my seat.

He leans against my desk and gazes down at me. Those perceptive turquoise eyes scrutinizing me.

"What's going on?"

"Nothing." I nonchalantly adjust my junk and glance at the computer screen. "Where are the girls?"

"Napping, finally." Jett drops his head back. "London was up with Layla all night again."

"Sucks, man." I attempt to make casual conversation. "I remember my mom complaining that I didn't sleep through the night until I started crawling."

"Yeah. Well, we are almost there, so here's hoping." Jett chuckles. "Anything going on I should know about?" He nods at the monitor.

"Nope. All quiet on the western front."

"Nice. That's what I like to hear."

"Don't we all." I fiddle with Tara's flower distractedly.

Jett sighs. "Why don't you just go see her?"

"Who?" I whip my head over at him.

He shoots me a *don't bullshit me, brother* look.

"The owner of that flower," he says directly.

I scoff. "Don't be ridiculous."

"I'm being serious." He's stern.

Not that I haven't considered it, but what would it accomplish? Another weekend, at most, of complete and utter bliss that has a foreseeable end? A tease of happiness? No thanks. I'd rather just get past it on my own.

"I don't think so." I brush him off.

"You've been moping around here since Tara left."

"I don't know if moping is the right word," I grumble.

"Yearning then? When I walked in here, you were just about to jerk off to that flower."

"I was not." I glare up at him. "I was *adjusting*."

"Sure, we can call it that if it makes you feel better." He calls bullshit.

"Kayne would hang me off Diamond Head by my ankles if he found out I went to see her."

"Don't tell him." Jett shrugs. "What he doesn't know won't hurt him. Besides, he's so wrapped up with Ellie, he won't even notice you're gone."

"That makes me feel so loved." I bat my eyes at him sardonically.

"If I tell you that *I* love you, will your balls grow back?" He puts his hand on my shoulder, messing with me.

I smack him away and laugh. "My balls haven't gone anywhere. Trust me. I think they've turned into rocks."

"Someone needs some pussy. Perfect reason to go see Tara. Fuck her out of your system."

I curl my lip. "You actually kiss London with that crass mouth?"

"I do way more than kiss her." Jett leers at me like he just sprouted horns. "Don't you want to do more with *your* mouth than just blow hot air?" he goads me.

I cross my arms and exhale, half envious-half conflicted; my chest muscles stiffen as I reluctantly succumb to my raging hormones. As much as I hate to admit it, Jett is right. I do need pussy, and Tara's is definitely worth flying clear across the country for.

"You'll cover for me with Kayne?" I raise an eyebrow, actually considering it like a crazy man.

"I promise he won't have a clue," Jett responds insidiously, his eyes glittering like a pair of precious stones. I swear he gets off on fucking with Kayne.

"Well, then . . ." I smile presumptuously. The fact this trip will be covert as well as illicit adds even more of an appeal. "I guess someone is going to New York."

ABOUT THE AUTHOR

M. NEVER RESIDES IN NEW York City. When she's not researching ways to tie up her characters in compromising positions, you can usually find her at the gym kicking the crap out of a punching bag, or eating at some new trendy restaurant.

She has a dependence on sushi and a fetish for boots. Fall is her favorite season.

She is surrounded by family and friends she wouldn't trade for the world and is a little in love with her readers. The more the merrier. So make sure to say hi!

Visit my Website: *www.mneverauthor.com*

Or find me on:

Goodreads

Facebook

Instagram

Twitter

Pinterest

BOOKS BY

DECADENCE AFTER DARK

Owned

Claimed

Ruined

Lie With Me ~ Coming Soon

CPSIA information can be obtained
at www.ICGtesting.com
Printed in the USA
FFOW01n2241161215
19741FF